THE CITY OF DUSK

BOOK ONE OF
THE DARK GODS

TARA SIM

HODDERSCAPE

First published in Great Britain in 2022 by Hodder & Stoughton
An Hachette UK company

This paperback edition published in 2023

1

A CIP catalogue record for this title is available from the British Library

Hardback ISBN 978 1 399 70409 0
Trade Paperback ISBN 978 1 399 70410 6
Paperback ISBN 978 1 399 70413 7
eBook ISBN 978 1 399 70411 3

Printed and bound in Great Britain by Clays Ltd, Elcograf S.p.A.

Hodder & Stoughton policy is to use papers that are natural, renewable
and recyclable products and made from wood grown in sustainable
forests. The logging and manufacturing processes are expected to
conform to the environmental regulations of the country of origin.

Hodder & Stoughton Ltd
Carmelite House
50 Victoria Embankment
London EC4Y 0DZ

www.hodder.co.uk

'Tara Sim's adult debut is a glorious tapestry
of magic and murderous gods'
BuzzFeed News

'Lovers of epic, dark fantasies, rejoice!'
BookRiot

'Tara Sim proves herself again to be a talented
worldbuilder and detailed storyteller'
Locus

'A delightful, complex, intimate yet
explosive debut adult fantasy novel'
Strange Horizons

'Recommended for fans of large-scale fantasy sagas
with diverse, frequently queer protagonists'
Booklist

'In the vein of *A Darker Shade of Magic* or *Gideon
the Ninth* . . . There's a lot to love here'
Kirkus

'A good fantasy, with a cracking ensemble
cast and a wonderful world'
Grimdark Magazine

To myself, because I deserve it

And to my parents, who always saw me reading doorstopper fantasy novels and knew it was only a matter of time until I wrote one thick enough to brain a man

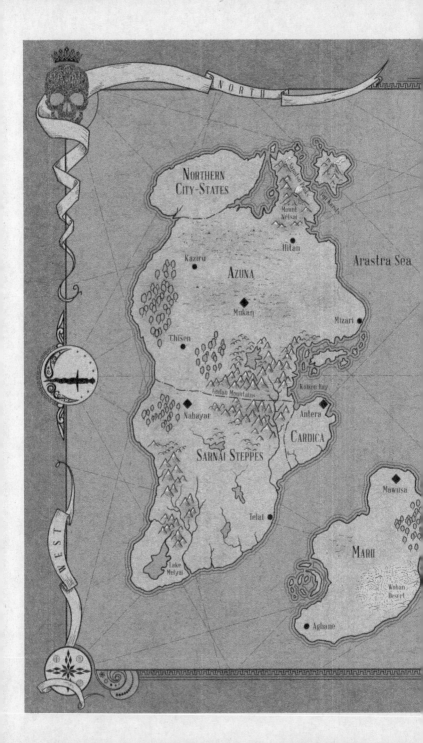

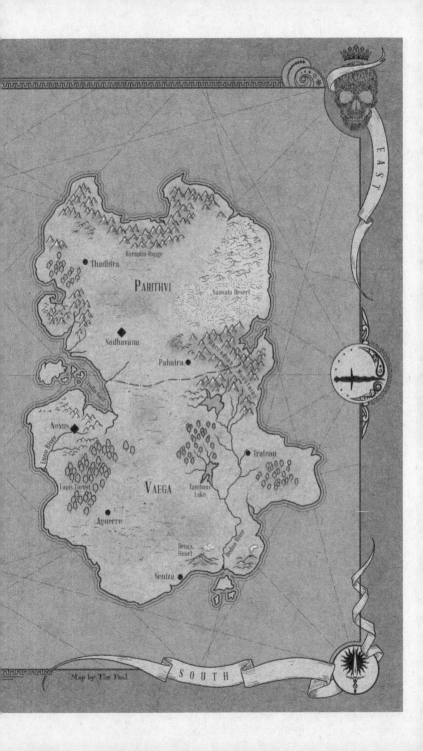

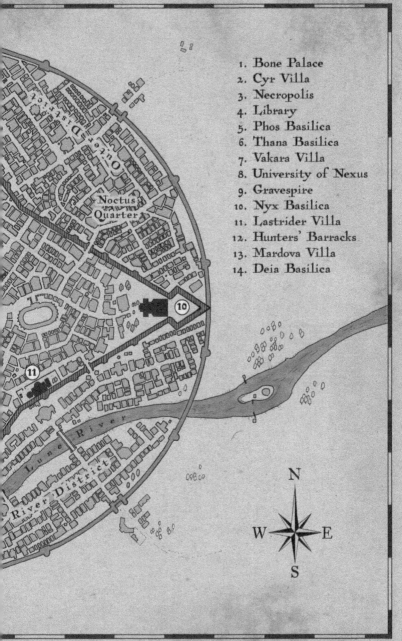

1. Bone Palace
2. Cyr Villa
3. Necropolis
4. Library
5. Phos Basilica
6. Thana Basilica
7. Vakara Villa
8. University of Nexus
9. Gravespire
10. Nyx Basilica
11. Lastrider Villa
12. Hunters' Barracks
13. Mardova Villa
14. Deia Basilica

Noctus Quarter

Lune River

River District

N
W E
S

Map by Tim Paul

THE FOUR NOBLE HOUSES OF NEXUS

House Mardova

Heads of House: Adela and August (deceased), Miko
Offspring: Angelica, Kikou (adopted), Eiko (adopted)
Blood: Vitae (Vaega)
Power: Elementalist
God: Deia

House Cyr

Heads of House: Waren and Madeia
Offspring: Nikolas, Rian (deceased)
Blood: Vitae (Vaega) / Solara
Power: Lumin
God: Phos

House Lastrider

Heads of House: Elena and Cormin
Offspring: Dante, Taesia, Brailee
Blood: Vitae (Vaega) / Noctus
Power: Shade
God: Nyx

House Vakara

Heads of House: Rath and Darsha
Offspring: Risha, Saya
Bloodline: Vitae (Parithvi) / Mortri
Power: Necromancy
God: Thana

Between the seams are where the monsters sing
Waiting for the fall of every man-made king
A curl of breath, a curl of light
The lure of death, the lure of night
They wait and writhe and plan and scheme
These gods of long forgotten things
To break their seams, to forge their mark
To draw all things living into the dark

—Marcos Ricci, *The Broken World*

DARK DAYS, DARK DEEDS

The flash of a dying star made the boy pause and look up.

Other than the streak of violent orange marking another star's passing, the sky was the same as it ever was: a somber mix of blacks and blues and purples, a cosmos unfolded. It was an inky darkness, almost cloudlike, purling out in fans of color as paint does in water.

He remembered paint. Thick and tacky on his fingertips, staining his clothes.

To the east, city lights winked in pale imitation of the silver stars overhead—those that had not yet faded, anyway. A palace rose golden and brilliant at its heart, a jewel within a bezel.

"How many more?" the boy asked. His words were faint and slurred, the half mumbling of a dreamer.

Do not fret, answered the Voice. It curled around him the way it always did, soothing his thoughts, his rising trepidation. *It won't be much longer. They do not yet know, but they will soon. Then . . . it will be time.*

Memories of paint faded, until all was calm and hazy again. His gaze traveled west, to the flat, dark land beyond. Where the others were waiting.

Not much longer now, cooed the Voice, a smile in its words.

The boy smiled, too. Turning to the dead body behind him, he grabbed an ankle and continued to drag it east.

PART I

Gods and Monsters

I

Taesia Lastrider had never considered herself a good person, nor did she have any intention of becoming one.

She was fine with that. Beyond the confines of her House's villa, she was freer to do whatever she wanted. Be whomever she wanted.

The last breath of summer's heat coiled around her as she shifted in the shadow of a market awning. Shoppers were buying melon juice and sarab, a clear Parithvian alcohol served with a pinch of orange-colored spice that cooled the body down. Jewelry on a nearby cart glittered in the sunlight, cuffs of hammered silver and brass sending spangles into her vision. Taesia blinked and retreated even farther into the shade.

It put her in view of the building she had been adamantly trying to ignore. But it was almost impossible to overlook the size of it, the swirling, conch-like design of shimmering sandstone, the length of the shadow it cast across the city of Nexus.

It was quite lovely, for a prison. But crack that pretty shell open, and all its filth would come pouring out, the discarded and condemned souls of Nexus's convicts.

Someone bumped into her as they passed by, and the shadows twitched at her fingertips. She was so jumpy it took her a moment to realize it was merely a common thieves' tactic: make someone paranoid enough to pat their trousers or their sleeves to know where to strike later.

An amateur trick. It didn't matter there were more guards than usual patrolling the marketplace; pickpockets would take any chance they could get.

At the next stall over, a man was prying open boxes with a crowbar, chatting with the vendor as they checked the wares inside. "Would've gotten here sooner if I hadn't been held at the city gates," the man with the crowbar said. "Guards were sniffing around me like the dogs they are."

"King's got 'em on alert." The vendor glanced at the nearest guards and lowered his voice. "Had an incident not too long ago. Some weird magic shit went down near the palace."

"What kinda weird magic?"

"Wasn't there myself, but sounds to me like it was necromancy. Folks say a buncha spirits came and wrecked shit."

"*Spirits?* Were the Vakaras acting up? I've heard they can kill with just a snap of their fingers."

This caught Taesia's attention like thread on a nail. It was well known throughout Vaega—as well as beyond its borders—that those who made up House Vakara, descended from the god of death, were the only ones who possessed the power of necromancy. It was also well known that once in a while, a stray spirit managed to wander from Nexus's over-crowded necropolis to cause trouble.

But the incident the two men were gossiping about had been different: a sudden influx of violent spirits converging close to the palace square, destroying buildings and harming those unfortunate enough to be in their path. People had been rightfully terrified—and confused about who to blame.

"No idea," the vendor mumbled. "But it was nasty stuff. Heard a man got his arm ripped clean off. Whole city's gonna be tighter than a clenched asshole from now on."

A tremor rolled across her body as Taesia turned back to the Gravespire. When the vendor beside her wasn't looking, she grabbed a glass of sarab and downed it in one go, wiping her mouth with the back of her wrist.

Citizens blaming the Houses for their troubles wasn't anything new. But the thought of Risha getting caught up in it made her want to punch something.

The shadows twitched again. Impatience crackled at the base of her lungs, made her roll onto the balls of her feet as if poised on the edge of something reckless.

"Follow me," a low voice whispered behind her.

She breathed a sigh of relief and waited a couple seconds before turning and following her brother through the market. Dante was dressed down today in a long, sleeveless tunic with a hood, the lean muscle of his dusky brown arms on display. A few people pretended not to stare as he stalked by. Not in recognition, but in appreciation of his features despite the hood's shadow. Or maybe they were drawn to the smooth, confident way he moved, the way Taesia never seemed to get quite right.

"Did you get the information you needed?" she whispered.

"I did. We should be—"

She nearly ran into his back when he suddenly stopped. He lifted a hand for her to stay put.

She soon saw why. A couple Greyhounds had descended on a confused vendor. They were inspecting jars from her stall, dropping what didn't interest them to the ground. The vendor flinched at the sound of breaking pottery.

Taesia cursed under her breath. Although the vendor had no horns, the bluish dark of her skin and the white tattoos on her forehead marked her as a Noctan. Perhaps a mixed-race offspring from one of the refugees. Mixed blood would explain how she could stand to be in this heat in the middle of the day; most of the night-dwellers from Noctus couldn't bear it, often getting sunsick if forced to endure it for too long.

"Please, I have no contraband," the vendor said softly. They were beginning to draw spectators eagerly searching for a distraction from the heat. "These were all fairly traded within Vaega."

"We're not looking for foreign goods," one of the guards said.

His partner waved a small pot in his direction. The guard took it, sniffed, and scowled.

"Sulfur." The single word was leveled at the vendor like an arrow. "A Conjuration ingredient."

Taesia sucked in a breath. While many were eager to call the incident last week necromancy, the Vakaras had never been shy to demonstrate their magic, and their methods didn't line up with the attack. For in the ravaged spot where the spirits had congregated, something had been left behind: a cleverly drawn circle containing a seven-pointed star and a ring of strange glyphs.

Conjuration. An occult practice that hadn't been seen in decades.

The vendor shook. "I—I didn't know! I swear, I—"

The Greyhounds didn't waste time listening to her stammer. They shackled her wrists as excited murmurs ran through the small crowd they'd gathered.

"Wouldn't have bought from her anyway," someone muttered. "Anything the Noctans touch is tainted."

"Did they say Conjuration? Isn't that demon—?"

"Shh! The Greyhounds won't hesitate to haul you off, too."

"She should have stayed in the Noctus Quarter."

Taesia curled her hand into a fist. Dante grabbed her as she took a step forward.

"Don't," he said. Not a warning, but an order.

"We're responsible for the refugees."

"They're cracking down on Conjuration materials," Dante whispered. "If you interfere, think about how it'll reflect on the House."

She didn't give two shits about that. "You're saying you're all right with this?"

"Of course I'm not. But we can't do anything about it right now."

Taesia watched the guards haul away the vendor, who was trying and failing to stifle her terrified tears. Dante didn't let Taesia go until the tension left her body. When he did, she spun to face him. "Are you sure you want to go through with this? You said it yourself: We can't have anything negatively impacting the House." She dropped her voice to a murmur. "Especially considering what the Vakaras are going through. Even if you manage to find what you need, what are you going to do with it?"

"Not summon a horde of spirits, if that's what you're concerned about."

It wasn't—not really—but there was so much about Conjuration they didn't understand, since all the old texts had been destroyed.

"You want to put a stop to these scenes, right?" Dante nodded in the direction of the vendor's abandoned stall. "To not have to worry about House politics when it comes to issues like defending the people?"

She swallowed, certain her hunger for that very thing was plain on her face. "What does that have to do with Conjuration?"

"Indulge me a little longer, and you'll see." He paused, then leaned forward and sniffed. "Have you been drinking?"

"Don't worry about it."

They walked past the beehive hum of the crowd and continued on to the edge of the market, where four children were playing with a couple of dogs. A gangly man was slumped over a counter. He watched the children with an air of someone who probably should be worried about their safety but couldn't muster up the energy.

"I don't *want* to be Thana," one of the children was complaining in a nasal voice. "Thana's scary. I want to be Deia!"

"*I'm* Deia," said another child, a tall girl with dirt smudged across her face. "I'm always Deia."

"Just because you have weak earth magic doesn't mean you can be Deia every time," mumbled a boy with Mariian black skin. Judging by the crown made of twigs and sticks resting on the tight coils of his hair, he was supposed to play the part of Nyx, god of night and shadow.

"It's not weak!" With a flick of her finger, she flung a pebble at his forehead, making him cry out.

"You can be Phos instead," said the last child, likely the Mariian boy's brother. He handed the girl who didn't want to be Thana his toy wings made of fluttering leaves, which made her brighten. "And I'll be Thana. I'll put her in a cage of bones."

Taesia smiled wryly. It was common for children to play at being gods; she herself had done it with her siblings when they were younger. That was before they'd understood only one god demanded their family's piety.

Dante rapped his knuckles on the wooden counter, making the gangly man start. "Heard you have good prices," Dante said, his cautious inflection almost making it a question.

The corner of the man's mouth twitched. "Come see for yourself."

Dante glanced at the children, the dogs barking and chasing after them when they ran. "Will they be all right on their own?"

The man shrugged and headed toward the nearest alley. They were led away from the market to a building that had seen better days, with a tarp-covered window and weeds sprouting along its base. The man eased the door open and ushered them inside. A second door on the far end of the room was open, revealing a set of stairs leading down. Taesia's nose wrinkled immediately at the smell, a bitter blend of ash and pepper.

"Ruben," the gangly man called. "Customer." He left to return to the market.

A heavyset man in shirtsleeves appeared on the stairs, wiping his hands on a handkerchief. "Hello, hello. This way, please."

Dante kept his hood up as he and Taesia descended into a basement. It might have once been a wine cellar, cramped and cool. But instead of racks of wine, the place was now stocked with sacks of herbs and roots, boxes of chalk, and jars of sulfur. There was even a display of small knives along the wall.

Dante's eyes lit up the way Taesia imagined a librarian's would at finding a rare book for their collection. He began to wade through the assortment, peering into sacks and running his hands through unknown substances. Taesia meandered toward the knives and inspected one with a serpentine blade.

The man, Ruben, cleared his throat. "Let's keep this brief, yes? No guards saw you come this way?"

"Not that I'm aware of." Dante's voice was distant, the tone he got when someone tried to interrupt him. He picked up a jar and shook it, the black specks inside rattling. "What's this?"

"That would be powdered lodestone."

"And what does it do?"

"It's a magnetized bit of mineral, known for attracting iron. Rich deposits of it along the eastern coast."

"I'll take ten grams, as well as loose chalk." Dante paused before pointing at a nearby sack. "Throw in some hellebore root as well."

Taesia grimaced. For all his intelligence and charisma, her brother wasn't particularly skilled at pretending to be something he was not. The order strung through his words might as well have painted a broadsheet across his face reading *I'm a noble, can't you tell?*

Ruben didn't seem particularly affected by it either way. Taesia obediently held the sachet of hellebore root Dante handed to her while he tucked the vial of powdered lodestone and pouch of chalk into his own pockets. Coins exchanged hands, the clink of gold loud in the cellar.

"A pleasure," Ruben said with a sickly smile.

Taesia took a much-needed deep breath once they were back on the street. "Again, are you absolutely sure about this?"

"I'll be careful." Despite Dante's light tone, she noted the divot between his brows. He was nervous.

Spotting the tip of the Gravespire rising above the buildings, Taesia thought about the Noctan who had been hauled away and swallowed.

Nexus had once prided itself on harboring people from every country, every realm, to form an eclectic microcosm of their broad universe. Now it seemed as if they were doing their best to eradicate those who *didn't belong*, whatever that meant.

She was jolted from her thoughts when someone slammed into her and sent her crashing to the ground.

"Stop her!" someone shouted.

Taesia gaped up at the face staring down at hers. The girl couldn't have been much older than her, with lustrous black skin and a cloud of dark hair. She winked and scrambled off Taesia in a flash, slipping into the startled crowd like a fish.

Dante helped her up as a few Greyhounds ran by in pursuit. Taesia stared after the girl, rubbing a sore spot on her chest.

"You all right?" Dante asked.

"Yeah, I'm—" She checked her pockets. "She stole the hellebore root!" Not an amateur thief, then.

Dante shushed her. "It's fine, I can get by without—Tae!"

She charged after the thief with a fire kindled in her chest, stoked and restless since Dante had stopped her from interfering with the guards.

Finally, some damn action.

The Greyhounds were slowed by the crowd, but Taesia easily evaded limbs and bodies. The thief hoisted herself onto the roof of a stall, so Taesia did the same. She rolled across an awning and leapt onto the next roof, which swayed dangerously under her feet.

She lifted her hand. To anyone else, the silver ring on her fourth finger bore an onyx jewel, but the illusion broke when her shadow familiar spilled from the bezel and into her palm.

"Do something for me?" she panted as she leapt the space between two stalls.

Umbra elongated, forming a snakelike head of shadow. It tilted from side to side before it nodded.

Taesia flung out her hand and Umbra shot forward in a black, inky rope. One end lashed around the thief's wrist, making her stumble. With a sharp pull on Taesia's end, the thief crashed through an awning.

Taesia jumped down. The thief groaned and staggered away from cages full of exotic birds flapping their wings and squawking at the disturbance. The vendor gawked at them as Taesia summoned Umbra back to her ring and took off after the girl.

The last thing she wanted was for rumors of a Shade tussling in the market to reach her mother.

Taesia dove into a narrow alley to try and cut the thief off at the cross street, only to be met with an arm that swung out from around the corner. It collided with her chest and Taesia fell onto her back with a grunt.

The thief stood over her, breathless and smiling. "Well! Gotta admit, this is a first. Never stole from someone like you before."

Taesia coughed. "You punched me in the tit."

"And I'd do it again."

Taesia braced herself on the ground and kicked the girl in the chest, sending her reeling backward. "Now we're almost even."

The girl wheezed around a laugh. "Suit yourself."

Taesia sprang to her feet and charged. The thief ducked and hit her in the back, dangerously close to her kidneys. Taesia caught her arm and twisted. The thief stomped on her instep, making her yelp and let go.

"Whew!" The girl's face was alive with glee despite the dirt and sweat streaked across it. "Must've stolen something you care about."

"Not really." The shadows trembled around her, ready to be called in, but she couldn't risk it. She'd already been too careless using Umbra. "Just needed to stretch my legs today."

The girl barked a laugh as they circled. Her dark eyes flitted to the alley over Taesia's shoulder before a blow caught Taesia across the backs of her knees, sending her reeling forward.

As Taesia fell, a young woman—likely the thief's partner—ran to the nearest wall and made a broad swirling motion with her arms. Both of the thieves were caught in a sudden cyclone of wind that lifted them up onto the roof.

An air elementalist.

Cheater.

"Better luck next time," the thief called with a mocking salute. Taesia gave a rude gesture in reply, and the girl laughed before she and her partner disappeared.

A moment later, Dante burst out of the alley. "Taesia, what the *fuck*—"

"She got away."

"I don't care! I told you it didn't matter." He ran a hand through his hair, hood fallen across his shoulders. "You're filthy. We can't let anyone in the villa see you like this." He pointed a stern finger at her. "Do *not* do that again."

She wasn't sure if he meant chasing after thieves or using her shadow magic out in the open. Before she could ask, he turned and began the trek home, not even bothering to see if Taesia would follow.

Like always, she did.

The black iron gates of the Lastrider villa were manned by House guards in black-and-silver livery. But Taesia had long since figured out a path over the tall adobe wall, through the gardens, and up the rose trellis her father had built when she was a child. It was easy as a song to slip into her bedroom and change into clean clothes.

She met up with Dante at the entrance to the vaults, the underground chambers where House treasures were stored. The two of them had often played here as children. Their younger sister, Brailee, had been too afraid to stay longer than five minutes, but Taesia and Dante had made games of the thick shadows and silent rooms. As heir, Dante was the only person aside from their mother who possessed a key.

"I know you said you don't plan to call down a horde of spirits," she said as he lit a lantern and led the way down the musty corridor, "but that still begs the question of what you *are* planning to do."

"I'm more interested in the origins of Conjuration rather than using it as a conduit for two-bit necromancy."

"Origins?"

"You'll see."

Umbra slithered up her arm as Dante shoved open a door at the end of the corridor. His own familiar, Nox, began to play around his shoulders, no longer required to stay hidden. Taesia wondered if they could feel the presence of Noctan artifacts down here, a tentative link to a realm they had never seen.

Dante lit candles in the stone-walled room. It had once been used for storage but now served as his workshop. Shelves bore jars and vials waiting to be filled, and the very center of the floor was covered in a thick rug.

He pulled the rug aside to reveal a hazy, stained area where he'd practiced drawing Conjuration circles. Taesia's breath caught, remembering the events of last week, the circle with its seven-pointed star left by people the king condemned as radicals. Nox brushed Dante's cheek as it peered over his shoulder.

"So," he said. "Lodestone. Typically used for its magnetism, but there was an ancient use for this that's long since fallen out of memory." He shook the vial. "It was used as an offering for Deia."

Taesia raised an eyebrow. "If you wanted to give an offering to Deia, you should have gone to her basilica."

He smirked and pulled out a jar of sulfur. He began to mix it with the loose chalk he'd bought, and Taesia fought against the urge to sneeze. "When we talk about Conjuration today, it's always associated with one thing: summoning demons."

Demons. Cosmic beings that prowled between the realms, in the pockets of the universe only the gods could access. There were countless stories told to children to make them behave, to warn others away:

"Narizeh will come and steal your voice if you don't stop screaming."

"Never follow a woman with lips tinged black. That is Vorsileh luring you to her bed, where she will turn you into a worm once she's done with you and slurp you up."

"The sound of coughing means Celipheh has visited to spread his plague."

But Conjuration had been outlawed over two centuries ago, the grimoires and texts burned in a massive purge of all things occult in Nexus. There had never been a case outside the city; why that was, no one could say.

Taesia grimaced. "What do demons have to do with an offering for Deia?"

He gave her a loaded Dante smile, silent secrets hidden under an ocean of charm. "What we call Conjuration today is a bastardization of an ancient ritual to commune with the gods. Back in the day, priests would draw a circle to replicate the shape of the universe, add offerings unique to the god they wanted to chat with, and there you have it."

Taesia felt cold as she watched Dante draw two circles with the laced chalk, one nested within the other. She leaned against the wall and crossed her arms. "So you want to talk to the gods, is that what you're saying? Why?"

He paused, staring at the diamond he'd just drawn within the inner circle. Quietly he said, "To understand why the Sealing happened."

Taesia's fingers tightened on her arms. "And you're certain it'll work? That we won't end up with some unsavory visitor?"

His laugh was tinged with apprehension. "Not at all." He poured the powdered lodestone around the diamond, then opened a jar and sniffed its contents. "I wish we had the hellebore root, but this should be a good enough substitute."

He sprinkled something that smelled like tobacco. When he looked back up, a lock of dark hair fell across his forehead.

"I figured trying is better than sitting around feeling helpless," he said, his voice gone soft again.

A wave of fondness washed over her despite the fact she was staring at her brother across a very illegal, very pungent Conjuration circle. Dante had more willpower than she did, but they both shared the desire to *act*.

He unsheathed the small knife at his belt and cut the pad of one finger. A drop of blood, trembling and infused with ancient power, fell into the center of the circle, over the upside-down horseshoe-esque symbol commonly used for Deia.

Nothing happened at first. Taesia braced herself, Umbra nervously coiling around her neck. Dante stayed kneeling, brow furrowed. Then a steady, low hum began to fill the room, the edges of the circle glowing red.

The offerings within the circle trembled, the hum traveling up the soles of Taesia's feet until it made her molars ache. Umbra hid itself in the crook of her neck, and it took all her strength to not make a run for the door.

"Deia, we beseech you to speak with us," Dante intoned. "Please bless us with your presence."

It was one thing to visit the basilica of Nyx, the god of Noctus, the founder of the Lastrider line, and feel a hint of night-touched breeze on her face. To sense the distant stars overhead and the depth of shadows in every corner. A reminder of where they came from, and what they could do. But this was Deia, god of elements, god of life, with the power to raise volcanoes and turn entire cities to ice. Attempting to summon her in this cramped room was perhaps not the best idea.

Yet as they continued to stare at the floor, waiting—for a voice, or the outline of a body, *something*—nothing happened.

A frustrated sound wrenched out of Dante's throat as the glow died, casting them back into dim candlelight. He scored the circle with a hand, and Taesia couldn't help her relieved exhale.

"I don't know what else to do, other than try different offerings." Dante glared at the wasted lodestone. "Or perhaps try to find a different configuration of symbols."

"Even if you manage to summon one of the gods, what good would it do?"

Dante worked his jaw, the tension fading gradually from his face. "It's not just about talking to them, or asking why they sealed the realms from one another. I want…" He ran a hand through his hair. "You're going to think I'm mad."

"I already do. Tell me."

He sat back on his heels. "I want to convince them to undo it."

Taesia waited a beat. Then another. Her mouth twisted to keep from laughing.

"It's not impossible!" he argued. "If we undo the Sealing, we reopen the realms and the natural flow of the universe will be restored. We can use our godsblood for good, to prevent our realm from dying." He lowered his voice. "It'll also give the Houses leverage over the king. We can gain support from the people to take away the Holy King's authority."

It was something they had discussed before, in the privacy of Dante's study. How he admired their neighbor to the north, Parithvi, and the Parliament they had instated with more populist beliefs.

"We can actually *use* our privilege for a change," Dante said.

They sat in the possibility a moment, familiars drifting between them, a couple more shadows in a room that smelled of forbidden magic.

It sounded stupidly heroic: going against the will of the gods, wresting control of their country from a man who believed himself untouchable. Again she thought of the Noctan refugee who had been seized in the market. Under Dante's watch, those scenes could disappear completely.

But there was one problem.

"I don't foresee myself with a political career," she said. "Once you've established this parliament of yours, what role would you give me?"

He wrinkled his nose. "Tae, you were *born* into a political career."

"Firmly without my say-so."

"Well, don't worry. Once the realms are reopened, I plan to restore the profession on which the Lastrider line was founded. I'll need someone to spearhead it."

Status came hand in hand with responsibility if you were a member of the Houses. Yet each household also had to contribute something to Nexus, to the kingdom, and to the throne in order to maintain that status. The Vakaras performed all things necromantic, the Mardovas cultivated powerful mages, the Cyrs produced and oversaw soldiers for the militia, and the Lastriders acted as inter-realm emissaries of trade.

Or at least, they had before the Sealing. Now, with resources both natural and Other-Realm dwindling in Vitae, the Lastriders worked with the surrounding countries to conserve what little was left.

Taesia felt cheated of a life of jumping from realm to realm, collecting artifacts and precious resources and exploring the wonders and dangers of other worlds. To not have to sit still. To have the freedom to go where she wished.

To not be a purposeless spare of House Lastrider, chained to a responsibility she'd never wanted.

"You're flirting with being labeled a radical for a hopeless plan," she said, though it sounded weak even to her.

He smiled at the greed suffusing Taesia's expression, his eyes glimmering with the same thrill she knew must be mirrored in her own. "But are *you* willing to flirt with it?"

Taesia glanced again at the forfeited circle. Dante wouldn't delve into something he didn't think was for the greater good. Dante believed in a better world, and she believed in Dante.

"Absolutely."

II

Risha Vakara asked for death to take her, and once again death declined.

The path was not smooth, nor was it straight. It ran in gentle serpentine curves, paved with jagged stone and glittering fragments of peridot and onyx. There were markers along the way, long, thin bones planted in the earth waving red ribbon from their tips. If she wandered off the path, she would forever be lost.

Her slippers scraped over the ground. Every footfall released the scent of grave soil. The wind blowing down the path was cold and stale, the musty air of a mausoleum hidden deep underground. No matter how hard she tried, she couldn't find the source of that phantom wind; everything outside the path was darkness, simple and unrelenting.

And within that darkness, the restless churning of spirits unable to move on.

She walked as long as she was able, as far as the path would let her. As it always did, it ended abruptly in a spiral of shadow she could not cross.

Risha placed a sprig of cypress on the path in offering before she pressed her hands against the barrier. She clenched her teeth as pain curled in her lower belly, squeezing around her heart. It stroked against the delicate skin at her throat, tracing the arteries across her body. A soft yet undeniable taunt, showing her all the ways in which she was vulnerable, all the gateways her body carried to death.

But the only gateway she cared about was before her, and it was sealed.

Behind her were three spirits she had found wandering the necropolis: sad, incorporeal things without purpose or direction. She wanted to bring them home. She wanted them to pass on before they turned to something worse, something festering and wrong.

"*He knew I was sleeping with someone else,*" one whispered, voice little more than the scrape of dry leaves. "*He was angry.*"

"*My daughter was tired of taking care of me,*" another whispered. "*I drank away the pain and fell out the window.*"

Risha closed her eyes and delved into the shush of her own blood to drown them out, listening to the uncertain rhythm of her heart. The darkness seemed to listen as well. She sensed the bone fragments in the earth, the quivering gems along the pathway.

And beyond the barrier, the dizzying expanse of Mortri. The power it kept at bay was colossal. Her pulse sang with it, the urge to burn a hole between worlds.

Like every time before, the urge went unfulfilled. No matter how hard she tried to break through, the barrier resisted her like a hand against her chest. Risha grunted and fought back, desperately searching for cracks. It remained firm, unyielding.

"Please," she whispered to her hands, to the darkness. To Mortri, one half of her birthright, the realm for which her powers cried.

The realm of death.

"Thana, can you hear me? Your blood is calling for you. Thana, I am here. Please listen to me."

Silence, even from the spirits hovering behind her. Her arms began to shake, but she kept pushing, pushing, subtly weaving her power into a pattern before her. It was a pattern her father had taught her, one for unbinding curses and opening seals.

The presence first came as a gentle breeze, carrying the scent of stone and rime. The barest caress on her cheek made her look up, a gasp caught in her throat.

Thana was lovely in her darkness—or rather, her illusion was. Risha knew the god was enmeshed within the heart of Mortri, would not deign to leave her seat of power to come so close to where her realm met Vitae. Risha saw her vaguely through the barrier, tall and barefoot, her skin a grayish brown, four arms splitting from her upper body. The god was covered head to ankles in a flowing, sheer black veil, kept in place by a crown of bone. The crown twisted into the thorns of rib points, sharp as a wolf's teeth.

Risha was sure if she so much as prostrated herself at the god's feet, touching the hem of her veil in deference, she would simply turn to dust.

Thana lifted a thin, skeletal hand toward her. Against her better judgment, Risha tried to reach for it.

And then her pattern broke.

"No!" Risha banged against the barrier. "Please, you must—"

But the god's illusion had already vanished. That invisible hand kept pushing at her, an impatient parent to a stubborn child. Sweat rolled down her neck as she focused on the hazy promise of Mortri on the other side. She just had to open the barrier slightly, had to forge some small bridge so the spirits could pass through—

Risha cried out as she was knocked back, stumbling across the path and coming dangerously close to crossing a marker. Her connection to the pathway dissolved; she'd exerted too much power to maintain it.

She fell to one knee on firm, plain earth. Dusk made ominous shadows of the mausoleums around her, a small city of the dead. The three spirits scattered, their incorporeal forms hiding once more between pillars of stone and marble.

She had failed. Again.

"I'm guessing it didn't go as planned?"

Risha started. Taesia lounged on top of a nearby mausoleum, arms pillowing her head, as if she'd been waiting there awhile.

"You shouldn't nap on top of graves," Risha said. "It's disrespectful."

"I'm sure they don't mind." Taesia sat up, rapping her knuckles against the mausoleum's roof. "Not like I'm disrupting them from their own naps."

Risha didn't bother asking how Taesia had known she would be here; she had found Risha in the necropolis enough times it had become one of their usual meeting spots. It had once spooked Taesia, being around the dead and decaying, but she'd since grown used to it. Maybe too much so.

"Were you trying the barrier again?" Taesia asked, readjusting her sword as she swung her legs over the side of the roof.

Risha stood, wincing at the soreness in her body. "I have to move the spirits on somehow. But no matter how many times I try, it's still the same."

"I did warn you about attempting it on your own."

Risha managed to keep her expression neutral despite the heat rising to her face. "I'm searching for weaknesses. I'm doing my part."

Taesia raised her eyebrows at the implication in her words. "And I should be doing...what, exactly? Going to the basilica and appealing to

Nyx on a nightly basis?" She mimed knocking on a door. "Hello, Nyx? Yes, it's me! Long time no pray. How rude of me. Allow me to put on a pot of tea while we catch up."

Risha turned her snort of laughter into a cough, not wanting to give Taesia the satisfaction. Taesia didn't fully understand, but Risha didn't expect her to. Not only was Risha an heir while Taesia was not, they were born of different powers, different worlds, different gods.

"Have you tried doing this at the actual Mortri portal?" Taesia asked.

Risha shook her head. "The barrier is strongest within the basilica. This is the only place I've been able to get as far as I have." She brushed the dirt off her salwar. "But not far enough. Now tell me what you want."

Taesia put an affronted hand to her chest. "I just wanted to ask if you've bought a dress for the gala."

"You mean the Autumn Equinox?"

"*No*, I mean the Godsnight Gala. I've had my equinox dress for ages."

Risha froze. Somehow she had completely forgotten about the upcoming celebration, despite it being the first—and last—Godsnight she would ever live through.

The phenomenon happened only once every hundred years. For one day, the Cosmic Scale of the universe, the cradle of the Four Realms, slid into perfect alignment. Channels of energy widened and magic became more potent. It had once been used as a grand demonstration by the Houses, showing off the might of their progenitor gods' power. And then the Sealing had cut off the Cosmic Scale's natural flow, severing the veins of energy that ran between each realm.

Yet the people of Nexus were nothing if not creatures of habit, and they did love a good party. The gala would be held a couple weeks before Godsnight, and on the actual day festivals would take place throughout the city.

"I haven't bought a dress," Risha answered. "It's still weeks away."

"Good. You can come with us when we get fitted." Taesia hopped off the mausoleum, and they both turned toward the necropolis entrance. "I have to admit, I'm actually looking forward to it."

"I can't imagine why. I distinctly remember you saying at the last party that you were tired of watching Dante get fawned over."

Taesia shrugged. "I just want the snacks." She peered at Risha. "By the way, I need a substance and you're the only person I can think of who might have it."

There it is. "What substance?"

"Calciphite."

Risha tried very hard not to sigh. Calciphite was the product of finely ground bones from a body that had been reanimated. "You do know that's illegal, yes? Especially with the recent crackdown."

Taesia shrugged again, unconcerned.

"I don't have any," Risha said. "Because, and stop me if you've heard this before, it's *illegal*."

"Then can you—"

"I am not going to reanimate a body for you."

"Not even part of a body?"

"No."

"What about an arm?"

"*No*, Tae."

Taesia leaned her head back and sighed dramatically. "Fine."

Risha considered asking why she wanted it but knew she wouldn't get a straight answer. Besides, Taesia had always been curious, especially when it came to Risha's power.

She could still vividly remember the day many years ago when Taesia had shown up at a restaurant where the Vakaras had been enjoying a long lunch. Risha had excused herself and followed Taesia around the back of the restaurant, where smoke and steam and irritated yelling leaked from the kitchen.

Taesia had pulled out a cloth bundle, unwrapping it to reveal a dead rat.

"You want me to reanimate it?" Risha had guessed.

"Is that what it's called when you bring something back to life? Then, yes."

Risha's training had been in its beginning stages then. But she had practiced in secret on bugs and insects around the villa. Her first reanimation had been a dead fly on her windowsill. Seeing it buzz around her room had been a great source of pride for her.

A rat, though?

It was already starting to smell, its fur mangy and its body stiff. Still, she'd wanted to know if she could do it, so she had tapped into the enigmatic power within her. It first started in her bones, a buzzing that made her teeth ache. She seemed to create her own wind, a small torus of cold air that gave off the scent of dark, dank things. She was connected to the earth, and to something far more distant—a hub of untapped energy, an unused channel between this world and another.

She had sketched the pattern for reanimation through the air with her finger. Her father had told her she would have to use string to assist with shaping certain spells, but not this one, not when it came so naturally in the Vakara line. When she'd tapped the dead rat on the back, it had trembled and jerkily pushed to its feet, leaning one way and then the other. Taesia had let out a scream of horrified glee.

And then Risha's father had found them and put the poor undead rat out of its misery. Taesia had been returned to her villa, and Risha had been punished by being confined to her own family's villa for a week.

"Waking the dead is not a casual sport," Rath Vakara had warned her.

"But you do it all the time," she'd argued. "It's your *job*. And it'll be mine one day, too."

"My path will not be yours, meer piaara. If I ever catch you doing it again without supervision, there will be a steeper price to pay."

He had also cautioned her to keep her distance from Taesia, but both his warnings had been in vain. Risha had still practiced on dead bugs, and she had still found ways to meet up with Taesia, both of them fascinated by the other's abilities.

They walked in silence, following the path between marble and sandstone, statues and archways. When Taesia pictured death, she no doubt thought of bones and rot, of dark soil and yellowed teeth in a weathered jaw. But when Risha pictured death, she saw old marble and hallowed ground, the shape of something beyond its original purpose. She felt the empty space of ceased breaths, of potential gone unfulfilled, and the smooth shape of finger bones tucked against her palm. Death was lovely and sad, and never quite an ending.

Nearby, Risha could make out the wooden structure of a watchtower. It was a new feature, standing at the edge of the necropolis and manned day and night by sentries. If reanimated corpses escaped the necropolis, her House was immediately called upon to deal with it.

But no one had been prepared for last week, when a storm of spirits had descended on a square near the palace.

"I—I heard a sound, first," the sentry had stammered when Risha and her father had questioned her. "This terrible groaning, like the earth was gonna split in half. Then they all just sort of...surged." The sentry had been shaking, her eyes distant. "They formed this cloud over the necropolis. There were all these *whispers* and howls and writhing limbs, only they weren't really *limbs*, it was kinda like churning water—"

"We can picture it," Rath Vakara had said firmly yet gently.

The sentry had nodded, sweat beading at her temple. "There was an odd, blackish glow, and then they all rushed east. Like a hive mind."

And convened upon a focalized point, where they had torn doors off hinges, broken windows, and collapsed roofs. Risha vividly remembered standing at the scene, awed and unnerved, unable to ignore a puddle of drying blood on the pitted cobblestone or the morbidly curious onlookers on the sidelines.

Although her family had been questioned, King Ferdinand had proclaimed it was the work of Conjuration, citing the remnants of the large circle the spirits had been drawn to. Risha herself had knelt at the edge of the circle, unable to interpret it one way or another.

When they reached the tall marble archway of the entrance, Taesia turned to Risha. "You can't kill people with a snap of your fingers, can you?"

Risha stopped short, yanked out of her thoughts. "*Taesia.*"

"Uh-oh. You only call me by my full name when I've said something stupid."

"Because that's the most horrible question you've ever asked me! Of course I can't." She had never tried, anyway. "What is wrong with you?"

"Sorry, sorry. It's just something I overheard."

"Why would anyone even speculate that?"

Taesia slipped her hands into her pockets. "You know why."

Risha did. There were a few who whispered that maybe the Vakaras *did* have something to do with the incident, that it was tied to some power grab for Ferdinand's throne.

Seeing the dismay on Risha's face, Taesia bumped their shoulders together. "But hey, if you could snap your fingers and make these Conjurer bastards keel over, you could use them to make some calciphite."

"Why do you want—? No, never mind. I don't want to know." Risha turned back to the carriage, where House Vakara guards in black-and-gold livery stood waiting for her. "I deal with people *after* they've died, not before. Have fun with whatever you have planned, but leave me out of it."

"You're missing out!" Taesia called after her.

Risha was helpless against a small smile. As the carriage began to make the journey home, she glanced out the window in time to see her oldest friend swallowed by evening shadows.

The Vakara villa was a stunning example of Parithvian architecture, found in echoes throughout the city from immigrants who had long held influence over Nexus. The main house sat in the center of the villa with four short, fat towers in each corner, the building austere yet beautiful in its flowing lines and repeating detailing. When the footmen opened the gates to her, Risha swept through the entrance and under the open arcade, the blue-and-gold tile flowing to the main house like an artery.

What Risha loved most about the villa was the wide, open courtyard in the middle of the main house, where she often napped in the afternoon sun or lazed upon a chaise while reading a book. It was where they held intimate parties in the late spring and early summer, sitting on cushions around a low table while the kitchen staff brought out course after course of traditional Parithvian dishes: curried cauliflower with slivered almonds, stewed lentils dolloped with herbed yogurt, saffron rice studded with chicken and pomegranate seeds, and desserts made of nut paste and dusted with decorative silver leaf.

A covered walkway surrounded the courtyard, leading to different areas of the house. Risha was heading for the eastern door when her mother called from the opposite side.

"Risha? Come here, please."

Darsha Vakara sat in the main sitting room, situated on a pile of cushions and surrounded by garlands. The scent of marigolds and lilies permeated the air, thick and cloying. Risha was more than familiar with the smell.

"Who's died?" Risha asked.

Her mother barely paused her work sewing flowers onto stalks of thick white string. Interspersed with the flowers were bundles of bay laurel and sage, as well as tiny bells that chimed softly as she moved. Petal debris was strewn over her mother's blue ghagra choli.

"People die every day in Nexus," her mother said. "More of their loved ones are requesting burial wreaths, is all."

"Do they think some flowers and herbs will prevent their loved ones from running off or being stolen?"

Within the past few weeks there had been odd reports made to House Vakara: corpses were going missing. Fresh ones, and always those of people who had died in accidents or by illness. They ranged in ages, but none had been older than their forties.

The truly odd thing was that the bodies always came back. A little more decomposed, but otherwise none the worse for wear. Except for one case a couple weeks ago when a returned body rose of its own accord and attacked its family.

"These sorts of situations are rare," her father had said after dealing with it. "But sometimes the dead refuse to stay dead. Unfulfilled desires, vendettas, revenge...Strong wills have a habit of lingering. When they happen with the recently departed, it's always the body's own spirit that takes possession."

"What does that mean, then?" Risha had asked. "That it's happening so often, and with random spirits?"

Her father had sighed. "I do not know yet. It could simply be that the more spirits accumulate here, the more restless they become. Either that, or someone is taking them."

Darsha glared at her now from under long lashes. Her eyes were rimmed with a fine line of kajal, an unnecessarily dramatic touch to an already beautiful face. "Burial wreaths blessed by the Vakara family will give them some comfort."

Not to mention line our pockets. To the Vakaras, death was a business. Risha had spent many hours of her childhood sitting on the floor beside her mother, stringing garlands together and learning calligraphy to write out blessings and spells.

"Do you need my help?"

"No, I called you in here because I wanted to give you a bit of news." Her mother put down the garland she was working on. "It seems King Ferdinand has extended an invitation to a few lords of the Parithvian Parliament to discuss strengthening our alliance."

Parithvi was Vaega's on-and-off ally when it came to matters of warfare. Even though there had been border disputes far back in their history, they remained ever eager to keep the trade routes between them open.

That, and the Vakara family had something no other House could claim: They had strong Parithvian blood running through their veins. Their line had been created centuries ago when a distant Parithvian relative of the then-late king had been handed the crown when the remaining two successors had fatally dueled one another for the privilege.

"That doesn't sound like him." The king frequently ignored outside counsel, choosing instead to cling to his carefully chosen and cultivated advisors.

"Recent events have . . . inspired him to take action. He wants to make sure we can rely on Parithvian support, should we need it. But that's not all." Darsha's eyes crinkled with barely concealed delight. "I've heard one of the Parithvian lords has an eligible son."

Risha fought not to sigh. "Amaa, is now really the time? I'm close to—"

A servant entered and Risha shut her mouth, waiting for the woman to refill her mother's teacup. Once the woman left, she went on in a softer voice. "I'm close to figuring out how to deal with these lingering spirits."

"Oh, yes." Somehow her mother made even the act of sipping tea a wry gesture. "Gaining access to Mortri. And how is that progressing?" Her mother looked pointedly at the grave soil staining the knees of her salwar.

A few months ago, the remarks would have cut deeper. Darsha had argued Risha was wasting her time and her powers, that she could potentially get hurt. But Risha was now used to her mother's vague disapproval, considering her mother vaguely disapproved of everything she did.

"I just have to keep trying," Risha insisted. "I'll punch a way from Vitae to Mortri if I have to."

"And what then? Even if the spirits and Conjurers are dealt with, where does that leave you as the heir to House Vakara?"

She hadn't thought that far ahead. Everything in her was too focused on Mortri, on her responsibility to take care of the dead plaguing Nexus.

"You know," Darsha said, setting her cup delicately on its saucer, "being married to a foreign dignitary comes with certain benefits."

Risha knew exactly what her mother was getting at. It was no secret the Holy King, whose line had long ago been blessed by the gods, had no heirs to speak of. As the descendants of Vaegan monarchs who had lain with the gods—and who had never held the monarchy themselves—the heirs of each House were therefore in contention for the honor.

"I'm talking about protection," Darsha said. "His Majesty has thankfully absolved us of suspicion from this attack, but that won't stop the citizens from whispering that it was some traitorous stunt." Her voice softened. "Risha, I want this plan to work, but it's unrealistic—and quite frankly, naive. Besides, you're twenty-one. When I was your age I'd already been married a full year."

Like that's something to aspire to? Risha thought, but didn't dare voice.

Darsha picked up the garland in her lap and resumed her work. "I'll discuss the idea with your father. I won't do anything until he agrees."

"So it's all right to get his permission, but not mine?"

Darsha gave her a pointed look. Risha knew it was meaningless to argue. Meaningless to tell her mother she had never cared about things like romance and partners and tying her life to another person.

Her legs ached as she climbed the stairs to her bedroom. She could still feel grit in the creases of her palms, her feet sore after traversing the unruly path to Mortri. Also lingering was her annoyance at Taesia for disturbing her in the necropolis and catching her in a moment of failure.

Risha paused on the landing halfway up the tower. The door to Saya's room was ajar, so she peeked inside to find her younger sister hunched over a giant tome spread across her desk. Its pages were yellowed with age, and Saya turned them with the care of one who often handled brittle things.

Risha knocked on the door. "Studying?"

"I have an exam tomorrow."

"What subject?" Risha drifted into her sister's room. It was well furnished, save for a tattered green armchair Saya had "rescued" from the university's library before they could throw it out.

"Planar properties." Saya hid a yawn behind her hand. "It's mostly theoretical work."

Risha leaned against the desk to get a better view of the book. It was open to a spread of the Four Realms, a sketch done by one of the first planar researchers. It depicted the realms—Vitae, Noctus, Solara, and Mortri—as points on a circle, the pathways connecting them forming a geometric pattern called the Cosmic Scale.

Four worlds, four realms, four gods, all on the same plane of existence.

Except now the roads between those realms were cut, the Cosmic Scale no longer in alignment. Each of them floated independently of one another, abandoned by the gods that had birthed them.

"I hated planar properties." Ironic, all things considered. Risha stole a glimpse of the next page, filled with blocks of text awaiting Saya's analysis. "Do you need help?"

Saya shook her head. Her dark, thick hair was starting to curl under her ears. Ever since she had been comfortable enough to publicly announce she was a girl, she had started growing it out the way she'd always wanted to. "I should be fine, but thanks. I just need to get all the theories straight." Yawning again, she reached for the plate of carob cakes sitting on the desk. Saya had the kitchen staff wrapped around her little finger.

Risha's stomach gave a loud grumble, and she snatched a cake for herself. Using her power in large doses tended to give her the appetite of a bear waking from hibernation. "I can bring up some tea," she offered around a mouthful.

Saya looked her up and down. "You're worrying about me when you should be worrying about yourself. You tried the barrier again?"

"I just need more time with it."

Saya didn't seem convinced. She set down her half-eaten cake, tracing the line between Vitae and Mortri in the book. "The planar points will align in a couple of months at Godsnight. What if you can't open the path even then?"

Risha threw a chunk of cake at her sister, hitting her square in the forehead. "First Amaa, now you. I'll get it open. And if I don't..." She thought of the souls she had found in the necropolis, that she'd tried and failed to cross over to Mortri, and wondered if it was only a matter of time until they, too, rained destruction on the city.

A knock sounded at the open door. A footman bowed on the threshold.

"The city guard is here. They're saying there's a rogue spirit near the basilica in need of banishing."

Their father was out on business, which meant the task fell to them. Darsha—having married into the family—had no necromantic magic to speak of.

"We'll be down shortly," Risha said with a pounding heart. As much as she didn't want to waste time, she needed to change into clothes more befitting her station.

"Being a Vakara means not only being a messenger of Thana, but a protector of the people," Rath had often told her. He was always striking in his necromancer gear: a black leather jerkin with gold buttons, bracers on his forearms over loose black sleeves, and dark leather trousers tucked into knee-high boots. A belt with necromantic tools and weapons always hung at his hips, identical to Risha's own.

Saya was already waiting for her at the bottom of the tower. They found one of the gray-clad city guards shifting uneasily on his feet in the courtyard. Seeing the two of them, he bowed.

"We have need of your services, my ladies."

"Our carriage will follow your horse," Risha answered.

Darsha had come out of the main sitting room, gripping two garlands in her hands. She hurried to her daughters and threw the garlands over their heads. Risha opened her mouth to protest as Saya kicked her ankle to stay quiet.

"Leave them on," Darsha pleaded. "And be careful. If your father comes home while you're gone, I'll send him to help."

"I'm sure we'll be able to take care of it ourselves." Risha turned toward the gate. Saya hugged their mother before trotting after.

"You're being cold," Saya muttered.

"I'm not. I'm being professional in front of the messenger, like Paaja would."

"Just because she cares about your safety—"

This time it was Risha who kicked her to be quiet as the carriage rattled up to the interior gate of the villa. They climbed inside in silence.

The carriage swayed and rattled on its way to the basilica of Thana. The small space was flooded with the scent of their garlands, syrupy and medicinal and making Risha nauseated. She raised a hand to pull hers off, then let it drop with a sigh.

Nexus was shaped like a four-pointed star, with a basilica in each point. When the carriage rolled to a stop in the western point and the door was pulled open, Risha saw the basilica ablaze with torches burning back the dark. Its tall stone buttresses led up to an impressive dome, figures of skeletons in various positions of prayer sculpted around its perimeter. The wide stone steps led to three sets of closed doors, barred and locked for the night.

Once, this had been more than a place for those who worshipped Thana to make offerings. Once, this had been the portal house to Mortri, where priests would lay out bodies within the stepwell to ensure their spirits would journey to the realm of the dead and find peace, torture, or rebirth.

But the portals had been sealed for five hundred years, and they were no longer able to make that journey. Vitae was overrun. Even though the Vakaras could keep the spirits dormant for a time, keep them lingering in that blackness between Vitae and Mortri, there was still no way to disperse them until the portal reopened.

The residue of its power still lingered. That pathway, that connective tissue between realms, with its scent of dark soil and aged things.

Members of the city guard stood around the basilica square. They were all on high alert, looking to the steps with hands on their sword hilts.

The rogue spirit shifted from the shadows into flickering torchlight. There was something off about it, something she couldn't quite discern from this distance.

Before she could approach, a guard with a black mustache blocked her path.

"Watch out, my lady. It's already harmed two of my men."

"I'm well familiar with the dangers, sir. But if we are to do our work, we must know what we're up against."

The officer nodded and sheepishly dropped his arm.

Risha and Saya drew closer to the shambling, shivering thing on the basilica steps. When they could finally make out its shape, Saya inhaled through her teeth.

"How did it manage to do that?" she whispered.

The spirit wasn't merely a rampaging ghost—it had taken hold of a heavily decayed body, mostly bone with a few hunks of gray, tattered meat. Risha wondered how it hadn't fallen to pieces yet when she noticed the vines strung through the skeleton like sinew. The plant fibers were threaded across its rib cage and twined around its arms and legs, some of them bearing fang-like thorns.

The skeleton shuffled up the steps, or tried to. Its bony hands scrabbled ineffectively at a buttress. Its moan sent a shiver down Risha's spine, hollow and echoing. No matter how often she witnessed a violent spirit, their voices still cut through her, into whatever animal instinct told her to *run*.

Saya trembled beside her. Risha took a deep breath, and then another.

"Let's bind it," she whispered.

They both opened pouches on their belts and pulled out pieces of red string. Risha allowed her fingers to work in familiar patterns, threading the string between them much like the vines through the skeleton's body. She created the pattern for binding and immediately felt a warm rush of power, concentrated into the spell between her hands.

But Saya was a little slower, not as practiced at creating the patterns. At the sensation of Risha's power flaring up, the spirit turned and fixed them with dark, hollow eye sockets. Its jaw lay slack, and from beyond it issued a high, terrible scream that made everyone in the square flinch.

The skeleton lurched toward them, stumbling off the basilica steps with hands extended. The officer with the mustache drew his sword and stood between them and the approaching spirit.

"*MY EYES*," it screeched. "*HE TOOK MY EYES*."

The string slipped from Saya's fingers.

"Saya," Risha said firmly. "You can do this. Focus on the pattern for binding." She turned to the spirit as it shuffled closer. She could smell the rot emanating from its bones. "Who took your eyes?" she asked to buy time for her sister.

"*THE PRIEST*," the thing hissed, and another, softer scream was layered over it. "*I STOLE HIS GOLD. HE TOOK MY EYES*."

"Perhaps you oughtn't have stolen his gold, then," she said. The officer gave her a pained expression over his shoulder.

"Got it," Saya said as her power flared. With both of them concentrating on the binding spell, the skeleton froze in place with hands outstretched. It shuddered and keened, fighting against them. Risha felt it knock up against her power, desperate to break the connection, but she clenched her jaw and focused harder.

Then the skeleton's head snapped back. Risha followed its empty gaze to the roof of the nearest building and twitched in surprise. A shadow was crouched above the eaves, watching the events unfold in the square.

"Someone's up there!" she shouted.

The guards reacted immediately, racing toward the shadow. The figure darted across the roof and jumped down to the street, rolling to soften its fall. On the fringes of torchlight, the figure resolved itself into the shape of a man.

He glanced her way. Covering his face was a mask in the likeness of a skull.

Giving her a quick salute, he turned and fled.

"Risha," Saya gritted out.

Risha shook herself. She and Saya pulled their strings taut in unison, the pattern stretching to its limit, before they each twisted their hands and let the string snap.

The spirit gave one more vengeful wail before the skeleton collapsed in a heap of bone and vines. Risha felt the spirit dissipate, retreating toward the inter-realm void.

Saya rested her hands on her knees to catch her breath. Risha approached the dead thing, frowning. Whenever a corpse happened to be raised by a spirit, it was usually a body freshly dead. She had never seen a skeleton animated this way before.

She skirted around the skeleton. Under the eaves where the masked man had crouched was a circle of chalk. Torchlight flickered along its outer edge, barely touching the design of a seven-pointed star contained inside, triangles layered over one another.

Risha went cold. It reminded her of Saya's textbook, the Cosmic Scale upon which the realms sat. Of the circle drawn too close to the Bone Palace for the king's comfort.

Old, forbidden magic. Demonic magic.

Conjuration.

She stared down the street where the man in the skull mask had disappeared. If he'd used this symbol, this magic, to raise the skeleton . . .

That meant Conjurers really could replicate necromancy.

The officer with the mustache drew up at her side. "Thank you, my ladies, for your service tonight. We will dispose of the body in whatever manner you suggest is best."

"Burn it first, then separate the remaining bone fragments. Bury them in different plots." Risha took the garland from around her neck and handed it to him. "Place this on top of the body before it burns."

"Very good, my lady."

"Did you happen to catch that man?"

"Ah . . . no. But you can be sure we'll be on the lookout for him. I'll add it to the incident report."

She almost told him not to bother. She would report this to her father as soon as he returned home, and tomorrow he would relate it to King Ferdinand. But the high commissioner's guards seemed to love paperwork.

Risha hesitated as she passed the skeleton again, Taesia's request for calciphite taunting her. It would be easy to snap off a rib and put it in her pocket.

Instead, she wrapped an arm around Saya's waist—once again finding it unfair how much taller her little sister was—and watched the guards bundle the bones in canvas to haul them away. She couldn't shake the oily, queasy feeling the spirit's presence had left within her. She had built herself around that feeling over the years, the sweet yet sickening release of her power. Some days it came as a soft song, a clear chime she couldn't help but follow. Today, it came as a low, pealing gong, a reverberation through her hollow spaces.

The Vakaras were the only necromancers in all of Vitae. The spells were in their blood, their marrow. The thought of others using it, wielding it so haphazardly, set her teeth on edge.

The basilica stood cold and quiet and empty. There was no telling how much worse this would get before she could open the way to Mortri. When or where the Conjurers would strike next.

She and her sister were quiet on the carriage ride back until Saya suddenly groaned and put her face in her hands.

"I'm going to fail my exam tomorrow," she muttered.

III

Angelica Mardova, stuck in a meeting she'd long tuned out of, wanted badly to play her violin.

But that wasn't in the cards for her this morning. Wasn't supposed to be in her cards at all, according to the university mage.

Angelica scratched her forearm and glowered out the window of the Bone Palace. The city was drenched in morning sun, people bustling through the palace square. The longer she went without playing her instruments, the itchier and hotter her skin felt. The mage assured her it was normal, completely normal. Every time he said so, Angelica wanted to take one of the many paperweights on his desk and smash it through the window.

"My lady?"

A servant bowed and offered a glass of cut crystal. Angelica took it without peering at what was inside; it was too early to hope for alcohol.

Her mother's voice carried over. "Storms in the north have been delaying merchant ships, and now they want air mages to journey with them for protection."

Angelica forced herself to return to the conversation. They were standing in one of the palace's receiving rooms, large windows high-lighting plush furniture upholstered in shades of white and green. All the receiving rooms had a theme. Angelica had thought it clever when she was younger, but now regarded it as gaudy. The room they'd been led to was Deia's Chamber, an unsubtle nod to the Mardovas. The walls were plastered with paper embossed with golden flame-like designs against a crimson background. Beyond the crown molding, the ceiling was lacquered blue with a golden setting for the chandelier, as if to mirror the sun in the sky.

Adela Mardova stood before a large pastoral painting of northern Vaega, the ridge of the Daccadian Mountains a dark, distant silhouette. She too held a glass in her hands as she faced the king, not daring to take a sip before he did.

Ferdinand Accardi was in his middle years, his dark hair and beard liberally seasoned with salt, a webbing of lines around his mouth and at the corners of his eyes. He sat flanked by two of his beloved advisors standing with hands clasped behind their backs. Like dogs awaiting orders from their master.

He was called the Holy King, which only added to Vaega's greatest insult to the surrounding countries: their connection to all four gods. Because no one else—not the empress of Azuna, not the heads of Parliament in Parithvi, not the prime minister of Marii—had been given the same honor. So Parithvi and Marii kept their prayers solely to Deia, and Azuna didn't pray at all anymore.

Seeing the way Adela hesitated, Ferdinand smiled slightly and lifted his own glass. "How many air mages can we spare?" he asked once he swallowed.

"We can pull a dozen from the elementalist division, but it'll thin their numbers," her mother answered.

"Air is the rarest element to master," Angelica added. "We can spare a few, but better to ask for volunteers from the university."

Adela gave her a pleased nod as one of Ferdinand's advisors scoffed.

"The university mages aren't used to labor," Don Soler said. He was a balding man with thick sideburns who often reminded Angelica of a hissing ferret. He was not only one of the king's most trusted advisors, but also his spymaster. "One day aboard a merchant ship would make them faint."

"It's either that or sending our battle mages," Angelica said coolly. "And who's to say if the Conjurers will strike again?"

Don Soler's brow furrowed, but Ferdinand nodded at this solemn reminder. "We can't take too many risks," the king agreed.

Angelica hid her satisfied smirk by finally taking a sip of her drink, which was light and lemony. She was always pleased when the king sided with her, but even sweeter were the moments she could step on one of his beloved advisors in the process.

As one of the four Houses—the first to be established, in fact—the Mardovas were called upon to deal with anything concerning the elements, the natural gifts Deia had long ago given to the realm of Vitae. Not everyone was born an elementalist, and those who were could only master one or two elements. Three, in rare instances.

Only the Mardovas, blessed by Deia's blood, could master them all.

But beyond their powers, the Mardovas held a long tradition of keeping close to the ruling seat of Vaega. Angelica had been groomed for it by her mother, who had taught her deference and decorum, strategy and servitude. The Mardovas were known for breeding the best mages, sending them to the court, to the university, to the battlefields. For twenty-one years Adela had filled her head with possibilities, promising greatness. Esteem.

"A scepter of ice, a throne of obsidian, a cloak of storm wind, and a crown of flame," her mother used to whisper as she tucked Angelica in at night. "They'll be yours, someday. The king will have no choice but to name you as his heir. You'll be the strongest ruler this realm has ever seen."

Angelica realized she was scratching her arm again and dropped her hand back to her side. It didn't escape her mother's notice.

"My ladies, what about the use of corona sails?" asked the other advisor, Don Cassian. He was tall and thin as a rail with a head of prematurely gray hair. Angelica supposed that was the effect a lifetime of politics had on a person. "Do they not convert the light of the sun into energy?"

"No access to Solara means no corona silk," Angelica said. "It's a resource even more precious than our battle mages." The inter-realm import had once been common enough, but after the Sealing five hundred years ago, the precious little left now drove ever-increasing prices on the market.

The king turned to Don Cassian. "Send a letter to the Lastriders asking if they know of any reserve of corona silk. Send one to the Cyrs as well, just in case." Don Cassian bowed and left. The king continued, "The Vakaras have given me a troublesome report."

"Oh?" Adela's tone was careful. Her mouth had thinned at the mention of the other Houses.

"The Conjurers have made a second attempt at the Thana basilica. Not to summon multiple spirits as they did the first time, but to raise a single one using their occult methods."

Angelica exchanged a look with her mother. "I thought only the Vakaras were able to do such a thing?" Adela asked.

"I think it's safe to say that is no longer true."

And in a city infested with the dead, that could only mean more trouble on the horizon. Though Angelica couldn't help but notice the tic of her mother's eyebrow, her chance at casting further suspicion on House Vakara come and gone.

"Do you believe they are indeed radicals?" Adela asked. "Rebels?"

Don Soler clucked his tongue. "Such a display so close to the Bone Palace? What else could they be?"

"Then what was the purpose of the spirit at the basilica?"

Don Soler hesitated. "We are not yet sure. I am working to identify who their leader is and what they want."

"Do you believe they have anything to do with Tambour Lake?" Ferdinand asked.

Reports said the eastern lake had entirely dried up, leaving nothing but a large bowl of mud and rotting fish behind. While there had been incidents like it in recent years—the oceans receding bit by bit, the edges of Vaega's dense forests withering, and now crop fields hit with disease—this was the most recent instance of Vitae's slow decline.

What was especially damning was that it had happened the same day as the spirit attack.

"I'm not certain how they could be involved, Your Majesty," Adela said. "Considering how far Tambour Lake is from the city."

Angelica cleared her throat, gaining their attention. Her mind had been churning with some way to explain the connection between the two incidents, and she knew she'd regret not sharing her theory while she could.

"The Sealing has resulted in a blockage of the Cosmic Scale's energy, creating a buildup along Vitae's barriers with nowhere to go," Angelica explained. "Without that energy, Vitae suffers."

Ferdinand nodded gravely. The king was not an elementalist, had no magic to speak of, and so had to rely on the Houses' input.

"However, the Conjurers have found a way to tap into that energy in order to perform their...rituals," Angelica went on. "I believe the more pent-up energy their rituals feed off of, the faster Vitae feels the effects. Tambour Lake drying up the same day as their attack isn't a coincidence."

Don Soler inhaled sharply. Adela tried and failed to hide her frown.

"If this is truly the case, then it is imperative we prevent the Conjurers from making further attempts," the king said. "Vaega is already feeling the effects of the Sealing. I won't have them making it worse."

Adela bowed slightly. "Your Majesty, are we sure we should be holding the Autumn Equinox Festival next week? It could be an opportunity for them to strike."

We, Angelica noted, not *you.*

Ferdinand sighed. "We will have the full force of the militia at our beck and call. I'll also be calling upon the Hunters. They'll work closely with the city guard and the militia."

Adela quickly covered her surprise with a gracious nod. "Very well, Your Majesty."

Militia. That was House Cyr's territory, meaning more opportunity for the Cyrs to put themselves in the position the Mardovas most wanted: at Ferdinand's side.

"And what happens once the Conjurers are caught?" Angelica couldn't help but ask.

"That's been a subject of debate," Ferdinand replied with a sideways glance at Don Soler, who pursed his mouth. "I've been speaking with Prelate Lezzaro, who believes these people are simply misguided. Like us, he wants to figure out why they're doing this."

Angelica had met Prelate Lezzaro many times, a genial man in his late middle years who oversaw the four basilicas of Nexus. Although he wasn't considered as holy as the king and Houses, his status and enduring benevolence gave him a reputation as someone who could do little wrong, helped by the fact he came from a long line of devoted priests.

Showing compassion to the Conjurers, however, might put a strain on his relationship with the public, if not the Holy King himself.

"If they truly are rebels, they will be dealt with swiftly and severely," the king said. "Still, the prelate has asked to speak at the Autumn Equinox, so we will learn more about his intentions then."

By the time they wrapped things up and said their goodbyes, Angelica was exhausted from maintaining her bland, polite expression. She was all too glad to escape the offensive chamber and the king's hard-to-read gaze.

"Don't think one or two smart comments will be enough to maintain your current good graces with His Majesty," her mother said once they were far enough away. Adela Mardova was the epitome of graceful as she strode through the white halls with hands clasped before her, all gentle curves with a refined face and dark, hooded eyes. Angelica was proud to say she had inherited most of her mother's features, from her sorrel-toned skin to the wave in her hair, but it was offset by her late father's contributions of a small, pointed nose and a petite stature matched with a thick waist. "Or chiming in with *theories* you haven't run by me first."

Angelica's arms were beginning to tingle. "It was stuffy in there. I couldn't concentrate."

Adela raised an eyebrow. "Angel, my darling, must I remind you what exactly is at stake here?"

A scepter of ice, a throne of obsidian, a cloak of storm wind, and a crown of flame.

"No," Angelica said, voice low.

They emerged into the atrium. It was wide and spacious, sunlight from the overhead glass dome bouncing off pristine white walls and marble floor. Guards in dark blue livery stood attentive in the corners, some with pins upon their lapels to denote if they bore an element.

There had once been lavish displays of art strewn through the hall made of silver and gold and gemstone, all long since sold when Vaega had needed to finance past wars. The starkness of the atrium made its morbid architecture stand out all the better, from the columns composed of vertebrae in the vestibule to the vaulted ceiling supported by massive, stark ribs. The ribs fanned out and curved like hooks, giving the appearance they truly were in the belly of some beast.

There was a myth the Bone Palace was built from actual bone. That when a horde of Other-Realm beasts had descended upon the young city, the gods had worked together to slay them, and the remains had been broken down and sculpted in the Vaegan style.

Angelica had a feeling it was merely marble put together with ox blood mortar to help preserve its structure.

"The king needs to see you as invaluable," Adela said softly as they passed under those monstrous ribs. "You can't afford to be distracted."

Their voices were too quiet to carry, but Angelica still spared a wary glance at the guards along the walls. This sort of talk under the roof of the Bone Palace was surely courting danger.

Adela had always positioned herself and Angelica to readily accept orders and carry them out quickly and efficiently. To be seen as irreplaceable. That way, Ferdinand, heirless, without even bastards to inherit the throne, would have no choice but to appoint the Mardovas as his successors.

"We'll work on air when we return to the villa," her mother said. She reached out and brushed Angelica's hair back over her shoulder. "We'll use the bridge over the pond, as the currents are stronger there."

Angelica was suddenly pricked with shame. This was something elementalist children did: go out into the gardens or the fields to grasp the fundamental principles of their elements, the most basic skills that laid the foundation for their later careers as mages.

She stepped out of Adela's reach. "There's no need. I'm perfectly capable of using air."

"With an aid," Adela reminded her bluntly.

"Father didn't have a problem with my instruments."

"Because your father, Thana guide his soul, was far too indulgent with you. I receive reports on the other Houses, you know. The Vakara heir is strong, reliable, and highly intelligent. The Cyr heir seems to be lacking in power, but he is consistently polite and graceful, and the gentry is fond of him. And as for the Lastrider heir, he is formidable and influential, as is his sister, and they do not hesitate to use their shadow magic as it pleases them."

Angelica gritted her teeth. For as long as she had known her, Taesia Lastrider had always been a rough-and-tumble creature who reminded her strongly of a time she'd seen an overactive monkey at a carnival. How could Angelica be so inadequate in her own powers when an utter fool like Taesia was so fluent in hers? "I'm stronger than they are."

"Are you?"

It was worse than a slap. Angelica's throat tightened, the crease where her palms met slippery with sweat.

"They see you as a stray spark in a field of dead wheat," Adela went on. "In light of this new threat, it's imperative we do all we can to prove House Mardova is capable and ready for rule."

Before Angelica could nod, a peculiar sensation crept up her spine. Her footsteps faltered, and she turned around.

Above the atrium was a mezzanine linking the eastern and western wings of the palace. As soon as her eyes landed on it, a figure darted out of sight.

"When is the last time you played?" the mage asked, skimming his notes.

Angelica ran her tongue across her teeth and didn't answer. Of course he knew she'd broken his rule.

"My lady, I'm here to help, not hinder," said the mage. Eran Liolle was one of the top elementalist professors from the university, and the cadence of his voice was perfect for giving lectures, smooth and unwavering. "If there is no communication between us, I'm afraid I cannot help you. I doubt you would like to see all your effort—and funds—wasted."

Hiring a man like Eran Liolle was admittedly costly. She had done her best to hide it from her mother so far—a bribe here and there never hurt—but it wouldn't be much longer until Adela found out.

"We've had five sessions now, and barely made any progress." Eran pushed his glasses up his nose, all the better to show the exaggerated disappointment in his gray eyes. He was typical Vaegan stock, with brown skin and thick, dark hair. Although in his midthirties, he had made a name for himself by mastering three elements when most mages only mastered one or two.

They were in his office at the University of Nexus. His desk was piled with paperwork and gifts that students had given him over the years—mostly paperweights. But he never sat there; he always chose the blue armchair across from hers, beside a wide window with a view of the campus below.

She had never attended the university. Her mother and father had insisted on homeschooling her to keep her away from prying peers, always wary of exploitation and gossip.

She wondered how much of a difference it would have made had she been taught by someone like Eran much sooner.

"Two days," she finally said. "Since I played."

Eran made a note of it. "Which instrument?"

"The piccolo."

"And what was the purpose?"

Angelica tapped her fingers on the armrest. "There was a hornet's nest in a tree in the garden. I used the piccolo to dispose of it."

"How did that go?"

Angelica had stood a good distance from the tree in question, piccolo poised at her lips. She'd begun with a quick trill, forming a current of air and directing it to the tree using the notes of her song. It had plucked the hornet's nest from the branches and sent it flying over the garden wall, but not before a few hornets escaped. Angelica had gotten rid of them with a couple more trills, then ran back inside in case they had a mind for revenge.

"They're gone," she said simply.

The mage leaned forward, bracing his elbows on his knees. "Do you think you could have done the same without the piccolo?"

She sneered. "Is that not why I'm here?"

Eran nodded and gathered his notes. "Good point. Let's move on to practical, then."

The university was one of the many prides of Nexus. The campus consisted of long buildings fanning out in a circle with the main hall at its center, surrounded by well-manicured gardens where students could relax or study if the weather was nice enough. A statue of the university's architect stood between two symmetrical lawns, scrolls of bronze tucked under one arm as the other pointed in the direction of the main hall.

Angelica spotted a cluster of students sprawled on the grass as the mage led her through a colonnade mostly blocked by ivy. Some were half-heartedly attempting to do schoolwork as they chatted, enjoying a peaceful moment together. They couldn't have been more than a few years younger than her, but somehow she seemed so far away from them, as if she were observing through a telescope.

One of them spotted her through a gap in the ivy, and their conversation ceased. She was every inch the proper lady in her lilac dress, the front of her bodice embroidered with silver leaves under a tapered half jacket. They stared at her as she had been staring at them, sneaking a glimpse into another world.

Then one of them pointed two fingers down in a V shape, a gesture that would have made Angelica's mother roast her on the spot were she to use it. A couple students gasped and the others sniggered behind their hands, watching for her reaction.

Doing her best to ignore the heat rising to her face, she dismissed them with a simple turn of her head.

Eran led her down the stairs to the familiar underground practice arenas. It was cooler here, and the smell of grass and pollen was replaced with something heavier and darker. Angelica took in a lungful of it, shivering like a horse shaking off flies. There was no mistaking the scent of life magic, the way the elements braided together into something complex and divine, soil and ozone and smoke.

And something ephemeral that reminded her of the first stages of dawn, or the quiet creeping of fog over a valley. Expansive and intangible.

Eran found an empty arena and gestured her inside. Angelica greeted the large stone chamber with something she convinced herself wasn't dread, only impatience. The arena was vast, with a high ceiling and a circular depression in the floor used as a stage for students during exams.

"You used the piccolo to shape the air you needed to remove the hornet's nest," the mage said. "Walk through it with me."

"A quick succession of higher notes gets the current to form. Sharp notes move it upward and forward, and flat notes move it down and back."

"Can you feel the current as you play?"

"Yes."

"And if you don't play?"

She pressed her lips together.

"Let's see if you can re-create it." Eran took a step back and pointed to a round target hanging from the ceiling, painted with a red bull's-eye. There were several of them in the arena, but this one was the closest, and Angelica had the distinct feeling he was going easy on her.

Bastard.

"People assume air is the easiest element to master," Eran said. "That it's as simple as blowing a breath and making a ship sail. We both know there's more to it, just as we know earth is stubborn and water is unruly." He cleared his throat. "And fire is fatal."

Angelica's fingers twitched.

"Air comes from the part of an elementalist that rests below the breastbone and above the stomach. It expands and recedes with the rhythm of your lungs, and the stronger your core, the more refined the technique. Focus on your breathing, and let it guide your power."

Angelica breathed. Whenever her mother attempted to practice with her, Angelica always grew too irritated to focus. It was especially difficult when they worked with air, as the element was her mother's favorite.

In, out. She could almost trace the shape of her lungs, the weaving of veins around them. Her vision narrowed as she concentrated on the air before her, attempting to sort it into individual strands. She just needed one to form a current.

But they kept slipping away from her, dissolving tauntingly back into the flow of the room. She tried again, forcefully grabbing whatever she could. They snuck through her fingers, whispered teasingly against her palms.

"My lady," Eran warned her, but she ignored him, violent heat spreading through her.

With her piccolo, she could have easily done this test ten times by now. But her instruments were considered an impediment by elementalist standards, far too bothersome to bring wherever she went.

Only those who were weak in their power required a conduit, whether it be music or writing or dance. She had been ten when she realized a single note on her violin could produce a lick of flame. It had been revelatory, satisfying, but one look at her mother's dismayed face had forever linked her passion with shame.

It had become a joke among the mages: she was a Mardova capable of using all the elements and yet was so limited in their use. She was an embarrassment to her line who could never hope to become a professor or court mage.

Never hope to be a queen.

As she dug her nails into her palm, something popped and flared. Her eyes flew open. The target was on fire, smoke spiraling toward the vaulted ceiling.

Eran ran to one of the water barrels lined up against the wall and siphoned its contents into a wet, rippling ribbon that shot across the room and doused the flames with a hiss. The target fell to the floor, charred and crackling.

Angelica fought to catch her breath. She reached for the itchy skin of her forearm, but Eran caught her wrist. His fingers lingered a moment too long against her burning skin, and Angelica glared at his hand until he let go.

"You need to learn patience, my lady," he said. "Forcing the elements never gives you the result you want. You must work in tandem."

Patience. She had been told to be patient all her fucking life, and it had gotten her nowhere.

Eran removed his glasses, now flecked with water, and cleaned them on his shirt. "We'll end a little early today. Until we meet next week, I don't want you to play any instruments, even ones not associated with your elements."

"But—"

"You'll have to use your powers organically, or not at all." Eran replaced his glasses and gave her the look that typically ended their sessions, exasperation mixed with pity. "Except fire."

Angelica stormed out of the arena, not bothering to wait for his offer to escort her. There was no relief from burning the target; on the contrary, it made the itch within her worse, maddening and painful and no closer to relief.

When she returned to the Mardova villa, Angelica stopped within the antechamber made up of noble dark woods and black marble. Light from the upper windows filtered through the gloom, striping the long, curving staircase with wheals of amber. Her stepmother stood under a fresco of the four main elements, a looming, blatant reminder to guests of which House they were calling upon.

Unlike the colorful frescoes displayed in fine establishments throughout the city, this one had abandoned beauty for truth. At the bottom was a depiction of earth, solid and heavy, the world's foundation. Soil pressed against a figure futilely attempting to not get caught between it and the jagged rocks at his back, hungry as teeth. To the left was water, gushing violently down a valley as it broke free of its dam, towering above a sleepy village in its path. To the right was air, bending trees in a turbulent storm that wended into a cyclone, people and animals caught within its might.

And at the top: fire, red and resplendent, eating a man alive as he burned within his house of splendor, his priceless possessions made useless as the fire consumed them. Its source came from the open mouth of a gilded wyvern curled around the fresco, its body forming a connective circle between the elements.

Angelica had often stared at the fresco as a girl, morbidly drawn to it. The Mardova line was not one of gaiety; they had come from ruthless stock, tracing their origins all the way back to the Headless King, a monarch of singular cruelty who had condemned hundreds of people to the chopping block, later deposed by his god-blessed son and subjected to the same fate.

Her stepmother's smiling face proved a startling contrast to the brutality depicted behind her. The guards closed the front doors as a serving girl hurried forward with a glass of mint water balanced on a silver tray. Angelica took a long, bracing sip to rid the bitter, ashy taste from her mouth.

When she lowered the glass, her stepmother was standing before her. Miko was lovely, with a heart-shaped face and straight black hair beginning to turn silver at her temples. Although she had emigrated from Azuna thirty years ago, she still wore traditional Azunese clothing of a wrap dress with a silken waist sash and long, trailing sleeves.

"You're home later than expected," Miko said, her accent a curious blend of her native Azunese and adopted Vaegan. "Adela came back hours ago."

"I had things to see to." Angelica swept past her toward the stairs. That blast of fire in the arena hadn't been enough, and she achingly thought of her violin stored away in the recital chamber.

"How was your meeting with His Majesty this morning?"

Angelica half turned, the last of her patience worn to a single frayed thread. "Didn't my mother already tell you? What use is it asking me?"

Miko's warm smile fled. She opened her mouth, then shook her head with a sigh as she thought better of it. "Very well. I will leave you to rest." She strode off in the direction of the gardens.

Angelica exhaled forcefully, pushing out the hint of guilt. Once Miko's footsteps faded, she walked to the fresco.

Four elements. Four gods. Four Houses. Each of them was like these elements, all the good and bad of them. Risha Vakara was earth—stubborn, as Eran had said. Nikolas Cyr was air, flighty and unpredictable. Dante and Taesia Lastrider were water: wily, unruly, adaptable.

And she...

Angelica touched her fingertips to the fire coming from the wyvern's mouth. She traced the golden curve of it, a familiar hunger gnawing at her gut.

Angelica was fire, ready to burn whoever stood in House Mardova's way to ash.

IV

Nikolas Cyr tested the weight of the sword in his hand and briefly fantasized about plunging it into his father's neck.

He figured it probably wasn't the best thought to have when standing in the middle of a basilica.

The priests approached carrying pieces of gilded armor. They wore long tunics of yellow silk and baggy white trousers, their eyes rimmed in shimmering powder. The oldest of them bore shaven heads to show the sun tattoos inked onto the base of their skulls.

A few of them were Lumins. Their light familiars hovered at their shoulders like large fireflies, steadfast and calm. Not like Nikolas's own familiar, which flitted around his head in excitement. Nikolas sent Lux a sharp reprimand, and it pulsed in resignation before drifting toward his collar.

The Lumin priests had Solarian blood, their hair whitish blond and their skin golden brown. It wasn't an uncommon thing to find those of mixed blood in Nexus, particularly with the influx of refugees after the Sealing. It was generally expected they should enter into the service of the basilicas.

When they were constantly turned away from other trades, they often had no choice.

Nikolas held his breath as they began to buckle armor onto his body. The nave echoed the creak of tightened straps, the snapping of a clasp. The cuirass sat heavy on his shoulders, clamping around his ribs like a jungle snake. Greaves locked his knees in place, vambraces weighing down his arms. Pauldrons rose from either shoulder in imitation of wings.

When they were done, the priests stepped back, heads lowered. Nikolas looked beyond them to the watchers on the sidelines, the novices, curates, and curious worshippers lingering between colonnades of gold-veined marble. Among them stood Prelate Lezzaro, overseer of Nexus's basilicas and the leading word in all things devout.

Nikolas hadn't known the prelate himself would be here. But when Lezzaro caught his eye, the man gave him his most reassuring smile with a dip of his chin.

Any comfort that would have given Nikolas was broken when his father stepped forward. The sword in Nikolas's hand was taken away, unbalancing him.

Waren Cyr unhooked the weapon from his back and held it out to his son. Nikolas had seen it thousands of times, whether resting upon its rack or wielded by his father during demonstrations and military parades. But now it was being pushed toward him—*him*, as if Nikolas had ever been considered worthy enough to touch it.

The Sunbringer Spear was long and sleek, its gilded stock enforced with metal alloy. On either side of the foot-long blade rose golden wings much like his pauldrons, arcing into points as deadly as the blade's tip. Each harbored a feather from Phos's wings. There were Solarian myths of people using the god's moltings to achieve astonishing feats of magic, like the peasant girl Vrinä leading the people of her ravaged village through the Shadow Sea.

To possess one was a miracle. To possess two was a grand testament to the power of Cyr blood.

Nikolas raised a shaking hand toward the spear. When his fingers wrapped around the stock, a faint hum tickled his palm. The two Phos feathers sheathed within the metal let off their brilliant glow, briefly pulsing in time to Nikolas's heartbeat. He almost thought he could sense their fine fletching under the nimbus, the shafts of translucent white, the vanes long and delicately curved.

"Nikshä," his father said, using what he insisted was his true Solarian name. "Are you ready?"

His father's expression spoke to the enormity of the task at hand. The messy feeling in the pit of Nikolas's stomach unfurled so swiftly he thought he would double over and vomit in front of everyone. He would have preferred that over what was about to happen.

For the first time in his life, he was going to commune with his god.

They passed rows of tapered candleholders and thuribles that smelled of amber and teak. His body was wooden under the weight of the armor, the hand curled around the spear grown numb. It was heavier than his sword, more persistent in its presence.

He knew, to some degree, what to expect. His father had performed this very ritual over thirty years ago, and had told Nikolas the story many times.

"My father brought me to the basilica when I was barely older than you are now. There, I was outfitted with my lieutenant's armor and approached the dais of Phos, and when I prayed to him, he spoke to me. His voice rattled my bones and filled my entire body. I understood, then, the call of worship. When his blessing was laid upon me, I felt immortal. Indestructible."

There had been a faraway look in his father's crystal-colored eyes, one Nikolas hardly ever saw. Waren Cyr was hard in both appearance and personality, a man chiseled out of the unrelenting substance of responsibility. Like almost all Cyr children, he had been given to the Vaegan militia at a young age. As a comandante, he trained his own squadron, but the title was mostly honorific at this late point in his career. His main focus now was maintaining his household and preparing Nikolas to take over in his stead.

Rian would have been the one to fulfill what Nikolas could not. His younger brother would have gone into the militia already, would have quickly risen through the ranks, would have inherited the weapon Nikolas now held awkwardly at his side.

But Rian was dead, and had taken all their father's pride with him.

The pain of his brother's absence was acute as he ascended the steps to the apse. He imagined Rian below, bouncing on the balls of his feet while he watched on with a grin, unable to keep still. Even his familiar had always been in constant movement, twirling through his fingers and around his legs. Nikolas breathed out a small, sad huff of laughter.

"You hide your fear as well as you hide your contempt," his father mumbled.

He glanced at his father, tall and stern and clad in his comandante uniform. The medals on his chest gleamed in the candlelight, familiar obediently hovering above his right shoulder.

"I'm not afraid," Nikolas lied.

Waren's jaw tightened. "Then focus."

The apse featured floral and geometric designs along its dome, sheltering the tall, golden sculpture of a vast sun. Candles had been placed along its rays to make it shine brightly. Two priests knelt on either side of the apse, diligently waiting to relight the candles or replace the ones burned down to stubs.

His father stepped away, leaving Nikolas alone at the dais where the sculpture loomed before him. Lux drifted forward in curiosity. Perhaps it was called by the power of this place, to the spot where Phos once stood to command the construction of his basilica.

Nikolas took as deep a breath as he could manage and knelt on one knee, balancing the Sunbringer Spear against his upraised thigh. His armor creaked and clanked, and the dizzy heat of embarrassment filled him as the sounds were magnified in the apse.

Everyone watched. Everyone waited.

Nikolas imagined his brother kneeling beside him, pale eyebrows raised at the display. "You look like an actor in a poorly budgeted stage production of *The Four Knights of Cardica*," he'd say.

He fought against a smile lest one of the priests think him a heretic. Sweat rolled down his ribs under the stifling armor, and he clutched the spear tighter to still the tremors in his hands.

"What am I supposed to do once I'm up there?" he'd asked in his father's office.

"You pray" had been his answer.

So Nikolas ducked his head and prayed to a god he had detested his whole life.

Light is life, light is longevity, he began to recite in his mind. *Light is the point in which we find ourselves whole. Phos, deliver me a blessing, and in return I will shed light where there is darkness.*

The apse was quiet save for the stutter of his breathing, the rapid *thud* of his heart, the rustle of the candle flames above him.

Please, he added. *Please help me.*

"Phos's power filled me for only a minute, but it felt like a lifetime," his father had said. "It was . . . intoxicating." He'd claimed light had filled the basilica, warm and radiant, and when he'd stood and turned, luminous wings of gold had burst from his back to halo his body. "Against the other gods, Phos's might is strongest. Once you have accepted his gift of power, His Majesty will see we are the most fit to be named his successors."

Nikolas laid himself open to that power. He waited for it to fill him with warmth, with assuredness, to drive away the sickening despair in his gut. He at least wanted to know Phos's intentions, to be able to recognize the arrival of his presence if it came again.

But there was only darkness and cold realization.

His god was refusing to bless him.

Nikolas didn't know how long he knelt there. Long enough to start shivering with exertion, to listen to the first startled whispers at his back.

Then a hand hauled him to his feet.

"We're leaving," Waren growled.

"But—"

"There's no use in prolonging this."

His father descended the stairs without looking at anyone. Nikolas trailed after him, Lux shivering under his chin.

The spear was pried from his stiff fingers, armor stripped off in silence. He still felt weighted down, his movements clumsy.

"My lords."

Nikolas hadn't thought the day could get any worse. He nearly laughed out loud at his unfaltering ability to be proven wrong.

Waren froze at the familiar voice before bowing low. "Your Majesty."

Nikolas mirrored his father's bow. When he straightened, King Ferdinand was giving them a benevolent smile, flanked by royal guards. Behind them, the priests and onlookers had fallen to their knees in deference. Although it was expected for the king to visit the basilicas from time to time, it was mainly a shallow show of piety, and he hadn't made it a habit.

Which meant he had come specifically for Nikolas.

"I apologize for intruding," Ferdinand said as they moved to a more private corner of the basilica. "I must admit, I was rather curious about this ritual." Waren's golden-brown skin paled to an ashen hue, but the king went on, "I seem to have missed the crucial moment. Pity."

Waren's expressions were so restrained it was difficult for others to tell what he was thinking. Nikolas, who'd had to learn the hard way, saw the corner of his father's mouth twitch in relief.

"I'm sure there will be plenty of opportunity in the future for Nikshä to show off his skill for His Majesty," Waren said with another bow.

Ferdinand smiled. "I look forward to it." He turned to Nikolas. "Actually, the reason I came is twofold. It's because I'm so curious of

Lord Nikolas's skills that I wonder if he could assist with an important mission."

"Of course," his father said a bit too quickly. "Whatever His Majesty orders, the House of Cyr will execute."

"I'm glad to hear it. Ah, perfect timing," Ferdinand said as Prelate Lezzaro joined them. "I was just filling them in."

"Then by all means," Lezzaro murmured in his soft voice.

"I'm working with the militia and the Hunters to put together a task force," Ferdinand explained. "A special unit that will focus primarily on tracking down and arresting Conjurers. Although the guards are doing their part, I believe a smaller, dedicated team might prove to have better results. The Conjurers will then be handed over to interrogation by Prelate Lezzaro and Don Soler." Lezzaro inclined his head in acknowledgment. "I would like Lord Nikolas to head this task force."

Nikolas fought to keep the shock from his face. Though Waren had trained him hard all his life, Nikolas wasn't a soldier. Entering the militia was something his father had been putting off for years, afraid of revealing to others that Nikolas's range of power was far from what it should be.

Which meant he would hold a rank solely because of his House, his blood.

The king was silent, staring expectantly at him. Nikolas realized he'd been waiting for his father to respond for him. But this was a direct request for *him*, not Waren. An order, really.

Nikolas bowed again. "I'm honored, Your Majesty. I—" He was about to say *I'll do my best* but shifted to "I will not fail you."

"I know you won't." The king nodded to Waren. "My lords. I will see you at the Autumn Equinox."

Once the king left, Nikolas swayed on his feet, light-headed and unsure if this was merely a ridiculous dream fueled by inhaling too much incense.

"Lord Nikolas." Lezzaro briefly touched his arm. "I hope you take some time to rest after this. Remember it is harder now for the gods to hear us. All we can do is keep trying."

Nikolas fought to swallow. "Thank you," he whispered. Lezzaro smiled before returning to the priests.

To his surprise, the Sunbringer Spear was handed back to him. Nikolas took it slowly, waiting to see if it was a test of some sort.

"It's yours now," Waren said in response to Nikolas's confusion.

"What the king has given you is a high honor, and you are not prepared for it. You will do all you can to not bring shame to House Cyr. You will *not* ruin all my years of effort to see us on the throne."

Waren walked out of the basilica without another word, leaving Nikolas and the softly glowing spear in the shadow of a colonnade.

The Bone Palace sat within Nexus's center like a watchful eye. It rose white and triumphant beyond large black gates, surrounded by lush gardens and encompassed by a tall stone wall. The main palace was topped with a dome, flanked by towers with elevated, pear-shaped pavilions. It was bright in the late-morning light, finials of gold winking like sunbursts.

The courtyard before it was massive, a round pool with a fountain in the center and plots of grass in swirling designs. Laurel and palm trees lined the walkways and the promenade leading to the palace, along with bushes of thyme and lavender trimmed in neat, even rows.

From where Nikolas stood by the grove of lemon trees, he could make out the festivities in the palace square beyond the gates. The king had provided meat and vegetables for their tables, and there was dancing and cheap wine, but nothing close to the lavishness in the courtyard.

But in this place, the gentry ruled; old families with rich histories tied to the Holy Kingdom. Tables and divans had been moved outside by servants earlier that morning, and drinks and food were passed around like money exchanging hands. One woman had a domesticated beast perched on a shoulder, a monkey-like creature with talons and folded wings, which she continuously fed bites of canapé to. Laughter peppered the air, chased by murmurs amid the clink and rattle of glass and porcelain. Somewhere a string quartet crooned songs above the gentle din.

Ferdinand Accardi was not a particularly popular man, but what he lacked in tact he made up for in pandering to the pious citizens of Vaega, of which there were still surprisingly many. Today's party was another string in the tapestry of tradition he had to maintain. It helped that he had invited Prelate Lezzaro, the unspoken guest of honor. Perhaps that was why the guards were in excess today, the courtyard ringed with both royal soldiers and those of the elementalist division.

Surrounded by partygoers, the prelate was dressed in robes of solemn colors that clashed with his gentle, smiling face. By his side was Camilla Lorenzo, Taesia's aunt. Nikolas had never known Camilla to be religious, yet in the past year she had joined a small contingent of nobles who helped Lezzaro raise funds for the basilicas' upkeep. As Nikolas watched, Camilla laughed heartily at something and put a hand on the prelate's arm as if for balance.

Nikolas raised an eyebrow. Camilla had been unmarried her entire life; was she setting her sights on Lezzaro? He'd have to ask Taesia.

But there was no sign of her as he searched the crowd. Although they were celebrating the Autumn Equinox, summer refused to relinquish its hold on Vaega, and sweat dotted the back of Nikolas's neck as he stood with hands behind his back, attentive yet begging for no one to ask anything of him. There were frequent surreptitious glances at the Sunbringer Spear peeking over his shoulder, though. The bandolier felt foreign across his chest, digging into his white-and-gold jacket.

"Onion tartlet, my lord?"

Nikolas started. His back had been to the trees so no one would sneak up on him. But someone had, a young man around his age wearing the dark gray-and-blue uniform of a server. He was handsome and fine-boned, with dark curling hair and piercing blue eyes made all the brighter against his brown skin.

Seeing Nikolas's surprise, the server grinned and lifted the silver tray he carried. It was strewn with tartlets of crispy pastry holding pools of caramelized onions and sprinkled with crumbly cheese.

"Ah...no, thank you," Nikolas said.

"Are you certain? I've snuck in a few myself, they're quite good."

When the server lifted the tray higher with a suggestive hum, Nikolas couldn't help but laugh and pick up a tartlet. "All right, you've sold me. Thank you."

The server grinned again, not even remembering to bow before scurrying off with his tray. Maybe to eat the whole thing himself.

Nikolas nibbled on the tartlet as he resumed watching the festival. Camilla lingered by the prelate, but her gaze had drifted to the king. Ferdinand must have been aware of her attention, because at the same time she made her move, he turned in the opposite direction.

Straight toward Nikolas, in fact, with a handful of soldiers in tow. Nikolas hastily brushed crumbs from his hands.

"Your Majesty," he greeted with a bow, hoping his flush wasn't too apparent.

"Lord Nikolas." The king gestured to the soldiers behind him, who bowed to Nikolas in turn. A couple of them weren't wearing traditional uniforms of blue and white. Instead, their outfits were tan trimmed in green. "Forgive me for mixing business with pleasure, but I wanted you to meet the members of your new task force."

The soldiers stared back at him, either unimpressed or nervous. He wouldn't fault them either way.

"In addition to the soldiers under your command, the Hunters have also sent a couple of their best to aid you," Ferdinand went on.

The two men in tan uniforms stepped forward. One was tawny and stern-looking, his dark hair shorn short along the undersides. The other was tall and lanky with an easy smile.

"My lord," said the stern-looking one. "My name is Julian Luca, and this is my partner, Paris Glicer. Please know we're yours to command, should you need us."

"Thank you. I hope we may get to know one another better in the coming days. We have a growing situation on our hands, and Nexus will not be safe until the danger is put to rest."

The soldiers saluted, forming a fist over their sternums. Nikolas nodded to dismiss them.

"Well put, Lord Nikolas," Ferdinand murmured. "I am eager to see the results of this task force." Before Nikolas could respond, one of Ferdinand's advisors hurried up to him and whispered in his ear. The king blanched and uttered a quick goodbye before walking purposefully toward the palace. Nikolas let out a tense breath once he was gone, a little confused by the exchange but largely relieved.

"*We have a growing situation on our hands*," came a voice behind him, deep and unmistakably mocking. "*Nexus will not be safe until the danger is put to rest*." A snort. "I've read pornography with better lines."

Nikolas turned. "You've read what, now?"

Taesia stood grinning and glittering under the late-morning light. She wore a dress of black crepe, its simple design purposefully drawing attention to the silver belt around her waist, upon which hung charms of moons and stars. It matched the crest of silver at her breast, the Lastrider sigil of a crescent moon crossed with a dagger amid a field of stars. Her black hair was pinned in an elegant bun, leaving a few loose locks to curl against her neck. With his golden-brown complexion and hair so pale it was practically white, he felt like the morning to her midnight.

"A girl gets lonely sometimes," she said without a hint of shame. She reached up to touch his golden Cyr crest, a sword against a sun. "Nice spear, by the way."

He first thought it was a euphemism until he remembered the Sunbringer Spear on his back. The weight of it seemed to double.

"Congratulations," Taesia said. Her fingers lingered on his House crest. He knew firsthand how calloused those fingertips were from years of swordplay. "You've spent a long time ogling it. Now it's finally yours."

If he had once ogled it, it was only because it had been promised to Rian. He'd felt freer, then, to pine for a thing he knew was not his.

The failed ritual was a bitter taste in his mouth. He longed to spit it out, to unravel it in words she would understand. But she couldn't understand, not when she was so fluid in her powers, Nyx's silent blessing. Not when she came from a rival House.

Not that she would ever use his words against him. But too many years of his father's caution had infected him.

Both his and Taesia's familiars always knew when the other was near. Lux uncurled from Nikolas's wrist as Taesia's bangle of shadow slithered into her palm, a featureless blob of darkness. Lux twirled around Umbra, prompting a playful chase.

"Come here," Taesia whispered.

He followed her through the trees as their familiars trailed behind. The sounds of the party dwindled as they meandered through the lemon grove, stepping over fallen fruit not yet picked by the gardeners.

Once they were far enough away, Taesia pushed him up against a tree. He grunted as the spear's stock dug into his back.

"For creeping around like you do, you're strangely lacking in subtlety," Nikolas grumbled. "What would the people say if they knew a Lastrider and a Cyr were involved?"

Her ringing laugh soothed him, made him feel pride that *he* had been the one to cause it. He was always trying to chase that laugh, ever since they had first met and she had set off a smoke bomb at a party, in the washroom where he had been trying to scrub a stain out of his shirt.

She could have left him there to take the blame. Instead, she had taken his hand and *run*. She had laughed as her raven hair tumbled out of its bun, filling Nikolas with light.

"They'd say 'lucky girl.'" She grinned at the heat rising in Nikolas's cheeks even as he reached out and held her by the waist. His hands slid over the smooth crepe of her dress.

"You look lovely," he murmured before she kissed him.

He had kissed Taesia a hundred times, a thousand times, and it was always this warm. Although he was the one descended from the god of light, holding her was akin to holding a blanket heated by the sun. He wanted to relax against her, let the warmth crawl into his bones until he knew neither of them would ever be cold again.

"Ugh," came a familiar voice. "I escape for one moment of privacy, and *this* is what I see?"

Nikolas and Taesia sprang apart. Angelica stood like a scowling lawn ornament under a branch drooping with lemons, arms crossed. Her burgundy dress highlighted the auburn threads in her dark brown hair. The Mardova crest glinted near her collar, a symbol of all the cardinal elements.

"I can't believe you left the house in that, Mardova," Taesia said.

Angelica sputtered as Nikolas sighed and pinched the bridge of his nose. "Not today, please..."

Angelica stabbed a finger at Taesia. "If you're not nicer to me, Lastrider, I won't hesitate to go out there and announce I found you in a compromising position."

"Oh, I'm terrified," Taesia deadpanned.

Admittedly, it would cause a large enough scandal Nexus would be talking about it the rest of the year. The Houses were expected to work together, but that didn't mean they were in league. The fact they were all descended from the line of Vaegan monarchs—and thus each had a claim to the throne—fairly prevented it.

"I thought I saw you all come this way." The words were chased by the recognizable chime of bangles. "Has the duel already started?"

Risha ducked under a branch. She was every inch the figurehead of her House today, dressed in a sari of black and gold, a spill of flowers embroidered across the fabric. Her black, shining hair had been twisted into an elaborate braid over one shoulder. Golden earrings hung from her ears like miniature chandeliers, accenting the Vakara crest she wore: a skull surrounded by marigold petals.

"It will soon if you don't get one of them out of here," Nikolas said.

Angelica scoffed. "No need to chase me away. I'd rather die than spend one more moment with these canoodling idiots."

Taesia cracked her knuckles. "That can be arranged."

Too late, Nikolas realized Umbra had drifted away from Lux and had slithered around a fallen twig. The shadow familiar raised it and began to poke Angelica's arms. Angelica swatted furiously at it.

"I'd advise you not to use your little shadow tricks on me," Angelica growled.

"Oh yeah?" Taesia drawled as Umbra continued to poke. "What'll you do, open the earth below my feet? Don't you need a cello or an oboe for that?"

Angelica bristled. Risha sighed and grabbed the twig, snapping it in two.

"Enough," she said. "We're not children anymore. The both of you need to show more deference to one another."

"I'd rather leap into a volcano," Angelica declared.

"I'd desperately love to see that," Taesia said.

Nikolas shared a look with Risha and shook his head. The two of them had been like this since they were old enough to start attending galas. It was a lost cause.

Risha's gaze trailed up to the spear. "Congratulations, Nik. For that, and for your new mission."

Taesia frowned. "Mission? Is that what the king was talking to you about?"

Angelica had turned to leave, but at this she froze. Nikolas hesitated, wondering what she would relay back to her mother, but he supposed it would become public knowledge soon enough. He told them about the task force as a breeze rustled the branches overhead. "I don't know why His Majesty would choose *me* to head it. He should have asked my father."

"No kidding," Angelica muttered.

"You're the Cyr heir," Taesia insisted, poking him in the sternum. "You have power. Influence."

"It's a test," Risha agreed. "His Majesty still hasn't chosen which House will succeed him. You've undergone your god's communion ritual. He wants to see what you can accomplish."

He nearly cringed at the reminder of yesterday, kneeling in the basilica and hollow of his god's strength.

Seeing his expression, Taesia squeezed his arm. "I'll do whatever I can to help."

"You'd be helping another House gain the king's favor."

"Hey, I'm not the Lastrider heir. What I do doesn't matter."

He was surprised by the resentment that pricked him. He couldn't tell if it was Taesia's reminder that she didn't carry the same weight he did or her offer of help, as if she saw him the way he saw himself: weak.

"You're not getting *my* help," Angelica said, as if anyone had asked or expected it of her. "But I do hope you succeed. I guess." She inclined her head to Risha and Nikolas, then made a rude gesture at Taesia before she swept out of the grove.

Risha shook her head at Angelica's back. "I'll provide you with whatever information I happen to find. It already feels like the Conjurers are testing the limits of their borrowed abilities." She told them about the shambling skeleton, the circle with its seven-pointed star, and the one who'd drawn it.

"A man in a skull mask," Nikolas murmured. "I'll keep that in mind."

Risha nodded in thanks before they turned back to the main courtyard, leaving the lemon trees behind. Taesia kept a hand on his lower back, as if to support him.

Outside the grove, something crunched under his boot. He lifted it and found a braided string of black, gold, silver, and red—the colors of the Four Realms. Dangling in the middle was a silver charm in the shape of a tree.

He picked it up. It was dirty from the ground, and he could tell it was old, the strings frayed and the charm scuffed with years of wear.

As he looked around, searching for who might have dropped it, he felt a curious sensation on the back of his neck. Slowly he peered up at the looming structure of the Bone Palace. The pavilion-topped towers on either side of the dome gave it the appearance of a crouching spider, the finials like gleaming eyes staring down at him.

No, he was sure there *were* eyes staring down at him. Nikolas squinted at the windows, but it was impossible to make out anything beyond the sun's glare.

"Everyone! Please direct your undivided attention to His Majesty, Ferdinand Accardi!"

The call came from the middle of the courtyard, near the fountain. One of King Ferdinand's advisors slunk away with a deep bow as Ferdinand stepped forward, holding a flute of bubbling wine in one hand. Nikolas supposed whatever had called him away earlier had been dealt with.

"Thank you all for coming on this day to celebrate the waning of summer, the promise of upcoming harvest. By Godsnight we will surely be reaping the rewards of our land's bounty."

Polite applause. Nikolas noted the uneasy shifting within the crowd of dons and doñas. Ferdinand refused to acknowledge that the harvest he spoke of was in danger, that with each consecutive year it grew sparser and sparser. But the subject of the Sealing was taboo at parties such as this, when frivolity and excess were the day's goals.

"Let us raise a toast not only to our hardworking citizens and farmers, but also to our most esteemed Houses, who are each doing their part to bring peace and balance to our city, our kingdom, our realm." Ferdinand held up his glass, and others followed suit. The citizens within the square began to crowd the gates, listening in. "These are trying times, and certain members of our society have taken to troubling pastimes in response."

This time there were murmurs among the crowd; the gentry was just as unnerved about the Conjurers as the commonfolk.

"To that end," Ferdinand went on, gesturing for Prelate Lezzaro to stand beside him, "our dear prelate has an announcement concerning these individuals."

"Thank you, Your Holy Majesty, for the honor," Lezzaro said, the picture of serenity even when addressing so many people. On the sidelines, Camilla watched on with a pleased smile. "It is indeed troubling that the long-outlawed practice of Conjuration has resurfaced. As you all know, the practice has a morbid history tied to the summoning of demons." More uneasy murmurs. "But so far we have seen no demons. Instead, we have seen desperate people dabbling in magic. And of course, as magic tends to be unruly, there have been some unforeseen complications." He nodded toward the House heads as if to get their sympathy on this. Nikolas noted his father's quickly stifled scowl.

"There has been speculation that these people are radicals, but I believe not every motive is purely spiteful," the prelate went on. "I believe there is more behind this than fervor for the occult. That is why, starting today, anyone who has been or will be arrested as a Conjurer or holds ties to them will be granted asylum under my care."

Taesia inhaled sharply as a roar of disbelief came from the citizens in the square. Though the gentry had been trained to contain such dramatics, Nikolas spotted several dropped jaws and heard more than a few startled exclamations.

"What is he saying?" Risha hissed. "They're *criminals*. Citizens have been hurt because of them!"

"Maybe he wants to round them up in one place before they can do more damage," Nikolas guessed. It was clear that Ferdinand had not been anticipating the prelate's announcement to go this way; his face was carefully neutral, but his neck was flushed.

"And do what with them?" Risha demanded.

Nikolas himself felt misgivings stir in his chest, wondering where this was coming from, if the prelate knew how much his words would displease the king and the public. But then he remembered Lezzaro's gentle reassurance in the basilica, the balm he'd needed against his father's ire. Perhaps the man had a plan, knew precisely what he was doing.

He had to hope so.

V

Taesia was already seated at the private table when Risha stepped onto the balcony. The server who had escorted her bowed and murmured he would return to take their orders shortly.

Taesia sat as she normally did: trying to take up as much space as possible. Her arm was flung out so that it rested on the railing, one long leg sprawled under the table. When she turned to Risha, her smile was aborted by a yawn.

"Morning," Taesia mumbled. "Think you chose an early enough hour?"

Risha sat across from her with a glance at the mostly gray sky. It *was* early, but she didn't want to risk anyone overhearing them. Besides, it was always best to ply Taesia with food during serious conversation.

Café Daphne was situated in one of the richer districts of the city near the Bone Palace. The tables outside were already filling with people who wanted to enjoy a leisurely, if expensive, breakfast. Stores were beginning to pull back drapes to reveal window displays, and the sounds of a child throwing a tantrum rose from the street.

Looking at the scene, it was almost impossible to think a growing threat lurked in the cracks of their city, or that beyond its walls the earth was starting to rot.

"My sleep's been poor since the Autumn Equinox," Risha said, spreading the white linen napkin over her lap. "I've already been up for hours."

Taesia, no doubt realizing this was why Risha had lured her here, huffed. When Taesia was serious, she grew quiet and formed a divot between her brows. But now she was restless, tapping her fingers on the railing, fiddling with her cutlery.

"How are you?" Risha asked in the hopes of softening that uneasiness.

"As well as can be expected," Taesia answered vaguely. "Better than you, at least." Risha rolled her eyes but was heartened by Taesia's short laugh. "Tell me what you're worried about."

She opened her mouth and was interrupted by the server. They ordered quickly—Risha an egg cocotte, Taesia a plate of assorted pastries with coffee—before she tried again, leaning in and keeping her voice down.

"I'm worried the prelate has some ulterior motive for granting clemency to the Conjurers." She thought of the man in the skull mask and wished, not for the first time, that the guards had been able to chase him down.

"He probably just wants to figure out their plot and decide punishment from there."

"But it sounded like he didn't want them to face *any* punishment." Risha fiddled with the silver bangles at her wrist, comforted by their soft chimes. "Who knows what else these Conjurers are capable of, if they can replicate necromancy? Why stop there at all? What if—" She lowered her voice even more. "What if they bring the demons back?"

Now the divot was forming on Taesia's forehead. "Ri. Slow down. You told us the most they can do right now is, what, raise a spirit within a skeleton? That's a far cry from an army, let alone a demon."

Risha made a shushing motion as their food was delivered. Taesia plastered on a charming smile that was so much like Dante's and thanked the waiter as Risha stared miserably at her plate.

"You're leaping to conclusions," Taesia said once they were alone again. She took a sip of her coffee. "Maybe this is a good thing."

Risha picked up a piece of toast and stabbed it into her egg cocotte, stirring it around without eating any. "How is this good?"

Taesia chewed on her lower lip. "Maybe...the Conjurers are trying to do something beneficial?"

Risha dropped her toast. "*What?* How is ripping up a street, stealing bodies, and harming citizens beneficial?"

"They're experimenting." The way she said it gave Risha pause, and she had the feeling Taesia was keeping something from her. "Lezzaro doesn't want to pass judgment until he knows what they're experimenting *toward*."

"I think their demonstration near the palace made that clear."

"Maybe." Taesia peered into her coffee thoughtfully. She hadn't even touched her pastries yet. "In any case, it's safe to say folks aren't happy about it. I understand why you're not, too."

"And you are?"

"I didn't say that."

Risha took a deep breath. "I wanted to speak to the prelate, but my father told me not to. He said the king's going to be watching the prelate closely, and if the Vakaras are seen with him, it could cast suspicion on us."

Taesia snorted. "And jeopardize a bid for the throne? Ever the filial daughter."

Risha didn't know why this gave her embarrassment instead of pride. She chose not to examine it too closely.

"The Houses should be working *with* each other, not against each other," Taesia went on.

"They're already working together." *Or we are, at least.*

"Not the way they should. The heads all hate one another, and they regard their children as little more than future seat-warmers for the throne." Seeming to remember Risha was one of those so-called seat-warmers, she added, "Sorry."

Risha quickly banished the memory of her mother mentioning a marriage alliance. "Even so, we're bound to serve the king."

Taesia opened her mouth, then closed it again. A sort of grayness settled around her even as the sun began to break through the clouds.

"Sure," Taesia murmured. "You're very loyal, you know that?"

It sounded more like a criticism than a compliment.

When Taesia returned to the villa, the dining room was warm with early sunlight streaking across the long mahogany table. Her mother was eating breakfast while poring over a news tattler, which she put down as Taesia threw herself into her usual chair.

"And where were you, so early in the day?" Elena demanded. Her black hair had been styled into a chignon, showing off the gold earrings that shone enticingly against her rich brown skin.

"Thought I'd take a nice, brisk walk. Get the blood flowing. Enjoy being alive until a rogue spirit grows jealous."

Taesia took a modicum of delight in her mother's withering look as she popped a piece of melon in her mouth. Even though she'd already eaten with Risha, she crowded her plate with soft-boiled eggs sprinkled with black salt, thick slices of herb-smothered tomatoes, a potato omelet, and a sweet roll dusted with cinnamon and sugar.

"The hour's far too early for you to be sacrilegious," Elena muttered before going back to her tattler. They were printed broadsheets of the juiciest bits of news in Nexus, usually distributed to the wealthiest households. Elena, with her proud shoulders and elegant bearing, seemed the exact opposite of someone used to rumormongering.

"The nobles have been muttering nonstop since the prelate's announcement," Elena said after a while, sighing as she put the tattler down. "Doña Bianca's recently departed husband was one of the bodies stolen by those heretics."

"You mean her fifth husband."

"Taesia, please. It was traumatizing for the poor woman." Elena shook her head. "They're saying his body reappeared on the manor's doorstep with its neck broken. Which makes no sense, since he died of an aneurysm."

Taesia frowned and thought back on her conversation with Risha, her friend's anxiety over what the Conjurers had already done and could potentially do. Thought of Dante's workshop below and his repeated failed attempts to call upon the gods. Risha had a right to be anxious.

"Do you think old Freddie will call off the gala, considering what happened at the last party?" Taesia asked as she nibbled at a sweet roll.

"Don't call him that," Elena admonished. "He's your *king*. And no, of course not. The Godsnight Gala is far too important to cancel."

"Of course. I completely understand risking a Conjurer uprising to gorge on finger foods."

Quiet footsteps approached the dining room, heralding the arrival of her younger sister. The both of them took after their mother, all cool dark tones and fine bones, but where Brailee was petite, Taesia had inherited her father's height and broad shoulders. Brailee had also snatched the lion's share of Elena's gracefulness and manners, which was why Taesia had always suspected she was their mother's favorite.

Brailee kissed Elena on the cheek before she sat down and helped herself to fruit and cheese.

Taesia leaned forward. "Morning, Bee."

"Morning." Her voice was clipped. Elena sent a questioning look at Taesia, who shrugged.

Their father walked in next. He was dressed for the day in trousers and a dark blue doublet under a fashionable coat Taesia was sure her mother had picked out for him. Left to his own devices, he would likely pull on a grain sack and call it fashion.

"Good morning, my doves." He stooped to kiss all of them on the cheek, the bristles on his unevenly shaved chin tickling Taesia's jaw. Cormin Lastrider—originally Cormin Lorenzo—was from a reputable noble household in Nexus. Out of three suitors, Elena had chosen him, admittedly the weakest of her three options, due to his good humor and easy demeanor.

"You're going so early?" Elena asked as her familiar slithered across the table to fetch the apricot jam. "Our meeting with His Majesty isn't until this afternoon."

"No, I moved up our conference with the western merchant guild. They're a little wary of doing business now that certain, ah…proclamations have been made." He cleared his throat. "Don't worry, I'll handle their complaints. Pray to Nyx I return with both ears still attached."

"I'm sure Nyx has better things to occupy his time than worry over the state of your ears," Elena said. "If you wait a moment, Taesia can accompany you."

Taesia nearly choked on her coffee. She'd rather jump into a shark's maw than have Don Kermin insist, yet again, that she ought to marry his pockmarked son—considerably more awkward due to the fact she had once snuck away from a dinner party to kiss his daughter instead.

"I was planning to go over those letters from the Parithvian minister of commerce," she said smoothly. "They're being stingy about their frost stone quarry, so I'm drafting a response to negotiate a trade for our ember crystals."

Elena pursed her lips, then nodded. "Fine. But I want to see it once I return from the palace."

"That can happen."

"I mean it. End of the day, not end of the week."

"Why, Mother, it's like you don't trust me at all. Even a lowly spare such as myself is capable of paperwork." Taesia bared her teeth in not quite a smile, knowing exactly which barbs got under Elena's skin. She had decided long ago, being the most frequent recipient of their mother's ire, she might as well draw it away from Brailee and Dante. Besides, there was an oily feeling in her stomach that wasn't helping. She probably shouldn't have had that second cup of coffee.

Elena set her teacup down with a definitive *clink* that made Brailee and Cormin flinch. "Dante may be heir, but you'll still be helping him with House duties. You need to take those duties more seriously, especially now that Nexus faces such a grave situation."

"I take them plenty seriously. I went to that fundraiser, didn't I?"

"The one where you stabbed Don Geraldi with a fork?"

"I wouldn't have had to resort to fork stabbing if he'd kept his hands to himself. Besides, Dante is much better at talking to the dons and doñas than I am."

As if she had summoned him via Conjuration circle, Dante sauntered into the room. "Talking about me behind my back again?"

"Always."

He kissed Elena and Brailee on the cheek, though Brailee scowled. Their father clasped his shoulder before leaving to take care of the merchants.

Instead of taking his seat at the table, Dante grabbed one of the sweet rolls and poured a mug of coffee. "Busy day. Need to get started."

"Surely you can spare a moment for breakfast," Elena wheedled.

"We can meet at lunch." He saluted them with his steaming mug and retreated to his rooms.

"Well," Elena said, trying to mask her disappointment. "At least he's pulling his weight."

Taesia wondered what would happen if she revealed that Dante was so *busy* because he split his days between his duties as heir and Conjuration experimentation.

The room grew progressively darker, the shadows in the corners inching inward. Brailee looked nervously between her mother and sister. Taesia downed her coffee and followed after Dante, taking some of the shadows with her.

She climbed one of the long, curving staircases in the entrance hall, the banisters spotted with silver in the reflection of light off the chandelier. The interior of the villa was darkly elegant, with black stone and marble interrupted with bright tile and touches of silver.

All the doorways in the residential halls bore keystones of moons in their different phases. She glanced at the shrouded new moon above Dante's study door before barging inside.

"Busy, huh?"

Dante started. The window at his back was darkened by heavy

blue drapes, laying the bookshelves on either side of him in shadow. A book was spread before him on the desk. "What have I told you about knocking?"

"This is your study, not your bedroom. Should I be worried about what you do in here?"

He snorted and closed the book. "How was your chat with Risha?"

"She's on edge. Understandably so."

"Did you ask about the calciphite again?"

Taesia blinked. She had completely forgotten to bring it up. "She'd just say no. You know how she is. And what with everything going on, it would make her too suspicious."

"I guess that's true. Still, would've been nice to have. Thana couldn't ignore an offering that strong."

"She could, and would. Dante..." She sat on the edge of his desk and crossed her arms. "Are you sure you should be continuing with this?"

His frown softened in understanding. "What are you worried about?"

"I'm worried these experiments of yours might get out of hand. I mean, what if you slip up one day and a horde of spirits descends on the villa?"

"I'm not—"

"I know you're not trying to replicate necromancy or anything like that. But the practice itself is dangerous. It was outlawed for a reason. The reason being demons."

The corner of his mouth ticked up. "You think I'll accidentally summon a demon?"

"*No*, but..." She sighed. Dante's familiar, Nox, uncurled from his wrist and went to circle Taesia's, teasing Umbra until they began to chase one another through the study. "I don't want you getting lumped in with them."

Dante walked around the desk and sat beside her. He nudged her shoulder with his. "This isn't like you. All this sincerity creeps me out."

"Your face creeps me out."

"Seriously, Tae, I'll be fine. And you heard Lezzaro. Anyone suspected of being involved with the Conjurers won't be persecuted until he gives the say-so."

"Don't you find that odd, though?" Nyx's piss, Risha had gotten under her skin. "After all the stunts they've pulled?"

"Maybe he wants to give them a second chance, or reform them."

She hadn't considered that. "Ferdinand isn't happy about the idea."

"Ferdinand is rarely happy." His face hardened in a way she wasn't used to. "But even he knows he has to appeal to the pious masses."

Worship in the country of Vaega was compulsory, children learning about the gods by the time they were barely out of the crib. It wasn't enough to worship Deia, the god of their realm, alone. They had once been blessed by all four, and so each god deserved their prayer.

Their northern neighbor, Parithvi, only valued the elements gifted to them by Deia. The western empire of Azuna was much the same way, though multiple wars and internal conflict had split it into parts, ruled by an empress whose ancestor had publicly renounced the gods after the Sealing five hundred years ago. Heralds and newsboys had shouted her infamous speech through the streets of Nexus: "If the gods cannot and will not hear us, then we have no choice but to turn our backs as well. We are on our own. They have made it so."

But Vaega was the Holy Kingdom, the Houses exemplars of the Four Realms. Nexus was the sole portal city of Vitae, the singular point on which the realms aligned, called the City of Dusk for its positioning between Noctus and Solara on the Cosmic Scale. Ferdinand wasn't shy to tout this honor, and other lands weren't hesitant to pick up the implication that this somehow made Vaega superior.

"We can't keep living in a dying realm," Dante said softly. "We can't keep pretending the king is the best person to lead Vaega to a better future. If the prelate and the Conjurers are searching for solutions, we shouldn't dismiss that."

Some of her doubt receded. She admired her brother's ideals, the desire to see a new Vaega birthed from the old, rigid country that presumed to call itself *holy*, so bound to the model of piety that they barely strayed from the basilicas.

The gods had abandoned them. It was time to follow Azuna's example and cast them off for good. With the destruction of the throne, the Houses could then rise to form a parliament like Parithvi's, a delegation for the people. Taesia quite liked the notion of no longer being a political pawn, of the Houses no longer being played against each other.

That she, tied to her House on the sole circumstance of carrying godsblood, could be free of a system she'd never wanted any part of.

She suddenly remembered what Risha had said about wanting to speak to the prelate and her father forbidding it. Risha's loyalty to her

House and the throne had not yet been tested, but she and Dante didn't have such qualms. "What if we asked him directly?"

Dante turned to her. "What?"

"Lezzaro. We want to know what he's thinking, right? So let's confront him. We're Lastrider heirs. He has to give us an audience."

Her brother stared at her, and she waited for him to dismiss the idea as ridiculous. Instead, he threw his head back and laughed.

"Why didn't I think of that? It's so simple. And if he's reluctant to cough up an explanation, we'll know there's an ulterior motive." Dante's eyes sparked with reawakened excitement. "You'll come with me?"

"Of course." She was her brother's right hand. "But be prepared to be disappointed. I doubt a man devoted to the gods will be susceptible to threats or bribery."

"You never know." He held out his hand, and Nox settled into his palm. "We are, after all, descended from a god."

Taesia hid her displeasure at the reminder.

VI

Dante Lastrider woke up thinking about demons.

Once again they had infested his dreams, restless dark figures with sharp teeth and burning eyes. Of course, no one quite knew what a demon actually looked like, as the grimoires and occult texts had been burned and subsequently banned long ago, but the common consensus was that they were vaguely human-shaped. How vaguely was left up to the imagination.

Unfortunately, Dante's imagination was more than sufficient, and he had to settle his frantic heartbeat as he lay in bed and stared at the ceiling of his bedroom, painted in the likeness of a night sky brilliant with purples and blues. He could still feel phantom claws on his arms, his thighs. His hands trembled as he got ready for the day.

They were still now as he and Taesia stepped out of the carriage and made their way toward the prelate's rectory. It wasn't far from the Bone Palace, an appropriately equidistant amount from the four basilicas. To have his home anywhere but the center of the city would be inviting people to wonder if he favored one god over another.

"You're oddly quiet," Taesia remarked as they walked down the cobblestone avenue lined with iron lampposts. Passersby were dressed in finely tailored light jackets or shirtsleeves with the newly fashionable double-breasted vests, a couple women carrying parasols to block the sun. The inner districts surrounding the palace were the nicest to be found in Nexus other than the coveted river quarter.

"I'm thinking," he answered. "This is my thinking face."

"You look constipated."

"I can do both."

He was gratified by her stifled laugh. He loved to make his sisters laugh. Brailee was admittedly tougher, but he'd discovered she had a weakness for weird voices, of all things. There was an impression he did of frog-throated Don Geraldi that always had her in stitches.

"Seriously though, how are we going to spin this?" Taesia asked. "Intimidation? Polite implication? Persuasion of a forceful nature?"

"You are *not* going to put the prelate in a headlock."

"Then what good are these for?" She patted her upper arm, firm with lean muscle. "Other than making Nik swoon."

"You're also prohibited from discussing the carnal nature of your relationship with me."

"Pretty soon I won't be allowed to do anything."

"That's the point." He stopped in front of the rectory at the end of the avenue and gave it an assessing once-over. It was smaller than the homes around them, adorned with nothing but a humble whitewash and stone trim. Windows sheltered by hoodmolds had been thrown optimistically open despite the day's humidity.

A moment of uncertainty froze him in place. He cast a surreptitious look around, but nothing seemed out of the ordinary. Just the cobwebs of his dream breeding monsters where there were none.

He drew himself up and approached the two guards flanking either side of the short flight of steps that led to the front door. Someone as important as the prelate had to be protected at all times, even in his own home.

Like flipping over a card, he switched into the role of Dante Lastrider— beguiling, unflappable, confident. "Good morning," he greeted the guards, his words light and warm, as if seeing old friends. He gestured to Taesia and himself, drawing the guards' attention to their attire. They had strategically donned formal clothes of black and silver, their House colors. "My sister and I were wondering if we could call upon Prelate Lezzaro for a bit of tea and conversation."

The guards eyed the silver crest on Dante's collar. "He's already with a guest, but you might be able to wait in the foyer," one said eventually.

Dante grinned widely. "Perfect, thanks so much." The guard flushed and cleared his throat as Dante swept past, Taesia lingering behind him as he knocked on the front door and was ushered in by a footman.

"I wonder who else is calling on him," Taesia said. She paced the foyer, picking up various little knickknacks and then putting them back down when they didn't hold her interest.

"He won't have any shortage of visitors after his announcement." Dante sat on the edge of a blue couch. "People like us who want to wheedle information out of him. Or those who might try to sway his mind."

Taesia grabbed an apple from the silver bowl on the table and took a bite. "Has Ferdinand summoned him to the palace?"

"Not that I know of. I'm surprised the Vakaras haven't made a move."

"Rath prevented it," Taesia answered. "Risha told me."

Dante frowned. If the head of House Vakara was being that cautious, their presence here today wouldn't go unnoticed.

He was about to warn Taesia—for the third time—to be on her best behavior when they heard footsteps coming down the hall. He shot to his feet as Prelate Lezzaro's guest came into view.

"Aunt Camilla?" Taesia blurted.

Their aunt nearly stumbled at the sight of them. "What in Thana's grave are you two doing here?" She cast a critical eye over their House colors.

Camilla Lorenzo was his father's older sister, and just as ruggedly handsome. There had always been a certain sort of strength to her, the force of her personality repelling or attracting others in equal measure. Her eyes, though, were her true asset, an arresting shade of blue from their late grandmother. Dante was a little disappointed he hadn't inherited them.

"We could ask the same of you," Taesia shot back. Their aunt quirked a single yet economical eyebrow, making Taesia shift on her feet and, not knowing what else to do, set her partially eaten apple back in the bowl. Dante held back a sigh.

Camilla strode farther into the foyer and dropped her voice. "Did your parents send you?"

"No," Dante said. "We're here on our own to ask the prelate some questions."

"Such as?" When Dante hesitated, she poked him in the chest with her closed fan. "Do I look like the high commissioner? Tell me."

Haltingly, he did. Their aunt listened silently, her face betraying nothing. Once he was done, she took a deep breath, nodded, and turned on her heel.

"Come," she ordered. Dante and Taesia exchanged a glance before obeying.

They were led to a more private receiving room. It was as humble as the rectory's outsides, other than the thick blue-and-green rug taking up most of the floor. A servant was clearing away a tea service as the prelate himself helped.

"Ah, Camilla. Did you forget something?" Lezzaro spotted Dante and Taesia and bowed. "My lord, my lady. To what do I owe the pleasure?"

Dante executed his grin again. "It would be *our* honor if you granted us a measure of your valuable time." He sent out Nox to discreetly poke Taesia. She tried to copy his smile, but it came out more of a grimace.

"Tea?" Lezzaro asked as they sat.

"No thank you," Dante answered.

"Ugh, enough with the niceties," Camilla complained once the servant left. She opened her favorite Azunese folding fan, decorated with painted grassflowers. "It's too warm for all this back-and-forth. They're here to ask about ulterior motives behind granting asylum to the Conjurers."

Taesia hissed at being outed so suddenly. Dante could only curl his hands into fists on his thighs and wait as the prelate looked to Camilla for confirmation, surprisingly calm. But Dante had long ago learned how to read what wasn't said, and noticed the strain at the corners of the man's eyes.

Lezzaro cleared his throat. "Camilla? Are you certain?"

Certain of what? Dante wondered, noting the informality between them.

Camilla studied them a moment longer. Dante's spine straightened under her undivided attention, sweat beginning to tickle his ribs. "They weren't sent here by their parents. They want answers."

"Not to rat you out to the king or anything like that," Taesia hurried to say. "We—"

"Tae," Dante interrupted softly. She shut her mouth. "Prelate, you must understand how dire our situation is here in Vitae. We've felt the effects of the Sealing within the last hundred years, but recently it's gotten infinitely worse. The barriers *need* to be taken down, or else we're all living on borrowed time. I've taken inspiration from the Conjurers to attempt the old methods of communing with the gods, but they've proven ineffective. If you know anything that could help us, anything you may have learned that led you to make your announcement, we need you to share it."

Dante only got a sense of Lezzaro's hesitance in the way he clasped his hands together, silently considering.

"We need to involve the heirs sooner or later," Camilla told him. It sounded like they'd had this conversation before.

"Very well." Lezzaro was more solemn than Dante had ever seen him, including leading worship in the basilicas. "Your aunt trusts you, so therefore I will as well. If you've taken the initiative to come for answers, I shall provide them."

To Dante's growing surprise, the prelate walked to one corner of the rug and began to roll it up, uncovering a hidden door. Once lifted, it revealed a set of narrow stone steps.

"Are we about to be murdered?" Taesia whispered as they watched first the prelate, then their aunt descend. "Told you I should have worn my sword."

"Hush."

Still, Dante was also perturbed as he kept one hand against the rough stone wall and followed the other two down. The stairs were dark, yet beyond them came faint lantern light. He blinked to adjust his eyes when he reached the bottom and took quick stock of the room. It was cold and barren save for a small round table and a chair in the middle, as well as a wide bookcase creaking under the weight of archaic-looking tomes.

"It's supposed to be my safe room," the prelate explained. "But considering I've inherited quite a number of important records that don't mix well with humidity, I've had them stored down here to better preserve them."

"A fun little summer library, one could say," Camilla drawled.

Lezzaro smiled wryly. "Just so. There have been several ancestors of mine who entered into religious careers and passed down texts of historical importance. For example, my great-grandfather Vadius Lezzaro lived through the Vaegan-Parithvian wars, and—"

Camilla snapped her fan closed. "Not the reason they're here."

Lezzaro blinked. "Ah, right. Yes. Well, I say this only as an introduction." Here he hesitated again, eyeing Dante and Taesia. Specifically, their House crests. "What I am about to reveal to you is not common knowledge, my lord, my lady. I ask for your most fervent discretion."

Taesia's eyes widened as Dante bowed. "Of course."

The prelate removed something from the bookcase with slow care. Camilla gripped her fan as she watched, gaze flickering to her niece and nephew with a silent warning. Dante knew that if they so much as breathed any of this to their parents, there would be a price to pay.

He loved his aunt dearly. He was also terrified of her sometimes.

The prelate returned carrying a large book. He placed it on the table as if it were a newborn, or an explosive substance. The cover was gilded and studded with gems that winked in the dim lantern light, outlining a design of two interlocking circles.

"This was penned by my ancestor, a man who devoted himself to the Deia basilica." Lezzaro swallowed. "Marcos Ricci."

The name tickled Dante's memory. He stared at the cover until the design made something click, and he took a step back with a hitched breath.

"Yes," Lezzaro said. "This is the last surviving grimoire. In fact, it is the original grimoire. Marcos Ricci was the one who discovered demon summoning."

The tattered threads of Dante's dream hung in his mind, shapeless threats that pressed teeth against his exposed throat.

Dante slammed his hands on the table, making it rock. "What are you doing with this?" he growled. "This book should have been destroyed!"

"Dante," Camilla snapped. "Hear him out."

Taesia gripped his elbow. Not to draw him back, but as silent reassurance. Nox sat within the bezel of a silver ring on his right hand, and it crept out slightly at his distress.

"Is this why you want to grant asylum to the Conjurers?" Dante demanded. "You want to teach them demon summoning and restore your ancestor's lost art?"

Camilla sighed, near the end of her patience, but Lezzaro gestured for her to be calm. He himself was considerably calmer than Dante would have expected.

"I understand," Lezzaro murmured. "This grimoire is...a haunting reminder of the atrocities my family have committed in the past. I believe that is why so many of my forebears entered in the services of the basilicas and did their best to distance themselves from Marcos Ricci, even changing surnames." He spread out his arms. "I have no interest in bringing the demons back, nor do I have any intention of revealing such methods to others. No one besides myself has read the book." Camilla nodded to back up this claim. "However, the grimoire reveals far more than that."

He opened the book. Dante and Taesia braced themselves, as if a demon would claw its way out of the faded, yellowed pages. As the prelate flipped through them, Dante spied various diagrams, sketches, and Conjuration circles amid blocks of text.

"The realms were designed precisely within the universe, on a grid of geometric tethers that make up the Cosmic Scale," Lezzaro said. "But those tethers have been severed by the gods for reasons us mortals cannot begin to understand. However, they—and we—still lie within the Cosmic Scale. The tethers still flow with energy, but are blocked, like a dam holding back a flood."

He met Dante's gaze. "My lord, you know what the ancient ritual of Godsnight once was?"

Of course he did. Every hundred years the Cosmic Scale slid into perfect alignment, bringing about Godsnight, when magic was more potent and the gods could convene in one place. It had been a spectacle of divine magic when the heir of each House was inhabited by the god that had produced their line. They'd used the gods' power for enchantment and wonder, for *miracles*, their bodies conduits for cosmic energy.

"The hundred-year mark has arrived," the prelate went on. "The fifth since the Sealing. The realms will align, but the energy will have nowhere to go. The barriers will thin but not disappear completely." The grimoire was open to a spread of the Cosmic Scale, so much like the design of a Conjuration circle, a veritable map of the universe. Lezzaro pressed a hand against the center. "And that is where the Conjurers come in."

Dante's heart beat fast enough that he could feel its reverberations in his throat. Taesia's fingers tightened around his elbow.

"In reading Marcos Ricci's...findings," the prelate said with a slight wrinkling of his nose, "I've discovered something that I believe was lost with the purging. Something stricken from history, both oral and written: the original construct of Godsnight, and how exactly it was achieved."

He looked between Dante and Taesia, the set of his mouth grim.

"Godsnight was a Conjuration ritual."

For a moment, Dante stopped breathing. Nox fully slithered from its ring and twined around Dante's wrist, peering up at him in confusion.

He'd been right, to some degree. Conjuration *was* a bastardization of a method once used to communicate with the gods. He just hadn't known to what extent.

"And then it was ruined by Marcos Ricci," Camilla picked up, smacking her fan against her open palm. "Who witnessed the ritual and came up with the brilliant idea to do it all backward. We haven't had a true Godsnight since."

"Do you think..." Taesia forcefully cleared her throat. "Do you think that's why the gods caused the Sealing? They were mad we discovered this power?"

Lezzaro sighed and closed the book. "It's impossible to guess at the will of the gods, my lady, but it's not a bad theory. Whatever prompted it, it doesn't change that the realms are still cut off from one another. That they—or at least Vitae—are dying because of it."

"But what can we expect the Conjurers to do?" Dante asked.

"We shared certain bits of Marcos Ricci's studies with an interested group," Lezzaro said. "Their role will be to weaken the barriers further. By performing Conjuration, they siphon some of the built-up energy gathered at the barriers. By Godsnight, the barriers will be at their thinnest in five hundred years."

"And then what?" Dante pressed. "The Godsnight ritual was performed by the Houses, wasn't it?"

"Yes," Camilla answered. "Which is why we've decided to let you in on this. If all goes to plan and we convince the other Houses to cooperate, we can reproduce the ritual."

"And use it to undo the Sealing," Lezzaro added softly.

Dante's head swam, the stone chamber sliding in and out of focus. He stared down at the book, the *grimoire*, and felt a familiar teeth-gnashing hunger. He wanted to know more. He wanted to learn *everything*.

His mouth was too dry to speak, so Taesia picked up the conversation for him. "What does all this have to do with necromancy?"

Lezzaro clasped his hands together. "Summoning spirits isn't ideal, but it's a far better alternative to summoning demons."

"And what if they decide their results are lacking and want to start calling in demons after all?"

"I can only hope that will not be the case. Their goal has always been to open the barrier to Mortri. If they do not succeed, I've informed them their efforts won't be in vain, if we can indeed go through with the ritual."

"But they've *hurt* people. The king thinks they're rebels."

Lezzaro made a face. "That was...indeed unfortunate. Since Nexus lies upon the severed pathways to the other realms, I thought it might produce the best results to work at the heart of the city equidistant from the basilicas and their portals. His Majesty has regrettably considered this to be a threat."

"Well, he's not *wrong*, exactly," Camilla murmured.

Dante finally pulled himself out of his fugue. "What does that mean?" he asked her. "How do you even factor into all of this?"

Lezzaro coughed politely as Camilla grinned.

"Our dear prelate seems to be of a mind that the Holy King isn't as holy as some believe," she said. "And that Vaega would be better served without him."

"A rather aggressive way to paraphrase it, but yes." Lezzaro sighed. "I do not wish the king ill. I have no desire for the Conjurers to harm him. I do, however, believe that if we view those who rule as infallible—touched by the gods, and therefore sacred—we will continue to set a dangerous precedent for ourselves. It is one thing to show devotion for the gods. It is quite another to devote yourself to your people."

Dante was certain the stunned revelation on Taesia's face was a mirror to his own. He couldn't speak under the weight of it.

"We found we had similar views," Camilla said simply. "We've been working together since. We weren't sure how to approach the Houses with the idea for the ritual, but luckily for us, you two took care of that."

Dante let Nox weave through his fingers. "The Godsnight ritual involved a representative from each House inviting their gods to inhabit their bodies." Lezzaro dipped his chin in agreement. "I'll do it."

"*What?*" Taesia spun him around to face her. "Do you have any idea how that sounds? You're saying you want to *offer yourself* to Nyx. A god that's abandoned us."

"Do *you* want to do it?" She grimaced. "I don't see any alternative. The heads of Houses aren't thinking about sustainability. They care about the throne, and power, and a way to prove they're the only House that matters. Mother is trying her best, but everyone knows the king would rather listen to his advisors and fatten the Crown's treasury." And when it came to which Houses he favored, the Mardovas were at the top. Adela had no interest in a new method of rule; nor did Waren Cyr.

"Mother and Father mean well, but if we go through with this, we can't involve them," Dante said. "The heirs will have to take things into our own hands. If we work together and execute this ritual on Godsnight, it could very well be the thing to break the Sealing. To bridge the Four Realms. To get enough leverage over the king to phase out the monarchy and instill a new order."

"It's still Conjuration," she pointed out. "You know, the thing that's illegal?"

"When's that ever stopped you?"

"I don't care what happens to *me*, I care about what happens to *you*."

"If I may," Lezzaro broke in quietly. "It is a gamble, but the risk is necessary. If we miss our chance, we won't get another for a hundred years. How much more will our realm degrade by then? Will we even be around that long?"

Dante's chest tightened. Yes, it was a risk, but it was one he had to shoulder. Not only as heir to his House, but because he'd been born into a place of privilege, of power, that ultimately meant nothing if he didn't use it for the benefit of those without it.

The gods had refused to speak to him so far. But one way or another, he would make sure he was heard.

VII

Within each of Nexus's four points stood a basilica—one for each god, each realm. The basilicas of Nyx and Phos were largely visited by Other-Realm refugees, and the basilica of Thana was tended to by priests under the care of House Vakara, mostly used for blessings and funerals.

But Deia was and had always been the ruling god of Vitae. She was the god of life, the mother of the elements, and the founder of Angelica's bloodline.

When the country of Vaega had been little more than overgrown forestland, the Headless King had ruled. He'd initiated a war with Parithvi and sent raiders across the Arastra Sea to pillage the coastlines of Azuna and Cardica, even venturing into the Sarnai Steppes to steal prized horses and slaughter their handlers. He had been grooming his eldest son to take the throne, while his second born, Agustín, was sent to the basilica of Deia to become a priest.

Agustín had taken to priesthood willingly, hoping his devotion would prove a counterweight to his father's atrocities. He had not anticipated the god herself to visit him one night, to speak of his father and plant the seed of rebellion in his heart.

With the advantage of a god's blessing, Agustín had beheaded the Headless King and sentenced his brother to imprisonment. Agustín had become the first Holy King, cleansing his father's blood-washed throne.

Deia had lain with Agustín before disappearing. A year later, she returned with a child bristling with power, with the ability to rope all the elements around its body as if to swaddle itself with the earth's bounty.

But a legitimate heir was already swelling in Agustín's wife's belly. Agustín had no choice but to rear his two children together, only one of them bearing the title of heir. Once they were old enough, the second child, Deia's child, was presented with a choice: become a mage for the court, or relinquish all status and devote themself to the basilica.

Mardovas had always favored ambition over piety.

Despite the day's warmth, Angelica wore a hooded cloak to avoid recognition. Two House guards accompanied her, their red-and-blue livery exchanged for street clothing. As she crossed the basilica's square, she took in the facade of light gray stone forming a massive archway in the middle, topped with a dome and a golden spire in the shape of a flame. Patterns of waves and air currents streamed downward, expertly carved so they flowed in and out of each other.

Within the center of the archway stood a thick, living tree, its branches spindling out like fingers and connecting to the top of the arch in a wooden web. There was a myth that Deia herself had planted the tree when the basilica was built. Although it had lived for years too numerous to count, it never reached higher than the apex of the arch.

"Wait here," she told the guards, her wrapped offering held tight against her stomach.

She passed under the tree's branches, reaching out to brush her fingertips over its bark. The tree hummed beneath her touch. Every time she came near she felt its strength radiating across the square, as old and sacred as the first sunrise.

Yet it lived and grew at the whim of the god who had planted it, never able to sprout farther than the walls containing it.

Growing up, Angelica had often seen the basilica filled with hordes of devotees, had heard their pleas to reopen the portals, to heal their withering crops. Today, there were only a few worshippers kneeling before a statue of Deia, candles casting light against the underside of their chins. By their patched clothes and sun-touched skin, they were from the farmland surrounding Nexus.

The priest posted at the door was dressed in a traditional wrap of brown and blue, his sash embroidered with patterns of the four cardinal elements. Angelica removed her hood so he could anoint her with water and earth.

He paused as he reached for the clay bowls. But he said nothing as he dipped his fingers into the water and touched her forehead, followed by a thumbprint of cool soil.

The Mardovas, as part of their House duties, were expected to make offerings to Deia every month. As usual, a priest named Mateo gestured her to follow him to a private offering chamber. She always made sure to visit when he would be in service, appreciating that he never asked unnecessary questions. In fact, he never spoke at all.

On their way to the chamber, they passed a cordoned-off stepwell. It was a geometric wonder, a steep basin of sandstone shelves leading down to a square-shaped floor inlaid with the same patterns embroidered on the priests' sashes. The stairs were cracked and worn in the middle where thousands of feet had trod.

Once, this had been the portal into Vitae, where Other-Realm peoples would appear and ascend the steps into Nexus.

Now it was nothing more than a relic.

Angelica paused beside the rope warning worshippers away from the stepwell. There was a power here that felt out of reach, a craving she couldn't discern.

Mateo waited at the entrance to the chamber. Angelica brushed past him, and the door closed quietly behind her.

Then it was her and the altar. Angelica's pulse quickened at the sight of it, at the familiar mineral scent permeating the room. Clay bowls were laid out in a wide circle on a brocaded sheet, each containing elemental sources: water, soil, a lit candle, incense of ambergris that wafted thin ribbons of smoke, powdered lodestone, hellebore root, salt, a hunk of bone, and congealed blood.

As well as a bowl that always remained empty. Angelica spared it a long look, thinking of the stepwell outside the chamber.

She knelt before the circle, her offering clutched tightly between clammy hands. She unwrapped the cloth and placed it carefully within the center.

It was a piece of glittering fluorite, purple and green with a streak of cloudy gray. Angelica had found it when her family had visited the southern coastline of Vaega. She had been walking near a limestone deposit and felt the thin call of the gem, as if the earth had longed to give her a gift.

And now she was giving it back.

"Blessed Deia, I call upon you," she murmured. "Take my offering and grant me your presence."

Silence. Angelica's heart was in her throat, in her ears, in the very walls around her—maddening and confining, bearing down like judgment. She stared at the bowl containing the candle, its flame dancing seductively before her.

A faint rustle almost made Angelica scurry back.

Slithering into the circle was a sleek gray-green snake. It made a circuit around the bowls, closing in on the piece of fluorite. Its tongue scented the air—scented *her*—as its two beady black eyes turned to the gem.

"A GOODLY PRIZE TO GIVE UP," said the snake in the hushed, sibilant voice of Deia. "FOR ONLY THE HONOR OF MY PRESENCE."

Angelica exhaled shakily. "Blessed Deia, I am afraid it is not only your presence I desire, but a granting of my request."

The Conjurers resurfacing had made a pressure well up within her, ultimately inspiring her to return to the basilica. If her theory about the Conjurers using energy from the Cosmic Scale was correct, then another large-scale attack would lead to more environmental disaster.

She wanted—no, needed—more tools at her disposal. Power with which to target not only the Conjurers, but the barriers from which they siphoned off energy to fuel their rituals.

The snake regarded the fluorite a moment longer. Then it moved toward her, silent and sinister. Angelica trembled as its lithe, strong body coiled around her, curling over her shoulders.

"IT HAS BEEN MONTHS SINCE YOU LAST CAME TO SEE ME," the god whispered in her ear. "YET NOW YOU COME WHEN A DEMAND BURNS LIKE A COAL UPON YOUR TONGUE."

Angelica remained silent, head down, penitent. Deia chuckled.

"TELL ME WHAT IT IS YOU DESIRE," the god whispered. "MY BLOOD. MY HEIR."

Angelica opened her mouth, the words blazoned across her mind but frozen on her lips. She thought of Eran Liolle's pitying eyes whenever he realized she couldn't be taught. The way the other heirs perceived her, silently judging. The way she kept dashing her mother's hopes.

The presence of the god rested on her shoulder, heavy and expectant.

"I want natural access to the elements," Angelica said in a fierce whisper. "Using my own power, without the need to rely on music."

The god was silent, mulling this over. Angelica's skin itched so badly she nearly sobbed at the sheer burning discomfort of it. At the yearning that coiled deep within her, echoed in the dance and flicker of the candle's flame.

"YOU ASK FOR WHAT YOU DO NOT NEED," Deia crooned in her ear.

Angelica tried not to frown. "I...I do need this, blessed Deia. My instruments are an impediment, something others show contempt for. If I am to prove I'm strong, that I am *worthy*, the king will take more notice of our House until we are one day planted on the throne. It would be a victory not only for us, but for you, blessed Deia."

The body of the snake wrapped tighter around her neck. Angelica didn't dare move.

"AND WHAT SORT OF SPECTACLE DO YOU INTEND TO GIVE, TO PROVE SUCH THINGS?" the god whispered. "TO BREAK DOWN THE BARRIERS, PERHAPS? TO UNDO WHAT WE HAVE DONE?"

Angelica curled her fingers into her palms until nails bit skin.

Everyone had turned to the Mardovas when the gods had sealed off the Four Realms. But every time a Mardova asked why, Deia refused to answer. Angelica herself had tried, and Deia had responded by shattering the offering room in which she had knelt.

"YOU WISH TO PROVE YOURSELF ABOVE THE WILL OF THE GODS?" Deia asked.

"N-no, I—"

The snake hissed and disappeared. In its place stood a figure of a woman within the circle's boundary, brilliant and ephemeral.

Angelica shrank back from the true form of Deia. She was tall and pale as ice, her skin a web of cracks like hollow veins in dry earth. Her hair fell to her waist in a sheet of blazing red, the top half of her face concealed by a swath of black lace. She was bare breasted, her hips wrapped with a skirted loincloth. A sword of molten fire was clutched in one hand, and upon her chest lay a single blue eye.

"YOU CANNOT HIDE YOUR TRUE DESIRES FROM ME," Deia said, her voice—like her presence—magnified tenfold. "THIS IS ABOUT PRIDE. YOU WISH TO BE RID OF THIS INFATUATION. THIS WEAKNESS, THIS SICKNESS WITHIN YOU. BUT THIS IS THE PRICE OF TRUE POWER, MY BLOOD. YOU WILL DO WELL TO CULTIVATE IT, TAME IT, BUT NEVER TO LOSE IT."

Angelica's mouth dried. "What good am I as your heir if I'm constantly subjected to this infatuation? To be controlled by so base an instinct? Blessed Deia, please—"

Deia stepped forward, onto the piece of fluorite. It dissolved beneath her bare sole.

"YOU HAVE LAID DOWN YOUR REQUEST, AND I HAVE GIVEN MY

ANSWER," Deia said, the single eye upon her chest unblinking as it stared at her. "ONE DAY I WILL SHOW YOU HOW TO TURN THIS SICKNESS INTO STRENGTH. BUT IT WILL BE ON MY TERMS, NOT YOURS."

The god disappeared, leaving the circle empty and dark.

Angelica knelt there a moment, stunned and panting. Then anger began to swirl in her gut, gathering strength until it flickered over her skin and the offering bowls flew into the walls. They cracked and rattled, spilling their contents across the stone floor. The candle guttered out.

Strength, she thought. *What good is strength without control?*

She felt sick and hollow as she made her way back to the Mardova villa, the hunger in her bones fighting against the nausea in her belly. Everything was off balance. Her skin kept fucking *itching* and she had no way to scratch it, no way to dive under her flesh and rip at the muscle and sinew of herself, to drag this ugly feeling out and stomp on it with her heel.

The guards escorted her through the villa gate and into the main house. Once inside, she was informed that her mother wished to speak with her.

Fuck.

To her surprise, she was led to the gardens. They were bright and colorful under the early autumn sun, the plum trees near the wall still laden with fruit. Miko and her twin daughters were going from tree to tree plucking ripened plums, the girls carrying a basket between them.

A white iron table and chairs had been placed in the shade of a stone pine. Her mother sat there now, ignoring the paperwork she'd brought outside in favor of watching Miko and the twins fondly. Angelica sat in one of the abandoned chairs, eyeing the half-empty glasses of pear nectar juice and palm wine.

"Angel," her mother greeted. "How was the basilica?"

It was Angelica's duty to give offerings every month. She hadn't told her mother it was a duty she'd been neglecting recently. "The same as it ever is."

"Did Deia say anything of importance? Anything about the Conjurers, or the energy they're using?"

This weakness, this sickness within you.

Angelica swallowed. "No. She only took the offering."

Adela sighed as her shoulders slumped, a laxity she only allowed around her family. "I suppose I shouldn't hold my breath. You didn't happen to hear anyone talking about the prelate, did you?"

"No. Has something else happened?"

"A couple of things." Adela straightened her paperwork into a neat stack. They all bore her mother's looping signature at the bottom. "And both upsetting. The first being that he was visited by the Lastriders."

Angelica stiffened. Her mother had decided they wouldn't approach Lezzaro directly, as the king would likely set Don Soler to watch him after his controversial announcement. She'd figured the other Houses would follow suit.

"The eldest and middle child," Adela went on, contempt written in the set of her mouth. "They went directly to his home. In the middle of the day. With plenty of witnesses."

"Is it some sort of statement? Or do they just not care about their reputation?"

"Likely both. I'll be keeping a sharper eye on Elena at our next meeting." Adela rolled her neck, rubbing at one shoulder. Angelica stood and came around the back of her mother's chair. When she dug her thumbs into long-carried knots, Adela groaned in appreciation.

"Thank you, Angel." She went back to watching Miko and her stepdaughters, who were laughing over some shared joke. "Either way, it looks like the Lastrider children are more ambitious than we thought."

Angelica jabbed her thumb into her mother's shoulder, making her flinch. Taesia, ambitious? Taesia didn't give a shit about politics, about power. How could her mother consider that little monster *ambitious* when Angelica was doing everything she could to grow stronger?

Dante, on the other hand…

She thought back to Deia's words, the hard stone of the basilica under her knees, her request gone unfulfilled. Someone like Dante Lastrider could accomplish far more than she could based solely on his standing with the dons and doñas, the easy use of his power.

"What's the other thing?" Angelica forced herself to ask.

"Hmm? Oh." Adela shifted, more relaxed thanks to Angelica's ministrations. "The day after the Lastriders visited, there was an attempted burglary at the prelate's rectory."

"A *burglary*? Why?"

"The motive isn't clear yet, but the high commissioner is investigating as we speak. The most damage the perpetrator caused is a broken window and minor destruction to one of the rooms. The high commissioner believes they were attempting to find something."

"What would the prelate own that's so valuable?" Lezzaro had always been a modest man who refused to live in luxury.

"That's where we're stumped. Even he doesn't know what they could be after."

Angelica thought back to the Autumn Equinox. "Do you think it could be the Conjurers?"

Adela hummed in thought as a breeze smelling of wild bergamot wafted past them and fluttered the papers on the table. "It would be odd, considering his statement about granting them clemency, but certainly possible. You're not in communication with any of the other heirs, are you?"

"Why would I be?" The idea combined with her reawakened bitterness toward the Lastriders made the restless heat crawling under her skin worse. She yanked her hands back before her mother could sense it, shaking them out as if they had cramped.

"Just making sure. Tensions are high, and we need to use this as an opportunity. No matter what happens, we need to side with the king."

Of course. That's what it always came back to, what would always matter most.

Her trembling had gotten worse. She excused herself and made her way back to her rooms on unsteady legs. Weak—she was so weak. But once up the stairs, she wavered, her veins crying and her heart beating fast.

She turned to the recital chamber.

Angelica found her violin case in the cupboard of the practice room. She drew it out with shaking hands and unlatched it, groaning at the sight of the sleek, polished figure of spruce and maple. With a delicate touch, she ran her fingertips over its curves, down the strings, shivering in ecstasy at the soft, ringing sound they made.

The practice room's walls were padded. No one would be able to hear her.

You wish to be rid of this infatuation, Deia had whispered.

Angelica took out her violin and picked up the bow. She impatiently tuned it, but even that tedious act sent a delicious frisson down her spine, already taking the edge off.

Finally, finally, she put the bow to the strings and played.

A sweep of her arm, the bow swooning across the strings. A major chord. The thrill of fire. She closed her eyes and breathed and played, each glissando fueled by the flames licking up her arms, the embers popping around her feet. Just as a breath through her piccolo could produce a gale, each full, mourning note of the instrument in her hands called for heat, for the agony of the element that made her want and crave, never knowing when enough was too much.

Elemental addiction. When too much was never enough.

This weakness, this sickness within you.

The song was lust. The song was grief. And she, caught in the middle, clenched her teeth and kept playing, even as her skin began to burn and peel, even as the ends of her hair turned to ash.

VIII

Nikolas met his new unit in the Bone Palace's adjacent military compound. The yard—a stark, functional space for soldiers to train under an open sky—was scuffed from years of weapons handling, the archways chipped and scratched.

Nikolas eyed the three soldiers' dark blue uniforms. One wore a pin for water, another two pins for earth and fire. The elementalist division had their own practice areas, far enough from the main bulk of the palace to hedge potentially hazardous mistakes. The remaining soldier wore a sword, plying their trade in steel rather than magic.

And then there were the two Hunters. Nikolas had been surprised at their inclusion, but considering they were dealing with magic commonly linked with demons, he supposed it was more out of a sense of precaution.

The soldiers glanced from Nikolas's face to the Sunbringer Spear on his back. When he'd put it on this morning, he had hoped to feel like it belonged there, that it would impart him with confidence. Instead, he felt like an ill-fated fraud. He'd even wrapped the bracelet with the tree charm around the stock, as if it were some sort of luck trinket, but it didn't do much other than jingle from time to time.

"Greetings," he said. "And thank you for your continued service to His Majesty and the Kingdom of Vaega. As you well know by now, you've been hand selected by your superior officers to lend aid to the investigation of the Conjurers. It is imperative we find them before they cause more havoc."

Nikolas hated talking like this, especially when he thought of how

Taesia would tease him for it. But twenty-two years as the Cyr heir had conditioned him to use clipped, refined words to hide how incompetent he was underneath.

It usually worked. The soldiers nodded earnestly, focusing on his speech with undivided attention. Even their posture was impeccable, and Nikolas found himself pushing his own shoulders back.

No doubt this was a dream many officers in the militia had, a dream his title had snatched from them. Nikolas didn't want glory or prowess. He didn't want to lead, or be considered an expert in anything. He had never been ambitious, or even particularly determined. He wanted quiet, and solitude, and maybe a dog.

He cleared his throat and went on, "I hope I don't need to stress how much trust His Majesty is putting into this unit. It will be dangerous, and difficult. If you do not feel up to the task, I would advise you to leave."

No one stirred. Not even a waver of emotion on their faces. Nikolas wondered what it was like to have such conviction.

"Good," he said. "Now, you all know who I am, but I have yet to learn your names. Let's fix that."

The soldiers' rigidity faded somewhat, and a couple of them even smiled. Nikolas spoke with each one personally, learning their names, division, where they were from, and what abilities and techniques they excelled at. The swordsman was named Taide, a young man with floppy brown hair and a scar near his chin. The elementalist who could wield water introduced themself as Gem, their shoulder-length hair pulled back into a ponytail and their face dotted with freckles. Though they were short, Nikolas couldn't mistake the muscle under their uniform jacket. The other elementalist, Komi, wielded earth and fire and came from one of the liberated Azunese colonies of western Marii. His accent was musical and lilting, and though he had dark skin and hair rolled into short locs, his eyes were Azunese.

Nikolas was most interested in the Hunters. They weren't officially part of the military, but they weren't law enforcement either. Their main goal was to protect the city and its surrounding lands from beasts that had turned menacing.

"I have to ask," Nikolas said slowly. "We're working in hypotheticals, but...if the Conjurers do manage to rediscover the practice of demon summoning, is this a threat the Hunters can handle?"

The taller one, Paris, grinned easily while the other, Julian, barely stifled his scowl. "We're more than up for the task," Paris said with a bravado Nikolas envied. "You should hear some of the stories we have. This one time, a kiril was attacking travelers along one of the southern roads, but when I chopped the damn lizard's arm off, it grew *two more* in its place—"

"Paris," Julian murmured.

"What? It was disgusting!"

Nikolas bit his lip to hide his growing smile. "I'll take your word for it."

He was about to give everyone their first orders when the back of his neck prickled, and he glanced up at the windows overlooking the yard. It wasn't unusual for those within the palace to get a glimpse of the activity below, from the servants to the king himself. But the thought of King Ferdinand watching, evaluating—

"My lord?" Komi said. "Where should we start our investigation?"

Nikolas shook himself. "I received word that Prelate Lezzaro might have been targeted by the Conjurers. Someone broke into his home, and they're asking for us to examine the scene."

He'd felt a sickening lurch in his stomach at the news. The idea of someone like Lezzaro potentially coming to harm, let alone being the victim of a home invasion...

Gem frowned. "I thought the prelate was advocating for the Conjurers?"

"Only to the extent that he wants to better understand their motivations," Nikolas said. "Which will first require us catching them."

The others nodded. As they prepared to head to the prelate's rectory, his neck prickled again, but he didn't bother to peer up at the windows. Whoever it was, he might as well let them watch. He was used to scrutiny by now.

Nikolas was silently thankful he had an excuse to see the prelate. He'd wanted to speak with him ever since the Autumn Equinox, too aware of the growing speculation surrounding Lezzaro to risk it on his own, lest it get back to his father.

But now his new unit spread throughout the rectory in search of evidence while the prelate himself watched on at Nikolas's side, eyes pinched. Nikolas was so used to seeing him with a benevolent smile that this new unease heightened his own.

"I appreciate you coming to oversee this, my lord," Lezzaro said. Even his voice was strained.

"Of course, Prelate. I'm only sorry you had to see the task force in action under such circumstances."

A shadow of Lezzaro's smile returned, lessening the tension in Nikolas's shoulders. "I can't fully say I'm surprised. I was aware my announcement might cause anxiety."

"Do you believe this was done out of malice?"

"If so, that was not their only motivation. The high commissioner's men informed me there were signs the perpetrator was attempting to find something."

"What would they be trying to find?"

Lezzaro shook his head, looking older and more fatigued than Nikolas had ever seen him. "I have no clue. As you can see, my household is sparse in ornamentation. All I possess of value are family relics, and those were left behind."

"Do you think it was a Conjurer?"

Lezzaro hesitated before he spoke. "It very well could be. What they hoped to gain from this, I don't know." He clasped his hands together, but not before Nikolas noticed they were shaking.

"They could be suspicious of your offer of asylum," Nikolas said, aching to reassure him somehow. "Perhaps they wanted to find proof that it wasn't a trap."

"That's certainly a possibility." Lezzaro's eyes brightened with something like pride. "Good thinking, my lord."

The warmth in Nikolas's chest was oddly foreign. He allowed himself only a moment to appreciate it before he walked into the sitting room to join his soldiers.

"Just the usual signs of a break-in, my lord," said Taide. "Scuffed floors, broken window."

The window had been broken from the outside, with jagged pieces remaining. Whoever had done this hadn't bothered with finesse. He carefully inspected the sharp points of glass, but there was no torn cloth or blood left behind. Agile, then.

The rest of the room was in a mild state of destruction. The table had been turned over, pottery smashed, and couch cushions ripped open to expose their stuffing. One of the chairs even had a broken leg. The rug was littered with debris.

"Anything out of the ordinary you two can determine?" he asked the Hunters.

Julian inspected the scuffs on the floor. There were two gouges near the window, which he touched with a frown.

"Could be knife marks," Julian said. "Or left by something the intruder threw. Although they're oddly deep."

"This was definitely the work of a human," Paris said. "The damage is too careful. Almost calculated."

"And you're certain that nothing was taken?" Nikolas directed to the prelate, who stood watching from the doorway.

"I checked four times," Lezzaro said. "But I'd be happy to check a fifth, if you so wish."

Nikolas shook his head. "No need, so long as you're sure. Did the breaking glass wake you?"

"Yes. I was upstairs in bed when I heard it. I believe it was past midnight, though I can't be sure of the exact time. I opened my window and signaled to the guards below. But by the time they reached the room, the intruder was gone."

"They've also been questioned?"

"Yes, by the high commissioner himself."

"And...the Lastriders." Nikolas fought to keep his face neutral as his mind filled with images of Taesia, smiling and vibrant and beautiful. "They visited you the day before?"

"They did. But I do not believe they had any hand in this."

Despite his relief at this, the first tendrils of panic began to creep higher. A dead end, and everyone turning to him for what to do next. His mind raced as he stared at the broken chair, then a corner of the rug that had been flipped over. Lezzaro followed his gaze to the rug and swallowed.

"We'll search the outside of the house as well," Nikolas said.

As his soldiers left through the front door, Nikolas hung back. He turned to Lezzaro, who patiently waited for him to formulate his question.

"Forgive me, Prelate, but it's my responsibility to ask: Are you working with the Conjurers?"

"Of course I don't begrudge you this, my lord." Though Lezzaro's smile failed, there was still fondness in his voice. "You've been tasked with protecting the city and its people. I am not working directly with the Conjurers, no. But I have a feeling we may have similar desires."

Nikolas noted the use of *directly* and tucked it away. "Desires?"

"To protect our realm." Lezzaro took a deep breath, knuckles paling from how hard he gripped his hands together. "It's my theory they're experimenting with the occult in order to reopen the portals."

The words nearly knocked the breath out of him. "Wh— How? Is that even possible?"

"At this point, it's hard to say. This is why I wish to speak with them more. However..."

He grasped Nikolas's arm with surprising strength, eyes slightly wild.

"Lord Nikolas, please stay vigilant," Lezzaro whispered with a glance at the door. "Conjuration is fascinating, but also incredibly dangerous. If there's even a sliver of a chance it could bring demons back to our realm..."

Nikolas stood frozen under Lezzaro's bruising fingers. Perhaps this incident had rattled Lezzaro more than Nikolas first thought.

"I will do my best to protect the city," Nikolas said. "Be it from demons or otherwise."

Lezzaro inhaled and nodded, letting him go slowly. "Once everything has been cleaned up," he said with a gesture toward the sitting room, "I would like you to return, my lord. Without your soldiers."

"To discuss this matter further?" he asked carefully.

"To share more insight about the threat we face, and your role in preventing it." Lezzaro put an unsteady hand on Nikolas's shoulder. "There is more you need to know."

Your role in preventing it.

He thought of his father in the basilica, the shame and humiliation he wore as blatantly as one of his gleaming medals. How despite Nikolas being heir, Waren was loath to give him more responsibilities lest the king get wind of his potential failures.

Nikolas inclined his head. "I will return in a couple days, then. Alone." The flash of relief on Lezzaro's face gave him a mix of satisfaction and disquiet.

Outside, the soldiers were studying the spot where the intruder had climbed in. Nikolas was about to join them when a now-familiar prickling sensation erupted over the back of his neck.

His gaze snapped to the rooftops. Crouched on an eave with the sun at their back was a figure dressed in black.

"Hey!" Nikolas shouted. He immediately regretted it when the figure tore across the roof.

He ignored the surprised cries behind him and ran down the street below the figure. As soon as they dropped into an alleyway Nikolas made a sharp turn and barreled forward.

Nikolas delved hard and fast into his power. Lux flared above him as his fingertips glowed, a tingling warmth spreading through his limbs. The Sunbringer Spear pulsed against his back, the pull of Phos's feathers distant yet persistent.

Come on, he thought furiously, tapping into his lightspeed ability, urging his body to disappear and rematerialize farther ahead. *Come* on!

He thought of wings, luminous and golden.

A pop and spark within him, the *crack* of lightspeed taking hold of his body and flinging him through space and time. Nikolas's feet hit solid ground.

He had only jumped a couple feet forward.

"*Shit*." He flung Lux out like a cannon blast, hitting the figure between the shoulder blades. They stumbled and bounced off the nearest wall, something clattering to the ground before they tore off again, out of sight.

Nikolas summoned Lux back to him and caught his breath. The pounding of footsteps announced the arrival of his unit.

"My lord?" Gem ventured. "What happened?"

"I don't know. But we were definitely being watched." He approached the spot where Lux had hit the culprit. Lying against damp brick was a mask in the shape of a skull.

He knelt and picked it up. Paris made a sound of recognition behind him.

"Aren't the Conjurers said to be wearing those?"

"Yes," Nikolas said slowly. "Which means they're aware of our mission."

This should have been confirmation enough that they were the ones who had infiltrated the prelate's house. But despite his wariness, his desperate plea to Nikolas, Lezzaro still wanted to protect them. Why?

There is more you need to know.

Nikolas frowned at the mask in his hand. For all he knew, the break-in could have been orchestrated by Lezzaro himself to throw off suspicion.

Nikolas shoved the thought away. He would return on his own to get answers, to learn what role Lezzaro intended for him—and whether or not he could accomplish it.

IX

The public library of Nexus was as beautiful on the inside as it was the outside, multiple levels of shelves arranged neatly beneath a wide dome from which hung an elaborate chandelier. All of the Houses were patrons of the library, and Dante was glad to see their money didn't go to waste.

He inhaled deeply, savoring the smell of paper, vellum, and binding glue. Beside him, Brailee did the same.

"I wish I could bottle this," his youngest sister said, hugging a couple of brightly colored books to her chest. She'd picked them up only a few days ago and had read them cover to cover already. "But maybe that would make it less special."

Dante grinned. "Ever insightful, Bee."

She rolled her eyes. "I'm surprised Tae didn't want to come."

"She's pestering Nik today. Besides, I'm pretty sure she's been banned for not returning books." Brailee huffed in agreement. "What are you reading these days, anyway?"

He plucked one of the books from her grasp despite her protests. The cover was a belligerent shade of green featuring silhouettes of a man and woman in an embrace underneath the title's flowing script.

"*The Doña's Secret*, huh? I didn't know you liked romances."

Brailee grabbed it back, flushing. "Aunt Camilla gave me some recommendations."

"She does have good taste," he admitted. He was gratified by the smile this earned him.

But mention of their aunt reminded him of the purpose of this visit. He'd already exhausted the villa's library for more information on ancient rituals and Godsnight. Ever since speaking to Prelate Lezzaro, he'd wanted to study it, but found his resources frustratingly limited.

There was so much he didn't understand, and he had a suspicion Lezzaro was purposefully keeping answers from them, answers that could be found within that grimoire. But not even Dante's most charismatic wiles would convince Lezzaro to let him have a peek.

Maybe it didn't mean anything. Maybe Lezzaro wanted to wait for all the Houses to agree to the ritual before divulging more.

Still, Dante wanted to be prepared. After hearing about the break-in, he and Taesia had exchanged a long, meaningful look. Lezzaro was in league with the Conjurers, but that didn't mean they were beholden to him. What if they slipped out of his control?

"Dante?"

He automatically reached out to ruffle Brailee's hair. She swatted his hand away with a vexed sound.

"It's warm in here," he complained. "The library needs better cross breezes."

"Right. I'll be over in that section. I'll come find you when I'm done."

She wandered toward the novels while Dante headed for the reference books. He made efficient use of a librarian, who helped him locate several tomes on planar properties, ancient Vaegan history, and myths collected from the Four Realms. Once he was armed with an imposing yet promising stack, he claimed a table and got to work.

Four books and one paper cut later, he had a whole slew of notes written out yet nothing of much use. The books largely covered things he already knew: myths of how the gods were born—his favorite being Nyx formed from a moon's tears, though he supposed he was biased—how the portals were connected along the Cosmic Scale, and that Godsnight was once used as a day for the Houses to perform grand feats of magic.

Brailee had long since come to join him, engrossed in something titled *The Beastly Affair*. Dante was afraid to ask. He took a break to watch her dark eyes skim over the pages, the prominent bags underneath them telling of another difficult night of sleep. Her familiar, Somnus, was tucked against her neck.

As he stared at Somnus, Dante's tired mind kicked back to life. Not all Noctans were Shades, but all Shades carried shadow familiars. They were regarded as extensions of the Shade who bore them, tools with which to perform their magic.

Tools.

Dante sat back. The book spread out before him was on planar properties. He flipped back to the sketch of the Cosmic Scale, the universe's map, and narrowed in on the thread connecting Vitae to Noctus.

"This isn't going to be easy," he'd told Taesia after meeting with Lezzaro. "If it hasn't been accomplished in five hundred years, there's little chance of us accomplishing it now unless we create fail-safes."

"Fail-safes?"

"Additional steps taken to ensure we succeed. The prelate is already using the Conjurers to thin the barriers by using up energy. What if we can do something like that, too?"

Brailee started when he stood. He gestured for her to keep reading and found the librarian again, who pointed him to the shelf he needed. He climbed the ladder and pulled out a yellow-bound book, the cover illustrated with fantastical animals. A bestiary.

He sat on the lowest ladder rung and turned to the section on Noctan beasts. Turning the pages, he reached a particular image that made him pause.

It was a wolflike beast, its fur long and bristling, its eyes pure, milky white. A constellation burned bright on its brow, with sharp lines around its body indicating an ethereal glow.

The page's header called it an astralam. Wayward stars broken off from their constellations, fallen to earth and turned to creatures imbued with cosmic power. Whenever one happened to be captured, the hide, teeth, and bones were all harvested for magical purposes. They could produce gravitational forces, some so strong they could replicate the lightless hollows left by dying stars, as well as manipulate celestial energy to form temporary portals.

Dante's breathing grew thin. Making sure the librarian was gone, he tore out the page with an apologetic wince and tucked it into his pocket. He replaced the bestiary and returned to the table.

"I'm done," Dante said cheerfully. He collected his stack at the table's edge for the librarian to put away; they got fussy about patrons doing it wrong. "Ready to head home? We can stop by that bakery you like on the way back."

Brailee studied him a moment, brow furrowed. Like she could see straight through the lightness of his voice, the beaded sweat on his forehead, and what was clearly a bribe. But eventually she closed her book and gathered up the others she was taking with her.

"All right," she said. "But you're buying me an entire almond cake."

"Deal."

The bestiary's page burned in his pocket. He'd been planning to check on Prelate Lezzaro anyway, but now he had something new to bring him—a fail-safe, the seed of an idea that could end up ensuring at least one barrier was destroyed come Godsnight.

Dante made his way to the prelate's rectory on foot later that night. He couldn't risk using the carriage; over dinner he'd told his mother he was going to a wine bar to have drinks with a don's son.

"You're supposed to finalize the minutes from the merchant's council," Elena had argued. "Your father needs notes by tomorrow morning."

Dante had caught Taesia's eye. Her face had hardened in displeasure, a look that meant *You owe me for this.*

"I'll do it," Taesia had drawled while spearing a piece of chicken on her fork.

Elena's eyebrows had leapt toward her hairline. "You will?"

"Sure. It's important for Dante to make connections with the gentry." Her grin had been a shade too mean for his liking. "He'll need to think about marriage someday soon."

Dante had quickly wiped away a scowl as their mother turned back to him with a sigh.

"I suppose that's true," Elena had conceded. At her side, Brailee had given him the same odd expression she'd worn in the library. "Just don't drink too much and make a fool of yourself in public."

Dante yearned to actually be in a wine bar right now, with a glass of something red and rich in his hand. A crawling restlessness had been itching under his skin since the library, since gazing on the sketch of that beast. He hadn't had an opportunity to share it with Taesia yet—had been hoping to bring her with him tonight—but this felt too important to put off.

Godsnight was less than two months away. If they wanted to be prepared, they had to act *now.*

The guards at the entrance stopped him. "The prelate is usually preparing for bed around this time, my lord," one of them said.

Dante employed a disarming smile with just the right amount of remorse. "I'm deeply sorry for troubling him at such an hour, but I'm afraid it can't wait. I was hoping to get his input regarding a sensitive matter by tomorrow morning."

The guards hesitated. No doubt they were under orders from the high commissioner to be more obdurate in who they let inside. But being heir to a House had its advantages, and Dante wasn't a stranger in using them to get his way. The guards granted him entry without further questions.

The footman didn't answer Dante's knock, having likely retired for the night. Dante tested the door and found it unlocked. He frowned at the laxness but was grateful for it as he stepped inside and closed the front door behind him.

The foyer was lit only by a single lamp, casting twitchy, misshapen shadows across the walls. The rectory was oppressively silent, without even the common noises of a house settling. Dante strained to hear the creak of a floorboard or the groaning of a rafter, but in addition to the silence was an eerie stillness, as if the building held its breath around him.

He found himself doing the same and forced the air from his lungs. Sensing his disquiet, Nox unspooled from its ring, another shadow in the gloom.

Dante didn't like the idea of waking and potentially spooking Lezzaro, but he couldn't wait. Touching a hand to where his notes were concealed, he turned to the stairs and paused at the sight of the doorway to the sitting room.

His heart tapped nervously against his breastbone as he looked between the stairs and the doorway. With a dry mouth, he advanced toward the sitting room.

He hadn't seen the wreckage of the break-in, and it had since been repaired so that it looked as if it hadn't happened at all. But it smelled strange, like sawdust and something unpleasant—almost sulfurous.

That was when he noticed the corner of the rug was flipped over, revealing the closed door to the underground safe room. Was the prelate down there? Or had he simply forgotten to straighten the rug when leaving?

Dante slowly knelt and gripped the door's flat metal handle, pulling it open with a faint creak. The sulfurous stench grew stronger, making his nose wrinkle. The stone stairs were utterly dark except for a flicker of light on the very last step.

A strange, garbled sound echoed up the narrow passageway, raising the hairs along Dante's nape. Nox formed into a dagger of shadow in his hand in response to the spike of his pulse.

He opened his mouth to call down, but his vocal cords were a tangled knot. Warily he lowered himself onto the stairs, arms prickling with goose bumps at the next wet, choking sound.

Dante reached the last step and lost his footing. He landed hard, but the pain barely registered over the shock.

Pressed up against the opposite wall was Lezzaro. He feebly struggled against the hand that held him several feet above the floor, face swollen with blood, eyes bulging in their sockets. He scratched at the fingers choking him while scrabbling uselessly at unforgiving stone.

Dante stared. Stared until he realized what he was seeing, but even then understanding eluded him, because the person choking the prelate— no, the *thing*—was straight out of Dante's nightmares.

Underneath a hazy red aura was a figure that was humanoid and wrong, its angles too sharp, its presence teeth-aching. It gave a low, rasping laugh as Lezzaro twitched in its clutches, eyes rolling to the back of his skull as blood trickled from his mouth.

A loud *crack* reverberated through the small chamber.

The sound startled Dante to his feet, Nox held out before him. Lezzaro's choking had stopped; the only sound left was Dante's harsh, panting breaths.

The thing tossed Lezzaro's body aside. The prelate rolled limply, lifelessly, his neck bent at an alarming angle.

And then the creature looked over its shoulder at Dante with too-black eyes. The eyes of a monster.

The eyes of a demon.

Dante pressed his back against the wall as it slowly turned and stalked toward him. Its skin was deep crimson, dark hair rippling from its skull and over the sharp spikes curving up from its shoulders, over its breasts. Thin black chains wrapped around its forearms.

As it drew nearer to Dante, its mouth widened in a grin. It reached for him with unnaturally long fingers, black-nailed and sharp, and Nox trembled apart in his hand to flee up to his shoulder.

Then the chains around the demon's forearms jerked, making it step back with a hiss. The chains grew taut, and Dante followed them to the corner, to the cloaked figure he'd been too distracted to notice until now.

"Enough," they said.

The demon bared its teeth. The chains yanked again, and it growled low in its throat before crouching beside Lezzaro. It glared at Dante over the body with the same smugness of a cat who brought its owner a dead bird. *This is how you hunt. This is how you kill.*

Dante's head had grown dangerously light, his mind longing to disassociate from his body, to wake up in bed and stare at the ceiling and remind himself it was just a dream.

The cloaked figure stepped toward him. Dante's fingers twitched, gathering shadows to him, ready to conceal himself and run for the stairs.

"That won't be necessary," said the person—the Conjurer—from within the darkness of their hood, their words gravelly. "You'd be no match for Shanizeh."

Shanizeh? Dante glanced at the demon, who was staring at Lezzaro's body as if longing to devour it.

"If..." Dante's voice was little more than a croak. "If you've come for the grimoire—"

"The grimoire isn't here," they said with an audible sneer. They gestured to the shelves, once lined with books and now sitting empty. "He must have hidden it after last time."

The demon was now trailing one long, black nail over the broken blood vessels on Lezzaro's face. Dante fought to swallow. "Wh...What do you want from me?"

The barest whisper of a laugh came from the Conjurer's hood as it turned back toward him.

"Your cooperation," they said.

Taesia hid within the bower of her shadows as she leaned against an archway and watched Nikolas run his unit through drills.

She should have announced her presence, but she enjoyed observing him when he was focused and misty with sweat. The sleeves of his shirt had been rolled to his elbows, showing off his forearms. With the Sunbringer Spear resplendent over his shoulder, she felt drawn to him like a devotee to worship.

She wondered if he had used the ancient weapon yet. He refrained from doing so now, instead pairing soldiers up to go over grappling moves.

"If we run into another Conjurer, we have to be prepared to engage with both weapons and hand to hand," Nikolas said. Normally when he spoke his voice was quiet, gentle, but now it was firm and clear in a way that made her smile. "We need to restrain them quickly. Considering you haven't been given the same training as the city guard, there are a couple techniques I'd like to show you."

He demonstrated on one of the Hunters, the one with shaven undersides. He was shorter than Nikolas, but their build was similar. The Hunter obediently moved where Nikolas positioned him, slowly going through different takedowns that all ended with the Hunter on his knees or on the ground. The last ended with Nikolas straddling the Hunter and pinning his arms behind his back. Taesia raised her eyebrows, storing the image away for later.

Nikolas walked toward the archways while the soldiers practiced on one another. He grabbed his waterskin and leaned his head back to drink, and she hungrily watched a bead of water escape the corner of his mouth and hang off his jaw.

She crept forward and waited for him to lower the waterskin before she grabbed his ass. He jumped and reached for his spear as Taesia let the shadows dissolve with a laugh.

"I'm sorry," she gasped, leaning her forehead against his shoulder and shaking with giggles. "The opportunity was too good to pass up."

His sigh was long-suffering. "Have you been here this whole time?"

"Maybe." She wrapped her arms around his waist. "You're good with them. I can tell they respect you already."

Nikolas hummed, uncertain. "Even after watching me let a Conjurer get away?"

He'd told her about his visit to Lezzaro the other day. "They took you by surprise. You'll be better prepared next time. But speaking of, did you see the prelate today?"

He turned fully to face her, and she let her arms drop back to her sides. "I went in the morning, but he wasn't home." He frowned. "No one seemed to know where he was."

She mirrored his frown. That was odd, considering Lezzaro almost always had guards nearby. They should have been more attentive after the break-in.

She wondered if it had anything to do with Dante's visit the night before. She'd waited up for him, eager to hear what they'd discussed, but dozed off before he could return home. And no matter how persistently she'd knocked on his door that morning, he hadn't answered.

He could just be sleeping in. But it wasn't like Dante to ignore her.

"He might be at one of the basilicas," she said.

"Maybe. The footman said he hadn't even taken breakfast." Nikolas shook his head. "I'll try again later this afternoon."

He glanced at the soldiers, then took her hand to draw her behind the archway. Their familiars stirred and began to circle one another like orbiting planets. "He said he had something to tell me, that I should come alone. But you and Dante spoke to him already. Did he ... Is there anything you can tell me?"

She hesitated under his imploring expression. She was usually weak to it, but something like this was too delicate to whisper behind an archway with strangers only a few feet away. On the grounds of the Bone Palace, no less.

"It's better if he explains it," she said while patting his hand. "I'd come with you, but we have to deliver goods to the refugees tonight."

He nodded. After a moment he lifted her hand to kiss her knuckles, and the heavy feeling that had been growing in the pit of her stomach lessened.

Soon Nikolas would be tied into their plans, then Risha, and hopefully (though she wasn't holding her breath) Angelica. Dante would be one step closer to achieving his goals.

And she'd be one step closer to being free.

The Noctus Quarter was tucked in the eastern corner of the city, close to the basilica of Nyx. Once a slum, it had been converted after the diaspora created by the Sealing, when roughly two thousand Noctans had been abandoned in this realm. With no way to return to their own realm, they had been shoved into crooked, crumbling tenements and forced to call Nexus their new home.

As emissaries to Noctus, the Lastriders had taken on the responsibility of providing supplies for the displaced Noctans. Jobs, food, and medicine were often difficult to come by for the refugees when so many Vitaeans distrusted and despised them. Beyond that, new diseases had sprung up among their population, forced to live in a realm their bodies were not adapted for.

Taesia thought back to the half-Noctan girl at the market taken away by guards and wondered where she had ended up.

She and her siblings walked alongside the supply wagon, Elena sitting up on the bench with the driver. House guards flanked them, more watchful than usual. Taesia kept glancing at Dante, his face unnaturally strained, his color off. If he felt her attempts to get his attention, he stalwartly ignored them.

"It always smells like cloves here, don't you think?" she asked, hoping to bait him. To her, though, the smell of the Noctus Quarter was similar to that of the basilica, something more complex than cloves; something velvet and sweet and dark, like the latest hour of a crisp, fall night, when the air was filled with both the decay of leaves and the growth of harvest.

It was fitting, she thought, that it smelled like the border between life and death.

He made a noncommittal noise. Undeterred, Taesia turned to Brailee on her other side. "What do you think, Bee? Does it smell like cloves to you?"

Brailee shot her a glare and pulled her hood over her head.

"Everything all right?" Taesia ventured, making sure her voice wouldn't carry to their mother. "Can't help but notice you've been in a sour mood lately."

"Everything is *fine*."

"Sure doesn't sound like it. Anything we can do?"

Brailee huffed, the sound more tired than indignant. "The two of you can stop sneaking off all the time and tell me what you're up to."

Taesia swallowed a surprised cough. "What gives you the impression we're up to something?"

"Please." Taesia realized her sister's eyes were veined with red. Her familiar was lazily draped over her shoulders like a thin shawl. "You might be able to fool others, but I know you."

"Are you having sleep problems again?" Taesia asked, mostly out of concern but partly to shift the topic. Sleep had never been easy for Brailee. Ever since she was young she had been prone to vivid, surreal dreams that left her exhausted come morning. She'd tried sleeping draughts, but claimed they made her muddled and cotton-mouthed.

The muscle at Brailee's jaw jutted out. "If you're not going to tell me what's going on, fine. But don't pretend I'm clueless." She lengthened her stride to walk ahead of them.

"Nyx's piss," Taesia muttered. "We can't tell her, right? We shouldn't risk getting her into trouble."

Dante ran a hand slowly through his hair, a wavy lock settling against his forehead. "She doesn't understand, but she will."

Even his voice was washed of color, all the liveliness drained out of him. His gaze was eerily distant, and he was twitchier than she ever remembered him being.

"What happened last night?" Taesia whispered.

He tensed, then shook his head. "Nothing."

"It doesn't seem like nothing."

"I'm *tired*, Tae."

She couldn't help a twinge of annoyance. The two of them were keeping secrets from Brailee, but the thought of Dante keeping secrets from Taesia as well was...unpleasant.

Taesia's body was strung as tight as one of Angelica's ridiculous instruments as they made their way through uneven streets. City guards were patrolling even here, as if expecting occult dealings between these derelict buildings. Taesia suspected the Solara Quarter was being given the same treatment; suspicion always targeted outsiders first, and the Other-Realm refugees got the brunt of it.

And it wasn't as if King Ferdinand did much to protect them. If anything, his silence encouraged the animosity.

They passed the tall, imposing structure of the Nyx basilica. It had been crafted with black stone, cornered by towering minarets, its facade studded with gargoyles of Noctan beasts amid engravings of constellations. Coming here always transported her back to her childhood, when her family had paid their respects to Nyx on a weekly basis. Back when the three Lastrider siblings had only argued over who got to eat the last cream puff at dinner or who got to light an offering candle during prayers.

Cobblestones glittered in the solemn dusk light, the walls of white-washed brick tinged lavender and ruby. Brick arches above their heads formed natural bridges between buildings that each housed a family on both the top and bottom floors. From the arches hung garlands of paper and gemstone, amber and amethyst winking in the fading light, paper stars and moons twirling in the warm breeze.

"You'd think they'd sell those," Taesia had said when she was younger, pointing to the garlands.

"Stones are sacred to them," her mother had explained. "To *us*. They use them to store dreams and memory."

Being a Shade meant the ability to wield shadows, but there were certain talents unique to certain Shades. Taesia had always naturally been drawn to shadow manipulation, whereas Dante was clever with shaping shadows into objects. Elena herself specialized in retrieving and storing memories, her office at the villa filled with glittering hunks of rock and jewel that contained moments of joy and sorrow. She often helped aging dons and doñas who had dementia, and those who had suffered trauma or head injuries.

Despite it being dusk, the refugees who stood under the awnings to greet them still blinked and squinted against the waning daylight. White markings stood out starkly from their ink-dark skin, some of their eyes so pale they rivaled the gemstones hanging from the arches overhead.

Elena straightened with a smile as a Noctan man came forward. He was tall, with horns curving back in S shapes. White tattoos had been etched into his skin, two straight lines plunging from his hairline and trailing over his eyebrows that marked him as a leader.

"My lady." The Noctan man bowed, his long black hair falling over his shoulders. "It is always an honor to see you."

"Thank you, Balwith. I trust you're well?"

"Well enough, my lady. However, there have been more and more cases of sunsickness among us. Summer is a difficult season, as always."

"I understand. We've brought medicine and extra food rations for your stores. There are also blocks of ice packed in straw for you to keep in your cellars. Hopefully that and the approaching autumn will provide your people some relief."

Balwith bowed in thanks. The structure of Noctan society in Nexus was tenuous; they did not acknowledge Ferdinand Accardi as their ruler, but they honored the god Nyx, which meant the only authority they recognized was the Lastriders, descended from Nyx himself.

Elena helped the Noctans sort supplies, divvying up the work between her children. Taesia hefted a crate of ice and followed a Noctan woman to an unevenly plastered building with a door painted black.

"Through here, my lady." The Noctan woman bowed. When she straightened, Taesia noticed the tightness of her mouth and the trembling of her hands, as if she were exhausted, hungry, sick—or perhaps all three.

Sensing her scrutiny, the woman dropped her gaze. "We appreciate all the Lastriders do for us, my lady. The summers seem to keep getting hotter, and our elders and youngest have been hit the worst. We've already lost a few of our own. I . . . we thank you for this. Truly."

Taesia's throat tightened. It wasn't their fault they were stuck here, not their fault no one else in this city wanted to take responsibility for them. The king did nothing. The guards did nothing. The other Houses did nothing.

Dante was trying to clear a path forward when everyone else was content to keep things as they were, lingering year by year until the whole realm of Vitae fell to decay.

They didn't need the gods. They didn't need the king. They didn't even need the Houses. They needed to protect their people, and somewhere along the line, that had been forgotten in exchange for salivating over a rusty throne.

Taesia inclined her head to the woman and crossed the threshold. The smell of Noctus was stronger here, warm and heavy. There was hardly any light, and Taesia had to blink furiously to get a good sense of her surroundings. Figures came into focus, seated on threadbare sofas and rugs, in wooden chairs that creaked as their occupants leaned forward.

They were all Noctans. Many sported white tattoos coiling up their cheeks and across their foreheads. Their hair was either black, white, or silver; the only way to tell who was an elder were the wrinkles on their faces and hands. Those hands bore long, knobby fingers and sharp nails. Several had horns growing in graceful, curling arcs.

Taesia hadn't expected so many of them. Their eyes were precious stones in the shadows, from garnet to sapphire to agate. They focused on her, on the ring that bore Umbra, sniffing the scent of nighttime in her blood. A few of them were Shades like her, with familiars worn around their wrists like bangles in the traditional style.

She resisted the urge to shift on her feet, to turn away after she set the crate down. How could she possibly consider herself one of them when they were so much *more* than she was?

Dante joined her and set down his own armful of supplies. He gave the Noctans a small smile. Some of them smiled back.

Taesia grabbed his arm on the threshold. "What aren't you telling me?"

"What?"

"You and the prelate. What did you talk about last night?"

"Tae...let's not do this here."

He gently pried himself from her grip and walked back into the street. Nox hovered above Dante's shoulder, curious or perhaps comforted by their surroundings.

"We're in this together, right?" Taesia demanded as she followed. "So you need to trust me."

"I do. But..." He sighed and rubbed his hands against his bloodshot eyes. "There's been a...complication."

"What sort of complication, Dante?" She accidentally raised her voice, making their mother look over with a scowl.

"Later," Dante muttered as he turned back to the wagon.

Elena handed off the last of the supplies and turned to Balwith. "Please let us know if you require anything else in the upcoming weeks. Once the harvest comes in from the surrounding farms, we should have quite a bit more for you."

Provided they don't fall to sudden blight, Taesia thought.

Balwith bowed deeply. "Your kindness is as infinite as the night sky, my lady. We are forever indebted to you." Elena accepted the familiar reverence with a graceful tilt of her chin. "Would you care to step into the basilica before you go?"

The question was mere formality; they were expected to display some semblance of piety whenever they visited. As they turned to the large, dark structure wreathed in sculpted beasts, Dante's arm brushed Taesia's.

"It's not that I don't trust you," he whispered. "It's that...something happened."

Her heart thudded. "Tell me."

He took a deep breath, making sure they trailed behind everyone else. Sweat dotted his temples. Her brother was *scared*—and if Dante was scared, that made her terrified.

"It's Lezzaro." He swallowed. "He—"

"Halt!"

Their congregation froze at the voice that carried across the basilica square. A flurry of movement at the far end revealed a small troop of royal guards in crisp blue uniforms. At their forefront stood Don Soler.

Elena put a hand on Brailee's shoulder. "Don? What are you doing here?"

Instead of answering, he gave an order to the guards at his back. "Seize him." He pointed, his finger sweeping through the air.

And landing on Dante.

Balwith and the other Noctans scrambled back as guards surged toward them. Elena moved to stand between them and Dante.

"What is the meaning of this?" she demanded.

"Dante Lastrider was seen entering Prelate Lezzaro's rectory last night." Don Soler's voice rang through the square. "The guards who stood watch after the midnight shift change did not see him leave. Earlier today, the prelate was found dead in his own home. Right beside a Conjuration circle."

Brailee gasped as shocked sounds rippled through the onlookers. Taesia whipped around to stare at Dante, watched the blood drain from his face.

Don Soler went on, "Dante Lastrider is hereby arrested for conspiring with the Conjurers and committing treasonous crimes against the Holy Kingdom of Vaega."

The guards moved around Elena to grab Dante, wrenching his arms up behind his back as Nox flitted anxiously through the air. Dante didn't even fight them, his face wild with confusion. Taesia could barely breathe as he was dragged across the square.

"This is absurd!" Elena cried. "My son is not a Conjurer, and certainly not a murderer!"

"I'm sure a trial will shed more light on this, my lady," Don Soler said. "But our prelate is dead, and we must take action."

Taesia finally broke through her stupor and sprinted forward, heart in her throat. She didn't know what she was doing, her mind wiped blank, but she had to stop this, stop *them*. She reached out to grab Don Soler by the collar, lips peeled back in a snarl.

"*Taesia.*"

She staggered to a halt. She had never heard her brother say her name that way, cutting through the air like a knife to a major artery. Dante's eyes were hard with warning as he gave a barely perceptible shake of his head.

Don't.

Her vision blurred as the guards swept out of the basilica square as violently as they'd swept in. Elena was still yelling, the Noctans muttering among themselves.

Umbra zoomed around her fitfully, matching the frantic pulse under her jaw. But as Dante was shoved from sight, she couldn't move, couldn't think of anything other than her brother's final command.

Don't.

She was always the one receiving orders, his partner, his general.

And now she was on her own.

XI

Thana's Chapel had already been wrecked by the time Risha and her father arrived.

For the Holy King's convenient and frequent prayer, four chapels had been built in the Bone Palace—one for each god. It was common for soldiers, advisors, and royal relatives to have their bodies laid out on the viewing dais of Thana's Chapel for at least a day before burial or burning, the latter of which was far more uncommon these days. Monarchs were a different story; they were doused in embalming fluid and herbs, then entombed within the mausoleum below the Bone Palace.

The walls and columns of layered bone had been scoured as if by a beast's claws, and tall silver candelabra had been knocked over. The black marble floor was dusty with the ashes of past famed nobles and generals of Vaega's history, spilled from broken vases and urns.

Looking at the vessel that had once been Prelate Lezzaro, Risha direly wished the king would allow the citizens at large to start burning their dead again.

Her father was grim yet calm at her side, dressed in his necromantic gear. Ferdinand was nowhere to be found; instead, they had been led here by a twitchy advisor with bulging eyes.

"How long has he been like this?" Rath asked as he pulled string from his pouch. A short black beard softened his strong jaw, his eyes so dark they were nearly black.

"A-about an hour," the advisor croaked from the silver doors, wincing as Prelate Lezzaro punched a column, making the room shudder. "Or a little more."

The prelate's body was swathed in fine robes embroidered in thread of red, gold, black, and silver to pay homage to the four gods. He was supposed to lie in Thana's Chapel for two days while the priests under his care came to say their goodbyes with burial wreaths and gifts for the afterlife.

Now his robes were dusty and torn, and his grayed skin still bore the faint tracks of broken veins. His neck, having been reset, bulged oddly with broken bones. Lezzaro had been a gentle, kind man in life, yet now he'd come back steeped in resentment, as if unable to move on from his violent end.

Did Dante really do this? she wondered as she copied her father's movements and wove her string into a complex shape between her fingers, the spell for binding. To say everyone had been shocked at the news would be an understatement. She couldn't reconcile the young man she knew with the injuries made to the prelate's body, couldn't understand how he'd be capable of such cruelty.

Once Lezzaro sensed their presence, he turned to the Vakaras with blank eyes and a slack jaw. He made a rattling moan and lunged, much quicker than the skeleton at the basilica had, his body far fresher.

He froze in a grotesque contortion as their spells took effect, teeth bared and those horrible moans echoing against bone and marble. Behind them, the advisor squeaked.

"I will keep him contained," her father said, ever calm. "You release his spirit."

Risha changed the shape of her spell, murmuring a prayer as she did. She stepped closer to the prelate's quivering body, his filmy gaze following her movements. She smelled the preserving liquid on his skin, the faint scent of death under sachets packed with lavender and thyme in his robes. Lezzaro's jaw moved, teeth clacking together, the rattling of bone.

And then he spoke.

"—ealing," he wheezed from a throat already tightened with rigor mortis.

Risha paused. Even her father stopped.

"Se—ee—ling," the body moaned.

"The . . . Sealing?" Risha ventured even as a chill rushed up her spine.

"Wait outside," Rath ordered the advisor, who needed no further reason to scuttle out the doors and close them. "Prelate, please tell us your message."

Lezzaro's head flopped back, the shape of his thyroid cartilage pressed up against mottled skin. "Gods...night. See...eee...De...mo..."

Risha glanced at her father, who nodded for her to continue. "You want to say something about Godsnight and the Sealing?"

"Wanted...open," Lezzaro said in a creaking, dusty voice. "Seal... Like old..." He shuddered violently, a high, shrieking sound leaking from his mouth. "Conjure...No! Don't let...! De—!"

He thrashed against the binding spell. Risha quickly finished her prayer and twisted the string, snapping it between her hands. She felt Lezzaro's spirit depart, wrenched from his decaying chest into the black void between their realm and Mortri. The body fell to the marble floor in a vulgar heap.

Risha steadied her breathing before she turned to her father. He stared at the prelate's body, mouth a thin line.

"What did he mean?" she whispered. "What was he talking about?"

Her father shook his head and returned to the doors to let the advisor back in. "I do not know. But don't speak of it to anyone."

The advisor sighed in relief once he saw the prelate fully dead once more. "Our deepest thanks, my lord, my lady. His Majesty would have come, but his guards insisted on moving him to the safe room."

"As they should," her father said gravely. "We'll likely see more of this in the coming months. We need to take greater preventative measures."

As he spoke to the advisor, Risha laid the body out straight, mulling over the prelate's message. Eventually her father waved her off, insisting he would do it. So she wandered toward the viewing dais instead, moving the candles so the gauzy black curtains wouldn't go up in flame.

Lifting the last one, Risha froze. She knelt on the floor, putting her head close to the marble. She had stepped in what she thought was more spilled ash, but in the light of the flame the color was different, white as chalk. Her heart began to pound.

A Conjuration circle had been drawn with the viewing dais at its center. It was the same seven-pointed star configuration she had seen outside the basilica.

She'd thought the prelate's spirit had raised his body of its own accord. Had the man in the skull mask found a way inside the Bone Palace? How? *Why?*

She steadied herself against the dais and her hand brushed something soft. A long-stemmed rose, its petals completely black.

*   *   *

Risha double-checked her hair in the mirror, frowning at her reflection. The puffiness under her eyes spoke to a night of restlessness, her mind whirring nonstop since hearing about Dante's arrest two days ago.

She'd wanted to visit Taesia as soon as they'd returned home from the Bone Palace, but her father had stopped her.

"We cannot be seen speaking to them. This is a scandal fit to ruin their House. Distance is prudent."

A rebuttal had curdled in her mouth even as Saya didn't hesitate to argue; she was friends with the youngest Lastrider sibling and wanted to make sure she was all right.

Risha had waited, and now she was close to crawling out of her own skin. She had to see Taesia. She had to ask if she had seen this coming, if she needed anything, if...

If she had known. If it was true.

The back of Risha's dress swept dramatically behind her as she descended the tower stairs toward Saya's room.

"I hate this," her sister whispered. She had dressed in somber colors today with a touch of silver. "Brailee must be devastated."

"The best we can do for them right now is give them support." Risha put a comforting hand on Saya's shoulder as they walked side by side. Rath was currently at the necropolis, the Vakaras needing to refortify the perimeter at least once a week now. Their mother had gone with him to distribute burial wreaths and written prayers. It was the perfect time to leave the villa without being spotted.

A crash sounded from above.

Risha stiffened as Saya's head whipped around. "What was that?"

Risha squeezed Saya's shoulder. "Go on. Brailee needs you." Saya hesitated before continuing down the stairs.

Bracing herself, Risha returned to her room and pushed the door open. One of her hands instinctively drifted toward the handle of her bone knife.

Her bedroom was lavishly decorated with paneled walls in the scalloped archway designs native to Parithvi, and a black tile floor was softened by a round rug in the very center. It matched the black velvet drapes of her western-facing window.

Drapes that Taesia was currently tangled in.

The decorative teapot beside the window had toppled from its column, pieces scattered across the floor. Taesia made another wild kick, trying to dislodge her leg from the drape. She had somehow climbed up the tower and through the window, and yet a simple piece of fabric was her undoing.

Something ripped and Taesia fell to the floor with a muffled "*Fuck.*" Risha hurried forward, careful not to step on stray teapot fragments.

"Are you all right?"

Taesia pushed herself to her knees, swaying and coughing. Her hair was snarling out of its braid, a few strands stuck to her face with sweat.

"Sorry," Taesia muttered once Risha helped her up, leaning against her. "Knew you liked that teapot."

Risha smelled alcohol on her breath. Taesia's eyes were fever bright. "How in Thana's grave did you manage to get up here *drunk*?"

"Mm? I'm not drunk." She toddled away from Risha, toward the nearby cabinet. "Not yet."

Risha's concern plummeted toward frustration as she watched Taesia throw open the cabinet doors, root around, and retreat with a bottle of sarab that Risha had infused with lavender and valerian. Risha kept it in her room in case she couldn't sleep.

Taesia threw her head back and took a big gulp.

"All right." Risha gently wrestled for the bottle, but Taesia was taller and physically stronger, holding it out of reach. "You're grieving. You're in shock. That doesn't give you the right to destroy my bedroom."

"It does." Taesia stole a smaller sip. "You have to be nice to me right now. It's the law."

Risha made another pass at the bottle, but Taesia's familiar wrapped around the glass and lifted it higher into the air.

"You're making this extremely difficult," Risha said. "I was on my way to see you. You didn't have to do...this."

Taesia's expression darkened. "I couldn't stay there anymore. Brailee hasn't stopped crying. My mother is furious. My father's barely said a word. It's like he fucking *died*."

She snatched the bottle from her familiar and sprawled out on the bed. Risha glanced despairingly at where Taesia's dirty boots touched her sheets before coming to sit by her.

"I'm so sorry, Tae." Risha brushed some of her friend's hair from her forehead. Her skin felt hot, too hot. Maybe she did have a fever. "I can't imagine what this must be doing to you. When I heard, I..."

She'd been shocked, yes; that wouldn't be a lie. But there had always been some part of her that wondered what Dante was hiding from the world. No one could be so perfect and precise all the time.

"Is it true?" Risha whispered.

Taesia glared up at the ceiling. "Dante was studying Conjuration. That part's true."

Risha closed her eyes, thinking back to the skeleton at the basilica. The masked man couldn't have been Dante ... could it?

"But he wouldn't have used it to kill the prelate," Taesia spat. "He wouldn't have killed the prelate at all! He *didn't*, he ... They were working to help us. To help Vaega."

Risha frowned. "Help how?"

Taesia wrapped a clammy hand around Risha's wrist. The expression on her face was so stark, so needy, that Risha's stomach clenched. "Get the others. The heirs. Bring them here."

"Here?"

"Can't do it at my villa. Being watched." Taesia's breathing had slowed, as if now she'd gotten this off her chest, she was beginning to relax. Or maybe it was the lavender and valerian infused in the sarab. "Need to talk to them here. All of you."

"About Dante?"

"About what he was doing." Her grip loosened on the bottle, and Risha quickly took it before it spilled over. "His plan. He had a plan, and now he ..."

Her voice hitched. Risha cupped the side of her heated face, ready to wipe any tears that fell. But she found rage, not despair, in Taesia's eyes.

"I don't know what to do," Taesia whispered.

Risha didn't know what to say. She waited for Taesia to fall into an uneasy doze before returning the sarab to the cabinet and sweeping up the teapot fragments.

Then, after a good five minutes' hesitation, she descended the stairs and sent two summonses.

By the time Nikolas and Angelica arrived, Risha had convinced Taesia to move from the bedroom to a sitting room, where Taesia collapsed onto a settee and flung an arm over her face. Risha asked a passing servant to order tea from the kitchens.

Taesia was sipping at the spicy, milky beverage when Nikolas arrived, out of breath. He hurried to kneel before Taesia and took her hand in his. Their familiars drifted toward one another, making eclipses as they moved.

"I went to your villa earlier, but you weren't there," Nikolas said. "Tae...Shit. I'm so sorry. I don't even know what to say."

Taesia freed her hand and used it to cradle his face, thumb digging hard into his jaw.

"Who found the prelate's body?" she asked quietly, barely a whisper. Her dark eyes, usually so expressive, were dull and flat. The space between Risha's shoulder blades prickled.

Nikolas stared at her until his expression cleared with understanding. "It wasn't my unit. Don Soler had people watching the prelate's house, and searched it top to bottom when they realized he was missing. He was..." His voice wavered, and he swallowed hard. "His body was in a basement. A safe room."

Taesia held on to him another moment, Nikolas silently accepting the pressure, before she let go.

"You don't need to say anything," she said at last. "Just listen."

"Listen to what?" came Angelica's drawl from the doorway. The Mardova heir's face was a thundercloud above a pristine cream-colored dress. "Some harebrained scheme to break your brother out of prison? I always suspected he'd end up there eventually."

Taesia's lips curled at the challenge. Risha stepped between them.

"Angelica, please," Risha urged. "This is a difficult time."

Angelica snorted and plopped into an armchair, but miraculously had no retort. Risha took the other armchair as Nikolas sat beside Taesia on the settee. He put a hand on Taesia's knee, and she covered it with her own.

"You wanted us all here, Tae," Risha said. "Why?"

Taesia took a deep breath. Now that the alcohol had worn off, she seemed exhausted. Wrecked.

Nikolas squeezed her hand. "Dante wouldn't have done this," he said, as if prompting her.

"No, he wouldn't." Taesia's voice was hoarse. "But he did go to Lezzaro's house that night."

Risha sucked in a breath, ignoring Nikolas's warning look. "Why?"

"Because he was learning about ancient rituals tied to Conjuration."

A moment of stunned silence passed, broken by Angelica's bark of a laugh. "Wonderful," she muttered. "The Lastrider heir really is a demon worshipper. How is this my business?"

"One House's business is *all* the Houses' business," Taesia snapped. "And this isn't about demons, it's about Conjuration's original purpose, which was communing with the gods. Dante and the prelate had the same goals of using it to break the Sealing. So we can reopen the portals."

"Break the Sealing?" Nikolas repeated at the same time Angelica said, "I'm sorry, *we*?"

"Lezzaro had an idea. Godsnight is happening soon, right? Before the Sealing happened, the Houses would gather the gods' power to them, tapping into the raw energy of the Cosmic Scale." Taesia swallowed. "And in order to do that, they used Conjuration."

Risha's eyes widened. She was suddenly back in Thana's Chapel, facing the decaying body of Prelate Lezzaro as he stumbled over the words *Sealing, Godsnight, Conjure.*

"This was what Dante wanted to accomplish," Taesia went on. "Not to bring the gods back, exactly, but to borrow their powers. To wait until the moment when the Cosmic Scale perfectly lines up to break down the barriers. To save our realm from dying."

Angelica's lips were pressed together. Nikolas stared at the floor, visibly trying to process what they were hearing.

"You're claiming Prelate Lezzaro was also a Conjurer," Risha said quietly.

Taesia leaned back. "He wasn't. Not really. But he had a grimoire—"

Angelica choked. "He had a fucking *what*?"

"A grimoire?" Nikolas insisted. "Are you sure?"

"Yes. I saw it." She tightened her hold on Nikolas's hand, gazing earnestly into his eyes. "This is what he wanted to talk to you about, Nik. He'd already told me and Dante, and he wanted the rest of you in on it, too."

"The Conjurers," Risha whispered as a chill stole through her. "He was working with them, wasn't he?"

"Yes, but—"

"That's why he made that announcement. Why he wanted them under his care. He was— And you didn't tell me?"

Taesia's pained look only fueled the horror and anger brewing in Risha's gut. For as long as she'd known her, Taesia had been all too willing to divest herself of responsibility at any given opportunity. Anything she did for her House was due to her mother's demands, her brother's need, and society's expectations as a member of the nobility whose veins ran with godsblood. She cared about people, but she didn't care about *serving* the people, dismissing her influence and status as meaningless rather than the tools they were.

So of course she chose to ignore the harm caused by the Conjurers. Of course she decided to follow Dante's path without bothering to consider the implications.

"Lezzaro didn't want them hurting anyone," Taesia said. "He said he only wanted them to perform Conjuration so that the barriers are thinned."

Angelica sat up at this. "So they *are* taking the energy built up at the barriers."

"Yes."

"And the prelate didn't stop to consider what this would mean for the rest of Vaega?" Angelica flung her hand out. "The same day they Conjured all those spirits, Tambour Lake dried up. By leeching the energy and thinning the barriers, they're weakening our own realm."

Nikolas swore. Risha continued to watch Taesia, silently begging her to put this to rest. Instead, she only doubled down.

"Once the portals are reopened, Vitae will heal," Taesia insisted.

"Tae," Nikolas said softly. "The prelate is dead. Your brother's been taken to the Gravespire. You might not..."

"Might not what?" Taesia asked in her low, midnight voice.

"Be thinking logically," Angelica finished for him. "You want us to believe that one of the holiest people in this kingdom was going against the king's wishes to perform occult magic. And now you want *us* to do it, too."

"That's not—"

"You know my current circumstances," Nikolas said, reaching again for her hand. She withdrew it. "The king placed his trust in me to stop the Conjurers."

"What we'd be doing isn't what those careless idiots are doing," Taesia argued. "We wouldn't be playing with the dead, we'd be using the gods' power to save our realm. To save *all* the realms."

"Even if we were to entertain the idea," Angelica said, far more calmly than Risha expected from her, "you're missing a few steps. For one thing, with the gods withdrawn as they are, how do you plan to summon their power?"

"I...I don't know the details about the ritual," Taesia admitted. "Dante was going to learn more, but he..." Her voice nearly broke, and she curled her hands into fists. "Lezzaro's grimoire. I'm sure if we found it, it would—"

"Stop it," Angelica snapped. "Listen to yourself. You're asking us to commit treason on little more than maybes. Wasn't your brother's stunt enough for you?"

Taesia banged a fist against the table, rattling her teacup. It made the others jump, and Risha's pulse quickened at the rage returning to Taesia's eyes.

"My brother was arrested because he was trying to do what was best for everyone," Taesia growled. "Whoever really killed Lezzaro must have framed him."

"Convenient," Angelica huffed.

Taesia ignored her and turned to Risha. "You want to find a way into Mortri, don't you? The dead are piling up. They're going to cause more destruction if they're not released."

Risha thought of Lezzaro's risen body, his filmed-over eyes and enraged moaning. The circle drawn with chalk and ash, the black rose at its heart like a taunt.

"Not like this," Risha said. "Playing with the dead is far too dangerous. We can't allow the Conjurers to continue meddling with them."

"Forget the Conjurers for a minute," Taesia said. "If we don't do this now, it'll be another hundred years until the next Godsnight. What will our country look like a year from now, five years, ten, if things continue this way? What will our realm look like, with resources dwindling and crops withering more and more every year?"

Risha dropped her gaze as the others fell silent. She couldn't ignore the faint voice telling her that Taesia had a point, that they were all heading toward certain extinction. By then it wouldn't matter how many of the dead had piled up; no one would be around for them to terrorize.

"Just think about it," Taesia urged her. In her words Risha heard what she couldn't say out loud: *Don't let Dante's sacrifice be for nothing.*

"With your brother locked up, you're the Lastrider heir now," Angelica reminded her. "You'd be better off dedicating yourself to learning your new duties and spare your family another heartache."

Taesia's lips twisted in a sneer. "Of course. Anything to lick Ferdinand's boots, right? You can't sit on a throne when you're prostrating all the time, Mardova."

Angelica stood with a flare of her nostrils. "Fine. Do your duty or don't—I don't give a shit."

She slammed the door on her way out. As if she were the only thing keeping Taesia upright, Taesia slumped back against the settee.

"Tae," Nikolas said carefully. "I'm sorry about Dante. I really am. And maybe... maybe this could be possible. But I don't see how the four of us can do it alone."

"We'd have the gods' power during Godsnight," Taesia said. "That's the whole *point* of Godsnight. Or at least, it used to be."

Nikolas opened his mouth to say something, then seemed to backtrack and cleared his throat. "Are you sure this is what Lezzaro had planned?"

"*Yes*, Nik. Why don't you believe me?"

"I do believe you. But think about my position. How would it look if I were caught doing Conjuration when I'm heading the task force meant to stop it?"

"Of course. Your House's status is far more important than the future of our realm."

Nikolas sighed and exchanged a helpless glance with Risha. They were both heirs; they both understood the severity of what the consequences would be.

"Let me know if you need anything," he murmured, squeezing her hand before he also left.

When it was just the two of them again, Taesia stared at the ceiling. Birds chirped outside the window, and a servant's footfalls shuffled down the hall. Though Taesia hadn't cried in Risha's bedroom, Risha noticed a shimmer in her eyes now.

"I don't know what to do," Taesia whispered again.

Risha didn't know either. Still, she knew firsthand how much Taesia admired her brother. How often she had gone running after him, begging to be included in whatever he was doing. Taesia wasn't shy to fling requests at others, but with Dante, she was always following his lead. Always willing to stand back so he could shine.

And now he was gone.

Risha sat beside her. Taesia slowly leaned into her shoulder, dampening the fabric of her blouse as Risha put a steadying hand on her arm.

This, at least, she could do.

XII

Angelica didn't miss the satisfaction on her mother's face as the Houses settled in for a council meeting with the king, the room stark and severe enough to match everyone else's mood.

Rath and Risha sat to the king's left and Adela and Angelica to the king's right. Waren and Nikolas stood with arms behind their backs among the military officers lining the walls, the Sunbringer Spear peering over Nikolas's shoulder. The only ones missing were the Lastriders, and Angelica was fairly certain this was the cause of her mother's smile.

Ferdinand sat at the head of the table, flanked by Don Cassian and Don Soler. His other advisors stood along the wall, ready to step forward should they be needed. Even Don Damari, the high commissioner, was present with a couple of officers from the city guard. The king's face was grave, and he kept fiddling with his wedding ring, a golden band set with rubies.

Though his wife had passed over a decade ago, he had never remarried, not even to secure himself an heir. Others might call it romantic, but to Angelica it was sheer absurdity on his part. Maybe, if he'd managed to squeeze out an heir from a consort at least, the Houses wouldn't constantly be at each other's throats. Then again, that meant the Mardovas not having a shot at the throne themselves.

"What has your unit collected so far, Lord Nikolas?" the king asked.

Nikolas glanced at the door, as if unsure whether to begin the meeting without the Lastriders. He cleared his throat and stepped forward with a small bow.

"We found no new information concerning the attack at the prelate's residence," he began. "Like Don Soler reported, there was indeed a Conjuration circle within the prelate's safe room. But the shape of it was... different."

"Different," Ferdinand echoed with a deepening frown. "How so?"

"Until now the Conjurers have been using a seven-pointed star within a double circle. But this one used a five-pointed star, and the glyphs weren't the same. We submitted them to the linguistics department at the university for further study."

"Good," the king said. "It's clear now the Conjurers are not merely occultists, but insurgents. It is vital we—"

The doors to the council room burst open, making several of the advisors yelp. A roiling fog of shadow seeped from the open doorway. Those at the table surged to their feet, hands bristling with magic or going for weapons.

The teeming shadows parted to reveal the Lastriders. Darkness trickled from every perceivable corner and purled across the shoulders of Elena and Taesia. Cormin stood behind them, and Angelica couldn't help but notice the glaring absence of their only son.

Nikolas sent Taesia a panicked look while Risha bit her lip. Angelica merely sighed; she should have known this was coming. At her side, her mother's smile grew wider.

"My lady!" Don Cassian hurried forward. "You—this commotion is quite—"

"Oh? You're worried about me making a commotion?" Elena strode toward the king's seat. Waren Cyr tensed, as did the officers at his back, but Ferdinand lifted a placating hand. "You didn't seem so concerned when Don Soler made a spectacle at the Nyx basilica."

"I would hardly call meting out justice a spectacle," Ferdinand said evenly.

"Justice!" Elena drew herself up. "Is it justice to publicly arrest a House heir on false charges?"

"The charges are not false." Don Soler didn't raise his voice, but he didn't have to; everyone else was deathly silent. "There were witnesses who saw Dante Lastrider enter Prelate Lezzaro's rectory mere hours before his time of death."

"The guards—"

"There were not only guards," Don Soler interrupted. "I've had my people watching the prelate since his announcement at the Autumn Equinox."

Elena clenched her jaw. "My son is not a Conjurer, or a murderer."

"Then would you be willing to offer up your villa to a thorough search, my lady?"

Angelica kept her gaze on Taesia. In fact, all the other heirs were staring at her, no doubt thinking about the other day at the Vakara villa. If Taesia sensed their stares, she ignored them in favor of focusing on the king and his advisors.

"Of course," Elena said. "You will find nothing of the occult in our household."

"We will see." Don Soler's tiny smile made the shadows across Taesia's shoulders writhe. She began to take a step forward when her father grabbed her arm.

"Do not make it worse," Angelica heard him whisper. "You're acting heir."

Taesia's breath caught.

Angelica had never particularly liked Dante Lastrider, but at least he had been capable and responsible. Even the youngest child, Brailee, was quiet and polite. But the middle Lastrider child had always been a wild, unpredictable thing.

Angelica's first memory of Taesia was when the Mardovas and Lastriders had accidentally run into each other many years ago at a performance of *The Gossamer Road*, Angelica's favorite opera about star-crossed lovers caught between the realms of Vitae and Solara. Angelica hadn't noticed the Lastriders at all, too invested in the plight of the lovers onstage and enraptured with the soprano's powerful vibrato.

But her attention had kept slipping at the sound of laughter in the next box. Taesia and Dante had been making fun of the actors and the way they sang, spiraling into fits of suppressed giggles when their parents scolded them. Dante had settled down eventually, but Taesia had gone so far as to try to stand on the box's railing, pulled back down by her harassed mother.

"They can barely keep their brood in check," Angelica's father had muttered with a smirk.

Angelica had glared at Taesia as the girl wriggled restlessly in her seat. Then their eyes had met. Taesia, with all the aplomb of a child, had stuck her tongue out at her.

Since then, Angelica had been witness to countless more of Taesia's antics, whether it was putting diuretic into wine decanters at a ball or challenging young men to duels. As if she thought she had something to prove every minute of her life.

Now, when she had everything to prove, she suddenly looked as if she wanted to leap out the window.

Taesia hadn't been groomed to be heir. Wasn't the least bit prepared for it. Even Angelica knew her place was in the shadows, out of sight.

"My lady." King Ferdinand stood, his broad hands splayed on the varnished table. "I understand your vexation. Perhaps we could have conducted this another way. But in the end, I decided it had to be public."

Elena's fingers twitched, as if she longed to rake her perfectly manicured nails across his face. "Please indulge me your reasoning, Your Majesty."

Ferdinand straightened with hands tucked behind his back. "We live in perilous times. Cultists hide within our city, and these heretics are happy to watch our faith plummet even as our realm falls to disease and starvation. I cannot risk them gaining more strength than they already have. I must cull every danger that shows its face. Every facet of evil that dares make an appearance."

Cormin stifled a sound, no doubt at the insinuation Dante was something evil. Elena's shadows thrashed like a fire in the wind.

"It had to be done publicly," the king went on, "as a warning to the rest of you." His gaze landed on each House, the room utterly silent. Adela's smile, which she hadn't bothered to conceal, finally fell. "We serve our Holy Kingdom and the gods. To go against them—against *me*—is the greatest form of treachery, and will not be tolerated.

"That is why, effective today, Conjuration will be punishable by death."

Someone gasped. Angelica felt sweat begin to gather under her bodice as Elena grew deathly still. Taesia's eyes were locked on Don Soler's self-satisfied smile, the pulse at her neck racing as shadows wove through her hair. Her father's grip tightened around her arm.

"Your villa will be searched, and our findings may or may not help in Dante Lastrider's sentence. Until then..." Ferdinand gestured to the empty chairs at the table. "If you would?"

Nobody moved for several seconds. Then Elena stiffly found her seat, the shadows still roiling over her body in silent protest. Cormin followed, grasping his wife's hand under the table.

Ferdinand met Taesia's stare and nodded to the seat normally reserved for Dante. Everyone waited to see what she would do.

Eventually Taesia forced herself into the seat. There was a collective sigh of relief, but Angelica didn't share in it. She knew better than to trust the deferential bend of Taesia's head, hiding the wild fury dancing in her eyes like a flame against the night.

XIII

Balancing the round, pink fruit in his hand, he studied the mound of bodies before him. He hoped they were enough.

They are enough, said the Voice. It sounded content, and perhaps also amused. *Why don't you test it?*

Yet he kept his feet stubbornly planted in the grass, unwilling to move. His mouth was dry. His stomach hurt. His head was spinning, spinning, like the top he used to play with.

Why the hesitation? the Voice whispered. Every syllable caressed the inside of his mind, driving away the fragmented memory beginning to form. *You were made for this.* I *made you for this.*

He had been made, forged. Which meant he could also break.

He did not want to break.

But when he asked himself what he *did* want, all that greeted him was the darkness of the sky overhead. He could not remember.

Let us test this power, the Voice suggested. *And then you might learn.*

Stuffing the fruit in his pocket, he knelt and drew a circle around the mound, following the Voice's instructions. Geometric shapes followed, symbols and writings he could not interpret, but that felt right.

This is an ancient and terrible magic, the Voice explained. *Birthed with the creation of the universe, the aligning of the realms, the beginning of everything. It used to represent harmony. Stability. And now it is broken, causing all the realms to wither.* A pause, long and ringing. *But not for long.*

He closed his eyes and concentrated on the bodies, on leeching the magic from within them to fuel the circle. Warm, golden energy coursed through his body.

That's it, crooned the Voice. *Very good.*

A rip and a crack, energy pulsing vibrantly through him. He rounded his back and clenched his jaw as his fingers dug into the dirt, feeling the crack grow larger, pulling his prize through.

I don't want this. The thought blared through him the way the stars overhead streaked then fell. *This is not what I want.*

He wanted the rest of that fragmented memory, of a spinning toy against polished wood, of a laugh echoing through time. He tried to pull his hands back, but they were seared into the earth. He cried out.

The energy flared, then died. Panting, he opened watery eyes and found a statue looming over him. The shape was of a man with a feathered cap and scrolls tucked under one arm, the other pointing west. It was cast in bronze, and gleamed under the starlight.

It seemed familiar. Another fragment of another lost memory.

Oh, yes! the Voice crowed. *This will do nicely, very nicely.*

He stood on weak legs and licked his cracked and peeling lips.

There is more work to do, but today you've done well, the Voice said. *You may reward yourself.*

Relief coursed through him as he took the fruit from his pocket. It sat round and cool on his palm, its solid weight a comfort.

He bit into its flesh like a god devouring the world.

PART II

What the Dead Say

I

The Gravespire from up close was far less lovely than it was from a distance.

Two massive metal doors stood closed and locked at the building's base, manned by guards in dark gray and black. They were flanked by tall walls topped with spikes, a deterrent to anyone seeking to escape. Up higher, the sandstone glimmered in the sunlight, but down here in the shadows was nothing but dreadful austerity.

The thought of Dante being forced through these gates made Taesia want to use the shadows to smash them apart.

You're acting heir. Her father's words, a desperate warning.

Forming one hand into a fist and tucking it behind her back, she made her steady way toward the guards. She had chosen an outfit of black and silver, her double-breasted blazer flaring sharply at her shoulders and displaying an unmistakable crescent moon and dagger at her breast. But the guards were far less intimidated than the ones outside Prelate Lezzaro's rectory had been, eyeing her every movement.

"I'm here to visit Dante Lastrider," she said, flat and low. As much as she made fun of Nikolas's "heir voice," she had one, too—they all did.

"Dante Lastrider is not allowed visitors," one of the guards said.

She kept her face carefully blank. She had been prepared for hemming and hawing, not outright refusal.

She wasn't aware the nearby shadows had begun to pool at her feet until the guard's eyes narrowed and he put a hand on his sword. Taesia forced herself to take a deep breath and clenched her hand tighter.

"I am Taesia of House Lastrider, and I've come to see my brother," she tried again. "If you won't grant you access, fetch your warden."

The flash of contempt on the guard's face was unmistakable. "The warden will only tell you the same, my lady." The way he said those last two words made her molars grind together. "This order was passed down from His Majesty. If you seek to challenge it, I'd advise you take it up with him."

The shadows at her feet spread farther. Two more guards noticed and tensed, one even going so far as to clear an inch of her sword.

Taesia turned back to the carriage, heart hammering. It wasn't until she'd closed the door that she let out her breath and held her head in her hands.

She had to talk to Dante. She had to *see him*, to know he was all right, to ask him what had happened so she could clear his name and…

And what, restore him as heir?

The scandal would follow him the rest of his life. There were already murmurs of *Traitor House* on the streets, the same cautious hostility the people had shown the Vakaras after the first Conjuration attack. Even if Dante was decreed innocent and released from the Gravespire, by the time he became head of their House, the city would show them as much contempt as these guards had shown her.

Unless they managed to perform the ritual at Godsnight. If the Houses were seen as heroes of their realm, no one would be able to touch Dante's reputation again.

He would be reinstated as heir and set up his parliament, and she would be free to do whatever she wanted.

Don Soler would be making his investigation of the villa later that day. Dante could have told her what to do, what to hide. But most importantly, he could have told her the truth.

Did you really kill Lezzaro? she wondered, guilt churning her stomach at even questioning her brother's innocence. *What were you about to tell me?*

She feared she might never find out.

Taesia didn't have the key to the villa's vaults—had no idea what had happened to Dante's—so she coaxed Umbra out of its ring and into the lock.

"Come on," she whispered, bouncing on the balls of her feet. "Come on, come on."

Umbra fiddled with the tumblers until there was a telltale metallic clunk and she could shove the door open. She didn't bother to light the lantern as she made her way to the workroom, full of damning evidence.

She pulled everything into a large pile in the middle of the room, on top of the ugly rug. The darkness didn't hinder her; if anything, it made the heavier loads lighter.

"Never thought I'd say this, but I could really use Angelica's powers right about now," she muttered as she surveyed the pile of Conjuration tools. "Shit."

But she couldn't burn it without making a suspicious mess. Besides, the room itself stank of Conjuration, a heady mix of cloves and herbs and sulfur. Adding smoke would make it worse.

Umbra kept drifting away from her, toward the floor. Frowning, she followed it to the corner and knelt down. "What is it?"

Her familiar spun a few inches off the floor and Taesia finally felt what it had found: a pocket of deep shadow underneath her.

She scrabbled at the floor until her nails caught on a hidden door. Beneath the stone slab was a crawl space for extra storage.

Taesia quickly pushed everything inside, flinching at the sound of something breaking. She hesitated when she reached for the chalk.

But she wasn't a Conjurer. She had no clue how to do the things Dante had been doing, and any chance of asking Lezzaro had been scorched up along with his broken body.

Taesia's throat burned. The same helpless rage she'd felt in the council room came flooding back, making the darkness around her writhe.

How was she supposed to continue on with his plan if he wasn't *here*?

Taesia let the shadows slam the stone back into place. Then she climbed out of the vaults and went to Dante's study.

She quickly searched the shelves for his favorite books to see if he'd hidden anything in them. Then she turned to his desk, rifling through the drawers and banging them shut when they yielded nothing. One of them, however, was locked.

She knelt and sent Umbra into the lock. It was smaller than the one to the vaults, making it more difficult for her familiar to maneuver inside. Minutes passed as sweat trickled down her neck. Don Soler and his people would be arriving soon. He could already be here, sniffing around like some fucking dog on a leash—

Growling, Taesia grabbed the drawer handle and wrenched it open. The drawer exploded out of the desk in a shower of splinters and broken wood.

The only thing she saw inside were loose papers filled with Dante's handwriting. She almost dismissed them, but figured if her brother had kept them behind a lock, they might as well be worth reading.

"What are you doing?"

Brailee stood in the doorway. Taesia quickly slipped the papers under her shirt.

"Uh…" Taesia tried to push the drawer back in, but it was woefully misshapen. "Nothing, Bee."

Her sister stepped into the room, and Taesia couldn't stand to see how gaunt she was. "They're going to search his rooms first, you know."

"I know." She stared at the drawer, fighting down a sudden spell of manic laughter. "Guess I wanted my chance before they did."

Brailee crossed her arms tight against herself. "You think he's guilty?"

"I think he was keeping secrets." She swallowed. "From both of us."

"Right," Brailee muttered. "Both of us."

The sound of the villa's main doors echoed up the stairs. The two of them exchanged a look.

"I suppose we'll see if they find anything," Brailee whispered.

They reached the entrance hall as Don Soler and a handful of soldiers crossed the threshold. Taesia held the banister in a white-knuckled grip, resisting the urge to fly down the stairs and wipe the smug smile off the don's face.

"His Majesty thanks you for opening your villa to us," Don Soler drawled. "And for your continued cooperation during this difficult time."

Elena's expression was cold. "We'll escort you to whichever rooms you wish to search. There is nothing we'll keep locked from you."

Don Soler's smile was greasier than a fried bun on a festival day. Sensing her glare, he briefly made eye contact with Taesia. While Brailee was on her way to perfecting their mother's frigid displeasure, Taesia blazed too hot to hide her loathing under an icy mask. She let him see her hatred, but it didn't faze him; if anything, it made his smile grow.

"Tae," Brailee whispered, pulling on her wrist.

Reluctantly Taesia followed her to the main sitting room. She received a small shock when she saw that the long blue couch was already occupied.

"Aunt Camilla," she breathed, relief washing through her.

Her aunt snapped her fan closed and stood, wordlessly holding her arms out. Brailee ran into them and Camilla held her tight.

"Disgraceful," Camilla muttered. "Forcing your parents to open up their villa like this when they're clearly grieving. What a spineless weasel of a man. Someone's going to give him a lesson someday, and he'll deserve it. Probably won't take long with all the enemies he's accrued."

Taesia hadn't had time or presence of mind to talk to her aunt about Dante. Everything since his arrest had been a whirlwind, and now she felt as if she stood in the eye of the storm, Camilla's knowing look over Brailee's head grounding her.

She read in her aunt's strained eyes and pinched mouth what she couldn't say in front of Brailee: She'd had no notion of the attack or Dante's possible involvement. They were equally in the dark.

Taesia let her aunt comfort Brailee on the couch as she paced the sitting room. When she made sure they weren't paying her any attention, she slipped Dante's notes out.

One page was filled with his handwriting, the other torn from what had to be a bestiary. It showed a detailed sketch of a Noctan wolflike beast called an astralam, its eyes white under a glowing constellation. They were extremely rare—so rare that Noctans made use of their entire bodies if they hunted one down.

Puzzled, she turned to Dante's notes:

Bears some measure of cosmic energy when they fall: gravitational pulls, force fields, etc.
 Potentially: portals?

"Oh no," she breathed.

When portals open, Other-Realm beasts could sometimes cross over. Ever been a case with an astralam? Or a trader from Noctus?
 Could be tool strong enough to force portal open. Would need to find sample. Bones preferably.

Taesia stared at the drawing of the beast. Was this what he'd gone to tell Lezzaro about?

She turned to find Brailee asleep on their aunt's lap, exhaustion having finally caught up with her. Mouth dry, she approached Camilla and silently handed her the papers. She watched as her aunt's brows furrowed and then rose.

"I think this is what he wanted to discuss with the prelate that night," Taesia whispered. How that had led to Lezzaro dying, she had no idea.

Camilla read the notes again. "How viable do you think this plan is?"

"I...don't know." The room spun around her. This was supposed to be Dante's plan, his grand design for a better Vaega. It wasn't supposed to fall on *her*. All she'd wanted was to help him and be rewarded for it by being cut loose from her obligations.

Undoing the Sealing was perhaps the only thing that could stop the decay of their realm and be used as leverage against the king to wrest power from him. Then Dante could be exonerated.

It was a narrow, near impossible target, but she had to hit it one way or another. Having a tool strong enough to break a god-made barrier would increase her chances of doing so.

"Where would I even find astralam bones?" Taesia whispered. It was hard enough for Noctans to find them in their own realm.

Camilla pondered over this a moment, then drew in a small, sharp breath. "I might know a place you can search. You'd have to be incredibly careful, though."

"How come?"

"It's a black market."

And if another Lastrider heir were caught snooping around a place that would undeniably be selling Conjuration materials, she might as well stand on top of the Bone Palace and announce their plan to the entire city.

Taesia fetched a pen and brought it to her aunt so she could write down the address. "I'll be careful. How do you know about this, anyway?"

"I was doing research of my own for Lezzaro." Camilla paused, fingers tightening around the pen as if the name caused her pain. Taesia put a hand on her aunt's shoulder, and she received a grateful, tired smile in response. "I'm glad to know it won't be a waste."

Once she had the address and the papers were tucked back inside her shirt, Taesia resumed her pacing. Umbra twirled restlessly around her. On the couch, Camilla stroked her hand over Brailee's hair as she continued to sleep.

A commotion suddenly sounded in the entrance hall. Brailee stirred, but Taesia stood rooted to the spot.

Their father walked in moments later, hollow-eyed.

"They found the remains of a Conjuration circle," he said softly. "In the vaults."

Camilla went to comfort her brother as Brailee covered her mouth and sobbed. Taesia's insides frosted over.

The rug. She had forgotten about the stain under that fucking rug.

Dante's notes were pressed close to her frantic heartbeat. This was her fault, and she was going to make it right.

No matter who stood in her way.

II

Although Julian Luca knew the minds of monsters, he took solace in the fact he wasn't one himself.

The difference was plain as he laid eyes upon the headless man, feeling disgust instead of hunger. The body was bloated, lying sprawled near the banks of the Lune River. The water was low after the summer months, but the river was notoriously deep, and even from where he stood on its shore, Julian heard it passing by in a sinister whisper.

He pulled up his shirt to cover his nose as he crouched beside the body. It barely did anything to alleviate the too-sweet stench of decay that sat on his tongue like a confectionary gone bad. The body's clothes were torn and askew, the tailoring fine. Likely the merchant who'd gone missing when a caravan had been set upon by beasts outside the city walls.

Julian waved the flies away in order to peer at the exposed neck. The flies had been hard at work; maggots were already beginning to worm their way into the cavity. The beheading had not been done by a human. The tear of the flesh was too ragged, and there were deep gouges on the shoulders and back. There were also strange burn marks on the skin around the neck.

Judging by the claw size and the way the head had been removed, Julian guessed there was a banri close by. They were similar to jungle cats but sported six muscular legs, and their mouths were horrifically wide, teeming with fangs sharp enough to easily part a head from a human's body.

Julian sighed. Banris were possessive; getting the don's head back was going to prove a challenge.

He stood and whistled to let Paris know he'd found the body. While he waited he surveyed the field. He was on Nexus's southwestern perimeter, where the river flowed to the sea and the gentle southern hills gave way to the Lapis Forest. The grass at his feet was yellow and brittle, but would turn lush when the winter rains came.

Vaega was a large country, wild and pastoral. There were four major cities including its capital, and dozens of larger towns, but the villages and farmland outnumbered them all. Civilization only took up half the kingdom; the rest was dominated by the elements, from the snowy caps of the Daccadian Mountains in the northeast to the volcanic land of the south.

But there was now brown speckled in with the green. Julian eyed the edge of the forest, adding up the number of dead trees until there were too many to count.

His partner came trotting up a minute later. Like Julian, he was clad in the traditional tan-and-green uniform of the Hunters, collar unbuttoned due to the warmth of the day. Their forearms sported green-and-black vambraces fortified with metal alloy, their canvas trousers tucked into calf-high boots.

The biggest difference between them was their weapons. Paris bore two curved blades on his back, the hilts rising above his shoulders almost like a Noctan's horns. Julian carried a sword at his hip as well as a longbow on his back. Paris had poked fun at the longbow at first, not understanding why Julian would choose a flimsier weapon over the superior crossbows most of the other Hunters favored.

He'd shut up when Julian had shot ten marks dead center in the time it took Paris to shoot three. Julian's father had been an officer in the Vaegan militia, and an expertly skilled archer. The longbow he carried had been made with his father's teachings—the only thing Julian had left of him.

Paris gagged at the smell of the body and held his nose, green eyes wide at the sight. "Deia's tits, how long has he been out here?"

"The report came in yesterday, so likely a couple days. I'm thinking it's a banri."

Paris, still holding his nose, crept closer to the corpse. "A banri this close to Nexus? I thought they preferred the desert?"

Julian shook his head, equally stumped. But the Hunters had been receiving more and more reports of dangerous beasts outside the walls lately, waiting to pounce on unsuspecting travelers.

It didn't take much work to find the banri's tracks; with six legs, it was nearly impossible for the beast not to leave a trail in its wake. But more than that, Julian sensed a pale echo of its heat from where it had trod. As he concentrated, he could hear the buzzing contentment of the beast's thoughts, momentarily driving out his own.

He clenched his jaw and forced the sensation away before it could overwhelm him.

The two of them were quiet as they slunk through the grass, Paris focusing on the trail while Julian primed his bow, scanning the surrounding field. Other than a few birds overhead and the quiet scurry of moles, he didn't find anything out of the ordinary.

He felt it, though. It was near.

Paris held up a hand, signaling them to stop. He pointed ahead at an outcrop and tilted his head. Julian nodded and they split up, Julian going right and Paris going left. Paris grabbed a clay ball from one of the utility pouches along his bandolier. Julian's fingertips pressed against the string of his bow, thumb brushing the goose fletching of his arrow.

Paris chucked the clay ball toward the rocks. When it broke, white smoke billowed out and a confused roar broke the quiet of the field. It was high and otherworldly, like the wailing of wind through a hollow reed.

The banri leapt over the outcrop, shaking its head and rubbing it against the grass, desperate to get the sting of peppery smoke out of its eyes. Julian aimed and loosed his arrow.

It hit the banri in the foreleg. The beast whirled toward him, its massive, terrible mouth lolling open. The yellow and white hairs along its back stood on end, three-inch-long claws springing out of paws the size of his head. But what Julian found most unsettling was the saliva dripping off its fangs, making the ground sizzle and steam where it landed.

"Keep away from its mouth," Julian shouted before the banri charged. He grabbed another arrow and aimed at the beast's head, but the banri lunged and the arrowhead grazed its cheek. Julian jumped to the side, rolling through the grass and popping back to his feet in time to see Paris coming at the banri from behind, twin swords gleaming in the sunlight.

Paris hacked at the tendons of its back legs. The banri screamed and thrashed, but its bulk made it slow to turn, and Julian took the opportunity to shoot two arrows at once. One hit it in the side, the other near its shoulder. Enraged, the banri threw its head back as a gurgling sound emanated from its long throat.

"Look out!" Julian shouted right before the banri aimed its acid spit at Paris.

Paris cursed and dodged, the spot where he'd been standing now a hissing mass of yellowish ooze. It had been close; the heel of one of Paris's boots was smoking.

"Fucking overgrown house cat!" Paris yelled. "I just bought these!"

Julian fired two more arrows. The banri growled as each one landed, but they didn't penetrate the hide deep enough to bring it down. He tossed the bow aside and drew his sword instead.

"We need to provoke it until it does that again," he called to Paris. "When it draws its head back, go for the throat."

"Simple enough," Paris said, twirling his dual swords. "If there's one thing I'm good at, it's provoking."

Julian hung back while Paris dashed in, dodging a swipe of the banri's claws and retaliating with a hit near its underbelly. The beast's tail whipped in a frenzy as its fangs snapped at Paris's head. His partner leaned back to avoid it with a laugh.

"Almost got me that time, you miserable bastard!"

"Don't get cocky." Julian stalked the edges of the fight as his partner flitted from one side to another, nicking the banri and dancing away from its head.

Come on, he thought, nipping at its mind. *Spit at us again. You know you want to.*

Between Paris's attacks and Julian's taunts, the beast was getting angrier and angrier. Julian finally found his opening when Paris grabbed one of the arrows in the banri's side and yanked.

The banri shrieked and threw its head back. Julian dashed in with sword at the ready. As the gurgling noise filled his ears, he lifted his blade and swung as hard as he could.

His sword chopped through the vulnerable skin of the banri's neck, changing the gurgling noise to an even worse choking one. Black blood spattered his face and jacket. The banri tottered, its mouth directly above him. A drop of saliva fell onto Julian's shoulder and he yelled as it ate through his jacket and burned the skin below. He abandoned his sword and jumped away as the banri collapsed, its throat steaming.

Julian sprawled on his back and caught his breath. Paris appeared upside down above him.

"It got you, didn't it?" He knelt to examine Julian's shoulder. "I've seen worse. I'll dump you in the infirmary and get this reported. The disposal team can take care of the rest."

"Wait," Julian panted, getting back to his feet. He stumbled toward the outcrop where the banri had made its nest, coughing when he inhaled the strong odor of animal musk.

And a familiar, too-sweet scent of decay. Julian found it beside a plot of churned-up earth: the merchant's severed head. The skin was gray, cheeks shredded with tooth marks. One of his eyes was missing, leaving a hollow socket, and the expression frozen on his face was one of rictus-preserving horror. Julian gathered his resolve before picking it up by what remained of its dark hair.

Julian reached for a bag to stuff it in and realized it had gotten shredded during the fight. He'd have to carry the head all the way back through the city, and suddenly he very much wanted to lie down and never get back up.

"We'll give it to the captain and she'll figure it out," Paris said. "Then we should probably report to His Brightness."

"Don't let him hear you call him that," Julian warned.

They stopped by the banri on their way back. Julian pulled his sword from the beast's neck, but part of the blade had been eaten through by acid. He sighed and tossed it to the ground before retrieving his bow and whatever arrows weren't damaged.

"I'll get you another one," Paris promised, patting his uninjured shoulder.

"Save the money for repairing your new boots." His partner swore at the reminder and kicked the banri's rump.

Captain Kerala couldn't quite hide her disgust when Julian held up the head for inspection. He and Paris had trudged through the Hunters' barracks to get to her office, stained with dirt and blood and the merchant's head swinging between them. The captain's assistant had taken one look and admitted them without question.

"I'm fairly certain that's him," the captain said, consulting the charcoal sketch they'd been given. Her skin was Mariian black, the light from the window highlighting her cheekbones in gold. "Guess I'll throw this in a sack and bring it to the high commissioner. You said it was a banri?"

"Yeah, and I got half a missing heel to prove it." Paris wobbled on one foot to show the ruined sole of his boot. "Oh, and Julian's got a burn."

Kerala eyed Julian's shoulder. "Head to the infirmary, Luca. And you'll need to get that jacket mended."

"Yes, Captain." With the adrenaline wearing off, Julian felt the burn full force, a throbbing heat radiating across his arm and chest. He tried to salute but realized he still held the merchant's head.

"Here." Kerala came around the desk, braids swaying with the motion. She grabbed a canvas sack hanging on the back of her office door and Julian carefully packed the head inside, wincing as some of its flesh sloughed off. The captain pulled the sack's drawstring tight and set it gingerly beside her desk.

"Why do they have to *play* with their food?" she muttered.

A knock came at the door before the Cyr heir walked in. The three Hunters immediately stood at attention, bowing in his direction.

"Ah, please, that's not necessary," Nikolas Cyr said. He wore simple and sturdy clothes today, more uniform than outfit. He could have blended in on the street if it weren't for the glowing spear that gilded his pale hair. "I'm sorry for interrupting. I was told you wanted to discuss something with me?"

"Yes, my lord." Kerala's tone smoothed into something far more polite than what she used for her Hunters. "And no apology necessary. In fact, this is perfect timing, since Luca and Glicer are here. We've been having more and more beast-related incidents within the last few weeks, and some believe they could be reacting to the Conjuration being performed within the city."

Nikolas's brow furrowed. "How so?"

Kerala met eyes with Julian, and he swallowed.

"You don't have to tell Lord Cyr about your abilities if you don't want to," she'd told him when she had chosen him and Paris for the task force. "But you can't hesitate to use them if you think they'll be useful."

He didn't mind the other Hunters knowing, but he had no desire to explain to a noble that he was the only person in recorded knowledge with this power. That he was a beastspeaker, and cursed to know the minds of monsters.

Thankfully, Kerala only ordered him to repeat their report. Julian related the fight with the banri, as well as the state of the body they'd found.

"Banris don't typically come near Nexus," Julian finished. "They prefer more arid climates."

Nikolas inclined his head. "Thank you for explaining, Julian."

Behind Nikolas, Paris mouthed, *First name basis with His Brightness!* accompanied by a thumbs-up.

Kerala gave Paris a warning look. "Since we've seen a few nonregional beasts recently, this has led us to believe that they're being...well, *lured* by something. The biggest change we've seen is the emergence of the Conjurers. Therefore, the two might be related."

Julian watched the Cyr heir, waiting for him to scoff or show contempt for the idea. Instead, Nikolas nodded slowly and solemnly.

"That very well might be the case," he agreed. "I'd be happy to discuss further safety protocols with you, if you wish."

"I do wish," Kerala said. "Luca—infirmary. Glicer—give the cleanup crew the coordinates for the body."

Julian gratefully left the captain's office. He longed for his bed, but it was all the way across the compound in the Hunters' boardhouse. Beyond that, the burn was becoming intolerable. He slowly made his way through the corridors of the barracks until he found the infirmary, a long stretch of curtained beds and examination tables that smelled of herbs and alcohol. A couple of pained groans came from the beds, no doubt Hunters who had been less fortunate in their recent encounters with beasts.

"You again," muttered the medic on duty, whom Julian recognized by face if not by name. "Shirt off, sit on the table."

Julian managed to shed his jacket while hissing through his teeth, but he couldn't manage the shirt. The medic had to cut it off, shaking his head the entire time and clucking his tongue at the sight of the wound. Julian could now see it was a large, shining blister, red and welted against his tawny skin.

"What abomination is this one from?" the medic asked.

"Banri secretion. It's acidic."

"Hm. It's not that bad," the medic said as he prodded the area. Julian's knuckles paled as he gripped the edge of the table. "Could have been a lot worse had it met skin directly. Should have something for it if those damn thieves haven't run off with my stash."

The infirmary had recently been the target of petty thievery. Julian shifted at the reminder.

"Won't get another stipend until the end of the month," the medic muttered, more to himself than to Julian. "Even though we *told* them we've got missing ingredients, and more and more Hunters getting hurt every day. King really has nothing better to do than fawn over those godspawn."

The medic applied a cooling ointment on the burn, then packed it with comfrey and aloe before wrapping it in a clean linen bandage. He handed Julian a cup of medicinal tea that made him cough and sputter.

"That should do it. Come back tomorrow morning to get the bandage changed."

Julian set the cup down and weakly pulled his jacket over his uninjured shoulder. He hesitated by the shelves lining one whole wall of the infirmary. While the medic leaned over his desk to write the patient report in Julian's file, Julian scanned the various vials, bottles, and boxes they held.

"Hey." The medic snapped his fingers. "No loitering. Out with you."

Julian hastened out of the infirmary, hiding his grimace.

So close.

With a new shirt on and a loaf of bread tucked under his arm, Julian struggled to take out his key and unlock the door to his mother's apartment one-handed. All along the residential street windows displayed banners bearing circles with four quadrants in the colors of black, red, gold, and silver to represent the Four Realms, each harboring a symbol for its respective god. Julian had seen many of these mourning flags in the city since the announcement of Prelate Lezzaro's death, and the basilicas had become flooded with grievers making offerings to the gods in the prelate's name.

Julian had never been very pious, and wasn't sure how to feel at the news. What he cared about more were the growing whispers about the Conjurers, the more noticeable fear. People were beginning to set up small shrines to the gods along the streets or outside shops and homes, superstitious passersby stopping to pray at them or give small donations.

If the gods couldn't protect a holy man, I doubt they'd protect you.

As soon as the apartment door swung open, he was greeted with the smell of rosemary and roasted chicken.

"About time," his mother called from the kitchen. "Did you bring the bread?"

He brought the loaf to the sweltering kitchen. Marjorie Luca didn't seem too affected by the heat as she determinedly basted the chicken before throwing it back in the oven. She wiped her forehead as Julian kissed her damp cheek.

"Don't overdo it," he said. "I don't want to come in one of these days and find you fainted on the floor again."

"That happened *once*," she said. "But since you're here, go ahead and clear the table."

The scarred oak table in the front room was cluttered with papers and used cups, and he shook his head at his mother's habit of never finishing her tea. Reaching for some of the papers, he frowned.

"You're still reading this garbage?" he called toward the kitchen, picking up one of the gossip rags his mother favored. There were several issues on the table, all sporting different covers done by the same artist: a woman in a cage of bones, a man cowering under the sun, and a woman wreathed in flames as she laughed maniacally. The one Julian held was a dramatic sketch of a woman with a fearsome grin and a face hidden in darkness, shadows pooling at her feet.

"It's the best way to keep up with what's happening." Marjorie stepped out of the kitchen to catch her breath. "Aren't you fascinated by all this?"

He gathered the papers into a messy pile. "No, I'm not." Why would he be invested in nobles' affairs when he was busy trying to clean up the streets of the city they neglected? It was bad enough he was taking orders from one of them.

"It's a pity what happened to House Lastrider." Marjorie nodded to the gossip rag on top of the pile he'd made. "They're saying the Lastrider heir is the Conjurers' leader."

"It's also a pity what happened to the prelate," he pointed out. "Dante Lastrider deserves to be locked up." Of course someone with too much money to throw around and too much time on his hands had dipped his toes into clandestine practices.

"That's true. Can't help but feel sorry for the family, though." Marjorie bustled back into the kitchen. "Now come and slice this bread before I eat it all."

The bread was still crusty and soft. He snuck a piece while his mother rambled about what the gossip rags had told her of the new Lastrider heir, her relationship with the other heirs, her powers.

"Tell me, what's it like working with the Cyr boy?" she asked as she checked the potatoes.

"The same as working with the captain, I suppose."

"But what's he like? Is he kind? I've heard he's kind."

He rolled his eyes. "Ma, come on."

"Well, I'm curious, is all. He lost his younger brother a few years ago, the poor thing."

"You don't even *know* these people. They're rich folk who love their status."

"They're also the descendants of *gods*." She tapped her knife against the cutting board. "His Majesty is without an heir, which means one of them will take up the throne someday. If I were a betting woman, which I'm not, I'd probably put it all on the Vakara girl. She's got a good head on her shoulders."

Julian tried to drown her out as he worked. But the motions of using the knife pulled on his burn, making him wince.

"What's this?" Marjorie snapped out of her musing and pointed at his shoulder. "Are you hurt?"

"It's nothing."

Marjorie was a soft woman, both physically and in spirit, but a simple glare paired with the crossing of her arms made him sigh and set the knife down.

"Paris and I took down a banri today," he admitted. "Their saliva is acidic, and some got on me. But it's all right," he said quickly as she gasped. "The medic fixed me up. It'll heal in its own time."

Marjorie shook her head. "I don't know why you go out and put yourself in harm's way like this. You're just like your father, always running first and thinking later."

Julian smiled slightly. Though he suspected she meant it as a critique on his character, to him, being compared to his father was a compliment.

Benjamín Luca had been with the Nexus militia since the age of eighteen. He had risen through the ranks until five years ago, when he and his men had been ambushed in the night by feral beasts near the Parithvian border. There had been few survivors; Benjamín had not been one of them.

His mother always said he took after his father. Except Julian wore the uniform of a Hunter, not the uniform of the militia. A month after his father's body had been found, Julian had walked into the Hunters' barracks to test for an apprenticeship.

Beasts had taken his father from him. He'd do everything he could to return the favor.

Julian stared at his father's medals—proudly displayed above the window lintel—as they ate a dinner of roasted chicken with crispy skin and boiled potatoes with fennel, as well as bread with a thin scraping of butter. Julian had no medals or honors attached to his rank as a Hunter—just scars on his body and a monthly stipend that included room and board.

His mother dramatically retold her morning's excursion to the laundry well and what gossip she'd heard. The more she spoke, the more winded she became, until she began to cough gently into her fist.

"Ma, take your time," he reminded her. "Don't tax yourself."

"I know my limits. Don't you worry about me."

A rush of anger made his hand tighten around his fork. He wasn't angry at his mother; he was angry at her body, that the things once easy for her to do were now difficult and draining.

Marjorie had been sick since last winter, when a sudden spell of fatigue had laid her out. Julian had spent a frantic two weeks at her bedside, barely eating or sleeping, possessed by the terror that his mother was about to leave him, too. But though she had regained some of her strength, she hadn't been the same since.

The medic who had examined her called it languor, a low-simmering sickness swimming through her blood and weakening her body. There was no cure for it, but a certain type of medicine could stave off the worst of the symptoms indefinitely.

For the past year, Julian had put the majority of his pay toward that medicine. But it was expensive and not easy to come by. When his savings began to run dry, he had resorted to stealing from the Hunters' infirmary to try and make the stuff himself. Now the medics monitored their stock like sparrows defending their nests from crows. And though he had been selected for the special unit under Nikolas Cyr, it was a temporary position promising more promotion than reimbursement, the extra pay a hillock compared to the mountain he needed.

He could tell his mother about the wound on his shoulder. He couldn't tell her about his near-empty pockets—or that they had been emptied for her sake.

"You're scowling," Marjorie said, putting a small bowl in front of him. He hadn't even realized she had gotten out of her chair. "Does the burn hurt?"

"A bit. You shouldn't be on your feet anymore. I can fetch whatever you need."

"No matter." She put a spoon beside the bowl, and he saw now it was a dessert of semolina and raisins, one of his childhood favorites.

She kissed the top of his head, ruffling his dark hair and scratching at the shaved undersides. "You ought to grow your hair back here, it looks silly."

"Only you think so. Now go sit down."

"Yes, sir." Marjorie sank back into her chair with a barely concealed groan, Julian's heart weighted with worry.

He glanced at his father's medals, wondering how much they would sell for if they were melted down.

"What are you thinking about, Jules?"

He picked up his spoon and turned to his dessert. "Nothing, Ma."

III

A headache had formed by the time Angelica made to leave the university after another disastrous training session. She'd been distracted in the earth arena, her attempts to lift three blocks of hardened clay resulting in them only shaking as if mildly inconvenienced by a passing earthquake.

She blamed Taesia and her mad ramblings about Godsnight. She kept thinking about that awful meeting, the desperation in Taesia's eyes that had made her so uncomfortable.

On her way to the carriage outside the gates, she spotted Nikolas among a small congregation. He was kneeling on the ground before the spot where a statue of the university's architect stood. Except the spot was now empty, leaving nothing but a blank stretch of stone with blackened lines running across it.

It wasn't until she came closer that she realized those lines extended beyond the stone, burned into the grass of the lawns. A Conjuration circle.

Nikolas looked up at Angelica's gasp. He stood and brushed off his hands.

"Angelica," he greeted. "What are you doing here?"

Her face burned. "Nothing that concerns you. What are *you* doing here?"

He gestured to the circle. "A report came in that the statue was missing and this was left in its place. The staff thinks it must be a prank done by the students."

It sounded like the sort of prank bored teenagers would pull off. But as she studied the circle and the symbols along the outer ring, they seemed too intricate, too precise. The middle, too, was different; instead of a seven- or five-pointed star, it bore four quadrants. She recognized some of the symbols as those of the gods, such as Deia's upside-down horseshoe and the crescent moon of Nyx.

There was also an uneasy feeling in the air, as if it still lingered with power. It itched at her.

"What would Conjuration have to do with a missing statue?" she asked. So far as anyone knew, it had only been used to replicate necromancy. "And why would they draw it like this?"

Nikolas shook his head. "I have no idea. But the university's been searched, and no one's found the statue yet. Even the plinth is gone."

As he spoke to a soldier in his unit, something about making a sketch, she studied it again. Within the circle's inner ring were intersecting lines with strange shapes in each section, much like the four quadrants of the elements represented in the Mardova crest.

"I'm glad you're here, actually," Nikolas said as he turned back to Angelica. The spear glowed softly on his back, earning stares from curious students and staff. "I wanted to talk to you about something."

Angelica was instantly on guard. "Let me guess, you want me to help with your investigation?"

"What? No. I have it handled." He took a deep breath, looking profoundly uncomfortable. "It's about Taesia. Or rather, what she said."

Her headache throbbed. "About Godsnight?"

"Yes. I... I feel like it's something that we shouldn't dismiss right away. Especially if it was something Prelate Lezzaro was backing."

Angelica held back a scoff. She'd expected Nikolas to fall first, out of simple loyalty to his... whatever Taesia was to him. "You really think Conjuration is the key to fixing our problems? You didn't strike me as *that* much of a fool."

"What other choices do we have?" he demanded. "Conjuration taps into the blocked-up flow of the universe. If we can open the barriers and undo the Sealing, they'll have less ammunition. Every time they do their magic, something bad happens. Even beasts are starting to be drawn to the city because of them. Besides..." He swept an arm across the university grounds. "How many years do we have left, cut off from the rest of the universe as we are?"

Angelica gritted her teeth. Her body was tired and sore from practice, her mind hazy with irritation.

"You don't have to make a decision now," Nikolas said. "But will you think about it?"

The Mardovas only serve themselves, Adela had told her throughout her childhood. *They do not rely on others. One day, we will surpass the other Houses, so there is no purpose in being friendly.*

She was about to refuse when her gaze returned to the Conjuration circle, the damning black lines scorched into earth and stone. The empty space where the statue should have been. The lingering feeling in the air.

She realized where she had felt it before: down in the practice arenas, the intricate braiding of elements.

"I'll do more research on my end before I make a decision," she said slowly.

Surprise flashed across his face. "Oh. Of course. Um...thank you."

"Don't thank me." She strode over to where the soldier was sketching the shape of the Conjuration circle and plucked the paper from their hands.

"Hey!" Nikolas called after her.

"Draw a new one," she said, tucking the sketch into her pocket.

Before heading home, she stopped by the jeweler's. With the Godsnight Gala fast approaching, Angelica had to put a considerable amount of thought into her appearance, how to best represent House Mardova.

The man who ran the shop offered her tea, which she sipped slowly as she perused the collection. Long strands of pearls and mountainous rings of diamond winked back at her.

What do you want? Eran Liolle's question, posed to her in the arena today, tugged at her hem. *Learning to use your power without instruments is a goal, not a dream. What do you want?*

She hadn't responded, because the answer was too large to package it into words.

A scepter of ice, a throne of obsidian, a cloak of storm wind, and a crown of flame.

Her hand tightened around the teacup, savoring the heat of it. For many years, she thought what she wanted was a glimmering ascent to something greater. A golden band on her head.

"The ruby necklace," she ordered.

The shop owner hurried to fetch it as the tea in her cup began to boil. Angelica set it down.

"How is this, my lady?" The man returned with the necklace, a fat ruby hanging off a silver chain.

"Do you have anything with sun quartz?" The Solarian gem had a mesmerizing ability to glow in warm colors, from orange to yellow to scarlet.

The owner's face fell. "Sadly, no, my lady. With the portals as they are..."

He didn't need to finish. The sketch in her pocket rustled as she shifted on her feet.

"The garnet choker," she ordered. The owner bowed and rushed to obey.

Half an hour later, Angelica finally settled on the choker and a diamond bracelet connected to a ring by a fine chain. As the owner packed them up, her eyes strayed to the top of the cabinet she had been trying to steadfastly ignore.

She pointed to a tiara encrusted with tiny diamonds and red spinels. She could already hear the whispers of the dons and doñas, wondering where she'd found the gall.

Her heart sped up as it was placed upon her head, as she studied her reflection in the mirror. Her face was wiped of emotion, stern and unforgiving under the radiance of the tiara.

It was over her budget, but she had it wrapped up with the other pieces anyway. Tucking the box under her arm, she returned to the carriage and headed home.

What do you want?

Angelica sat at her desk and stared at the pile of books and papers she'd assembled, her study drenched in the scarlet glow of sunset. She took the sketch from her pocket, staring at the Conjuration circle, the four quadrants within it. If it wasn't a prank, then what did this configuration mean? How did it differ from those who were replicating necromancy?

She pulled the nearest stack of books over. She had scoured the Mardova library for anything referencing Godsnight or ancient practices, but as she'd suspected, there was little of the occult to be found. Most of those writings had been destroyed in the demonology purge long ago.

She skimmed through the book, making notes as she went. Distant birdsong came through the tall window, the clock on the wall ticking away the minutes.

Angelica set her pen down.

What am I doing? she thought. *Am I really going to be roped into this ridiculous scheme?*

To partake in Conjuration would be considered treason. She could face what Dante Lastrider was now facing, and bring shame upon her House. Her mother would lose any chance of succeeding King Ferdinand.

What do you want?

She leaned back and closed her eyes. She wanted to not be used as a pawn against the other Houses by a man who considered himself holy and untouchable. She wanted the authority to make decisions that would benefit the country, whether it was trade agreements or treaties or laws to protect Vaega's most vulnerable citizens.

Power. She wanted power.

And beyond that, to be followed simply because she was someone worthy of being followed. To be smiled at the way her father used to smile when she sang, the only way she could express what she was feeling without having to construct it into a sentence.

Adela saw the throne as a goalpost, but Angelica knew it was merely a tool. What mattered more than a divine title was intent, and loyalty, and confidence to run a kingdom not through the whispers of advisors, but one's own knowledge and capability.

What will our country look like a year from now, five years, ten, if things continue this way? Taesia had asked of them. *What will our realm look like, with resources dwindling and crops withering more and more every year?*

It had been easy to dismiss Taesia's ramblings as absurdity, a belief instilled in her by her traitorous brother. But the more Angelica thought about it, the more she realized this was something she could use to the Mardovas' benefit.

If her power could truly be greater when the Cosmic Scale aligned, she could have natural access to her elements, without the need to rely on music. She could impress the king, and perhaps even sway the citizens' opinions of her and her House.

In cooperating with the other heirs and undoing the Sealing, what if she gained their allegiance to back the Mardovas to the throne?

She was shaken out of her thoughts by a familiar low drone near the window. Angelica sat up with an annoyed sigh.

"Fucking *wasps*," she muttered, opening a drawer to get her piccolo. "How many nests did they make?"

Her piccolo wasn't in the drawer. She searched her sleeves and the inside of her bodice, making sure she hadn't stuffed it inside her dress and forgotten about it. With a sinking stomach, she headed for her bedroom.

She could immediately tell something was off. Angelica stepped inside and glanced at the jeweler's box she'd placed on her bed, but it was the window seat that caught her attention; its pillows were slightly askew.

She hurried to the window seat and lifted the bench, revealing the secret compartment below.

Her lute was gone.

Heat prickled across her skin, the hairs along her arms standing on end. Angelica slammed the bench down.

A servant jumped out of her way as she marched down the hall, toward the practice room of the recital chamber. She threw the door open and startled the two girls inside.

"Where did you put it?" Angelica demanded.

Her two younger stepsisters knelt before the cabinet where she kept her violin, gaping at her. Eiko and Kikou took after their mother in many ways, from their straight black hair to their pale skin. As twins, they would have been difficult to tell apart aside from Eiko's hair stopping at her shoulders and Kikou's long enough to reach her lower back.

They shot to their feet. Kikou flushed and looked at the floor as Eiko put her hands defiantly on her hips.

"Mother's orders," Eiko said firmly. Angelica knew she meant Adela; to them, Miko was Maa.

Angelica took a few steps inside. "And what exactly were her orders?"

Eiko swallowed but lifted her chin; she'd always been the more stubborn one. "To take away your instruments. Put them somewhere you won't find them."

All the things she wanted to say, to scream, grew tangled and thorny in her throat. The air warped in front of her. The twins scurried back, wide-eyed.

"Angelica."

Her mother stood in the doorway, face like steel.

"You know this has to be done," Adela said. "You are a Mardova mage, and cannot keep using your instruments if you want to be seen as an asset to His Majesty. Accept that."

"What I'll accept," Angelica growled, forcing herself to speak, "is making my own decisions in how I handle my power."

"I know about your lessons with Mage Liolle. I know he's told you to not touch your instruments. Why are you wasting House funds if you're going to simply ignore his teachings?"

The center of her went ice cold even as tongues of flame danced along her fingers. Adela gave them a scornful look.

"Father gave me the piccolo and violin," Angelica whispered. "At least give me those."

"No."

"They're *mine*."

"Don't test me, Angel." Adela walked to the cabinet and wrapped her own burning hand around the lock, melting it. Once it was broken, Adela retrieved her violin case. "You won't like where it leads."

Angelica had a brief fantasy of turning all three of them to ash, to be rid of the agonizing anger, to give over to release. Instead, she stood rigid as her mother walked past her, out the door. Eiko and Kikou quickly followed, Eiko glaring at her as she went.

Angelica turned, wooden, and went back to her room. Humiliation sat sharp at the base of her throat.

She blacked out, or perhaps her mind simply went somewhere else. When she came back to herself, half her room was destroyed, the window broken, the bed smoldering with embers.

Angelica panted and stumbled into the dresser. Her body shook as if she had a fever, her throat dry and in need of water.

Her instruments were gone. She had nothing, nothing other than the meager tethers she held to the elements.

As she wiped sweat from her forehead, she noticed the jewelry box had been smashed open, the pieces scattered like fallen stars across the floor.

She picked up the tiara. The metal warped and melted in her hands, staining her skin silver.

IV

Julian couldn't sleep.

It wasn't the restless moon crawling across his window, or the humidity in his small room in the Hunters' boardhouse. Uncomfortable thoughts kept cycling through his mind, between his mother's health, the merchant's head, and the threat of Conjuration luring beasts toward the city.

Sitting up with a sigh, Julian pulled on his clothes and slipped into the compound.

The Hunters guarding the entrance to the pens stepped aside for him without a word. Julian walked through the wide doors and waited for his eyes to adjust to the dim lantern light. The pens weren't afforded windows; there was no telling what manner of beast could smash or crawl through them.

The indoor pens were massive, designed to hold any type of non-elemental Vitaean or Other-Realm beast. The dangerous ones were killed outright, like the banri in the field, particularly if they had a mind to maim and slaughter the humans around it. But some species were considered No Kills, whether because they were going extinct or because they were useful in their realm's ecosystem. So long as they didn't pose a threat, the Hunters captured and often treated the beasts for injury before releasing them back into their native habitats.

Julian walked toward the large iron cages that stood empty—except for the one at the end. The beast inside was roughly the size of a horse, its hide covered in steel-gray fur, its four massive paws ending in sharp claws. A wreath of jagged, broken antlers crowned its lupine head. It was currently asleep, its head tucked down between its forelegs and giving Julian a good view of the mess of broken antlers.

The beast was a fenris, typically found in the forests of northeastern Vaega. Yet Hunters had found it running rampant in the streets just the other day, clearly agitated and showing signs of abuse.

"Do you think this has to do with the Conjuration problem?" Julian had asked the captain. "Did the fenris break into the city somehow?"

"There were no sightings at the gates," Kerala had demurred. "But witnesses clearly saw it near Filigree Street. Maybe you can check it out, see what you can find."

The report said it had killed a civilian. He couldn't help but think of his father, mauled and maimed, surrounded by the bodies of fallen beasts. Beasts who had somehow been hacked and torn apart, as if they had attacked each other.

Julian studied the thick scars in the fenris's hide. The beast had endured torture of some sort, likely while in captivity. Of course it had taken its anger out on the people of Nexus at the first opportunity.

The fenris's head suddenly shot up, turning to stare at Julian. Its eyes were much like a wolf's, its round, black pupils surrounded by large amber irises. Those pupils contracted at the sight of him, upper lip curling to reveal yellowed fangs.

The burn on Julian's shoulder throbbed dully as he lowered himself to kneel before the cage. The fenris followed his movements, muscles taut. But as Julian remained still and barely blinking, the fenris gradually began to relax, lowering its lip and even giving an exhausted huff.

"I know," Julian murmured. "It's not fun being in there. Once your wounds heal, you'll be brought home."

He never spoke like this to the beasts they captured. They were his duty to kill or subdue, to protect the people from their claws and teeth and horns. To prevent any more deaths like Benjamín Luca's.

But he couldn't find it in himself to be cruel or dismissive of a creature with such haunted eyes.

The fenris blinked at him. Julian reached his hand through the bars.

"I'd like to know what happened to you," Julian said softly. The fenris's ears flicked. "I won't hurt you."

The fenris, calmed by his voice, allowed Julian's hand to come in contact with its fur. It was soft and parted easily under his fingers, allowing him to touch the paler skin hiding beneath.

His mind clouded and thinned. The small statements that made him human—*I am a man, my name is Julian, I live in Nexus, I am not a monster*—dissolved into nothing, until the world was made up only of sight and smell and sound. Julian breathed slow and even, his pulse and breath matching the rhythm of the fenris's.

Show me.

The pens faded around him. The floor was rough stone, gritty and holding too many smells, so many it made him dizzy. A dull and persistent roar all around him, making his hackles rise.

Then the painful *snap* of bone, ringing through his head and down his body. Blood in his mouth, splashing across his tongue. Thrashing against the ground as a lean figure loomed above with something sharp in its hand, so sharp—

The slam of something heavy, the smack of a whip against his hide. He snarled and twisted even as he was corralled into a cage to bleed and lick his wounds.

Enemy, standing on two legs, lips parted to reveal teeth as it stared down at him.

The fenris shifted and Julian came back to himself with a small gasp. He withdrew his hand, warmed from the beast's side, and tried to remember all the details he could. What he latched on to most was the last image—a man, Vaegan by the look of him, with a wicked saw and blood on his forearms.

"Thank you," Julian said.

The fenris turned and tucked its head down, heaving a sigh as it went back to sleep.

Julian pressed a palm against his forehead. *I am a man. My name is Julian. I live in Nexus.* He could still taste blood in the back of his throat.

I am not a monster.

He told the captain about the fenris's memories the next day. She nodded grimly and handed him the report so he could double-check the area where it had been found. "No one saw where exactly it came from," she said, "but maybe these memories can help fill in the gaps."

Julian mulled them over as he and Paris did paperwork in the back offices. Julian's shoulder was tight and hot, and a headache had wormed its way behind his forehead from lack of sleep. If Paris noticed his black mood, he chose not to acknowledge it.

When Paris was finished, he leaned back and stretched. "The place they found the fenris. I think it's near a rumored black market."

"So?"

"*So*, who do we know likes to use all sorts of weird ingredients?" Paris traced a circle in the air. "Maybe powdered fenris antler is one of them."

Julian frowned, thinking of the hazy image of the man holding the saw. "If so, then Lord Cyr should be told."

"Or we could investigate ourselves and save His Brightness the trouble." At Julian's raised eyebrow, Paris shrugged. "What if I see something good and want to buy it?"

"You're a *Hunter*. You work for the Crown."

"I'm a man with needs the Crown can't fulfill."

"Wha— No, I don't want to know." Black markets in Nexus were few and far between, thanks to the high commissioner's efforts to weed them out, and Julian had never visited one before. The idea wasn't appealing.

But his mother's latest dose of medicine was running low. What if he could find some at a cheaper rate? Or the ingredients to make his own?

Julian swallowed. "Let me send out a missive."

Julian glared at the ground wet with runoff dribbling out of a nearby pipe. It was dusk, the sky a pale purple that turned everything an unreal shade—even this derelict corner of the city with its crumbling buildings and corners smelling of piss.

Paris stood beside him, hands tucked into his coat pockets. Both of them had dressed down for the investigation. Julian's back felt exposed without the weight of his bow.

"Twitchy lately," his partner observed.

Julian sighed and rubbed the back of his head, fingers rasping against the shorter hairs. "Just anxious."

"That's obvious." Paris made a twirling motion with his finger and Julian warily turned around. Paris grabbed his shoulders and began to dig his thumbs into the sore muscles, removing the left one when Julian hissed in pain. "Sorry, forgot you're recovering. Point stands you're *very* tight and need to work yourself loose."

"I'll get right on that," Julian muttered.

"I know this place on Cascara Street where they walk on your back with bare feet," Paris said. "I don't know if you're a foot sort of man, but let me tell you, those feet are the most tantalizing I've ever seen."

"Please stop saying *feet*."

A cough sounded nearby. "Am I interrupting something?"

Paris let go of Julian and patted him on the back. "Nope! Just trying to get my friend here to loosen up."

Julian shot him a withering look before turning to the man who'd approached them. He was one of the Hunters' contacts, scruffy and middle-aged, his beard patchy with white and his trousers covered in sawdust. His hair hung long and loose, and seemed to be in need of a wash.

"Malcolm," Julian greeted, shaking the man's calloused hand. "How are you?"

"Fair enough," Malcolm rumbled. "What is it you're looking for?"

"Just wanted to get a read of anything illicit going on in this area."

"You implying something?"

This was the usual dance they had with their informants, and Julian went through the steps patiently. "No, sir. Merely asking if you've seen anything of the sort."

" 'Course I have. Impossible not to. Back alley trades, drug exchanges. Thought your type would be on top of that shit."

"Not quite our department," Paris said cheerfully.

"Have you seen anything particularly strange recently?" Julian went on. "Anything involving animals or beasts?"

Malcolm studied him, craggy face hardening. "You're paying me, right?"

Julian silently held up the small bag of coins.

"There might be a shop that'll interest you." Malcolm twitched and peered over his shoulder, as if expecting a whole squadron to come down on him. "Of the . . . beastly nature. Off Filigree Street and where Mar and Sulivad meet."

"Thank you, Malcolm." Julian handed him the bag and Malcolm bit one of the coins. Satisfied, he didn't bother with a goodbye before he limped off.

Julian and Paris set out. The sun was now well on its way to setting, making blades of shadow of the buildings on either side. There were plenty of people out, as vendors in the central markets tended to slap discounts on the remainder of their wares around this time, unwilling to haul it all back after a long and sweltering day.

They turned off the main thoroughfare and through a damp alley until they reached the well-hidden corner of Mar and Sulivad. It opened into a cramped street where smoke rose in hazy ribbons from brick chimneys and the normal din was reduced to murmurs. There was a distinct smell here, something coppery and ashy, ozone cut with man-made metal.

"I think this is the place," Paris murmured.

The stalls and dingy shops around them were definitely unconventional. One advertised a variety of shrunken body parts both animal and human, and another held jars filled with teeth. Most of the vendors wore masks for anonymity. One noticed Julian staring and flexed his bulky arms in warning.

"Split up?" Paris suggested.

Julian nodded. "If you see beast parts or Conjuration ingredients, don't make a move. We only need enough information to bring back to Lo—His Brightness."

Paris went left and Julian went right. He passed stalls with normal wares—sachets of herbs, fragrant teas, foreign-styled knives—and Julian paused, wondering if he should ask one of the apothecary vendors what could best counter languor.

But after paying Malcolm, the amount of coin in his pockets had dwindled significantly.

"It's you."

Julian looked up, startled.

Standing beside him was a tall young woman, her black hair tied into a braid. Her clothes were plain yet stylish: red hose, tall boots, white shirt. She had a hand braced on one generous hip, perhaps to direct others' attention to the sword hanging at her belt, held in a scuffed-up scabbard. A silver ring glinted with an onyx stone on her fourth finger. Strangely, the stone didn't seem to catch the light at all.

He drew his eyes back up to hers. They were a rich, dark brown, and unnervingly attentive.

"I'm...sorry?" he said. "Do I know you?"

"No. Not yet, anyway. But I know what *you* are."

Julian searched for Paris, but of course he was nowhere to be found. "I'm not sure what you mean."

"I know you're in a certain task force," she said in a voice like midnight, low and melodic. "And what division you come from."

She knew he was a Hunter, and working with Nikolas Cyr. Violent heat stole through his chest.

"I could use your help right about now," she went on. She bent down and pulled a velvet purse from her boot, which she shoved into his hand with a telling jangle. "Since I'm guessing we might be searching for the same thing."

"I..." The purse was surprisingly heavy in his palm. "I don't understand."

"There's a proprietor of beast parts here. Bones, mostly." She lifted an eyebrow. "Could be one of the Conjurers' suppliers."

Julian's lips parted, but his ability to speak had momentarily fled.

"So here's the deal," she went on. "I bring you to the proprietor and let you ruin this man's whole career, but in exchange"—she poked the purse—"you let me take one thing from the shop."

His fingers tightened around the purse. He could hear the taunting echo of his mother's cough.

But...no. He had no idea who this woman was or why she was looking for beast bones. It stank of something south of legal.

He barely managed to swallow his greed and handed the purse back. "I'm sorry, but I can't."

She stared at him, as if waiting for him to realize his mistake. When he did nothing but stare back, she huffed and snatched up the purse.

"Fine," she said. "Then let's see what happens once I tell these fine people there's a Hunter in their midst."

She opened her mouth and drew in a breath. Julian slapped a hand over her mouth.

"What are you *doing*?" he hissed.

She licked his palm, and he drew it back in disgust. "Trying to blow your cover," she answered as he wiped his hand on his coat. "It's called extortion." Her eyes held a glimmer of victory, mirrored in the smirk teasing the corner of her lips.

"Fuck," he breathed. "*Fine*. I'll help you, but don't say anything unnecessary. And you have to tell me what you plan to take."

She ran a thumb over the hilt of her sword. "It's a surprise."

Julian gritted his teeth. But finding this dealer, a potential supplier of Conjuration materials and undoubtedly the man with the saw in the fenris's memories, had to come first. He could deal with this woman after.

She tucked the purse into his coat pocket and patted it. "What do I call you?"

"Do you really need to know?"

"It's only polite."

He exhaled. "Julian. You?"

The smile that crossed her face was reminiscent of early winter nights and the cool weight of deep water. All silent killers.

"Tae," she answered.

V

Taesia studied the Hunter out of the corner of her eye as they walked. He was attractive, his face clean-shaven and finely sculpted with a slightly hooked nose and dark, thick eyebrows. The underside of his hair was shaved. He couldn't have been much older than she was; in fact, she'd be willing to put down money there were only a few months between them.

He had the carriage of a soldier, shoulders back and spine straight. It was all too easy to remember him in his Hunter's uniform, standing with the rest of Nikolas's unit.

"So what exactly are you doing here?" she asked. "Wanted to make a bust on your own, get ahead of your peers?"

"*No.* I came to investigate."

"Really? That's so boring."

"Then I'd hate to know what you'd find interesting."

"I can absolutely guarantee you would." She laughed inwardly at his sour expression, thankful for the bit of levity, the first she'd felt since Dante's arrest. Under the smoke and odors of the market was the scent of a dying summer given way to early autumn, warm and golden.

If they couldn't reopen the portals and restore the Cosmic Scale, the color and life would drain out of their realm bit by bit, until there was no such thing as summer or autumn.

They found the shop after a quarter hour of searching. The front was bare and unremarkable. Taesia opened the door warily, hand drifting to her sword.

She hadn't known what to expect, yet somehow the sight that greeted them was exactly what her imagination had first invoked. The shop was dim and murky, and crowded with beast paraphernalia: skulls in all shapes and sizes, twisting antlers and horns, pelts of fur in various patterns and colors—one sporting rings of bright, contrasting purple, reminding her of a poisonous dart frog—and jars filled with misshapen blobs in liquid.

Organs, she realized with a rush of nausea.

Julian cursed loudly. She turned and immediately reached for her sword. In the back of the shop lurked a fully formed beast, held to the wall with chains that rattled as it attempted to lunge at them. Its bat-like wings flared out on either side of a slim yet muscular body, its skin white as alabaster. Although its smooth, oval head was featureless, halos of light circled its skull and wrists.

Although her mind screamed *monster*, there was something beautiful in its feral design, in the way the light caressed it like the sun sinking into the horizon.

"What the fuck is that?" Taesia hissed.

"A volucris," Julian said. His gaze didn't waver from the beast; similarly, the volucris cocked its head toward him. "They're from Solara. How did he manage to capture one?"

"Good evening," came a silken voice from the shadows. "I see you've met my pet."

A tall, lanky man stepped out behind a row of shelves. He wore an apron covered in old, rust-colored stains, his sleeves rolled up to his elbows revealing a collection of scars on his forearms, deep and ragged enough to have been made by claws and talons. He wore spectacles low on his nose, his eyes a distant, unnerving gray above a wide smile.

Julian breathed in sharply beside her, as if he recognized him. And from the way he was looking between the volucris and the dealer, he clearly wanted to act. But she couldn't let him be a Hunter right now— not until she found the bones.

She stepped between them with a smile of her own and put on the voice she used when dealing with the dons and doñas. "And it's certainly a remarkable one. Gave me and my friend quite the scare."

His smile stretched wider. "That is its purpose, yes. Encourages customers to keep their sticky fingers to themselves."

The beast's talons pricked the floor uneasily, like a dog begging to be let off its leash. A deep, primal horror formed in her gut the longer she stared at it, an instinct that she—or rather, it—shouldn't be here.

"How may I help you?" the dealer drawled.

"I'm searching for a specific type of bone," Taesia said before she lost her nerve. "From a Noctan beast. I'm told it's very rare. I'm not even sure if you'd have it." She let skepticism color her tone, and the man's mouth twitched in challenge.

"Follow me," he said, then turned toward a thick curtain that led to a back room. They had to skirt around the volucris, which, despite being eyeless, followed their every move with a slow turn of its head. As they got closer, Julian suddenly stopped and pressed his fingers to his temple.

She grabbed his elbow. "What's wrong?"

"Nothing. I...I don't like this. The volucris is clearly being abused. What if it escapes, like the fenris did?"

"What fenris?"

"Never mind. I have to get my partner, get backup—"

"Not yet," she hissed. "I need the bones first."

When they passed through the curtain, the dealer stood waiting for them with hands clasped behind his back, smile unfaltering. He stared at Julian for a lingering, silent moment, then nodded to the shelves lining the walls.

The entire place was a bone emporium. There were twisted finger bones and ulnae, neat stacks of humeri and radii, scapulae and heels ranging from hard and white to spongy and yellowed. She picked up a nearby jawbone bristling with fangs.

Flitting among the shelves were about a dozen Other-Realm creatures. They were small and pale as grubs, their amphibian-like skin swathed in brown fabric and carrying tiny lanterns of white light in their clawed hands. They were currently organizing piles of bones, shepherding a rib here, a skull there, with quick whispers of a language she couldn't decipher.

They stopped and peered up at her and Julian with large black eyes. One by one they began to pull out small bone knives.

The dealer lifted a hand. "They're all right. Let them browse." The creatures slowly put their knives away. "Bone snatchers," he said to their bewildered expressions. "From Mortri. Excellent little helpers. If you tell them what you need, I'm sure they'll help for a small fee." With that, he stepped back through the curtain.

Taesia stared at the bone snatchers. They stared back. Julian made a small choking sound.

"Well," Taesia said, taking a silver solsta from her pocket, "let's see if you can find me some astralam bones." She handed the coin to one of the bone snatchers. It grabbed it with its tiny clawed hand and tucked it in its robe before shuffling off to search. Taesia turned to the opposite shelves.

"What are you planning to do with these bones?" Julian murmured at her side. "If it's for Conjuration—"

"Relax. I'm not a Conjurer." She tried to keep her voice light as she inspected a curved rib. "What I need them for is my own business, just as what you need my money for is your own business."

Julian scoffed. "Fine. But don't say I didn't warn you. If Dante Lastrider can be thrown in the Gravespire, anyone can."

Taesia froze, the smile on her face turning brittle. The shadows in the corners of the room inched closer. She could almost hear whispers within them, encouraging her to use them.

Julian didn't notice. He picked up a femur and scowled at it as she watched him from under her lashes. Even Umbra quivered from within its bezel.

A high, keening groan came from the front of the shop, followed by the sound of chains. Was the volucris sensing her shadow magic?

Julian started at the sound. When he put the femur back, he winced and reached toward his left shoulder.

"What's the matter?" she asked. "Nyx's piss, are you injured?"

"It's nothing. Had a little run-in with a banri."

Before she could ask about it, there was a tug at her leg. Looking down, she met the unblinking gaze of the bone snatcher she had paid.

Her heart leapt. "Did you find it?"

The creature led her deeper into the room, to a tall, dusty set of shelves set into a niche, and pointed up at one it couldn't reach. Taesia quickly moved bones around, ignoring the bone snatcher's weak protest as a couple fell to the floor.

Eventually she spotted black amid all the white. She pushed away an assortment of femurs and pulled out an entire row of vertebrae, black and glittering in the light from the bone snatchers' lanterns. The bones were cold against her skin, but a tingling warmth went through her, the buzzing of some unknown energy.

A relieved smile broke across her face. Astralam bones, what remained of a fallen star turned beast. The first step in potentially discovering how to break the barrier to Noctus.

For a moment she lost herself to the warm satisfaction purling through her chest. It was like living out one of her daydreams, hunting through the terrifying landscape of Mortri or the light-blasted lands of Solara or the night-drenched kingdoms of Noctus in order to uncover treasure beyond imagining.

With these bones, perhaps that would finally be possible.

"You got what you wanted," Julian said. "Now let me do my job."

"Unfortunately, I cannot allow the two of you to leave."

They turned toward the dealer's voice. He stood in the doorway, smile still in place, though now he held a serrated saw in one hand and a cleaver in the other.

"I know a Hunter when I see one," the dealer went on as the curtain at his back parted, revealing the hulking, pale shape of the volucris. Its chains dragged freely from its light-encircled wrists. "And I know better than to let them live."

Julian watched with dawning horror as the bone snatchers scattered and the volucris lunged at Tae.

Julian had brought a brace of daggers with him. He drew one and attacked the beast from behind. It twisted and swiped at him with its talons, catching him across the stomach. Julian danced away in time to avoid the worst of it, but the talons had cut cleanly through his shirt, leaving thin red lines on his skin.

Sword in hand, Tae darted in and struck the junction of the beast's arm and shoulder. Black blood spurted as it made a high whine of displeasure. Julian moved to help and just managed to dodge the man's cleaver. Off balance, he tripped over one of the scurrying bone snatchers and fell onto his back.

The dealer pinned him down. He was grinning madly now, his glasses opaque with the light shining off the volucris. "I knew it was a matter of time until you lot came sniffing around." He pressed the edge of the saw against Julian's throat.

Julian gritted his teeth and bucked up, disrupting the man's seat and striking him with his dagger. The dealer fell back with a wild laugh even as blood bloomed across his apron. Wetness trickled down to Julian's collarbone; the saw must have nicked him.

Even with the whirling confusion of the room Julian could sense the volucris's hot, molten anger. All it wanted was an open sky, and instead it had been locked up here for weeks, in the cramped dark, being fed whatever scraps the dealer couldn't sell.

It wanted violence, to remember what it was to kill something, to have power.

"Tae!" Julian shouted as he staggered back to his feet. "You take him, I'll take the beast!"

She nodded and dodged the volucris's next attack, spinning effortlessly toward the dealer and stabbing her sword at his midsection. He caught it between the cleaver and the saw.

Julian unsheathed his second dagger and faced down the beast. It lurched forward with talons fully extended. He ducked and blocked them with one blade, aiming his second dagger at its wing. The volucris made that high whine again and flapped its wings hard enough to send the dagger spinning, bones scattering from their shelves. Then it grabbed him.

Julian gasped as they launched upward, talons breaking through the skin of his shoulder. The volucris hit the ceiling, twisting and scrabbling at the wood as Julian dangled from its other hand. He choked as his collar tightened around his neck and reached up to wrap his free hand around the beast's forearm.

Let me go, he thought, practically shouting into its skull. *Let me go and kill your captor!*

The volucris keened and rammed itself against the ceiling again. It was too far gone in its madness, its thirst for freedom.

The room seemed to get darker, or perhaps it was his vision. Julian struggled and was about to raise his dagger when the volucris suddenly let him go. He fell to the floor in a heap, coughing and cringing at the pain of his injured shoulder.

Then the volucris dove toward him.

"Not many people looking for astralam bones," the dealer murmured as he and Taesia circled. Bones crunched and snapped under her boots. "Not a lot of folks in Vitae who know about astralams."

"Not a lot of folks who'd chop up beasts either," she retorted before she attacked.

She had been trained since she was seven years old. But the man was uncannily fast, and she cursed as she came dangerously close to losing a hand to his cleaver. She danced back as shadows trembled at the edge of her consciousness, so terribly eager to be used.

I can't. Not where the Hunter can see.

But a sudden crack made her look up at where the volucris had rammed against the ceiling, Julian within its grasp. Using the distraction, the dealer opened a gash on her arm.

Taesia snarled and twisted, returning the favor. The man laughed, glasses sliding down his nose.

"Tell me what you wanted to do with them," he breathed, licking her blood off the cleaver. "The bones."

Taesia lifted her sword even as her heart thundered. *The bones.* Where were the bones?

There—they'd fallen near her foot. She dove and closed her hand over one of the vertebrae just as the dealer pounced.

The bone pulsed. It was like a fishhook tugging her heart, ripping a gasp out of her throat as the tingling, buzzing warmth she'd felt before stole through her.

Bears some measure of cosmic energy when they fall, Dante's notes had said. *Gravitational pulls, force fields, etc.*

Potentially: portals.

She clutched the vertebrae tighter. A restless, dark energy sang through her own bones. With a mere thought the shadows sprang out like a trap and latched around the dealer's body. He stumbled with a cry, clawing at the tendrils around his neck.

The volucris let go of Julian, and the Hunter fell. But the beast wasn't through with him; it dove with talons extended, desperate to claim a life. Julian lifted his dagger and winced.

Taesia held out the bone and the restless energy within her spilled out. She *felt* the cosmic energy shift and alter above them, a small vortex of power just below the ceiling.

With a violent wrench of her arm, she forced the opening wider. It lasted a second, maybe even less, but it was enough. The volucris was snatched up in the column of dark, cosmic energy, pulled from the room and sucked into the fragile, flickering portal.

The bone tumbled from Taesia's numb hand as the vortex resealed itself tight, leaving nothing but an empty stretch of wood.

Julian stared at the empty space, panting. "What— Where did—?"

She couldn't answer, dazed with disbelief.

Dante had been right. If she and the other heirs channeled their powers during Godsnight, when the Cosmic Scale aligned and the barriers would be at their thinnest, they could potentially re-create a similar breach in every realm's barrier. They could undo the Sealing.

We can do this.

A choking sound diverted her attention. The dealer was no longer smiling, staring first at the ceiling and then at Taesia.

"What are you?" he coughed out around her shadow's garrote. "What did you do?"

This man, this monster in his own right, was now looking at her as if *she* were the thing to be feared.

A searing, brutal heat spread through her. She was suddenly back in the council room, the king stating that Dante's arrest was a warning, that the Houses had to follow every order without question or complaint. She was back at the Gravespire, the guards ready to draw their weapons even as contempt danced in their eyes.

Breathing hard, Taesia opened herself up to the darkness already swirling within her from using the astralam bone, swelling as the shadows lengthened and deepened. Umbra coiled around her wrist as she lifted a hand.

"What are you doing?" the dealer gasped. "What are you—"

She clenched her hand into a fist. The shadow around his neck twisted, and a loud *crack* thundered through the room.

It was so easy. Just her and her power, the deep dark well of it, the endless night sky of it. She wanted to swim in it forever.

She wanted it to never end.

Julian sat stunned on the floor amid bones and debris as he stared at the dealer's body. At his eyes, wide and gray, and the broken glasses lying beside his snapped neck.

Julian lifted his gaze until it landed on Tae. She was wreathed in living shadows, her eyes gone completely black and her arms and legs wrapped with tendrils of dark air. Her hair had come loose from its braid, and her face was splashed with blood like war paint.

Then she turned those all-black eyes on him. She looked like a god standing at the end of the world.

His mind turned back to his mother's gossip rags, the sketch of a woman in shadow grinning viciously at the reader.

He had thought it a gross exaggeration, but he saw now that wasn't the case. They had only captured the truth of Taesia Lastrider.

Slowly, the shadows inched inward until they disappeared, her eyes returning to normal after a few blinks. She swayed on her feet, and suddenly she was transformed from god to exhausted young woman.

She stared at him. He stared helplessly back.

"Well," she croaked. "The bones work."

VI

Nikolas was used to his mother dropping things. Her tea, her reading glasses, her commitments. Lux had learned to unwind from Nikolas's wrist and return whatever had fallen back to its proper place.

But when Lux caught her ball of yarn and placed it gently back in her lap, she didn't thank the familiar as she usually did. She merely stared out at nothing, as if gazing upon another world.

Nikolas sat with her in the morning room, a parlor in the Cyr villa outfitted with massive windows along the far wall. They faced the sprawling gardens with their hedge maze and patchwork plants, the gardeners below moving through the footpaths as they worked. The furniture was white trimmed in gold, the walls and floor pale. When the sun rose at dawn, the entire room was flooded with light.

It was meant for prayer and meditation, a place where Cyr Lumins gathered strength at the start of their day. Waren had always made his two sons kneel with him on the rug and mutter quick blessings to Phos before going down for breakfast.

Nikolas hadn't prayed since Rian died.

Still, the sun felt nice. That's why household staff liked to bring Madeia here, to sit and absorb the sunshine, to cast some brightness around her.

Nikolas touched his mother's wrist. "What are you making?"

Madeia took a deep breath and blinked a few times. She seemed surprised by the unfinished knitting project beneath her hands.

"Oh." She lifted the circle of green yarn she'd crafted, the interlocking loops tight and even. Every row she added expanded the circle, but unlike the hats she'd made for him and Rian during the winter, she didn't seem to be following any particular pattern. "I'm not sure."

"It'll be beautiful no matter what it is."

She smiled faintly. "Such a flatterer."

Madeia Cyr was from a noble family in southern Vaega. Her marriage to his father had been out of convenience, as her family held power in Seniza, a large city in the volcanic region. Nikolas often wondered if she wanted to return to Seniza and never set foot in Nexus again. Or maybe Seniza was also too painful for her, memories buried within the ash that fell from Deia's Heart.

For a moment he felt the volcano's heat on his skin, the echo of his brother calling his name. Nikolas closed his eyes tight.

"Perhaps I'll go back to bed," Madeia murmured. "I'm a little tired."

The staff were on strict orders to prevent his mother from crawling back into bed, where she would have spent the majority of her day had Nikolas not insisted otherwise.

"We could take a turn around the gardens," Nikolas suggested. "The bugle lilies are still flowering."

"Not today," she said. Her most used phrase.

Grief was not a simple thing. It crushed and gnawed, turning you to gristle between its teeth. When it eventually spat you out, it left you broken down and stripped into layers, left you to carefully rebuild what had survived and discard what no longer fit.

Nikolas had spent the last few years rebuilding, reminding himself who he had once been and who he now was. He wasn't fond of the latter—probably never would be—but at least he could go whole days without mourning his ghost.

He was terrified his mother had been stripped of too much. That she couldn't rebuild with the scraps left in the wreckage. She had haunted the halls of the villa after Rian succumbed to fever, more specter than woman.

Some days it was better. Some days she laughed, and ate, and her eyes gleamed like they had when she'd played with her golden-haired sons.

But most days were like this: quiet, forgetful, working the muscles into a routine to keep her moving.

A quiet knock sounded at the door. A servant in white-and-gold livery bowed at the threshold.

"Pardon, my lord and lady, but there is a guest in the receiving room."

There were no meetings scheduled for today, or at least, none his father had told him about. "Who is it?"

"Lady Risha Vakara, my lord."

Risha didn't normally visit him, instead choosing to meet outside of their villas. He suspected his father was the reason.

"I'll be down shortly. Thank you." Nikolas turned to his mother. "I'll see you for luncheon?"

She nodded absently, picking up her knitting project. "Perhaps I'll know what this is by then."

Nikolas followed the servant downstairs. The Cyr villa was an ornately gilded spectacle, all frill and unnecessary flourish. From the ornate crown molding to the sculpted friezes to the wall paneling, everything was styled to the point of gaudiness.

"It's like a golden sarcophagus," Rian had once said. "And we're all trapped inside."

Risha stood waiting by the window in the receiving room, fingers loosely laced before her. Nikolas quietly dismissed the servant.

"What happened?" he demanded.

"Nothing *happened*. Or rather, something did, but I've also been thinking."

"Uh-oh."

She managed a small smile, but it quickly fell. "Gardens?"

He led her to the hedge maze. The gardeners waved to him and he lifted a hand in greeting. He wondered if his mother could see them, or if she was too busy with her knitting.

Either way, he and Risha were obscured from view as soon as they entered the maze. The hedges were at least seven feet tall, constructed into a square geometric grid with a fountain waiting at the center for those who found their way there. It was a good place to wander with his thoughts—or for dampening sound.

Risha spoke without preamble. "Something was stolen from the Bone Palace."

He nearly stumbled. "What?"

"From the Hall of Antiques. Leshya Vakara's necklace." She took a steadying breath. "Which holds necromantic properties."

"The Conjurers?"

"It must be. But how they were able to get it, let alone get into Thana's Chapel before, I have no idea."

Nikolas would have to bring this up with his unit, do a sweep of the Hall of Antiques. The idea of the Conjurers having secret access to the palace was beyond disconcerting.

At least the king was surrounded by attentive guards who shepherded him into the palace's safe room at the first sign of trouble. Nikolas remembered the chamber from his youth, when a group of magic users had thrown projectiles at the palace, displeased with a new law that all elementalists were required to be documented by the government. The nobles inside had been guided to a wide, heavily fortified chamber. Rian had clutched his hand while their mother whispered soothing nonsense in their ears until they could leave.

"I've been thinking about what Taesia said," Risha went on. "About the true origins of Godsnight. About how it might be the way to undo the Sealing."

Nikolas reined in his surprise. "And?"

She seemed to struggle with her next words as they turned a corner. "This situation with the dead is getting worse, and it's only a matter of time until the Bone Palace is targeted again." She fiddled with her silver bangles. They sparkled with sunlight and made reflections on the hedges, which Lux chased playfully.

"The problem won't fix itself," she said softly. "I've been trying to break the Mortri barrier, even just a little, but I *can't*. Not by myself. I... I want to make a difference."

"It's Conjuration," he said carefully.

"I know. But what else can we do? I hate to admit it, but Taesia's right. If we miss Godsnight this time around, it'll be another hundred years until our descendants can attempt it again."

He thought of running into Angelica at the university, how she'd called him a fool for even indulging the possibility. But she hadn't been able to hide the same uneasiness that Risha was now baring to him, the same tentative hope that wanted to bloom wild in his chest.

Lezzaro had told Nikolas he'd have a role to play. This was it—and it was his decision whether or not to accept it.

"I've been thinking the same thing," he admitted. "I don't want to go against His Majesty, but..."

There was only so much the king and their families were doing, and still there was no solution, no forward momentum toward saving their realm. It had first seemed like such a slow track, but in the last couple of years plants withered faster, winters bit colder, and animals died sooner. There were the wildfires in southern Vaega last year, the plague in Marii last spring, and the draught in Azuna.

And the gods watched on and said nothing. Did nothing.

It was easy to feel helpless, standing under the open sky only a hairsbreadth away from a sprawling universe. There were other beings facing what they faced.

As if sensing the encroaching doom settling on Nikolas's shoulders, Risha reached out and held his hand. It helped a little.

They spent another hour in the gardens until Risha left and Nikolas went to his study to see if his father had left anything for him to review. He wasn't expecting to run into his father in the corridor, Waren's arms crossed and a cold glare in his eyes.

"What was the Vakara heir doing here?" Waren rumbled.

Nikolas swallowed his sudden panic. "We were discussing the matter of the Conjurers." Which wasn't a stretch, really.

His father took a step toward him. Nikolas instinctively flinched, though all Waren did was point a calloused finger at him.

"The Lastriders are already falling apart," he said, his voice a barely restrained warning. "Soon there will be one less House in contention for the crown. The other heirs are your rivals, Nikshä, not your peers. They are not welcome in this villa. Remember that, or I will remind you myself."

Waren backed off and made for his own study. Nikolas didn't move until he heard the distant slam of his door.

Knees weak, Nikolas returned to his bedroom. He had enough to worry about without throwing his father's resentment into the mix.

Like how Taesia was currently sitting on the edge of his bed.

Nikolas barely bit back a yelp. He scrambled to shut the door and pressed his back up against it.

She winked. "Hello, gorgeous."

"Tae," he said slowly, "what in Thana's grave are you doing here? And what *happened* to you?" She was absolutely filthy, covered in dust and— "Is that *blood*?"

"Hardly any of it is mine," she said. "Actually, that's why I'm here. Can I wash up before going back to my villa?"

Nikolas pinched the bridge of his nose and took a deep breath. He should have been used to this. It was one of the greatest tragedies of his life that he wasn't.

"Now's not a good time," he said, his father's warning ringing through his mind. Lux crept away from his shoulder and Umbra coiled out of her ring, the two familiars twirling through the room.

"It never is." Taesia flicked a flake of dried blood from his counterpane. "But if I walk through the villa gates like this, my sister will suffer a stroke. Now can I use your washroom or no?"

"If you tell me why you're like..." He gestured to her from head to toe. "This."

"I saved a kitten from certain doom. It got messy."

He couldn't tell what he felt more: exasperation or relief. Seeing Taesia after Dante's arrest had unnerved him. Scared him. He could still feel the indent of her fingers digging into his jaw, dark eyes boring into his own. If she was making jokes, that meant her mood had lifted.

How it had lifted, he wasn't sure.

Taesia made for the washroom, leaving her sword and some dirt smudges behind. The sound of pumps was followed by the splash of running water. Nikolas glanced at the open archway, though Taesia and the tub were out of sight. He stifled the urge to slip in there with her, to see her face flush and her dark hair curl from the steam.

Instead he leaned her sword against the wall, next to where he'd hung the Sunbringer Spear. He took a moment to touch the tree charm he'd wrapped around the spear's stock, as if asking for strength. Beside it, his outfit for the Godsnight Gala hung on the back of his closet door. When it had been delivered, he'd had to resist the urge to go outside and burn it.

Nikolas turned away and sat on his bed, a lavish acre of linen and far too many pillows for one person's use. This wasn't the bedroom of his childhood; he'd been moved from the nursery wing when he was ten, away from the pale blue walls painted with the shapes of clouds, away from his toys and his small writing desk. "You're going to be an adult soon, and need to act like one," his father had told him. So Nikolas had had to get used to empty spaces on the walls and expensive things he could only look at, never touch.

"I'm in," he said.

He hadn't meant to blurt it. But he was tired, and his mind was spinning.

The sound of water stopped. "What?"

"Godsnight. I want to try it." He swallowed. "If it's the only way to help our realm, then I'm in. Risha is, too."

Another ripple of water, followed by soft footsteps padding toward him. He kept his gaze on the floor as Taesia's bare feet came into view, arching up into the gentle curve of her ankles. Beads of water dripped down her legs.

"Are you sure?" Her voice was the sweet night air after a rainstorm, the kind he could never get enough of.

His laughter held no mirth. "No. But even if we try it, I..." He glanced at the Sunbringer Spear. The glow of it seemed dimmer, as if it too were disappointed in him.

"Phos refused to bless me," he whispered. He'd been wanting to tell her, tell *someone*. If they really were going to attempt Godsnight, she needed to know there was a chance he couldn't do his part.

Couldn't fulfill the role Lezzaro had chosen for him.

"What do you mean, refused to bless you?"

"I tried to commune with him." He swallowed. "He didn't answer."

"But he answered your father."

"Yes."

Her thin fingers touched the underside of his chin, lifting it. She was still bare, her hair wet, water caught in her eyelashes. She looked as if she had emerged from the ocean, a goddess of the dark, quiet depths. His next breath was needle-sharp, the eager gasp of someone drowning.

"No matter what happened, it doesn't change the fact that you are powerful," she whispered. "The rightful Cyr heir."

"Rian was—"

"No, Nik. You have to move beyond that. Phos didn't bless you? Fine. You don't need his blessing. You're enough on your own."

It was such an easy thing for her to say, when the shadows bent to her merest whim. He stared at her, a girl of darkness and desire, and wondered what it was like to be so certain of yourself. She didn't understand his situation, couldn't begin to fathom how far he was from the person she saw in him.

But he wanted to be that person. Would do anything to be that person.

Slowly she straddled his lap. Nikolas's hands instinctively went to her hips, the soft, devastating curve of them. He watched as a bead of water trailed down her neck, toward her collarbone.

Their mouths met with the rough eagerness of the starving. There was no grace to it, simply an opening up, the inevitable resignation. Nikolas wanted to remember when they had once been gentler and shier, when intimacy had been punctuated by laughter and soft murmuring.

There was none of that as he dug his fingers into her flesh, skimming his lips across her throat, following the path the drop of water had taken. Down over her collarbone, between her breasts. She shivered in his arms and it was a kind of power—he felt mad with it, like he always did. Stunned and selfish at being the only one who got to eke this out of her.

It didn't matter there were scrapes and cuts along her arms. She wouldn't explain them even if he asked.

She pressed her damp body to his clothed one, pushing him down. She made quick work of his shirt and trousers as he marveled over her surefire movements, hard muscle giving way to softness. He couldn't help but touch her, shuddering as the ends of her wet hair dragged over his burning skin.

Taesia kissed the center of his chest and looked up at him from beneath her lashes. He watched in awe as she moved down, over his stomach, breathing against the inside of his thigh. He gasped, cupping the back of her head as his hips arched, as goose bumps erupted over his arms.

It was easier when they didn't talk. When everything was boiled down to rough breaths and half-formed moans. When he eventually rolled on top of her, he allowed himself a weak grin as she grabbed him by the backside, pulling him insistently closer. Her face was open and sweet, eyes half-closed, lips swollen. He moved and she rose to meet him, and he allowed himself to feel powerful, to grab her by the hip and make her gasp and swear, unraveling her until she became the girl he knew and loved, a thing he could actually touch, not just admire.

Long minutes later he was catching his breath against the mountain of pillows as Taesia rested her head on his chest. For one moment, everything was peaceful, his burdens mercifully lifted.

Then all too soon she was rolling away and getting dressed. She reattached her sword and called Umbra back to her, the familiar retreating into its bezel.

Nikolas sat up, not bothering to pull the blankets over his lap. "So? How do we prepare for this?"

Taesia slipped off her pack and drew something out. It was small and black, glittering like mica. When she handed it to Nikolas, he nearly dropped it. It was freezing.

"Is this...bone?"

"Astralam bone, to be precise. It comes from a powerful Noctan beast." Seeing it was hurting him, she plucked it from his fingers. "I'm going to make something out of it. A tool, of sorts, to help channel my power through. You could probably use the Sunbringer Spear for the same purpose."

He rubbed his numb fingertips. "Tae..." He examined the bloodstains on her clothes, finally pulling the blanket over his lap. "Where exactly did you get these bones?"

"I'll tell you later. I need to head back to the villa." She bent down to kiss him. "You should have someone paint you like this, by the way." She indicated his naked body. "It would look good over the mantel."

She opened the window and crawled out onto the roof, and just like that, she was gone.

VII

Taesia waited until the shadows grew long with afternoon to scale the wall of the Lastrider villa. Once up the rose trellis and over her balcony, she stumbled into her room with all the exhaustion of a ninety-year-old woman returning home from a day haggling at the market.

At least she'd been able to wash up at Nikolas's villa. She hadn't planned to sleep with him, but she'd been so relieved he was agreeing to her plan, had needed to be worked loose, to relieve the adrenaline sitting stagnant in her veins. And his touch had grounded her, made sure she knew there were types of power other than the one that commanded her.

She'd thought of telling him about the way her shadows had obeyed her, the mesmerizing vortex they'd created. The terrifying pleasure of it, better even than the feeling of him inside her.

Which reminded her to root around her cabinet for the jar of wild carrot seeds. She crunched on them as she changed out of her filthy, torn-up clothes and examined her injuries.

The bone dealer was dead because of her. He had deserved to die—would have been executed regardless of Nikolas's task force bringing him to justice—but the fact it had been her, and her alone, made an odd weight form in her stomach. She had almost been able to feel the snap of his neck reverberate through her, and the longer she thought of it the more nauseated she became.

And then there had been the Hunter, looking up at her with a mixture of awe and terror, giving her the same thrill her power had.

Longing to put it out of her mind, she curled up in bed and slept for a couple of blessed hours until she was woken by a malevolent presence. She opened her eyes to her mother leaning over her, nostrils flaring.

"Where were you?" Elena demanded.

Taesia tried to clear her throat. "Ah...out?"

"And you didn't take the House guards."

"No."

"Why?"

"I wanted to be alone."

"You don't get to be alone," her mother snapped. "Not when the entire city—gods, the entire kingdom, the entire *realm*—has their eyes on us. Not when we're under such scrutiny. I know you don't want to be in this position, but we all have our parts to play. It's past time you do yours."

When her mother stalked out, Brailee tentatively poked her head in. Her eyes were red, the bags under them pronounced.

"Nyx's piss, did you sleep at all last night?" Taesia asked.

Brailee hesitated, then reluctantly said, "I had a dream."

Taesia scooted to the edge of the bed and patted the space beside her. Her sister stood rigidly by the door a moment longer before she relented, Somnus drifting lazily above their heads.

"Tell me about it," Taesia said.

"I was exhausted. I was out as soon as I lay down." It wasn't uncommon for Brailee to fall asleep suddenly, sometimes even while sitting up. "I thought I heard a voice telling me I was right on time, and then I was in a field at night. But the sky had so many stars. It was like...a cosmos. Some of them were falling."

Brailee's gaze went distant, her upper body swaying. Taesia put a hand on her back to steady her.

"There was a city in the distance," her sister murmured. "All bright and gleaming. But there was something else, something closer. A shape of a person. A...boy. My age, I think. It was hard to tell. Usually my dreams are so clear, but this one was fuzzy. He was underfed, and he was dragging something. A...a body. And then he noticed me."

Taesia stared at her in concern, wondering if she should mention this dream to their mother. If Brailee should start taking the sleeping draughts again.

"He asked me who I was, said I couldn't be there. He came toward me, and I tried to back away." Brailee's eyes fluttered closed. "Then I saw what was behind him. A mound of bodies, their limbs all tangled. The boy pushed my chest, and I fell, and woke up."

When Brailee opened her eyes, they seemed a little clearer. "But I saw something else, before I fell. Something at the base of the mound. A statue. I think...Taesia, I think it's the missing statue from the university."

"What missing statue?"

"The architect. It went missing. Saya told me about it." Brailee's voice had gone quiet and slurred, her breathing growing deeper. "I don't know what it means."

Taesia didn't either, and she hated not having answers. She gently pressed Brailee toward the pillows, making her lie down before she could fall. She swept Brailee's hair away from her face as Somnus settled on the pillow beside her.

"Mother's trying to help you," her sister mumbled. "Let us help. Don't be like Dante."

A bright pain struck Taesia's chest. She wanted to tell her sister she had wielded her power and it had felt *good*, that she was capable of so much more than anyone thought possible.

Instead, she said, "You have to trust me, Bee. Please."

Brailee sighed, and tried to mutter something before sleep claimed her.

Taesia and Dante had been born with teeth and claws, and Brailee had been born with the sensitivity neither of her older siblings possessed. Taesia loved her for it, but with Dante gone, it wasn't the same.

Gods, she missed him. She thought of him in the Gravespire, wondering if he was too cold at night, too hot during the day, if they were starving him or beating him.

Swallowing the painful lump in her throat, she slipped out of her room.

Nexus was bustling as afternoon crawled toward evening. Clouds sailed across the sun, and the shadows lengthened all around her. Her fingers twitched, and Umbra sent out a curious tendril.

Something had changed since she used the bones. A mindfulness, a knowledge she wasn't completely sure she wanted. A newly awakened hunger.

And then she remembered Julian's face. The horror, the shock. The fascination.

Taesia took a deep breath and let the memory go. She couldn't be shackled to things that had already happened. Forward—always forward.

She entered a quieter district, gated and manned by guards. They recognized her and let her inside, though she didn't miss the woman's scrutiny of her plain outfit. It wasn't quite in theme with the neighborhood, a boulevard of mansions ringed with black iron balconies and wide bay windows wreathed in decorative molding.

Her aunt's home had grown wild with ivy, the window planters bursting with untrimmed flowers. The neighbors were not shy with their disapproval, even going so far as to send Camilla letters asking her to please consider hiring a gardener, and would she like to make use of theirs, as he was quite skilled with plant-based earth magic and had turned one of their shrubs into the likeness of an elephant?

Camilla threw the letters straight into the trash. "No one appreciates the aesthetic of nature reclaiming mankind's creations anymore," she'd complained.

Taesia knocked and waited for the doorman to let her through. She found her aunt reclining with a tumbler of sherry and a book in the sitting room, her feet bare and her hair down.

"Let me finish this chapter," Camilla said without looking up.

Taesia poured her own glass of sherry and plopped into her favorite green chair. The whole room was done in greens and golds, a massive mirror hanging above the mantel giving the illusion the room was bigger than it actually was.

This was the house her father had grown up in. It had belonged to the Lorenzos for generations, but her father had been unable to inherit due to marrying House Lastrider. When Taesia's grandparents had passed on, Camilla had become the sole owner.

It was too large for her aunt alone, but Camilla had never married, and seemed to have no intention of doing so. There were live-in suitors now and then, but they never lasted long. She claimed to enjoy travel too much to settle; she had even taken a yearlong trip to Cardica twenty years ago, where she'd commissioned the rug beneath their feet.

"All right," Camilla said, setting the book facedown on the table to mark her place. Taesia briefly read the title: *The Risky Gentleman.* "How did it go?"

Taesia took a sip of sherry and let it burn on the way down. "I don't know whether you'll applaud or throw that book at me."

"I won't throw the book at you. I haven't finished it yet, and I want to see if Emilio will finally quit his roguish ways and propose to Riara."

"But has Emilio proven himself a capable lover?"

"Oh yes, quite a few times. Once on a rowboat. But you're avoiding the question."

Taesia hesitated. Her stomach clenched, her heart suddenly beating harder. Umbra uncoiled from her ring and slithered around her neck.

Her aunt had always been understanding, so ready to forgive Taesia for the things her mother despised. When Taesia had first begun to bleed, it was her aunt she had gone to, not Elena. Camilla was matter-of-fact, practical, open-minded. She wasn't the sort who asked unnecessary questions.

And with Lezzaro dead and Dante locked up, she was the only one Taesia could fully confide in.

The urge Taesia had to confess to Brailee was finally sated as it came spooling out of her: meeting the Hunter, their encounter with the dealer, the volucris. She reached into her pack and drew out the bones, their coolness a welcome sensation against her skin.

Camilla had sat up while Taesia spoke, setting her glass beside her book. At the sight of the bones, she picked her glass back up and drained it.

"You got them," her aunt breathed. "But how did you get out of there?"

Taesia swirled the sherry in her glass and downed the rest of it. It sent a plume of heat into her chest. "We fought."

"Taesia."

Like Cormin, Camilla did not easily anger, but there was a line that, once crossed, lit a slow-burning fuse.

"I used my power," Taesia admitted. "But it was different. *Bigger.* I can't really explain it. When I held the bones..." She stared at her hands. Umbra uncoiled from her neck and twirled around her fingers. "I ripped open a portal. It was so fast, and small, but it happened. I made it happen."

The shadows in the corners of the room hummed softly. Taesia slowly closed her hands into fists. Umbra struggled between her fingers.

"A portal," Camilla repeated, almost as if to herself. "Is it still there?"

"No, it sealed itself almost immediately. But I can do it again, I know I can." Camilla nodded absently, eyes distant. "And the dealer...he..."

"You killed him," her aunt guessed.

Taesia exhaled forcefully. "I didn't intend to, at first. But the power made me feel..." Strong. Invincible. *Right.* "The Hunter saw the whole thing. He made me leave the body where it was." Julian had been silent and wary afterward, even as he agreed not to speak of her to his task force. He had called her *my lady.* "What do we do about him?"

"We do nothing except keep watch on him from afar." Camilla got up to pour them both more sherry. "If he admits to visiting an illegal market with the heir of House Lastrider, how will that look for him?" Her aunt grimly saluted Taesia with her glass. "It may have been reckless and foolish, but at least this is a step toward blasting apart those barriers. Toward freeing your brother."

Taesia's tension eased. She released her hands and Umbra sulkily wrapped itself around her wrist.

"But you must be careful," her aunt went on, returning to the couch. "The other heirs might be interested in trying the Godsnight ritual, but they all have a claim to the throne. The more people know a secret, the less chance it has of staying a secret."

"They're my friends. Or at least, Risha and Nik are."

"Yes. But sometimes friends are outgrown."

Taesia frowned but didn't reply. The light was fading outside, which meant the Noctans would be awake. "What should I do with them? The bones."

Camilla thought about it as they savored their drinks in silence. Taesia wondered how Dante would have fashioned the bones, what he would have forged with them.

"What makes you feel strong?" her aunt asked.

The question was simple, its answer anything but. Taesia considered it, imagined herself facing down a god-made barrier like she'd faced down the dealer and his volucris.

"I might have an idea." Taesia stood to leave. "Thank you for... for the sherry."

Camilla picked up her book again. "Of course. You know I have an endless supply of it."

It was full dusk by the time she arrived at the Noctus Quarter. She took a moment to admire the wreaths of paper stars children had made to hang on doors, the gems twinkling from the arches between tenement buildings.

As the city settled into evening, the Noctans were beginning to leave their homes. One spotted her and jumped. "M-my lady!" The others on the street fell into hurried bows, long hair slipping over their shoulders.

Taesia cleared her throat. "There's no need for that. I'm sorry to bother you so early."

"You are no bother to us, my lady."

She turned at the familiar voice. Balwith greeted her with a small smile and a polite bow.

"To what do we owe the grace of your presence, my lady?" he asked. He was taller than her by half a foot, more so if one were to count the tips of his curving horns, but he kept his chin lowered in respect.

"I was hoping you could direct me to your best blacksmith."

If he thought the request strange, he didn't show it. "Of course. If you would follow me?"

Taesia nodded to the refugees they passed. She ought to have been used to bowing and scraping by now, but it was one thing to be on the receiving end of a bitter don's posturing versus someone who regarded her family as if they were gods themselves.

"Will you be holding a festival for Godsni—er, Starfall again this year?"

"Should we have the supplies for it, yes, my lady. Also, I must thank you again for your latest delivery. The fevers are finally waning now the weather has begun to cool. The ice and medicine helped considerably."

"I'm glad to hear it. And if you need anything for the Starfall festival, please don't hesitate to ask it. We'll be happy to supply you with whatever you need."

"My lady is too gracious."

This city and this realm have failed you, she thought. *It's the least we can do.*

Balwith hesitated before speaking again. "Forgive me if this is impertinent, but I feel you should know we don't believe your lord brother is guilty."

The sharp pain that had struck her with Brailee hit her again, harder this time. She didn't have the words to tell him how much this simple gesture meant, that the very people her brother wanted to keep safe were the people who would support him no matter what.

She quickly blinked the prickling from her eyes. "Thank you," she whispered. They walked the rest of the way in silence.

The blacksmith's shop was nestled at the far end of a quiet street. It smelled of ash and steel, and it was humid inside, the windows screened to keep sunlight out. Candles had been arranged to provide enough light to work by, and the forge—built into a hollowed-out pit, supported by brick walls—emanated a brilliant orange glow.

They walked across a stone floor littered with bits of grit and sawdust until they reached the empty counter. Balwith called for the owner as Taesia studied the large anvil before the forge and the metal tongs resting on its surface. The forge's flames were low and banked with no one to stoke them to life. She couldn't help but think of Angelica, wondering if she'd made a mistake trying to bring her into this. Angelica had always tried to distance herself from the others.

But the Houses couldn't afford to be insular. Not anymore.

Taesia snapped out of her thoughts as a Noctan woman emerged from the back of the shop, wiping her hands before she slipped on a leather apron. She was tall and impressively dark, with thin, pointed horns emerging from sleek silver hair. White dots in the shape of stars had been tattooed over the arches of her eyebrows. When she spotted Taesia, she did a double take.

"Mirelle," Balwith greeted. "Lady Taesia has requested your talents."

With Taesia's identity confirmed, the woman swallowed and bowed. It was difficult to tell a Noctan's age, as they tended to live roughly fifty to eighty years longer than Vitaeans, but Mirelle looked young, at least thirty by Taesia's guess.

"I'm honored," Mirelle murmured. The words contrasted with the furrow of her brow, and Taesia wondered if she was annoyed or nervous. "What services would my lady request of me?"

Taesia slid the pack off her shoulders and set it on the countertop. "Well, for one thing, you can stop calling me 'my lady.' Just Taesia is fine, or Tae, if you're into that." Balwith's eyes widened at the mere notion of such informality. "And second, I have something I think you're going to enjoy very, very much."

She opened the pack and meticulously took out each of the astralam's vertebrae. There were thirty pieces in all, cervical and thoracic and lumbar and sacral. She laid them out in the shape of the wolf-beast's spine across the countertop, grinning at the way Mirelle's jaw dropped.

"This is—!" The Noctan woman looked up at Balwith, then at Taesia, her black eyes shining. "How did you find astralam bones?"

"Found a clueless trader," Taesia lied. "Didn't know their true value, poor fool."

Mirelle didn't question it, instead reaching a shaking hand toward the edge of a vertebra.

"My mother told me stories about astralam," Mirelle murmured. "What constellations they fell from, how those constellations came to be formed in the first place. How the royalty of Inlustrous would form grand hunting parties for them." Taesia unconsciously leaned forward, hungry for those stories, but Mirelle misread the gesture. "Ah, I'm sorry, I'm babbling again."

"No, no, please go on."

Mirelle chewed her lower lip as she stared at the bones. "We come from a long line of reputable blacksmiths, dating even before the Sealing. One of my ancestors forged astralam fangs into a crown for the then-queen of Inlustrous, who used it to create a protective shield around the city of Astrum. To think I would have the opportunity to live up to our legacy..."

Taesia's blood fizzed with possibility. Dante's notes had been right. She was following his plan, doing what he couldn't.

Mirelle met Taesia's gaze with unsuppressed excitement. "What would you have me do with these, my—Taesia?"

What makes you feel strong?

Taesia grinned again. This time, the blacksmith mirrored it.

VIII

After twenty-one years as a daughter of House Vakara, Risha knew firsthand the power of a well-tailored gown. Of stepping into a pool of silk, or satin, or chiffon, and letting it hug her body as a sheath hugs a knife. Everything had to be precise—the cut, the length, the color, the accents. Gloves or no gloves, a necklace or a bracelet, her hair up or her hair down.

Over time, she had come to realize they were their own sort of armor.

She knew Taesia felt the same, judging from the way she smiled inside Violetta's, Nexus's most renowned dressmaker's shop. It wasn't a joyful smile; it was calculating, like a general evaluating her soldiers.

Risha was surprised by it all the same. Taesia had been an absolute wreck after Dante's arrest. She could see the fine cracks running through her, something dark having settled behind her expression.

Still, there was the gala to consider, meaningless as it was. The Lastriders had to act carefully, Taesia most of all. She was the new heir. She had to represent her House accordingly.

Risha thought it cruel.

She watched their younger sisters browse, Brailee and Saya drifting between mannequins draped in the season's latest designs. They were speaking softly, Saya often putting a hand on Brailee's arm. The poor girl looked heartbroken, but it seemed as if the dresses and Saya's company were lifting her mood somewhat.

"It seems rather pointless, doesn't it?" Taesia said suddenly.

"What does?" Risha asked carefully.

"This shopping trip. The gala. All the fanfare they make in the weeks leading up to it." Taesia studied a mannequin wearing a shimmering gown of topaz. "Ferdinand should be devoting resources and efforts to better things than appeasing the gentry. Our farms are struggling, but his advisors just encouraged him to invest in more mining trades with Parithvi." She laughed humorlessly. "The rich get richer and the poor get poorer, all while our realm dies."

Risha clenched her hand in the crepe of a salmon-colored gown, the material rasping against her knuckles. "There's nothing we can do to change his mind."

Taesia watched Brailee be measured in the back by Violetta herself, an elderly woman with astonishingly steady hands. "Isn't there?" She glanced at Risha. "You'll have to purchase that if you tear it. And, no offense, salmon isn't your color."

Risha released the gown and went to find Saya, leaving Taesia to her mood. Her sister was in the Parithvian section, ogling the different cuts and styles.

"Do you think Amaa would let me wear this?" Saya pulled a sheer lavender sari from the rack, the accompanying blouse so short it would leave a long expanse of midriff bare.

"Not at a gala."

Saya pouted and put it back. She glanced at Brailee being measured. "I feel terrible. Their brother is in prison and we're shopping for dresses."

Risha rubbed a calming circle over Saya's back. "The Houses still have to uphold tradition."

"Why?" Saya muttered. "It feels useless."

"It won't be useless. It..." She briefly thought about telling her of the ritual, then decided against it. "It'll be all right," she finished awkwardly.

She hid her disquiet as well as she could while she helped Saya choose a lehenga choli in a shade of blue so dark it was almost black. Perusing the anarkalis, her mind drifted back to Thana's Chapel, the smell of ash and blood, black rose petals, Lezzaro's body.

Shortly after, they'd received notice that something from the Bone Palace's Hall of Antiques was missing: a necklace made of the finger bones from the founder of House Vakara. Risha had gone to double-check, but sure enough, the glass case where the necklace of finger bones had lain on black velvet was empty.

As she'd stood there, uneasy at the notion that the same person who had drawn the Conjuration circle in Thana's Chapel could have also done this, she'd thought someone was staring at her. But a quick look around had revealed no one but the guards and her own anxious reflection in the glass.

As Saya set up an appointment for a fitting, Risha drifted aimlessly between the racks until she found Taesia again.

"I thought you didn't like these colors," Risha said, gesturing at the pastel gowns.

"You never know," Taesia said. "I'll need to surprise people, won't I?"

Something in her friend's tone made her reach out and squeeze her wrist. "Tae...I need to tell you something."

Taesia fixed her gaze sharply on her.

"It's about Godsnight," Risha whispered. "What you said at the villa. I think...I think we should try."

Taesia's mouth parted before it curled up in a smirk. "Oh? Why the sudden change of heart?"

Risha narrowed her eyes. "Did Nik already tell you?"

"Maybe. But I want to hear it from you."

"You know the situation with the Mortri barrier. The more time passes, the more spirits congregate, which means more fodder for the Conjurers. If Dante was on track to discovering how to reverse the Sealing, we should continue his work. To break the Mortri barrier, if nothing else."

"Even if we need to use Conjuration to pull this off?"

The man in the skull mask flickered through her memory.

"Yes," Risha whispered. *Forgive me, Paaja.* "But we must be careful. After what happened to the prelate, all the villas are being watched, particularly yours."

Taesia stiffened. The unsettling thing behind her eyes flashed.

"I'm with you. But you can't..." *You can't end up like Dante. Please.* "You can't make impulsive decisions anymore." When Taesia nodded, she asked, "What are our next steps?"

"Research, mostly. I recently found a tool that could help us during the ritual."

Before Risha could ask what it was, Violetta bustled up to them. The woman bowed and gestured to the mannequin before them.

"Surely this is not to your taste, my lady," she said to Taesia. "I have an idea of what you prefer."

Taesia quickly wiped the grim expression off her face. "Lead on, then."

The first option was bloodred velvet, sleeveless and immodest. The front plunged so far the space between the mannequin's breasts was bared down to its navel, held in place with crimson string. The back was just as scandalous, dipping in a dramatic U.

Risha blushed and Saya, who had wandered over, coughed to hide her laugh. Taesia pretended to think it over.

"Perhaps not this time," she said at last.

Violetta's second choice was a handsome gown of black and gold that was the inverse of the first, with long tapered sleeves and a high collar. The full-length skirt had a slit where the mannequin's plastered leg stuck out at a sultry angle.

"Closer," Taesia said. "Something jaw-dropping, but not as revealing as the first."

Violetta tapped a finger against her lips. She then urged Taesia toward the back rooms, where the unfinished designs were kept. Risha was about to follow when the doors to Violetta's opened, the cerise light of dusk spilling through.

A gray-clad member of the city guard rushed in. Upon seeing Risha and Saya, he fell into a hasty bow.

"My ladies, you're needed at the necropolis at once," he gasped.

Risha's heart skipped a beat. "What happened?"

"It's Lord Vakara, my lady. He's been injured."

Evening had fallen by the time the carriage rattled to a stop. The necropolis rose before them, a small mountain of bones and souls. Rising from the alleys of marble and stone was the orange gleam of torches.

An officer with curling sideburns bowed to them. "My ladies. Please follow me."

Risha could already hear it: a scraping, lowing, animalistic din coming from the heart of the necropolis. Saya kept close to her side as they passed under the wooden guard tower. The woman at watch had a spyglass to her eye, no doubt the one who'd rung the bell to summon her father.

Injured.

Risha followed the scent of rot and let the necropolis swallow her. Statues and monuments, mausoleums and tombs—the dead within them grasped for air, for life. Saya grabbed her arm with a small whimper.

Guards ran back and forth, some calling orders, others with weapons drawn. The torchlight spun and danced.

Then she saw them.

Some were mid-decomposition, their flesh splitting and shedding off lumbering bodies, and others were freshly dead. Those without bodies were simply bone and sinew, and where muscle had eroded away were the same thorny vines that had strung together the skeleton outside Thana's basilica.

They congregated in the spot where she had last tried to break the Mortri barrier. A spot now overtaken with a Conjuration circle containing a seven-pointed star.

Saya's grip on her tightened. Risha couldn't help the terror fermenting in her own gut, the ache of their desire shooting up her spine, into the roots of her teeth. Some bodies bore the sign of trauma—a caved-in chest, a missing arm, a slash across a throat like a second smile. They moved with purpose, with single-minded drive, to the spot where the barrier to Mortri stood firm. Their gray, bony hands scrabbled in the air, dug through the dirt in frustration.

Rath had been taken to the steps of a nearby mausoleum, the medic crouched before him winding a bandage around his midsection. Scarlet blossomed against the white fabric.

"Paaja." Risha had planned for the word to be stern, sure, a soldier awaiting orders. It came out in a ragged whisper.

Rath's eyes were pinched. "I've never seen this many before. It's as if they have a hive mind."

The same words had been used to describe the congregation of spirits the Conjurers had called down. Was their goal, then, to create an army of the dead?

If so, this was certainly a good start.

The medic finished, and Rath lowered his shirt. "They aren't attacking, but they are violent when interfered with." He gestured to his bloody shirt. "At least none of them have magic." No one but a Vakara had the skill it took to resurrect a spirit that had possessed magic in its life.

Saya sat beside him on the steps. "What can we do?"

"We need to drive the spirits out of the risen bodies and pacify them, let them settle back into the void."

"And if we can't?"

"We must. If they enter the city…"

There was no point finishing the sentence. They'd already seen a preview of what would happen.

Guards had set up a ring around the dead, unwilling to cross the Conjuration circle drawn with chalk and red paint. Some held torches, others stood at the ready with swords and shields. The spirits had begun to rip into each other in vexation, their growls vibrating through Risha's chest. A hunk of gray flesh landed on a guard's shield and he jerked back with a cry.

The sound drew the attention of a nearby skeleton. It turned, its lower jaw missing, and Risha noticed the threads of plant fiber woven across its bones. The sound it issued was high and echoing, two octaves overlapped.

"Get ready." Rath fetched red string from his belt pouch.

Risha did the same. The skeleton advanced on the terrified guard, phalanges extended, as if itching to touch living flesh.

"G-get away!" the guard wailed, backing up between the headstones.

Another guard rushed forward and swung her sword. It lopped off the skeleton's skull, which flew through the air and landed near Risha's feet. It turned its death grin up at her, screeching, before she shattered it with the heel of her foot.

But the body still reached for the guard. Rath weaved his string into an intricate design and pulled it tight. The skeleton fell to the ground, the fibers within it slackening.

"We can't bind them all this way," Risha said. "It'll take too long, and others will get hurt."

"Then we have to work fast," her father said.

The three of them spread out, pulling and winding their string, weaving the spells for binding. Risha focused on a nearby spirit within a mostly intact corpse, opening her well of power, the air freezing around her. She sent out her spell and halted the spirit in place, its eyes rolling in fury before Risha pulled her string taut and let it snap. The body collapsed.

Her kurti was damp with sweat and she was gasping for breath by the time she got to her fifth spirit. There were still so many of them, and her head was *pounding*, and the cold air drove daggers into her lungs every time she took a breath. She could sense the dominating barrier of Mortri, so close and far.

Were the spirits trying to do as she had done, and break it by force?

Why? she thought as she kept unspooling string from her pouch. Twist—snap. Another spirit driven from a body. *What do the Conjurers want them to do?*

Taesia had mentioned that Lezzaro wanted the Conjurers to thin the barriers for Godsnight. But she couldn't imagine the prelate sanctioning something like this.

Saya was already flagging, hair sticking to her skin with sweat. This was too much for them to tackle on their own. There had to be another way.

"We need more torches," Risha said to the nearest guard. "And oil."

The guard nodded and took off. Risha wove more string across her fingers, leaving dark trenches in her skin.

The space between her shoulders itched. At first she dismissed it, thinking it was sweat. But the feeling persisted, tugging at her awareness.

Someone was watching her.

Risha looked around. The sky was a purplish gloaming that cast everything in a surreal light.

It was in that light she saw him. He stood a distance away on top of a mausoleum, a dark figure cut against the falling night, his skull mask limned in torchlight.

Risha's stomach lurched. Before she could think it through, she was passing the guards who ran toward the spirits with barrels of oil, throwing herself deeper into the necropolis and away from her family. Away from the growling and shrieking and uneasy longing of the spirits locked out of their final resting place.

The man jumped down. Risha gave chase through the avenues of the dead, her hip barking against a tomb and her slippers filling with pebbles. She only caught a glimpse of his shoulder here, a whisper of running feet there. She tripped and caught herself on the arm of a statue.

He led her away from the main entrance and to the lesser paths, past the gently sloping hillocks and the field of small tombstones for those who couldn't afford the larger plots. He slid down a gravelly slope and she didn't hesitate to leap after, the satin trousers under her kurti ripping.

She expected to follow him into the city, but when she rounded a large tree, she found him standing in the middle of the empty path. His chest rose and fell with heaving breaths, his arms loose at his sides.

"You're persistent." His voice was muffled behind his mask, and carried a slight Parithvian accent.

Risha's head throbbed, her stomach swirling with nausea. "Who are you? Why are you doing this? You're not a necromancer."

"Unfortunately, no."

"You have no right to be making a mockery of it with this...this dishonest magic. You—"

She cut herself off as more shadows joined him. Not spirits, but people, dressed in black and wearing skull masks similar to his. The man spread his arms in a casual gesture.

"We may not be necromancers, but I assure you we're not trying to make a mockery of it," he said. "In fact, there are some tricks we've picked up. Tricks you might be interested in. We could teach them to you, if you like."

Risha's fingers twitched toward her bone knife. "I have nothing to learn from Conjurers."

Another figure stepped up, this one with a slighter build. "We're Revenants, not Conjurers," she said, her voice low and hoarse. "We're not like those fools who salivate at the thought of demons."

"But you're using Conjuration! You just manipulated it into imitating necromancy. How?"

The woman *humph*ed. "We don't answer to godspawn."

"But it *would* be beneficial for both parties to form an alliance," said their leader.

"An alliance?" Risha repeated. "For what?"

"To find a way into Mortri."

"That," Risha said coolly, "is something you need to leave to the Vakaras."

"Why?" the woman demanded. "You haven't made any progress."

Had these people, these *Revenants*, been watching her? Risha stared at their leader, who'd shoved his hands into his pockets.

"There are strict rules to necromancy," she said. The words were her father's, and she recited them from memory. "If you do not follow them, you might end up in a situation you can't control." She gestured behind her.

"That's what you've been taught. But there are new rules now." She could hear the smile in his words. "I could show you, if you come with us."

"I'd rather swallow hot coals."

"That's a shame. We're eager to show you."

A loud *whoosh* erupted behind her, followed by the unearthly scream of the dead. Risha whirled toward the conflagration rising above the necropolis.

When Risha turned back, the Revenants were slipping away into the dark. Their leader made to follow, but Risha was far from done with him.

She tackled him from behind, sending them both to the ground. He let out a surprised *oof!* and quickly shoved her off. His mask had fallen, lying in the grass nearby.

But what her eyes landed on wasn't his face. A necklace had slipped from under his black shirt. A row of long, spindly finger bones.

Risha had only ever seen them against black velvet, but there was no mistaking it.

"Where," she said slowly, "did you get that?"

Finally she took in his face, highlighted in orange by the fire. He wasn't much older than she was, dark eyes framed by long lashes, hair thick and black. His dark brown skin was so smooth the doñas would be falling over themselves to demand to know what he used to gain such a flawless complexion.

The man grinned, showing off a set of strong teeth that mirrored the curve of the necklace on his chest.

"Ah, my secret is out," he said.

"Answer me," she growled. "Where did you get that necklace? What are you planning to use it for?"

"Those are good questions. However, I'm afraid I don't have the time to answer them. Not unless you'll reconsider our offer and join us?"

She opened her mouth, but nothing would come out. She could feel the spirits writhing and biting, eaten up by fire, dissolving into ash. Her throat convulsed in a cough.

"Thought not." He picked up his mask and fitted it back over his face. "I hope you'll reconsider, though. The world is more than rules and regulations. There are hidden pockets that would fascinate you."

She tried to follow and catch him again, grab the necklace from around his neck, but she had already exhausted herself. After two steps, she was falling, the edges of her vision dimming.

Her body pulled her under as a wave of spirits spiraled into the sky like embers.

In the darkness, their voices flitted by.

"—hated him, wanted him to suffer like I had—"

"If my daughter knew she has a sister in the south—"

"—couldn't tell them the jewels were fake—"

"Does he think of me still? Has he found someone new?"

She woke as she was being carried back to the carriage by a guard. Her father walked beside her, stone-faced and silent. Saya was on her other side.

"What happened?" Risha croaked.

Her father said nothing, so Saya spoke up. "The fire worked. We were able to burn the bodies, though the skeletons still had to be bound. The spirits retreated."

Away to that dark void between Vitae and Mortri, unable to go any farther.

The guard carefully deposited Risha in the carriage. She was shaking like a newborn kitten, all her strength depleted. Saya climbed in after her.

"I'll stay and help the officers," Rath said. "Get your sister home." He closed the door, and the carriage took off with a sudden jolt.

Risha closed her eyes with a grimace. "He's mad."

"Of course he's mad! You ran off without a word. We found you lying in the grass."

Risha wanted to explain, but it would take too much out of her, so she only sighed. Saya rustled beside her.

"We also found this. It was on your chest."

In Saya's hand was a single rose, its petals deeply, impossibly black.

IX

By the time Nikolas Cyr's unit arrived at the necropolis, the brightness of the day washed over what had to have been a horrifying scene the night before. The Vakaras weren't there, but guards prowled through the mausoleums and shooed away boldly curious citizens wanting to get a peek. There was even one enterprising individual trying to make a sketch, and Julian wondered if it would show up on the cover of his mother's next gossip rag.

Other guards were busy raking up the lingering embers of a bonfire. When Julian made out the contents, his stomach flipped. Corpses and bones, all piled up together in a horrible mound.

"Eugh." Paris held his sleeve to his nose. "It smells worse than a den of xachs. Why do we always get stuck with the malodorous missions?"

"That's a big word for you," Julian said, though his voice was distant. Paris was right—it smelled awful, of smoke and char and burning meat, but there was also a faint underlying scent of something metallic and acrid.

He knelt beside the Conjuration circle, a mixture of red paint and chalk that traveled over ground and stone uninterrupted. He tried to make sense of the odd geometric shapes, the glyphs and symbols surrounding a seven-pointed star in the center.

It was different than the one they'd found in the prelate's rectory, which had been drawn with a five-pointed star. When Julian had gotten close to that one, he'd stumbled and would have fallen if Nikolas hadn't caught him.

He'd seen a flash of images he couldn't understand: a burning red glyph, a towering cathedral, pale lips whispering a name. Thoughts had lingered like an echoing scream, fear and rage infusing the air. Julian had closed his eyes, his mind one low snarl.

"Julian?"

He'd tensed and bared his teeth. Then it had all fled out of him at once and he'd been simply Julian again, swaying dizzily.

"Sorry," Julian had gasped. *I am a man, my name is Julian, I live in Nexus, I am not a monster.* "I'm fine."

Nikolas hadn't looked so sure, and had ordered him to wait outside while the rest of them finished up. Since then, Julian had wondered what exactly he'd been picking up in that underground room—what the Conjuration circle had been trying to tell him.

But this one didn't feel the same. Against his better judgment, he touched the outer circle and a shiver traveled through him.

Nikolas knelt beside him. "Can you tell what components were used to make it?"

Julian licked his dry lips, concentrating. "It f— It looks like ground-up bone. Maybe sulfur as well."

"Bone," Nikolas echoed, brow furrowed.

"There's blood here, too," Paris said nearby. "Human."

Julian turned and nearly lost his balance when a vision came to him: a hooded figure, a flash of black light, the cry of something otherworldly.

Once again he had the embarrassing ordeal of Nikolas steadying him. "Are you all right?"

He opened his mouth, but no words could describe the itching oddness the circle left in him. Like peering into the mind of a beast, but wholly different. "Yes. I think…I think the Conjurers use their own blood to activate these circles."

"Gross," Paris muttered.

The Cyr heir's usual gloomy disposition somehow became graver. He stared at Julian, who fought not to look away. To not remember how it felt to face down a volucris at Taesia Lastrider's side, or how she had threatened him not to speak a word of their encounter, with the implication she could ruin his life with a snap of her fingers. It was all he could do to agree; after seeing what she'd done to the dealer, it was a miracle she hadn't killed him, too.

Slowly Nikolas released him. "We'll search for signs of where they've gone. Julian, take a break."

He didn't bother to argue, still rattled from the vision and from the wariness beginning to creep into Nikolas's eyes.

A light rain fell over Nexus as Nikolas made his way to the Solara Quarter at dusk. He'd felt the shift in pressure today, the heat of early autumn giving way to a swampy buzz of humidity before finally splitting the sky apart.

The necropolis had been an alarming reminder that if left to their own devices, the Conjurers' attacks would only escalate. They had killed Lezzaro even though the prelate had given them the fundamentals with which to perform their magic, wanting him out of the way so they could move on unimpeded.

And with the threat rising higher and the city tense, Nikolas grew all the more aware that he was lacking the power he needed for Godsnight.

The sodium glow of lanterns refracted off crystals hanging above doorways painted white, limned signs and bulletins written in slanting Solarian text, and made shadows along the stone shrines dedicated to Phos with offerings of sage and fruit and piles of rock salt.

Nikolas hadn't been here in months. Summer was the time the Solarians thrived, nourished by the sun's glare and the heat that stayed baked into the cobblestone long after sundown. But as they ventured deeper into autumn and the dreaded winter months, the Cyrs made sure to send supplies and medicine like the Lastriders did for the Noctan refugees. Unlike the Lastriders, though, the Cyrs rarely came to visit, and instead delegated the task to House servants.

Lux flared at his wrist, as if it knew where they were. Its presence comforted him. He'd toyed with the idea of asking Taesia to come, then laid it to rest. She showed up for him time and time again. He was grateful—and ashamed. As much as he wanted her help, needed it, he couldn't constantly rely on it. He wasn't someone who needed saving. He was someone who had been born to protect and serve.

He felt foolish for it now when he sensed the presence of a thief behind him.

Nikolas sighed. He then used lightspeed to close the short distance between them, catching his pursuer off guard.

The thief's eyes turned luminous as Nikolas's glow ringed their irises in gold.

Nikolas grabbed the thief by their lapels and pushed them against the nearest alley wall. The thief squirmed, the ground beneath them quivering like the aftershock of an earthquake.

An earth elementalist. Interesting.

"Stop that," Nikolas snapped. Lux lashed the thief's wrists together behind his back. This close, he could see the thief was a young man. But the way the rain was dampening his curls, making them stick to his fearful face, gave him the appearance of a boy who'd been caught sneaking candies from a jar. Something about him was familiar, though Nikolas couldn't put his finger on what.

The thief cleared his throat, eyes wide in alarm. "Hello again, Sunshine."

Sunshine? Nikolas frowned. "You know who I am?" He'd left the Sunbringer Spear at home, choosing instead a sword at his hip. "Wanted to jump a House heir, is that it?"

"No! No, nothing like that, I swear."

"Then why were you following me?"

The thief hesitated. Nikolas waited a moment before lifting a finger in silent command. Lux tightened its hold around the thief's wrists, making him yelp.

"All right, I'll tell you!" Nikolas dropped his finger and Lux loosened its viselike grip. "Deia's flaming tits, how does a bit of light hurt so much?"

"Lux isn't a bit of light."

"Lux?" The thief tried to look over his shoulder at the familiar. "Didn't know you named them."

"Don't change the subject."

The thief hesitated again, still clearly panicked. He had fine features, his nose straight and small, his cheekbones high. Though his ears were pierced, he wore no earrings.

"What's your name," Nikolas ordered.

Surprised laughter tumbled from the thief's mouth. "Fin. I'd ask for yours, but I already know it."

"Well, Fin, you're not asking the questions here. And you still haven't answered mine. Why were you following me?"

Nikolas stared at him, waiting. Drops of water trailed down the young man's face and hung off his jaw. When he swallowed, Nikolas watched the bob of his throat.

"The bracelet," Fin whispered. Nikolas leaned in to better hear him, and Fin's breath hitched. This close, Nikolas felt his tempestuous heartbeat. "I—I saw you pick it up, but didn't have the chance to get it back. Didn't know when I'd see you again, so..."

The bracelet with the tree charm. Nikolas *had* seen him before, in the courtyard of the Bone Palace during the Autumn Equinox Festival. The server who had offered him tartlets.

"You work in the palace?"

Fin winced. "Y-yes?"

"Why not send a missive to my House instead of following me around like a crook?"

Fin licked water off his lips. "I..."

He glanced over Nikolas's shoulder and his eyes widened.

Nikolas called Lux back and erected a shield of light. Projectiles bounced harmlessly off its surface. They weren't arrows or rocks; they were whips of light, glowing as bright as Lux.

The ground rumbled and Nikolas's grip slackened. Fin broke free and scaled the wall like a lizard, his magic pulling out bricks to make hand- and footholds as he went.

"Hey!" Nikolas shouted, but the barrage of light projectiles kept coming. "I'm not done with you!"

His attention divided, Lux's shield flickered. One of his attackers cried, "Stop!"

The projectiles ceased. Nikolas waited another moment before dropping the dissolving shield. He glanced at the wall, but the bricks were sunken back in, and Fin was gone.

Swearing under his breath, he turned his full attention to his attackers. A group of three Solarians stood at the mouth of the alley wearing hooded cloaks. All of them were Lumins, light familiars sitting sedately in their palms.

One stepped forward. "M-my lord." All three sank to their knees. "We did not know it was you. Forgive us."

Nikolas wiped the water from his face. "It's all right. Are you the night patrol?" They nodded. "I need to talk to your primary."

Before Nikolas and Rian had been allowed within the Solara Quarter, they had first been taught the culture, such as learning Solari and the structure of society.

Beneath the Imperators—warriors who had risen to power by Phos to maintain total autocracy over Solara—were various dignitaries and heads of state. Within the smallest communities, such as towns or a string of villages under a fiefdom, there were primaries.

The primary of the Solarian refugees was named Maddox. He'd been primary since Nikolas was ten, after the previous one had succumbed to a particularly bad winter.

The night watch brought him to a meetinghouse, past a lopsided table, and up a flight of stairs to a room on the landing. After a knock and some murmuring, one of the night watch members bowed and said he could go in.

Nikolas expected an office of some sort, but what he stepped into was a bedroom. It was simple and sparse, with a bed in the corner and a dresser under the small window. But there were a few personal touches here and there: a paper streamer from some bygone festival, a crystal hanging in the window to catch the sunlight, an incense holder shaped like a wyvern.

Maddox stood by the dresser. He was a well-muscled man who looked to be in his thirties, though age could be deceiving with Solarians. His hair was pure white, long and pulled back into a queue. Eyes the color of candlelight through glass stared at him in confusion.

"Lord Nikolas." Maddox bowed and gestured to the small round table situated before a fireplace. There was a fire in it now, the rainfall already too cold for Solarian blood. "Please, sit."

After he gave an order for someone to bring them water and towels, Maddox's familiar slunk up to his shoulder and perched there. It pulsed in warning as Lux attempted to come near.

"The night watch tells me you were having an altercation in an alley," Maddox said. "Are you all right, my lord?"

"Yes, I'm fine." Nikolas pressed his lips together as one of the Solarians came back with a tray of two glasses, both containing water with sprigs of mint. They also handed Nikolas a towel, and it was only then he realized he'd been dripping water everywhere. He dried his hair to hide his embarrassment.

Once they were alone again, Nikolas took a deep breath. "I apologize for the late hour. I've been tasked by His Majesty to eradicate anything related to Conjuration in the city, and it's proven to take up quite a bit of my time."

Maddox inclined his head. "Of course. We've heard about the attacks and find them appalling. Is there anything we can do to assist you?"

Nikolas cleared his throat. "In a sense. I want to speak with your best Lumins." He infused as much austerity in his voice as he could while soaked and wearing a towel around his shoulders. "To see if there's any aspect of my powers they can help me reveal or…make stronger."

Maddox's eyes widened slightly. "I understand, my lord. I will bring you to them."

Nikolas waited for Maddox to confer with one of the night watch. He heard Maddox ask "Why would they be there?" before another bit of murmuring, and then he was gesturing for Nikolas to follow him outside.

The rain had lightened to a faint mist. The glow of lanterns fleeted over doors and across darkened windows, making the crystals blush. Maddox glanced at him often but remained silent.

"You'll be celebrating Cosmica in a few weeks," Nikolas said. Just as the Noctans' version of Godsnight was called Starfall, the Solarians called theirs Cosmica.

Maddox nodded. "The children are looking forward to it. Things have been rather bleak this summer." He glanced at Nikolas again. "Forgive me, my lord, but I know your brother passed around the time of Cosmica. We had a day of mourning when we heard the news."

Taesia had tried to get him out of the villa to see it: vendors selling honey candy and large granules of salt sparkling like sand along the streets, for sweet and salty things were ways to appreciate what the dead could no longer enjoy; banners of pale blue and gold to honor the recently departed soul in case it happened to sweep by, drawn by the sugar and salt.

But Nikolas had stayed home. His grief was for himself, and no one else was entitled to it. He would let others mourn their own way so long as they gave him the same courtesy.

And he hadn't been able to face them, knowing what he had done.

"I…The Cyrs appreciate it," Nikolas said. They lapsed back into silence.

Eventually they came upon a butcher's shop, empty meat hooks smiling in the window. Even though it was closed for the day, Maddox opened the front door as if he owned the place. Nikolas frowned in mild confusion before following.

At once Nikolas heard muffled voices behind the far wall, a strip of light emanating from under the door. Maddox opened this one, too, and all chatter ceased as Maddox froze. Beyond was a room harboring a beaten-up couch against one wall, and a collection of weapons hung opposite. Nikolas quickly counted four Solarians before he noticed what they were kneeling around—and what had startled Maddox.

It was a Conjuration array, a circle within another containing a diamond surrounded by symbols, the centermost one for Phos: a circle with curving lines radiating from it like a small sun. Candles were lit along the perimeter of the outer circle, and the room carried a musky scent of myrrh and cinnamon. The four Solarians looked between him and Maddox with blank, terrified faces.

Nikolas reached for his sword as Lux spun excitedly around his head. Maddox stepped between Nikolas and the Solarians, hand outstretched. "My lord, please wait. This... This looks suspect, but perhaps it's not what you think."

Nikolas's pulse raced. He thought back to the necropolis, the red circle and the remains of bodies. Bodies that had injured Rath and Risha. "It's exactly what I think."

One of the Solarians scrambled to their feet, their familiar darting behind them. "My lord! We—we are not using Conjuration to raise spirits. We are using it to try and speak to Phos."

"What?"

Seeing Nikolas wouldn't attack, Maddox lowered his arm as the others rose to standing. Their skin was golden brown, their eyes ranging from crystal to citrine, their frames tall and willowy. Some of them even had ears elongated into points. They were all Lumins, their familiars worn as bangles and chokers.

"Conjuration is something that is... not known in Solara," the first Lumin went on. "It is only here, in Vitae—in Nexus, specifically—that this magic works. It is tied to ancient customs of communing with the gods. With the right offerings, and the right array, a god may be called upon to answer questions and prayers."

Nikolas vaguely remembered Taesia saying something along those lines. That it was something Dante had been trying on his own. The other Solarians were staring at him with a mix of fear and greed.

"And have you succeeded?" he asked slowly.

"We've been unsuccessful so far. But you..." They stepped forward eagerly. "You are the Cyr heir. You own the Sunbringer Spear, which contains two of Phos's feathers. It could be enough to gain his attention."

"I..." Nikolas's mouth went dry under all their stares. Lux came to huddle by his collar. "I've tried to speak with him. I receive no answer either."

A collective breath went through the room, a mix of shock and dismay. Nikolas was again filled with the bright, prickling shame he'd felt in the basilica.

One of the others stepped forward, his pale hair worn long and loose. "Nikolas Cyr," he said, his voice far from reverential. "Sired by Phos."

"Sired by Waren, but yes," Nikolas said.

"You want us to believe godspawn cannot hear the voice of their own god?" The man sneered. "The Cyrs truly have abandoned us."

"Vedari," Maddox snapped. "Apologize."

"No." Nikolas held up a hand. "He brings up concerns, and I will address them. It's true the Cyrs have not been as attentive to you as I would like. I humbly apologize on behalf of both me and my father."

Waren was not the sort to apologize easily. If he knew Nikolas was doing this, that his son was making him lose face...

Still, he went on. "I understand your desperation. You wanted to plead with Phos to bring you back to Solara. Is this correct?"

Vedari's pale eyebrows twitched. Maddox's gaze dropped to the floor.

"In a few weeks, Godsnight will be upon us," Nikolas said. "When it comes, I will force Phos's power to run through me, and I will open the barrier to Solara."

Another gasp from the Solarians. Even Vedari's lips parted in surprise.

Nikolas had a duty to report any and all Conjuration activity to the king, to capture anyone seen participating in the occult. But for being a Holy King touched by all four gods, Ferdinand clearly didn't care about the Other-Realm refugees. Nikolas wouldn't give him the satisfaction of sentencing his own kind to death.

These were his people. His responsibility.

"You must promise me not to continue this practice. It's unsafe, and illegal. Instead, I will do everything in my power to break the barrier, to restore balance to the Cosmic Scale and allow you to return to your own realm. But in order to do that..." He thought of Taesia's conviction in him, how much he wanted to prove her right. "We will need to work together, if you will allow it, to prepare for Godsnight. To see if there's a chance of communicating with Phos, or of channeling his power through mine."

The Solarians bowed to him, murmuring their willingness and fealty. The heaviness in Nikolas's stomach began to ease.

"Thank you, my lord," Maddox said quietly. "Is . . . is it truly possible? What you intend to do?"

Nikolas took a deep breath that shook.

"I will make it so," he replied.

X

Angelica caught a glimpse of herself in the mirror as she dried her hair. The bath had added more color to her cheeks. Drops of water still clung to the curves of her body, hiding in the crooks of her elbows and rolling down the backs of her knees. She smelled of jasmine thanks to the soap they'd provided.

The young woman on the bed behind her smiled at Angelica's reflection. She was tall and lithe, with warm brown skin and long dark hair in pleasing curls. She lay in repose like a cat caught in a sunbeam.

"I hope the bath was sufficient," the woman said in the subtle accent of southern Vaega.

"More than sufficient." Angelica let her wet hair hang over her shoulder. "Thank you."

The girl—Rosemary, though of course that wasn't her real name—lifted a hand in a partial shrug. A gesture that meant *Nothing to thank me for, it's included in the service.*

Angelica took stock of the room as she dressed. She hadn't been paying much attention when she arrived, but now she noticed the small charms hanging from the window, the closet full of southern-style dresses with sleeveless bodices, and a painting of ruins on a mountainside. Angelica had come to the Garden often enough to see the touches of personality in each girl's room, and this room told her Rosemary was homesick.

She wanted to ask when she had come to Nexus, and why. She always wanted to ask, and never did. Angelica came here for one purpose, and when that purpose was met, there was no reason to linger.

Except the way the girl was laid out on the bed kept drawing her eye. She really was beautiful, reclining with one long, smooth leg pulled up, her chest rising and falling gently with her breaths. She watched Angelica through half-lidded eyes, smiling indulgently as Angelica crept back, a silent call being answered.

Angelica's fingertips roamed over her warm skin, buried themselves between her legs. The girl made a soft sound and arched her back. Angelica watched, hypnotized, as Rosemary came undone again, her red-bitten lips parted.

After a shudder and a long sigh, Angelica removed herself and cleaned her hand with the leftover bathwater. Rosemary stretched lavishly with a groan.

"So generous," the girl crooned.

Angelica gave her a parting nod and headed for the door. She had to leave now or else risk losing the entire morning.

Coming to the Garden had become a necessary if expensive habit to relieve the maddening itch of not having her instruments. She craved her violin, wanted to be encased in rich, burning flame that ate and then rebirthed her. Using her body in other, less destructive ways took the edge off for at least a little while.

Angelica descended the staircase of the Garden. The proprietor saw her and came out of the main den, where tea was being served to customers who had stayed the night. "Do you wish for a full or half breakfast, my lady?"

"Not today." Angelica pushed a coin into the woman's hand and brushed by her, aiming for the back door the more noteworthy clientele used.

"I hope the services were to your liking, my lady!" the woman called.

"They were." Angelica paused on the threshold. "Give Rosemary some time off to visit home."

House guards collected her and she settled into the carriage. She filled herself with thoughts of last night, the way Rosemary had touched her, kissed her. They fed the burning in her veins as she opened and closed her hands, keeping herself contained.

She was on her way to the museum on her mother's orders. They had set up a memorial exhibit for Prelate Lezzaro, displaying all sorts of religious artifacts he had inherited. Since it was being funded by the king, their House needed to make an appearance. She planned to visit right when it opened, hoping the hour was early enough no one else would be there.

The museum was located near the university, a long building of white marble and stone. While appreciating its architecture, she couldn't help but think fondly of the opera house in the northern district with its arcades and its clerestories, its marble vaults and its rose windows. The Mardovas had their own balcony there, paid for by her father when she was young. Adela had complained when he'd done it, but August had thrown her his usual disarming smile with a broad hand on Angelica's shoulder.

"She loves the opera so much, how could I not? That way she'll learn more songs other than that *Gossamer Road* one."

"I thought you liked that song?" Angelica had pouted.

He'd laughed. "I do, I do! Can you sing it for me now?"

It had been ten years since she sang it.

Shaking off the memory, Angelica climbed the wide steps with a House guard on either side of her. The space beyond the open doors was wide and echoing, with a vaulted ceiling and pristine tiled floors. Rare pieces sat in glass cases or roped off on pedestals. There was even a set of leathery wings hanging above the entrance to an exhibit named *Beasts of the Four Realms*.

A woman approached her with a smile, her square glasses accenting the shape of her jaw. She was dressed in white as if to match the building around her, her hair tied up in a bun.

"Lady Angelica, it is a pleasure," the woman said with a bow.

Angelica inclined her head. "You must be the curator."

"You can call me Cynthea, if it pleases my lady. I'm more than happy to provide you with an exclusive tour." The curator gestured to the nearest wing. "Shall we?"

Cynthea's voice droned on as she described how to tell the age of bone weapons from Mortri and explained the properties of nightstone from Noctus. Angelica made sounds to indicate she was listening, but really, she was trying to figure out where her mother would have hidden her instruments. She had a small yet acute fear they might have been destroyed. But the violin and piccolo had been presents from her father; surely Adela wouldn't have thrown them out.

Would she?

They finally arrived at the memorial exhibit. Pedestals had been erected to show off the late prelate's treasures, from an ancient thurible to scrolls written in a Noctan language to a hair ornament worn by priests in Solara.

"We were quite surprised when the prelate decided to donate so many of his artifacts," Cynthea said. She bowed her head and whispered a quiet prayer, which Angelica did not partake in. "We came into possession of them only a few days before... before his passing."

Angelica frowned, thinking that odd. Almost as if Lezzaro had anticipated dying.

Cynthea went on to explain the collection of books when one of them caught Angelica's eye. It was wider and taller than the standard printed books in Vaega, and its cover was a hard shell of gold and gemstones. A complex metal lock had been threaded between the front and back covers.

All the breath rushed out of her at once as her knees threatened to buckle. She was suddenly back in the Vakara villa, learning that Lezzaro had owned a grimoire.

Lezzaro *had* been anticipating his own demise at the hands of the Conjurers. And instead of giving them an opportunity to snag the grimoire, he'd kept it safe by donating it along with his other relics. Hidden in plain sight.

When Cynthea realized Angelica was no longer following, she quickly backtracked. "Ah, that is a true prize," the curator said. "The prelate told us this tome dates back centuries, and holds a detailed history of Nexus with extensive notes on our oldest traditions. Most of its pages are damaged, unfortunately, which is why no one is allowed to open it."

Sure, that's *the reason.*

Angelica studied it a moment longer, thinking about the Conjuration circle at the university, the recent chaos at the necropolis.

Just as the first Conjuration attack had been followed by the draining of Tambour Lake, news of a recent series of cave-ins had traveled up from southern Vaega. The kingdom got most of its ore from a town called Aguerre, where mines studded the southern ridge. But many of those mines had collapsed in a sudden earthquake, and earth elementalists had been deployed to save the miners who were trapped.

If the Conjurers attacked again, what other devastation would they cause?

"I would like to borrow this book," Angelica said.

The curator paled. There was a flash of something familiar in her expression Angelica had seen in the jeweler, in the Garden's proprietor, that she saw no matter where she went.

The citizens of Nexus could laugh at the Houses and king all they wanted to behind closed doors, but faced with the real thing, their fear overcame their contempt.

Cynthea's mouth worked soundlessly. Then, as if remembering she was in the presence of nobility, she bowed.

"M-my lady, I'm sorry, but we cannot part with it."

"Name a price, then."

The woman winced. "It's not an issue of price, my lady. The late prelate and His Majesty commissioned this exhibit, and—"

"How. Much."

"My lady!" It was nearly a sob. "I cannot."

Angelica's nostrils flared as she glanced at the grimoire, sitting there as if waiting for her to smash the glass and take it. Looking deceptively innocent while holding secrets that could change the course of their history.

That could lead to them undoing the Sealing, and preventing the Conjurers from destroying any more of their realm.

She forced herself to calmly smooth out the skirt of her dress. "If you give it to me now, I can explain myself to His Majesty. I'll make sure you won't get in trouble."

But the woman was trembling, shaking her head. Everyone was afraid to tell Angelica Mardova *no*; of course the one person she needed to use that fear against resisted her. Heat licked up her ribs and stung her palms.

"Your museum is shit anyway," Angelica snarled before retreating to the exit.

She was going to get her hands on that grimoire one way or another. She just needed another plan.

"Well," Taesia said, "I honestly thought I'd never see the day."

"Shut up," Angelica grumbled. She pulled the fraying shawl tighter over her head, the dress she wore similarly roughspun. Taesia had no idea where she'd gotten it. "The sooner we get this over with, the better. How much farther?"

Taesia stifled her laughter. She'd been equally amused and concerned as soon as she'd received Angelica's blunt missive:

T—

Time to call in the favor you owe me.

—A

PS You're still a piece of shit.

"We're here, actually." Taesia nodded to a building across the way. They had crossed over into one of the seedier outer districts near the city's perimeter, marked by the higher quantity of trash on the ground and the amount of people who were already drunk before nightfall. The few signs she could see were for gambling halls and drug dens; the one hanging from their destination bore a suit of cards under the name KING'S CORNER.

Once in a while, there had been nights when she and Dante dressed down and explored the darker parts of the city like this one. Taesia used to think of it as a game, pretending to be common for the span of a few hours in order to escape the name *Lastrider* and all that was required of it. Then she'd noticed the way Dante would interact with commoners, treating them as he would any other member of the gentry: as equals.

To Dante, it hadn't been a game. He was familiarizing himself with the city from the inside out in order to best comprehend how to fix it, maintain it.

She didn't know how to pick up where he had left off, or if she even could.

But when she'd met up with Angelica and learned about the grimoire sitting in the museum, excitement had nipped at her, telling her this was the obvious next step in preparing for Godsnight.

As Angelica stepped forward, Taesia grabbed her arm. "Let me do the talking. You're not exactly..."

Angelica tensed under her hand. "You really want to finish that sentence, Lastrider?"

Taesia sighed. It was going to be a long night. "See, that's what I mean. Don't use my real name. Don't talk like...well, like you grew up in a villa."

"I *did* grow up in a villa."

"Nyx's piss," Taesia muttered as she let her go. "Follow me, and *keep quiet*. And if you can manage it, try not to stick your nose up in the air."

"You don't give me enough credit." Angelica kept her voice low, eyes darting across the street. Lamps were being lit by children running around with flint, and down the way a group of men erupted into raucous laughter over a shell game. Like the growing threat of the Conjurers couldn't touch this boisterous corner of the city.

"I'm just saying, some shabby clothes and unwashed hair won't be enough of a sell. It's unlikely anyone here will recognize us, but we have to be careful." She altered her accent slightly, letting crisp consonants fall into a softer burr. "So don't talk like a damn noble, all right?"

"Don't make me regret this."

Taesia snorted. "If you hate this so much, why not ask someone else to help you?"

Angelica looked away. Then, quietly, "Risha is still recovering from the necropolis, and Nikolas is too busy. There was no one else."

Taesia wasn't sure what to say, so she kept silent as they crossed the threshold into the King's Corner. Two goons flanked the front doors inside, giving her and Angelica a once-over before going back to scanning the floor.

The card house was not yet lively, but she was certain more patrons would spill through the doors as the sky grew darker and the wind blew colder. Despite the grand name, it was a modest setup, the bottom floor consisting of ten card tables and a desk in the back to exchange chips for winnings. There was a flight of stairs nearby, which led to a bar and the more exclusive games, the ones patrons got to play through invitation only.

"Some of the city's best thieves come here," Taesia whispered. "They like to visit the Soldiers' Standing table."

"They allow thieves in here?"

"They have an agreement with the owner. They get to gamble their illicit money, and in return they don't filch anything."

"They're *thieves*."

In response, Taesia nodded to the wall above the bar, where wooden plaques displayed pairs of severed hands. "They know better."

Taesia led Angelica to the Bluff table overseen by a bored-looking dealer. She worried Angelica wouldn't know how to play, then relaxed as Angelica eased into the game, calling out card suits she may or may not have. Taesia flirted with the dealer, which improved the woman's mood somewhat.

Angelica raised an eyebrow. "What are you doing?"

"Having fun?"

"Won't Nikolas be jealous you give out your favor so readily?"

Taesia's cheeks puffed out as she tried not to laugh. "*Give out my favor?*"

"You know what I mean," Angelica snapped.

"We're trying to blend in. Loosen up a little."

Angelica's gaze shifted between her cards and the dealer. She cleared her throat. "Do you...work this table often?"

The dealer shrugged, expression unchanging. "Couple days a week."

"Ah," Angelica said. "I see."

Taesia rubbed her forehead. "Terrible," she muttered. "Absolutely abysmal."

Angelica threw her cards down. "I'm getting a drink."

Taesia followed her, unwilling to leave Angelica on her own. She leaned against the bar, the wood stained and warped from years of spilled drinks. Angelica stood with her arms crossed, glaring at nothing, as the bartender poured her a glass of red wine.

"So tell me," Taesia said, keeping her voice down. More patrons had come in, creating a lively din behind them. "Is getting this...book... for research on the ritual, or are you planning something on your own?"

"I haven't decided yet."

Taesia sighed and flagged down the bartender, ordering a whiskey. "There's bound to be useful information in there. Information we need if this is going to work."

"I'm aware."

"Then...you're interested in joining us?"

Angelica pressed her lower lip against the rim of her wineglass. "It'll depend on what I find."

When Taesia got her whiskey, she flipped a coin at the bartender and clinked her glass against Angelica's, making her start. "To treason, then."

Now Angelica was the one shushing her. "You really are a fucking idiot."

Taesia took a small sip, letting the whiskey linger on the back of her tongue. "But here's something to consider. You and your mother have worked hard to gain the king's favor. We can use that to our advantage."

"In other words, you want me to sacrifice that favor."

"What? No. I don't want the throne."

"Bullshit. Everyone wants the throne."

"*I* don't. And even if I did, any chance I had would be shot because of…" She swallowed Dante's name, a bright pain in her throat. "Why do *you* even want it?"

"None of your business. You wouldn't understand."

"Try me. Unless you don't *really* want it, and you're just following your mother's ambition." Taesia leaned in closer. "Am I right?"

"I said it's none of your business!"

"I think you should consider what *you* want, and what's been drilled into your head." Taesia took another sip, savoring the smooth burn. "So? What does Angelica Mardova want?"

The question seemed to hit a sore spot. The wineglass in Angelica's hand shook, ready to break into pieces.

Giving Angelica a moment to compose herself, Taesia turned to study the Soldiers' Standing table. The breath caught in her throat.

Sitting at the table was the Mariian girl who had stolen Dante's hellebore root, the one Taesia had tussled with outside the market what felt like years ago. Her cloud of dark, wiry hair framed a smirking face, exuding the confidence of someone who believed no matter where she trod, the ground would be solid beneath her.

"What are you doing?" Angelica hissed, grabbing her arm as Taesia started forward. "I thought we weren't going to approach yet?"

But the air in Taesia's lungs crackled, her fingertips buzzing with the need for action. After the dealer's shop, everything had been too quiet, too slow—the preparations for the ritual would take time, the forging of the astralam bones would take time, waiting for the creeping date of Godsnight would take time.

Taesia needed to *do* something.

She yanked out of Angelica's hold and made straight for the thief. When she placed a hand on the Mariian girl's shoulder, Taesia knew the exact moment she was recognized, relishing the flash of panic and excitement in the girl's eyes.

"Round two," Taesia said before she lunged.

The thief spun away from her chair and sprinted for the front doors. The patrons cried out in alarm, and Angelica cursed as they gave chase past the goons and into the newly fallen night.

The shadows in the streets sang at her presence. They rose up, joyous, whispering like the blood rushing through her veins.

"Why are you laughing?" Angelica panted, her shawl fallen to her shoulders. "Is she even a thief?"

"Oh, she's a thief, all right."

The girl's shoe disappeared over the edge of a roof. Taesia glanced between the alley and the main street and signaled for Angelica to take the street.

"Split up," she said. "Pincer her."

Taesia dove into the alley and let the darkness swallow her. It was cool and welcome against her body, like sliding into a lake of clear water in the height of summer. Umbra uncoiled from her ring and formed a rope in her hands. When she broke out of the alley, the thief was jumping from the roof onto a balcony. Taesia let Umbra fly, reaching for the girl's arm.

The thief narrowly avoided it, hanging from the lip of the balcony before dropping into the street. Then Angelica was there, charging at her like a bull.

Instead of dodging, the thief used Angelica's momentum against her, kicking up and sending Angelica flying over her head. Angelica landed on her back with a pained grunt, the wind knocked out of her.

The Mariian girl winked at Taesia before taking off again. Angelica struggled to all fours, coughing.

"Stay here," Taesia ordered. "You're slowing me down."

Angelica spat and wiped her mouth. "The fuck did you say to me?"

She didn't bother to answer, following the thief with determination sharp as a bolt loosed from a crossbow.

They crossed a large square, paper lanterns strung between the buildings to illuminate an open market. It was cluttered with vendors' blankets spread in a grid over the cobblestone. Taesia leapt over them and ignored the indignant cries, accidentally smashing something apart under her heel.

A group of people were gathered around a caged chicken stall, demanding the vendor squeeze the chickens' necks and prove he hadn't fed them rocks to make them weigh more than they were worth. People and poultry alike erupted into startled squawking as the thief grabbed a chicken and threw it at Taesia.

Taesia cursed and fumbled with the distraught bird as it beat her face with its wings. Using the most of the distraction, the girl darted into the nearest side street. Taesia gathered the shadows to her as she followed, Umbra vibrating against her wrist. The whispers in her ears were sibilant and coaxing, like that day in the bone dealer's shop.

The thief threw open a door and Taesia rammed into it, pain sparking against her forehead as the thief vanished into the building's dim interior.

The acrid smell of opium assaulted Taesia as soon as she crossed the threshold. The den was murky with smoke, a far cry from the red plush and gilded panels of the dens the gentry visited. Here, patrons sat or lay on thin cushions in an otherwise bare room, their eyes glassy and their breathing slow.

"Hey!" someone yelled. "What're you doing?"

The thief scrambled up a flight of stairs. Taesia chased her into one of the private rooms, a couple crying out in alarm as the thief launched herself through the open window.

"Shit!" Taesia leapt after her and caught the windowsill of the next building over. The thief had managed to grab on to a drainage pipe leading down to the alley.

Taesia released her shadows, and the thief's eyes widened before she let go of the pipe and dropped. Taesia did the same, landing on top of her and sending them sprawling across ground wet with drainage. The thief got in a couple of punches before Taesia kicked the inside of her hip to dislodge her.

"Damn, you're persistent!" The thief struggled to her knees. "You must really like me."

Taesia laughed and wiped the back of her wrist across her mouth, smearing blood. "Why don't we make this next part nice and quick, huh?"

The thief shook out her hands and formed them into fists, one tucked under her chin and the other gesturing for Taesia to come at her. "I like the way you think."

The shadows writhed and whispered around her, but Taesia didn't want an easy victory. She wanted the satisfaction of a fight, a way to unleash all the pent-up fear and fury inside her.

The fistfight was quick and brutal. Taesia lost track of where they were, forgot even the shadows twitching around her as she focused on dodging, blocking, striking. Her knuckles barked with pain and everywhere the girl hit promised a new bruise, the ache delicious and hard won. Taesia grinned even as the thief drove her fist into her solar plexus, even as her retaliating punch made her hand throb.

"What, no elementalist friend to help you out this time?" Taesia goaded.

She shouldn't have wasted her breath. The thief darted in and feinted to sweep Taesia's legs out from under her.

Taesia landed on her back as the girl sprinted away. She raised her hand to finally let the shadows descend, to plunge the thief into disorienting darkness.

Before she could, there was a crackling sound as the ground underneath her froze over. The thief slipped and fell, hitting her head against the side of the building and slumping at its base.

Angelica walked into Taesia's line of sight, out of breath and hands stretched out before her. Taesia sat up and realized the water from the drainage pipe had turned to ice.

"Well," Taesia said, "look at you. Not even a ditty or a chord."

"Shut up." Angelica's face was strained with exertion. "Bind her wrists before she wakes up."

Taesia hesitated. The shadows were still inching forward, ready to be unleashed. She felt them under her skin, echoing in the pounding of her heart.

Angelica glanced at the swirling darkness growing beside her. "*Taesia.*"

She reluctantly let the shadows go, shivering at their loss. The whispers faded, leaving hollow silence and the farseeing stars overhead.

By the time they rented a room at a nearby inn, the adrenaline was already wearing off. Taesia's arms shook as she set the thief's unconscious body into a chair and pulled her arms back to better tie them together. The thief had stirred after hitting her head in the alley, remedied by Angelica pulling some sort of vial from her sleeve and passing it under the girl's nose to make her pass out again.

Angelica had been the one to spot the inn, had been the one to pay for the room. The place was far from spotless, yet Taesia was surprised Angelica hadn't immediately wrinkled her nose, or that when the innkeeper had given the thief a questioning look, Angelica had said, "Our friend got drunk. Needs to sleep it off."

"You're getting the hang of this already," Taesia said.

Angelica rolled her eyes and poured water into the basin on top of the dresser. "Clean up. You're filthy."

They waited several minutes for the thief to rouse. Once she did, she started hard enough to make the chair scrape against the floor.

"How's your head?" Taesia asked, standing over her with arms crossed.

The thief squinted up at her. "It's been better, that's for sure." She studied Angelica with interest. "A Shade and an elementalist working together. Interesting."

"What *I* find interesting," Taesia said, using her foot to drag the other chair closer so she could sit across from her, "is why you stole that hellebore root."

The thief's eyebrows rose. "You know how much those ingredients sell for right now, what with the crackdown?"

"Careful," Taesia drawled. "The punishment for Conjuration is death. Pretty sure that goes for suppliers, too." Her mind echoed with the sound of bone snapping.

Angelica huffed and grabbed the back of Taesia's chair, dragging her away from the thief so she could stand between them. "That's not why we're here."

"Gonna torture me for information?" the girl asked, batting her lashes. "Without even buying me dinner? Pretty sure the guests in this here inn'll hear my screams."

"We're not going to torture you." Angelica took out a pouch and threw it onto the table beside them, the gold coins inside rattling. "We're going to pay you. *I'm* going to pay you. For a job."

The thief's full lips parted, the bottom one split from their scuffle. She looked between them and the pouch and asked slowly, "What sorta job you in the market for?"

Taesia and Angelica had agreed they couldn't be the ones to steal the grimoire; their magic was too recognizable, and if they were caught, it would bring disaster down on their Houses. More disaster, in Taesia's case.

"You know the museum by the university?" Angelica asked the thief.

" 'Course."

"There's a book in the new exhibit, the one they've set up to honor Prelate Lezzaro. I will give you a full description of it, and you will steal it for me. In return, I'll give you a hundred soles now and five hundred after."

The thief nearly choked. "*Soles?*"

Angelica took out a small knife and unbound the thief's arms. The girl rubbed her wrists and continued staring at the money pouch. Taesia tensed and Umbra uncoiled from her ring, ready to pounce if the thief decided to start another chase.

Instead, the thief laughed and shook her head. "Suppose I've taken on stranger jobs," she said. "You can call me Cosima."

XI

King Dalvinder, also called the Foreign King, had been terrified of rule. The Vaegan people had been uneasy under the influence of a Parithvian, the royal blood in his veins barely a trickle. So the Foreign King decided he needed an heir to secure his tenuous throne. He had prayed fervently to Thana for years until she finally came to him, veiled and vexed.

"What is it you wish of me?" the god had demanded.

"The Vaegan people do not trust me," Dalvinder had claimed. "I am considered an outsider, a stranger to their ways. But the gods are what connect us, the one thread uniting all the realm of Vitae. Every god has provided unique progeny who have been reared within this city. Every god except you."

"And so you desire to make me a conquered thing," Thana had responded with a sneer. "To fill the star of my womb with a creature that responds to death."

"Only if you also desire it, blessed Thana. I merely ask you consider it. I will humbly await your answer, whatever it may be."

The story went she considered for three days before she returned. The other gods had done this deed, she reasoned—why not her as well? It was curiosity that drove Thana to lie with him, and obligation that brought her back a year later, a child of rare and frightful power in her arms.

"I believe this is yours, now," the god had said as she unceremoniously left the child with the king. "Do with it as you will."

Thus was the House of Vakara established.

That child, Leshya Vakara, had grown up to become the singular necromancer of Vitae. She'd accomplished great feats, such as facing the four undead kings of Mortri when they sought to make war upon Vitae. When she died, she'd stipulated she wanted some part of her to remain with her House, for her heirs to have access to her power once she was gone.

Now the relic hung around the neck of a Conjurer.

"My lady? Did you hear me?"

Risha came back to herself with a jerk. Don Ferro and his wife were staring at her, anxious to begin.

"Yes," she said. "I needed a moment to get settled."

When she was younger, Risha had dreamed of performing magnificent feats of magic like Leshya Vakara: resurrecting old kings, learning new stories from ancient heroes, perhaps even a parade of skeletons who had learned to do an impressive jig. She had not daydreamed about performing séances for minor nobles.

It was an idea from one of her ancestors, back when the Four Realms were still open and Nexus didn't have to worry about wayward spirits. With need for something to do, the Vakaras had begun loaning themselves out to those who wished to speak with the dead. But it wasn't enough to open the thin gate of communication between the living and dead; no, somehow that was deemed too boring, too simple.

Her House had a reputation to uphold, even if it meant putting on theatrics.

Lighting incense did wonders for atmosphere, and now Don Ferro's dining room was flooded with the scent of lotus blossom. Candles, too, were essential, especially those with the most dramatic buildup of melted wax. Risha finished her preparation by laying out bowls of rose water, their surfaces speckled with pale pink petals, as well as a few roughly cut crystals that did absolutely nothing but enhance the aesthetic.

The six nobles clustered at the rosewood table were practically vibrating with excitement. It amazed Risha to see this morbid curiosity, this bizarre desire to brush up against the dark and uncertain. Everyone feared death. To come so close, to examine it without succumbing to it, gave them something of a high.

Was this why the Conjurers—the *Revenants*—were so eager to learn necromancy?

Don Ferro sat to her right, his wife to her left. The don seemed eager, but the doña was pale. Beyond the candlelight, Risha caught sight of the room's decorations, a collection of Azunese woodblock printings and Mariian ritual masks. It gave her the uneasy sense of gazing upon a hunter's trophies.

From the way the nobles were eyeing her Parithvian jewelry, perhaps that assessment wasn't so far off.

"We will begin," Risha intoned in her séance voice, slow and dreary. She laid her hands out before her. "Please join hands." The nobles shifted to comply. Don Ferro's grip was relaxed and dry, his wife's tight and clammy. "Speak into the air the name of the departed."

Don Ferro glanced at his wife. When she said nothing, he replied, "Casir Gioni."

Risha breathed in, breathed out. Incense filled her head and lungs.

"Casir Gioni," she repeated. "Casir Gioni. Casir Gioni. Come to us, Casir Gioni, and use my body, my voice, to speak to those you have left behind."

She bowed her head to better concentrate on the actual magic required. It had taken her years to learn it, years of stubbornness to prove to her father she could do anything he could, years of hard work and opening herself up like a revolving door to spirits only to become a mere puppet for bored nobles.

Casir Gioni. Power awoke in her core, deep and dark and desiring. She felt the faint tug of Mortri, still locked. Risha gritted her teeth and pressed on, expanding her awareness out of the incense-choked room and into the graveyards of the city, the necropolis, the half-remembered bones resting underneath.

The difference between locating a body and locating a spirit was the difference between a glass ball and a soap bubble. Risha had learned the hard way that sifting through the pinpoints in her awareness was a waste of time; all she had to do was keep herself open, inviting, the name of the departed in her mind.

Eventually he came to her, lured by the call. An older man, his presence reserved yet willing. Risha opened her mouth.

"Lilia?" It was not her séance voice. It was hoarse and deep, trembling slightly.

The doña gasped and gripped her hand tighter. The nobles across from her murmured in surprise.

"Are you there, Lilia?" Casir called.

"I-I'm here, Father," Doña Ferro warbled.

"My darling," Casir sighed.

When a spirit came to her, Risha never let them have full access to her body. She could still move her hands, her arms, her legs. But her voice was seized from her, so she couldn't tell the doña that her hand was on its way to breaking Risha's.

"Father, I've missed you so much," the doña sobbed.

"What is death like?" blurted one of the nobles from across the table.

Casir sighed again. "It simply is. I have no notion of time or place or thought. I simply remain tethered."

Risha couldn't help but frown. Had the Four Realms remained open, his spirit would have eventually left this place and gone on to Mortri. Instead he was left to languish here, shapeless and purposeless.

"My dear man," said the don on her right. "I want you to know your daughter is well taken care of. In fact, we are trying now for a child."

Risha's lips quirked in Casir's smile. "That is wonderful news indeed."

"However," the don continued, his voice a little too bright, "we still seem to be paying off the, ah…lingering debt. I—*we* were wondering where exactly the family's funds were allocated."

The spirit within her turned suddenly cold. Risha's skin prickled in alarm.

"Father—" the doña began, but a rattling laugh had begun in Risha's throat.

"I knew that was all you ever cared about," Casir said with a sneer of Risha's mouth. "Money. *Luxury.* Is my house not enough, boy? You have taken it all."

"Now look here—"

"The funds are *gone*, lost to gambling and poor investments."

Don Ferro scoffed. "Of course it is. You could never keep your vices in check."

"Raoul!" the doña wailed. "Don't speak to him that way!"

"It is up to you to make whatever wealth you desire," Casir went on. "Stop depending on others to cushion your life for you, boy."

Don Ferro scoffed again as the nobles whispered among themselves. The spirit was already leaving her, his energy spent on anger. That was likely for the best; an aggravated spirit had a better chance of overcoming her. Her father had once told her of a great-aunt who'd summoned a spirit that had latched on to her permanently, forever riding inside her head, and the woman had been forced to speak with two different voices.

"It's all right, Father, we'll be all right," Doña Ferro was saying. "He doesn't mean it. We love you, truly."

"And I love you, my darling. If you've a son, name it after me."

"I will, I will!"

And then Casir drained out of her, a cold, sinking feeling that made her shudder. When Risha opened her eyes, her vision spun.

"Why did you have to interrogate him like that?" the doña snapped at her husband.

"We've both been trying to figure out his ledgers—"

"Excuse me," Risha interrupted, her throat raw, "but we must close communication for the séance to end."

"Oh, yes, of course..."

They didn't actually have to do anything—Casir was well and truly gone—but Risha didn't want to be literally in the middle of a domestic dispute. She murmured some nonsense phrases and let go of their hands, her left one aching.

As she packed up, the married couple thanked her and assured a payment would be made to House Vakara by the end of the day. Then they took their leave, raised voices echoing down the hall.

"That was incredible," breathed one of the noble women left behind. "Can anyone learn to speak with the dead?"

Risha extinguished the last candle and packed it away, hiding the twitch of her eyebrows. "I'm afraid not. But if you would like to host a séance of your own, simply call upon House Vakara."

"But the Conjurers are doing so," the woman pointed out, the others nodding.

Risha's hand tightened on the strap of her bag. "The Conjurers," she began slowly, as calmly as she could, "are heretics who use occult methods. Not so long ago they were stealing bodies for nefarious purposes. Or have you forgotten what happened with Doña Bianca's husband?"

That chastened them enough to bow their heads and mutter apologies. Risha inclined her head back and swept out without another word.

She dozed on the ride home, a headache sitting behind her forehead. She had spent the last couple days holed up in the villa, recovering after the necropolis attack, and exerting herself even this much was proving to be strenuous.

But at least they knew where Leshya Vakara's necklace had gone. Risha had told her father about her interaction with the Revenants, who'd then relayed it word for word to the king, Don Soler, Nikolas, and the high commissioner. Apparently Don Soler wanted to come and speak to Risha himself, but Rath firmly denied him from disturbing her, which Risha was thankful for; she didn't much like the thought of the don hovering over her bed.

She knew why he was frustrated, though. Other than identifying the Revenants' leader as a Parithvian man, it had been too dark and her body too exhausted to clearly make out his features. Still, they had more now than they had before.

When she arrived at the villa, she was surprised to find her father sitting on a bench in one of the side gardens. Risha sat beside him.

"How did it go?" he asked.

"The same as it always goes." She sat back and enjoyed the sunshine hitting her face, letting it relax her. The garden here was verdant and soothing, with spills of trailing purple blossoms and spiky fronds. The bench sat across from a banyan tree, its roots spreading in a wild tangle. The smell of summer, of dry sunshine and the bright growth of leaves, had faded. Now she smelled the sweet rot of autumn.

"There was a spat between husband and wife," she went on. "I got out of there as soon as I could."

"Perhaps for the best," he said. "Spirits tend to bring out the worst in others."

Risha nodded. "I think we should start training Saya to do the séances instead."

"Saya hasn't been able to hold on to a spirit for more than thirty seconds."

"But she's already more accomplished at summoning them than I was at her age. She'll learn quickly."

"Why are you bringing this up?"

Risha tried not to sigh. "You know why. I despise the séances, the wreaths, the funeral rites."

"They're a necessary part of being a Vakara."

And that had been enough for her, once. But with Godsnight approaching and the others counting on her to do her part, Risha felt as if she were walking in mindless circles instead of carving a path forward.

"You are doing well, meer piaara, but you make mistakes when you exhaust yourself. So long as you keep yourself out of trouble, nothing

will befall you. You don't need to fling yourself into every small disturbance to prove your worth to the people, or the king."

"That's not..." Risha rubbed her aching head. "That's not it."

She couldn't tell him about Godsnight. It still felt too tenuous, too
uncertain, too *forbidden* to do anything but rile him. A man as committed
to the rules as Rath Vakara wouldn't understand what they were trying
to do.

Clouds began to roll across the sky when her father left to help refortify the wards at the necropolis. Risha stayed outside a moment longer
before finally entering the main house. Across the courtyard, her mother
spotted her and headed over, trailing a purple muslin dupatta behind her.
"Where has your father gone?"

"The necropolis."

"Oh." Darsha grimaced, no doubt remembering the injury he'd sus-
tained from that harrowing night. "Well, how did the séance go?"

It was a poor attempt at nonchalance, but Risha humored it. "As well
as any other, I suppose. The husband—"

"Good, good. Anyway, I have some excellent news for you."

Of course. "Which is?"

"Do you remember when I said a visiting lord has an eligible son?"
Darsha's chest swelled like a bird contentedly fluffing its feathers. "Your
father and I discussed it at length, and he's finally agreed we can set up a
dowry meeting."

"Amaa...we're far too busy to consider this right now. The dead—"

"You can still maintain your duties if you're married, can't you?" Darsha argued. "You'll need to be married sooner or later. It's better for us to
make allies now."

But Risha knew that wasn't merely it. If her father had only now
agreed to have a dowry meeting, that meant her stint at the necropolis
had swayed him.

She was losing his trust. And once she took part in the Godsnight
ritual, willingly participating in Conjuration, it would be shattered for
good.

This upsetting revelation was interrupted by the arrival of a messenger in the white and gold of House Cyr. Darsha's eyebrows did a strange
dance at the sight of them, but Risha politely took the missive they
offered her and quickly read it.

"Nik needs me for an investigation," she said, her headache pulsing in protest. Still, after the triviality of the séance, she longed to be useful in some way.

"Well, make it quick," her mother muttered. "You still need plenty of rest. The lord and his son will be attending the Godsnight Gala, and I want you to look your best for it."

"Yes, Amaa." Knowing Nikolas, it was likely just a means to get them alone to talk about the ritual, or the recent necropolis attack. Simple enough.

It was not simple.

The shop was horrific, from the ominous jars containing floating body parts to the rows of various beast and animal horns and antlers. Nikolas's unit was already here, three soldiers scouring the front of the shop. They bowed and introduced themselves.

"Terrible, isn't it?" the swordsman named Taide said with an odd twinkle in his eye, like he was secretly thrilled. "Like, look at this." He shook a jar containing an organ of some sort. "What even is this? What would the Conjurers *use* this for?"

"Hey," the elementalist named Gem barked. "We're supposed to be taking inventory, not gawking." They bowed again to Risha. "Lord Cyr is in the back, my lady."

Risha made her way to the parted curtain. The other elementalist lifted a broken-off chain and asked the others, "What d'you think this was for?"

"Probably a sex thing," Taide muttered.

Risha wanted to breathe a sigh of relief as she stepped through the doorway, but the air she met with was so putrid she had to cough and cover her mouth.

"Sorry," came a familiar muffled voice as Nikolas trotted up to her. He handed her a handkerchief. "Forgot to warn you."

Risha quickly tied the handkerchief around the lower half of her face, though she could still smell the telltale scent of decomposing flesh. The room they stood in was littered with bones, and the two Hunters in Nikolas's unit, also wearing handkerchiefs, were busy shepherding a handful of little creatures into a cage. Bone snatchers, clinging possessively to the lanterns that housed their life forces.

"Yeah, I know you like this stuff, but you can't bring it with you," the taller Hunter was saying to one of them, trying to pull a femur from its grip. It keened unhappily. "Fuck, you know what, fine. If it brings you joy, why the fuck not."

"What..." Risha didn't realize she was swaying until Nikolas steadied her. "What is going on?"

"We got an anonymous tip saying there was a Conjuration supplier here. But when we came to arrest him, he was already dead." Nikolas gestured to a shrouded figure on the floor. "Several days dead, at least."

Which explained the smell. And also why Nikolas had called her here. Steeling herself, she knelt and uncovered the body. The man had died with his eyes wide open, sunken now in their sockets, the sclera turned gray. His neck was twisted at an alarming angle, and she couldn't help but remember Lezzaro's broken neck lolling on his shoulders.

Had the same people who killed Lezzaro killed this man? It wasn't too far of a stretch, if they'd both dabbled in Conjuration.

There were ragged bites taken out of his flesh, and she glanced at the bone snatchers scuttling around in their cage.

"Poor little bastards were trapped in here," said the taller Hunter, noticing her put two and two together. At his side, the other Hunter stared at the body with a haunted, wan expression. Then for some reason he turned his gaze toward the ceiling, as if expecting it to crash down on them.

Risha's headache fueled the nausea eddying through her. Nikolas knelt at her side.

"Can you revive him for questioning?" he asked.

Risha gingerly put her fingertips to the man's cold forehead and closed her eyes. A small torus spun around her, knocking away a nearby piece of bone. But try as she might to call forth the man's spirit, like she had with Casir Gioni, nothing came to her.

"He must have gone straight to the void," she said as the torus died out. "I can try to read his memories, but depending on how many days he's been dead, they'll be hazy at best."

"I can work with hazy."

She again put her fingertips to the man's forehead. This time she pulled from inside his own body, teasing out memories hidden within muscle, tissue, and nerves. She shuffled through sensory memories first— the smell of blood, the feel of bone, the sound of rattling chains.

Gradually she worked up to the sunken eyes, coaxing out images of red-tinged water, a saw, meat that split between his hands. Risha kept going even as her nausea spiked.

And then there was a beast. Large, white, winged, straining at its chains. Two people, blurred and moving. Darkness in the edges of his vision.

A hole. A *vortex*. Swirling and mesmerizing and utterly terrifying. She must have made a sound, because she heard Nikolas's distant voice—but it wasn't *her* sound, not really, it was this man's, feeding her his terror and elation and dread through memory alone.

And then—

No.

His thought, not hers, at the encroaching instinct that he was about to die, that the tendrils (shadows?) that gripped him were not natural, not a thing he could cut or maim, that the bitch (girl) who wielded this power wasn't human—

No.

Her thought, not his, at seeing the girl who controlled the shadows, her eyes gone completely, horrifyingly black, her hand held out before her ready to pass judgment, her mouth pulling wider into a grin—

SNAP

Risha yanked herself back with a strangled scream. Nikolas caught her as she touched her neck, trembling fingers mapping tendon and unbroken bone. But the sound was trapped inside her, echoing, endless.

"Risha!" Nikolas was practically yelling in her ear. "You're all right. It's all right."

She tried and failed to speak. Even the smell was forgotten as she pulled in deep breaths, forcing herself to calm down.

"What happened?" Nikolas whispered. His pale eyes were wide above his handkerchief. "What did you see?"

Risha looked meaningfully at the Hunters.

"Wait with the others up front," Nikolas ordered.

The taller one nodded and grabbed one of the cage's handles. The other hesitated, staring at them as if trying to categorize a new type of beast.

"Julian," Nikolas said, a warning.

The Hunter started and helped his partner carry the cage full of bone snatchers out to the front. Once they were alone, Risha covered the body back up. Nikolas put a hand on her shoulder.

"Tell me," he said softly. "The way he died is almost like Lezzaro. Do you think...?"

But her ability to think had been stripped away from her. All that remained was a low, frantic buzz, making her fingers twitch.

"Risha." Nikolas's voice grew louder, urgent.

She closed her eyes, but every time she did she saw the images desperately passed on to her, saddling her alone with their burden.

When she met Nikolas's gaze again, it was pleading, begging her to get it over with. Like he already knew. Like he already suspected.

"Nik," she whispered. "It was Taesia."

XII

The chairs in the council room were truly uncomfortable. Angelica thought it must be on purpose to keep the dignitaries and officers on edge.

She was on edge sure enough, but her focus kept slipping as her mother and the king discussed the distribution of the elementalist division around the city in the coming weeks. Angelica watched the beaded condensation on her glass roll down to the table's surface. She similarly felt the tickle of sweat across her chest, under her arms, down her thighs.

She kept telling herself it was nerves. The thief, Cosima, would soon lead a small team inside the museum to retrieve the book. Lezzaro's grimoire.

But it was more than that. Angelica had searched the entire villa for her instruments with no success. Every passing day without a tuned string or a lilting note was a day Angelica's skin tightened and burned hotter. She tried whistling to relieve the worst of it, but it only produced light breezes and a thin ribbon of roaming water, not nearly enough to suppress the yawning ache inside of her.

A sharp pressure on her foot brought her back to the present. Her mother sat beside her, staring intently at the king even as her foot pushed down on Angelica's.

Angelica took a sip of lemon water. It relieved the burn in her throat enough for her to speak.

"Your Majesty, are you certain you would like to continue with the gala despite what happened at the necropolis?" she asked. Adela had urged her, on their way to the palace, to be the one to bring this up. "These Conjurers have killed the prelate. They must be radicals."

Ferdinand gave her a smile a shade too patronizing for her liking. Behind him, two of his advisors frowned. "Of course. Godsnight traditions mean a great deal to the public, and the people of Nexus need something to celebrate amid all this chaos."

"The gala will be held here, within the Bone Palace," Don Soler added. "We have already established guard rotations, royal and city alike, as well as units from the militia and elementalist division both inside and outside the palace. The necropolis will also be refortified by the Vakaras right before."

"It will be quite safe," Don Cassian added.

"Then may I ask His Majesty if these precautionary measures will be the same for the actual day of Godsnight?" Angelica went on. "There will be many people celebrating in the streets. It's imperative to keep them safe."

Ferdinand inclined his head. "We are planning to distribute guards and soldiers to the districts where the festivities will be confined to, as well as the palace square where the nobility will be gathered."

You and your mother have worked hard to gain his favor, Taesia had told her in the King's Corner. *If we're going to perform this ritual, we can use that to our advantage.*

"Your Majesty," Angelica said slowly, "I was wondering if I may propose an idea for Godsnight."

Adela stiffened, but Ferdinand seemed intrigued. "I would love to hear it, my lady."

"Godsnight is an ancient custom that has existed long before the Sealing. In those days, the Houses would put on grand feats of magic as their gods' power traveled through them when the Cosmic Scale aligned perfectly."

Her mother stared at her. The two advisors shifted as they exchanged an uneasy glance.

"Of course, with the Sealing, this is no longer the case," Angelica went on. "However, the Houses could still celebrate with individual displays of magic. I believe the gentry and citizens alike would be pleased with such a spectacle. As you said, Your Majesty, our city has been rampant with chaos lately. The least we could do is entertain them."

And position the heirs to enact the ritual. Perhaps, if they were to hide the Conjuration circle in some way—make it large enough to have the palace square at its center—no one would be the wiser.

She was positively drenched in sweat as Ferdinand sat speechless for a moment. Then, to both Angelica's and Adela's shock, he began to laugh.

"Oh, my lady, you must forgive me," he said once his chuckles had died down. "It's just that I happened to have the same thought not too long ago."

"You . . . did?"

"Yes, and I was planning to announce it at the gala, though I see you've beaten me to it." His advisors exchanged a bewildered look, as if this were news to them as well. "I was thinking of how to best celebrate something so grand and rare. A way to please not only the people, but the gods as well."

His next smile held no warmth, and it reminded her of the day the Lastriders had barged in here, how he'd warned the Houses to play by his rules—or end up like Dante.

"I can think of no better way to honor Godsnight than a public demonstration of the Houses' abilities," he said. "A reminder that Vaega holds true power in this realm."

Angelica was too stunned to say anything, so Adela swept in and thanked him on her behalf. Once she and her mother were dismissed, they were halfway down the hall when Adela grabbed her wrist.

"Do you understand what he's doing?" her mother whispered. Angelica had expected her to be irritated for not bringing the topic up with her beforehand. Instead, she found trepidation, which was far worse.

Speechless, Angelica shook her head.

"He wants a demonstration because he wants to see the public's reaction." Her mother's grip tightened, digging between tendons. "To begin the process of choosing his heir."

Angelica barely made it to her bedroom in the villa by the time the shaking intensified. It began at her core and radiated outward, a starburst of nauseating tremors. She collapsed against the closed door.

She craved fire. Needed notes of heat and destruction, a blissful moment to simply burn, burn, burn.

Begin the process of choosing his heir.

It was something Ferdinand hadn't made concrete steps toward, to the chagrin of the heads of the Houses. He had tested them throughout the years, of course, to gauge their dependency. But this—a spectacle, a display of divine power, a fucking *audition*—would be the biggest chance they had to prove themselves.

All she had to do was give the public and the Holy King a demonstration worth remembering.

Gasping, she held out her hands and tried to ignite a spark between them, but only the barest of cinders escaped her fingertips. Angelica sobbed and tensed as the tremors racked her body, her jaw locking up until it passed.

This weakness, this sickness within you.

With her powers so lacking, she had no chance. Her mother would never let her take a stage with instruments in hand—provided she ever got them back.

Then there was the ritual. Working together with the other heirs rankled her, but if they *could* undo the Sealing, wouldn't that give Ferdinand the spectacle he craved?

But then they'd be right back at the starting line, with all the Houses equal in his eyes. Unless she could get the others to agree to bow out in exchange for her help.

Her skin was damp and smelled of noxious smoke. Raking hair away from her face, she wiped her mouth and went to draw a bath.

Later, after dressing in a simple lounging dress, she hummed the melody of an aria from *The Gossamer Road* as she brushed out her hair. The aria was sung by the main character mourning her lost love, trapped forever between two realms, unable to meet again.

The notes vibrated tenderly around her, simple yet encompassing in their resonance. Her heartbeat slowed, lost in the music she created, allowing it to take up residence in the spaces between her ribs and shoulder blades. It almost seemed to prop her up, to elongate her spine and loosen her jaw, to smooth the divot between her eyebrows.

"That's a pretty little tune."

Angelica jumped and threw her hairbrush across the room. Cosima, reclining on the bench beneath her window, caught it with one hand.

"How did you get in?" Angelica demanded even as she noted the open window behind her. Her bedroom had been cleaned up after she had raged at it, her broken furniture and window replaced without questions. Angelica hadn't ordered the staff to do so, and knew her mother hadn't either, or else she would have heard about it.

"You need to invest in tighter security," the thief said as she fiddled with the brush's pearl handle. "Those House guards of yours are real easy to distract. Like tossing a turkey leg to a pack of dogs."

Angelica's heart beat like a galloping horse. "What are you doing here?"

In the daylight Cosima's skin glowed. Angelica found herself visually tracing the arches of her eyebrows and the curve of her full lips, plump like summer-ripened fruit.

"Have you already forgotten? I'm here to settle our arrangement." Cosima sat up with a stretch and grinned, and something about it reminded her of Taesia, a smile wielded like a weapon.

"You have the book?"

"Indeed I do. And I'd like to see the rest of what I'm owed before I hand it over."

Angelica dug a purse from her trunk and tossed it to the thief. While Cosima examined it, she realized her hair was half brushed and tried to smooth it out with her hands, wincing as her fingers got caught in tangles.

Cosima looked up from counting. With a sigh, she set the purse down and picked up the brush again. "C'mere, my lady."

"Why, so you can conveniently fit a knife to my throat?"

"Such dramatics. Don't you have maids to do your hair for you?"

She had, growing up, but only used them now when preparing for a major public outing. She hadn't liked the feeling of being molded and shaped beneath other people's hands.

Cosima waited, expectant. Perhaps it was the exhaustion that made Angelica come closer. Cosima gestured for her to sit on the floor, and Angelica's face heated as Cosima's legs bracketed her body.

"There, now," Cosima said. "Let's get you presentable."

The heat in her face intensified as Cosima carefully ran the brush through her hair, holding it at the roots to better tackle the snarls at the ends. Every time Angelica shifted or fidgeted, Cosima poked her in the back. She felt like a child again, in need of someone to care for her.

It made her wonder: When *was* the last time she'd been cared for?

"Can't believe you managed to catch me with a bit of ice," the Mariian girl murmured above her. Her voice was light and melodic, the smooth resonance of a flute. "Then again, suppose it makes sense. You seem to be made of the stuff."

Angelica stiffened.

"But I bet there's something under all that ice," Cosima went on, her voice dropping as if speaking to herself. "Some hidden fire."

Angelica swallowed. "You're talking nonsense."

A small huff of laughter. "Guess I am. Sorry, my lady."

They fell into soft silence. Angelica closed her eyes as Cosima ran fingers through her still-damp hair, over her scalp. The shivers across her shoulders faded away until she was merely sitting within a moment of much-needed calm.

"Hypericum," Cosima said suddenly.

Angelica's eyes shot open. "What?"

"For the shakes and the sweating. Hypericum powder may help. I recognize the signs."

Humiliation ran like a silent river through her. This girl saw not just an heir, but an addict. Something base and common.

And yet, she was trying to help. Why?

"How do you know about it?" Angelica asked, peering over her shoulder.

Cosima shrugged. The top button of her shirt was unfastened, revealing a triangle of smooth skin at the base of her throat. "I've known addicts. When they went through withdrawal, Hypericum helped."

She thought Angelica was addicted to opium, not an element. Angelica forced herself to nod, to do something other than sit there and gape at her. "I . . . I'll look into it."

Cosima began to braid her hair, separating it into strands and weaving them together, making sure the base was tight enough. Angelica's breathing was slow and even.

When the braid was done, Cosima hung it over one of Angelica's shoulders. The girl stood suddenly, reaching into the pack sitting beside her on the bench. Angelica stood as well, pulse fluttering at the sight of the jewel-toned book.

"I have to admit, I'm a little sad to see this end," Cosima said. "But I'm a woman of my word. Your tome, my lady." She gave an exaggerated bow, presenting it to Angelica. "I hope whatever's in there proves interesting."

Angelica took it with both hands, surprised by the weight. She almost wanted to handle it with gloves, as if touching it with her bare skin would stain it in some way.

The thief climbed up to her window, and Angelica bristled. "That's it?"

"That's it."

"You . . ." Angelica wasn't sure why she was so reluctant to let her go.

"You can't reveal anything about this. You breathe a single word, I'll find you."

"Promise?" Cosima's eyes shone as Angelica scowled. "Corner of Belmin and Kelle. Feel free to call on me for future rogueries. Enjoy your read, my lady."

With a two-finger salute, the thief was gone.

Angelica stared at the grimoire and wondered if it was even real. If she'd been tricked by Taesia somehow, wrapped up in an elaborate con.

She supposed there was only one way to find out. Angelica sat on the edge of her bed, her braid a comforting weight on her shoulder, and began to read.

Angelica moved through the world like she were made of glass. One wrong move and she'd shatter, unrepairable, in too many pieces to fit back together.

She left long scratches in her arms. She shook and vomited smoke. She sometimes reached up to feel the braid of her hair only to remember it had long since been taken out, the gentle curls now lying straight and limp.

The twins brought her meals as she sweated in bed. Her mother and Miko came to check on her, Adela's worry tempered with impatience. Even as her mother pressed a cool cloth to her forehead, she muttered about Godsnight and the upcoming gala.

"He's being adamant about carrying this out," Adela explained when Miko scolded her. "The Mardovas need to make a strong impression, not only at the gala but at whatever demonstration he's planning. We need time to *train*."

Angelica's teeth were chattering, or else she would reply with something along the lines of Ferdinand being a fool, of there being no point to it. Instead, Miko sighed.

"She needs rest, not more stress," Miko murmured. "Perhaps, with her instruments—"

"*No.* I refuse to have her be laughed at." Adela took a deep, steadying breath, her fingers gentle on Angelica's warm forehead. "We'll figure it out. We must."

But Angelica had no way to release the burning ache. The Garden was out of the question; she was too physically weak, and she didn't want to put anyone in danger.

She convinced a servant to find and bring her Hypericum, remembering Cosima's recommendation. The little vial made the worst of the shaking and dizziness fade, enough that she dragged herself to her study to pick up where she'd left off reading the grimoire.

The first third had largely referenced the early days of Vaega, things Angelica already knew from historical books and her homeschooling. It was written in a dry, stale style, and there were several instances where she couldn't translate the antiquated language. She forced herself to squint down at the words with her burning forehead propped on one hand, the window at her back lighting the study in pearly gray. The past few days had seemed dimmer; perhaps they would have an early winter.

She turned the pages faster, her headache and impatience growing with every useless sentence she read.

She stopped when she saw the word *Godsnight*. Her breath stuttered as she dragged the grimoire closer.

The developing of autumn brings the turning of the leaves and ripened harvest, the intersection of things coming to life even as they come to an end, the aligning of the Realms within their place, the certain flow of their might and magic. This has always been a sacred time, a coming together of power and peace. So we give thanks and take, and give back. We began with simple offerings: cloves and camphor, benzoin and hellebore, myrrh and saffron, cypress and mandrake, salt and sulfur. We descend the stepwells and walk in worlds dark and light and terrifying, as others ascend into our elements.

It was not until the coming together of the gods' get that the tradition began to gain shape and weight. With the creation of the Houses we saw in them the gods' power, and we feared them, and loved them, and wanted more. It was no longer enough to give thanks, but to draw together the Realms in ways we never had before, never had been able to.

And so it began with the construction of that great and potent circle, with its language of doorways and windows. Each of the offerings laid out upon its five points: Noctus, Vitae, Solara, Mortri, Ostium. There each heir stood, and there the power of the Realms converged, and there was witness to magic unspeakable and beautiful, the calling in of miracles.

Angelica narrowed in on one word: *Ostium*. She'd never heard of it, but here it was, lumped in with the Four Realms. Why?

> Only those of the Houses will ever experience this joy. Those without magic are left to wonder and be satisfied with their normality. Yet that does not stop some from seeking it, such as those who journey to acquire quintessence. Some claim it impossible, that the only transference of power comes from death and consumption. Some even seek to ingest a mage's flesh as if to take on their power. But it is a fool indeed who would meet the gaze of a god and attempt to eat of their flesh. And it will be a grim day indeed should the gods devour their kin.

Angelica shuddered. The gods had certainly turned on one another, but *devouring*? Did people really use to think that eating a mage would give them their powers?

The next page revealed a large, two-page spread of the Cosmic Scale. There were the Four Realms in their own quadrants, the lines connecting them forming a diamond. They were contained within the circle of the universe, and in the middle was a smaller circle with lines spreading to each realm. It looked like the shape of Nexus, the four-pointed star with the Bone Palace at its center.

She nearly skipped past it. But the sketch was labeled, and within the middle circle was written a barely legible word, one that was becoming increasingly familiar:

Ostium.

Angelica pushed the book away. Her throat was so fucking dry she couldn't stand it. She downed the rest of the tea and, when that wasn't enough, crushed the cup in her hand.

This couldn't be right. It had to be a work of fiction, or else Lezzaro was playing some posthumous prank, or...

Or the Four Realms had not always been four.

It's not possible, she kept repeating like a mantra. *It can't be possible*.

Ostium. A possible fifth realm no one knew about, or remembered. How? *How?*

Angelica might have passed out. She couldn't recall what happened next, and within the span of a blink the sky beyond her window was dark with evening. She didn't move. She couldn't.

Godsnight truly was an ancient ritual. It had used Conjuration, or the earliest form of it. It had not used four heirs, but *five*.

Taesia had been so certain they could undo the Sealing with this. But how could they, if the ritual was incomplete? If they didn't have something to represent Ostium, whatever that actually was?

Where the fuck were they going to find a fifth heir?

XIII

Julian watched the carriages pull in through the Bone Palace's open gates. A contingent of curious citizens were being held back by the city guard, all trying to get a good look at the Houses as they made their way to the Godsnight Gala. Julian couldn't help but think how badly his mother wanted to be in that crowd.

"What a racket," Paris muttered at his side. "At least we'll see His Brightness all shiny and coiffed."

"Is that something you want?" Taide asked with an arched eyebrow.

"What, can't a man engage in light mockery of his betters from time to time?"

"Why would you mock Lord Cyr?" Gem demanded in genuine outrage.

Paris rolled his eyes. "*Endearing* mockery, *endearing*."

Komi had pulled out three small balls of clay, a toy he'd made for when he got fidgety. The elementalist wiggled his fingers, letting the clay balls orbit one another above his palm. "We need to be more focused on the courtyard than Lord Cyr."

Julian silently agreed, peering up at the palace's towers standing stark against a lavender sky and then scanning the soldiers ringing the courtyard. The commotion at the necropolis had put them on high alert, and there were more soldiers guarding it at that very moment, but Nikolas had asked his unit to secure the palace instead. There was still the possibility of a Conjurer attack here, if they decided to call in a horde of spirits like they had that first time.

A black carriage with silver trim trundled by, the crest of House

Lastrider on its doors. A flush traveled up his neck during a sudden onslaught of memory, tendrils of lethal shadow and a low, menacing laugh.

It was a miracle Nikolas hadn't asked him about his behavior in the bone dealer's shop. Although Taesia Lastrider had threatened him not to tell anyone what had happened, he'd still been racked with guilt, unable to get the shop out of his mind. So he'd sent in an anonymous tip, hoping it was enough to skirt the Lastrider heir's warning while fulfilling his duties.

He hadn't been prepared for the visceral reaction he'd had, standing in the place he had nearly died days before. Where a vortex—a *portal*—of impossible magic had bloomed before his eyes. Where a man had died violently at the hands of a woman who didn't seem to fathom her own strength.

The Vakara heir had read the man's memories. What had she seen? Had she seen *him*?

"Ohh, looking *good*," Paris murmured appreciatively as the Houses left their carriages one by one.

Julian glanced over, curious despite himself, and spotted the Sun-bringer Spear as the Cyrs slipped into the ballroom. He caught a glimpse of the Lastrider carriage again and wrenched his eyes away.

You have a job to do, he berated himself. *Focus*.

Umbra coiled around Taesia's fingers as she stared at the congregation below.

The ballroom was lavish and gleaming, a pearl nestled in the shell of the Bone Palace. The vaulted ceiling was a graceful curve over a floor of polished black granite, a small dome of glass admitting the last of the evening's light.

Guards lined the staircase and lurked in the corners of the balcony where the Lastrider family waited to make their entrance. Taesia glanced at the nearest one, a woman with the underside of her head shaven. It reminded her of the Hunter, Julian Luca. She'd briefly spotted him outside with the rest of Nikolas's unit.

King Ferdinand stood in the back of the hall, surrounded by guards and his usual retinue of advisors. Don Cassian stood at his side and helped facilitate the dons and doñas who fought for the king's attention, battles warred with sideways glares and forced smiles. The king's attire was surprisingly understated, his outer coat a rich emerald with golden embroidery, a demure circlet of gold atop his head.

Sensing her stare, Ferdinand glanced up at the balcony. Taesia retreated into the shadows.

"Put your familiar away," Elena said as she styled her husband's hair. Cormin sat obediently on the balcony's chaise and smiled ruefully at Taesia, though it seemed strained. Even her mother was grim, the lines around her eyes having deepened over the past couple weeks. "And, Brailee, I know this is difficult, but please try to smile tonight."

Brailee didn't seem to hear. Her sister leaned against the wall nearby, staring at nothing. She wore the gown she had purchased from Violetta's, deep purple with a flaring skirt and a laced-up front. She'd been reclusive for the past few days. Whenever Taesia went to check on her, her sister's room was empty. Even the bed didn't seem slept in. Perhaps that was why the bags under her eyes were tinged purple like bruises.

"Bee?" Taesia leaned against the wall beside her, feeling her forehead for fever. "You seem off."

"Worry about yourself tonight," her sister muttered. "I'm sure it won't be hard."

"Cheeky little gremlin, aren't you? Come on, Bee." She lowered her voice. "Is it because Dante isn't here? Or... have you been having those dreams again? The ones about the boy?"

Brailee frowned, meaning she'd guessed correctly. "It's fine."

"It's obviously not fine if you're like this." Taesia crossed her arms. "Tell me about the dreams."

Brailee hesitated. Then the stiffness of her shoulders deflated, as if shucking off a weight. "He's just... dragging bodies. I don't know where he's getting them, or what they're being used for. I've tried asking him, but he always seems surprised and afraid when he sees me."

"You're in the dream as yourself?"

"Yes." Her sister rubbed a knuckle between her brows. "Once or twice he's tried to talk to me, but something always stops him."

"Have you been taking the sleeping draughts? Maybe Mother can—"

"Don't tell her," Brailee said quickly. "It'll be fine. I'll handle it."

Taesia was about to argue when the attendant returned for them, bowing.

"Remember, don't overdo it," her mother directed at Taesia. "We're already being targeted. Don't paint the target larger."

"You'll be great," her father added before offering his arm to Elena. Brailee trailed after them and spared Taesia a nervous glance.

Beyond the curtain, she heard the attendant cry: "The House of Lastrider, descendants of Nyx and Queen Arcelia, of the realms Vitae and Noctus!"

The names of her family were called after. Applause rose from below, the gala's revelers feasting their eyes on the Lastriders. Except one was missing. She felt Dante's presence like a ghost, imagined him loping down the staircase with an easy grin and making the young dons and doñas alike vie for his attention.

Instead he was holed up in the Gravespire, awaiting the sentence they all knew was coming, and she was in his rightful place. A place that should never have been hers. A place she had never wanted.

Taesia's pulse sped wildly. Before she had been full of frantic energy, ready to show off, but now...now, it felt hollow. Exploitative. She wished her aunt had come, but Camilla had sent a missive stating she'd eaten something off and would rather not retch before the king. Taesia wondered if she was still mourning Lezzaro and didn't like the thought of attending without him.

She walked up to the still-swaying curtains. Taking a deep breath, she nodded to the attendant.

The curtains parted, and her name was announced. As she stepped out and paused at the top of the grand staircase, she took in the sea of upturned faces, all trying to figure out what to make of her, this spare-turned-heir.

A soft murmur ran across the hall. Taesia allowed herself a moment to enjoy it, to feed off their astonishment.

Really, Violetta had outdone herself with this one. The entire dress was made of thin black mail, the cool metal linking together to form a skirt with a slit that revealed a tasteful amount of leg as she walked. Black tassets hugged the width of her hips, flaring out from the belt of silver cinching her waist. The collar hung low and loose, revealing a large onyx necklace that gleamed beneath her collarbone. A silver, diamond-studded torque around her neck connected to the black pauldrons on her shoulders, from which hung the loose chain mail of her sleeves. After some thought, she had decided to attach a sword to her belt to complete the effect.

It was her declaration that she was Taesia Lastrider, a girl made of shadows and whispers, sharp as a scraped knuckle and guarded as the new moon.

She descended the stairs, hands held open on either side of her body. She indulged in the crowd's attention, silently prompted them not to look away. *This is the good part*, she wanted to whisper in their ears. *Don't miss it.*

A shiver and a sigh, and the darkness came to answer her call. It folded around her as a cloak would, a piece of night turned to cloth. It could have gagged her, blinded her, made her wretched and senseless. But this darkness was as soft as it was forgiving, covering her hands like gloves, circling her throat like a velvet choker, brushing her lips with the worship of an indulgent lover.

The crowd gasped and shifted, and her smile broadened as the darkness flared into a cloak of writhing shadow. The train behind her was impossibly long and wide, curling down the sides of the stairs and wending around ankles like fog. She filled up the entire ballroom with an expanse of glittering black, mirroring the night sky with subtle swirls of purple and navy and garnet, studded with twinkling bits of silver.

Applause rang through the hall, but even she could hear how hesitant it was. Taesia hit the bottom step and reluctantly let the shadows disperse, returning to their nooks and crannies. Despite the way the gentry flinched back, one glance at her parents—her father's grin, her mother's scowl—told her she had done well.

"What a stunning magic you possess."

Taesia's spine turned to steel. Turning, she came face-to-face with Don Soler. His face was impassive, but his lips quirked in a bland imitation of a smile. He held two flutes of sparkling wine.

"Don," she said in greeting. "I thought you would be too busy handling security measures to attend."

He handed her one of the flutes, the liquid a pale gold. She reluctantly accepted, holding it as if it were filled with Nyx's actual piss.

"I'm handling things from the inside," he drawled. Music filled the hall with mournful strings as Don Soler glanced at the corner where King Ferdinand held court. "I don't believe I formally gave my condolences to you and your esteemed House."

You don't give a shit about us, she thought with a tight, polite smile.

"In any case," the don went on, "you're already a fitting representative to your family. Your entrance was quite impressive."

It had been her mother's idea to fashion a cloak of shadow, and Taesia couldn't help but give in to the moment, thoughtless in her desire to impress. A reminder that House Lastrider was powerful, and not to be underestimated.

"I'm sure you'll succeed where your brother did not," Don Soler said, every word a kick to the ribs. "Perhaps his passing will even be a relief."

She went absolutely still.

"Oh," he said, his tone far too casual, "I suppose it hasn't been announced yet. How careless of me."

"If you would please elaborate," she forced out.

"Your lord brother has confessed to killing Prelate Lezzaro." He spread his arms in a helpless gesture that was anything but. "I am afraid he is to be executed, my lady. Again, my deepest condolences."

The floor tilted, the ballroom a blur. She did her best not to seem affected even as a voice screamed in her head, *It's not true. He's only trying to get a rise out of you.*

Well, it was fucking working.

"I must check on my guards. If you'll excuse me." He bowed and slipped back into the crowd. Taesia followed him with her eyes, still unable to move.

The interaction seemed too targeted. Too precise.

As if he was baiting her. Were they beginning to look at her in the same light as Dante?

Dante wouldn't confess because he didn't do it, she thought fiercely. Umbra coiled around her upper arm, sensing her distress. *He's lying.*

She thought of telling her parents, but they were busy mingling with the dons and doñas, and Brailee was nowhere to be found. Servers approached her like bees to a pollen-rich flower, offering delicacies like scallops with hefty flakes of black truffle, salmon mousse on seed wafers, pickled fig with tart cheese, tiny green cakes flavored with bitter Azunese spices. She denied all of them.

She searched the crowd for the king, thinking he, at least, could verify Don Soler's claim. He was flocked by an entirely new group of nobles hoping to prostrate themselves into better social standing. Ferdinand was not a popular man, it was true—his foreign diplomacy and taxation rates were often the subject of grousing—but there was no denying the power he held as the ruler of the Holy Kingdom of Vaega. At least he wasn't as greedy as Queen Geia, who had killed five thousand citizens with hard labor when she'd ordered the construction of a temple dedicated to herself. Or mad like King Muradad, who had declared war on the Arastra Sea and forced his soldiers to stab the water.

She wondered what he thought of the citizens outside his gates, the ones who considered themselves lucky to catch a glimpse of excess without ever experiencing it.

Those gates were another barrier Dante had longed to break.

The king's gaze fell on her, and Umbra tightened around her arm. She was taking a step forward when the attendant on the steps gave another cry.

"The House of Mardova, descendants of Deia and King Agustín, of the realm Vitae!"

They were the biggest House of all, with Adela and her wife Miko plus their twin daughters. One of the twins seemed embarrassed while the other grinned broadly, their black hair adorned with dazzling ornaments in the shapes of the elemental symbols, both wearing Azunese wrap dresses like their mother. The one who was grinning waved at the congregation below.

Then Angelica appeared. She certainly *looked* the part of heir; her throat and fingers glittered with jewelry accenting her crimson dress. The gown was fitted to her torso, the neckline plunging, with a skirt that danced like flames. Her sleeves were of a similar flowy fabric, with a cape fanning out behind her for an added touch of drama.

But it was her face that gave Taesia pause. Her rouge-touched lips were pressed together and trembling, her kohl-lined eyes bloodshot. No amount of makeup could cover the fact Angelica Mardova was exhausted—and scared.

Still, she descended calmly, hands held out before her. In one rested a perfect sphere of water, and above the other rotated a hunk of red clay. Polite applause went through the crowd, although Taesia felt their apprehension like the drawn-out note of the cello in the corner. At first she thought it was because they feared Angelica suddenly lighting up like a torch, but then she realized it was because the clay was being shaped into a crown.

Bold of them, she thought as she eyed the earthen crown levitating above Angelica's palm. *And stupid.*

Once Angelica was reunited with her family, Adela opened her reticule. Angelica quickly dumped the clay inside and poured the water into a glass Miko provided. Her face was already studded with sweat.

Angelica turned and their gazes met. Taesia swallowed her wine too quickly, coughing as the bubbles fizzed in her throat. Angelica's expression darkened, but not in her usual dour way. There was something almost haunted about her.

Taesia shook it off and slipped into the crowd, allowing herself to be preyed on by the dons and doñas, desperate to take her mind off Don Soler's words. They cooed over her entrance, and Taesia pretended to be flattered. She didn't overlook the nobles whispering as she passed, the flash of coins exchanging hands. Part of her wanted to go right up to them and ask what her odds for inheriting the throne were—unless they were betting over whether or not she'd end up like her brother.

There will be no heir, she wanted to tell them, if only to watch their eager faces fall. *My brother will help reform this country until it's unrecognizable.*

"The House of Cyr, descendants of Phos and Queen Mabrian, of the realms Vitae and Solara!"

She turned to find Waren Cyr walking down the stairs. Taesia wondered where Nikolas's mother was. She knew the woman hadn't been well since Rian's death, but thought she'd at least come to the gala.

"The heir of House Cyr, Nikolas Cyr!"

She shoved her empty flute into the hands of the nearest server and stepped forward to get a better view. He appeared at the top of the stairs, dressed in a suit of white and gold.

He was beautiful. His pale hair shone in the lantern light, crystal eyes scanning the crowd below. The collar of his suit was connected with a golden chain, and unlike the real versions on Taesia's outfit, his jacket was stitched with golden embroidery in the patterns of pauldrons and tassets. The Sunbringer Spear shone over his shoulder.

Where Taesia had darkened the staircase moments before, Nikolas lit it up, driving the shadows away.

Her bones ached with the urge to have that light touch her.

As Nikolas descended, he held out a hand. Lux moved and shifted until Nikolas held a sword of pure light. The crowd murmured in appreciation, and Taesia smiled. He looked like a Solarian holy warrior.

She drifted toward him as soon as Waren took off in the direction of the king. Nikolas froze when he saw her.

"Nik," she said.

He took in her dress, lips parted. Lux re-formed into a bangle around his wrist.

Then he averted his eyes. There was something stiff and sad in his expression, a distance she wasn't used to.

"What's wrong?" She came a little closer, as close as she dared with so many eyes on them. "Is it about your mother? Why didn't she come?"

"She's tired, and my father didn't think she should exert herself. I..." Nikolas frowned, and her gut squirmed nervously. Something was definitely wrong.

"Nik. What is it?"

Coming to an abrupt decision, he took her elbow and steered her to one of the side rooms. It was dim and smelled of rose oil, the window casting yellow stars upon the ground. The light of the spear's blade formed a halo about him, the last evanescent ray of sun in a night-choked sky.

He took a deep breath, then another. Taesia didn't dare say anything before he did, even though she longed to tell him about Don Soler, to excise the dread rising up in her. Eventually he mustered up the words.

"I know what you did," he whispered.

"What I...did? What did I do?"

"Where did you get those astralam bones, Tae?"

Her heart picked up a sickening rhythm as she suddenly understood. Understood it the way she knew thunder came after a lightning strike.

A soft, hollow laugh escaped him as he shook his head. "I can't believe it." He rubbed a hand over his mouth, staring at the wall. The silence prickled against her skin. Eventually he turned back to her.

"Or maybe I can," he said softly. "I don't know who you are anymore. Since Dante...No, it started before that. You stopped telling me the truth. You stopped telling me much of anything. You're so invested in your own schemes that you don't make time for anyone or anything else."

She said nothing, because it was true.

There was a specific pain when one was reminded of what could be lost. A fracture in the chest, stealing breath with the promise that one day soon, this beloved thing—this beloved person—would be gone.

Taesia felt that pain as she looked at Nikolas, as she thought back to all their time together, everything they had been through and everything they had been ready to face.

"He was going to kill me," she said slowly.

"Even if it was done in self-defense, why didn't you tell me the truth? You came to me afterward covered in his blood, you even *showed me* those bones, and you didn't say anything. Why?"

She didn't know.

He stepped closer, hesitated before running the backs of his fingers against her cheek. She closed her eyes and focused on the sensation.

"You wear masks, Taesia," he whispered. "One day you're the hero, the next you're the thief, the fool, the killer." His voice broke on the last word, and Taesia's breath caught. "What will you do when all your masks fall? Who will you be then?"

Again she said nothing, because she didn't know. Her heart was a starving inmate in the prison of her rib cage, and it was easy to remember the boy who had shyly held her hand and pressed his lips to her cheek. It was easy to think back on the times where they had lain in bed talking, eating, slowly making love.

But that wasn't who they were anymore. It hadn't been for a while, and she'd been too stubborn to acknowledge it.

And now this—this one stupid decision—had made him see her fully.

Nikolas stepped away, and still she said nothing. She didn't know if the right words even existed.

She couldn't stand to see him walk away from her, so she fled the side room before he could. Her throat was too tight to inhale a proper breath.

"The House of Vakara, descendants of Thana and King Dalvinder, of the realms Vitae and Mortri!"

Taesia's head snapped up. Risha's parents and sister made a handsome family as they made their stately way down the staircase, and her heart stuttered when the curtains parted and Risha herself appeared. It was the first time Taesia had seen her since hearing about the necropolis. But Risha seemed fine, not like someone who had overextended her powers by taking out a horde of angry spirits.

She was dressed in a Parithvian anarkali of black, with golden embroidery spiraling up the wide skirt in vine-like designs. A long, gauzy scarf was draped around her body from shoulder to opposite hip, sheer black trimmed in gold. Her sleeves were long and transparent, more gold crawling up her arms to wrap around the base of her throat. Strangely, her upper body was plain.

Then she lifted her hands and something came from the parted curtains. Bones. She clapped her hands before her, fingers interlocking, and the bones locked around her torso in the same manner. They constructed a corset that finished her outfit, a rib cage encasing her own.

The crowd applauded loudly as Risha descended. Her hair was done up to better reveal the massive gold earrings brushing her neck, her eyes set within a thick ring of kajal. Even Taesia was struck by the sight of her, more goddess than queen.

She made her way toward the Vakaras. Darsha held a hand to Risha's face, smiling proudly as Rath went to greet the king. Saya immediately slipped away, no doubt to find Brailee.

"I need to talk to you," Taesia blurted as soon as she was close.

Risha jumped. "Taesia." She looked to her mother, who pursed her lips but nodded as a handful of doñas surrounded her like sharks. Taesia took Risha's wrist and pulled her into one of the side rooms, far from the one she'd shared with Nikolas, batting away the drapes and peering through the star-shaped latticework to make sure they hadn't been followed.

Risha gently extricated her wrist from her grip. "What's this about?"

"What's this *about*?" A dark feeling brewed in Taesia's gut. "I know it was you."

"What—?"

"Nik. He's turned against me, he . . . He asked you to extract the bone dealer's memories, didn't he?"

Risha turned away and crossed her arms, her bone corset emphasized by the lantern light. Taesia moved to stand before her.

"You knew," Taesia said. "You knew, and you didn't bother to come talk to me, didn't bother to ask why I did it." Risha stared at the floor, and that black feeling was up to her throat now, searing and painful. "What have I done to make you write me off so completely?"

"What have you *done*?" Risha's voice held none of its usual placidity or patience. It was hard and angry, her black-rimmed eyes bright with blame. "Do you not even realize the scene was too similar to how Lezzaro died?"

Taesia stared at her blankly until it clicked. "You think . . . You think I killed the prelate? Even though he was the one helping us?"

"I don't know! I don't know what to think anymore."

She was too furious to properly feel how much that hurt. "The *Conjurers* killed him, Risha. Not me. Not Dante. So far as I know, my body count's only one."

Risha grimaced. "But you hid it from us even after all that talk about working together. Like you're—you're hiding something else, some other motivation behind all this."

The only reason the heirs had warily agreed to invest in the ritual at all was because she'd left out the rest of Dante's plans. "What would I be hiding? The lunatic was going to kill me!"

"So you thought it was fine to kill him instead, and in such a horrible way?"

Those whispers in the shadows had overwhelmed her, feeding the anger in her blood. The days afterward had been odd and fragile, but the more she thought about it, the more she knew she'd made the right choice.

"He deserved it," she growled in Risha's face. Risha flinched but stood her ground. "What I don't understand is why you and Nik are making such a big deal out of this when Don Soler is giving my brother a *death sentence*."

Risha's anger finally cracked. "He what?"

"He told me. Just now." Taesia's ears rang. "He wants to execute my brother. My *brother*, the only heir who gives a shit about our future and is being punished for it."

"The only heir—?" Risha clenched her hands into fists. "But you said Dante was innocent. Why would Don Soler be set on executing him?"

"Because he's a fucking *bastard* and a peon for the king! Because Ferdinand knows he has the upper hand in everything and uses it to his advantage against us."

She forced herself to take a shaking breath. "You want to know why Dante was really so invested in the ritual? It's not just because our realm is dying. It's because if we manage to break the barriers, it'll put the Houses in a position of power greater than Ferdinand. Under the combined efforts of each House, the monarchy wouldn't stand a chance, and we can create a better system not under some"—she flapped her hand toward the crowd—"so-called Holy King. We can forge a better nation that prioritizes the people and not the gentry."

Dante had been so fervent when he told her his plan, and Taesia had been caught up in it for one simple reason: She was tired. Tired of politics, of posturing, of pretending to be someone she was not. She had wanted action more than paperwork, adventure more than meetings with merchants.

But this had gone beyond her simple desire. This wasn't merely about her; it was about all of Nexus, all of Vaega, all the people clustered beyond the palace's gates who yearned for better.

The words didn't have the same effect on Risha, who finally took a step back. The look on her face was a dagger to the neck, and immediately Taesia regretted saying anything at all.

"You lied," Risha whispered. "You were using us all this time to... what, usurp the king?"

"We don't care about the throne! It's hard to explain, but—"

"No, I think I've got it." Risha took another step back, holding up a hand as if to keep Taesia at bay. "You have your vision, and I have mine. But they don't align anymore. Maybe they never have." Risha swallowed, her eyes wet. "We will undo the Sealing, but I'm not going to be a traitor to my kingdom."

Then her oldest friend was gone, the curtains swaying silently behind her.

XIV

Risha forced herself not to give in to tears as she stormed away. Taesia's words, her look of betrayal, twisted into her like a screw.

How could Taesia have done this? Did she revere her brother so much she wanted to follow in his footsteps, all the way to the gallows?

Undoing the Sealing was one thing—to protect their city, their country, their realm—but an insurrection against the king?

Risha crossed the hall, wanting a quiet place to hole herself up in before the dons and doñas had their way with her. She spotted her mother searching the crowd.

"Your fiancé and his father will attend tonight," Darsha had told her at the villa. "You probably shouldn't see each other until the arranged dowry meeting, but he's so handsome, you simply must catch a glimpse of him."

Risha did not want to catch a glimpse of him, or even be in the same room as him. The bones around her torso seemed to tighten, shortening her breath as the enormity of everything crashed down on her.

We can create a better system not under some so-called Holy King. We can forge a better nation that prioritizes the people and not the gentry.

A touch at her shoulder made her jump. She turned and came face-to-face with Angelica.

"Sorry," Risha breathed. "You startled me."

She realized Angelica looked as disoriented as she felt. As if she hadn't slept, hadn't had a peaceful thought in days.

"Where are the others?" Angelica demanded.

"I . . . don't know. Why? What's wrong?"

"I need to talk to you. *All* of you."

* * *

Nikolas had always hated gatherings. It was exhausting to put on smiles and airs. It was exhausting to be part of House Cyr.

It made him miss Rian like a phantom limb. His brother hadn't been big on gatherings either, preferring to keep parties small and intimate, but he had always handled himself with a grace Nikolas envied. A joke here, a compliment there. Rian Cyr had been the jewel of his House.

Nikolas stayed in the side room after Taesia left, sitting on the cushioned bench and holding his head in his hands. He wanted to go home to his mother, to check she was all right, though it would mean risking his father's ire. He'd already felt the beginning of it on the carriage ride here.

But it wasn't only his father that had made him squirm. It had been the looming confrontation with Taesia, the truth weighing on his heart.

She was a murderer. He hadn't wanted to believe it—had been prepared to deny it. But Risha wouldn't lie.

Taesia would, and did, over and over.

Nikolas wiped away a tear on his cheek as voices passed the latticework window.

"Put down ten for Mardova?"

"Not a chance. Twelve for Vakara, and then another five that Cyr goes out in a Conjuration attack."

The voices faded, and Nikolas closed his eyes and reached into his pocket, where he'd put the bracelet with its tree charm. Thoughts of the Solarian refugees had circled his mind for days, but every so often he also thought of the server from the palace. Nikolas had no idea whether or not he would be working the gala, but in case he saw him, at least he could give the bracelet back.

A new shadow darkened the latticework window. Nikolas tensed, ready to have someone come in and spot him, more fuel for gossip—*I saw the Cyr heir crying in a side room, can you believe it?*

But whoever it was didn't enter. It was two men conversing in low tones, and Nikolas found himself straining to hear them.

"He confessed a little too easily, in my opinion." Nikolas recognized the voice of Don Cassian. "As if he's trying to cover for someone. The true leader, perhaps?"

A circlet of gold glinted on the head of the other man as he nodded. *Ferdinand.* "We'll have to wait and see, I suppose."

After a pause, Don Cassian said, "Excuse me for the observation, Your Majesty, but you don't seem particularly worried."

"I have other things on my mind." He lowered his voice even more. "You've made sure they won't come tonight?"

"Yes, Your Majesty. We even have extra guards posted. He will not be a problem, nor will that woman."

"Good."

Nikolas waited until they left to breathe properly again. What in Thana's grave had that been about?

He was still pondering it when the drapes were yanked open. Angelica stood backlit from the hall, a concerned Risha behind her.

"Come with us," Angelica said.

Angelica's hands shook as she stared at the hall below. At her mother in her shimmering turquoise gown, a complement to Miko's deep blue. The twins had run off, no doubt to pilfer the food trays.

She no longer felt that confining fury toward them. Her fingertips brushed the back of her dress, feeling the outline of her piccolo hidden under the large bow.

She had woken up from her recent fever to find it lying on the bed beside her. She'd wrapped her hand around it immediately, afraid it would disappear like a dream, but it had been solid and real. Angelica had had a feeling Adela wouldn't get rid of the instrument, considering her late husband's connection to it. Now it was back where it belonged.

A truce, perhaps, from either her mother or the twins.

"What's this about, Mardova?"

One of the attendants had found Taesia, who now strolled onto the balcony with a dull expression. Nikolas shifted awkwardly and Risha pointedly ignored Taesia's entrance.

"What's this, the dream team's dead?" Angelica drawled.

"We have obligations to speak with the dons and doñas." Risha nodded to the balcony's railing. "We can't afford to be away for long."

"I wouldn't call on you if it wasn't important," Angelica said.

"Tell us, then," Taesia snapped. She darted a glance at the others, but remained ignored.

Where had their willingness to work together gone? Something had definitely rattled them, and here she was, about to make it worse.

"You won't like it," she said at last. "What I'm about to tell you. But you have to know."

Risha lost some of her rigidity and stepped forward. "Angelica? What's happened?"

Short of breath, Angelica turned and grabbed the railing, leaning her weight against it.

"It's useless," she whispered. "This. All of it." She gestured at the gala below them, the mingling gentry who knew no better.

"We admit it's a little over the top, but you know this comes with the territory of being heir," Taesia said. "The parading about, the demonstrations—"

"I mean the ritual." Angelica whirled around. "Godsnight. We can prepare and plan as much as we like, but it won't matter."

"You're not making sense," Risha said gently. "What are you talking about?"

Taesia sighed, long and slow. "You're getting cold feet. I knew this would happen."

"That's not it." Angelica again touched the hidden piccolo at her back. "I got the grimoire. I've been reading it. Doing what research I can."

Excitement spilled back into Taesia's expression. "You got it already? What does it say? What did you learn about Godsnight?"

Angelica licked her cracked lips, tasting rouge.

"I learned it won't be possible," she whispered. "Because we have nothing to represent Ostium. The fifth realm on the Cosmic Scale."

Angelica's statement was met with silence. Taesia uncrossed her arms as Nikolas and Risha shared an uneasy glance, but they still wouldn't turn in her direction.

"How much wine have you had tonight, Mardova?" Taesia finally asked.

"Don't you dare start on one of your little *jokes*," Angelica hissed, poking a finger hard into Taesia's chest. "This isn't funny."

Nikolas dragged his incredulous gaze away from Risha. "Angelica—"

"*Shut up*, Cyr." Angelica took a moment to compose herself, the temperature around her growing hotter.

Then, in words that were stilted and hoarse, she explained what she had read in Lezzaro's grimoire. The sketch of the Cosmic Scale, of something called quintessence, and Ostium—a supposed fifth realm burned out of the universe and everyone's memories.

"Which means Taesia's bullshit plan won't work," Angelica finished. "Because the ritual doesn't require four heirs, it requires *five*. And we have no fifth heir to represent Ostium."

"This...this can't be right," Nikolas murmured. "We would have known about this, wouldn't we? This should have been in all our history books, findings from planar scholars—"

"Unless the gods wanted the knowledge gone," Risha whispered with growing horror.

Taesia scoffed. "After all the planning and work we've done so far, you really want to sabotage this?"

"*I'm* not the one sabotaging it," Angelica spat, eyes narrowed. "If anything, it's *you* who's set us up for sabotage by making us follow your brother's senseless plan!"

"It's not senseless," Taesia growled. "It will *work*."

It had to. She couldn't have done all of this—getting the bones, the grimoire, losing Nikolas and Risha in the process—only for things to fall apart now. For her to lose her chance of making a difference and freeing Dante.

She had nearly died for this. She had *killed* for it.

"If there really was a fifth heir, then performing the ritual without them would backfire," Risha said. "It would end up becoming another Conjuration attack. And like Tambour Lake and the Aguerrean mines, there'll be consequences."

"There's something else," Angelica said.

But before she could speak, a loud clinking sounded from below. King Ferdinand stood upon the dais where the band had been playing. Guards were positioned all around him, not letting anyone close.

"I thank you all for coming," Ferdinand began. "We've had some trying times as of late, including mourning our beloved late prelate, may Thana guide his soul."

"May Thana guide his soul," the crowd murmured back.

"But I know he would have wanted us to honor tradition, and Godsnight will soon be upon us. Every hundred years as the Cosmic Scale aligns, we celebrate the riches of our realm, and the awe-inducing splendor of the larger universe. It also used to be a phenomenon of divine magic, when the Houses used the gods' power for miracles."

The other heirs tensed beside her, sensing what was coming.

"Although the Sealing prevents this ancient custom from coming to fruition, I am certain our revered Houses can and will provide us with the enchantment we so desperately need in our lives." He nodded, and the four House heads, who had been standing at the fore of the crowd, stepped forward. "Godsnight will once again be a show of divine power, a reminder to those who embrace the heretical practice of Conjuration what true magic looks like!"

Applause broke out, some even whistling or shouting their approval. The heads of the Houses bowed, ever subservient to the Holy King's wishes.

Up on the balcony, silence fell between the heirs as, one by one, they realized what this meant. Taesia felt it like a rake through sand, a sudden erecting of barriers that, if they had been smart, they should have put up a long time ago. They were heirs of disparate Houses. Heirs to a throne. Heirs to a universe divided and broken.

Heir. The word had haunted Taesia since Dante was taken. Her grip tightened on the railing as the truth crackled and settled along her veins like hoarfrost. If the ritual couldn't be completed without a fifth heir, then the others would no doubt bend to their families' wishes and take part in Godsnight as the king wished it—not as Dante and Lezzaro wished it.

The tension drew out tighter than a string on Angelica's violin when it was suddenly broken by a resounding crash.

Dons and doñas screamed as the dome above them shattered, fracturing the young night with shards of glass. A particularly long and jagged piece struck a man at the base of his throat and sent him to the floor in a spray of bright blood.

Shapes crawled from the broken dome and onto the ceiling as others began to punch up through the floor, cracking the black granite apart. Shapes made of sinew and curving bone, with grinning teeth and hollow eyes.

"No," Risha gasped.

Guards had been posted along every wall and door, along hallways and the courtyard and the ballroom, and all throughout the necropolis.

No one had thought to guard the royal mausoleum below their feet.

XV

Julian was only half listening to one of Taide's bawdy jokes when they heard the screaming. A second later, warning bells began to clang.

"It was too much to hope for a peaceful fucking night, huh?" Paris griped as he unsheathed his twin swords. All around them soldiers were getting their weapons out, gleaming in the torchlight.

Julian primed his bow, and not a moment too soon. An eerie wail sounded from above before something leapt off the roof and into the courtyard. Julian fired an arrow into its chest, but it did little to slow its progress.

"Oh, fuck me," Paris muttered as the thing came into the light, more dropping behind it.

It was a half-rotted skeleton, jaw agape and sockets staring blankly at them. A soldier swooped in to attack and it turned with alarming speed, digging its fingers into the soldier's eyes. Balls of fire came to life within Komi's palms, which he shot at the corpse until it screamed and fell back. Julian abandoned his bow for his sword, hacking at the skeleton's ribs until it fell apart.

"We need to get to Lord Cyr!" Gem called.

They ran for the ballroom. Julian could *feel* whatever was wrong— a swirling, sickening maelstrom. He clenched his teeth and ran harder, tugged forward by that sinister call.

Nikolas was pushed back from the railing as something rammed into him. It reached for his chest with bony claws as a putrid stink filled his nose.

He couldn't grab his spear. Instead, Lux formed into a blade of light and he stabbed it through the creature's ribs. The thing twisted and hissed, but didn't seem much affected. He soon realized why—it was a corpse, its clothing in tatters, skin so old it had adhered to bone like leather.

Another blade punctured its neck, black point sticking out of its withered throat only an inch above Nikolas's forehead. The corpse shrieked and writhed as it fell to the balcony's floor. Taesia removed her shadow dagger.

Nikolas opened his mouth to thank her, but the words stuck in his throat. When she held out a hand to help him up, he ignored it and got to his feet on his own.

"How is this possible?" Angelica demanded of no one, her face drained of color. "Where did they come from?"

"The mausoleum," Risha whispered. "Saya. I have to find her." She bolted for the stairs, Angelica following behind. Taesia hesitated, glancing at him one last time before she also took off.

Corpses scuttled over the ceiling and down the walls of the ballroom, more ascending from the mausoleum through the broken-up floor. Lux was still formed as a blade of light. With his other hand he grabbed the Sunbringer Spear, glowing and ready for a fight, to finally be wielded.

Down on the main floor, dons and doñas were screaming in panic, chaos overtaking the masses as guards rushed in. The elementalists used chunks of broken granite, water from the refreshment table, fire from the lanterns, anything they could reach to do damage to the shambling and shuddering dead. Even the servers were cowering and attempting to flee, and Nikolas wondered if Fin was somewhere in the mayhem.

His father battled back the corpses, his familiar a shield of light in one hand, a sword of steel in the other. A true comandante fighting for king and country while Nikolas stood numb and dazed in the middle of the fray.

"My lord!"

He turned to his unit with a surge of relief. Gem's eyes were round and Komi was whispering prayers in Mariian-Azunese pidgin.

"My lord, what do we do?" Taide asked.

Nikolas gripped the spear tighter. *You are their leader. Give them orders.*

"The Conjurers have breached the palace," he said. "Find them and subdue them with any means necessary. Or else find their Conjuration circles and destroy them. Split up to cover more ground."

They nodded and took off, but Julian paused. He was staring at the staircase—specifically, at Taesia slamming her sword into the skeletons attempting to grab her and her sister's ankles.

Nikolas didn't have time to wonder about it. The air around him gave off an energy that raised the hairs along his arms and neck. *Lightspeed.* Lux pulsed as Nikolas opened himself up to it, the fight-or-flight instinct tickling his ribs, urging him into action.

A shriek cut through the air as a woman across the hall was dragged back by her hair. The corpse that had hold of her clicked its teeth together as if laughing.

Nikolas ran forward. *Go. GO.*

He let the warmth spread through his body, legs alighting with adrenaline, Lux's glow enveloping him as he shot forward with a crack. He stumbled as his feet reconnected with the ground a couple feet away, but he kept going, kept holding on to that lightness, that warmth.

Go!

Another crack and pop, another couple of feet forward. The young woman screamed as blood trickled down her scalp. She was still so far away.

He wouldn't make it.

Wings, he thought, *luminous and golden, wings, give me wings, please*—

The light sputtered around him even as he shot forward another foot—then half a foot—

A roar and a burst of light. A loud *crack* reverberated through the hall as Waren Cyr used his lightspeed to step out of time, reappearing before the corpse with sword at the ready.

From his back sprouted two large, golden wings of light.

Waren lopped the corpse's head off, catching the woman before she could fall to the ground. Once she was set down, Waren turned.

Nikolas stared at his father's wings shimmering as bright as his shield. He wore a mask of rage that made Nikolas think for one terrifying moment his father would turn his sword on him next.

But his father's glare moved past him. "Nikshä!"

Nikolas turned, blocking the downward swing of a weapon with his spear. The clash jarred his arm and made him gasp, but he maintained his position.

When he realized what had attacked him, his knees nearly buckled.

He had only seen portraits and statues of her, but she bore enough of a resemblance even after centuries underground. She had been entombed within a fortified crypt, after all, her body doused with the strongest embalming fluid and blessed by the earliest necromancers to slow the rate of decay.

She stared at Nikolas with cloudy eyes, the skin of her face pressed close to her bones and her lips shrunken inward. Her hair fell in black curls, the dress she had been buried in ripped and stained with dirt.

Queen Mabrian, the Warrior Queen of Vaega, the one blessed by Phos to bear his god-touched child.

The sword she held against the Sunbringer Spear was long and brutal, a blue vein running through the fuller made of lapis lazuli. Mabrian had worn that sword everywhere. She had famously used it to behead a Parithvian ambassador who had attempted a coup.

Now she wielded it against her own descendant.

When Risha found her family, Rath was standing before Darsha and Saya, string held between his fingers.

"Get your mother and sister out," Rath ordered without even a glance in her direction, focused on the congregation of the dead. Risha had no idea so many nobles had been buried in the mausoleum.

"I can help you fight," Risha stressed.

"You're not fully recovered."

"I *am*." And to prove it, she turned and held her hands before her as if clutching on to an invisible ball. The bones of her corset stirred, and as she pried her hands apart, they followed the motion, releasing her torso like an opening claw.

She slid one foot back and shot her arms out before her. The rib bones hurtled through the air, stabbing into the nearest corpse. With a shriek it tumbled to the floor.

"Whoa," Saya breathed.

Rath twisted the string in his hands to force spirits from the bodies they had claimed. "Risha, please. Get your mother out of here, then you and Saya can help the guards at the front."

"All right," she agreed. "Amaa, follow me. Saya, do you have your string?"

Her sister took out a ball of string from the pocket of her lehenga. Risha found the loose string she had purposefully left in her sleeve and pulled, gathering the golden thread in her hands. "Do as I do."

Darsha pressed a desperate kiss to Rath's grim mouth before following her daughters. Risha felt loath to leave him; though his sherwani was dark, she could detect a bloodstain where his injury from the necropolis lay.

But he wasn't the only one fighting. Waren Cyr flew above them on wings of light as Adela Mardova used whips of water and air to blast apart whatever corpses came near. On their way to the staircase, Risha spotted Elena Lastrider weaving a blanket of darkness around a group of corpses. When one tried to attack her from behind, she stepped into her own shadows and disappeared, reappearing with a blade she used to lop the corpse's head off.

The king was nowhere in sight. His personal guard must have already helped him escape to the palace's safe room.

Risha hurried her mother and sister onward, preparing string across the loom of her fingers. Saya copied her as best she could as they ran.

A shrill neigh rent through the air, making them cringe.

"Is that a *horse*?" Saya gasped.

There was, in fact, the undead body of a horse galloping through the ballroom. But it wasn't a normal horse—it was an equille, a beast with a long, spiral horn on its head and a taste for flesh, likely the famed war steed of an old monarch. It was going mad skewering as many people as it could.

Risha sketched a spell with her string. As she concentrated, dons and doñas rushed past for the exit. Saya huddled close to her as Darsha fervently prayed behind them, jeweled hands clasped before her, bangles rattling as she shook.

The equille jerked and slowly turned to Risha as her claiming spell took hold, its white eyes farseeing. Gradually she strengthened her connection to it, its sinew and bones, its joints and cartilage. With a twitch of her finger, Risha sent out an order for the equille to charge, skewering a corpse in the entryway with its long horn.

With the equille guarding the stairs and clearing a path for frightened dons and doñas to escape, they navigated the entryway. From here Risha could see the courtyard, washed in darkness relieved by torches and moonlight glinting off weapons and bone. The gentry flooded the area where the carriages were parked, fighting one another to climb into them first, shoving people to the ground in their haste to escape.

Risha spotted a House guard and whistled to get their attention. "Take Lady Vakara back to the villa!"

Darsha reached for Saya's wrist. "Saya, come!"

"No, I'm staying to help."

There was no time for this. Risha got between Saya and their mother, and Darsha stumbled back.

"Go!" Risha ordered before dragging Saya back through the entryway.

"You didn't have to do that," Saya said as she fumbled with her string.

"You can berate me later. Focus now. Follow my lead."

"Brute."

"Wretch."

She and Saya searched for corpses to reanimate, using them as shields to protect the guards from oncoming attacks. Their clothing had once been lavish, a glint of gold here, a swing of a tassel there. Sweat ran in rivulets down her body as she worked, Saya out of breath at her side.

A faint, persistent sensation unfurled inside her. It was larger than the spirits surrounding them, not a single point of bitterness but rather a whole galaxy's worth, endless and cold and terrible. Risha's concentration flagged as she turned toward it, unable to pinpoint its origin but knowing it was near. Near enough to call to her with resentment laced with urgency. The longer she focused the more her power flared and reached, searching, grasping, wanting to break that galaxy open and spill all the stars it hid.

"Risha!"

She followed her sister's gaze toward the middle of the ballroom. Three corpses were pulling themselves up from the cracks in the floor and rolling their necks grotesquely. Immediately she noticed their state of decomposition was less, their clothing much finer, as if more care had been put into their burials.

One of them lifted his head and a riot of shadows emanated off his body. Another encased herself within a nimbus of bright light. A third held out his emaciated hands as hunks of granite flew to them, whittling into sharp points.

No.

"They're wielding magic," Saya whispered. She was trembling, the string between her fingers slackening. "Aren't those...the House founders?"

Three out of four, at least. The founders of Lastrider and Cyr and Mardova walked purposefully into the chaos. The founder of Vakara House was nowhere to be seen.

This was impossible. Spirits who had possessed magic in their life weren't able to be reanimated unless a Vakara performed the spell, and all three Vakara necromancers were fighting the dead.

A flash of bone in her memory, strung across a black-clad chest like a smile.

Leshya's necklace.

The Revenants had learned a new trick.

Angelica found Miko and her daughters huddled in a corner, Miko standing protectively in front of them with her arms held out, long sleeves trailing nearly to the floor.

"Where's my mother?" Angelica demanded.

Miko nodded toward the center of the hall. Adela had surrounded herself with a ring of water, tendrils lashing out in sharp whips. When a corpse got too close, Adela shoved her palm forward and a blast of air sent it hurtling into the wall hard enough to make it crack. She followed it with a blast of fire that made the surrounding enemies stagger back.

"Angelica!"

Miko's scream made her refocus. There were corpses headed right for them. Kikou yelped as Eiko yanked a knife from her sleeve with a grimace.

Angelica reached behind her to undo the dress's bow. Pulling out the piccolo, she played a trill that sent a wave of air crashing into the corpses. They screeched as they went flying.

The trill caught Adela's attention, and her nostrils flared at the sight of the piccolo. But all she said was, "Get them to safety!"

Blood pooled over the floor, bodies lying at haphazard angles. Angelica swore and ripped the skirt of her dress to better run, then gestured at Miko and the twins to follow her.

She kept the piccolo at the ready, blowing sharp notes every time the dead came near. By the time they reached the courtyard, Angelica was gasping for breath. As a corpse turned toward her, Angelica pulled off her shoes and stabbed a heel into its jellied eye.

"Find the House guards," Angelica said as she turned back to the ballroom.

"What about you?" Kikou demanded. Eiko's knife trembled in her hand. "Your elements—"

"*Go*," Angelica growled even as a prickling heat began to build in her palms.

Miko squeezed Angelica's shoulder. "Be careful." She grabbed her daughters and ran for the House guards.

As Angelica returned to the ballroom, something struck her side and sent her crashing down the stairs. She landed hard on her back, the breath knocked from her lungs. Wheezing, she looked up to find the corpse of a man staring down at her.

She knew his face. It hung in the Mardova villa, the portrait of a man with a dark goatee and piercing blue eyes, as piercing as the single eye upon Deia's chest.

Cordero Mardova, the founder of her House.

He lashed at her again with water. She dodged and it fractured the stone beneath her. Scrambling to her feet, Angelica fumbled with her piccolo and played a single sharp note.

The air she shot at him was easily batted away with a spear of granite he held in his hand. The dark spike was red with blood that dripped off its point. Angelica backed away, breathing hard.

"L-Lord Cordero," she tried, her voice wavering under the din of screams and the shrieking of the dead. "I'm a Mardova. Please, put down your weapons."

But he advanced again, mindless in his pursuit. Angelica fueled her power into the piccolo, hardening the air into a shield before her. He crashed through it as if it were no stronger than a mild breeze.

She dodged and attacked as well as she could. His granite spikes tore into her arms and punches of air sank into her stomach, making her double over. Sweat and blood tickled her skin, and her entire body lit up with heat, fierce and delicious and taunting.

Desperate, Angelica held up the piccolo and channeled all her power into its notes.

Cordero turned it against her, her own attack slamming her to the ground. The piccolo spun from her grasp. A hunk of granite landed on top of it with a terrible, sickening *crunch*.

"No!" she screamed. She scrambled to her knees. "No, no, no—"

The sound of it breaking apart echoed through her body.

Her father had given it to her when she was ten. He'd winced at her first shrill notes, then clapped when she could perform her own songs.

Now both were gone.

"Angelica!"

Someone stood behind her, shielding her. She turned and found Risha facing down Cordero Mardova, golden string wrapped so tight around her fingers they had begun to bleed.

"What are you waiting for?" Angelica shouted. "Get the spirit out!"

"He's—strong," Risha panted. Cordero was paused in the middle of his next attack, bloodied spikes ready to rip Angelica apart. "You—need to help me!"

Angelica's hands were empty without the piccolo, but heat swirled under her skin, begging for release. Her palms shone with an orange aura, like the sun behind a mountain. She forced herself to breathe, to settle herself and get back to the fight, but something in Risha's expression, her tone, had further ignited the wick inside her.

Angelica wondered what would happen if Cordero killed Risha here, if she had one less heir to worry about come Godsnight.

Risha bared her teeth as her arms shook. "Angelica!"

Cordero finally broke out of her hold and charged. Angelica raised her glowing hands and let go of the fury building heat around her heart.

Flames fanned in all directions, uncontrolled. They caught Cordero Mardova within their unruly trajectory, barely giving him time to stumble before his body was charred beyond recognition.

"Stop!" someone was screaming. "*Stop!*"

Angelica closed her hands into fists as the fire sputtered, resisting the urge to release more of it. She let loose a small, pathetic sound, relief flooding her veins.

She turned away from the smoking, blackened corpse and saw Risha clutching her arm, face screwed up in agony. Saya Vakara was holding on to her sister. She shot Angelica a half-terrified, half-furious look.

"Get away from her!" Saya yelled.

The fire slowly died as Angelica took in the angry welt on Risha's arm, half her sleeve burnt away. Tears stained Risha's cheeks and smudged her kohl, and Angelica felt a terrible swoop in her belly.

She turned and fled deeper into the fight, seeking bodies to decimate.

Taesia's first instinct was to get her sister and father to the carriages. Brailee cried out her name as soon as Taesia slammed the carriage door in her face. She knew Brailee wanted to stay, but her grasp on the shadows had never been particularly strong. Taesia gritted her teeth, her sister's fright drilling holes into her newly awakened rage.

Lezzaro, you sadistic bastard, she thought as she headed back for the entryway. The cool mail of her skirt brushed heavy against her thighs. *You knew about a fifth realm, didn't you? If your corpse were here, I'd shove my sword so far up its ass—*

Her thoughts were interrupted by the appearance of more corpses. Taesia let herself fall into familiar movements as she spun her sword in a blur of steel, biting into decayed flesh and bone. Umbra remained a dagger of shadow in her other hand, a complement to her blade as she followed through with her attacks. The shadows inched toward her, wanting to envelop her, to do her bidding.

Her dress was quickly covered in the white powder of bone debris. The dons and doñas huddled in the entryway took one frightened look at her before running into the courtyard where she'd cleared a path.

"You're welcome," she grumbled.

Umbra trembled in her grip as the shadows quivered around her. Taesia's heart pounded as the whispers pressed in close. They spoke nonsense words, or a language she couldn't translate, but their intent was clear enough: They longed to be used. They longed for her to control them.

A familiar voice broke through the tide of whispers. Don Soler was barking out orders to the guards, getting them in formation.

I'm sure you'll succeed where your brother did not. Perhaps his passing will even be a relief.

Taesia's grip on her weapon tightened as opportunity opened up before her. She breathed in, breathed out.

She remained hidden until the don turned back toward the entryway, flanked by two guards. It was quick work to fling out her shadows and slam the guards against the nearest wall, letting them drop to the ground unconscious. Before Don Soler could react, she grabbed him and pulled him into her darkness.

A high, thin noise left him as he scrabbled at her hands. It was just the two of them in this lonely little pocket of the courtyard, and she parted the shadows to reveal his wide, terrified eyes. They landed on her face, her spreading grin.

"Don," she greeted.

"What do you want with me?" he snarled. "If His Majesty knew of this—"

"I don't give a shit about him." Taesia's fingers tightened in his jacket. "Tell me how my brother supposedly *confessed.*"

His breaths came fast and shallow, gaze fixed on the mesmerizing churn of shadows around them.

"That is a matter of confidentiality," he said. "It's my duty to the Holy King to—"

"I said I don't give a *shit* about him!" The shadows wrapped around Don Soler's limbs, slithering up his body like living snakes. He whimpered as one wound around his neck. "How. Did. Dante. *Confess.*"

The don's attempt at a sneer was weak. "There was never any hope for him after the evidence at your villa. That brat couldn't even cover up his own crimes."

Taesia's fingers threatened to rip through the fabric of his jacket. The shadows similarly tightened their grip, making him choke.

"Careful, Don," she whispered. "You've ripped apart House Lastrider. Do you think I'll let you get away with that?"

"Dante Lastrider is a dangerous individual!" he spat. "The seed of a god, killing a prelate? Willing to harm a god-appointed ruler? Could you imagine the horror that would wreak on this realm? You should be glad I put a stop to what he was planning. The Houses ruin this city with the poison they call politics. If one of them is locked up, all the better!"

"Poison," she repeated. She leaned in. "You'd do better to look to your own so-called *Holy King* if you want to draw the poison out of this city."

"You—!"

"Go on, tell me I'm wrong."

The shadows crept closer, blocking out the stars, the moon, whispering secrets of what they hid in their depths. Umbra shivered as blood roared in her ears.

"Heretics," Don Soler rasped, "deserve to die. Dante Lastrider is no exception."

Taesia closed her eyes and felt the shudder of the night pressed close, the rattle of the cosmos far above her. It sang in her blood and urged her heart to beat a war march. She could have become a new star with how hot she burned.

When she opened her eyes, her smile was bright as the glint off a blade's edge.

"You've miscalculated, Don," Taesia whispered. "Dante isn't the dangerous one."

He didn't have time to scream before the shadow around his neck severed his head clean from his body. His arms and legs were sliced away as easily as a knife through fat. Blood, red and bright, sprayed her as he fell in a dismembered heap.

"I am."

XVI

There was a reason Mabrian had been called the Warrior Queen. As she fought against Nikolas, he was quickly brought to his limit, his arms screaming at the strain. He sent Lux to push her back, creating openings for the Sunbringer Spear to do what it did best.

It was his first time actually wielding it, spinning it in his hands as the glow of the metal wings created a nimbus along the blade. Although it was largely meant for combat in the air, aided by wings, it gave him a longer reach at close distances.

The queen was determined to slip through his attack radius. He let her come, angling the spear across his chest to catch the fall of her blade. He twirled it to disarm her, but she flowed with the motion rather than fought against it, retreating slightly with sword still in hand. With the distance regained, he switched to offensive, keeping her at bay. She easily dodged and skipped aside, sometimes using the flat of her blade to bat him away.

His father had also joined the fight. He still bore his wings, and when he wordlessly held out a hand, Nikolas tossed him the spear, using Lux as a sword as his father used the advantage of the air to strike at Mabrian. Waren tossed the spear back once there was another opening and Nikolas swept low, trying to cut her legs out from under her.

"How is this possible?" Waren asked as he landed beside Nikolas, watching Mabrian recover and ready her sword again.

They were about to rush back in when a flash of light hit them both in the chest, sending them sprawling. Waren righted himself by flipping through the air, but Nikolas rolled painfully over the ground before coming to a stop.

A woman had come to stand beside Mabrian. While the queen was short and muscular, the woman bathed in light was tall and willowy, her hair pale gold and the tips of her ears pointed. Her eyes burned yellow all around.

"Avestra," Waren breathed, looking as if he were about to fall to one knee. Nikolas, already on one knee, gaped at the corpse of Avestra Cyr, daughter of Mabrian and Phos, the founder of their House.

The original owner of the Sunbringer Spear.

Mother and daughter lunged at the same time. Nikolas took on Avestra as she attempted to reclaim her spear, pulses of golden energy flooding the ballroom. Wings of light burst from Avestra's back before Waren got between them and they took to the air, god-given power against god-given power.

"Nik, get out of the way!"

Risha. He dove to the floor as something slammed into Mabrian from behind, the point of a weapon driving through her chest and lifting her into the air. No—not a weapon, but a horn. The undead equille that had skewered the former queen of Vaega tossed her aside like a rag doll.

Risha and Saya hurried toward him. Risha was in a rough state, her fingers bleeding and a large, angry burn mark on her arm. "Are you all right?"

"I should be asking you that," Nikolas panted. "Thanks." Above them, his father and Avestra kept colliding with brilliant flashes of gold. "I can't believe Conjuration did this. I thought magic users couldn't be resurrected?"

"They can't." Risha swallowed. "But I think I know what's causing it. I have to go down to the mausoleum."

He got to his feet. "I'll go with you."

"No, I need you to stay and keep Saya safe. Some of the other monarchs were born elementalists, and Damarion Lastrider is running around somewhere."

Indeed, he found a tall man wreathed in shadows fighting against Elena Lastrider on the other side of the ballroom, their darkness pitted against the light from this end. Where was Taesia? Why wasn't she helping her mother?

"I can handle myself," Saya argued, and Risha put a hand on her sister's back.

"I know, bhina, which is why you need to look after Nik as well. Take control of the equille. I'll put an end to this."

"Risha—"

But she was already running toward the largest crack in the ground, where the dead had crawled out like insects, and she leapt into the mausoleum below.

Taesia stared down at Don Soler's body as the shadows swept over her. Distantly she thought of Risha and Nikolas, their disappointment at her killing a madman. What would they say if they knew she'd done this?

But it was irreversible. Don Soler was in pieces, bleeding over her shoes, and she couldn't stitch him back together even if she wanted to.

Her mind was curiously blank—relieved or satisfied, or maybe shocked—but her body was another story. It was still twitchy, still eager for action, still wanting a *fight*.

Slowly she turned back for the entryway. If there were corpses to clear out of the ballroom, she was more than up to the task. Her power was liquid and sweet, filling her veins like starlight.

But as she entered the cleared-out entryway, footsteps echoed off the walls, step-*clunk*, step-*clunk*. Taesia stopped and appraised the corpse making its way toward her, limping along the red carpet runner. Her face, though waxy with death, was long and bore the hints of former beauty.

Taesia had grown up with stories of the woman before her. How Nyx had come to her in dreams, seducing her slowly, quietly, leaving her breathless and aching in the morning. When Vaega had gone to war with Cardica over trade with Marii, she had called upon his help, and he had answered by unleashing beasts called Nightmares within the enemy's camps. In return, he asked to lie with her—not in dreams, but in reality.

When her stomach began to swell, she and her consort had made the most of it by proclaiming it far and wide—"Queen Arcelia is with child by the god Nyx! Holy seed ripens in her womb!"—which had the citizens abuzz with both the scandal and the honor of it all.

The child was raised in the palace as Arcelia and her consort made children of their own. When one of them attempted to stab a dagger through the holy heir's heart, Arcelia had reluctantly banished her first child to found the third of Nexus's Houses, Lastrider.

One of Arcelia's hands gripped an elegant cane she must have been buried with, a necessity after a childhood injury had left her in constant pain. Stories said she had concealed a blade inside.

The stories became true as Arcelia pulled a thin, devious rapier from the cane's handle.

Grinning, Taesia gratefully sank back into a fighting stance. "Pardon me, Your Majesty. Or can I call you Great-Great-Great-Great-Grandmother?"

Arcelia did not speak—or rather, the spirit possessing her did not speak. She attacked all at once, her speed and strength a welcome distraction. Though Taesia's blade was bigger, Arcelia was an expert in hers, moving it in quick flashes of steel.

"Good to know I inherited this from you," Taesia panted as she blocked and evaded. Umbra, still in dagger form, slashed at Arcelia's arms as Taesia waited to go on the offensive. Instead, she found herself with her back against the wall.

Arcelia was no longer alone. A trickle of corpses spilled from the ballroom, skeletal fingers reaching, mouths agape, their fine clothes torn.

Taesia ducked as the rapier's tip plunged toward her chest. It embedded in the wall instead, and Taesia took her chance to call in the eager shadows around her.

Her shock was beginning to trickle back into rage at everything she'd learned, everything she had been denied, the precarious position she was in thanks to the woman who bore down on her. If only she hadn't lain with Nyx—if the House of Lastrider had never been formed—

The shadows whispered and jumped forward. She caught each and every one she could find, baring herself to the very bottom of her well of power, as if ripping open her own chest.

The world around her slowed, then blasted apart with darkness.

She was in that darkness; she was its master. It plunged the entryway into a night so thick it was suffocating. Taesia's whole body shook as it scraped against the boundaries of her control, demanding more, demanding everything from her.

In the shadows, she was beyond death and life—she was the breath tentatively connecting them. Delicate as gossamer. More powerful than crowns or wars or blades. Unseen, patient, devastating.

Although her family dealt in death, Risha had never been inside the royal mausoleum.

As she fell into the vault where the dead had congregated, she managed to land on a body and break her fall, as well as their rib cage. She winced at the crunch as the burn on her arm throbbed.

Risha staggered out of the archway of the vault. Beyond was a much wider hall, supported by white stone bricks and inlaid with precious jewels. Tombs had been built along the walls, marble and stone and wrought iron broken apart under the vicious strength of the raised dead. Lamps flickered against the floor and low ceiling, across the cheeks of statues and ancient weapons forgotten in the mad scramble to annihilate the living.

Standing in the middle of the hall was the man in the skull mask. He wore the necklace of finger bones, which shone with a black radiance. One hand was held out before him, braced against the back of a corpse.

Leshya Vakara.

The House founder's head was tilted back, eyes wide open and glowing black. A dark mist traveled over her body, weaving around her arms that ended in fingerless hands, even spewing out of her slack mouth. Both she and the man were standing within a gently pulsing Conjuration circle.

"Ah," the man said, his voice muffled behind his mask. "I was wondering when you'd show up."

Risha prepared her string. Her sleeves were ragged and torn by now, the golden threads she'd been using needing to be replaced once they snapped.

"So the necropolis was a test run," she rasped.

"Yes."

"You're using the necklace to reanimate bodies that held magic."

"Also yes."

"Why?"

He didn't answer at first. The black mist spooled around Leshya Vakara, tendrils snaking across the floor and ceiling, fueling the undead above.

The man bent his head. "I told you before: We're trying to find a way to Mortri. Believe it or not, we have the same goals as you and your family. The dead are a problem. They need to move on."

"How is *this* the way to do it?"

"We need a strong gathering of spirits to force the barrier open. The necropolis wasn't enough, so this became our target. And thanks to your ancestor here, I found a way to get them all to wake up at once."

"And attack innocent people!"

"I . . ." He made a small, pained sound. "I don't know why they became so fierce. As soon as I came down here, this acted up." He gestured to the necklace. "I called in the spirits, but they were all resentful. We only meant for the spirits to clear out the ballroom. We didn't want them to *attack*."

"Then you have to stop!" Risha stepped forward, cut-up hands extended with her new thread.

He stayed put, and she could hear the regret in his words. "I can't stop. Not until the spirits' energy culminates and the barrier is forced open. They're resentful enough that it should work." Then quieter, almost to himself: "It has to work."

"It's *not* working," Risha growled. She took a few more steps, sensing the strange energy of the circle, the bitter cold emanating off Leshya's corpse. "Stop this. *Now*."

"You can work with us instead of against us," the man insisted. "Ensure no one else will get hurt."

"No."

"There's so much more to necromancy than you or I know, secrets that have long since died after she did." He pushed lightly on Leshya's back and she swayed. "We can figure them out together."

"I said *no*."

The string between her bleeding fingers shivered. There was too much energy in this hall, emanating off of Leshya, feeding the spirits above. Risha's breath quickened, her lungs aching.

She was closer, now. From this distance she could sense the pathway of the man's veins, the map of his bones. Something jerked awake inside her as the string unraveled and fell to the floor. Her blood flowed under the echo of another pulse, all around her the forceful pounding of a wild heart.

Some primordial instinct took over. She closed her hands into tight fists, keeping her eyes on the man's skull mask as that bright, pounding sensation between them tensed and the second heartbeat faltered.

The man stumbled back and gasped, releasing his hold on Leshya to clutch his chest. Risha ran forward and entered the circle, crying out as its power whipped at her legs.

She wrapped her arms around Leshya's body. Within the cold torus of her power, power that had been handed down from this woman, she let their energies combine. Risha screamed as it ripped into her, out of her, up into the night where the undead reigned.

Together, their power forced all the spirits out of their reanimated bodies. Risha felt them collapse one by one. Leshya shuddered in her arms.

And then the founder of House Vakara turned to bone and dust, falling between her fingers like sand.

Risha sank to the floor after her, letting her world go dark. She was asleep but not, aware but not. She could hardly feel it when a pair of strong arms lifted her up, a quickened heartbeat beneath her ear.

"I'm sorry," said a shaking voice above her. "I didn't mean for it to go this far. I...hope I can earn your forgiveness. Lillum Street. We'll be waiting for you."

Risha's wrecked fingers twitched, but she couldn't speak, couldn't answer.

"I have no idea what you did," that voice whispered, "but please never do it again."

Her father had given her so many lectures over the years it was sometimes difficult to remember them all, but she knew first and foremost that necromancy was a magic used only against the dead, a way to manipulate, seal, and recover.

And yet she had nearly killed a living creature with that very power.

You can't kill people with a snap of your fingers, can you? Taesia had once asked her.

I can, she thought before she went all the way under. *I can.*

Julian heard the corpse behind him and jabbed his sword backward, skewering it through the stomach. It screeched and fell as he yanked his sword out. He quickly switched his sword for a crossbow, aiming at another corpse running toward the palace gates. The arrow struck it between the shoulders and it went down.

His stomach clenched. And yet his mind was clear, his heart pumping steadily, his blood spiked with adrenaline. He felt *alive*.

Paris was no longer at his side, the both of them having been caught in the tide of the dead. Julian took a moment to lean against the nearest wall. His blood roared in his ears, the rush of it like the river's current.

Deep in his stomach he felt the stir of hunger.

I am a man, my name is Julian, I live in Nexus, I am not a monster.

He hadn't found any Conjurers or circles yet. Shouldering the bow, he tightened his grip on his sword and hurried back to the entrance chamber.

Only to be met with a wall of pure black.

Julian skidded to a halt. The air before him seemed to warp, a darkness so consuming it was like wading into ink.

There was one person he knew who could do this. One person who, in his memory, gave the same deep laugh he was hearing now.

The sword shook in his hold. Swallowing, Julian took a step into the darkness.

He'd expected to feel malice and pain; instead, the shadows brushed against him like a friendly cat, like the cool embrace of water in a still lake. His senses were utterly dampened—he was at the mercy of these shadows. But they did nothing more than card through his hair and tickle his neck, affectionate in their touch.

Then the shadows began to dissipate, moving away like fog rolling down the valley.

Taesia Lastrider sat straddling a corpse, with more in crumpled heaps behind her. Some of its limbs had been ripped off, and as he watched, Taesia finished sawing through the leathery neck until the corpse's head rolled away from its body.

Her chest heaved for breath, sword held in one hand and dagger in the other, hair loose and wild about her shoulders. She was wearing black-and-silver armor—no, a dress—and her eyes were as they'd been in the bone dealer's shop, a deep, malevolent black that absorbed sclera and iris. Blood was splattered all across her front.

She grinned. "Coming to my rescue?" she asked in her midnight voice.

He watched her breathe, the way her ribs expanded with it, the way the shadows still clung devotedly to her, caressing her skin like a jealous lover.

His lungs burned. His blood burned. He didn't know if he was staring at a killer of monsters, or a monster herself.

"What..." He cleared his throat. "What happened?"

Taesia looked back down at the dismembered corpse. "Mm. I may have gotten a little carried away."

She rolled gracefully to her feet and approached him. His whole body tensed.

"I warned you, Julian Luca," she murmured. Her warm breath hit his lips. "Not to say a word about what we did."

He dropped his gaze. But the tip of her sword kissed the spot under his chin, lifted his eyes to hers once more.

"I didn't," he whispered. "But I had to report the shop. I didn't know..."

"Didn't know Nikolas Cyr would call on the help of Risha Vakara," she finished for him.

His mouth dried. He tried to nod, forgetting her blade was there until it pricked his skin. "Did you tell them what happened?" *That I was involved?*

"No." The word was flat, cold, but it gave him a measure of relief, selfish as it was. The shadows around him crept closer.

"Your *report* cost me," she said softly. The shadows brushed his hands, his arms, his throat. "How will you make up for it?"

A bead of blood trickled down to his collarbone. He swallowed. "A favor."

He didn't know what possessed him to say it. He was already mired in something he wanted no part of, something *she* had instigated. But he couldn't allow Nikolas Cyr to know of his involvement with Taesia Lastrider. One word and he'd be out of the task force, out of the Hunters, with no way to care for his mother.

"A favor," she repeated, as if savoring the words on her tongue. Her dark smile returned, and it set his blood to burning again. "Well, the gods have their plans, and they've somehow included you in them, Julian Luca."

She held out her bloody hand. He considered ignoring it, turning away, pretending none of this had happened.

But he didn't want to forget. He didn't want to ever underestimate what the Houses could do—or how easy it would be for them to crush all of Nexus beneath their power, finishing what the gods had started.

Slowly, Julian reached out. His palm eclipsed hers, her calloused fingers brushing the underside of his wrist.

Julian had the sudden, distinct feeling he had made a terrible mistake.

XVII

The circle was bigger than the one he'd drawn before. He stopped to sit back on his heels, catching his breath. His head was woozy, his stomach cramping.

Keep going, the Voice ordered.

He continued to draw the circle. The hill of bodies had turned into a mountain, and it stunk. He kept having to swat flies away from his face, their buzzing filling him with a sudden, gnawing anxiety.

His chest grew warm as his vision blackened. Closing his eyes, he thought back to the strange girl who had spoken to him. Her body had been covered in a long, flowy shirt that outlined the shape of her body when the wind blew, her black hair fanned out around her.

"Who are you?" he whispered out loud, as if she could still hear, still answer.

Do not worry about her, crooned the Voice. *She is merely a figment, a casting of your delirious mind. Perhaps you are lonely. Perhaps you need someone to speak to. Perhaps you need more to eat.*

He held a thin hand to his cramping stomach.

All in due time, the Voice said. *First, you must finish.*

He tried to get up, arms shaking.

GET UP.

He gasped and rocked forward, his body moving seemingly on its own. Trembling, he filled in the circle's gaps with symbols he could barely understand.

Test it.

He planted his palms within the circle. Bowing his head, he opened himself once more to the sensation of reaching and pulling, of dragging something heavy across a room.

A shudder traveled over his shoulders as he groaned. Golden light flooded the circle, glutted on the bodies' magic, washing over him.

The prize was bigger this time. It took even more of an effort to pull it through, but he finally managed it with a broken-off scream and the very last of his energy.

Drained, he fell to the ground. Sweat dampened the back of his neck as pain lanced through his stomach and into his chest.

You've done it, the Voice said, satisfied as a crow cracking open a walnut. *Stunning.*

He opened his eyes. Looming over him was a stone arch that cast a half circle of shadow across the ground. On either end were lampposts, their lights flickering.

Look inside the bag.

He turned over and crawled to the pack nearby. When he opened it, he nearly sobbed in relief.

There you go, the Voice whispered as he drew out strips of dried meat and took his first, enormous bite. Tears ran down his cheeks as his mouth flooded painfully with saliva. *You'll need to keep up your strength for the next one.*

He curled up on the ground and ate at the foot of the mountain of corpses, his mind again drifting to the girl.

Who are you? he thought as he ripped the meat apart with his teeth. *Who are you?*

PART III

The Queen of Lies

I

When Risha received an urgent summons to come to the Thana basilica, she prepared herself for one of the Revenants' tricks, yet another vie for her attention after the disaster of the gala.

She found something worse.

"Blessed Thana, merciful Thana, we ask for your forgiveness!" cried a man standing in the middle of the basilica square. He was ringed with worshippers, all with the same wide-eyed, haggard look, rhythmic in their swaying. Priests in dark robes stood huddled within the basilica doors, watching with a mixture of confusion and fear.

"It's been like this for an hour, my lady," said the guard at her side, her mouth pinched.

"Are they attacking the priests?" Risha demanded. "What's happening here?"

"No, they're just..." The guard waved a hand at them. "Doing that."

"Forgive us for not giving sufficient offering!" the man in the middle wailed. "We are in sin! We are at fault! Forgive us!"

"Forgive us," chanted the others in disturbing synchrony.

"The dead speak for you and they speak of anger! We are tortured as they are tortured! Forgive us!"

"Forgive us!"

Risha's scalp prickled. The past few days after the Godsnight Gala had been quiet and tense, like an indrawn breath not yet exhaled. King Ferdinand had declared a state of mourning for those who had fallen, but the citizens weren't grieving—they were spooked.

"Paaja says he's going to attend every funeral, not just Don Soler's,"

Saya had told her once she'd woken from her restorative sleep. They'd found Risha lying on top of a marble tomb under the hole in the ball-room's floor, holding a black rose to her chest. "He told the king to order the families to burn their dead instead of burying them. They didn't like that very much." Many still adhered to the tradition that a body should be connected to the earth and therefore brought closer to Deia, that the god would reuse them in some way. "There's also a curfew, now. Every-one has to be indoors by sundown."

But these people seemed adamant on staying right where they were despite the sun's slow descent. The City of Dusk lived up to its name as the shadows grew longer and the light dimmed to an otherworldly shade of violet.

Risha took a deep breath. "We need to disperse them. They—"

"Blessed Thana, we call on you for protection!" the man wept. He lifted his hand, and Risha's insides turned to ice at the glint of a wide knife. "Please take our offerings to satisfy your retribution!"

"No—!" But even as Risha started forward, she knew it was too late.

The man swung the knife down on his wrist. His howl of pain rang through the square as the other penitents drew their own weapons and began to mutilate themselves, a horrifying tableau of blood and scream-ing. The guards who'd been warily watching on the sidelines sprang into action to disarm and restrain them.

The man hadn't succeeded in chopping his hand off; the knife was wedged halfway through, blood spraying from a severed artery as he continued to yell nonsensical things at the basilica's cold facade. The priests had scurried back inside, guards standing between them and the penitents.

Risha stared at a woman on her knees, her face drenched scarlet from her ruined eye, and had to turn away. She closed a hand over her own wrist, thumb pressed against a cut from the gala. Above lay the burn Angelica had given her, whether intentionally or not, wrapped in bandages packed with aloe and honey. Its throbbing pain made her nausea worse.

"My lady?" The guard from earlier approached, face screwed up in disgust. "What should we do with them?"

Risha took a moment to settle herself, to become a Vakara first and foremost. She straightened her spine. "Turn them over to the high com-missioner. I doubt they have anything to do with the Conjurers, but they'll need to be watched so as to not cause further harm to themselves."

The guard nodded as another ran up and, out of breath, handed them a piece of paper. "This was found on their leader," they said.

It was a broadsheet, or something like the news tattlers her mother pretended not to read. Ignoring the specks of blood in the corner, Risha read it only to find more of the same nonsense the man had been yelling, calling for others to appease Thana's wrath for protection against the Conjurers and the dead.

Guilt wove tightly around her throat. Risha hadn't put a stop to the Revenants, hadn't been able to prevent the attack at the gala and the resulting deaths, including one of the king's most trusted advisors.

The mines in Aguerre had collapsed after the necropolis attack. She'd been braced to hear what would fall apart after the gala, but so far there was nothing noticeable—which made her apprehension all the worse.

You want to find a way into Mortri, don't you? Taesia had asked when she'd brought the heirs together, revealing Lezzaro's plan. *The dead are piling up. They're going to cause more destruction if they're not released.*

Risha knew, she *knew*, but after what Angelica had told them of a fifth realm—after confronting Taesia, learning of Dante's ulterior motives—how were they supposed to go through with the ritual? How was she going to take away the Revenants' methods of necromancy?

She handed the broadsheet to the guard, who scowled after reading. "Gods' bones. If they wanted to make offerings, they could've done it the normal way. Light a stick of incense, for fuck's sake." Remembering who stood before her, the guard murmured, "Apologies, my lady."

Risha shook her head. She didn't fault her, and she couldn't even fault the penitents. Fear was like a disease; once caught, it spread quickly. She understood their frustration, their helplessness, their desperation to give away parts of themselves in exchange for safety.

She hadn't been able to grant them that safety, and that was her burden to bear.

Lillum Street, the man had whispered. *We'll be waiting for you.*

Whatever it took, she was going to get answers.

Risha followed the markers of bone, red ribbons fluttering as a strong wind cut through the valley of darkness. She stood her ground as the gale did its best to push her into the void, eager for her flesh, her beating heart. She thought she heard the click of bone, then realized her teeth were chattering.

The ground beneath her winked with bits of half-buried onyx, like the wet, beady eyes of insects. All around her were fragments of things forgotten and discarded.

In her hand she held a black rose, one of the three she had collected in a vase in her bedroom. Although they hadn't shown any signs of decay, the petals now began to wilt and wither, curling in on themselves as the stem browned. Then the petals unfurled and became whole once more. Over and over, a mockery of death and life.

She reached the thick spiral of darkness preventing her from going any farther. Her stomach ached from being so close to it, her body struggling to remember how to function—air in her lungs, blood in her heart. Or maybe it was the other way around.

Risha held out a trembling hand. Mortri waited on the other side of this barrier.

Risha began to construct her spell. She rarely crafted her own patterns, instead following those her father had taught her. But this was different. This was desperation in the wake of disaster, a question that needed an answer.

A circle, and then a seven-pointed star. The wind howled and tugged at her hair and clothes, her eyes watering from its force.

She pressed a thorn against her thumb and let a drop of blood fall. The spell flared and writhed before her. The barrier moaned, darkness rising up to claim her.

She went flying back with a scream. She hit the ground and nearly rolled off the pathway. Her leg fell into the void and something cold and slippery touched her calf. She snatched it away.

"How dare you."

The voice cut straight to her marrow. Thana stood before the barrier, not an illusion but the god herself, impossibly tall and veiled in black. Four arms hung at her sides, wreathed in clasps of gold and silver and bone.

"I have no use for these games," Thana said, her pale lips still even as the voice boomed around her. "This is an ugly magic, and you will not bring it here again."

Risha struggled to get to her knees as her body shook. "Th...Thana." She bowed, pressing her forehead to the ground. "Please forgive me. I was only trying—"

"I know what you were trying. And you will not try again."

"Blessed Thana, please, you can't keep Mortri locked away. There are spirits who need to pass on. If this... If this is the power of Ostium—"

"DO NOT SAY THAT NAME." She stepped toward Risha, bare feet a grayish brown, her long veil swaying in the wind. She cradled Risha's face in her wintry, skeletal hands. "IT SHOULD NOT BE YOUR CONCERN, NOR IS IT MINE. MY ONLY CONCERN IS THE VESSEL OF MY BLOOD. YOU."

Risha couldn't breathe. Couldn't move. She stared in horror at Thana as the truth lay thick and venomous between them.

Angelica had been right. There had been a fifth realm, and the gods wanted everyone to forget it.

"Why?" The word came out as a trembling whisper.

Thana's fingertips pressed harder into Risha's cheeks. Her skin smelled of rot and ruin. "IT IS NOT YOUR POWER TO WIELD," the god breathed, and it was the sigh of the wind through barren branches, the last breath of one who readily accepted death's embrace. "IT WILL BE MINE. FOR I DESERVE MORE THAN A REALM OF DEAD AND DYING THINGS. I DESERVE THE LIVING AND THE LIGHT AND THE SHADOW AND THE DOORWAY."

The doorway. Ostium? Risha didn't understand what she was saying, but she knew this: If there had been a fifth realm, they were missing an heir with which to complete the ritual.

Which meant she needed another way to open the barrier.

Thana let her go. The god returned to Mortri as the wind picked up speed, stinging her skin numb.

When Risha blinked, she was kneeling in the necropolis, the black rose in her hand. It was half dead, frozen in the process of rebirth.

"Whatever it takes," she whispered.

Nikolas and his father had walked away from the Godsnight Gala with only minor injuries, but it had been enough to send Madeia into a fit of weeping. "My boy," she had sobbed, clutching on to Nikolas so hard her nails had left crescent marks in his skin. "I'm so sorry. I'm so sorry..."

Waren had holed himself in his office for the next few days, servants running back and forth to deliver messages to the other comandantes. Every so often he ordered Nikolas to help, such as organizing a meeting to discuss further protection for the king.

"Will I be attending?" Nikolas ventured to ask. He quickly realized his mistake when his father looked at him as if he were a fish asking to be given legs.

In the night he still woke in a clammy sweat, surrounded by screams and a pressure in his chest as if Queen Mabrian were trying to crush him beneath her foot. His wounds healed clean, but they ached at the reminder of panic and destruction, the threat of something far beyond his competence.

Nikolas stared out the window of the villa's conservatory as his mother hummed under her breath. The sky was a ripe shade of blue, hard and clear like sapphire. It was a sure sign that autumn had finally settled over Vaega, the breathlessly hot days easing into chill, the wind knocking against the windows carrying a hint of decay.

Only two weeks until Godsnight, when the planes intersected, when Ferdinand would make the Houses demonstrate their powers for Nexus's entertainment. When they would have performed a forbidden ritual were it not for one integral missing piece.

"You're cold," Madeia said as he shuddered.

"I'm all right." He wondered how many times he'd said those words to her in the past few days. "Just thinking."

She reached across the table and held his hand, abandoning the sketchbook in her lap. Her fingers were chilled, and he tried to warm them between his palms.

He'd sent Risha and Angelica messages, but they went unanswered. Taesia...well, he gave her space. Nikolas sometimes dreamed of her hands around his throat, her eyes black and depthless.

Madeia's fingers warmed between his hands. She smiled slightly, a sliver of gray sunlight amid winter clouds. She turned back to her sketchbook where she was drawing an abstract shape, a series of circles interconnecting, shaky lines running through them like spindly spider legs.

"What's that supposed to be, Mother?"

Madeia hummed and blinked down at the circles. The edge of her palm was stained black where it had smudged the charcoal.

"I..." She stared, lips parted, until she suddenly shoved the sketchbook away. "No! *No!*"

"Mother?" Nikolas knelt before her. "Mother, it's me, it's Nik. Look at me."

Her eyes were wide and wild. They roamed the conservatory before settling on him.

"Breathe," he whispered. "You're home, you're safe."

Once her breaths evened out, he stood to fetch her calming tea. Before he could, the doors opened and a servant bowed on the threshold, holding out a missive.

"Sorry to interrupt, my lord, but this came for you."

These days, a missive always harkened something sinister. He forced himself to take it, and when he turned it over and saw the high commissioner's seal, he held back a curse.

What now?

At first Nikolas had no idea what he was looking at.

He thought the summons might lead to a Conjuration den, perhaps something related to the gala. Instead, he stared at Lune River snaking through Nexus on its way to the Arastra Sea, water gleaming in the mid-morning light. A small crowd had formed on the banks as soldiers with pins marking water proficiency scoured the shore where thick iron studs had been ripped from the ground.

It took him a moment to realize what was missing.

"Lune Bridge," Nikolas said slowly, disbelieving. "It's supposed to be here."

"Yes." The high commissioner, Cristoban Damari, was roughly his father's age, gray streaking his brown hair and his forehead etched with deep lines. He had a strong chin and steady eyes, the sort of quiet, confident demeanor that made him appear more handsome than he naturally was.

He was also missing a right ear, but that wasn't new. Everyone loved making up their own stories as to how it had happened. Nikolas had heard a serial murderer with a shine for human flesh had bitten it clean off.

"An entire bridge is gone, and no one knows how or why," Damari murmured. "It seems to have occurred near the time of the gala."

Nikolas watched Gem talk with the other water elementalists, Komi working with the earth elementalists to clear recent mudflow. There were no scraps of metal or wood, no damaged buildings, nothing sticking out of the water. But as the mud was cleared away, he saw scorched black lines, the arc of a circle. It reached from shore to shore, the majority of it lost beneath the river.

Nikolas inhaled sharply and hopped down. He slipped a little as he joined the water elementalists.

"Part the water here," he ordered, pointing where the bridge would have been.

Gem nodded, but the others hesitated before noticing the Sunbringer Spear and realizing who he was. They lifted their hands and the water stirred, moving in surges like a restless ocean. The earth elementalists helped by creating mud-hardened walls for the current to splash against. A small maelstrom formed as they swirled their hands through the air and slowly, carefully parted the water down the middle.

Even under the river the circle was undisturbed, perfect.

"How?" Nikolas breathed. "How could any Conjurer manage this?"

Gem shook their head, face flushed with exertion. "I don't know."

"It's like the statue at the university," Komi said on his other side. "They chalked that one up to some sort of prank."

"Are you seriously making a pun right now?" Gem grumbled.

Komi blinked. "It was completely unintentional, but I stand by it."

The crowd above was leaning over to get a look. Nikolas wiped clammy hands on his trousers as Taide gave a thumbs-up that he'd managed to sketch the circle. Nikolas nodded to the elementalists that they could bring the water back down. The last thing he needed was for bystanders to get ideas about Conjuration.

When Nikolas returned to the street, Damari had his arms crossed and brow lightly furrowed. "They're still managing all this even with their leader gone," Damari murmured. "No matter. The erstwhile Lastrider heir has been sentenced to hang. Hopefully it will send the right message to others who wish to follow in his footsteps."

Nikolas's stomach churned like the water below, reliving the flash of fear and hurt on Taesia's face in the side room when he'd accused her. Had she known, then, that Dante would face execution?

"You haven't unearthed anything more about the gala?" Damari asked, unaware of Nikolas's discomfort. "Your unit searched the mausoleum."

"The initial search yielded nothing beyond the Conjuration circle and Leshya Vakara's remains."

"And what about Don Soler's death? Any leads on the possible cause?"

Don Soler had perished in the gala attack, but the manner of his death had been different than the handful of nobles and soldiers who had been overwhelmed by the dead. He'd been fully dismembered, the cuts clean, precise, as if by an expertly sharpened blade.

It had seemed…intentional.

Nikolas swallowed, again seeing Taesia's panic, her desperation.

"No, Don," he whispered. "Not yet."

★　　★　　★

A missing statue and a missing bridge. A dried-up lake and collapsed mines. A necropolis and a gala overrun by corpses. Conjuration linked them, but he didn't know *how*. All he knew was the more he saw of the forbidden magic, the more he understood why it was forbidden.

By leeching the energy and thinning the barriers, they're weakening our own realm, Angelica had told them. Had Lezzaro known about this side effect of Conjuration? Or had he been willing to sacrifice part of their realm in order to save the whole of it?

He had two weeks to figure out what to do: take part in the ritual and potentially do nothing but spark another Conjuration attack, or else refuse and throw away their last shot of undoing the Sealing for a hundred years. When he was younger, a fortnight was an impossibly long stretch. Now, knowing what potentially waited for him at the end of it, every day seemed to pass in the span of a blink.

Maybe Vitae would make it a hundred years. Maybe it would make it to two hundred.

Maybe he was just a coward.

He was having a nightmare about Taesia standing on top of a bridge when he was woken by his father at dawn.

"Come with me," Waren ordered.

It was the first time he'd seen his father outside his office in days. Nikolas followed him up the stairs of the tallest tower in the Cyr villa, any drowsiness he'd otherwise feel at this hour washed away in pounding, unrelenting dread.

They walked onto the tower's balcony, the dawn air making him shiver. From their vantage spot, they had a clear view of Nexus as sunlight washed over roofs, and he could even see the tip of the Gravespire poking up among the chimneys belching the first wisps of smoke as shops and homes slowly roused.

Nikolas waited for his father to say something, do something. He held his body rigid in anticipation. But Waren did nothing other than stare grimly at the horizon, at the golden disc of the sun as it rose, hardly even blinking.

Just as Nikolas was about to shatter apart with nerves, to finally ask what was happening, he noticed it.

"The sun," he whispered.

Waren nodded. "It's fading."

Nikolas gripped the icy railing. The sky was clear, pale blue, cloudless. No haze, no fog.

Yet the sunlight that reached them didn't do much to counter the chill; it was vague, distant, more an idea of warmth than the actual thing. And the sun itself—the round ball of fire said to have been birthed from Deia's womb after consuming one of Phos's feathers—was dimmer than Nikolas had ever seen it.

The people of Vaega likely wouldn't be able to tell for another few weeks, another few months, but Nikolas *felt* it. Lux sluggishly unwound from his wrist, slithering up to wrap around his neck. His familiar trembled as if it, too, were cold.

Nikolas didn't have to ask what it meant. They were finally seeing the side effects of the Conjuration performed at the gala, what their energy had consumed.

Vitae was dying. They knew this already.

What they hadn't known was how little time they actually had left.

II

"Sit down before you wear a track in my rug," Camilla scolded. "It's from Cardica. It was expensive."

Taesia ignored her and continued to pace the length of her aunt's sitting room. She hadn't known what else to do, where else to go, to get this terrible weight off her. They were having their first truly cold day of autumn, and a fire smoldered in the hearth. Every time one of the logs popped it made her flinch.

"When's the last time you've eaten?" Camilla asked when Taesia's stomach gurgled unpleasantly. "You sound like an irritated cat."

But she had no appetite. Her stomach was crowded with panic, her insides bitten raw.

"You don't seem disturbed by this," Taesia shot at her. "Dante's officially been sentenced to *hang*. How can you sit there and accept that?"

Camilla was sitting in her most comfortable armchair, which had started out stiff but had sagged and softened over time. "Just because I'm being calm doesn't mean I'm not affected," her aunt said softly as she plucked at the loose fabric on the arm. "Dante is my nephew. You think I want to see him dangle off a noose?"

Taesia now noticed the strain in her aunt's face, making her appear older than usual. Discomfited, Taesia turned away. Umbra gently squeezed her wrist, but it only made her more aware of her erratic pulse.

The official sentencing had been carried out quickly, quietly, without a member of House Lastrider to witness it. Don Soler had been right. The only thing she couldn't wrap her mind around was that Dante had somehow *confessed*. Confessed to what, exactly, and why?

But there was no getting answers, now. They had died along with the man who had baited and taunted her—rather successfully, to his detriment. And because of her indulgence, the high commissioner had taken up an investigation, as Don Soler's fatal wounds didn't match those who had been caught by the dead.

Careless.

News of the confession was gradually becoming public, and with it, more murmurings of the phrase *Traitor House.* Yet the Noctans were still supporting Dante and the Lastriders, and Taesia couldn't help but be nervous for them. She didn't want them coming under suspicion for any reason, not when they were already so targeted.

Camilla's hand came to rest on her shoulder. "You showed me those astralam bones. With the power in them, you might be able to break your brother out of the Gravespire before..." She rubbed calming circles over Taesia's back. "Or perhaps during Godsnight. I can cause a distraction for you. I'm very good at those."

Taesia's laugh was strangled. "The bones won't be ready for another couple of days."

"Then we'll wait. Until then, you focus on your plan."

"There's been a complication." When she finished telling her about Angelica's discovery, her aunt's eyes widened.

"Oh," she whispered. "Complication seems a...mild way of putting it."

"Did Lezzaro not tell you about Ostium?"

"No, he barely shared anything about the grimoire with me. Hardly even let me lay eyes on it." Her aunt sat back down, silently processing. Taesia couldn't blame her; for days now she'd been turning the thought of a fifth realm over and over, and no matter how she looked at it, it didn't seem real.

"Have you considered she may be lying?" Camilla asked eventually.

"Who, Angelica? Of course I've considered it." Taesia started pacing again. "This could just be some way for us to drop the whole thing, to focus instead on this Godsnight presentation the king's so adamant about. She seemed to know about that before the rest of us did. But if it's true, and if we need something, some*one*, to represent Ostium for the ritual..."

She shuddered; she was cold to her bones, and not even the fire helped. "I don't think Risha and Nikolas are willing to try it anymore."

It wasn't until the morning after the gala that Nikolas's and Risha's words had sunk through. She had boiled with anger—a deep, rattling fury that made her grab the porcelain ring tray Nikolas had given her when they were eighteen and smash it against the wall.

Then the anger had washed away into heavy, unavoidable grief, haunted by a guilt she couldn't shake. She'd still had flakes of Don Soler's blood on her skin. She'd stared at them for hours.

Camilla sighed. "I did tell you friends are sometimes outgrown. There had to come a day when you put duty before each other."

"*Fuck* duty." It was a sentiment she had carried for years, but it held a different flavor in her mouth now, tinged not with adolescent rebellion but weary disillusionment. Dante had shaped duty into something that worked for him—prowling the city and learning it from the inside out, learning how to best serve it. But the Houses carried duty like a chain. Those chains all led back to the palace, to the throne, to the fear Ferdinand held over them like a thrall.

What good was something like *duty* when it amounted to little more than unchallenged obedience?

"Even if I can talk them around again, it won't do any good if we don't have something to represent this fifth realm," Taesia said.

Camilla sat on this some more. Taesia took it upon herself to grab the sherry decanter from the drinks cart and drank straight from the crystal spout, relieved by the warmth that settled in her chest.

Eventually her aunt made a small, startled noise. "The fulcrums."

"The what?"

"Fulcrums." Camilla's gaze sharpened. "Lezzaro told me about them. One of the only things he was willing to discuss at length. The gods rule over their respective realms, yes?"

Taesia blinked, unsure where this was going. "Yes?"

"And each realm is therefore infused with their respective powers. There are points within each realm where these powers align along the Cosmic Scale, creating the ley lines, creating the portals. Nexus sits upon those ley lines."

Taesia already knew this—everyone did—but she decided not to interrupt as Camilla tapped her fingers eagerly against her knees.

"But where do those ley lines *come* from, exactly?" Camilla said. "They travel along the Cosmic Scale, yes, but they originate from the gods. From their power suffused into the realms. How does their power become so integrated into their realms in the first place?"

"You're asking a lot of rhetorical questions," Taesia murmured. "Can you please get to the point?"

Camilla stood and yanked the decanter from Taesia's hand, taking a big swig for herself. "The point," she gasped once she lowered it, "is that in Lezzaro's fucking grimoire, it theorized the gods are connected to their realms via a fulcrum. A...core, of sorts, that they planted in each realm. That is where they store their power."

Maybe it was the sherry, but it didn't seem far-fetched. Most people were content with not knowing how the gods functioned, unwilling to dive into the existential turmoil required when theorizing about the universe and the beings that ruled it. They were happy to let it be at *the gods have dominion, the end.*

The more she thought about it, though, the more it made sense. Just as magic needed focal points—the Conjuration circles, for example—the gods would have needed focal points from which to birth their domains.

"Does that mean Deia has one here, in Vitae?" Taesia asked. "Where is it?"

Camilla shrugged. "If the fulcrums exist, I imagine they'd be a weakness to the gods, and therefore hidden at all costs. I didn't think it was particularly useful when Lezzaro told me about it, but if there was a fifth realm..."

"Then it also had a fulcrum," Taesia breathed. "And if we could somehow get the fulcrum—"

"You'd have something to represent Ostium for the ritual," her aunt finished.

They stood in silence broken only by Taesia's harsh breathing and the crackle of the fire. Camilla handed her the decanter again, but Taesia's throat was too tight to take a sip.

"How could we possibly do that, though?" Taesia demanded. "We don't have access to any of the other realms, let alone one that's been forgotten or potentially destroyed for half a millennium."

"Your astralam bones. You said they created a portal."

Taesia's heart thumped painfully at the memory. "Yes. You think I can...what, summon the Ostium fulcrum using the bones?"

Camilla laughed, spreading her arms out. "I'm not the one with magic, darling. I just come up with ideas."

Taesia chewed the inside of her cheek. She didn't know if it was possible, but it was a *chance*, and she was going to grab at any chance with both hands. But would the other heirs still be willing to try the ritual based on a theory?

"Even if this works, Ferdinand wants us to perform for the public on Godsnight," Taesia said slowly. "How are we supposed to do both at once? Or . . . or maybe if the king's incapacitated before then . . ."

Camilla laid a hand on her arm. "One problem at a time. The Sealing first, then the king. You don't have to fulfill all of Dante's goals."

"I do."

"Why? You said it yourself: fuck duty. Unless this isn't about the greater good. Unless this is first and foremost for *you*."

A list of rebuttals rose to Taesia's tongue, but she quietly swallowed them. Her aunt knew her well—knew of Taesia's longing, her impatience, her desire to be free of the web of politics and journey into something grander. Camilla was much the same way, traveling from place to place, even having the freedom to spend a year abroad in Cardica.

But it wasn't just about that anymore. It was also about saving Dante, and ensuring Brailee could grow up in a realm that wouldn't perish.

If she had to break the kingdom to set it straight, she was more than ready for the excuse.

"If you're certain, then," her aunt murmured when Taesia said nothing. "But you shouldn't overextend yourself. I worry about you."

"I'll be fine. There's a lot more you should worry about before me."

"Oh, darling." Camilla touched her cheek. "I will always put my family first."

She'd forgotten the new curfew.

The sun had begun to set when she left her aunt's house, and by the time she came across Greyhounds on their patrol route, it was well and truly dark.

Holding her sword to her hip to prevent it from jostling, she ran through the alleys hoping to eventually lose the guards' interest. Umbra flew out of her ring and floated beside her. "Fine," she panted, and the familiar spread across her face in a half mask. It was better to be mistaken for a criminal than to be recognized as the Lastrider heir.

She skidded against cobblestone as she made a sharp turn, the streets still wet from yesterday's rainfall. One of the Greyhounds cried out and she briefly turned to gauge their distance. She'd lost one of them, but two were still on her heels. At this point she wasn't even mad, just impressed.

She ducked into a narrow alley, the walls scraping her clothes, and emerged in a residential district.

"Stop!" a guard called. "By order of the king, everyone must be off the streets by sundown!"

She held out her hands and drew the shadows toward her. They rushed forward with whispers of joy like the night of the gala, eager to do her bidding.

Then she stumbled. Halfway down the street, Julian Luca was climbing a set of stairs leading to a second-story apartment.

She'd thought he lived at the Hunters' barracks, but she didn't have time to question it. As she barreled toward him, he noticed her with the hopeless shock of someone about to be stampeded by beasts.

"What are you—?" he began, but she launched herself over the railing and grabbed the lapels of his coat.

"Take me up to your apartment," she gasped. "*Now.*"

"What? Why?" He tried to peer around her, but she pushed him up the stairs. "What's going on? *Ow,* gods, do you do nothing gently?"

"Do you always ask pointless questions?" She pushed him toward the door as he fumbled with his key. "You owe me a favor, and I'm calling it in. Come on!"

He muttered to himself as she watched the street. As soon as the door creaked open, she hustled both of them inside, slamming it behind her.

"Shit." She shakily wiped the sweat from her forehead. Julian stared at her, eyes flitting across her face, and she realized she was still wearing Umbra as a mask. With something dangerously close to embarrassment, Taesia flicked her fingers and peeled Umbra off, letting her familiar settle back into its ring.

She cleared her throat. "I, uh...didn't know you have an apartment."

Julian blinked a couple of times, as if coming out of a trance. "I don't." He pointed to the table in the middle of the room. "It's my mother's."

Taesia froze at the sight of the middle-aged woman standing by the table. She was short and round, with a pleasant face currently overtaken with alarm. A cup fell from her slack fingers and crashed to the floor.

"Ma!" Julian hurried to her, but the woman batted him away.

"*Jules,*" she hissed, "do you know who this is?"

Julian glanced back at Taesia with a pained expression. "Yes, I do." *Unfortunately,* his posture added.

"Why didn't you tell me you knew the heir of House Lastrider?" Julian's mother wailed.

Taesia, her back against the door, fumbled for the knob. She very much wasn't in the mood to have a random citizen cursing her or her supposed Traitor House out. "I see this is a bad time . . ."

"No, no, you're more than welcome!" The woman stepped toward her. "W-would you like anything to drink, my lady? Tea? Brandy? Both? I have some leftover almond cake."

Taesia looked helplessly at Julian. He shrugged.

She had to make sure those guards were well and truly gone before she braved the streets again. With a tight smile, Taesia nodded. "Tea and brandy is exactly what I need, Miss Luca."

The woman flushed and tried to curtsy in her woolen dress. "Of course, my lady! And please, do call me Marjorie."

As she shuffled into the tiny kitchen, Julian knelt and began to gather the broken cup pieces. Taesia went to help.

"Can you *please* tell me why you barged into my mother's apartment past curfew?" he muttered.

"What are *you* doing visiting her so late?" she countered.

He cut her a small glare. His hazel eyes were browner in this lighting, like freshly tilled earth. She realized she was staring and returned to picking up shards.

"Hunters are exempt from curfew," he finally murmured. "I got off duty and came here to spend the night. I need to take her to a medic appointment in the morning."

Taesia sat back on her heels, a small mound of porcelain in her palm. "Is she sick?"

He clenched his teeth. It made the lines of his cheekbones stark, complementing the precise corners of his jaw.

"She has languor," he said quietly as his mother bustled around the kitchen. "It's a slow sickness, but it doesn't have a cure. That's why . . ." He sighed and stood, grabbing a trash bin and dumping the debris inside. "That's why I took your money, to buy her medicine. I've already scraped the bottom of my savings."

Taesia had grown up in a villa, surrounded by wealth and power. Folks like Julian . . . well, they had not. She could now see the driving necessity that had led him to take on a profession as dangerous as his, to accept her money in exchange for silence.

They shared a common language, then: desperation.

As she tossed the porcelain into the bin, Julian caught her wrist.

"What were you doing tonight?" he asked. His eyes were unwaveringly focused on hers, the heat of his body intense, warming her chest and stomach and thighs in a way the fire in her aunt's sitting room hadn't.

"We agreed you owe me a favor," she said softly. "Be grateful I'm using it to take up your mother's offer of cake instead of something else."

His fingers tightened painfully, but she didn't move to break his hold. She sighed.

"I was visiting my aunt and lost track of time." She raised an eyebrow. "Unless you have reason to believe I was doing something more nefarious?"

"I—"

"Here you are, my lady!"

They sprang apart as Marjorie returned. The woman cleared off a portion of the cluttered table and set down a cup of steaming tea and a slice of honey-colored almond cake.

Taesia dug deep into years of handling the gentry to pull a polite smile to her face. "Thank you, Marjorie."

The woman blushed with a grin, then started to cough into her fist. Julian stepped forward, but Marjorie waved him away.

"I'm fine, Jules, I'm fine," she croaked. Aggressively clearing her throat, she pulled a seat out for Taesia. Dutifully, Taesia sat. "Let me know how it is, my lady. It's a recipe handed down from my grandmother."

Julian's gaze bored into her as she picked up the fork and took a bite. The cake was light and spongy, with a hint of cinnamon. An odd sensation began to bubble in her chest, like water boiling to the point of spilling over.

Unless this isn't about the greater good, her aunt whispered in her mind. *Unless this is first and foremost for you.*

Maybe she was doing this first and foremost for herself. But it was also for Dante, Brailee, the refugees, and—she was now realizing—people like Marjorie Luca, who deserved better than what they were handed.

"It's delicious," Taesia said. "Truly."

Marjorie pressed her hands to her heated cheeks. "I'm so glad! Oh, before I forget…"

Marjorie searched through the debris on the tabletop and emerged with a pamphlet. She held it out to Taesia along with a charcoal pencil. The cover of the pamphlet was an artist's rendering of herself, grinning maniacally amid a storm of shadows.

"Would you sign this?" Marjorie breathed.

"*Ma*," Julian groaned.

Taesia stared down at the pamphlet. At her own crude likeness, painting her as some sort of villain. Some sort of legend.

That bubbling feeling in her chest released itself as laughter. Her shoulders shook as she roared with it, hitting the table with the palm of her hand.

"You don't have to sign it if you don't want to," Julian muttered.

Taesia wiped her eyes and caught her breath. "No, I want to." She took the pamphlet and pencil from Marjorie, who beamed. Taesia's answering smile was genuine. "Anything for an admirer."

III

Julian's soul had left his body. It was floating somewhere along the barrier to Mortri, crying to be let in and escape what was happening at his mother's table.

Taesia Lastrider and his mother were laughing. Joking. Trading stories like cards in a fast-paced game. It didn't matter that Taesia had burst through the door in a shadow mask during curfew; Marjorie Luca saw an heir, a member of royalty, a carrier of godsblood.

And she was currently telling that carrier of godsblood about the time he'd accidentally shot one of the neighbor's pigs with an arrow.

"You should've heard the squealing," Marjorie said with a chuckle that turned into a wet cough.

"From the pig?"

"From *Jules*. He was so upset, he was weeping for days. Even offered to help rake up pig dung for a month. We didn't bother to punish him, the poor lad did it himself."

Taesia's eyes crinkled as she glanced at him. Julian put his head down on the table and wished for death.

He'd told Taesia about his mother's appointment in the morning, which was true. But he had also come to sleep here because the silence of his room at the compound was getting too loud.

And there was also the conversation he'd had today, while on duty with Nikolas Cyr's unit.

"Jules? Are you all right?"

He sat up. "Why don't you go to bed, Ma? It's getting late."

Marjorie hesitated, looking between him and Taesia. Taesia smiled, and the softness of it almost made him question if she was the real Lastrider heir.

"I should be heading back as well," Taesia said. "Thank you again for the tea and cake."

"You're absolutely welcome, my lady. I'll provide you with tea and cake whenever you desire."

"I'll certainly take you up on that."

His mother gave a weak half curtsy before Julian led her to her room. "Do you need help, Ma?"

"Oh, I'm fine," she whispered. "You worry about the beautiful girl who keeps looking your way."

Thana, please take me. "Ma. Stop it."

She closed the door with a wink. Julian came back to the main room, sighing.

"Well, you've thoroughly won her over," he said. "I hope you're pleased with yourself."

Taesia's straight posture was gone. She sat slumped in her chair, long legs spread out before her, arms crossed over her chest.

"I would die for that woman," Taesia said with alarming sincerity.

"There's no need for that." He returned to his own chair. "Though, speaking of dying..."

She tensed. "Careful how you finish that sentence."

"What happened at the bone dealer's shop... What did Risha Vakara see?"

Her arms tightened against her chest. "She saw me. Killing him." A sideways glance. "She didn't see you, if that's what you're concerned about."

It was. He felt braced at all times for guards to seize him, or for Kerala to dismiss him. He figured the reason Taesia hadn't been punished in any perceivable way was due to her status and the Houses' discretion. Still, she'd said it cost her something. What exactly had she lost?

"I guess I could use this against you as leverage in some way," Taesia said. "But then who'd take care of your lovely mother if you were locked up?"

She was joking, but there was a strain in her too-casual voice. For a moment he mourned having brought it up, if only that it had created a troubled divot between her eyebrows.

Tonight he had heard the clear ringing of her laugh, saw the gleam of amusement in her eyes, but solemnity had stolen over her. There was still color in her cheeks, her lips darkened to red from the tea. A smudge of dirt slanted over one high cheekbone.

"I'm surprised," Taesia said, staring in the direction of his mother's room, "that she reacted that way toward me. Not a lot of people viewing the Lastriders favorably right now."

Julian scoffed. "Gods know why, but she's fascinated with the Houses. With you. No amount of scandal would change that." He hesitated, knowing he treaded on unstable ground. "I'm sorry. About your brother."

She closed her eyes. It reminded him of the aftermath of the dealer's shop, when her power had withdrawn and she'd been left drained and stunned, when she'd turned to him and asked if he was badly hurt. As if she hadn't just snapped a man's neck. As if she contained something far bigger than herself and didn't know how to come to terms with it.

Godsblood. To Julian, it meant nothing. To her, it meant everything.

"You searched the prelate's rectory," she whispered, keeping her eyes closed. "You probably heard the witness reports from the guards. Do you think he's guilty?"

His head filled with the sound of the alarm bells at the Hunters' compound that rang if a beast escaped the pens. Why *wouldn't* Dante Lastrider be guilty? What did it have to do with Taesia, with the bones she'd been so adamant for?

"Never mind," she said quickly, waving a hand. "You're just following orders, doing your duty. It's not like you're the one who arrested him."

No, but the man who *had* arrested him was now dead. Julian was skeptical when it came to coincidences.

"Don Soler died during the gala," he said quietly. "He was dismembered not too far from the entryway to the ballroom. Did you . . . happen to see anything? Hear anything?"

Taesia finally opened her eyes. They were oddly flat, oddly dark. The candles in the room flickered, shadows leaping across the walls.

"No," she said. "I was too busy catching up with my dear great-grandmother. Which you saw."

He had. He could see her there still, sitting astride that corpse, clad in a dress turned armor and a smile turned sinister.

She turned to him then, surprising him once more when she asked: "Why did you become a Hunter?"

Julian sat back. He knew the answer, of course, but he needed a moment to decide which version he should tell her. She'd trusted him, in some way, with a truth about her powers. He felt compelled to return it.

"I'm a beastspeaker," he said. "Or at least, that's what I call it. I don't know of anyone else with the ability."

Her solemnity faded as she perked up, grief overtaken by curiosity. "Beastspeaker? What's that?"

"It's like a—a sense, sort of." His neck flushed; he'd had years to figure out how to best explain it, and he still did it abysmally. "I can connect to the minds of beasts. Not animals, or other humans. Just beasts. It's like . . . reading their emotions. They don't have thoughts like we do, but I can tell what they're thinking all the same."

"Huh." She studied him from head to feet, as if reevaluating him. His flush spread to his face. "I've never met someone with a skill that wasn't tied to an element or the other realm-based powers."

"It's not a *skill*."

"What is it, then?"

He didn't know. No one did. In the darkest hours he thought of it as a curse, something as forbidden and abhorrent as Conjuration.

But the way Taesia was looking at him didn't make him feel ashamed of it. She'd even leaned forward, as if begging for the rest of an exciting story.

"How did you find out about it?" she asked.

He glanced at his father's medals. "It was my first real mission. My partner and I were assigned to a senior Hunter who brought us to take down a mustador terrorizing the local farmers." Taesia whistled; mustadors were a much larger and deadlier version of a buffalo crossed with an elephant. "I kept getting this strange feeling, as if I could shut my eyes and point to its exact location. When we found it, I froze. It wasn't fear, it was . . . anger. The mustador's anger was *in* me, somehow, or I was tapping into it. I warned my partner to get out of the way before the mustador could gut him with its tusks."

Julian took a deep breath. "I told the captain, and she's been making use of it ever since."

"Which is why she put you on Nik's task force," she guessed.

"Yes."

She nodded, not quite meeting his eyes but rather staring at his chest. He let her be lost in her thoughts, taking the time to study her back: the fall of an errant lock of hair against her cheek, the dark ring on her finger he now knew contained her shadow familiar.

Suddenly she asked, "Were you hurt?"

"We managed to corral the mustador before it could injure anyone."

"No, I meant at the gala."

Julian swallowed at the thought of those raised corpses and their grasping hands. "Some gashes. Nothing major."

"Let me see."

He waited for her to say she was joking. But she'd turned solemn again, patient. It felt like a challenge, like she was testing him in some strange, cryptic way. It made no sense how his heart skipped at the thought, razing the carefully nurtured fields of caution in his chest.

And it made no sense that he slowly, painstakingly pulled his shirt up to oblige her. Her gaze dropped to the muscles of his chest and abdomen before focusing on the bandaged gashes in his side.

They looked worse than they were, and though they stung and itched, the medic had claimed there was no infection. Taesia skimmed a finger along the edge of the bandage around his ribs. Julian shuddered as a flash of heat engulfed him.

He had been groomed to hunt beasts and yet somehow he had become the hunting ground, a land wrecked by tooth and claw and one woman's arrow tip pointed between his eyes.

"Conjuration caused this," she murmured. "There's still so much about it we don't know."

The words broke him out of his daze. Clearing his throat, he pulled his shirt back down. "Do we need to know everything? The important thing is to put a stop to it."

The twist of her mouth was barely a smile. "You're right."

Julian walked her to the door. The night was thick beyond the landing, pushing fingers of darkness into every nook and crevice. "You never told me what you ended up doing with those astralam bones."

She grinned. It was the same grin she'd used on him before, one made to disarm. He was beginning to see it for the shield that it was.

"You just focus on taking care of that sweet woman," she said. She started down the stairs, throwing over her shoulder, "This doesn't count as my favor, by the way."

He sighed loudly, and her laugh echoed in the shadows.

Taesia Lastrider seemed to have a habit of smashing into his life, stirring it up, and jumping back out. But that wasn't the only reason his head was swimming, or why he'd wanted to spend the night at his mother's.

Earlier that afternoon, he had been on patrol with Taide. The soldier had kept glancing at him until Julian snapped, "What?"

Taide had flinched. "Sorry! Um, that is, I wanted to ask you something. Your surname is Luca, right? Are you the son of Benjamín Luca?" Seeing his surprise, Taide had nodded. "I thought so. I wanted to ask because my own father served with him, back in the day."

Julian wasn't sure what to make of this, until Taide continued: "He was there when the beast attack happened."

Julian's throat had closed up. The beast attack near the border, where his father had been stationed five years ago. Where he had died.

"I'm sorry for your loss." Taide had shifted on his feet. "My da's told me some stories, and it sounds like he was an incredible soldier. Even when the assault happened . . ."

He'd trailed off, and Julian had stared at him in a silent plea to continue. To give him something, a shred more, of what had happened.

Taide had obliged. "My da said your father was ruthless. Nearly unstoppable. He managed to shoot down most of the first wave on his own. But more and more of the hill beasts came, and they were outnumbered."

Julian already knew this. Knew his father's body had been found surrounded by the bodies of monsters, matted with red and black blood, sword nowhere in sight.

"But his bow broke," Taide had gone on in a whisper. "And he . . . well, my da said . . ."

"Said what?" He'd barely recognized his own voice.

"He said Benjamín Luca started to fight them with his bare hands. And he was *winning*. Da said he'd never seen anything like it. It was almost as if—these are his words, not mine—it was almost as if Benjamín were a beast himself."

Julian had closed his eyes then, and he did the same now, standing in his mother's quiet apartment with the echo of Taesia Lastrider's laughter and his father's medals gleaming above the lintel.

He turned toward his room, then paused when he saw the light under his mother's door. "Ma?" he called softly, in case she had fallen asleep with the lamp on.

"Come in, Jules."

He eased the door open. Her room, like his, was a small square barely large enough for a bed, let alone her dresser. She was lounging against the pillows, a book propped open before her.

"I told you to get some rest," he admonished.

"I am resting." She gestured to the book, her nightgown, the bed. "I take it Lady Taesia left? I hope you acted like a gentleman."

He sat on the edge of her bed. "You were a good host, Ma."

Marjorie grinned at the praise and pinched his cheek. "She's welcome anytime. But what's this for?" She pressed a fingertip to the furrow on his brow.

"I wanted to ask you about...about Dad."

Marjorie's hand fell back to her lap. "Oh. What about him?"

But he didn't know what to ask, really. Or how to phrase it. It wasn't as if his mother had been there. It wasn't as if she could confirm what Taide had told him.

"How did you meet him?" he asked instead.

She raised her eyebrows. "I thought I told you this story? I was a laundress at the military compound. Your father came in every so often. He was so shy." She laughed at some distant, cherished memory. "I kept waiting for him to talk to me. Eventually I snuck a note into his clean uniform, and the next time he came in, he blustered through asking me for a night in the city together."

Julian began to smile, too. His father must have grown out of his shyness, because he recalled Benjamín as a man who was sure and steady.

But as much as he racked his memory, he couldn't think of any instance where his father had displayed anything close to inhuman strength.

"Did he ever act strange?" Julian pressed. "Did he ever do anything you couldn't explain?"

Marjorie frowned. "Where is this coming from all of a sudden?"

"Please, Ma."

His mother sighed. It was a while before she finally said, "There was one time something strange happened. To this day I can't really explain it. Do you remember my cousin Fabrian, in Jerica?" Julian nodded; Fabrian had died when Julian was ten. "We visited him when you were less than a year old. It was a nice little holiday. But on our way back to Nexus, your father was restless. We had rented a small wagon for the trip, since I don't know my way around horses like he did. You and I were in the back, and he was driving. He kept looking all around, frowning. As if he could sense something."

Her voice grew hoarse until she fell into a coughing fit. Julian brought her a cup of water and had her take tiny sips until it passed.

Marjorie exhaled and wiped her mouth. "Where was I? Right, he was driving the wagon. He suddenly pressed a knife into my hand and told me to stay put. You started crying, and that's when the beast showed up."

She shuddered, and Julian put a hand on her shoulder. "I'm not sure what it was, but it was big, bigger than a horse. Almost like a bull, with horrible twisting horns and a rough hide. Your father wasn't surprised at all, as if he knew it was coming. He met it in the field with his sword."

When she trailed off, Julian asked softly, "What happened?"

"He killed it. I was holding you in the wagon and watched the whole thing. I'd never seen him fight before. He was . . . fast. *So* fast. And strong. He could lift me like I weighed nothing even though I've never been particularly small, but this was different. It was . . . merciless."

Julian's mouth dried as he thought back to Taide's words, relating what his father had seen.

"He wrestled the beast into submission and ended it." She swallowed. "The beast didn't fight back much. Maybe it was sick? I don't know. But you stopped crying as soon as it was dead."

Julian tried to keep his breathing under control, squeezing his mother's shoulder a little harder to still the tremor in his hand.

"Jules?" Marjorie looked from his hand to his face. "Why did you want to know?"

He forced himself to shake his head. "Just curious," he whispered.

Taesia had asked him about his abilities, but he'd never known their origins, or understood the strange circumstances of his father's death. But now he had one more piece to fit into the puzzle of himself.

Benjamín Luca had also been a beastspeaker.

IV

Are you paying attention, my lady?"

Eran Liolle sat across from Angelica in his blue armchair, eyes pinched behind his spectacles. She thought she could hear thunder grumbling in the distance, the air sharp with ozone. It mirrored the storm building inside her, building within Nexus, between the Houses.

She couldn't stop dreaming about an unblinking blue eye, the terror of the gala. She and her mother had encouraged the king to cancel his plans for a House demonstration at Godsnight, but he'd refused.

"We need to remind those within our city who wields the power," Ferdinand had claimed. His voice wasn't its usual polite blandness, but something rich with annoyance. "No Conjurer is going to make us cower."

"Your Holiness," Adela had said, a title she only used when she was desperate, "we understand completely. And we would be more than honored to display our magic for you and the public. But these heretics are growing more and more powerful. It won't be safe for you."

He'd looked at her oddly then, and the space between Angelica's shoulder blades had prickled. It reminded her of a time she was younger and had attended some doña's dinner party. The woman had owned a cat, and it had stalked over to Angelica slowly, back arched, leaning toward her in a way she didn't like. The tension had drawn out until the cat clamped itself around her leg, making her shriek.

That same tension had seemed to flood the room until the king smirked.

"Don't worry about that," he'd said at last. "I'm planning a little demonstration of my own to dissuade them."

Angelica had exchanged a quick glance with her mother, baffled.

"The people need a spectacle of divine magic now more than ever," Ferdinand had went on. "Something to believe in. Something to pray to."

Angelica knew firsthand praying didn't do shit. Her fingers twitched as the storm inside her brewed, hot and humid.

"My lady, have you been playing your instruments?" Eran said. "Is that why you are suffering?"

Angelica choked on a laugh and hung her head, driving her fingernails into her skin. If only she had her violin, or her piccolo, or *anything* she could play to take the edge off this burning fever.

But her piccolo had been destroyed. She could still hear the crunch of it, the obliteration of one of the last few precious ties to her father.

A knock at the door startled them both. Eran excused himself and went to answer it.

"Georgina, what can I do for you?"

Angelica looked over her shoulder. A girl stood in his doorway, at least a first- or second-year university student, judging by the vest she wore with the university's crest. The girl was grinning, her face flushed.

"I...wanted to thank you." The girl's voice was little more than breath. "For your help after class." She shoved a paperweight shaped like a turtle into his hands.

Eran took the gift from her with a wide smile. "Someone told you I collect these," he said teasingly, balancing the paperweight in one hand. "It was my pleasure. If you ever want another private session, let me know and I can check my schedule." He winked.

The girl blustered her way through a goodbye. Eran stared after her retreating form before remembering Angelica was there.

Recalling his fingers around her wrist in the practice arena, Angelica shuddered. She wrapped a hand around that burning wrist as she stared at all the paperweights on his desk, her veins humming like plucked violin strings.

"Apologies, my lady," Eran said as he returned to the chair. "Now, where were—?"

"Stop it," she snarled.

Eran sat back, stunned. She took in a gulp of air, sweat beading along her forehead.

Instead of responding, Eran got up and poured a glass of water from a carafe behind his desk. When he placed the glass before her, all she did was stare at it, her throat paper dry.

"Having a relapse is completely normal," he said. "But we should really get to work, if you plan to have a presentation suitable for Godsnight."

She knew that, was haunted by it at all waking hours, and yet this deplorable man kept telling her all the things she already knew, and he couldn't help her, and the ritual was futile, so what was the fucking point?

"Let's try with something small," he said. "The glass of water before you. Can you form three balls of equal volume from the contents?"

What was the point? *What was the point?*

"I understand it must be difficult for you," Eran said. "It will be painful at first, but it will pass."

She stood abruptly, making him start. She grabbed the glass and hurled it at the wall, shattering it.

"My lady!"

"You are a disgusting little man," she seethed. Embers popped around her feet and sparked between her fingers. "You like having others feel like they owe you. I don't owe you anything."

He got to his feet slowly, hands held out before him. Genuine fear flickered in his eyes. "I... I apologize if you feel that way. I certainly had no intention of—"

"SHUT UP!" she screamed, and with the scream it was as if all the horror was ripping out of her, sloughing off her skin and hurling up from the bottom of her gut, all the useless rage and unfulfilled desire spiraling out, out, until it was nothing but a javelin of destruction.

Eran toppled over his armchair as the furniture in the room banged against the walls and the window exploded outward in a shower of glass. Angelica stood at the heart of the storm, breathing ash and smoke. The floor trembled beneath her feet as the wood groaned.

She walked toward Eran getting to his knees, every step leaving a footprint of charred rug in her wake. The mage fumbled for his glasses; once he slipped them back on, he looked up at her and paled.

"You are nothing," she whispered.

The doorway was crowded with people drawn by the commotion. They hastily parted as she walked by, smoke rising off her shoulders.

It felt as if the world around her was about to snap and break.

The mage was useless to help her. Her mother ran her through countless exercises, but it only resulted in frustration on both sides.

She wasn't getting better.

Yet somehow she'd managed to produce flame in Eran's office, as well as air. But she could think of nothing she'd done differently other than open herself to rage, letting it out as a ringing wail. It had felt *good*.

That feeling drained out of her with every step she took toward her rooms, waving away servants who inquired after what she needed. It was only after changing into a dress that didn't smell like smoke she noticed the window was open, letting in a cold breeze. Frowning, she eyed the vial upon the sill. It was made of cheap glass, filled with an unknown liquid. Underneath it was pinned a small scrap of paper.

Angelica carefully popped the cork off the vial and sniffed. She recognized the sweet, herbal scent of Hypericum. Frown deepening, she picked up the scrap of paper. A heart had been drawn on it.

"The fuck," Angelica muttered.

Then she remembered: Cosima. The thief had been the one to suggest Hypericum in the first place. She choked a little at the thought of her being here, in Angelica's rooms, alone. Maybe their House guards really were slacking.

She cast a cursory look around but didn't find anything missing or out of place. What kind of thief broke in and *left* something instead of taking something?

Her fingers curled, ready to crumple the paper and toss it into the trash bin. Instead, she stared at the inked heart before sighing and tucking it into her pocket. Then she downed the Hypericum and made for her study to read more of the grimoire.

She'd received a missive from Taesia this morning asking her to search the book for reference of fulcrums. The missive hadn't explained why, but Taesia's use of proper capitalization and punctuation meant it was something she was taking seriously. Whatever these fulcrums were, maybe they were related to their fifth realm problem.

Two servants were chatting quietly in the antechamber as they polished the floors. Angelica would have ignored them if she hadn't heard one of them say, "—going to the Godsnight exhibition?"

She paused on the stairs. The servants hadn't noticed her yet, their heads bowed as they scrubbed.

"Palace square's gonna be full up," the other one grunted. "It'll be impossible to see anything."

"There's gonna be a big stage, though. They're constructing it next week. One of my friend's cousins is helping build it."

The other snorted. "Making it all that much easier for the Conjurers, huh?"

"You think so?"

"If they've hit the palace and killed the king's spymaster, then nowhere's safe." The servant shook her head. "I barely get enough sleep as it is."

"It's so rare we get to see the Houses' magic, though."

"Especially this one," the other snickered.

Angelica drew herself up and descended the rest of the stairs. The servants, finally spotting her, scrambled to their feet and bowed with flushed faces.

"My lady," they whispered.

Angelica stared them down a moment longer before turning away, purposefully leaving a scuff in the floor with her sole.

In her study, she gratefully sank into her chair. Though the Hypericum was working, her head swam and her heart rate was elevated. Once she'd driven the servants' inane chatter from her mind, she unlocked the secret compartment in her desk and drew out the grimoire.

Fulcrums, she thought as she opened to where she'd left off. There had been an entire section labeled "Of Demons and Their Conjuring," which she had skipped, as if laying eyes on an actual demon's name was enough to summon one. She'd been eager to read anything else about Ostium, but so far the grimoire hadn't revealed more, as if the existence of a fifth realm was entirely commonplace and unremarkable.

A whole realm, *gone.* Did the other realms remember it, or had it been a joint effort by the gods to erase knowledge of it? And if so, *why?* Would Deia tell her, if she asked?

Familiar footsteps echoed down the hall, their pace quickened with anger. Angelica barely managed to shove the grimoire out of sight by the time her mother stormed through the door.

"Angelica," she growled. "Please explain to me why you destroyed a university mage's office."

Of course news had traveled quickly. Angelica hid her shaking hands under the desk, on top of the grimoire's jeweled cover. "He deserved it. He—"

"I don't care!" Adela leaned on the desk, the wood smoking under her fingertips. "Do you have any idea what this might look like to others? Don Damari is in the middle of an investigation into Don Soler's *murder.* We can't afford to give him any ammunition against us!"

Angelica tried and failed to swallow. The heat that had encompassed her earlier was gone, leaving her bitterly cold. "It's...it's officially been ruled a murder?"

Realizing she'd left burn marks on the desk's surface, Adela swore and stepped back, half collapsing into one of the velvet-lined chairs. She pinched the bridge of her nose, and Angelica was flooded with dread at the prospect of seeing her mother cry.

Instead, Adela gave a heaving sigh and dropped her hand. Her fury was gone, replaced with exhaustion that was worse than tears. Her mother seemed...vulnerable.

"Angel. I know there's a lot of pressure on you, but we just have to get through the king's exhibition."

Angelica picked at one of the grimoire's jewels. "And then what?"

Her mother huffed. "It'll depend on what happens. At least we'll know the Lastriders won't be the favored House."

"And what if..." Angelica took a deep breath, forced the words out. "What if there *is* no favored House?"

"What do you mean?"

"I mean that the king's persistence about going through with it is strange, considering the risk. Don't you think so?"

"Of course. But we've already tried to sway him." Her mother pursed her lips. "I wonder if Don Soler's death rattled him more than he's letting on."

A contributing factor, perhaps, but it had to be more than that. If Don Damari was including the Houses in his investigation, that meant Ferdinand didn't trust any of them, especially after Dante's arrest.

Was the king trying to punish the Houses, then? Or else publicly humiliate them in some way? The thought made her face sting with a sudden rush of blood.

The grimoire sat heavy on her lap. For a heady moment she wondered what would happen if she told her mother everything about the ritual, about Ostium, about the potential for the Houses to wrest more control from the king. Of turning the exhibition into a true miracle.

But the truth sat painful in her throat. She couldn't, not knowing how much her mother had worked toward the crown. How disappointed she would be seeing Angelica turn to Conjuration after everything they had seen it do.

"You should have never gone to that mage in the first place," Adela muttered as she stood. "Anything you need to be taught, I'll teach you. We'll work on a presentation for the exhibition. Something that will make the king and the public think twice before doubting us."

"Does that mean you'll give the rest of my instruments back?" Angelica asked.

Adela frowned. "Absolutely not. What do you mean, the rest of your instruments?"

Angelica had thought the piccolo had been some sort of apology from her mother. If it wasn't . . .

"Nothing," she whispered.

Her mother opened the door. "We'll practice this afternoon. Get some rest before then."

Angelica waited several minutes after Adela had left to lay the grimoire on her desk again. There was only so much she could learn from it, she realized.

If she wanted answers to her questions, she would need to bring them before her god.

V

Risha was becoming increasingly uncomfortable with desperation. She hated the way it held her by the throat, taking up all the space within her she wanted for other things—ideas, inspiration, insight. But the more she allowed the desperation in, the less she was able to focus.

Which was how she found herself on Lillum Street on a cloudy morning, a black rose tucked into her pocket. It was a narrow cobblestone walkway along the outer rim of the city. Little sunlight reached this place due to the wall's shadow.

"Where are you going?" her mother had demanded that morning as Risha headed out. Darsha had been busy writing out funerary dirges, calligraphy shining wetly on parchment.

"Saya forgot a textbook," she'd said, startled by the ease with which the lie had come to her. *You're becoming as bad as Taesia.*

Darsha had eyed her ensemble critically. Risha had chosen an understated Vaegan outfit rather than the more elaborate Parithvian clothing that filled her wardrobe.

"I'll embarrass Saya if I'm dolled up around her university friends," Risha had said. "Besides, I shouldn't draw attention to myself."

That, at least, her mother agreed with. The mood of the city was still somber, still tense. And yet somehow King Ferdinand thought a pretty demonstration of magic would be enough to appease the citizens and assuage their fear.

"All right," Darsha had said at last, scattering sand on the wet ink to make it dry faster. "But make sure you're home by noon so you can get changed."

"Why?"

Her mother's frown could have melted ice on the Daccadian Mountains. "Your dowry meeting! You're finally going to meet your fiancé. It's a little sooner than I hoped, but we can't risk distrust of House Vakara spreading any more than it has after the gala."

Risha had nearly laughed at the absurdity of something as inconsequential as an engagement. "All right," she'd played along. "I'll be back by noon."

Risha stopped when she found a wooden sign hanging above a door. The sign had been engraved with the likeness of a rose, the paint faded and peeled after several winters' worth of exposure.

A florist? The vases and planters in the window display were full of bright yarrow and purple barberry and starburst sunrays.

And roses. No black ones, but an ombre of white to pink to scarlet, flourishing and hale.

A garland of marigolds and bay laurel hung on the door, strewn intermittently with tiny bells. A burial wreath meant to keep spirits out—or keep them inside. It wasn't one from her House; she was more than familiar with her mother's wreaths, and this didn't follow Darsha's usual patterns.

The bells chimed softly as she opened the door. Inside, the floral scents converged into a harmonious note, clean and sweet. The shop was quiet, dim thanks to the wall's shadow, and for a second she wondered if anyone was actually here.

Then a lanky man at the counter straightened. He eyed her over, feigning disinterest.

"May I help you?" he asked. "If you need funeral bouquets, we have a special going on."

Wordlessly Risha took the black rose from her pocket.

The man nodded and moved away from the counter. Risha caressed the sharpened bone shards in her other pocket, ready to shoot them at the man's throat and eyes if he so much as twitched toward her. The longer she maintained contact with them the more she sensed the distant spirits they were connected to, faint echoes of violence and grief and illness.

He opened the back door and ushered her inside. She cautiously walked past him into a stockroom filled with terracotta vases and bags of fertilizer. A set of gardening tools were hung above a worktable, shears left out on its surface. The man cleared his throat and pointed to the floor, where a basement door had been propped up with a short shovel, revealing the top of a flight of wooden stairs.

Risha descended slowly, wood creaking under her soles, its grain tight with age. Every step she took revealed more of a wide, square room with a stone floor softened by an ancient burgundy rug. It smelled of mildew and soil, and something unpleasantly familiar.

Death.

Four people were milling around the basement, three sitting on stools and one pacing. The latter stopped and looked up at her.

It was the young man she'd seen in the necropolis. When he smiled, his dark eyes crinkled.

"You found us," he said.

One of the Revenants, a short Azunese woman with broad cheekbones, stood and flexed her muscles as if to attack.

"Easy, Nat."

"What, are we giving away names now?" his partner spat. Risha recognized her low, hoarse voice as the one who had called her *godspawn* in the necropolis.

"I suppose we haven't formally introduced ourselves." He bowed toward Risha. "Call me Jas. This cheerful creature is Natsumi."

Risha didn't say anything. The other two Revenants watched on, bemused and intrigued. They didn't offer up their names.

Their leader held a gloved hand out to her. Risha forced herself to let go of her bone shards and placed her palm on top of his, allowing him to escort her down the remaining few steps. Natsumi scoffed.

"I want to make one thing perfectly clear," Risha said. She tossed the black rose at his feet. "I'm only here to get answers."

Jas raised one sleek eyebrow. "We can provide you with those. But first..."

She took a step back as he sank to his knees and prostrated, touching his forehead to the floor in a traditional Parithvian gesture of respect—or contrition. The other Revenants shuffled on their feet before bowing their heads, though Natsumi kept her arms crossed with a scowl.

"Words alone can't convey how sorry we are," Jas murmured without lifting his head. "We knew there would be some risk with our methods, some collateral damage, though it wasn't our intention to take human lives. But lives were taken regardless, and that will forever be our burden to bear."

In Parithvi, someone who prostrated wasn't allowed up until the one being prostrated to touched the back of their head. But Risha stayed still and silent, unwilling to extend this gesture of forgiveness.

Jas, realizing this, sighed and slowly regained his feet. "We understand that our methods are unconventional. That they wouldn't be to your taste."

Unconventional? What they were doing broke every rule her father had laid out for her. Anger pricked the palms of her hands, one of the bone shards in her pocket jumping in reaction.

"You're putting people in danger, *yourself* in danger, all because you want to call yourselves necromancers," she said lowly.

"It's not as if your family is making any breakthroughs," Natsumi said. "If we leave this situation to the only three necromancers in Vitae, we're fucked."

"The city is swarming with spirits who're denied rest," Jas went on. "If we don't get the barrier open, they'll cause a lot more damage than we've done."

The anger burned in her chest. Before she knew it the bone shards had fanned out in front of her. They pointed their sharp tips at Jas, backing him up against the wall. Natsumi cursed and unsheathed a knife as the other Revenants cried out, but Jas held up a hand to stop them.

"You are a hypocrite," Risha growled. The bones angled around Jas like fangs waiting to pierce his neck. "You say you want to stop the spirits from rampaging, but look at what you've done. That stunt near the palace. The necropolis. The *gala.* What you're doing is irresponsible and... and impossible!"

"Not impossible," Jas said, oddly calm. "As you've seen for yourself."

"Because you stole an artifact with incredible magical properties," she said. "Leshya's necklace belongs to the Vakaras. Hand it over willingly, or I'll take it by force." Natsumi made a sound like a growling cat.

"I can perform many of the same spells as you, even without the necklace," Jas said. "I understand the fundamentals of necromancy."

"Your cult's found shortcuts." The bone shards inched closer to his throat. He swallowed. "A way to tap into a power beyond you."

"I don't think it's beyond anyone, so long as they apply themselves," Jas said. "And we aren't a cult."

"Then what are you? Why do you call yourselves the Revenants?"

"We've all died and come back," Natsumi answered.

Risha frowned. "What do you mean?"

"I had a terrible illness as a child," Jas said. "I was predicted not to make it past three days. In fact, my heart stopped for a few seconds." He shrugged, as if the matter of dying was a minor inconvenience. "Then it started back up again."

"I almost died of hypothermia," Natsumi added. "Like Jas, my heart stopped then started again."

"We're bound by our bodies' trauma." Jas laid a hand over his chest. "The memory of the barrier, of being unable to move on, the frustration and horror of it. That's what I mean when I say we're working toward the same goal. I know you'd do whatever it takes to see this through. We can help."

"Not if it means taking the lives of others."

"In that we agree," he said softly. His lashes brushed his cheeks as he looked down, repentant. "We want no more death, my lady. As I said before, we want to atone with action, not merely words."

Taking a deep breath, Risha reluctantly drew the bone shards back to her. When she tucked them into her pocket, the Revenants relaxed.

"Prelate Lezzaro helped you, didn't he?" she asked.

Jas rubbed his throat, though the bone shards hadn't touched him. "Yes. He and I...ran into each other, and had an interesting talk. He told me how Godsnight would be a time when the barriers are at their thinnest. That by performing Conjuration throughout the city near the portals, it would help thin the barriers even more."

She remembered the skeleton at the Thana basilica, the Conjuration circle with its seven-pointed star. Risha narrowed her eyes. "How did you run into the prelate? Why would he even talk to you about this?"

"We happened to be visiting the Thana basilica at the same time. He overheard me expressing my frustrations with the Mortri barrier." Jas shrugged. "We came into an agreement."

"But how can Conjuration replicate necromancy? What exactly did he tell you?"

"I'm not sure how he got his information. He only showed me a sketch of the original Conjuration circles, those that had been used to commune with the gods." Jas sketched one in the air with his finger, a circle with a diamond in its center. "Then a priest named Marcos Ricci experimented with the magic and learned demon summoning." Another circle, this time with a five-pointed star. "Different alignments and symbols to activate different sorts of magic. We weren't sure which one could give us the effect we wanted, so we had to experiment."

"The missing bodies," Risha said slowly. "You stole bodies to experiment on them."

"Yes. But we always returned them."

"One still housed a spirit that attacked their family!"

"Like you've never made a mistake," Natsumi muttered.

Risha bit back her retort. "If Lezzaro taught you all this to begin with, then why kill him? Did you need him gone so you could make your attack at the gala?"

The Revenants all seemed startled by this. "Why the fuck would we kill the prelate?" Natsumi snapped.

"He was killed by Conjurers. You..." But they'd denied being Conjurers in the necropolis. "Weren't you working with Dante Lastrider?"

Jas shook his head. "No. We're not sure why he's being lumped in with us, but we've never spoken to the Lastrider heir."

Risha's head spun. Had Dante really been a Conjurer? Had he really killed Lezzaro, or was Taesia right and he was being framed? It was getting harder to parse lie from truth, and she didn't know what to believe.

She couldn't take the Revenants at their word. But she couldn't take Taesia at hers anymore either.

The Revenants were staring at her. She felt suddenly hot, itching to remove her overcoat.

"The plants." She waved at the black rose. "These don't wither, and the color is unnatural. Also, the skeleton at the basilica was woven through with vines. Some at the necropolis were, too."

Jas walked over and picked up the rose, twirling it in his gloved fingers. "Little tricks I learned here and there."

"So you're an elementalist." Risha had guessed so, but felt better for having confirmation. "What are your elements?"

"Mostly earth, plant based." He brought the petals to his nose and inhaled. "A little air, but not much."

"Is this flower shop yours?"

"No, it belongs to the man upstairs and his wife." He smirked at Natsumi, whose frown deepened.

Risha blinked at her. "You're a florist?"

Natsumi tilted her head as if daring Risha to push her incredulity.

"They were kind enough to let us use their basement for our purposes," Jas said.

"For experimenting on the dead."

"We've been through this, my lady. We want to get the spirits to Mortri. For our loved ones to move on. We..." He glanced at the others. "We've all lost someone precious to us. For me, it's my mother. For Natsumi, her sister. Because of the barrier Thana erected, their souls haven't been able to move beyond the void. All we want is to break the barrier open and free their spirits. Let them move on to Mortri to rest or be reborn." He pressed a hand to his chest. "Including those we have taken from *their* loved ones. It's the only path I know toward redemption."

It wasn't, and they all knew it. Reading her expression, Jas huffed a quiet breath that was almost a laugh.

"Of course, you have duties to adhere to," he said. "You now know where to find us. What we look like. If you'd rather turn us in to the authorities, that's your decision to make."

"Jas!" Natsumi hissed, the other two exchanging looks of alarm.

Risha stared into Jas's eyes. They were a warm brown, framed by thick lashes. Risha had spoken to the gentry long enough to tell when someone was deceiving her, putting on airs to please her. There was none of that here, only conviction that the path he'd chosen was one he believed in wholeheartedly.

She remembered the cold soil of the pathway beneath her, Thana's fingernails digging into her cheeks. *It is not your power to wield*, Thana had told her. *It will be mine.*

Her god was constantly refusing her, had been furious at Risha's attempt at crafting a spell via Conjuration. There had to be a common thread between them.

"How..." Risha cleared her throat. "How do you do it?"

Jas visibly relaxed, then signaled to the others. There was only the slightest hesitance before the rug was rolled away, revealing a stretch of floor white with chalk dust. When Natsumi opened a deep wooden trunk in the back, fog billowed out. The chest was lined with frost stone, a material harvested in the north that emanated a burning cold. The kitchens at the villa had one to store easily perishable food.

But there was no food in this chest. A body lay inside, its skin unnervingly pale, covered with rime. The chest cavity was riddled with knife wounds crusted with frozen blood.

Risha glared at Jas, but he lifted his hands. "He was stabbed in an alley outside a gambling den. There was no family to claim him."

She knew of people who stole bodies for their own purposes—medics, cults, even those who took their worship of the dead to disturbingly ardent levels—but to see it up close made her shiver. Her father's rules had been etched into her since she was a child: how to respect and care for the dead, to listen to their stories if they felt like sharing, to burn their bodies or put them in the ground as soon as possible before the spirit claimed it.

Jas took a piece of chalk from his pocket and knelt on the stone floor. "Conjuration is the only way a person can tap into the natural power of the Cosmic Scale that's built up because of the Sealing."

Risha recalled Saya's textbooks on planar properties, the intersecting lines between the Four Realms making a geometric circle. As Jas sketched the circle, the other Revenants drew symbols and glyphs within the perimeter.

"At first the knowledge was contained to an insular cult that's been around since the initial days of demon summoning, but members began to leak their knowledge to others." Jas's brow was furrowed as he drew a seven-pointed star within the circle. He held the chalk like he'd held the rose, delicate and assured. "People who didn't have magic yet wanted a taste of it. Or those who wanted a certain kind of magic they could never perform otherwise."

"Like you?" Risha guessed. His short laugh rang like struck crystal.

"Like me," he agreed. Two Revenants moved the body into the circle's center, like a stamen surrounded by petals. "But I was fascinated by Lezzaro's ideas. If Conjuration had been used to call upon the gods, and then demons, what if it could call other things? A spirit, perhaps? What if someone could become a necromancer not through bloodright, but by practicing an unknown art?"

Jas gained his feet and dusted the chalk off his gloves. Natsumi handed him her knife. "The circles and their construction are integral, as well as an offering of some sort. In this case, blood."

He peeled one of his black gloves off with his teeth. He pricked one of his fingers and let a drop of blood fall into the circle.

It glowed an ominous black. Risha backed away, her stomach aching with the familiar sensation of Mortri. Expansive, distant, yearning.

The body in the circle jerked in the blackish light, ice melting off its skin and lashes, fingertips twitching as the effects of rigor mortis were reversed. A thin, clear fluid began to leak from his nose and mouth, filling the room with the odor of putrefaction.

Above the body hovered an indistinguishable outline. Risha couldn't tell if the spirit was the man's or another one entirely; all she could perceive was its anger. It dove into the body, fitting itself within the space of decomposing flesh.

The body jerked once, twice, then sat up. The man's eyes were blank and unseeing. When Jas commanded it to rise, it did so clumsily, listing to one side. The black glow left the circle, and the Revenants murmured happily.

Risha wanted to throw up. It went against everything she knew about her power, every rule a Vakara had to abide by. They wanted magicless people to learn this? *This?*

"What do you think?" Jas asked as the corpse began to wander the basement aimlessly. Natsumi kept an eye on it, ready to score the circle at the first sign of trouble.

The stink in the air made Risha nauseated, despite having smelled it so many times. It was because of whatever that circle had brought with it—the sulfuric aftertaste of something beyond even Mortri.

"I think this is crude," Risha said at last.

Jas glanced at the corpse bumping into the side of the stairs. "I'll admit, I could do better if I had the necklace on me. The trick will be getting them to not shamble around like a tipsy child."

"They shamble because they're dead!" Risha's head suddenly spun, and Jas reached out to catch her, his ungloved hand warm around her elbow.

"I'm sorry," he said softly. "I think we've overwhelmed you. I wanted to show you there's more to your power than you probably realize."

More to your power. The contact between them, even between the layers of her clothes, allowed her to sense the blood rushing through his veins as it fed into his heart, pumping out again to his organs, feeding a body that was young and healthy and harbored a delicious power.

Risha remembered the tight curl of her fingers against her palm. The struggle of the man's heart.

She broke away and tried to compose herself, taking deep breaths and regretting it as the smell of death burned in her nose. The corpse was feeling around the opposite wall, jaw hanging open.

Her halfhearted attempt at Conjuration before the Mortri barrier had incensed Thana. There had to be a reason why. Had to be a way to work around the obstacle of a fifth heir.

Whatever it takes.

"All right," she whispered.

Jas straightened. "All right?"

"You show contempt for those whose magic is a bloodright, but this *is* my bloodright, and I've spent my entire life learning it." Risha met the eyes of each Revenant. "You're right that our goals are aligned, however different our methods. But if you desire my cooperation, those methods must stop."

She took out some string and wrapped it around her fingers. "By using the energy of the Cosmic Scale built up at the barriers, you drain the only energy Vitae has to sustain itself. By calling out to the dead, you end up summoning spirits farthest from Mortri's barrier, the ones who linger in this realm because of unfulfilled resentment."

She twisted the string until it snapped. The corpse fell limply to the ground as the spirit shot out of it, sucked back to the middle of the circle as if by a strong wind. There it writhed and made a low hissing noise, fighting to get back to the body.

Risha raised her eyebrows at Natsumi. Scowling, the woman broke the chalk circle and the spirit disappeared to the void with another flash of black light.

"Whatever your plans are next, I will oversee them," she said. "As much as I want a way into Mortri, I won't endanger the city for it."

She turned back to Jas. He studied her a long moment, then broke into a radiant smile. He held out his ungloved hand for her to shake.

"You have a deal," he said.

Risha had to hurry home, running the last mile until she burst into the villa. Her mother paced the courtyard, dressed in rich blues and golds, enormous earrings swaying. The servants grabbed hold of Risha as soon as she skidded to a stop.

"Where have you *been*?" Darsha cried as they hustled her to her rooms. "You need to get changed! *Now!*"

Risha, sweaty and no doubt carrying some of that sulfuric stink on her, was shoved into a bathtub full of warm rose water. She washed as quickly as she could before her mother's retinue of maids descended on her, fighting to comb and style her hair while rubbing her skin with neem oil and lotus extract.

The outfit they chose for her was a lovely yet heavy lehenga choli in dark emerald, the skirt flaring to the floor in a riot of golden embroidery and beadwork. A silk dupatta hung from her elbows, sheer and simple. A necklace was clasped around her neck and long earrings brushed her jaw, her face touched with kajal and rouge.

Once she was deemed presentable, she was escorted back to the courtyard. The clouds had momentarily parted, a sheet of dull light striping the ground. As she walked toward her mother, she realized their guests had already arrived.

"It is an honor to be invited to the House of Vakara, meer rata," the older Parithvian man said with a deep bow over Darsha's hand. His accent was thick, his hair more white than black. He wore a sherwani of black and gold, an obvious nod to their House colors. "Even more of an honor is the consideration of my son to take your daughter's hand in marriage."

Darsha smiled with a polite dip of her chin. "The honor is ours, meer sirdar. I'm sorry my husband could not attend today. Duty calls, as usual."

"Yes, that is to be expected," the sirdar said with a grim nod. "Considering recent events." He then spotted Risha and his eyes sparkled. "My! What a vision you are, meer rata."

Risha held her heavy skirt as she curtsied. "It's a pleasure to meet you, Sirdar Chadha. My mother has told me much about you."

Darsha's nostrils flared; she had *tried* to tell Risha about him, but Risha hadn't bothered to listen.

"The pleasure is all ours." The sirdar gestured behind him, at the younger Parithvian man gazing up at the polished granite keystone shaped like a skull above the nearest archway. "Please allow me to introduce my son."

The younger man stepped forward at his cue, his air of trepidation giving way to a charming smile. He was dressed in a sherwani of silver with black trim, his hair thick and dark.

Risha stared, knowing her mouth was hanging open but unable to close it. His gaze trailed over her lehenga before moving back up to her stunned expression. Clearing his throat, the young Parithvian lord bowed over her hand and kissed the back of it, lips warm against her chilled skin.

"Jaswant Chadha," he introduced himself, smiling up at her with a challenge in his brown eyes. "But you, meer rata, may call me Jas."

VI

A bead of sweat rolled down Nikolas's face as he sat surrounded by Lumin refugees. The Sunbringer Spear lay across his lap, his thighs itching from its heat.

The blade glowed brighter than usual as he poured his power into it, using the spear as a conduit. Even Lux was drawn to the metal wings that housed Phos's feathers, pulsing gently as if encouraging Nikolas to keep going.

"Light is life, light is longevity," the refugees chanted around him. Maddox had joined them, following the prayer even as he watched Nikolas with worry. "Light is the point in which we find ourselves whole. Phos, deliver to us a blessing, and in return we will shed light where there is darkness."

Nikolas repeated the prayer to himself silently. Thought of wings, luminous and golden, sprouting from his back—the sure sign that he had earned Phos's blessing, his strength, his power.

He grunted as his solar plexus began to ache with it. His limbs were trembling at the strain of holding on to his lightspeed for so long with no outlet. The prayer started up again, and he tightened his hold around the spear's stock, breaths coming in sharp pants.

"Hold."

The Lumins' voices died at the sound of Maddox's order. Nikolas gratefully let go of his power, the spear's brilliance dimming as he caught his breath.

The Solarian primary ran a hand over his tied-back hair and sighed, and suddenly Nikolas was a boy again, standing in the training yards as his father instructed him in the ways of Lumin magic. Telling him how it was a gift and a right, and how he was expected to master it before proving himself in front of king and country. Yelling and shoving him when he got something wrong.

Nikolas had once been able to do what he was told. To create a shield blocking swords and fists alike, to throw Lux like a spear. To run across the villa in sporadic bursts of lightspeed as Rian tried to make off with his books and toys. It felt like another life. A fever dream.

Maddox didn't shove or yell. Instead he looked at Nikolas with patience that seemed as foreign to Nikolas as the consonant-heavy language of the Sarnai Steppes.

"Maybe we should try another approach," Maddox suggested.

Nikolas didn't miss the quiet scoff that came from one of the refugees, the same ones he'd discovered attempting Conjuration. They weren't in the butcher's shop this time, but rather the meeting house in the Solara Quarter, the table and chairs cleared away from the central room.

None of them had been surprised to see him. The sun hadn't yet dimmed to a degree that non-Solarians would be able to tell, and his father had been insistent on keeping it to themselves for now so as to avoid more panic in the city, but the refugees understood the severity. They understood that if Nikolas was going to strengthen the connection between Vitae and Solara, he would need help.

"Most of a Lumin's magic is linked to their familiar," Maddox said. His own familiar looped around one of his slightly pointed ears like a dangling earring. "The rest comes from our connection to Solara, to Phos. Every Lumin is touched with it in some way. You more so than us."

"Phos's wings," Nikolas murmured.

Maddox nodded. "A gift only the descendants of Phos possess, a sure sign of his blessing."

"I used to play Phos's wings with my sister when we were little," said a refugee with close-cropped hair. "We would make a sheet of light on our backs and pretend to fly."

The man who had scoffed glared at Nikolas, his shock of white hair falling against a forehead prematurely lined with frown marks. Vedari, the one who had been so outspoken the last time they'd met.

"Your lord father has them, doesn't he?" he demanded. "Then why don't you? Why is Phos ignoring his own descendant?"

The others turned to him, silent questions in their eyes. But Nikolas had no answer; he was just as in the dark as they were.

Maddox put a strong hand on Nikolas's shoulder. "We'll try again. This time, use your familiar as well as the spear."

Nikolas nodded and delved back into the unsteady reservoir of his power. His fingertips began to glow, and a similar light engulfed Maddox's cupped hands as his familiar floated above them. The other Lumins did the same, channeling power through their familiars as Lux twirled nervously before Nikolas, shining brighter.

He thought back to when his power had come easier, tried to remember how it had felt. He and Rian used to pelt things at one another—rocks, weapons, even furniture—to test each other at unexpected moments, to create a shield fast enough. It had pleased Waren, but Madeia had forbidden it when Nikolas had broken a chair on Rian's back.

A huff of laughter escaped him even as a dull pain closed his throat. Rian's cry of surprise and disappointment, the cracking of the wood, his brother grabbing a broken chair leg to retaliate.

Nikolas sank deeper into the memory. A spark in his chest crawled down his arms before igniting his hands, traveling up the spear, creating two points of heat near his shoulder blades. The light unspooled around him, a shaft of sunlight escaping a thick cloud.

But all of him was the cloud, and the sunlight that touched Nexus now was thin and feeble. His arms shook under the strain of magic gone uncast, sitting heavy and reluctant inside him as all the negative thoughts he tried to keep at bay surged forth.

Nikolas's power slipped away. He gasped and fell forward, Maddox catching him as the light dissipated.

"A fucking joke," Vedari muttered.

Nikolas squeezed his hands around the spear. He pulled a breath into his lungs and held it there, letting it burn and distract him from the queasiness in his gut.

"Let's take a moment," Maddox suggested.

Nikolas was all too glad to follow the primary up the stairs to his apartment, escaping the stares of the others. Maddox asked for someone to bring them tea as they settled at the small table before the fire.

"I hope you can forgive them," Maddox said at last. "Living in Nexus isn't exactly easy for us."

Despite Vedari's tone, Nikolas really couldn't blame them for being disappointed. He'd claimed he would find a way to get them home. They probably thought it was nothing but an empty promise, now.

"Did you originally come from Solara?" Nikolas asked.

"No, but our great-grandparents did. They were locked out after the Sealing." Maddox nodded in thanks as the tea tray was set before them. "We grew up as children of two realms, conforming to Nexus's society while keeping the traditions of our culture alive."

He indicated the blooming tea within the glass teapot. The tea buds were woven around lilies and Osmanthus, as well as a couple morning glories and the full head of a sunflower, their petals extended, suspended in the green-tinted water.

"We have our own plants and flowers for this tea in Solara, but we've adapted the recipe," Maddox said as he poured a cup for Nikolas. "It helps with concentration and the flow of your Lumin energy."

Nikolas accepted his cup with a quiet thanks. It smelled fragrant, the heat of the cup against his fingers exquisite. Maddox noticed his shiver.

"Is there anything we can do?" the primary whispered. "About..."

About the sun. Nikolas took a sip and barely winced as it nipped his tongue. "That's partly why I came to you today. Godsnight falls in little over a week. When the Cosmic Scale aligns, I hope to reopen the portal. But..."

But what chance did they have of succeeding with the ritual, if they needed a fifth heir? If the king was forcing them onto a stage, in front of so many witnesses?

He set this cup down but didn't let go of it, too enamored with its heat. "I don't know if I am strong enough to do so," he finished in a whisper.

Maddox took a deep breath. "It is a massive undertaking, one that no Cyr before you has accomplished. We will continue to help in any way we can."

Nikolas closed his eyes. "Thank you."

"It helps that you possess the Sunbringer Spear, and two of Phos's feathers." Maddox's eyes drifted toward the spear leaning against the wall behind Nikolas. "Miracles have happened with just one. Like Vrinä and the Shadow Sea."

Nikolas had read that tale in one of his father's books. How Vrinä had found one of Phos's molted feathers outside her village, which was suffering from drought and famine. Their land had been cut off from precious resources by the Shadow Sea, a cavern of endless dark made during an invasion of Nyx's minions. But Vrinä had used that feather to light the way for her village, crossing the darkness in their plight to find a new home.

Lux drifted closer to his cup, floating above the tea and turning it from green to gold. "I'm afraid not even two feathers will be enough to rip through the barrier," Nikolas said. "But I'll still try. I just have to find a way to keep my power stable without Phos's blessing."

Maddox hesitated before saying, "I brought you up here because I wanted to ask you something personal. When you try to tap into your power, what do you feel?"

"I feel . . ." Nikolas grasped for the words to describe it, something other than *empty*. "I feel like it's there, beyond my reach, unable to come to the surface. I used to be able to make shields that lasted hours, to phase myself long distances. It was easy. And now it's . . . not."

An uncomfortable flush traveled up his neck. Nikolas had long fallen out of the practice of speaking of these things; his father refused to hear it. Rian was gone, and he didn't want to worry his mother. He hadn't even explained it to Taesia, who came from a different magic source and wouldn't understand—and he'd always feared it would make her perceive him as weak.

Maddox hummed in thought. "Something must have happened between then and now."

Nikolas thought of the violent game he and Rian had played, laughter turning to yells or the other way around.

"An event as tragic and traumatic as death is certainly enough to stopper up your magic," Maddox said softly. "And in fact is not unheard of. I had an aunt who was a Lumin, but after the death of her Vitaean husband, she could not access the full capacity of her power for the remainder of her life."

"What are you saying?" Nikolas said slowly. "That if I stop grieving my brother, my magic will return?"

"You and I both know there's no end to grief. The solution is to find a way to live alongside it, rather than allowing it to lead you by its leash."

Nikolas's throat felt raw, as if he had been screaming for hours. He tried to take a breath and inhaled a broken gasp.

"Forgive me if I spoke out of turn," Maddox said quickly. "I'm only trying to help."

So that he and the others could get back to Solara. They didn't care about Nikolas, not really.

But that wasn't the point. The point was he could make a difference for these people—*his* people, no matter how much he felt an outsider in their presence. He could stanch their own grief by opening a door to their realm, attempt to heal decades' worth of generational trauma.

And, like Vrinä, he could use Phos's feathers to light a path.

"How…" Nikolas had to stop, try again. "How do you live alongside it?"

Maddox's face lost its tension. "First, you only have to accept it."

But that was something Nikolas couldn't do. Hadn't been able to do in the years he'd had to live without Rian's jabs and laughter, their arguments fizzling into meaningless conversations that lasted until the small hours of the morning, his quiet assurances that everything was going to be fine.

How could he accept that life? How could he ever hope to believe things would be fine if Rian wasn't there to say so?

Nikolas finished his tea and set the cup down. He stood and bowed to Maddox, making the man start. "Thank you for taking the time to indulge me. I'll return tomorrow to try again."

Maddox stood as well, his bow far deeper. "Of course, my lord. I believe you will set things right."

That makes one of us, Nikolas thought.

Late morning brought a sheet of heavy clouds. Nikolas considered it a blessing; every time he glanced at the sun it made the weight in his chest heavier.

Strangely, he also considered the missive he got a blessing, too—a much-needed distraction from the way his thoughts spiraled. He'd fully expected another summons by Damari. Instead, in messy handwriting he'd never seen before, he'd been asked to meet up with an informant at the library plaza.

Nikolas wasn't sure what he expected as he leaned against the side of the library. It was a few blocks from the university, a towering infrastructure of thick stone walls, ornamental arches, and flowering corbels. A bell sat in an open tower above the roof, ringing the hour of two.

"Sunshine! You came."

Nikolas reached instinctively for the knife at his belt. The young man who'd silently sidled up beside him raised his hands.

"Whoa," Fin said. "Didn't mean to startle you." His long gray coat was unbuttoned, his collar popped to shield his neck from the chill.

Nikolas relaxed. Lux tugged at his pouch, but he ignored it. "You're the informant?"

"Seems a little formal, but sure."

Nikolas waited for him to go on, but Fin only stared at him, eyes roaming over Nikolas's features. The silence was undercut by the low murmur of people in the plaza. Despite there not being as many out today as usual, hawkers walked around carrying wares that dangled from sticks over their shoulders, anything from bright red bundles of peppers to clinking charms promising protection from evil spirits. A couple children ran in a circle singing an old rhyme about monsters until their mother scolded them. From a nearby food cart came the smell of Mariian spicy tomato stew being ladled out with cassava bread. The afternoon was heavy with shades of pewter and slate, the wind biting at his exposed throat like a warning.

"Well?" Nikolas prodded. "You're the one who called me here."

Fin crossed his arms with a flush and a nervous laugh. "And you actually showed up. I'll admit, I'm surprised."

Nikolas suddenly understood what this was about. He'd been carrying the bracelet in his pocket ever since the young man's failed attempt to accost him. He took it out now and handed it to Fin, the tree charm shining a dull silver.

"I meant to find you at the gala and return this," Nikolas said. "I'm not sure if you worked that night. All the better if you didn't, considering what happened."

Fin's eyes widened as he took it. He caressed the charm between careful fingers.

"I . . . thank you." Fin attempted to retie it one-handed. Nikolas, seeing him struggle, reached out and did it for him. The young man's fingers were long and slender, the knob of his wrist bone a stark slope above the valley of his palm.

Fin let out a long, trembling breath when he was done, as if he'd held it the entire time. He grinned widely at the bracelet before his face turned grim. "The reason I called you out here is because of the gala, actually. About what I saw that night."

Any warmth in Nikolas's body leeched away. He took hold of Fin's elbow and dragged him into the alley beside the library.

"You were there?" Nikolas asked.

"Not in the main ballroom, but yes. I was traveling between the servants' hall and the ballroom when it started."

He trailed off, looking pointedly at the pouch on Nikolas's belt where Lux's light was emanating. Sighing, Nikolas opened the pouch and Lux zoomed out.

"Incredible." Fin held out his hands and Lux curiously drifted around them, like a dog sniffing a stranger. "You're much nicer when you aren't keeping me tied up."

Nikolas raised his hand and Lux stretched into a thin, glowing bangle around his wrist. "Please continue."

Fin cleared his throat. "Right. When I was walking from the kitchens to the ballroom, I noticed someone slip by. It happened so quickly I almost didn't register it, so I didn't stop to think about it until later. But I'm pretty sure I saw someone wearing a skull mask."

Nikolas recalled Risha's report of the Conjurer she'd met in the mausoleum—the same one who had been behind the necropolis attack. How could one person control so many spirits at once? Was Leshya Vakara's necklace truly that powerful?

"Why come to me with this?" Nikolas asked. "Why not someone in the palace?"

Fin shifted on his feet. "You're in a special task force, aren't you?"

"Yes." Still, Nikolas felt something was off. "You could have gone to your supervisor or one of the advisors, and they would have brought Don Damari to take your statement. Sending a message directly to an heir is something that could cost you your job."

Fin drew in a sharp breath, and Nikolas was immediately ashamed when he realized what he'd implied. He sometimes forgot the power he held at being a noble, of being connected to royalty, to the divine. It was a power to change people's lives with a simple snap of his fingers. It was a power his father wielded like a scythe.

"Sorry," Nikolas murmured. "I'm...just confused."

Fin nodded slowly. "Don't worry about it, Sunshine."

"Nik," he said. "You can call me Nik."

Fin inhaled again. He soundlessly shaped the name on his lips.

"Is there anything else about this person you remember?" Nikolas asked.

He needed as much information as possible for his next meeting with the king. If he risked Ferdinand's displeasure—or worse, his father's—there would be a price to pay. Waren had already made that clear when stressing Nikolas had to present the Cyrs favorably during Godsnight.

But after speaking to Maddox—*you only have to accept it*—he no longer knew if he could do that.

Fin had started to answer him. Nikolas shook himself and tried to focus.

"—necklace made of *bones*." Fin shuddered. "Other than that, what I thought was most peculiar was the direction he came from."

"What do you mean?"

"Well." Fin rubbed at his nose, as if it were cold. "Not sure how familiar you are with the ballroom's layout, but the only way to get in and out is through the main entryway unless you take the path between the main palace and the servants' hall attached. And since I saw him in the servants' hall near the kitchens, that means—"

"He came from the palace, not the ballroom," Nikolas finished. And not only that, but this person had also managed to break into the Bone Palace in order to raise Lezzaro's body and steal the necklace. Either they had someone working for them on the inside, or...

Or they were a noble.

He thought back to the aftermath of the first Conjurer attack, when speculation had spread wildly about the Vakaras having something to do with it. To the fact that Risha had been found in the mausoleum alone, unconscious, with Leshya's remains nothing but a pile of ash.

Risha wasn't involved with the Conjurers, was she?

The thought, the mere possibility, sent a dagger between his ribs. Throughout their lives, Risha had always been the most stable one, the honest one. So much in Nikolas's life had already turned upside down. He couldn't lose any more.

Rian. His power. Taesia.

You only have to accept it.

His breathing was choppy, his throat searing. He was colder, suddenly, and dizzy.

"Nik? Hey—are you all right?"

Nikolas's vision blackened. As it slowly came back, he realized he'd slid down the alley wall to the ground. Fin crouched before him, blue eyes narrowed in concern.

"What happened?" Fin asked quietly.

Nikolas crossed his arms tight against his chest as if to defend himself. Fin slowly put a hand on his forearm. The solid weight of it was overwhelming, an anchor landing on brittle earth.

"I can't accept it," Nikolas whispered.

"Can't accept what?"

There's no end to grief. The solution is to find a way to live alongside it, rather than allowing it to lead you by its leash. Maddox's words would never apply to him. Grief was not something he could shake hands and coexist with; grief *was* a leash around his neck, pulling him through each day. He wouldn't be able to approach Godsnight with his head held high. That leash would drag him before the king and gentry and commonfolk, their eyes landing on him like flies on a corpse.

"My power..." Nikolas flexed his hands. Lux, curled around his wrist, twisted around his fingers. "I can't access it the way I used to. Not now when I need it most. Everyone expects me to help, to put a stop to these attacks, but I can't. I *can't.*"

Fin was utterly still, perhaps surprised, perhaps perturbed. Nikolas had no idea what he was doing, what he was saying, why it felt like if he didn't speak, the words would consume him from the inside out and destroy what was left of him.

There was no one to talk to. No one who would understand, not in the way he needed them to. But Fin was a stranger, impartial, someone who didn't *know* him like the others did.

"Someone recently told me grief can block a Lumin from their magic," Nikolas murmured. "That if I make peace with it, my powers would go back to normal." A bitter laugh escaped him. "But it won't work."

Fin seemed to think carefully about his response. "How are you so sure?"

"Phos refuses to bless me. Refuses to speak to me. And I think I know why. Why he's severing me from my power." His eyelashes grew wet. "It's because it's my fault."

Fin's grip on his arm tightened slightly. "What is?"

"My brother's death."

It had been a simple decision, one of the myriad of stupid decisions he'd made throughout his life. His family had been traveling in the south, in the volcanic lands near Seniza, where his mother was from. Nikolas had found the cuisine too spicy for his palate, the air too humid. But he'd enjoyed the landscapes, the visits to the junglelike countryside and the salt flats shining white as diamond under the sun. He and Rian had even tried their hand at harvesting the salt that would make its journey up to Nexus.

Their estate was in the countryside, in full view of the volcano the locals called Deia's Heart. At night, they could see its peak spurting bright tongues of lava that ran in continuous rivulets down its slopes, drying into black crags before reaching the bottom. The air was hot and muggy, always carrying a whiff of sulfur.

Nikolas had wanted to get closer to Deia's Heart, so he and Rian had snuck out one night. They couldn't get near without coughing from ash rain, so instead they'd scouted the terrain around it, occasionally watching the slow crawl of stubby flows of magma. They had found slates of basalt and small ridges emitting odorous gases, as well as fire lizards that scurried away when they drew near, their cracked bodies revealing molten insides. There were all sorts of strange and fascinating beasts here, from the lizards to the stone giants disguising themselves in the shale to the fabled lava titan who dwelled beyond the rim of the volcano's mouth.

But Nikolas hadn't known about the ash flies. The insects in the south were various and disconcertingly large, and he hadn't been prepared for their bright red bodies and iridescent wings. At first he'd gaped at their luminescence. Then had come an instinctual dread at the sound of their droning, some evolutionary conditioning flooding his brain with a warning to get as far away as possible. But by then it had been too late.

Rian had been bitten three times. The bites rose swollen and angry on his neck, a triangle of pain. He couldn't hide them from their parents, earning them both lectures the next morning over breakfast, cut off mid-tirade when Rian fainted.

It was a fever known in the south as ash blight, and one of the reasons locals knew not to get too close to Deia's Heart. They tried to get treatment for Rian, calling in Seniza's best medics and apothecaries, shoving various vials down his throat and even wrapping his body in alcohol-soaked seaweed. But nothing had worked. Rian had burned with fever, the three marks on his neck spreading into one large, red rash that crawled over his skin.

They carefully traveled back to Nexus, but the same result found them there. All the medics, even the royal ones, were stumped. There was no cure. It was a fever the body had to fight on its own.

His brother had fallen into a coma.

Nikolas sat with him for hours at a time, listening to the breaths struggling in Rian's chest, his hair constantly damp with sweat. Nikolas had volunteered to bathe him, give him water, change his bedpan.

When he woke one morning and made his way to Rian's bedroom, he'd stopped at the sound of his mother's wailing. The noise had pierced him through, pinning him in place as servants and his father ran past.

Fin listened quietly as Nikolas relived the shrill heartache of his mother's scream. The way his father had never looked at him the same.

"I'm the reason he's gone," Nikolas whispered. Lux had come to settle between his palms, pulsing gently. "Phos is punishing me by taking away my powers." He inhaled shakily. "I'm sorry. I shouldn't have told you any of this." *I barely even know you, and now you probably think I'm pathetic.*

But Fin didn't seem rattled. Or at least, he didn't run off. His expression was soft, worried. "What happened wasn't your fault. He made the decision to go with you. You didn't know about the danger."

They were nearly the same words Taesia had said to him years ago, cradling him on his bed as she ran fingers through his hair. Those words hadn't comforted him then, and they didn't comfort him now.

Fin went on. "I get it, though. It wouldn't have happened if you hadn't been impulsive. We all do impulsive things, some worse than others. I've had my own fair share of mishaps. I'm still waiting for the one that knocks me on my ass, because I know it's coming—it comes for everyone. It just came for you a little early."

Nikolas hadn't realized he was crying. Fin stared at his chin, where a tear hung ready to fall.

"You were a child who wanted to have fun." Fin carefully brushed a thumb against his chin, dislodging the tear. "Gods, you're still a child."

"I'm probably older than you," Nikolas muttered. Fin breathed out a laugh.

"I'm saying what happened was shitty, and terrible, and can't be undone. But it's not your fault. You didn't kill your brother. Your god is not punishing you. You're punishing yourself, and maybe by showing yourself forgiveness, your powers will return."

That was as impossible as Nikolas accepting that Rian was well and truly gone. He deserved every harsh word from his father, every empty minute spent with his mother.

But he also knew this went far beyond him. Instead of banishing grief the way Maddox suggested, he could redirect it, use what he had learned of his own failings to protect others. The citizens of Nexus deserved to not live in fear any longer. The refugees deserved to go home.

He couldn't be like Vrinä with Phos's feather a blessing in her hands, but he could be Nikolas Cyr, wielder of the Sunbringer Spear and inheritor of his brother's legacy, leading his people home through the dark.

VII

"Taesia?"

She looked up from oiling her sword. She'd chosen an armchair by the balcony, weak sunlight spilling onto the naked blade. Brailee stood in her doorway with a book clutched to her chest. Her familiar, Somnus, was settled around her shoulders like a cat.

Taesia set her sword down. "What's the matter, Bee?"

Brailee stepped inside, chewing her lower lip. "I...I went to Mother, recently, to ask if there was something wrong with me. With my power."

Taesia frowned. "What are you talking about? There's nothing wrong with you."

"But I've never been able to call the shadows as well as the rest of you." Brailee shifted a book in her arms. "I don't know why. But Mother said every Shade is made differently. That her strength is storing and recovering memories, and yours is using the shadows to do things for you. That D-Dante's is turning shadows into objects. So I started to research what my strength could be. And I think I know."

Brailee handed her the book. It looked to be at least a century old, wrapped in the scent of decaying paper. She took it carefully, opening it to the spot where Brailee had left a slip of parchment to save her place.

Memory, Visions, and Dreams: The Mind of a Shade.

Brailee sat on the bed as Taesia paced and read. It was true what Brailee had said; Shades could wield shadows, but the most powerful, like her family, held special abilities passed down from Nyx's blood. Elena Lastrider was sometimes called on to help the aging dons and doñas with their memory issues. She could draw a certain memory into a glittering gemstone, capturing and containing it forever. Taesia had even heard of Shades who could let you daydream while awake, as marvelous a trick as it was dangerous.

And some Shades, the book told her, were more attuned to dreaming. To perceive past and present and future while asleep, opening the mind to what existed beyond one's immediate surroundings.

"Is this why you haven't been sleeping?" Taesia asked. "You think your abilities involve dreams?"

The bags under her sister's bloodshot eyes were more pronounced than ever, her skin ashen with exhaustion. "I have nightmares," Brailee whispered. "About the gala. Glass shattering, corpses screaming, blood on my slippers." Brailee shuddered. "The servants keep finding me passed out. I begged them not to tell Mother or Father or you."

"Bee."

"I know. I need to sleep. I need *real* sleep. The draughts don't do anything anymore. But I... I know. I know that if I sleep, I'll dream of the boy again. The pile of bodies. Tae, I think this is real. I think this is something happening *right now*."

Taesia didn't know what to say. She supposed it made sense, considering all the heavily detailed dreams Brailee had rambled about when they were younger. But how was she supposed to help her when she didn't even know how it worked?

Brailee's expression fell. "You don't believe me."

"No! No, I do." Taesia sat beside her. "I just don't know what to do about it. Have you told Mother?"

"Not yet. I wanted to... to ask you a favor. I want to try and transmit the dream to you."

"Is that even possible?"

"The book said something about sharing dreams between Shades." Brailee shivered. "I'm so tired, Taesia. I'm scared. I don't know who this boy is, or what he wants. What he's doing."

"All right." Taesia rubbed her sister's arms, trying to warm her. "All right, we can try." Even if nothing happened, she could at least watch over Brailee as she got some much-needed rest.

She drew the curtains as Brailee climbed under the covers. Taesia joined her and shifted until she was comfortable—or the closest she could get, considering this strange turn of events—and felt Somnus slither up her arm to twine around Umbra.

She thought it would take hours to fall asleep. It only took twenty seconds.

It was like shoving away from the shore onto a dark sea, letting the tide carry her out. It terrified her to surrender control, to not be able to turn back or go against the tide.

You're here, said a velvet voice, carrying a hint of surprise.

Taesia, through Brailee, opened her eyes to a universe of color. Swirls of peach happiness and tornadoes of vermilion warfare, cyan wonder and marigold revolution. Neither she nor her sister had a body here, only driving thoughts like fingers reaching into the vastness, sorting through emerald diamonds of success and violet birds of love.

What is this place? Taesia demanded.

I don't know, Brailee answered. *I see it, sometimes, as I'm falling asleep.*

Every time they brushed across a shape or color, images flickered through their minds. A woman crying over a body, a gardener admiring his vegetables, a troop's long trek up a mountain. Ice harvesters in the north and volcanic researchers in the south. Azunese tea shops and Parithvian food carts. Temples built in fantastic and otherworldly architecture, a throne of blinding light, rivers of blood and wailing ghouls, a tree covered in bodies, a city lit up like a jewel.

There.

Brailee seized that last image. The universe of color dissipated around them, filling in its absence with a dark cosmos overhead and long grass tickling their ankles below, the bright city in the distance. There was a sweetness in the air Taesia hadn't expected, and a hint of spice, like anise. Like the turning of leaves in autumn.

Taesia realized they had a body, here. Or at least, Brailee did. Her nightgown swayed around her legs and Brailee hugged her arms to her chest as though a chill stole through her, but Taesia couldn't feel it. Their vision was fuzzy and uneven, as if the dreamscape refused to give either of them a clear view.

Look, whispered the velvet voice.

Brailee turned and gasped. A large structure had been planted in the ground, like the rounded belly of a sleeping monster.

Even with their hazy vision Taesia realized it must be Lune Bridge. The one that had mysteriously vanished after the gala.

A figure stood in the middle of the bridge, gazing out at the dark land surrounding them. Brailee cautiously approached, noting how the bridge's lanterns were still lit, their flames guttering amid the shadows.

Her bare feet whispered in the grass. When she stepped onto the cold stone of the bridge, the figure turned its head.

It's him, Brailee thought. *The boy.*

Taesia couldn't quite make out his features through Brailee's eyes, but she could tell he was thin and haggard, his eyes wide as they took Brailee in.

"You." He stepped away from the railing. "How did you get here?"

Brailee opened her mouth to answer, then decided against it. Twisting her fingers together, she joined him in the middle of the bridge. He was taller than her, fairer than her. He was also barefoot.

"Who are you?" Brailee asked softly.

He looked away. "No one."

She turned to see what he was staring at. A city sat in the distance, its lights so bright it formed a corona.

"Where is this place?" she asked.

His lips moved soundlessly. Above him, a streak of a shooting star briefly brightened the sky.

"It must be difficult to get anything done when it's so dark," she ventured.

A quiet laugh escaped him. He seemed shocked by the sound, and Brailee smiled tremulously as she rested her hands on the bridge's railing.

"I know it was you," Brailee said quietly. "You stole the statue from the university. I saw it here the last time. And now you've taken this bridge. Why? How?"

The boy's teeth were white against his lower lip. "It's a forbidden magic," he whispered. "It requires life. Energy."

Brailee glanced over her shoulder, and Taesia cursed. Behind them sat a mound of corpses, as well as the bronze statue at its base. Taesia couldn't make out much other than their clothes seemed to be suited for traveling. Had the boy waylaid them on the roads?

"Why use it if the cost is so high?" Brailee asked.

"Because…" He frowned. "I have to. The realms…" He pointed upward as another star shot across the sky. "They're weakened. Eager. We have a lot of work to do."

We? Taesia thought. *Ask him who "we" means.*

Brailee ignored her. She raised a hand as if to reach out to him, then decided against it. "I'm sorry, but you'll have to explain this to me. What do you mean about the realms being weakened? Do you mean because of the Sealing? Does this have anything to do with Conjuration?"

He winced in pain. His hands flew up to grab his head as he groaned.

"I'm sorry," Brailee said quickly. "I didn't mean to overwhelm you."

He staggered away from her. Taesia told her sister to stay where she was, but she didn't have control over Brailee's body in this confusing blend of existence. Brailee followed, watched as he knelt before the barren ground upon which he'd made his tiny kingdom: the corpses, the statue, the bridge, the circle and its multiple layers of lines and symbols.

Fuck, Taesia thought. *So this* is *Conjuration. Where is this boy? Who is he? I need you to get answers, Bee.*

I'm trying, Brailee snapped back. *But I have to take it slow. If he gets too upset, he pushes me out of the dream. It's hard enough staying here—that's why it's so indistinct.*

So he's making everything hazy for protection?

I think so.

Carefully Brailee knelt beside him. The boy's breathing was strained. His lips were feathery with dead skin. A smudge of dirt marred his jaw.

"Please tell me your name," Brailee whispered. "I want to help you."

The boy stared at her, as if he'd forgotten she was there. "You. How…" He clutched his head again.

The back of Brailee's throat tasted metallic when she swallowed. They wouldn't be able to stay here much longer. "Are you going to take something else?" She glanced at the unfinished circle. "What will you summon next?"

"I…" His voice choked off, as if a hand were squeezing his throat. Brailee touched his arm.

"Let me help you. *Please.*"

He groaned again, shaking. He reached out and shoved her back onto the grass.

"Get out," he panted. "You have to get out."

He turned to the mountain of corpses, to the unfinished circle around them. Muttering to himself, he picked up where he had left off, his movements frantic and jerky.

Taesia sensed her sister's urge to pull him back and prevent him from finishing, but she didn't have the power here—he did.

I thought your powers would allow you to shape a dream? Taesia said.

They can, Brailee said, *but I don't know how!*

You know how, whispered the strange velvet voice.

Brailee's breath hitched as she lifted her hands. If she could siphon power from the universe of color, use it to transform the dreamscape into something more manageable…

A cage, Taesia thought. *Quickly!*

No, that's too cruel—

But a cage was the first image that came to Brailee's racing mind, and she was already pulling it through the universe of possibilities, constructing lines of metal around him, closing him in.

He cried out as the bars sealed him away from his circle. Brailee fell to her knees in exhaustion. The boy stared at her from behind the bars, aghast.

I did it. "I'm sorry," Brailee whispered. "I'm sorry, I didn't—"

Then the boy's face hardened and his eyes burned golden. Grabbing her construction, he ripped the bars apart with impossible strength, as easy as if they were made of paper.

"No," Brailee gasped, struggling back to her feet. "Wait, I'm sorry—"

We have to get out of here! Taesia yelled.

Brailee turned and headed for the bridge. He caught up to her at its apex, grabbing her wrist in a grip that ground her bones together. He loomed over her, eyes a bright, piercing gold. His face had transformed from haunted boy to a being of malice and rage.

"Go," he said between clenched teeth. "Now."

"But—"

"I said *go*," he growled. He pushed her off the bridge, and she went tumbling into the dark.

Taesia woke with a cry. It echoed oddly in her ears, her voice caught by the four walls of her bedroom and not the open expanse of the land lit by stars.

Umbra uncoiled from Somnus and drifted onto her chest. She leaned back against the pillow and caught her breath.

"Fuck," she panted. "You were right. I mean, I believed you, but to actually *see* it—or at least, sort of see it—" She yelped as Brailee hit her arm. Her sister sat up with tear marks on her face.

"Why did you have to do that?" Brailee sobbed. "A *cage*?"

Taesia sat up as well, her head pounding. "I didn't know what else to do! He's clearly out of his godsdamned mind, and he's planning *something* with this little habit of his. He's going to make something else in this city disappear."

Brailee wiped her face. Sighing, Taesia grabbed the water pitcher and poured her sister a glass. "I didn't mean to mess it up."

Brailee shook her head, holding the glass between her hands. "He would have found a reason to push me out anyway. It's like he gets possessed by something. I don't understand it."

"Do you know what he might target next?"

Brailee took a tiny sip of water. "No. But he seems to like landmarks."

Taesia nodded, still woozy from the dream. She took the glass from Brailee and downed the rest of the water. "Nik should be told about this."

"I agree. You should tell him as soon as you can."

Taesia cringed. She hadn't seen Nikolas since the gala, when her own deceit had wedged between them.

"I can't," she murmured. "You have to do it, Bee."

"What? Why me? You and Nik—"

"We're no longer together." The glass trembled in her hand. "I can't see him right now."

"Oh." Her sister was quiet as she processed this. "I'm sorry, Tae, but this is more important."

But Brailee hadn't seen Nikolas's look of betrayal and heartache. She knew they had to work together to prepare for Godsnight—hinging on whatever Angelica managed to discover about fulcrums—but every day that passed without word from the others ratcheted the tension inside her.

"You said you wanted to be included in what Dante and I did," Taesia said eventually. "This is me including you. It's *your* dream. You have to be the one to tell Nik."

Brailee seemed ready to argue more, but she deflated. "Fine. But speaking of Dante...I wanted to do this with you because maybe I can speak to him. Find him in a dream. To g-get the truth from him, before..."

Taesia found her sister's hand and gripped it tightly.

"We can do that," she whispered.

They weren't allowed visitation in the Gravespire. She had never learned about what had happened with Lezzaro, the thing Dante had been about to tell her before Don Soler had him arrested.

If they could find him in dreams, they could finally get answers.

The door opened so suddenly they both started. Their mother only spared them a second of confusion before her face hardened back into a mask Taesia knew well: the mask she wore when dealing with the king and his advisors.

"Don Damari is here," Elena said. "Come downstairs looking presentable."

Again? Taesia thought as Brailee grabbed her book and scurried back to her own rooms. Cristoban Damari was leading an investigation into Don Soler's death, but he'd already come around with his probing questions, asking each member of House Lastrider where they had been that night, what they'd been doing, how they had fought.

"I resorted more to my sword than my shadows," Taesia had answered smoothly. "As evidenced by the result of my tussle with Queen Arcelia's corpse."

"Yes," the high commissioner had said in that calm, unruffled voice of his. "As I recall, her head had been severed from her body."

Taesia had smiled with the same frost lining his words. "Quite messily, I'll admit. It was my first time beheading anything."

He had merely stared at her for a long moment until concluding his questioning. Was he returning because he'd found new information? Something she'd overlooked in that exhilarating moment of revenge, too keen on the fear in Don Soler's eyes, the fury trawling through her at his words?

Her parents were already seated across the tea table in the sitting room when she and Brailee entered, spines straight and faces grave. Damari sat on the couch opposite, legs crossed and fingers laced, two gray-clad guards standing at attention behind him.

Taesia gave a shallow bow to the high commissioner as Brailee curtsied. "Don."

Damari answered with a respectful dip of his chin. "My ladies. Please, sit and join us."

Taesia didn't miss the tightening of her mother's jaw. This was their villa, their family's legacy built on magic and godsblood, and yet a man who had climbed the ranks from a low noble station was giving them orders.

"To what do we owe this visit, Commissioner?" Elena asked. "Are there further questions you need to ask us?" To any common observer she would sound calm. Taesia, who had painstakingly learned the differences in her mother's inflections, stiffened.

Damari plucked a piece of lint off his trousers. "I've come at the behest of His Majesty to deliver a message. He regrets being unable to deliver it himself, but he's been hard at work setting up for Godsnight."

Taesia barely refrained from sneering. Ferdinand never made visits to the Houses, but he could have at least sent them a summons. Instead he'd sent one of his lapdogs.

"Understandable," Elena said as Cormin quickly smoothed away his frown. For as well as he handled the sensitive politics of the Houses, her father had always been an expressive man. "We ourselves are quite busy with preparations."

Which was only half a lie. After Taesia's demonstration at the gala, her mother wasn't worried about putting on an act that would stun the crowd. Instead, Elena was mired in all the possibilities the exhibition would invoke, whether this was a test of loyalty or if Ferdinand would decide who would succeed him based on magical prowess.

Beside her, Brailee nervously fiddled with Somnus, the familiar weaving through her fingers. When Damari's gaze fell upon her, Brailee cupped Somnus between her hands.

"His message concerns Godsnight," the high commissioner went on. "And your son."

Elena's eyes flashed as the muscle in Cormin's jaw fluttered. Taesia barely breathed.

"His Majesty has decided the exhibition should not only be a divine spectacle, but a pointed, public warning to the Conjurers," Damari said. "Which is why His Majesty has ordered Lord Dante Lastrider to hang preceding the demonstrations."

The room fell silent. All Taesia could hear was the mad thumping of her heart, the susurrus of the shadows inching toward her.

Elena stood slowly. "How dare you," she whispered. "How dare he not tell us *personally*—"

Damari also stood, fluid and unfazed. "Lord Dante confessed to the murder of Prelate Lezzaro and is believed to lead the Conjurers. This was the clearest choice of action."

Sudden pain made Taesia start as the shadows around her scattered. She met Brailee's red-rimmed eyes, wide and frightened, as her sister dug her nails deeper into Taesia's forearm.

"He—" It was testament to how rattled her mother was that she was letting herself stutter like this. "He's not—"

"I'm sorry, my ladies, my lord." Damari bowed low to them. "I regret not coming with better news. I can only hope this will give the city some measure of peace, and that you can one day understand it is for the best."

Brailee's fingers were still anchored around Taesia's forearm. Taesia put her hand on top of her sister's, conveying what she couldn't say out loud: that they were going to find a way to speak to Dante, that they would get answers.

That Taesia was going to make Ferdinand pay for this.

VIII

Risha couldn't recall what was said during the dowry meeting. Didn't know if she nibbled on the barfi and kala jamun laid out upon the table, or drank the tea served alongside them. She mostly sat and glared at Jas on the couch across from hers, darkly pleased whenever he fidgeted in discomfort.

A couple hours earlier she had seen him reanimate a body. Now he was playacting a Parithvian lord's son, with dimples and charm in his arsenal. It worked perfectly on her mother—Darsha was singing his praises by the time they left.

According to the rules of the dowry meeting, Risha and Jas hadn't been allowed to speak to one another. She had only managed to catch Jas's eye, the rueful shake of his head and his mouthed *later* before he and his father left. Risha had fumed the rest of the day, wondering how she'd managed to fall into such a strange predicament.

It was only a couple days later when they were able to share an afternoon together in the gardens, their escorts following at a safe distance. He was dressed in a sherwani of black and red this time, with small golden hoops in his ears. He kept clearing his throat whenever she glanced at him.

"When were you going to tell me?" she finally asked, fed up with the guilty silence.

"I didn't know," he answered. At her answering glare, he raised his hands. "I swear, I didn't!"

"How could you *not know*?"

He sighed and raked a hand through his thick hair, disheveling it.

She found she preferred it to the sleek style he'd put it in. "My father is a member of the Parithvian Parliament, as you know. When he was told to go to Nexus for trade negotiations with King Ferdinand, I asked to come along. He agreed only on the condition that I would meet with potential suitors. He told me he'd found one, but he was being... precious with it."

"Precious?"

"My father likes jokes and pranks. He was humoring himself at my expense. Whenever I'd ask, he would smile with that damn twinkle in his eye."

"So that's where you get it from," she muttered.

"Pardon?"

"Nothing." She rubbed a knuckle over her forehead. "Now I know how you were able to steal the necklace and reanimate Lezzaro." He didn't have to sneak into the palace; he was already staying in the guest wing for foreign ambassadors. "And find a way into the mausoleum. You realize this won't work, don't you?"

Jas looked over his shoulder to make sure their escorts weren't eavesdropping. "Don't be so hasty to dismiss working together. I have an idea for the basilica—"

"*No*, I meant this." She gestured between them. "This engagement. I'm only playing along for my mother."

"Oh." Jas paused. "Why?"

"Because she seems to think marrying a foreign ally will help our standing with the king. But I only care about opening the barrier to Mortri."

"Huh," he murmured. "And here I thought all Vaegan lords drooled over the crown."

"I don't."

They fell silent as they strolled through impeccably trimmed hedges and flowerbeds. Some of the plants had been shielded with burlap against windchill, and Risha missed the bright hues of summer.

Jas noticed her longing stare at the begonias, which had bloomed pink and white and then faded to yellow. The gardeners would soon remove their tops so the bulbs could sprout new ones next year. Necessary deaths to secure new life.

Before Risha could stop him, Jas reached for one of the begonias and gently caressed the wilted petals. Slowly they perked up, their drying edges turning soft, flushed with delicate pink. It stood boldly apart from its dying kin, a bloom of defiant color.

She wasn't aware she was smiling until Jas mirrored it, satisfaction in the curve of his mouth. Risha quickly schooled her expression.

"Why did you want to come to Nexus with your father?" she asked.

"To look into something."

"Conjuration."

"That's what it led to, but it wasn't my motivation. I…" He turned away, touching the begonia's stem. Each leaf ripened again to green. "I wanted to learn more about my mother's death."

Risha frowned. "You said the Revenants want to get the barrier open for your loved ones to move on, including your mother."

"And that's true. But I also want to know how she died in the first place." His brow furrowed, his voice dropping. "If it was truly an accident or something more."

Trepidation made the air nip colder. "What do you mean?"

"My mother was a member of Parliament before my father took her seat. She traveled to Nexus some years ago for… I can't even remember, possibly a border dispute. But her aide told us that halfway through the trip, something had shaken her. My mother insisted on going home early, but several miles out of Nexus, her carriage fell into a ravine." Jas audibly swallowed. "They brought her body back to us."

Risha put a hand on his arm. "I'm sorry."

He shook his head. "It seemed like an accident, but I kept thinking about what her aide said. My mother was… well, she wasn't easy to push around. I loved her as much as I feared her." He briefly smiled, a small, tenuous thing. "But something in Nexus had rattled her so much she wanted to come home early. It haunts me that I don't know what it was."

He finally locked eyes with her again. Risha couldn't look away even if she wanted to.

"My mother wouldn't have gotten involved in something like Conjuration," he whispered. "Whatever spooked her, I think it was political. Something she wanted to warn Parliament about. Something the king might have wanted to die with her."

Her trepidation rose higher. "You think the king assassinated her?"

"I don't know."

Risha's mouth was uncomfortably dry as she said, "You want to find her spirit. That's why you're so desperate to get the Mortri barrier open."

"If we're allowed access to Mortri, I have a better chance of finding her there than here, where we're overrun with resentful spirits," Jas agreed. "And once she tells me what happened, she can finally move on and be at peace."

She didn't know whether to laugh or cry. "You didn't think asking the Vakaras was a possibility?" After all, she was the one delegated to performing séances.

"My mother died outside of Nexus. From what we know of the Vakaras' powers, I didn't think your abilities went that far."

It was true she had only ever called upon spirits within the city. Was it possible to extend her range farther?

"I can still try," she said stubbornly. "Although it might require additional power."

He nodded. "We can provide that."

Her stomach knotted, but she did her best to ignore it. "Even if you're able to get answers from your mother, what would you do with them? If you're right and she learned something she shouldn't have, where does that leave you as an ambassador of Parithvi?" *Is it something a war would be started over?*

"I don't know." He stared again at the begonia, a single point of life amid a garden of withered things. "But if my mother died in order to protect it, surely it's something you deserve to know, too."

Shortly after Jas left, Risha was saved from her mother's endless questions— "What was he like? What did you talk about? How does he like Nexus?"— by a messenger from Don Damari requesting a necromancer's abilities.

"I will go," Risha said at once.

"You should really wait for your father to return," Darsha murmured, holding Risha back. "I don't like the thought of you going on your own."

"You don't like the thought of much, Amaa."

Darsha's grip on her tightened. "Remember there's an ongoing royal investigation. If we're not careful—"

"We have nothing to worry about so long as we're innocent."

"Sometimes the innocent receive worse punishment than the guilty." Darsha glanced at the open doors, the light muted in the overcast sky. "Just...keep things to yourself, and don't antagonize anyone."

Risha chewed over what Jas had told her on her way to the offices of the city guard, but it was driven out of her mind once she walked through the doors. The main floor was paneled with bright wood, guards sitting or weaving through a labyrinth of desks, the upper floor reserved for the senior officers.

"Welcome, my lady."

Don Damari was waiting by the doors. He gave a bow, which she returned with a tilt of her chin. She couldn't help but glance at the spot where his right ear was missing.

"I was told you were in need of assistance?"

"Yes. We have been looking further into the Don Soler incident and have been unable to follow any particular leads," Damari said. "His Majesty wasn't fond of this idea, considering recent events, but I'm afraid we've run out of options."

Now she understood. "Of course. Please lead on."

Guards stopped what they were doing to salute Damari as he passed, sparing Risha curious glances. Damari moved like a shark through water, cutting and graceful and calm.

Holding cells along the back wall were filled with people either passed out drunk, sitting in sullen silence, or leaning against the bars trying to get the guards' attention. One man snatched out a hand as if to grab her.

"Pretty dark flower," he slurred. "C'mere and I'll make you bloom."

I'll see your rib cage bloom, she thought.

Damari took her down a flight of stairs to an underground level. Risha immediately sensed the bodies, as well as a couple waning spirits who had not yet let go of their bitterness. She would need to disperse them before leaving.

"Here is where we hold our more dangerous prisoners," the high commissioner explained. In a show of perfect timing, an enraged wail echoed amid the clanging of bars. "It's also where we store sensitive evidence."

Damari and the guards who accompanied them didn't seem to notice the din coming down the stone halls. She wondered how long it had taken to become used to something like this.

She wondered if Dante had gotten used to life in the Gravespire.

Shaking the thought away, she stopped when Damari stood before a thick metal door and let the guards open it. When they stepped inside, Risha shivered at the cold.

Metal slabs were erected along the far side of the room between panels of frost stone, surgical instruments hanging from the walls. Two out of the four tables were occupied, both bodies shrouded in white cloth. Damari led her to the one on the left.

"We've been storing his body in deep freeze since the gala," Damari explained. "But I must warn you, he's reached a certain level of decomposition nonetheless. There are also multiple wounds on him."

He spoke to her as if she were a necromancer who had never seen a dead body before. She merely nodded her acknowledgment before peeling the shroud back.

It wasn't the worst she'd seen, but it was far from the best. The body was an eerie blue, the blood decaying as the organs within swelled with gas. The stomach was grossly distended, the fingertips swollen. His arms and legs and head had been sewn back onto his body, thick black sutures a startling contrast to his pallor.

One of the guards gagged and turned away. Risha leaned over to get a better look, noting how cleanly his flesh had been cut.

Risha carefully placed her hands on either side of the don's head. It was icy to the touch.

"Wait, my lady. In order to be properly used as evidence, we need more than a glimpse of his memories. He'll need to be reanimated so I can question him."

Risha hesitated, unsure how well that would go considering the don's vocal cords had been cut.

"I apologize. I know it must be asking a lot from you," Damari said, misinterpreting her silence. "If you would rather wait for your father—"

"Considering how long ago he died, I'll have less time to work with him," Risha interrupted. "I suggest you make good use of your questions, High Commissioner."

Risha sank into the dark pool of her power. It was sweet and seductive, like a self-indulgent stretch after waking from a night of pleasant dreams. Risha's spine straightened as the air twisted around her in a tight, cold torus. With one hand she sketched out the pattern for reanimation over the don's head, feeling the distant call of Mortri rush to answer her.

A mangled scream erupted below her. Don Soler's eyes flew open, darting between her and Damari, sunken and gray.

"Don Soler," Damari said. "Please focus on what I'm saying and try to speak, if you can."

The don's jaw sagged open, his tongue lolling. His eyes rolled.

"Do you remember the night of the gala?" Damari asked. She noted he refrained from saying anything about his death, which would have sent the don into more of a panic.

"Ga...la," the don repeated, nothing more than a hoarse, wheezing whisper. "Sha...Sha..."

Damari's expression didn't change, though the slight twitch of his eyebrow gave away his impatience. "Do you remember what happened?"

A low groan. "Nnn...hol...hold...m..."

"Someone was holding you?"

"Mon...ster!"

Damari glanced at Risha. "Would the dismemberment addle his mind?"

"It might," Risha said, "but that usually happens with major trauma to the skull."

Don Soler's neck began to undulate, as if it were trying to swallow. "Hold...Holll...Sha...!"

"Slow down, Don."

"Mon...ster," the don wheezed again.

"A reanimated corpse? A beast?"

Soler's moan made the back of Risha's neck prickle. "Sha...dow!"

Risha suppressed a gasp. With the don's rising aggravation, it didn't take much for his spirit to knock against hers—not the smooth transition like what happened during a séance, but a violent pounding, demanding to be let in.

Risha fought it. Damari said something, but she couldn't hear it under the roar of her blood, Don Soler's moaning.

The Bone Palace's courtyard. Flashes of the risen dead.

Shadows everywhere, walls of impossible black.

A woman's face before him, her grin a white scythe.

As soon as the images were transferred, the tug within her went slack, her connection to the don slipping.

"Can you tell me anything else?" Damari demanded, but Soler merely gaped at him, eyes flat and cloudy.

"It's no use," Risha said as the connection finally gave way. "He's gone."

"Damn it." Damari straightened, running a hand through his hair. It was the most agitated she'd ever seen him.

Risha's heart beat low and heavy in her chest. *Taesia.* She thought she'd known disappointment before, learning her oldest friend had lied and kept truths from her—but this was something else altogether. She had killed not once, but twice. Had killed the king's *spymaster*, the man who had sent Dante to the Gravespire and sentenced him to hang.

And she had done it with a smile on her face, full of chilling malice Risha hadn't known her capable of.

"The don said something about shadow," Damari said. "It seemed as if you were reading his memories at the end. Did you happen to see what he was referring to?"

Her pulse tripped. "I'm afraid the memory was too hazy to make out details."

The words were spoken before she understood their significance. Despite her outrage, her displeasure at Taesia and what she'd done, she continued to protect her.

But to do otherwise would make her a hypocrite, after joining the ones who had caused the destruction at the gala. Risha wasn't without guilt either.

Damari watched her, as if waiting for her to rescind her answer. When she didn't, he rolled his shoulders back.

"Shame," he murmured. "I was hoping there would be a stronger lead to follow. It would help, certainly, to have the Vakaras' assistance in this matter, considering..."

Risha tensed. They had been questioned about the gala, and Risha had given the truth: that she'd run into the Revenants' leader, that she'd destroyed Leshya's body to reverse the spell.

But it hadn't been enough to wash away suspicion.

"I know you wouldn't willingly withhold information, of course," Damari went on. "That you care about your family's reputation, and wouldn't do anything to squander it further."

She thought of her weary father, her worried sister, her mother frightened for them all. Doing what they could to avoid the king's wrath and the public's disdain while keeping the people of Nexus safe.

"Perhaps you simply need to think about it some more," Damari said. "To fully recall what the don may have shown you."

It was a struggle to swallow past her dry throat. After an unsteady moment, she whispered, "I...I think I do remember something, now."

Damari's smile was tiny yet triumphant. "And what would that be, my lady?"

"The shadows." Her voice cracked. "I believe they were caused by a Shade."

Even now she couldn't say Taesia's name.

But it was damning enough.

"A Shade," Damari repeated. His small smile sat at the corners of his lips, still not reaching his eyes. "I see. Thank you for your help, my lady. Your cooperation will be noted."

Risha couldn't answer, couldn't move. She felt outside her own body, marveling at her capacity for betrayal.

Damari pulled the sheet back over the body. "Who knows," he murmured. "Perhaps Dante Lastrider won't be alone when he hangs."

IX

The fenris radiated a familiar warmth as Julian knelt before its cage, as well as boredom from having to wait for its injuries to heal. Julian found it oddly comforting amid the questions that kept piling up without answers.

How had his father been a beastspeaker? Was it hereditary? Did Benjamín have abilities beyond it, some excess strength that had made it possible to fight all those beasts on his own?

He was still kneeling there when the captain found him. The fenris lifted its head at Kerala's approach, ears twitching forward.

"You know," Kerala said, "we're nearly ready to return it to its natural habitat. The wounds are looking good."

Julian nodded. The fenris, sensing no threat from Kerala, lay back down with a long sigh.

"It's a good thing you and the rest of Lord Cyr's unit were able to shut down that supplier." Kerala leaned one shoulder against the bars, arms crossed. "Speaking of, I heard about the missing bridge. Does Lord Cyr think it's related to the incident at the university? The missing statue?"

Julian hadn't been there for the bridge, but he'd seen Taide's sketches. "The Conjuration circles were the same, and both landmarks are nowhere to be found. I think it's safe to say they're related."

She nodded, watching the fenris's eyes slowly close. "It's odd, isn't it? These things disappearing, the prelate and spymaster killed in two very different ways. Actually..." She raised her eyebrows, the way she did when there was scandalous or titillating news to share. "This hasn't been made public yet, but I got a report from the high commissioner's office this morning about the Don Soler investigation. Apparently the Vakara heir managed to get some answers from his spirit."

Julian went ice cold, remembering the way the Vakara heir had read the bone dealer's memories.

"The don said something about shadows. Could be a Shade, right?" Kerala rubbed her jaw. "It makes sense, since the Noctan refugees are loyal to Dante Lastrider. Could be he roped them into his Conjuration schemes. In any case, they're going to issue a reward of ten thousand soles to whoever comes forward with information."

Julian swayed and gripped the cage bars. The fenris, sensing his distress, perked its head back up.

Ten thousand soles. That would be enough to buy his mother's medicine for the next two years.

A memory of laughter, of tea and brandy and cake, of Taesia Lastrider standing in his mother's apartment with her familiar pooling her face in shadow. The absolute darkness he'd stepped into at the gala, the unfathomable black of her eyes, the splatter of blood all down her front.

Ten thousand soles.

He'd wanted answers. But it was only now he realized they came with a price.

Taesia's sword sung through the air as she practiced her movement flows, needing some way to burn off the restless fury inside her. Her every waking moment leading up to Godsnight was lined with teeth after Damari's visit.

The city was flustered, on edge, and many muttered about Ferdinand's decision to present the Houses on Godsnight despite the horror of the gala. Others seemed keen to have a show, a much-needed distraction.

But it wouldn't only be feats of otherworldly magic. It would also be the eldest Lastrider heir dangling from a noose, a blatant warning to commoners and gentry alike.

Taesia yelled and spun through the air, plunging her sword into the neck of the training mannequin. She staggered back and wiped her wrist across her brow.

The training ring beside the gardens was cool and dappled with shade from the nearby trees. Fat bees hovered among the autumn flora, drunk with pollen. Soon the plants would wither and sleep.

And soon, the entire realm would follow.

She was still waiting to hear from Angelica, had half a mind to burst through the doors of the Mardova villa and demand she hand over the grimoire so she could do the research herself. If her aunt had remembered Lezzaro's words correctly, they had an opportunity to perform the ritual with the Ostium fulcrum, if it even still existed. If it didn't...

"My lady?"

Taesia came back to herself with a jolt. Turning, she glared at the House servant in black and silver who bowed in apology.

"I'm sorry for startling you, my lady," the servant said, "but you have a visitor. He's waiting in the sitting room. He wouldn't give me a name."

"Then why did you let him in?"

"B-because of his uniform, my lady."

Uniform? Taesia thanked the servant and headed for the sitting room. One of Damari's lackeys sent to deliver another crushing blow to House Lastrider, perhaps?

She flung open the door and stopped in her tracks. Julian Luca turned from the window overlooking the garden, dressed in his green-and-tan Hunter uniform. His face was wan, his hair disheveled.

"What are you doing here?" she blurted.

"You can barge into my mother's home, but I can't barge into yours?" His voice was cold, flat. Taesia frowned.

"Will you take some refreshments, my lady?" asked a servant in the hall.

"No," she said, trying to mask her wariness with a smile. "Just some privacy, please."

The servant nodded and closed the doors. Taesia turned back to Julian, framed by a room in rich blues and silvers with threads of yellow, the room her mother prided herself on when the dons and doñas complimented her taste. The room where Damari had delivered his damning message.

"What is this about? Has something..." She felt herself pale. "Has something happened to Nik?"

He said nothing for a long time. Her fingers twitched, and she realized she hadn't yet sheathed her sword.

He took a couple steps toward her, glancing at the naked blade.

"I know about Don Soler," he said quietly.

A flash of prickling shock turned the fingers around her sword's hilt numb. The line of his mouth thinned.

"Admit it," he said. "Admit you were the one who killed him. That the blood I saw on you the night of the gala was his."

For a second she was back in the bone dealer's shop making the decision to let him walk away, certain their paths wouldn't cross again. Perhaps this was what the priests at the basilicas meant when they talked about *fate*. The blending together of disparate events until they wove a tapestry that couldn't possibly be unraveled.

"Why do you care?" she said at last. "Are you moonlighting for the high commissioner? Do you get some perverse satisfaction at justice? You've seen what I can do. Why is this suddenly the breaking point?"

The muscle at his jaw twitched as he looked away. "I thought..." A hoarse laugh escaped him. "I thought maybe you were *good*. Terrifying, but good. I almost started to understand why my mother is so fascinated with you." His expression twisted, as if in pain. "But you're not good, are you? You only like to pretend you are."

Taesia's heart faltered, like a blade had pierced her there. It hurt as much as Brailee's tears, as Dante's absence, as Nikolas and Risha turning their backs on her.

It hurt because she knew he was right.

"Yes," she whispered. "I killed him."

Julian's eyes widened at the admission. There was something in his face, in his posture, that betrayed his disappointment. Maybe he'd hoped for something else, for her to keep denying so he could deny it himself.

"Why?" he breathed. "Is it because you're working with your brother? Was Don Soler next on his list of victims?"

"My brother didn't kill Lezzaro, and he had no intention of killing Don Soler."

"Then *why*?"

Her grip tightened on her sword hilt. "You wouldn't understand."

"Do you think so little of me? Go on—tell me what it's like to be a murderer. To willingly end someone's life."

His voice was rising, with a harsh edge she'd never heard before. She would be lying if she said it didn't disturb her.

"You put down beasts all the time," she countered. "It's the same thing."

"It's not!" he yelled, slicing his arm through the air in a violent gesture. "Taking human lives is not the same fucking thing!"

"Then go on," she said, entering a defensive pose with her sword held across her chest. Her grin was a taunt. "Try to turn me in. Try to throw me down at Cristoban Damari's feet and maybe he'll even give you a prize."

He winced, proving her right. Then he stalked closer until she could smell whiskey on his breath and something else, strong and sharp and sweet—a blend of everything that was Julian, from the polish he used on his weapons to the soap he used in his hair.

Perhaps she really was a beast being hunted.

"Don't," he growled. "Do not make light of this."

"I said *do it*," she said between clenched teeth. "Make me pay for my crimes. Put your conscience at ease. You'd be doing me a favor, really, sparing me from Godsnight. From having to see..." She swallowed painfully. "So come on." She tapped his chest with her sword, watching it rise and fall. "Be the weapon that ruins House Lastrider for good."

The rasp of his sword escaping its sheath was her warning to duck, the sitting room wide enough for her to dance back. They began to circle the blue rug. His face was set in hard lines, a reluctance in his eyes countered by the threat of steel.

Julian pressed his attack. She blocked and pushed back, swinging low only for their blades to kiss again and retreat. She wondered if the servants could hear the ringing.

"You'll have to pay my mother back for any damage you cause in here," Taesia said as she made a cautious step to the right. "Then again, whatever reward Damari hands out should cover it."

Julian scowled and fell for the taunt. She lured him in and caught his blade low, letting its point sink into the rug before she jerked her pommel toward his face. He twisted and caught it in the shoulder instead with a grunt. She used the advantage to press forward, their blades a flurry between them, skill matched with skill. But he was slightly taller, broader, stronger.

She lured him toward the furniture with her onslaught. She kicked him back and climbed onto the nearest chair, falling with it as she descended on him from above. He caught the downward swing of her sword and turned, making them roll over the back of the couch and crash to the floor. Something on the table fell and shattered. She leapt over the now-cleared table and faced him from the opposite side.

They stared at one another across the gulf, panting. There was a cautious knock at the door.

"My lady?" a servant called. "Is everything all right?"

Taesia didn't take her eyes off Julian. "Everything's fine. Please keep this area clear until my visitor leaves." Then, in a lower voice: "If I decide to let you leave."

Julian breathed out, sweat dotting his forehead. "Stop this."

"Stop what? Fighting you? Getting rid of people who want to degrade and destroy me?"

He opened his mouth, but whatever he wanted to say came out as a sigh. Instead he asked, "What are you doing with the astralam bones?"

"It's a surprise."

"If you're planning on harming more people—"

"I'm not using them for *harm*. It's..." But the thought of revealing everything here, while their blades were aimed at each other, seemed hopeless. "It's complicated. You have to trust me."

He laughed, the sound unnerving. "*Trust* you? After what I saw you do, after knowing what I know? How is anyone supposed to trust you?"

Again she was back in the ballroom, facing Nikolas's and Risha's misgivings. "I suppose you can't," she whispered. "I suppose no one can."

His eyes softened a fraction. They briefly fell to her mouth, where all her lies had spilled.

He abruptly shook his head, stalking around the table. "Taesia—"

She caught him by surprise as she lunged, reversing her grip on the sword so it was pommel-first, ready to strike his ribs in the spot where she knew his injury from the gala lay. He grabbed her arm in his free hand and swung down with the other, but she twisted and angled her sword across her back, allowing his blade to clash with hers. She gave him a lopsided smile before punching him in the shin.

He reeled back with a curse. They traded blows that became mere blurs of silver. Though they kept their movements tight, they scored gashes in the walls, the bookshelves, the chairs.

Their swords met in a cross before he grabbed hers with his bare hand and disarmed her. He tossed the weapon behind him as he pressed her against the wall, his blade to her throat. The snarl in her ear made her shudder down into her toes, and she choked on a gasp.

Then he froze. Looked down at the shadow dagger she had pressed to his ribs.

"And here I thought you didn't have initiative," she murmured. She reached up and grabbed a fistful of his hair, tugging hard enough to make him grunt as the dagger pricked through his uniform.

He glared at her with eyes the color of a forest floor, a blend of woody detritus and fallen leaves bright with spring. His chest brushed against hers as they panted, one broad hand tight around her arm while the other held his blade steady.

She pushed the dagger harder, parting the fabric of his coat and shirt to the skin beyond. One shove and it would be over. There would be one less person who knew her secrets.

But she couldn't move her hand any farther. She continued to stare at him, wondering what fate truly meant and whether or not she could sharpen it like a weapon.

His pupils had become pinpoints during their fight, but now they fanned out like a drop of ink hitting paper, darkening his gaze as warm breaths hit her face. Some primal element had taken over him, and it caused a fusion of fear and excitement in the pit of her gut—as if he had opened his mind to a beast and hadn't shut the door. The heat of him was intense, a star against the darkly curved horizon of her body. She wondered what he would do if she dared to touch his parted lips. The possibilities made her ache.

She released his hair to grab the back of his neck. Not to pull him down, but to keep him where he was. Her fingers dug into soft skin and muscle, a growl vibrating from his chest into hers.

"Kill me," she whispered in the space between their mouths, "or get out."

She let him go, and he stumbled back. His pupils shrank to normal as color rose to his face.

His lips moved silently. He took a half step toward her, then two back. Shaking his head, he hurried for the door, slamming it against the wall as he fled the villa.

Taesia let Umbra dissolve from its dagger form and leaned her head against the wall in relief. She could still feel the bruising impression of his fingertips around her arm, the warmth of his breath on her cheek, the wild beating of his heart against hers.

Julian's head ached so badly he thought he would throw up. When he staggered away from the Lastrider villa he did just that, purging all the raw emotions he couldn't put a name to, ferocious and clawing.

Why couldn't I do it?

He was still shaking by the time he reached his mother's apartment.

He didn't want to return to the Hunters' compound only to lie miserable and alone on his bed.

You're an idiot, he told himself as he made his way up the stairs. *A gods-damned idiot. You should have turned her in.*

But the way she had stared at him—the sound of her heart struggling against his—

Julian rubbed his face. He was so fucking tired.

When he unlocked the door, he found his mother kneeling before a large crate on the floor.

"Ma? What are you doing?"

She looked up at him with watery eyes. His alarm spiked until he noticed her brilliant smile.

"Oh, Jules," she breathed. "I can't believe it. I can't believe you did this for me."

Confusion replaced his alarm. Kneeling beside her, he peered into the crate and saw rows and rows of bright vials.

Medicine.

"I have no idea how you did this, but I'm so grateful, Jules." Marjorie cradled his pounding head and kissed his cheek over and over. "Thank you."

"Sure, Ma," he said faintly, the words nearly sticking in his throat. He could still feel Taesia's pulse on his fingertips, her scent clinging to him like fog on the northern hills. It was dark and velvet, the smell of a cold and starless night.

Taesia must have been the one to send the medicine. *I would die for that woman*, she had told him.

He thought he'd known the rules of the world, but they kept shifting beneath his feet, leaving him unbalanced and unsettled.

X

The priests were unnerved to see her again. Angelica told herself it didn't matter, that she had every right to visit the Deia basilica whenever she chose, but the widening of their eyes and the nervous bobbing of their throats sent something searingly unpleasant into her stomach.

Mateo was the one who shuffled forward. Sweet, silent Mateo. Angelica let him anoint her with water before marking the center of her forehead with soil. Incense floated from the thuribles on the walls, choking her with the smell of burning leaves.

Angelica followed him to an offering chamber but slowed as she passed the stepwell, the inactive portal. The sensation of it felt familiar—something like the first sign of dawn, or fog over a valley. Expansive. Intangible.

It was the same element she sensed whenever she walked into the underground practice arenas at the university. The same element symbolized by the empty clay bowl at the altar.

She glanced at that bowl as she knelt within the offering chamber, thinking of Conjuration. The congealed blood in the bowl nearest her gave off a fetid smell that made her instantly queasy, the candles causing shadows to dance along the stone walls.

Her offering today was a small vial of ambergris. After placing it within the circle of bowls, she closed her eyes.

"Blessed Deia, I call upon you. Please hear my prayer and answer. I am in need of your guidance." The room was hushed and suddenly far too small. "Blessed Deia, please. I need answers."

A rustle and a whisper. An enormous weight clogged the very air around her and made her ears pop.

"You make yourself small for me when others should make themselves small for you."

The god sat within the middle of the circle, large and impossible, glowing a reddish gold that lit the room in a brilliant sunrise. The molten sword she always carried lay across her bare thighs, bubbling and spitting like lava. Her cracked skin flaked as she leaned forward, the single blue eye above her breasts unblinking as it studied Angelica.

"I tire of these summonings," the god said in her deep, resonant voice. It pierced Angelica between the ribs. "I am not some maid for you to snap your fingers at."

"I—I apologize," Angelica stammered. "I wouldn't summon you if it wasn't necessary."

Deia cocked her head, the gesture more animal than human. What the black lace around the top half of her face concealed, Angelica did not know.

"What you deem necessary I deem inconsequential," the god said without moving her red slash of a mouth. Her voice was everywhere—in Angelica's mind, reverberating against the walls, the contents in the clay bowls shivering. "Is this about your sickness?"

"No. Unless you have changed your mind in helping me better connect to your elements."

"Such a bold little thing you are today. What else would you bring before me?"

"There was a fifth realm, wasn't there?"

She had read the grimoire and learned about fulcrums. Power hubs connected from the gods to their realms, a sort of umbilical cord that, if cut, stopped the flow of essential energy.

Angelica understood now why Taesia had wanted her to look into it. If their ritual required a fifth heir, or else something to represent Ostium, could they potentially use Conjuration to summon Ostium's fulcrum? Based on what she had seen at the university when the statue had gone missing—and then the bridge shortly after—it was possible Conjuration could transport objects.

Fortitude began to work itself back into her sinew. "And if there was a fifth realm, then there was a fifth god."

And a fifth magic.

"What happened to them?" Angelica whispered.

The silence that descended was so thick it nearly suffocated her. Deia stared at her, blue eye unblinking. The longer she stayed in the god's presence the more she began to go mad with it, twitching and panicked.

"YOU PATHETIC CREATURE," Deia drawled.

The offering bowls surrounding her burned in the god's summoned fire. They threw up sparks that stung Angelica's hands and thighs. The heat was too intense even for her, making her shrink back.

"YOU THINK BECAUSE YOU HAVE LEARNED OF OSTIUM'S FATE, THAT MAKES YOU FIT TO KNOW ITS SECRETS? FOOL. WHAT HAPPENS BETWEEN THE GODS IS NOT FOR YOU TO KNOW."

"Between the..." Was it true, then, that the gods had conspired to wipe out all knowledge of the realm? "What happened to Ostium? And what does it have to do with Conjuration?"

"CONJURATION," the god snarled, "IS A BROKEN WINDOW WHEN THE DOOR REMAINS LOCKED. SOMETHING MORTALS HAVE TWISTED BEYOND RECOGNITION."

"What do you mean by twisted?"

"ENOUGH." Within a blink the god stood. Deia's body morphed slowly, her limbs elongating and her torso cracking and shifting unnaturally. Her teeth grew long and sharp, her hair shrinking into bristling fur of gray and red. The wolf was enormous, taking up the majority of the room, looming over Angelica with a mouth that opened hungrily. On its face sat one solitary blue eye.

Angelica fought to stay where she was even as her heart climbed into her throat. She would not scramble away. She would not admit her fear to the entity that had placed her in this world and could just as easily erase her from it.

The wolf laughed, and it was the scraping avalanche of rock down a mountainside. The wolf's head lowered until Angelica was staring into its unblinking eye. "HOW EVEN SMALLER YOU LOOK NOW."

Angelica clasped her shaking hands in her lap and forced the words out. "I...need...to know. Was Godsnight only possible with the presence of a fifth heir or some other marker of Ostium?"

The wolf's hackles rose and it scraped a paw along the ground, claws screeching against stone. It took everything in her not to immediately prostrate and beg forgiveness.

"I SEE MUCH, AND HEAR MUCH," the god growled, upper lip curling to reveal fangs. "YOU ARE ATTEMPTING THIS MAGIC DESPITE MY OWN POWER FLOWING THROUGH YOUR VEINS."

"I—I wasn't—"

"MY BLOOD, MY HEIR," Deia crooned. "I KNOW WHAT YOU PLAN TO DO AT GODSNIGHT."

She was going to shake apart. She was going to be unmade in this room, piece by painful piece.

The tears finally spilled down her face as she said, "I have asked you for a way to connect with my true p-power, to understand it, but I have been denied. And so I must take a different path to help this city, my country, the realm which you have birthed. T-to undo the Sealing."

The wolf thrashed and snapped its jaws before Angelica's face. At first she thought Deia was furious, so the sound of the god's laughter sent goose bumps down her arms.

"WHAT FOOLISH BEASTS!" the god howled.

"Is...is this not possible? Without something from Ostium—"

"EVEN WITH AN HEIR OF OSTIUM, THEY WILL STILL FAIL." The wolf laughed again, its tongue lolling out in glee. "BECAUSE THEY WILL NOT BE IN THEIR RIGHT MINDS."

Pressure grew in her chest. The wolf loomed over her, casting her in its shadow.

"WHY DO YOU THINK THE REALMS WERE SEALED IN THE FIRST PLACE, MY BLOOD?" The wolf's breath washed over her, smelling of sulfur and pollen. "THE GODS ARE AT WAR. WE HAVE BEEN AT WAR. IT BEGAN WITH THE FALL OF OSTIUM, WHEN WE VIED TO EAT OF THEIR FLESH. IT CONTINUES FOR THE HONOR OF THEIR REMAINS."

Angelica's lips parted, but no sound came out. Her mind clouded with a panic so great it turned distant, elusive as smoke through her fingers.

"What war?" she whispered at last.

"THE WAR THAT HAS ALWAYS BEEN WAGED." The wolf's breaths were heavy and hot against her neck, its fangs dangerously close to her skin. "THE WAR THAT BEGAN WITH OSTIUM AND WILL END IN VITAE. THE WAR TO DETERMINE WHO AMONG US IS FIT TO RULE ALL THE REALMS."

Understanding bit her like a wild animal.

Godsnight.

"WE HAVE BEEN UNABLE TO FIGHT AS WE DESIRE TO. UNTIL NOW. NOW, WHEN THESE SO-CALLED CONJURERS HAVE WEAKENED THE BARRIERS SURROUNDING NEXUS. NOW, WHEN YOU AND THOSE SPAWN DESIRE TO TAKE

US INTO YOUR FLESH AND MINDS. NOW, WHEN WE SHALL FINALLY HAVE
OUR BATTLE, ONE THAT WILL DETERMINE WHO RISES . . . AND WHO FALLS."

"Why are you telling me this?" Her voice was barely a whisper.

"BECAUSE YOUR TIME HAS ALREADY RUN OUT." Her god chuckled.
"AND WHO WOULD BELIEVE YOU?"

Angelica tried to shake her head, her body stiff with terror. She was
too numb to feel the tear crawling down her cheek.

"WITH MY POWER TO GUIDE YOU, YOU WILL NOT NEED YOUR FRIVO-
LOUS INSTRUMENTS, YOUR SEDUCTION TO THE FIRE." There was a smile in
her words. "I WILL HELP YOU SLAUGHTER THEM WHERE THEY STAND. AND
WHEN THEIR BLOOD SOAKS YOUR FEET, THE CROWN WILL REST UPON YOUR
HEAD. THE FIRST OF MANY."

Angelica had grown up obeying her mother's orders, believing they
would lead her toward a better future. She and her House had done all
they could to resist becoming a king's pawn. But all this time she had
been a god's pawn instead.

They all were.

What Vitaeans called Godsnight, Noctans called Starfall.

It was observed in the realm of Noctus, when the sky of permanent night was lit up with the brilliance of a thousand shooting stars. As the Cosmic Scale aligned, the shadows grew stronger and the moon shone brighter, and Shades celebrated with playful bits of magic.

Of course, Starfall had also been used to wage wars. No matter the realm, no matter what race, power was always desired to the point of bloodshed.

But what Taesia remembered were strings of gems and necklaces heavy on her neck, the taste of fried pastries filled with currants and spices, the prayers ringing out in a Noctan dialect she half understood. As she walked through the Noctus Quarter now, she took a deep breath, inhaling the scent of cloves that reminded her of a dying autumn, when everything felt clean and dark. The hanging gems had tripled in number, streamers of cut-out stars linking building to building as if to replicate the great river of shooting stars that would blanket Noctus in a few days' time.

Dusk had fallen, casting the street in an ethereal blue. Tàesia stood and admired it a moment: the lamplighter making their way down the street; the restaurant opening its doors for the first patrons of the night; the vendors setting up small, crooked stalls to show off wares they had prepared specially for this time of year. A couple of children dragged their father toward one of the stalls, pointing at the wooden dolls and intricately carved flutes.

The children were so small, their horns not yet fully grown, dazzled by the way the light caught on the cacophony of gems above their heads. An ache settled at the bottom of Taesia's lungs, between her ribs, growing roots. She had come here with Dante and Brailee when they were younger, pointing at everything the way these children were. Somewhere along the way their wonder had dampened to grim reality, their closeness dissolving as games became unescapable duty.

She didn't want the same for these children. She didn't want them to grow up in a world that despised them, refused to protect them. Under Ferdinand, they surely would be forced to mature much too quickly.

I understand, Dante, she thought as she made her way down the street. *I understand why you fought so hard to make things different. We can take up that fight together.*

From one cart wafted the magnificent smell of cinnamon and sugar, no doubt selling moon pastries. She had always gone mad for them, often stealing bites from Dante's when he wasn't looking. Sometimes her father would give her the rest of his, claiming to be full.

The vendor smiled and bowed a few times as she ordered three. When he tried to insist they were complimentary, she firmly placed the money on the cart.

Something bumped into her leg. Looking down, she met the wide, pale green eyes of a Noctan child. She barely came up past Taesia's hip, her hair white as moonlight with green ribbons tied around the base of her growing horns.

A gasp sounded close by. "My lady! I–I'm so sorry for her, truly." The young woman who spoke grimaced in discomfort, possibly an older sister based on her likeness to the girl.

Taesia waved it off. "Don't worry about it." She knelt to be on eye level with the girl. "You were rushing to get these, weren't you?"

She held up one of the moon pastries, shaped in a crescent. The girl nodded shyly.

"I like them, too," Taesia admitted. "But I may have gotten too many. How about I give you one of mine?"

The girl's mouth hung open. They were beginning to draw attention from others on the street, whispers stealing through the scant crowd. Umbra uncoiled from her ring and began to twirl around the girl's head. The girl sucked in a breath and then laughed, the ringing sound breaking the tension of the onlookers.

Taesia knew dons and doñas who tossed coins to beggars, charities the Houses donated to, funds they reallocated to fix a broken street or venue. She'd once thought money was the only thing a noble could give others—a temporary, contemptuous remedy. But they could accomplish more beyond tossing money at problems.

Like handing a pastry to an eager girl or sending medicine to a sick woman, they could find ways to bring the people joy and relief.

"Thank you, my lady," the girl's sister whispered as she received her own moon pastry in both hands, like a supplicant. The girl was already devouring hers, getting sugar granules all over her mouth.

"Enjoy yourselves," Taesia said. "You deserve it."

The young woman bowed and, after a moment, hissed, "Naela!" The girl started before bowing as well.

Taesia smiled, her first true smile in days.

By the time she reached the blacksmith's, she was sucking cinnamon and sugar off her fingers. Mirelle perked up when she walked through the door.

"My lady. I mean—Taesia. Thank you for coming."

"Thank you for sending for me. I assume that means it's ready?"

Mirelle's expression melted at the edges, revealing a wicked curve to her mouth. "It's ready."

Taesia held her breath as the blacksmith went to fetch it from the back. By the time Mirelle returned, her chest was aching—but for a different reason, this time.

Mirelle set the wrapped package on the counter with all the care of someone handling the thinnest glass. She took a step back as Taesia came forward, unable to still the tremor in her hand as she pushed the wrappings away.

She had put all her trust in the Noctans' best blacksmith. She saw now she had been correct to do so. It was more beautiful than she could have possibly imagined on her own.

The astralam bones had been fused so seamlessly together it was difficult to remember them as separate pieces. The fuller was narrow yet deep, running nearly the full length of the blade. The hilt Mirelle had chosen was perfect—a cross guard of black steel and the grip wrapped in silver leather, the pommel a heavy counterweight in the shape of a waxing moon.

The blade was black and glittering. Anyone could tell it wasn't of this world, this realm. And Mirelle, clever Mirelle, had echoed the blade's origins in the sharp spinous processes traveling up each side like fangs.

Taesia caressed one of those little spinous wings, remembering how they'd poked into her hand, fueling her with a sensation wholly new and desirable. The bone was as cold as it was then, carrying the same promise of cosmic power.

The other heirs were still on the fence about Godsnight. Julian thought she meant to use the bones for destruction. But with this sword, the only thing she'd be destroying was the barrier to Noctus.

And these refugees could return to the realm they called home. Naela could celebrate Starfall as it was meant to be celebrated, and eat moon pastries the way they were supposed to be made, with ingredients they had no more access to here in Vitae.

"My lady?" Mirelle called, and likely not for the first time. "Is it to your liking?"

Taesia came back to herself with a shaking sigh and wrapped a hand around the hilt. Umbra traveled down her wrist to inspect the blade.

What makes you feel strong?

"It's perfect," she whispered.

Mirelle's face broke into a pleased grin. "I'm glad. Working with it was...incredible." She rubbed her fingers together, as if remembering the feeling of the bones against them. "Do you plan to name it? A weapon of this caliber should be named."

Taesia nodded in agreement. She had never named her swords before, as the practice was seen as vain and ridiculous in Vaega. But in Noctus it was completely normal to name your weapon, to forge a better bond between wielded and wielder.

Lifting the sword and savoring its weight, Taesia smiled as it glinted in the forge fire's light. She could hear the distant din of the street, taste the residue of sugar on her tongue.

"Starfell," she said.

A promise forged into the bones, into her own flesh and blood.

Risha hadn't set foot in the Thana basilica in weeks. The barrier was strongest here, the pinpoint of Thana's rage.

Yet here she was, lingering with Jas in the corner under a steep archway. He held his skull mask in one hand, his clothes dark and nondescript. She couldn't help but recall the sight of him in a sherwani, framed by flowers.

The other Revenants were preparing a Conjuration circle in the middle of the basilica. The air filled with clouds of chalk amid the scent of frankincense spilling from the thuribles along the walls. The priests, adhering to curfew, had already locked up and retired for the night.

"—this?"

Risha realized Jas was talking. "What?"

He eyed her critically, no longer a Parithvian lord's son—her *fiancé*—but the leader of the Revenants.

"You seem distracted," he noted.

She'd been distracted since her encounter with Don Damari, bracing herself for a hammer to fall. A hammer she had positioned perfectly to strike Taesia.

If Damari followed up on her lead, or found enough evidence, then she had condemned her friend to the Gravespire with her brother. The thought alone pressed a hand against her chest, pushing and pushing until she thought the bone would cave inward and slash her heart open.

I had to do it, she kept thinking to herself. *Damari was threatening my family. I had to do it.*

"Risha?"

She took an unsteady breath. The frankincense was giving her a headache. "I'll be fine. What I'm more worried about is you keeping control of the spirits."

He huffed. Leshya's necklace hung around his neck, bones glowing in the low torchlight. "That's why I wanted to do this in the basilica. What we did at the necropolis and the mausoleum ended up summoning resentful spirits, but the bodies that have passed through here were given proper funerary rites. They shouldn't be violent."

Risha hugged herself. "You better be right."

"And are you…" He cleared his throat, fiddling with his mask. "Are you certain you can reach her?"

His voice was soft, filled not with skepticism but hope. It made her heart clench.

From her pocket she drew a long, thin whistle of yellowed bone, taken from a Mortrian beast with an ability to call lesser spirits to consume. While the Revenants summoned and herded spirits, she would assist and use the combined energy to find Jas's mother.

"I'll try my best," she replied. "But I can't guarantee it. If we weren't preparing for Godsnight, I would travel out of the city to perform a séance, but…"

Jas's smile was small but genuine. "I know. Godly duties to attend to, and all that." He gave her a solemn bow. "No matter what happens, I consider it a privilege to be working beside you, my lady."

Risha flushed. "Let's just do this," she muttered.

The others had crafted a large Conjuration circle over the brown marble. They'd found a spot a stone's throw from the roped-off stepwell. Risha had climbed down those worn steps to the basin several times, trying to hack away at that black barrier.

Jas clapped Natsumi on the back as he surveyed the circle. It was similar in design to the one drawn under the flower shop, ringed with layers of symbols and geometric shapes, containing a seven-pointed star. "Well done, all."

Part of Risha couldn't believe she was indulging them, the other part sick with desperation. If the Revenants could help her achieve what she couldn't do alone, if they could bring down the barrier without a ritual, she had to try it.

"We'll try to draw as many spirits to the portal point as possible," Jas reminded them. "The more come, the more their energy will resonate with the barrier." He nodded in deference to Risha. "Correct?"

"Correct."

"I believe the spirits here will be less resentful, and easier to manage. At the first sign of violence, we break the connection." He took off his gloves, tucking them into his belt. He unsheathed a knife and held it to his hand. "With that in mind, let's begin."

The Revenants took their places around the circle and also drew their knives. Natsumi gave Risha a brief frown that either meant *good luck* or *don't mess this up.*

Jas slashed his palm. His blood dribbled into the circle, the other Revenants adding their own offerings to the spell. The chalk began to glow a murky black.

Risha put the bone whistle to her lips and blew.

As she walked back to the Lastrider villa, Starfell wrapped on her back, Taesia began to realize the delicate thing unfurling inside her was hope.

Perhaps it was the added presence of the sword. Over the last few weeks, she had been more attuned to her powers than ever, and it was even more so now—an awareness like a warm gaze settled upon her, or a comforting hand against her back.

Above her, the night was a tapestry of ink and navy, faraway stars seeming to burn closer. She remembered the stories passed between her siblings before they understood what waited for them between their realm and Mortri—that when you died, you became nothing but a whisper in the night sky, fitted into the quiet darkness between stars.

She almost wanted it to be true, to know for certain if her efforts would be rewarded with hollow peace.

Taesia breathed the darkness into her lungs like a drug. The shadows sensed her and moved closer as she walked, hugging her from all sides, content to be in her company. Umbra uncoiled to join them. She wondered if they could whisper how old the earth truly was. If she stood in perfect darkness, perhaps she could feel the ground miles beneath her, cold and wet and ravenous. Perhaps she could sense the other side of the world when it was bathed in night. Cradled in shadow, she could be anywhere and everywhere.

She could do anything.

But her peace was not meant to last. As soon as she entered the gates of the villa, she stopped at the sight of her aunt coming through the front doors.

"There you are!" Camilla rushed to her, which was Taesia's first warning; her aunt never rushed anywhere. Her second warning was her aunt's expression, the panicked tilt of her eyebrows. "I came to see your parents, but I was told they're at the palace."

To appeal to the king about not hanging Dante on Godsnight. Taesia took Camilla's wrist and pulled her farther from the House guards. "What happened? Is it Dante? Have you learned something?"

Camilla shook her head. "I was drinking with a couple of Don Damari's men—I happened to find them in a wine shop, so it wasn't difficult to get them talking—and . . ." Her aunt noticed the wrapped-up sword on her back for the first time. "Is that—?"

Taesia's grip tightened. "*What did you learn?*"

"Damari's convinced it was a Shade who kidnapped and murdered Don Soler. He's going to raid the Noctus Quarter. *Tonight.*"

The world spun out from under her. She had just been there, had just seen children laughing and playing—

"Taesia!" her aunt cried as she wrenched away, running out the gates and past the startled guards. "Taesia, wait!"

She couldn't wait. She was tired of waiting. The sword pulsed eagerly at her back, the shadows spurring her on faster until she was nothing but a dark blur against the silvery starlight.

The next time Angelica was aware of being in her own skin, she was slumped over a waste bin reeking of the contents of her stomach.

She shook so badly her teeth rattled. Tears collected at the corners of her eyes, frustration and helpless rage and horror. She could barely move for hours, simply focused on breathing her next breath, on keeping her heart from pounding out of the cage of her chest.

She considered destroying the grimoire.

No, she thought once the haze began to lift. *No. I have to tell them. They need to know.*

Which was how she hauled herself out of the villa and into one of the House carriages, her hair uncombed, her clothes askew, and ordered the driver to take her to the Lastrider villa despite his protests that curfew was approaching. She rubbed her arms during the ride, cold and burning at the same time. The itch had traveled into the very roots of her molars and she wanted nothing so much as to rip them out of her head. The grimoire sat on the seat beside her, wrapped in unassuming cloth.

It wasn't until the carriage pulled up to the Lastrider villa she realized she'd forgotten to take her next dose of Hypericum. It was too late now; she was already stumbling from the carriage, toward the open gates.

A woman stood before them, staring down the street. As soon as she noticed Angelica, she blinked.

"Lady Angelica? What are you doing here?"

Angelica narrowed her eyes at the woman. She seemed familiar; certainly a member of the gentry, considering the make of her dress. Then she remembered—Camilla Lorenzo. Taesia's aunt.

"I need La—Taesia." Her voice was so hoarse she almost didn't recognize it. "Step aside."

The woman slowly shook her head. "My niece just left."

"*Left?* Where the fuck did she go?"

Camilla Lorenzo hesitated, brilliant blue eyes glancing between her and the street beyond. "To the Noctus Quarter. But I'd advise you to not follow. This is Lastrider business."

"Lastrider business is my business," Angelica growled before turning back to her carriage. "Noctus Quarter, *now.*"

There was a storm inside her and it was raging to be let out. Angelica was not a stranger to monsters or to violence. It was the promise of her god that wove around her like razor-sharp twine, ready to cut her into pieces with the slightest tug.

She didn't want a crown because Deia desired dominance over the other gods. She wanted to win a crown with her own merit, her own power, her own competence.

She allowed herself a moment to think of it: Vaega having a true Holy Queen, one whose hands stretched across the realm until everything that fell under their shadow was hers.

Not like this, she thought as she closed her eyes, exhaling smoke. *Not like this.*

Nikolas stared up at a sky grown dark with night, wondering if it was merely his imagination the starlight seemed fainter than usual, the darkness more gray than black. Was it not just the sun that was fading, but all the stars?

Only a few days until Godsnight. He was running out of time.

But the king demanded progress on their hunt for the Conjurers still hiding within the city, and Nikolas was forced to put that before all else. Which was how he and his unit ended up in Haven Square, a hub in the eastern sector near the Nyx basilica and Noctus Quarter.

He was following a new—if questionable—lead. He hadn't expected Brailee Lastrider to come to him with information, nor the way in which she'd obtained this information.

"It's my specific Shade power," she'd explained. "I'm able to discern what has happened, what *will* happen, or...what's happening right this moment."

Slowly she'd described her dreams, how a boy had somehow Conjured first the university statue, then Lune Bridge, to wherever he was.

Nikolas hadn't been sure whether or not to humor her. He'd always liked Brailee, appreciated her steadfast calm compared to Taesia and Dante's chaos. She wasn't the sort to give false information, or play pranks.

So he'd chosen to take it seriously. "And you don't know where exactly this boy is? Or what his goal is?"

She'd shaken her head. "No. But he's getting ready to collect something else. I've tried to reach him again, but my power...I'm still not entirely sure how to use it."

He could tell she was flustered, possibly upset with herself, so he'd thanked her sincerely and told her he'd look into it. The dreams she'd described left him with an odd feeling in the pit of his stomach, the cloudy fear of something you couldn't see or hear, but knew was coming closer.

"We've cleared the square," Gem announced at his side.

"Good. Make sure no one comes through."

Gem nodded and went to assist the others. His soldiers were set up across the square, either redirecting citizens away from it or else pacing restlessly, waiting for something to happen.

Brailee had said the Conjurer liked to target landmarks, so he'd asked for Damari to send guards to various statues, fountains, and the like to watch for suspicious activity. Nikolas wanted to catch him in the act, to see how this impossible thing was done.

Nikolas resigned himself to the idea nothing *would* happen. He felt jittery, restless, like he was wasting time. He could be with Maddox right now, refining his lightspeed ability, or with his mother, who had been quieter than usual.

Instead, he stood staring up at the monarchs' monument in the middle of Haven Square. The monument was large, a marble memorial to kings and queens of the past. Ferdinand Accardi's father had been added to the list of names chiseled into the plinth, and his mother's before him. Ferdinand's own name was expected to join the catalogue of royal lineage, though the question was whose name would appear under his. A Cyr? A Mardova? A Vakara? A Lastrider?

Four figures stood upon the plinth, two queens and two kings. Nikolas studied each one—Agustín, the first Holy King, his ruthless father's head tucked in the crook of his arm; Dalvinder, the Foreign King, holding a persimmon in one hand to represent Vaega and a fig in the other to represent Parithvi; Arcelia the Cunning, a cloak flowing from her broad shoulders as she was frozen in the act of pulling a rapier from her cane; and Mabrian, the Warrior Queen, decked in armor and wielding her famous sword.

Nikolas shuddered, remembering his battle against that sword.

Sensing eyes on him, Nikolas turned and found Julian standing with Paris. At Nikolas's attention, Julian quickly averted his gaze to the crossbow he held, as he wasn't allowed to wield a longbow within city limits. He hadn't been acting right for days, oddly skittish when before he'd been stoic and calm.

"Julian," he said, perhaps a little sharper than he intended. "Come here, please."

Julian looked as if he had been called for his own execution as he peeled away from his confused partner and went to stand beside Nikolas. The Hunter's eyes briefly darted up to the monument.

"Yes, my lord?" Julian murmured. The night was cool, but he had been sweating all evening.

Nikolas hadn't fully considered what he would say. There was only a slowly building ire, a growing suspicion. "I wanted to know if you had anything new to report."

Julian frowned slightly, staring at the Sunbringer Spear instead of his face. "If there were, I would have reported it. My lord," he added like an afterthought.

"If you're feeling unwell, perhaps you should take some time away from the investigation."

"My lord?"

"I can't spare worry over a soldier who isn't fit to work or fight. Or," Nikolas said, stepping in closer, "is it simply that you're distracted? I heard about you visiting the Lastrider villa, Julian. Why did you go there on your own?" *What connection do you have to Taesia?*

Julian's throat bobbed. "I—that isn't—"

A low hum filled the air. The hairs on Nikolas's body stood on end as he turned slowly back to the monument.

A ring of gold burned around it, casting the statues of the four monarchs in bright, eerie light. Everyone in the square fell silent, staring.

Then the light flared into the shape of a Conjuration circle. The ground rumbled faintly and guards cried out as the marble statue sank into the earth as if being consumed.

And all the while the circle spread farther, gathering Nikolas and his soldiers within its maw.

XII

She could already hear cries of confusion and fear in the Noctus Quarter.

Taesia had left it in a peaceful state, the moon on its way to rising, the beginning of a new night meant for celebration. Now it was chaos, Greyhounds rounding up refugees and driving them toward the basilica square as if they were dogs nipping at sheep.

And in the center of it all stood Cristoban Damari. His face was set in its usual forbidding expression, one hand settled on the sword at his waist.

"Please, tell us what is happening," Balwith was imploring him. "Will you not explain yourselves?"

"I see no reason to," Damari said. "I'm simply carrying out my duty. Yours is to do what I say."

"We hold no duty to the authorities of Vaega."

Damari's eyes flashed. "His Majesty, as well as his ancestors, graciously allowed you to live here. I would rethink that statement, if I were you."

A woman screamed as she was dragged out of her house, a Greyhound pulling on her wrist. Balwith bristled and made to intervene, his shadow familiar forming into a whip in his hand.

"Seize him," Damari ordered the nearest guards. "He's a Shade."

Balwith fought, his shadow whip first snapping against the forearm of the guard hauling the woman toward the square and then pushing back the ones closing in on him. A couple refugees rushed to help, including Mirelle, armed with a saber.

Taesia wove through the chaos to try and reach them. Balwith cried out as one of the guards slashed the back of his calf.

"Stand down now or else more will get hurt," Damari said.

Balwith lifted a shaking hand, a silent order. The refugees reluctantly lowered their weapons, though Mirelle snarled as her saber was wrested from her.

"Damari!" Taesia bellowed.

He turned and appraised her, not at all surprised to see her there. "Good evening, my lady."

Balwith and the others were tied up and shoved toward the square. Balwith's eyes widened when they landed on her.

"I'll handle this," she told him. "I'll—I'll fix this, just hold on."

"My lady," he whispered, and she couldn't tell if it was acknowledgment or warning.

"What's the meaning of this, Damari?" Taesia demanded.

The high commissioner sighed and nodded at the two guards attending him, who stepped away to help round up stray refugees. "I'm afraid my investigation into Don Soler's murderer has led me here, though I wish that were not the case."

"What the fuck are you talking about?" She nearly winced at the sound of a vendor's cart being overturned as someone tried to flee. "The refugees are under the protection of House Lastrider. If you mean to harm them—"

"I don't mean to harm anyone. Anyone who doesn't attempt to resist, at any rate." Yet he kept one hand on his sword, the other tucked behind his back. "But I require them to obey orders and subject themselves to questioning. Anyone who is not a Shade will be released."

As if in response to the word, Umbra slithered into her palm, ready to turn to a dagger should she need it. "What do you need with the Shades?"

"We have reason to believe Don Soler was murdered by one. He mentioned shadows, and a monster. It was therefore likely an act of vengeance carried out by someone with strong loyalty to Dante Lastrider." The corners of his lips curled, though his gaze remained blandly fixated on her face. "Surely you'd like to see justice carried out, would you not, my lady?"

He knew. He knew, and yet he had chosen to goad her anyway. She took a deep breath, as deep as she was able, while the shadows shivered around her.

"I understand," he said softly, unmoving despite the turmoil around them. "It must be difficult to think of justice at such a time, when your brother is about to face his own."

It won't work, she thought even as the shadows inched closer, even as the sword at her back pulsed eagerly.

"Perhaps it will be a double hanging," Damari mused. "A proclamation that those who oppose the Holy King will be dealt with swiftly and mercilessly. Otherwise we will surely lose our city to the greed of those who hunger for magic and power. Don't you think so, my lady?"

A bead of sweat tickled her neck. "Some would say the greed of those already in power supersedes that. That the systems laid out by them would be better dismantled, and those who uphold them are just as complicit in ruining our city, our country."

If she hoped for a flicker of anger or annoyance, she was left disappointed. "A disquieting notion," he murmured. "If that is the case, one might have to go up against the gods themselves."

She smirked. "Oh, I plan to."

A scream forced her attention away from his frown. Taesia's stomach flipped as she recognized the little girl, Naela, and her older sister being manhandled by guards. Naela tripped, and the guard behind her grabbed her by a still-growing horn and yanked. Naela screamed again, tears running down her face.

Taesia sucked in a breath, and the shadows drew in as one. She'd been keeping them at bay, but now their whispers were too insistent, too loud, too *yearning* to ignore any longer. They wrapped around her limbs, the night all at once brighter and blacker, and her at its center like the new moon.

"Let them go," she said, and her voice seemed magnified somehow, carried through the shadows to all they touched. "You know this display means nothing."

At last there was a flicker of unease on Damari's face. He shifted to better face her, his stance that of a fighter, a soldier. "Are you willing to confess, then, my lady?"

The night shuddered. Taesia breathed in the cold starlight and hummed with its power. Slowly she reached behind her.

"I'll confess," she whispered.

The wrappings fell away as she brought Starfell forward, jagged and glittering. Damari's eyes widened a fraction as he took a step backward, perhaps recognizing the sight or feel of something Other-Realm.

He was afraid, and she loved every second of it.

The shadows swarmed her, ready to obey her every whim. Then there came something else: a distinct tug in her navel, a distant cry of magic. It traveled through her and spilled into the sword's blade, though it didn't feel like her power—it reminded her of the bone dealer's shop, of the spine digging into her palm and the churning window to the universe on the ceiling.

Something was here—happening—opening.

She heard nothing now but the whispers. They turned to sobs and pleas, to cackles and seductive murmurs. Taesia threw her head back and became their conduit, grasping for that secondary source of power, the blade pulsing and shining and so bitterly, wonderfully cold.

When she tilted her head back down, she gazed serenely at Damari.

"I'll confess," she repeated. "That I'm sick of looking at your fucking face."

Lifting the sword in an upward arc, the sky broke open above them. The whispers turned to screaming, enthralled and terrified and vindictive. It was as if some monstrous hand had driven a knife into the foundation of their world and torn it like cheap fabric. Beyond was nothing but a decaying blackness, a cosmos of all things hungry and loathsome.

Monster, she thought, wondering if that was truly the word Don Soler's corpse had used to describe her. If it was the word the bone dealer had thought in his last moments, when his expression had morphed from glee to terror. *Am I a monster, or a god?*

Who was to say they weren't the same thing?

At the call of the bone whistle, the spirits around Risha stirred.

They crawled out of the stepwell, where bodies had once passed through during rituals. They emerged from the walls and from the chambers that had been used as sick rooms during plague times. A few even descended from the vaulted ceiling while others rose from the floor.

Heart hammering, Risha tucked the bone whistle into her pocket and held out her hands.

"Come," she commanded them.

They listened to her Vakara magic. Their gray, pallid faces turned toward her, toward the circle luring them. The ghost of a man with a pockmarked face twitched violently as he moved, and another behind him had an axe wound in his chest and his mouth open so wide and black it was as if his jaw had been unhinged. A woman sobbed with a sound like wind through a valley as a girl around Saya's age walked with her scalp in her hands, the top of her head scraped to the bone.

Whispers filled the basilica as they crowded the circle. The Revenants stayed completely still even though Risha noticed a few of them trembling, Natsumi's eyes darting around in panic. Jas clenched his jaw as the ghost of a boy stopped beside him, tried to reach for his knife, failed, and continued on to the circle.

Risha's breath began to stutter. She had never seen so many of them in one place. The entire basilica was cold with their presence, their last remaining thoughts.

"—thought I could be cured, but I should have known the medicine was fake—"

"—what if I'll never be remembered, what if they toss my paintings out with the trash—"

"—didn't want to die, I didn't want—"

Risha didn't dare cover her ears. The whispers would find her anyway, seeping through her flesh and into the inescapable legacy of Thana's blood.

She edged toward the stepwell, opening herself up to the barrier between Vitae and Mortri. She couldn't easily access the pathway here, but she could sense it all the same, looming tall and foreboding. The more spirits entered the circle, the more the barrier began to lose its rigid shape.

"Keep going," she called, then bowed her head.

Jumari Chadha, she thought, cycling the name over and over in a mantra. *Jumari Chadha*.

Just like during the séance she had performed not too long ago, she opened herself to the specific spirit she called for, the others contained to the circle behind her. It usually took a few minutes to locate a spirit within Nexus with its proper name, but Jas's mother had died outside the walls, and Risha worried it might be too far after all.

Jumari Chadha, she kept trying. *Your son wants to speak with you.*

Her spine straightened as the core of her power unfurled, stretching, reaching for the spirit that did its best to answer the call.

"Jaswant?" The voice was deeper than her own, strained with yearning.

A hand anchored on her arm. "Amaa?" Jas's voice broke.

"Yes, I'm here," she breathed, and Risha realized the woman was speaking Parithvian. "I feel faint."

Jas's breath hitched, and his grip tightened. "It's all right, Amaa. We'll let you rest soon. I just want to know what happened when you came to Nexus."

A small sound escaped her, something like a choked laugh. "City of secrets," Jumari whispered. "City of lies." Her voice was already growing softer, Risha's grasp on the spirit weak to begin with. "Jas—be careful. Do not trust the king. Leave Vaega alone."

"Why should we not trust King Ferdinand?" Jas asked. "What did you learn?"

"He has—"

"Jas!" Natsumi shouted at the same time Risha sensed the spirits behind them struggling.

Risha gasped as a familiar feeling pulled at her stomach, similar to what she'd felt in the mausoleum. The basilica groaned under the spirits' sudden displeasure, dust and mortar raining from the ceiling.

"Amaa—"

But whatever had disturbed the spirits had also disturbed Jumari Chadha. She faded from Risha like water sliding off skin, and Risha nearly tumbled into the stepwell before Jas caught her.

"Concentrate on the circle!" Jas yelled. "They can't—"

But the murky light was already flickering, the spirits drawn to the new sensation. Jas ran forward and slashed his forearm, blood spraying onto the chalk symbols, but it didn't do any good. The spirits writhed and wailed, their hands reaching toward something Risha couldn't see.

"Risha, get out!"

She couldn't move as the circle lost its light and broke its connection to the barrier. The whispering grew into a high, hair-raising scream as the spirits surged up through the roof and wall and blasted them apart.

The entire east side exploded in clumps of stone and marble before collapsing, the basilica rumbling from the force of it. Risha lost her balance and clung to the edge of the stepwell as Jas fell on top of her, shielding her from debris.

Under the terrible din, she heard Thana's low laugh as the ghosts poured into the city to enact their newfound vengeance.

"Get away from the circle!" Nikolas yelled as golden light spread across the square. "Don't touch it!"

His soldiers danced back, weapons out despite not knowing who or what they were fighting. Nikolas pointed the Sunbringer Spear at the sinking monument. Strong Lumins could phase not only themselves, but physical objects. If he managed to move it—to break the Conjurer away from his prize—

"My lord!"

He heard them before he saw them: a groaning, shrieking tide of silver-tinged ghosts congregating above the opening circle. There was no time to wonder where they'd come from before they started to smash into the surrounding buildings, breaking them up with single-minded rage as the wreckage pelted toward the soldiers below.

All the power Nikolas was stoking rushed out of him in a shield. It covered them like sunlight, the buildings' debris bouncing harmlessly off its surface and tumbling to the sides of the square. Nikolas's knees buckled under the strain as he kept it intact, the spear glowing hot against his palms. Phos's feathers shone brightly, their strength feeding his own.

But he couldn't maintain the shield for long. Holes began to grow and spread, turning his barrier into moth-eaten fabric. One of the holes opened above Julian's head.

And a large piece of rubble was falling straight toward him.

"Julian!" Nikolas yelled.

The Hunter lifted his crossbow, but there was no chance he could move away in time, let alone shoot a bolt to divert the rubble's trajectory.

In one fluid motion, Julian brought his arm back and punched through the debris. The impact shattered it into bits and dust, raining around him as if he were caught in a miniature sandstorm.

Nikolas gaped as his shield stuttered and disappeared completely. Even Paris was staring at his partner as if he were a stranger, round eyes reflecting the glow of the circle.

Julian looked from his bloody knuckles to Nikolas, and in that moment, Nikolas knew he was dealing with yet another thing that went beyond his understanding.

The route Angelica's carriage took to get to the Noctus Quarter passed through Haven Square. When the carriage suddenly stopped, the driver's voice cut through the roof.

"What in Thana's grave *is* that?"

"Sir, you can't come through here, you have to turn around—"

Angelica grabbed the wrapped-up grimoire and hauled herself out of the carriage. The driver exclaimed as she staggered past him, and a soldier tried to stop her, but he laid one hand upon her burning arm and quickly let go with a yelp of pain.

The square was sheer pandemonium. The sky swirled with keening spirits, pieces of broken buildings crashed to the ground, and in the very center, the monarchs' monument was slowly being devoured by a Conjuration circle. The magic tickled her nose and made her spine ache.

"Angelica!"

Nikolas stood across the square. His spear was golden in his hands, his whole body glowing within its nimbus.

"We have to stop it!" he called out.

Angelica licked her dry, peeling lips. The fire within her was relentless, the truth burning at the base of her throat, but she was needed here, she was *needed*, and—

And she had no instruments.

That didn't stop her from taking her position on the outer rim of the glowing circle, the ground rumbling beneath her feet as the monument sank. But going where?

The air was muggy. A growling hunger swept through her, demanding something, anything, to subdue it.

It felt, strangely, like the training arena, a hint of impossible depth as hopeful as a newly rising sun, or whatever clung like verdigris to the stepwell in the basilica.

Angelica choked back a sob as her hands shook, dropping the grimoire.

Let me close the circle, she begged of no one, anyone. *Let me close the door that's been opened.*

Yet the sensation kept escaping her grasp, parting like fog between her fingers, stretching farther and farther away the more she approached it.

Instead, she only found the fire.

"No," she growled as it rose to scorch her throat. "*No*."

But there was no reasoning with obsession.

The flames crawling through her veins were better than any rendezvous at the Garden. She groaned as she finally gave in to the heat, her clothes catching fire, sleeves eaten up to her elbows and the hem of her dress burnt away to embers.

There were screams, inconsequential at first and then getting louder, her name shouted as if from the top of some distant cliff. Angelica's eyes shot open, taking in the sinister orange glow she'd added to the square.

And remembered the pain on Risha's face when she'd burned her in the ballroom.

When their blood soaks your feet, the crown will rest upon your head.

Everything shrank to a pinpoint. Angelica's ears rang as the world turned soft and dark, and for a moment, one blessed moment, there was simply *nothing*.

Then it all rushed back as rage and shame and terror.

Angelica opened her mouth and screamed.

It burst out of her and enveloped everything in its noise. Soldiers fell to their knees, dropping weapons to cover their ears. The scream was a single high note that ripped from her body, but it wasn't fueled by fire. It was something else, something foreign, expansive and intangible and *severing*.

The earth heaved and the circle's light suddenly cut off, throwing the square mercilessly back into night.

Angelica staggered and fell. Her chest heaved and she tasted blood. The circle's lines were now dark and cold, and where the monument had been was nothing but broken-up cobblestone.

No—there was one thing left. The head of one of the four statues. Agustín's marble eyes stared back at his descendant, the son of the Headless King now headless himself.

"Angelica!" Nikolas fell to his knees beside her. "Are you all right?"

Shakily she touched her fingertips to her throat. She couldn't respond, not because she'd broken her voice, but because her voice had broken something.

Damari stared up at the portal in stark terror. It nourished her on some primal level.

Taesia had one moment to meet his gaze. Then she spun the sword and stabbed it in his direction, aiming the shadows at him and the guards who had rushed to his aid.

With a yell of effort, she swung the sword up. Damari and the guards were caught in the torrent of black cosmic energy, cutting off their screams before they were sucked up through the hole.

She didn't know where they went. She didn't care.

Taesia slashed Starfell through the air and closed the portal. It sewed itself up tight, and as it did, that secondary power suddenly disappeared, leaving her weak-legged and empty.

The shadows slowly fell away as she stumbled against the nearest building, gasping. Starfell was heavy in her hand, Umbra urgently nuzzling her cheek.

The refugees. Taesia found that everyone had frozen, staring at her as if turned to stone. Naela tried to run to Taesia but was restrained by her wide-eyed sister.

It wasn't only the refugees. The remaining guards roused from their horrified stupor, half lifting weapons as they gaped at her sword.

In that moment, she understood.

She thought she could choose what to be—god or monster, the heir to a House or a free woman—but the choice wasn't up to her. It never had been.

She had always been and would always be Taesia Lastrider, carrier of godsblood and feared by the people.

Fine then, she thought, straightening to her full height as those around her flinched back.

Fear me.

XIII

*W*ell, said the Voice, *they tried their best to stop it, didn't they?*

Every spell took a little more out of him, left him more fatigued and hollowed out. His stomach clenched as he forced himself to look up.

The structure was whole, for the most part. A head was missing, and though the statue was carrying a head underneath one arm, he didn't think this was deliberate. A tear escaped the corner of his eye.

"I'm sorry," he whispered.

The Voice laughed. *It will still work for our purposes. This was not any fault of yours.*

He leaned back on his heels and swallowed, tasting copper and bile. When he wiped a sleeve under his nose, it came away bloody.

He wished he'd let that girl help him. She'd said she wanted to, but then she had put him in a cage. Clenching his hand into a shaking fist, he hit it against his thigh.

She cannot help, whispered the Voice. *Only I can help you, remember?*

"Yes," he whispered.

There's one more to go. One more before we both get what we desire.

He stared up at the ruined marble. Something wet tickled his upper lip.

One more, he thought.

One more.

PART IV

What Lives in the Dark

Ⅰ

The Lastrider siblings used to play a game called Sacrifice.

It was simple yet cruel: One would face a day of something they hated while the other two waited for them to crack. However many hours they'd make it was tallied into points. Whoever had the most points at the end of the month would be able to order the other two around for an entire day.

For Brailee, it was talking. The longer she went without a conversation, the more morose she got. For Taesia, it was food. Her Sacrifice days were fasts that barred her from the kitchens and dining table, causing her stomach to rumble angrily and her mood to rival a bloodthirsty beast's.

Dante's Sacrifice days involved shutting himself in his room with no books, no socialization, no puzzles or toys, no busywork whatsoever. They'd been absolute torture. Lying on his bed with his mind buzzing and frantic for stimulation, he'd been forced to turn inward on himself, collapsing like a black hole into thoughts that became increasingly dark and morbid.

The winner of Sacrifice would change often, but Dante had had the highest loss rate.

Sitting in the cell reserved for solitary confinement, he wondered how many points he had racked up. He didn't know how many days they'd kept him here in the pitch black. Sometimes he was convinced he was the only person alive. There was nothing beyond the Gravespire, or else it had all been destroyed—or maybe he had always been here, and the world was just a dream. Colors, shapes, tastes, sounds, had all been created within the genius of his mind, and he was the architect, the maker of this beautiful yet terrifying world. He felt a strong sense of possession at the notion, and comfort—like disappearing back into this dream would be all he needed to make himself happy, to forget about the walls of his cell closing in.

He had been calm at first in the unrelenting dark. It had surrounded him like an embrace, recognizing kinship between them. But though he was of Nyx's blood, he was also the product of several generations of Vaegan blood. He needed sunlight and fresh air and the sounds of life. Deprived of these things, he was nothing but a grub in the ground, directionless. Stuck. Dying.

They had moved him from his regular high-security cell to this one when Don Soler had died, despite Dante being locked up and shackled every minute with lightsbane, a material from Noctus originally used to dampen a Lumin's magical ability—until the people of Vitae had discovered it worked on all types of magic. They had shoved the restraints onto Dante's wrists the second he'd stepped into the Gravespire, scraping his knuckles raw. Nox had desperately slithered up his arm until the lightsbane made it shrink and disappear.

Some days he could pretend the shackles were merely an accessory. Other days he felt the cost of their weight in the empty pockets of his being, the holes and hollows where darkness had once settled and breathed. He missed the way the shadows had caressed his skin and fitted to him like armor. He missed the way the night had surrounded him with stars that shone brighter wherever he stepped, as if he were some lost prince they remembered and adored.

"The Lastrider heir," others would whisper. "He'll take over his House one day, but he could be chosen as the Holy King's successor."

That was no longer his fate.

He could have let Taesia be dragged away with him. But it was too easy to remember her Sacrifice days, the image of her sprawled before the kitchen doors, groaning and miserable. Dante would sit beside her and keep her company, make sure she was at least drinking water, not caring if he was helping her win points against him.

She was his sister. She was infuriating, and he loved her. The last thing he'd wanted was for her to suffer.

"I'll make this easy for you," Don Soler had said when he'd come to speak with Dante, looming over the chair where Dante had been chained. "Confess to murdering Prelate Lezzaro, or you won't be the only Lastrider to receive His Majesty's retribution."

The don was right; it had been an easy choice.

Dante rolled his shoulders, trying to ease the soreness out of them. He hadn't slept well since coming to this wretched place, but at least he made use of the hours he didn't sleep. He practiced late at night, his only company the slow rhythm of the guards' footsteps. He didn't have chalk, so he drew symbols and glyphs by feel alone, the swirls and lines he made in the dust easily erased with a swipe of his hand.

Sometimes when he did manage to sleep, he found himself back in Lezzaro's safe room, the man dead and broken beside him, listening to instructions as he watched the construction of a Conjuration circle. The five-pointed star, the symbols of the realms, the name that fell from shadowed lips that plagued Dante's days.

Dante knew demons dwelled in the spaces between realms, the unknowable, unreachable pits in the universe.

He knew they were summoned by using their true names.

He knew they required offerings for their service, lest their displeasure come out in violent ways.

He knew that summoning one was his only way out of here.

He had no idea what time it was when the door opened and Officer Ybarra stepped in. She had once greeted him with restrained smiles, the only guard who had treated him like a human being, had even let him have a shave when the stubble on his face grew intolerable. Now her face was stone.

"Lastrider," she said. "You're getting cleaned up today."

It took him a moment to remember how to form words. "You going to dump a bucket over my head again?"

"I'd prefer it, but no. We need to make sure you don't get sick."

"Even though I'm about to hang?" His voice was raspy, making him cough. "I *would* like to look pretty for my execution."

With a strained sigh she latched a chain to his shackles. Like a cow on a lead to be taken to the slaughterhouse.

Dante had taken to pacing his cell to keep his circulation going, but his legs still wobbled as he walked down the hall. Ybarra opened a door and nudged his chain, a silent command to walk in before her. The guards never turned their back on an inmate.

Dante quickly deduced the washroom inside was used only for those in solitary. It had a stale, musty smell, the ground and walls ringed with mildew and white, crumbling lime. A single tub sat in the middle of the barren room.

"I take it I'm the first prisoner in solitary for a while," he guessed.

"You're the first prisoner to stay in solitary long enough for a bath in a while," Ybarra corrected.

The tub was already filled with sudsy water. Two guards were posted at the door, and one came in to help Ybarra undress Dante and cut the shirt off his back. When they helped him into the tub, he sucked in a breath at how cold the water was. He didn't complain; like the gray, tasteless food they gave him, it was better than nothing. They stood watch as he awkwardly rubbed the soapy water over himself as best he could while shackled. He bent over to scrub fingers through his greasy hair as water trickled down his neck.

Out of his cell, his mind felt clearer, lighter. He didn't have chalk, and he didn't have an offering for his summons. If he was going to escape this place, he needed something that would please a demon into agreeing to a pact. Yet nothing within his reach was suitable, unless the demon liked dirty water or mildew.

He glanced at Ybarra. A silver wedding band sat snug on her fourth finger.

Dante put on his best smile, hair dripping over his forehead. "Your wedding band is lovely."

Ybarra raised an eyebrow.

"I know a thing or two about jewelry," he went on. "May I inspect it?"

"Absolutely not."

"Don't you want to know how much it cost?"

"Why, so I can sell it? You implying something about my marriage?"

"No, I meant... if you wanted to know how much your husband spent on it..." Dante tried not to cringe. Admittedly, it wasn't his best work. Being holed up in that cell had stripped away the natural rhythms of conversation, the ins and outs he had once expertly weaved to tease information from people.

"I know how much he spent," Ybarra said dryly. "Too much. We should have been saving for a house in the inner districts instead." She gestured for him to get up. "Let's get you back, Lastrider."

They roughly toweled him off, and Ybarra began to unlock his shackles to pull a new shirt over his head.

His heart raced. This was his chance. When Nox appeared, when his power briefly flared, he had to use it to knock the guards unconscious and yank that ring from Ybarra's finger. The thought of hurting Ybarra twisted his stomach, but he had no other choice.

Yet his power was a muscle he hadn't flexed in a long time. As soon as his familiar flickered before him, Dante let the shadows burst out of him. Ybarra cursed and the other guard whistled in warning to the guard at the door. Dante lunged forward, but he was too weak, his power too big for him to properly grasp.

Someone grabbed him around the waist and slammed him to the floor. He was manhandled by the three guards, the shackles bruising his wrists as they were shoved back on.

"Fuck you, Lastrider," Ybarra growled. "You can't hang soon enough."

The words hurt more than the spot where his head had hit the floor. Nox was gone; his power was gone. That surge of comfort had been doused like water over coals.

Back in his cell, he was caressed by darkness. He lay on his pallet and shook, fighting back his frustration, his fear, as shadows brushed through his hair.

He was running out of time. He had to call the demon one way or another.

And he knew there was one offering the demon would take without hesitation. The ultimate game of Sacrifice.

II

The sound of the city's alarm bells followed Risha into sleep.

The spirits had already descended on Haven Square when she'd caught up to them. Doors had been torn off hinges and street lanterns had gone flying through the air, hitting a man in the back of the head hard enough to crack his skull. And through it all, their frantic whispers rose like a wave.

"—*wasn't my time, I had so many more years*—"

"—*know the taste of belladonna, the wretch put it in my tea*—"

"—*sentenced to hang for stealing a fucking chicken*—"

Risha had tried to silence as many as she could with her string and her spells. Sweat had dampened her clothes and hair by the time her father and sister showed up.

"Nyx's piss," Saya had breathed at the sight of the spirits crawling over the houses like an infestation.

They had worked for hours. At some point Risha had found Nikolas staring at her across the square, standing in the barren circle where the monarchs' monument had once stood. She couldn't make herself go to him.

Back at the villa, Darsha had wrapped them all in a large hug. Rath waved her away before turning dark, furious eyes on Risha.

"Do you know what caused this?"

Risha's face had burned, her body shaking with fatigue and delayed shock. Darsha had made her sit down, but Rath hadn't relented.

"The spirits originated from the basilica," her father said. "The whole eastern section is demolished, and guards found the remains of a Conjuration circle."

She'd thought—she'd *hoped*—Jas would have kept everything controlled, that the worst-case scenario would have been only a couple of rogue spirits instead of a horde. But something had upset them, another Conjuration circle flaring to life at the same time.

It was too late for regrets. The basilica was partially destroyed, and it was her fault. Spirits had been set loose on the city, and it was her fault.

Everyone was so alarmed by what happened in Haven Square it wasn't until the next morning they heard the news: Taesia Lastrider had killed Cristoban Damari and a couple of his guards. The Lastrider heir was nowhere to be found, but anyone with information on her whereabouts would be rewarded handsomely.

Risha was not surprised about Damari, or that Taesia got away. Some weak, soft part of her was glad for it, but the larger, furious part of her crackled bitterly.

Although Risha only wanted to hole herself up in her bedroom, her father forced her to join him at the palace. They had to report the incident to the king and his advisors, as well as try to convince him to put a stop to the Godsnight exhibition.

"It isn't safe," Rath stressed. "It will put the citizens in danger."

But Ferdinand stood firm, backed by his cowardly advisors. "We need it now more than ever," he said. "The people need to be reminded of the power our city wields. And if any Conjurers think to act, we will show them what happens to their kind when Dante Lastrider hangs."

Rath seemed perturbed by that. "The Lastriders—"

"Confined to their villa until we say otherwise. They'll not be allowed to participate."

"But their son—"

"Will be our bait to lure Taesia Lastrider out."

Risha suppressed the urge to gasp. She kept her hands linked tightly under the table to still their shaking.

Ferdinand was grimmer than she had ever seen him. There was something like steel in his gaze, cold and sharp. As if he were no longer bothering to put on a pleasant air for the Houses.

Do not trust the king, Jumari Chadha had warned them. *He has—* Has what? What had the woman learned all those years ago? Risha had attempted another séance in her bedroom, calling for her to return, but it was likely Jumari's spirit had fled into the void.

On their way out, unsuccessful in swaying the king's mind, they passed Nikolas coming to make his own report.

"Nik—"

"I don't know where she is," he whispered, muted and tired and dismayed. "Or where she would have gone."

"Do you think she'll come to the exhibition?" she whispered as her father called her name down the hall. "It's a trap. She has to know it."

Nikolas shook his head. "I don't know. I can't—"

"*Risha*," Rath snapped.

She parted from Nikolas and rejoined her father. Rath studied her the same way he had after the necropolis, all suspicion and uncertainty.

"Do not speak to him," Rath ordered. "Or the other heirs."

"Yes, Paaja," she murmured.

It took her a moment to realize something familiar was tapping her on the shoulder, a persistent sensation that sent a frisson of cold through her body. She stopped and stared at the pale marble, frowning in concentration.

Was it coming from Thana's Chapel? No . . . it felt far more expansive, like a giant eye gazing down at her.

Her father called her name again. She reluctantly hurried after him, that eye following her every move.

Despite her father's warning, she received a message from Angelica that same day. It told her to come to the opera house at midnight, even though it was a risk with the curfew.

She received a message from Jas as well—to her mother's delight—full of apologies and inquiries if she was all right. She hadn't responded to it, too full of guilt and disappointment in herself.

Unwilling to add to her growing list of misdeeds, she debated not going to see Angelica. She even took a few swigs of her lavender- and valerian-infused sarab before attempting to sleep, resulting in little more than a half doze. She fully woke when moonlight slanted across her face.

Immediately she knew she wasn't alone. Risha summoned her bone shards and whirled around, aiming them at the figure beside her.

The shards froze midair and fell onto the counterpane when a familiar face turned away from the shadow and into the moonlight.

Just like after Dante's arrest, Taesia had managed to climb up through her window and onto the bed. She was sitting cross-legged over the sheets, elbows on her knees. Her clothes were dirty and scuffed. She looked exhausted.

There was a wrapped parcel strapped to her back. Witness accounts from the Noctus Quarter had claimed the Lastrider heir had held a strange weapon that night, a black sword.

"Hi," Taesia murmured.

Risha grasped the front of her nightgown. "Taesia, what... what are you doing here?"

"I was going to leave before you woke up." A long, slow blink. "I guess that sounds pretty creepy when you say it out loud."

"What do you mean, leave? Where do you plan to go?"

She shrugged. "It's a surprise."

Was she going to try to save Dante? "It's a trap," Risha blurted.

Taesia's eyes sharpened. "Obviously." *But that won't stop me*, her expression added. "What do you care? I thought you'd washed your hands of me."

"Don't be like that."

"Like what? Myself?" Her voice was a contradiction of hard and brittle. "You made it perfectly clear you don't agree with Dante's vision."

"I don't need to in order to perform the ritual." Although after seeing the king today, after Jumari Chadha's warning, she wondered if she was changing her stance on that.

Taesia frowned. "You still want to do it?"

"Only if we find a way around the Ostium problem. Only if it's safe." She didn't know if she could use the Revenants again after what had happened. She hated either option, but what other choices were there? It was either try now, or wait another hundred years.

Taesia nodded. "I think there is. I was having Angelica read up on it. But what about the exhibition? Your family and Ferdinand expect you to represent your House."

"This is more important."

They stared at one another. Taesia had never been comfortable with duty, likening it to a chain, whereas it was all Risha had ever known. To share this responsibility, this burden, felt oddly personal.

"Angelica asked me and Nik to meet her at the opera house," Risha said. "I wasn't going to go, but she might have answers. You should come, but... stay out of sight."

If Taesia found that hurtful, it didn't show. Instead, she slipped off the bed as Risha dressed in the most nondescript clothes she owned. At least she didn't have to worry about being spotted on the streets if Taesia cloaked them in shadows.

She couldn't stop the shiver that racked her as she did up her buttons. "Damari—"

"Deserved it."

They were the same words Taesia had spat at her in the ballroom, the same disregard. The same unrecognizable fury.

"I know he had you reanimate Don Soler," Taesia said behind her.

The air grew thick with uneasy pressure. Risha's fingers trembled against the button she couldn't loop through, waiting, keeping her back open.

A soft exhalation. "You had no choice," Taesia muttered.

Risha closed her eyes. Not forgiveness, not quite, but not condemnation either.

That was, after all, the difference between them: Risha staying on her straight, paved pathway, and Taesia wandering off to explore other roads.

Maybe they had never been meant to end at the same destination. Maybe they had never been meant to walk side by side.

There was something comforting about the opera house at night. Angelica was used to seeing it lit up handsomely, both on the outside and from the large crystal chandelier that cast a warm glow over the rows of seats and private boxes, but the curfew made it so that there were no shows at night anymore.

The only light now came from the hand torch Angelica had brought with her. The torch was nothing more than a wooden handle with a flare quartz affixed to it, a material from Solara that produced a short radius of light. It flickered worryingly and she tapped on it, the pale, wan light steadying.

It illuminated the Mardovas' private box overlooking the theater. She sat in her customary seat at the front, staring down at the empty stage and thinking back to a time she hadn't been able to see over the railing. Her father would place her in his lap, holding her secure even as she leaned forward to get a better view.

She wrapped her arms around herself now as if to replicate the feeling. As if that was all it took to believe she was safe.

She kept swallowing, her lips parting over and over as if wanting to speak—or sing. Maybe it was the setting. Maybe it was the memory of her father. Maybe it was Haven Square haunting her, that sharp, ringing scream somehow cutting off the flow of energy fueling the Conjuration circle.

Angelica didn't understand anything about what had happened that night. The city was murmuring about Taesia Lastrider, as faithless and traitorous as her brother. There were calls for a dual hanging, to find the Lastrider heir and bring her and her whole family to justice, to dismantle the so-called Traitor House.

But any satisfaction Angelica felt about Taesia's downfall was marred by the fact that when she had returned to her right mind, she'd realized the grimoire was gone.

She couldn't remember where she'd dropped it. If a Conjurer got their hands on it...

"Angelica."

She jumped as Risha stepped into the box. The Vakara heir hesitated before taking the seat at the end of the small row. Angelica was oddly grateful for it, as well as the silence they shared waiting for Nikolas to join them.

They only had to wait a few minutes. Angelica hardly ever saw him in the somber, dark colors he was wearing now, even his pale hair hidden until he pushed the hood of his cloak back. Glancing at the hand torch, he opened a pouch on his belt and his light familiar drifted toward the ceiling, illuminating them better. The shadows cast stark lines across their faces.

Angelica stood, and Risha did the same. She refused to think about who they were missing.

"You called us here," Risha said. "Why?"

Angelica looked at the worn seats, specifically the one her mother usually chose for herself.

After she'd come home from Haven Square, she'd locked herself in her room, huddling in the corner until her mother had found her. But no matter how perplexed Adela had been, no matter how often she asked Angelica what had happened, no words could pass her chattering teeth.

Deia's words had forged themselves into a blade above her neck. One wrong move and she would bleed out.

When their blood soaks your feet, the crown will rest upon your head.

Angelica had always been willing to be ruthless, to break apart the other Houses if necessary. It was what her mother had prepared her for, what the Mardovas had been doing in quiet, intentional acts for years.

But this was not mere scheming or political ruin. This was drenching herself in blood to ascend a throne already dripping with it. This was knowing she would be possessed with a violence beyond human understanding, a yearning for power as old as the Cosmic Scale itself.

As much as she desired power, she wanted it to be her own. As much as she wouldn't hesitate to turn her enemies to ash, these were not her true enemies.

They were victims.

Risha took a step toward her. "You were learning more about the fifth realm, weren't you? About how to do the ritual despite not having access to Ostium?"

Turning, Angelica grabbed the railing and leaned her weight against it.

"It won't matter," she whispered to the empty stage below. "None of it will."

"What do you mean?" Nikolas asked.

"I mean *us*. All four of us. Even if we do attempt the ritual, it won't amount to anything, because we are *puppets*. That's all we are. That's all we've ever been."

Saying it out loud for the first time shook something loose in her. Not quite anger, but a bitter *unfairness* that made her reevaluate everything. She had grown up with her mother's promises, thinking her bones were made of granite and her heart cut from diamond, able to withstand anything because she was a *Mardova* and she shared the blood of a god.

How surprising, then, to realize her own blood was a traitor—her granite bones turned to sediment, her diamond heart to glass. One strong grasp between immortality and ruin.

"What are you saying?" Risha whispered.

"I learned about something called fulcrums. They're anchors between the gods and their realms. We've seen that Conjuration can somehow transport objects." She nodded at Nikolas, knowing he must be thinking of the Conjuration circle in Haven Square and its four quadrants. Her hand slipped into her pocket and touched the sketch she'd taken from him at the university, where a similar circle had appeared. "I thought we could use this Conjuration circle to summon some of Ostium's power from its fulcrum, if it still exists. With that, we could complete the ritual."

"So we'd need to use Conjuration twice?" Risha asked, brow furrowed. "I don't like the idea. We've already seen the latest disaster it brought."

Nikolas shifted on his feet. "Risha…is it true the spirits escaped the basilica? That Conjuration was being performed there?" Something in

Risha's face made him huff. "Gods, you *are* working with them, aren't you?"

"I'm *not*. I've met with them, heard their side of the story. They want to break the barrier to Mortri, like I do, but I don't condone their methods."

"Then why didn't you report them? Why didn't you strike as soon as you met them?"

Angelica had never seen Risha so at a loss before. "I...I wanted to keep an eye on them. Make sure something like the gala didn't happen again."

"But it *did*." Nikolas kept staring at her as if waiting for her to say she was joking. "You know I'm required to share everything with the king. I don't know how long I can protect you."

"It won't matter," Angelica said. "We don't have much time left anyway."

"What?"

Her palms were hot, and she let go of the brass railing before it could warp under her touch. "The idea of using the fulcrum didn't seem plausible," she said. "So I went to ask Deia about it."

Risha visibly tensed. "What did you tell her?"

"She already knew." Her shaking grew worse, and again she hugged herself. "She knows we plan to use the ritual. And she told me it wouldn't matter, because the gods have their own plan. They are at *war*. And they will use this—the alignment of the Cosmic Scale, the barriers weakening because of the Conjurers, us taking in their power during Godsnight—to tear each other apart."

A short, punched-out sound escaped Risha.

"This isn't funny, Angelica," Nikolas snapped.

"Does it look like I'm laughing? This is the truth as told to me by my god, in the sacred walls of her basilica."

"Your god who wants us *dead*!"

They all reached for their weapons as a dark figure dropped into the box from the one above it, landing in a blur of darkness. The shadows eased away as Taesia stood to her full height, glaring down at Angelica with a wrath that went far beyond her usual antagonism. Behind her, Risha shut her eyes as if in pain.

"Tae?" Nikolas breathed, eyes wide. "What are you doing here? Where have you *been*?"

"How long have you known?" Taesia demanded, ignoring him. "How long have you been sitting on this?"

"I only just learned," Angelica growled. "And I was going to tell you, but you were too busy *murdering the high commissioner.*"

Taesia bared her teeth. "So the gods have been planning all this time to turn our ritual into a battle? And whoever walks away from it—"

"Rules the Four Realms," Risha finished. She turned away, covering her mouth.

"Is that why Phos isn't speaking to me?" Nikolas murmured, glancing up at his floating familiar.

"And why Thana is keeping the barrier to Mortri shut," Risha whispered. "She told me she was more concerned about me being her vessel than the spirits who haven't moved on. That she wanted the power of Ostium for herself."

"And Deia said their war was started over Ostium," Angelica said. "There was something in the grimoire about…devouring. That if you ingest a being suffused with power, you get some of that power for yourself."

Taesia's wrath turned to disgust. "They wanted to *eat* the god of Ostium?"

Angelica shuddered. *It will be a grim day indeed should the gods devour their kin*, the grimoire had read.

"This can't be right," Nikolas stressed. "We would have known, wouldn't we? Shouldn't they have told us?"

"Why would they?" Angelica muttered. "We don't matter to them, other than fulfilling our roles as pawns."

"Then we can't do the ritual," Risha said. "We can't even do the exhibition. It'll be far too dangerous."

"And how exactly are you planning to stop this?" Angelica demanded.

"We could run away," Nikolas said.

Angelica scoffed. "Of course that would be *your* plan, Cyr."

"I mean it. If we leave now, get as far from the other heirs as possible—"

"What good would that do?" Taesia interrupted. "Even if we're across the Arastra Sea, the barriers are the thinnest they've been in centuries. When the Cosmic Scale aligns, it'll be easy for the gods to break through to reach us. If Nyx, Phos, and Thana want to see Vitae suffer, they'll cause unimaginable damage no matter where we are."

"Then what can we do?" Risha's voice broke with desperation.

No one answered, because there *were* no answers. There was only the dawning, spreading horror of what they were about to face, what they'd been marching toward this entire time.

"No," Taesia growled, reaching for the wrapped weapon on her back. "I am not going to be a *puppet*."

"Who says Nyx will possess you?" Angelica shot back. "Maybe he'll take over Dante. Unless he hangs first. I'm sure it won't be easy to possess a corpse."

Before Taesia could lunge at her, Angelica aimed a tendril of fire at her face. The erstwhile Lastrider heir dodged and launched herself off the railing, disappearing back into her shadows.

Angelica clutched her hand with the other, forcing the heat down, *down*, lest she reduce the opera house to ashes. The other heirs remained silent, stricken.

"Pray, if it makes you feel better," Angelica said. "Whatever happens now will be between you and your gods."

Then she grabbed the hand torch and left her family's box for what was perhaps the last time.

III

Although Risha downed the entirety of her sarab bottle once she got back to the villa, she still tossed and turned through dreams of Angelica crushing her windpipe, or Nikolas and Taesia dismembering one another, snarling like beasts.

Risha couldn't face them. Couldn't face Taesia, the girl who had asked her to reanimate a dead rat and shrieked in glee when she succeeded, and cut her down. Couldn't face Nikolas, the boy with quiet words and quiet dread and quiet hopes, and spill a single drop of his blood. Couldn't face Angelica knowing she'd only ever wanted validation, thinking it came in the shape of a crown, and deprive her of a future.

And she couldn't enact the ritual without risking more damage to the city. No matter what she chose, she would lose.

Once weak sunlight broke over Nexus, the dawn of the last full day before Godsnight, Risha considered going to her father. But if he knew about Thana's plans, he would offer himself to the god instead and whatever fatal destruction that entailed. She couldn't allow him to do that; even the wound he'd gotten in the necropolis had frightened her in a way little else could.

After picking over her breakfast tray, Risha wandered down the corkscrew stairs to Saya's room. Her sister was curled up in the armchair she had liberated from the university's library, a large book in her lap.

"You look terrible," Saya said.

Risha shuffled inside, weighted down as if her insides were made of lead. "Could I have done something differently?"

"You mean with Taesia?"

She supposed that's where this had originated. She nodded, and Saya kicked out the chair's ottoman. Risha sat on its well-worn upholstery.

"It wasn't your problem to fix," Saya said.

"I know. But I'm still…" *Part of the problem.* She should have never gotten involved in Taesia and Dante's plans. Should have put a stop to the Revenants as soon as she'd located them.

"She killed Don Damari," Saya said fairly.

And Don Soler. And the bone dealer. Maybe even others Risha didn't know about.

"She changed," Risha whispered. "And she didn't take the rest of us with her."

"You've also changed," Saya pointed out. "All of you have. It's like…" Her sister traced the diagram in her book. It was the same two-page sketch of the Cosmic Scale she had been studying earlier, the Four Realms connected by roads and ley lines crafting a geometric shape. "It's like the realms. All different, all harboring different magic, but connected and part of a whole. Together, they're strong—they trade resources and allow for inter-realm communication. But separately, they'll continue on regardless of the other three. We've seen that thanks to the Sealing."

Saya shrugged. "You used to be close, but that was before you understood your roles. Then you drifted apart, your own personal Sealing. You continued regardless."

"But the realms are dying on their own," Risha said. "They can't live independently of one another. They *need* each other."

Saya sighed with a reluctant nod. "True."

Risha stared at the diagram. At the realm of Mortri, drawn as an empire of stark trees and tombs. Roads sprouted from it like veins, tracing back to the other three realms, to the smaller shapes within the Cosmic Scale—pockets within the universe where mysteries were born.

Risha's heart suddenly started pounding, though she didn't know why. The longer she stared at the diagram, the more dread pooled in her stomach.

The realms—the Houses—the heirs. They were all connected to one another, their own roads and ley lines sprouting from their bodies, their magic. Risha had sensed it in lazy afternoons spent with Taesia and Nikolas, even when making small talk with Angelica at a party. It wasn't merely their stations; it was the Cosmic Scale itself, made in miniature.

Risha thought back to the Godsnight Gala, facing Jas in the

mausoleum. The way she had found the small threads binding together his life and nearly snapping them the way she snapped her string.

"Risha?" Saya's voice was distant, muted, as if she were underwater. "What is it?"

A knock startled them both. A servant popped her head in.

"I'm sorry, my lady, but you have a visitor," she said to Risha. "Lord Jaswant Chadha."

Risha's mouth dried. Her words were little more than breath when she said, "Tell him I'll be down soon."

Risha made herself stand even as vertigo threatened to send her under. Her revelation sat inside her like spoiled meat, nauseating, invasive.

Her hair was disheveled and her dress was plain, but she didn't have the strength to go to her room. When she entered the inner courtyard, her mother was hurrying out of the adjoining tower.

"Risha!" she hissed. "You can't see him looking like that! He came all this way—"

"I need to speak with him now," Risha said flatly, approaching the sitting room. "Alone."

"Risha—!"

Risha practically slammed the door in her mother's enraged face and turned to find Jas pacing the length of the room, sweating slightly above a dark blue sherwani.

"Praise Thana," he breathed in relief as he reached for her. "Risha, I'm so sorry—"

She yanked her hand out of his. "I was a fool to believe you could actually do it. I should have known the rules of necromancy are too strict—"

"Fuck the rules of necromancy!" he said loud enough for her to wince. "If that circle in Haven Square hadn't been activated, it would have worked. We can try again. We can—"

"Enough, Jas!" She walked to the window, shivering despite the sunlight. "I can't condone this anymore. There are guards surrounding the basilica, anyway. Although I...I tried to reach your mother again. I think she's moved to the void."

He moved to stand beside her. "You can't give up that easily."

"I haven't given up. I've just learned my purpose lies on another path. One I have to face alone."

"What are you talking about?"

She turned toward the sunlight, letting it warm her skin as best it could as the words spilled out of her, unable to keep it contained to herself any longer. The more she sat alone with it the more finite it seemed, the ending to a tragic play the viewer hadn't seen coming.

"The gods are at war?" Jas repeated softly when she finished. "Then the Sealing...?"

She nodded, tightening her arms around herself. When he noticed her shivering, Jas laid a warm hand on her shoulder.

"I'm sorry," he said. "You should have told me before."

"What could you have possibly done about it? The gods will have their way with us one way or another. And if Thana really does possess me tomorrow, if she makes me face the others, if they...if they truly want each other dead..." Her voice caught. "I can't let any of them win."

A hesitant touch at her elbow. When she didn't pull away, Jas closed his other hand around her arm. She leaned into his warmth, smelling cedar and a hint of damp earth on his skin.

"Speak plainly," he said, though not ungently.

"There are...paths between us," Risha explained. "The heirs. Everything, really—everything that touches the Cosmic Scale. During the Godsnight Gala, I found a way to tap into them. I think I've always had this power. I used to kill insects in my room and then reanimate them, though I never had to hit them with a book or a shoe. I'd merely look at them and they would fall to the floor, dead. I nearly did the same to you."

He touched his chest, over his heart. The hand around her arm tightened as he realized what she was saying.

"I have to kill them," she said as her tears finally escaped. "All four of us. Before the gods can do it, before one of them walks away with all the power."

"You can't do that! Risha—"

"It's the only way to ensure the other three realms don't fall under the tyranny of a sole god."

"It's suicide!" he snarled. "You said the rules of necromancy are strict. Surely this goes against them!"

It did—it would—and it would bring more shame to her father, her family. But she had tried to peacefully negotiate, had tried to plead with Thana, had tried Conjuration. Either the realms stayed locked from one another and withered, or they fell under a ruthless god. It was easy to see which was the lesser evil.

She didn't want it. But she was the only one who could do it.

Jas was shaking his head again. "Don't do this. Please. We can try the barrier again, in the necropolis. We…" He cast his gaze around the room, lost. "We can leave Nexus like your mother wants, go to Parithvi and be married. We can study the barrier more there."

Risha was surprised to hear the laugh that tumbled from her lips. It sounded like a children's story. *And then the princess went off to marry the lord, and they lived happily together till the end of their days.*

But that was not her story. It never had been.

She put a hand upon his chest. The heat of him seeped through her palm, making her fingers unfurl like petals under the sun. His heart was beating, beating, eager to reach up and meet her touch. Risha leaned her forehead against him, her own heart beating a funerary march. The part of her not numb with terror was grateful for the way he held her.

"Maybe," she whispered, because she didn't want to tell him no.

Let this be what I remember, she thought. Jas's warmth, the way Saya rolled her eyes, the tinkle of her mother's earrings, the soft smile her father wore when praising her. She hoped they would remember her in a similar light, the good she had tried to do, the roses between the thorns.

Let this life not have been for nothing.

IV

The circle in Haven Square had done more than destroy a cultural monument. It had also fractured something in Nikolas that was still weak and starving, the first green shoot of a vine now trampled under a careless boot.

Julian set off a warning bell in his mind. Taesia was a criminal on the run from the city guard. Risha was working with the Conjurers. Angelica had delivered a fatal blow to them all.

The day before Godsnight was the anniversary of Rian's death. It seemed appropriate his mind was full of endings.

He imagined Rian beside him, arms crossed, hair fallen carelessly over his forehead. "You give up so easily it's embarrassing," his brother would sigh. "Aren't you supposed to be a role model for me? You should be thinking about how to stop this. How to fight it."

What was he supposed to do? What *could* he do?

"I am going to die," he whispered.

It was a fitting punishment. More so than his father's hatred and his mother's hollow existence. No matter what happened at Godsnight, he was sure he was going to face Phos's judgment.

I'm going to die.

All things died. Even their realm had fallen into its own autumn period, the slow yet sure transition from ripe harvest to shriveled flora. In a few decades they would cross into winter, their final days. Perhaps it wouldn't be so bad, then, to die now and be spared the cold.

His dread rose so high it snapped and dissolved, giving way to acceptance. Suddenly he felt lighter, calmer. The closest to peace he had been in years. Like finally letting go of a boulder he'd forced himself to carry for miles.

He still had several hours until Godsnight. A whole night in which he could truly appreciate this new lightness, this new freedom.

It was all he had, but it would have to be enough.

Under the awning of a closed bookshop, Nikolas surveyed the efforts the city guard had made to allow for one of the few festivals permitted in the city today. They had closed off an entire road and emptied all the surrounding buildings, guards and soldiers posted everywhere.

The children who ran past didn't seem too affected, but their parents were tired and grim. Though the city thrived on drama and revelry, it had been uneasy since the gala, and the death of the high commissioner had not relieved it. Not even the promise of the exhibition tomorrow seemed to lighten their spirits.

Nikolas couldn't allow the exhibition to go forward. Ferdinand had blocked all attempts at a meeting today, so he would have to try again tomorrow.

It was not yet sundown—not yet curfew—but lanterns had been lit overhead, and music drifted over the din of the crowd. Nikolas had made sure to dress in casual clothes with a cap to hide his hair. This was an event for the citizens, not an elaborate show like the gala, to celebrate when the harvest season was at its peak.

"Didn't take you for a festival man."

Fin had once again snuck up on him. He was dressed in a blue shirt open at the collar, showing a triangle of brown skin. His hair was tousled by the wind, lips a wine-touched red.

Fin's message asking him to meet here had been more than welcome. Though Nikolas was mortified at how much he'd revealed during their last meeting, he couldn't help but want his company.

"I'm not, usually," Nikolas answered. "But tonight is an exception."

"Yeah? How come?"

"I needed a distraction." He swallowed. "You know what happens tomorrow."

Fin's expression sobered. "Oh. Do you..." He bit his lower lip, glancing around as if in search for something. "Do you need anything?"

"An evening to relax," Nikolas said. There were quite a number of things he needed, but none of them were possible. This, though—honoring his brother's memory with light and fun—he could do.

And if it ended up being his last night, he wanted it to be a good one.

Tables had been set up with platters of food and casks of drink, money exchanging hands for pastries stuffed with dates and nuts, gooey almond tarts, and lamb skewers slathered with herbs and spices. Smoke rose with a hissing sound and carried the scent of charring meat while frying oil bubbled, ready for the next batch of dough. The adults held cups of sarab and red wine while the children guzzled citrus juices that made their chins sticky.

Fin nudged him and pointed out a little boy who had a pastry in either hand, his mouth coated with crumbs as he took turns biting into each one, a look of true bliss on his face. Nikolas laughed, remembering how Rian used to pile second and third helpings on his plate before even finishing his first.

Nikolas bought them a couple of skewers. The lamb was tender and rich with fat. A yellow-haired dog ran up and down the street, barking occasionally and wiggling its rump as children squealed and rushed to pet it. Nikolas couldn't help but feed the dog a bit of meat, scratching it behind the ears.

They stopped at booths that had been constructed for games. One involved shooting a dart at a target as the booth worker moved it back and forth with a crank. They watched a man shoot three darts that all missed—one nearly got the booth worker in the thigh—then stomp away grumbling. A young girl tried next, and got close enough to win a crocheted cat.

Fin turned to him with a glint in his eye. "Watch this."

Fin paid for three darts. He held the first one between his long fingers, rolling it as if to test its weight. He cocked his arm and let the dart fly. It landed at the edge of the target's center, and his next two came just as close.

The observers let out a happy "Ooh!" and clapped. The booth worker sighed and dug out Fin's prize: a silver bangle.

Fin returned to Nikolas with a grin and held it up. "Stick out whichever wrist is Lux's least favorite."

Nikolas raised his eyebrows and held out his left wrist. Lux was tucked away in the pouch at his belt, emitting a faint glow in response to its name.

He thought Fin would slip the bangle over his hand. Instead, to his surprise, Fin wrapped the woven bracelet with the tree charm around his wrist. Fin then squeezed the bangle over his own hand, where it gleamed in the mingling dusk and lantern light, a pale smile against his skin.

The bracelet and its charm were a foreign weight despite its lightness. Heat spiraled up through his stomach and to his face, as new and strange as the accessory.

"I thought you didn't want to part with this?" Nikolas asked, almost accusatory. "You tried to jump me in the street for it."

"I was *not* going to jump you," Fin argued. His eyes kept flitting between the charm and Nikolas's face. "Think of it as your token."

"Token?"

"You know, how lords and ladies would give presents to their favorite warriors to do well in tournaments? Not that tomorrow is a tournament, but you get the idea."

His heart sank. Nikolas wrapped a hand around his wrist, the silver charm warming from his skin. It suddenly felt much heavier.

"I…" A curious shiver began in his chest. "Thank you." Fin swiped at his nose and turned away, embarrassed.

But that heavy feeling persisted. As they neared the end of the street, they found a puppet show surrounded by children. The puppets were in the likeness of the four gods, the show little more than crude, violent humor as they screeched and fought one another. The children's tide of laughter washed over Nikolas even as bile rose up his throat.

"Nik?" Fin called as he turned away, hurrying as fast as he could from the lights and the laughter. The peace he'd found earlier began to fray at the edges, revealing the panic hidden underneath.

He stopped once it was darker and quieter, leaning against the nearest building to catch his breath.

"Nik!" Fin came up beside him. "What happened?"

"The exhibition," he croaked. "Don't go."

Fin frowned. "Why?"

"Just don't. Please. Promise me."

Fin thought it over before nodding slowly. "All right, if it means that much to you. But I think this is something more than stage fright."

Nikolas took the deepest breath he could. How could he put any of this into words? How could he explain his decision, his acceptance, in a way anyone could understand?

"Sometimes—" Nikolas's voice came out scratchy, raw. "Sometimes I get this feeling. It's terrible and irrational, but I...sometimes I wish I'd never been born. That I could have done everyone a favor by not existing and creating more problems. To not have to bother with the responsibility I've never been able to fulfill."

The words had been with him for so long that once they were in the open, he wished he could call them back. But they belonged to the night now, and to Fin, and to this one corner of his city.

He'd never been able to tell Taesia, had never worked up the nerve. Even in their most intimate moments when she'd admitted she worried her parents hated her, or she would never amount to anything beyond familial duty, he had kept this part of him quiet, hoping it would be enough to hold her and be held in return. He'd never told Risha, who would have grown concerned to the point of meddling. And he wasn't close enough with Angelica to consider it.

He expected Fin to say something reassuring, to argue, to question. Instead, Fin stared up at a sky beginning to freckle with stars.

"I've felt that, too," Fin said at last, as quiet as if they were in a basilica. "Wondering how less complicated things would be without me here. If the world would be a better place for it."

Nikolas frowned. The words didn't line up with what he knew of Fin, of his seemingly simple life. He realized, suddenly, that he barely knew Fin at all.

And now he might never get the chance to.

Fin turned back to him, his expression reminding Nikolas of what he saw in the mirror every morning. *Guilt*.

"For what it's worth, I'm glad you're here," Fin said. "And I want it to stay that way."

Fin's eyes were bright blue and solemn, staring at him so surely Nikolas almost felt himself crack open again. Not with destruction, but to let something out, a starving vine choked off from sunlight.

Nikolas's body was a contradiction. He was a blend of contentment and sorrow, a bright sky with the sun obscured. Fin's words couldn't change his grim reality, but for now they could be a balm, a stillness in the middle of churning water. Slowly the heaviness began to shed off him, pooling at his feet as Lux burned bright as a star at his hip.

They barely knew each other, but they understood each other. He wanted more nights like this, filled with light and food and games. He wanted to stop feeling as if nothing he did mattered, because somehow, it mattered to this one person, and maybe he could learn that was enough.

But Nikolas had never been good at getting what he wanted.

As soon as he entered the gilded body of the villa, he knew something was wrong. His heart kicked a warning as Lux flew out of his pouch, heading toward the stairs. Somewhere above came his father's raised voice.

Nikolas rushed to his mother's room. When he barged through the door, his legs nearly gave way under him.

Blood streaked the floor, a handprint of it stark against the cream-colored wall. It had been used to create a strange, wending shape, and his mother sat crumpled in the middle of it before his looming father. She was weeping as Waren continued to rage, his voice creeping into hysteria.

"—think it's so fucking easy," he yelled, his face nearly purple. "Is that what you thought, Madeia?"

She was crying too hard to answer. Her dark hair hung in wet strands on either side of her face, sticking to her gaunt cheeks.

Nikolas fell to his knees beside her. "Mother, what—"

"Don't touch her," Waren growled. "She has a sickness, Nikshä."

"What are you talking about?" Nikolas carefully turned over her cut-up arms, the ripped fabric of her dress dark and heavy with blood. "What have you done to her?"

"I've done nothing!" Waren bellowed. He grabbed the dresser behind him and threw it to the floor in a thundering crash. Madeia shuddered under Nikolas's hands. "I've given her everything she could possibly need, and *this* is how she repays me!"

Nikolas looked down and the center of him went cold. What he thought was a shapeless array was actually a too-familiar pattern drawn in blood, a double circle with a diamond at its center.

His mother had been creating a Conjuration circle.

Waren's breaths were loud and strained, his body taking up too much space, too much air for Nikolas to focus. The words he'd spoken to Fin earlier came back to him.

Sometimes I wish I'd never been born.

He knew the same misery bound his mother's body, a shattered piece of pottery glued back together with grief and fear. But to see it so plainly, to have it spelled out in narrow gashes and spilled blood, made him want to double over and be sick.

Nikolas cradled his mother's face in trembling hands. The silver charm of Fin's bracelet winked in the candlelight.

For what it's worth, I'm glad you're here.

"Mother," he whispered as tears began to roll down his cheeks. "Mama. Please look at me." She could hardly lift her head, much less open her eyes.

Why were you making a Conjuration circle? What were you trying to summon?

"Call for a medic." Nikolas began to rip up his coat, planning to wrap the strips around her arms. "She's still losing blood."

Waren's nostrils flared, the only warning before his father's fist collided with his head.

"Waren!" Madeia screamed, woken by the sight of her son in danger.

"How dare you give *me* orders," Waren seethed. Nikolas had fallen to the floor, clutching his ringing head as pain lanced through his neck. "I've given you both everything. *Everything*, despite what you took from me!"

This was Nikolas's punishment; he understood. He'd often wondered why the ash flies had chosen Rian, the best son, the future comandante, instead of Nikolas.

It wasn't due to any twist of fate. It was simply because the world was cruel, and filled with perilous things.

Madeia crawled over Nikolas's body to shield him from his father. Nikolas held on to her thin wrist, her skin cold against his.

"Why couldn't it have been you?" Waren growled as a tear clung to his jaw. Without another word he stormed out of the room, the door banging against the wall hard enough for the knob to dent it.

Nikolas slowly sat up and held his mother close, straining to hear her heartbeat, to make sure it was still working; in one way, at least.

Nikolas took his mother to the infirmary on Gowell Avenue, an unassuming building on a narrow road, which bore no signs or ornamentation to denote its use. It was designed specifically for the gentry, a place to be medically attended to far from prying eyes.

The medics took Madeia to clean her up and stitch her wounds. He sat waiting in the front, elbows braced on his knees, staring blankly at the floor. Fin's bracelet rested gently against the base of his thumb.

For what it's worth, I'm glad you're here.

The promise of loss was something that had become more acute since Rian's death, and sometimes he forgot his mother was terrified of the same things he was. That, like him, she wanted some way to dodge the strikes before they could land.

He thought it was his only strategy for Godsnight: to simply be an offering, to let it finally end, to feel the full might of Phos's rage before he never had to worry about it again.

"My lord," one of the nurses said. "Your mother has been seen to. She's asking for you."

Madeia's room had a window facing east, which meant she could enjoy the sunrise. She was laid up in a bed with thick blankets, her arms bandaged and resting over the sheets.

She struggled to keep her eyes open as he hurried to her. He gently squeezed her shoulder as the nurse closed the door to give them privacy.

"I'm sorry," Madeia whispered. Her lips were dry and pale, her cheeks wet with new tears. "I'm sorry, baby. I couldn't..."

Her chest hitched with a sob. Nikolas cradled her cold hand between his. Lux hovered above Madeia before nestling against her collarbone.

"I know," he whispered back. "I know, Mama. It hurts. I'm so sorry."

She shook her head, or tried to. "Not your fault, baby. Never been your fault." Her fingers twitched between his hands. "It was mine. I should have stopped..."

"You know you can't stop him when he gets like that."

Madeia turned her face into her pillow. She looked small. Frail.

"No," she whispered. "*Him.* Tried to bring him back. Tried to use the same way, but..."

Nikolas frowned. "What are you talking about?"

"They prepared his body," she murmured in a monotone, almost as if she had gone into a trance. "Anointed him with oil and dressed him in Cyr colors. And then he was gone, in all that light. He was...*gone.*" She shuddered violently. "We buried an empty casket. I never told..."

But Nikolas had seen his brother's body laid out in the casket of polished cherrywood and pine, a funerary wreath draped across it prepared by House Vakara, the small bells chiming amid the fragrant bundles of marigold and sage.

Had she been trying to use Conjuration the way those so-called necromancers did to resurrect him?

"Forgive me," she begged, her voice thick with tears. Her fingers tightened around his. "Please don't leave."

"I won't leave," he promised her, sitting in the chair beside the bed. "And there's nothing to forgive." *I'm the one who took him from you.* "I'm sorry, Mama."

"Not your fault," she whispered, and his chest tightened at the words. "Don't leave me. Don't go. Please. Don't go."

Accept it.

Rian wouldn't tell him to accept this. He would tell his brother to fight. To protect the things he had resigned himself to losing.

"I won't leave. And I don't want you to leave either." Nikolas kissed the back of his mother's hand. "I'm glad you're here, Mama."

The upward twitch of her lips seemed to clasp something in place, like the bracelet on his wrist.

No matter what would happen tomorrow, he would at least put up a fight. He owed his brother's memory that much.

V

Angelica swept through the doors of the Deia basilica. She didn't bother to stop for the anointment, passing flustered priests as she walked straight to one of the offering chambers.

Mateo stepped in front of her, wearing a vaguely alarmed expression. Angelica snarled, and the priest hurried to open the door for her.

Inside, she sank to her knees as her heart pounded. She wanted to grab each bowl and break them apart, melt them down, deface the room and the entirety of the basilica.

"Deia!" she shouted. "Answer me!"

A wave of heat blew over her, followed by a growling laugh.

"No deference?" the god whispered everywhere at once. "No prostrations? You disappoint me."

There was a prickling on her back, the sensation of a large, many-legged thing climbing over her. The weight of it pushed her forward, and she shut her eyes as soon as she saw the edge of the bulbous, black body.

"Tell me what has made you so impious," Deia crooned by her ear amid the wet clicking of pincers.

Her thighs tensed, eager to run. She had come here with purpose and with righteous fury, but all of it washed away in the tide of Deia's presence. A spindly, hairy leg draped over her shoulder and across her chest, a monstrous caress.

"You said," Angelica began, her voice shaking, "that there was no need for me to master my elements, despite the pain and humiliation it's caused. You abandoned me in my need."

"ALL I HEAR IS THE WAILING OF A CHILD," Deia said. "SPEAK DIRECTLY OR NOT AT ALL."

"You were saving me for this. For Godsnight. You didn't care about my lack of control because you *wanted* me to keep losing control, to keep feeding the fire." She forced herself to straighten her spine despite the god's weight on her back. "But I refuse to be a pawn in this. If you gain access to my body, then in return I demand the power of Ostium."

It was a gamble, a guess, but all her thinking had led to this conclusion. If Ostium was somehow the original source of Conjuration—if it was related to what she had done in Haven Square—

"Did you eat them?" she whispered. "The fifth god. Did you take some of their power for yourself?"

A crushing silence fell. Then the room filled with Deia's rasping laugh. The hulking shape crawled off of her, into the circle. A shudder racked Angelica's body as she finally saw the massive spider's form, its many eyes black and lifeless surrounding the blue one at their center.

"I WOULD HAVE TAKEN OF THEIR FLESH, BUT ALL I HAVE LEFT ARE REMAINS," Deia hissed. "AND YET YOU THINK THIS IS A POWER YOU CAN WIELD? YOU CANNOT EVEN WIELD THAT WHICH YOU CURRENTLY HAVE."

"Because you won't help me!"

"ENOUGH. WHEN WILL YOU LEARN THIS IS FOR YOUR OWN GOOD?" Deia lowered her hulking body to the ground so Angelica could stare into that burning blue eye. "THAT I HAVE DONE THESE THINGS FOR A REASON, THAT I DESIGNED YOU THIS WAY FOR A REASON."

For a moment Angelica forgot how to breathe. "Designed?"

"WHY DO YOU THINK YOUR POWER IS SO OBSTRUCTED? THAT YOU REQUIRE ARBITRARY THINGS TO UNLEASH IT, KEYS TO UNLOCK THE DOORS TO THE ELEMENTS?" The spider's pincers dripped translucent liquid, falling to the floor and making the stone hiss and smoke. "I FASHIONED THOSE DOORS, MY BLOOD. I PROTECTED YOU FROM YOUR OWN DESTRUCTION."

The blood drained from Angelica's face, leaving her cold despite the throbbing heat all around her.

"YOU ARE MY HEIR. I HAVE KNOWN THIS SINCE YOUR CONCEPTION." The spider scuttled closer, lifting one spindly leg to brush her cheek. "I FELT THEN HOW YOUR POWER WAS A SUN TOO CLOSE TO LAND, READY TO SCORCH EVERYTHING TO DUST. IT WOULD HAVE CONSUMED YOU ALIVE, AND MY STANDING IN THE WAR WOULD BE FORFEIT.

"SO I INFILTRATED THE WOMB, SHIELDING YOU. I CLOSED YOU OFF FROM WHAT YOU MOST DESIRE SO ONE DAY I WOULD HAVE MY PERFECT VESSEL."

So much her god had kept from her.

"How could you do this to me?" she whispered, thinking back on all the years of craving fire, the shame in using her instruments, the whispers and sneers from other mages.

"I WAS SAVING YOU."

"Saving my *body*," Angelica growled, glaring through the film of her tears. "That's all you've ever cared about!"

The spider chuckled, its leg pressing into her chest.

"I THOUGHT I MADE THAT CLEAR," Deia said.

The cold crept back, freezing her from the inside out. She had no ally in Deia; she never had. The god would never open the doors she had locked.

She would never have true access to her powers.

Angelica wreathed her hand in sputtering flame. She lunged at the circle, wanting nothing more than to burn the god out of existence, to reclaim what was rightfully hers.

The spider disappeared and Angelica was slammed onto her back. Her bones cried out as Deia's true form crouched above her, sword point aimed at her heart.

"I HAVE CODDLED YOU FOR TOO LONG," the god said. "YOU HAVE GROWN INSENSIBLE."

Angelica tried to thrash, but Deia held her tighter, searing into her skin. She screamed.

"DO NOT DISOBEY ME AGAIN," Deia warned. "YOU WILL NOT LIKE THE THINGS I CAN MAKE YOU DO."

And then the pressure was gone, and Angelica was left weeping in the middle of the offering circle. Mateo found her there moments later, a burning handprint scarring her arm and the ashes of the offering bowls staining her dress.

A scepter of ice, a throne of obsidian, a cloak of storm wind, a crown of flame.

The portals reopened, the love of a kingdom.

Meaningless. So far beyond her reach she couldn't even see the bend in its horizon.

Pain turned her feverish and panicked, the burn on her upper arm in the shape of Deia's hand surrounding her in spirals of heat and madness. The city twisted around her, jeered at her, despised her the way she despised it, a slumbering beast ready to part its mouth and devour her.

She knew she should go home. Tell her mother what Deia had revealed. What she had learned of Ostium, the gods' war. But the pain silenced her, buried her under a mountain of rage and fear.

The doors between her and the elements closed in, looming, begging her to open them.

I don't know how. I don't know how.

All she could do was scratch at them, clawing and gouging with her fingernails, screaming at them to open, open, *open, OPEN.*

Blood ran down her arms and she realized she was scratching herself, breaking her skin open as if to reach inside and draw out the locks weighing her down. Her fingernails crusted over brown and red, copper in her nose, in her hair. She smelled burned flesh. She swallowed embers.

I have to break them open.

A door stopped her in her tracks. She was breathless, ragged, strung through with razor wire. She pressed her hands to the door.

"Open," she whispered against the wood.

There was an iron knob. She reached for it, fumbling, staining it crimson.

It swung open.

Angelica staggered into the room, the familiar blue, the window open to the growing night. The last night she might see alive, if she allowed Deia to take her. If she had no strength of her own to combat it.

A figure standing at the desk whirled around. Eran Liolle's eyes widened behind his glasses.

"My lady!" He took a step forward, then more wisely, two steps back. "What...What happened to you?"

Angelica gaped at him, her chest heaving. Doors and doors and doors around her. An ocean of the things she wanted and couldn't have. Deia's laugh in her ear. The barren pocket where her father's love used to nestle, empty empty empty.

Reaching blindly for the desk, her hand settled on the heavy orb of a paperweight. It was the one she'd seen that girl give him at his office door, one of the many girls he had offered private sessions to.

"My lady," he said warily, holding out a hand. "Whatever you need, I can help."

He didn't even reach for an element. That's how weak he thought she was. The smile she gave him sat slanted and wrong on her face.

"Yes," she said dreamily. "You will."

She smashed the paperweight against his skull. Eran crumpled to the ground with a muffled cry, his temple blooming red. The reverberation shuddered up her arm, delicious and jarring. The mage began to crawl toward the back of the room, where crocks of water and earth were kept.

Angelica followed him, the bloody paperweight like a ruby in her hand. She pressed her foot against his back, pinning him to the floor. He choked as his fingers twitched, shaping the air above him in a cyclone that whipped the hem of her dress.

She kicked him in the ribs, severing his concentration. Eran coughed and struggled weakly as she turned him over, barely registering the fear twisting up his face. His glasses had fallen off, forgotten on the floor beside him.

She smashed the paperweight against his skull again, felt the crack and give, heard the squelch of violence meeting flesh. Was this how Taesia had felt when she'd killed Don Soler and Damari? Had she experienced this same strength, this dark satisfaction?

Some claim that the only transference of power comes from death and consumption. It will be a grim day indeed should the gods devour their kin.

I would have taken of their flesh.

Angelica dropped the paperweight and drew the short knife at her belt.

"It will be painful at first," she said, an echo of his own condescending words. She lifted his shirt to reveal the slope of his torso. "But it will pass."

She plunged the knife into his sternum. Eran grunted as blood bubbled and welled, spilling over her fingers in a hot geyser. As she tore him open, it came on like a wave, an endless sea. She thought of the congealed blood in Deia's offering bowls and wondered if it had ever felt this hot, this brimming with potential.

Angelica grabbed a rib and snapped. Thin, high noises escaped Eran as the light gradually left his eyes, as the blood spraying with every pump of his heart began to diminish. Angelica was drenched in it, a second skin, sticky and cooling.

The mage's body was a patchwork of organs, purple and red and glistening, woven through with snakelike intestines. She chose one at random, pink and slippery in her grasp. Eran was fully dead beneath her, his heart lying still in the enclosure of his chest. But the organ was so warm, so full of life and magic.

Angelica realized she was weeping as she brought the organ to her mouth. Blood smeared her lips as her teeth caught on flesh, meeting a slight give before they punctured the outer layer. Her mouth flooded, the meat chewed between her molars before she swallowed. Bitter and metallic and acrid.

Was this how power tasted?

She didn't know how she managed to get away from the university. She stuck to the private paths she normally took, staggering through the dark, wanting to get home and unsure how.

She walked for so long her feet ached as much as every other part of her body. She kept thinking the words *corner of Belmin and Kelle*, as if so long as she reached this unknown destination she would be safe. Eventually she heard the sound of the river and turned toward it, wanting to be clean, or perhaps to let it catch her and drag her down, where she could be still and quiet and alone.

"Mardova? What the fuck?"

Then a cool hand was touching her forehead, a familiar voice by her ear bringing to mind a Mariian girl in her window seat, clever fingers braiding her hair.

Corner of Belmin and Kelle. Now she remembered where she'd heard it before.

"What happened to you?" Cosima demanded. "You look like you've crawled out of a butcher's shop. Are you hurt?"

Angelica tried to answer, but words held no meaning, no substance. Her mouth was sticky with blood, sealing her tongue to the roof of her palate.

Gods, she had—

Her throat convulsed before she turned and vomited.

The doors Deia had constructed inside her were still locked. It hadn't worked. Nothing had.

Nothing ever would.

"Come here," Cosima said once Angelica was done heaving up everything in her stomach. She led Angelica toward the river, made her kneel at its shore. "Stay still."

Angelica closed her eyes and drifted as a cool cloth touched her face, wiping away the gore, her last desperate attempt to defy her god. Eventually the cloth moved on to her neck, then her hands and wrists. She swayed and listened to the gurgle of the water, let it lure her into a temporary state of unbeing.

"You're lucky I was coming back from one of the festivals," Cosima muttered as she continued to gently clean her. "Makes for easy targets, you know? Was gonna head straight home and— Is this even your blood?"

Angelica shook her head.

"So this is...someone else's blood."

Angelica nodded.

"Someone who's, I'm guessing, very dead. Were you attacked?"

Angelica opened her mouth, but it was still clotted and sticky. Cosima handed her a water skin, and she eagerly drained the whole thing. She tilted her head back and opened her eyes at last, peering up into a night sky more gray than black, the stars seeming so distant it wasn't fair.

"I tried," she croaked, and Cosima stilled beside her. "I tried so hard."

She didn't realize until she felt Cosima's thumb under her eye that she'd started crying again. That simple, sweet touch—the merest brush of her thumb—broke something open inside her, and suddenly she was heaving with sobs.

Despite the state of her, Cosima brought her in close. Angelica fell against her, wrapped in the cradle of her arms and weeping in a way she hadn't done since her father died. Cosima rocked her and hushed her, petting a hand down her head and through her hair.

"I don't know what to do," Angelica was babbling, "or how to stop it, I can't, I—"

"Stop." The single word was like a spell, stealing all her words. "Breathe. And keep crying, if it'll make you feel better."

So Angelica did. The wretched city fell away until it was only the two of them beside the river, the cold negated by Cosima's warmth, the arms around her securing her in place. She couldn't remember the last time someone had held her like this. Couldn't remember what it felt like until now.

"There you go," Cosima whispered when Angelica began to relax. Angelica heard her swallow. "Whatever happened, I'm sure you had your reasons. But Deia's tits, you scare me sometimes."

Yet Cosima still rubbed her back. Angelica was used to others' fear, their prostrations, their avoidance. She'd never had someone fear her and accept her within the same breath.

Slowly she reached up and grasped Cosima's arm. Angelica's face was nestled at the base of her throat, where she could feel the skip in her pulse.

"What do you need, Mardova?"

The question gave her pause. She had never asked herself what she needed. Only what she wanted.

What do you want? Eran had once asked her, and Angelica had repeated the question to herself over and over, desperate for an answer that didn't mirror her mother's. She'd thought she wanted power, and knew only now how bitter it tasted.

What do you need?

This, she thought. *I need this.*

VI

Taesia was exhausted after a full day of evading guards. Nexus was a city that had cradled and rocked her all her life, begging her to explore its corners and crannies, but now she felt like a stranger to its limestone walls and gently curving streets. Her body lay in some in-between state of denial and acceptance, a fugitive in the making suddenly turned public enemy number one.

Traitor House.

Yet any satisfaction she had stoked at Damari's demise fell apart like a fire-eaten log in the aftermath of Angelica's reveal, spraying embers everywhere.

She had tried as best she could to follow Dante's plans. Now Nyx would have his way with her if she so much as attempted to open the barrier to Noctus.

As she watched the sun sink toward the western horizon in layers of bloody orange and yellow, casting the rooftops around her in swirls of shadow and gold, she allowed herself a full fifteen minutes of despair before pulling herself back together. The long day was over, and in several hours the dawn of Godsnight would break.

I will be no one's puppet, she thought. *I am Taesia Lastrider and I serve fucking no one.*

She couldn't go to her aunt's house; the guards would be thorough. Instead, she turned to the Noctus Quarter.

The basilica of Nyx was cornered by towering minarets, its facade studded with stone gargoyles of Noctus beasts amid engravings of constellations. Torches flanked the front doors, the rest of the structure bathed in moonlight. Blessed by Nyx long ago, the building hardly needed to be lit at night, naturally drawing the radiance of the moon and stars overhead.

As a child, it had awed her to look up at the snarling stone snout of a shadow wolf whose eyes glowed with starlight. It had been a way to warn people, back when the portals still worked, that the realm to which they were about to travel was dangerous and wild.

The streets were clear, the square empty except for the guards stationed at the intersections. No one wanted to approach the basilicas after what had happened to Thana's. The priests had all been evacuated until it was deemed safe to return.

Yet there was a figure at the doors, locking them up. Taesia kept her presence hidden with roiling shadows as she slowly ascended the steps, until she came close enough to recognize Balwith.

He turned, lips parted in surprise. As a Shade himself, he managed to peer into her shadows, meeting her gaze unfailingly.

They stood like that for a tense moment. Taesia's fingers twitched, unwilling yet ready to reach for her nearest weapon. Then Balwith bowed low, long hair slipping over his shoulders.

"My lady," he whispered, low enough to not alert the guards. "Thank you for intervening."

A sudden warmth bloomed in her chest, so hot it was painful. Taesia choked it down and inclined her head.

"I'm sorry for the position it has put you in," Balwith whispered. "We are currently being watched, but if there is anything we can do…"

Silently, she gestured at the doors. He nodded and unlocked them, easing one of the heavy doors open for her.

Umbra coiled around her forearm as she crossed the threshold. Immediately the scent of cloves hit her, the rich decay of autumn's last days, forcing her to breathe deeper, to properly fill her lungs. Once Balwith closed the door, she leaned against it and stared into the darkness, finally allowing her body a moment of rest.

Everyone hated and reviled her. Everything she had done to protect them had instead pushed them further and further away.

There was no one left, and it was her fault.

She sucked in a breath and shut her eyes tight. She focused on the scent around her, the hint of candle smoke in the walls, the lavender oil waiting in a large bowl on top of a pedestal by the entrance. For a long while she couldn't move, just another gargoyle cast in stone, but eventually she lurched forward and touched her fingertips to the surface of the oil, speckled with dust.

Even that brought too many memories. Dante grinning at her over the bowl when they were younger, trying to splash her. Taesia touching the cold oil to the back of Brailee's neck to make her sister scream.

Taesia shoved the pedestal to the ground. The silver bowl clattered and rolled, spilling its oil over the black marble floor, slick and dark in the sheet of moonlight coming through the glass dome above.

Taesia was not wicked—she did not *feel* wicked—yet she was something out of a nightmare, the monster who ate children if they did not go to sleep when they were told, the being in the forest who whittled bones into arrowheads, the god who would send a flood to your village if you did not give proper offering at the shrine.

She longed to destroy the rest of the basilica, yanking candles from their sconces, tearing down the reliquaries, ripping up the stale, herbed flatbread the priests left out for the Noctans who came to pray. Only the thought of the refugees using this as a place of sanctuary stopped her from doing so.

The shadows quivered in the corners. The whole basilica seemed to be watching her, waiting to see what she would do. Her eyes swept over the Noctan-written prayers embossed in bronze along the walls, the ancient language she had been forced to learn when young and had since forgotten most of.

No, these comforts were for the refugees, and were not the source of her rage. Instead, she turned to the statue of Nyx. The god stood tall and benevolent with his hands outstretched, as if begging his children to return home.

Taesia's lips curled as the shadows drew closer. They coalesced around her, waiting, worrying. She extended a hand before her, the other holding on to Starfell's hilt as the sword hummed against her back. The shadows curled around the statue of Nyx, hugging his legs and torso, seeking the weakest points as they had done with Don Soler.

Taesia clenched her hand into a fist. The statue groaned as the shadows heaved, stone dust falling white as chalk in the moonlight. Umbra shivered against her as the shadows grew stronger, pushing harder, leaking out of the corners with curious whispers.

The statue slid off its dais and crashed to the floor in a spray of stone.

One of Nyx's hands skidded across the marble toward her feet, open and entreating.

She was catching her breath with an ember of satisfaction burning in her belly when the velvet voice touched her ears.

"SO MUCH HATRED YOU CARRY IN YOUR HEART."

The shadows scattered. Umbra tightened around her arm, clamping down like a warning hand.

Taesia yanked Starfell off her back as the voice continued to reverberate through the basilica. It sounded like a cold wind through tree branches, the expectant hush of the first snowfall. The darkness around her pulsed gently like a heartbeat.

Slowly she turned to face her god. Or rather, the projection of him. Only Deia had a physical form here in Vitae; with the portals closed, the other gods were limited in their influence.

Until tomorrow.

Nyx was tall and lithe, milk pale with inky hair slipping over cowled shoulders. He bore a golden circlet of moons and stars, his knobby, taloned fingers glittering with rings of garnet and pearl. His robe whispered over marble as he stepped toward her, the utter darkness of his eyes—no pupil, no iris, only unforgiving black with hints of purple and blue as if containing a hidden cosmos—calmly fixed on her.

Taesia held the point of her sword to his chest. It was instinct more than decision. It would do nothing, mean nothing, other than serve as a reminder of how helpless she was. After all, the power it contained was his.

Nyx smiled with pale lips. The shadows obediently drew toward him, whispering over him like a cloak flowing in a breeze. Taesia couldn't help but feel betrayed.

She mustered up her courage to deliver the first words she had ever spoken to his face:

"Fuck you."

"YOU ARE ANGRY. BUT THERE IS NO NEED." His lips did not move, and yet his voice echoed in her mind and she worried about ever getting it back out. "I HAVE PLANS FOR YOU, AND THEY DO NOT END HERE."

"What are you talking about?" Her voice was beginning to shake despite her best efforts to control it. He was merely a projection, and yet his presence was enough to hollow out her stomach and chest, making her feel smaller than she ever had.

"GODSNIGHT IS NOT YOUR BATTLE. THERE WILL BE OTHERS WAITING FOR YOU."

It was colder now in the basilica, and darker. Her breath came out as white fog. She stepped back and nearly slipped on a piece of stone.

"A WHOLE UNIVERSE OF BATTLES," he continued. He didn't blink as he stared at her, reaching for her with those inhuman fingers tipped in sharp black talons. "A WHOLE UNIVERSE OF WORLDS FOR US TO CONQUER."

Something fragile inside her split open. It shattered like the statue, hardness giving way to uneven pieces of debris.

She screamed. It was terror and fury and unwanted desire, the unfamiliar urge for power pitted against the more familiar urge to run and run and never once look back.

Taesia lunged with Starfell in both hands. She swung through his chest and wanted the bright, hot ichor of his blood on her skin and in her mouth, transforming her even as she ended him, a legend slain so another could rise.

But his image flickered and faded, a quiet huff of fond exasperation in her ear.

"MY GENERAL," he crooned as his voice faded. "SAVE YOUR STRENGTH FOR WHEN YOU NEED IT MOST."

Moonlight filtered back into the basilica as she fell to her knees, leaning on her sword as she choked down sobs. She pressed the cool pommel to her forehead as if saying a prayer, or vowing allegiance.

She could run. She could fight. She could let Nyx control her and secure their rule across the Four Realms. There would be a place for her by his side. She would have the power to save Dante, keep her family safe, and do what she'd always longed for: to skip across realms and discover, explore, with no duty or obligations to tie her down other than the will of her god.

The only price would be the lives of the other heirs.

Monster. God. General. Murderer.

Her hand tightened around the sword's grip.

No, she thought with all the vindication she had left. *I will not let you take me.*

"I won't let you take me," she breathed into the quiet basilica. "Do you hear me? I refuse your power. I'll refuse it until I die!"

Perhaps she had known all this time. Perhaps all her refusal and reluctance in the face of duty was because some part of her had known this was coming.

That she would finally become the monster everyone already thought she was.

The fenris was being transported the next day, when many of the citizens would be piling into the palace square to observe the Godsnight exhibition and the hanging. The Hunters would make the most of the empty streets and cart the beast outside the city, toward the northern forestland where it belonged. Julian was ordered to accompany them.

The news didn't come as a surprise, nor the captain summoning him to her office to say he was no longer on Nikolas Cyr's task force.

"I'm not sure what the reasoning is, since he didn't give any," Kerala said as she carefully watched Julian's reaction. "Did something happen, Luca?"

He shook his head, mouth dry and scraped knuckles aching. "Not that I can think of."

"Well." She heaved a breath. "Maybe escorting the fenris back to its habitat will be good for you. Get out of the city, commune with nature, all that shit."

Maybe it would. His dreams were twisting and dark, death waiting patiently behind doorways, a sky raining ash, Nikolas Cyr staring at him across a glowing circle with the Sunbringer Spear ready in his hands. He woke up sweating, his head hurting so badly he nearly threw up.

He found it easier to sleep at his mother's apartment, especially since the medicine had stifled her coughing. There was more color to her cheeks, a little more energy in her step. As glad as Julian was, he couldn't help the heaviness in his stomach when he remembered where it came from.

It was made worse with what else had happened that night in Haven Square. As Nikolas had spoken to the Mardova heir, something had tugged at Julian's consciousness, an uncomfortable awareness that grew sharper as he approached the wrapped bundle lying outside the circle. When he'd picked it up, he'd caught a whiff of sulfur and something *other*, feeling both right and wrong at once.

He didn't know what possessed him to take it. To hide it away in his bedroom. He hadn't yet unwrapped it, but it felt like a book, and he knew he wanted to be alone when he looked at it.

The autumn wind bit at the exposed skin of his face and neck as he walked to his mother's apartment. He couldn't face another evening at the Hunters' compound, the chattering and speculation flooding the halls as Godsnight approached. Even Paris was in on it, racking up bets on whether or not the Lastrider heir would show up and cause a scene. For every window displaying Vaegan flags—a crown within a diamond shape above crossed swords—there was an equal amount of new graffiti.

Holy is not honest

Houses breed Traitors

No kings no gods no heirs

Julian sighed and dug out his apartment key. As he climbed the steps to the door, he froze.

Taesia Lastrider was sitting on the landing, her back against the wall as she stared blankly at the street. At the creak of the top stair, she turned those dark eyes on him.

They bored into his memory, the searing glare as he held her to the wall, the way she had breathed rapidly against him, the tug of her fingers in his hair. His body flushed hot then cold.

"What are you doing here?" he demanded.

She stared at him. Her hair was limp and unwashed, her clothes stained. A wrapped parcel lay on the landing beside her. He waited for her to speak, and she seemed to be gathering the strength to.

Then her body curled in like a fist as a low, painful sound escaped her. Julian's heart lurched as he took an unthinking step toward her.

Don't, he warned himself. She was a thing that bit; he could still feel the prick of her dagger against his ribs.

He glanced at the door, hoping his mother was too busy cooking dinner to overhear. "You shouldn't be here."

She rested her forehead against her hand, closing her eyes. "I have nowhere else to go. I wasn't thinking."

Julian knew, of course, about Don Damari, killed at the same time they had faced the Conjuration circle in Haven Square. The price on Taesia Lastrider's head.

Instead of the fury of before, resignation lay like a low cloud around him.

"I'll leave," she rasped. "I know you want nothing to do with me."

Julian walked to the railing. He wondered how long it would take for a city guard to come if he began yelling. What she would do to him if he tried to arrest her himself.

But he kept quiet, watching the street. He was so tired.

"I don't know why you do the things you do," he said. "I don't know what made you this way." *I don't understand you, and it terrifies me that I want to.*

"My brother believed we deserved more," she said around the cracks in her voice. "That the world could be better. But what I wanted was so selfish in comparison. So I became the one who did the difficult, bloody work because I was strong enough for it. But it wasn't because I'm strong. It's because I'm *cruel.* I can't do good things because I don't know how to be *good.*"

She'd started shivering. He didn't think before he sank down beside her. Wordlessly he shucked off his jacket and handed it to her.

"Stop being such a fucking gentleman," she muttered. It sounded so much like her usual self he nearly laughed. Still, she took his jacket and slipped her arms through, popping the collar.

"Pretty sure gentlemen don't barge into your house and knock you against the wall," he said. He still couldn't believe he'd done that—or how the rage had grabbed hold of him so swiftly and deeply. No matter what amount of anger he felt toward her, he was ashamed of it.

"It's what keeps you interesting." Taesia held on to the edges of his jacket, pulling it around her. She inhaled deeply, and it made his stomach clench. She was already growing calmer. "You're upset with me."

"Astute."

"You're in a long line of people who are, and who deserve to be. You're just the first who hasn't driven me away."

Not yet, he thought, heart pounding at the thought of his mother behind the door, all the violent potential in the young woman beside him. But he couldn't voice it. He didn't want to end on anger and fear again; he wanted to see if there was any part of her that resonated with any part of him, if there was some chance at understanding. She didn't deserve it, but there were a lot of things he didn't deserve either.

"You're wrong," he said at last, his voice nearly eaten by the shadows. "You know how to be good. You didn't have to send us that medicine. I..." He faltered at the reminder of his mother's face, the relief as warm as a fire in winter. "Thank you."

Taesia squirmed, either embarrassed by his thanks or uncomfortable with the emotion in his words. "I didn't want her to suffer. But that doesn't mean I'm *good,* it means I know how to siphon money out of my House's coffers without getting caught. If you knew what all I've done..."

"So tell me," he said.

Her lips parted, full and dark in the moonlight. Ragged and weary as she was, she didn't seem like the product of a god; she was a girl who had messed up one too many times.

"You won't look at me the same," she whispered.

"I've never looked at you the same way twice."

The hint of a smile. Her chin dipped toward her chest as she considered.

She started from the beginning, from her brother learning Conjuration and how it had led them to Prelate Lezzaro. How that had blown up in their faces when her brother was framed for Lezzaro's death and was sent to the Gravespire, the guilt infesting her like a parasite ever since, leading her to kill Don Soler. How she'd needed the astralam bones to forge a weapon that doubled as a key. How the investigation afterward had put the Noctan refugees in danger, giving her no choice but to fight for them the only way she knew how: with violence.

And then she told him about Godsnight. About the gods' war being waged across realms, silent yet strengthening. The ritual she and her brother had thrown everything into, only for it to fall apart.

"I have no choice but to go," she whispered. Her shoulder was touching his, and he could feel her breaths as if they were his own, her pulse a steady rhythm in his ears. "When I save my brother, he can accept Nyx's power, and he can fight off the others to give me time to break the barrier." She reached for the wrapped parcel, which he realized must be the sword she'd been seen with that night. "If Nyx chooses me instead... I'd be forced to cut the others down, and it won't matter if I'm a wanted criminal. I would be god-chosen, a vessel of infinite power, a being fit to rule all the realms. I will not let that happen."

Julian couldn't fully comprehend everything he'd heard, but this parted his shock like a curtain. It suddenly made sense, her laying out everything like this, like a bedside confession.

He cleared his throat. "Is there anything I can do?"

She shook her head. "Just stay away from the palace square tomorrow. I don't want you to get caught up in anything."

I don't want you to see what I might be forced to do were her unspoken words.

"You don't have to worry about that," he murmured. "Nikolas Cyr kicked me out of his unit."

Her eyes flashed in confusion. "He did? Why?"

"Is it important?" Compared to what she'd told him, compared to a war waged between the gods, it was far too insignificant to put into words. "It's probably for the best. I'd get in the way."

They sat in silence for some time, watching the stars overhead. They seemed more distant than usual, less bright, but perhaps that was because of the woman at his side. Taesia belonged to the night, to the pitch-black sky and whatever lay beyond, the infinite celestial world. Somehow Julian found himself drawn to it, his body aching with an urge he couldn't name. A longing with no outlet.

Eventually she picked up her sword and slung it on her back. "Thank you. And I'm . . . I'm sorry."

"You can stay here," he said, so quiet he almost hoped she wouldn't hear.

He felt her eyes on him, dark and still as a lake. Somehow her scent grew stronger, something like cereus and lavender and cloves.

"I don't want to put your mother in danger."

"She'd be glad to house you. She thinks the accusations against you are a load of horse shit."

She gave a small laugh even as she shook her head. "I can't."

She got to her feet, and he did the same. She reached to tug off his jacket, but he stopped her.

"Why are you doing this?" she whispered. "I told you everything. You should be dragging me to the city guard."

Part of him wanted to. But he was tired, and she was facing death, and it didn't matter.

"You said I still owed you a favor," he said.

He was strangely proud of the smile on her face. Wordlessly she turned and descended the stairs, his jacket on her shoulders and her bone sword on her back. Her shadow familiar unfurled from its ring and waved at him. He lifted a hand before forcing it back down.

He was used to the mindset of beasts, the things they had to do in order to survive in a world filled with teeth and claws and ruthless elements. He told himself that was why he had to let her go, swallowed by the shadows like a predator hidden in the long grass.

Julian developed a headache as he mechanically chewed the honey-glazed carrots and fennel pork sausages his mother had made for dinner. Marjorie tutted and pressed the back of her hand to his cheek.

"You feel warm," she said. "Are you sure you're well enough for this new mission, Jules?"

"I was given an order." It hurt to talk, his jaw aching up to his temples.

"Well, you don't have to follow every single order, do you?" his mother asked in the tone that meant she'd already made up her mind. "We can go to a medic first thing in the morning before you leave."

"Yes, Ma." It would make no difference, but it was better to humor her.

She rubbed a comforting hand against his back before returning to the kitchen to wash the dishes. Julian had a sudden longing for his father to be here, to enjoy his mother's humming and the lingering smell of fennel in the apartment. A quiet and non-notable moment to be thankful for the small details of life, banishing fears and doubts for a minute of much-needed peace.

But the minute ended as he thought back to the story his mother had told him, the suspicion his father had also been a beastspeaker. His head-ache swelled with a vengeance.

He retreated to his room, the one he'd had since he was a boy. It hadn't changed much since then; the clay soldier figurines on his dresser still rattled when he opened and closed the drawers, and the wall above his narrow bed was plastered with pages he'd torn out of a bestiary, yellowed with years of sun exposure from his window. Marjorie hadn't under-stood why he'd wanted the sketches of beasts looming over him as he tried to sleep. He'd never told her it was because he wanted to memorize as much as he could, to be prepared to encounter any of them in the wild, to know how to best use his abilities against them. To make them pay for taking his father from him.

All Julian had wanted was to do what he was told. A life like his father's, obeying the laws and climbing the ranks until he retired or died an honorable death. It was simple and it was boring and it was stable, and it had crumbled around him the moment he'd laid eyes on Taesia Lastrider.

Sighing, Julian reached under his mattress and pulled the wrapped book out. He realized then he could have asked Taesia about it; he was fairly certain it had been dropped by the Mardova heir, but the thought of going to their villa made his skin crawl.

And besides, the longer he held on to it the more he sensed that earlier awareness, as if whatever was hidden within the wrappings was some-thing he was meant to find.

Julian steeled himself before untying the cloth. As it slipped away, it revealed a gilded book studded with gems, something distinctly old and costly. He pried open the cover and was greeted with the smell of sulfur and old blood.

He coughed, momentarily overwhelmed by the odor. It reminded him of the necropolis, of the prelate's safe room, of the circle in Haven Square.

No, he thought with rising horror. *It can't be.*

He flipped through stained and yellowed pages, skimming over segments discussing the realms and gods. He spotted Nyx's name. Taesia's god. The one who had instilled her with such fear.

Julian swallowed and kept skimming. The elements of Vitae, the light of Solara, the dark of Noctus, the souls of Mortri—they were all linked by the Cosmic Scale. The pattern that kept the universe in balance. He studied a sketch of the plane on which their realms sat, the lines and gateways between them, so very much like a Conjuration circle.

But there was something unfamiliar in the center. A circle labeled *Ostium*.

He frowned at the name.

Between the Realms are pockets in which the unwanted and the unknown go, like hidden seams in clothing. In these pockets are things not quite alive and not quite dead, the victims of the Universe given a new twisted shape. The residue of quintessence from Ostium, new stars burned into the sky. It is the occupation of this magical debris within these pockets that give birth to demons, the unsung beasts of the Realms.

The center of him turned cold, but he forced himself to keep reading.

Demons cannot travel into the Realms on their own, despite being able to traverse the Universe within their pocket dimensions. They must be called with Conjuration—their original magic—given an offering, and bound to their caller. It is only then they can maintain a form. In return, they grant power to the ones bound to them, the power they have carried from Ostium and warped by their prison of the Universe. The greater the offering, the greater the power—the ability to travel large distances in a blink, to call down storms with a snap of the fingers, to level entire cities with a mere command.

He began to turn the pages quicker, sometimes having to squint to make out the handwriting as his head throbbed. He jumped every time he heard his mother move in the room next to his; she was having her own restless night.

He paused at a section labeled "Of Demons and their Conjuring." Swearing under his breath, he examined sketches of circles and glyph charts and demon anatomy, names written in alphabetical order, lists of suggested offerings. He read one of the first entries at random.

> Azideh can be invoked using the same manner as the rest, but with the sigils for his name to better catch his attention alone. He enjoys pretty offerings, the more expensive the better. If one wishes to better learn and control the minds of living beings, Azideh is who to summon. Through his influence one can discern the wants and dislikes of other humans, and even speak in such a way to mold them to one's own desires. This power can be used on all things sentient, humans of every race and creed, beings of each realm, and every manner of beast.

His room grew fuzzy as the grimoire slipped from his hands and fell to the floor. He barely noticed.

Every manner of beast.

The rumors and speculation that had followed him around the Hunters' compound for years suddenly solidified into a hard, jagged truth: His abilities were linked to something demonic.

His father had been a normal man, his mother a normal woman. But Benjamín had fought a beast in the field single-handedly to protect his young family, had died surrounded by the corpses he had decimated with no weapon other than his own two hands.

A crash sounded in the main room. Julian jerked to his feet, instinctively grabbing the fallen book. "Ma?" he called. "Ma, are you all right?"

She must have gone to make tea, as she normally did when she couldn't sleep. It wouldn't have been the first time she'd fallen or fainted while doing so, but she had just taken a new dose of medicine.

Julian hurried to the main room. He didn't get far before he saw her: Marjorie's crumpled form on the floor beside the table, one hand extended as if waiting for something to fall into her palm. A mug of unfinished tea had broken beside her, the ceramic pieces scattered within a puddle much too large and dark to be tea.

Blood.

He stumbled, catching himself against the wall. A cloaked figure knelt beside his mother's body, holding a long, dripping dagger. When his feet scuffed against the floor, the figure looked up.

A woman stared back at him, calm and sorrowful. She sighed.

"You must be Julian Luca," she murmured in a rich, throaty voice. "It's a shame I found you here and not where you were supposed to be in the compound."

He couldn't react. Couldn't speak. His eyes bored into his mother's back and nearly collapsed in relief when it lifted with a weak breath. He rushed toward her, ignoring the woman and her dagger.

"Please don't make this harder than you've already made it," the woman said. She rose to her feet, body crackling with a red-veined aura. "The sooner this is over, the sooner you'll stop hurting."

Finally Julian's brain kicked in. This woman was going to kill him.

He ran for his bedroom as a high whine filled the apartment. The crackling aura grew as something whipped him from behind, slamming him into the wall. He caught himself on the door frame and grabbed the sword leaning beside it.

Something yanked him back by his collar. He went rolling across the apartment floor, the grimoire falling from his grip even as he kept one stubborn hand on his sword. When he came to a stop, his elbow landed in something wet—his mother's blood.

"Ma!" He grabbed her shoulder and turned her over. She stared up at the ceiling, mouth opening and closing. He fumbled to press her hands against the wound. "Hang on, just—"

That same force grabbed him again, flung him into the wall. The breath knocked out of him, Julian slumped to the floor, coughing as the edges of his vision darkened.

The grimoire flew into the cloaked woman's arms. She then strode toward him, though she was no longer alone. The crackling, reddish aura had twisted and morphed into a figure hovering beside her, all wild teeth and dark, burning eyes. Julian blinked furiously, trying to under-stand what he was seeing. The humanoid figure was half-formed, some-how both corporeal and intangible, with deep crimson skin and a skull crowned with tangled thorns. Thin black chains linked its forearms to those of the cloaked woman. When it laughed, Julian felt it in his chest.

A demon.

"Shanizeh likes it when she can taste fear," the woman murmured. "I have no stomach for it, so I will make this quick and spare the both of us."

The woman lifted a hand, and the demon tensed, ready to lash out with that crackling energy. Another high whine filled the apartment, the threat of lightning about to strike.

Julian shoved away from the wall and swung his sword up, nicking the woman's hand. She cried out as the demon rushed toward him. Julian barely managed to block her long talons from scratching at his face, the chains on her arms rattling. He tasted blood in his mouth and realized it was streaming from his nose.

He kicked at the demon and felt his foot connect with her chest. The demon snarled and morphed, standing on two strong legs as red-veined light twisted like smoke around her. Julian struggled to lift his sword in one hand, using the other to crawl across the floor toward his mother.

"Better to get it over with," the woman muttered as she cradled her bleeding hand to her chest, hugging the grimoire tightly in her other arm. "You shouldn't have meddled in something that doesn't concern you."

He cowered beside his mother's body, tears and blood on his face, a being of monstrous power descending on him like the fury of a falling meteor.

Outside, the night pressed against the earth in quiet rage, making the stars shiver. Beyond them was something intangible and expansive, some massive presence that turned its gaze on Nexus—on him. Julian's bones ached with it. He ducked his chin and inhaled as the edges of his mind grew cloudy.

He sent out his ability like an arrow, plunging straight into the demon's thoughts.

They weren't thoughts so much as all-encompassing sensations: the cries of thousands being tortured, the endless cold of the universe, the furious heat of hatred in his veins. The demon stumbled to a stop, pain and rage and sorrow spreading through him like a cloth absorbing ink.

Within this shared connection he realized she didn't feel like a beast; she was something else altogether, a child of some foreign magic.

They are said to grant power to the ones bound to them, the grimoire had said. *The power they have carried from Ostium and warped by their prison of the Universe.*

Had Shanizeh—and all demons—once been human?

His heartbeat began to slow, and the demon wavered. The energy she exuded thrashed like an agitated snake. Without quite knowing what he was doing, Julian began to exude his own energy, as steady as roots diving into damp soil. The high whine in his ears faded into a thin whistle.

The demon was frozen, crouched over him as her nostrils flared and sniffed, black hair falling over her spiny shoulders to tickle Julian's jaw.

"You are..." the demon whispered, eyes narrowing.

"What are you doing?" the woman demanded, pulling tight on the chains. The demon hissed in displeasure as she was yanked back.

"I can smell it on him," Shanizeh growled. "I smell Ostium."

The woman turned back to Julian, her eyes a searing, bright blue. "So," she murmured. "There's one after all."

Julian shook himself out of his stunned silence and lunged forward, stabbing the demon through the gut. A shriek pierced the air.

"No!" the woman shouted. She stepped forward and clutched her stomach, as if her link with the demon forced her to share its pain.

Julian abandoned his sword to scoop his mother off the floor and barreled toward the street. He nearly fell down the stairs, his shoulder banging against the wall before he regained his balance. The high whine faded as he staggered into the shadow-drenched alleyways, his mother gasping and shivering in his arms.

Far above him, the dawn of Godsnight began to creep into the sky.

VII

Taesia stared at the place where the rose trellis under her balcony should have been, the wall stained brown and black from years' worth of plant fiber.

Irritation nipped her, but it was a minor inconvenience. On the eve of Godsnight, her powers were stronger than ever. Umbra lengthened into a rope and wrapped around the railing of her balcony, curling back into its ring once she hauled herself over.

Taesia entered her bedroom and realized too late a candle was burning on her nightstand. Sitting in the middle of her bed in her nightgown was Brailee.

Taesia's fingers twitched as she stared at her sister, waiting for the inevitable lecture, the questions, the threat to go fetch their mother.

But Brailee didn't speak, didn't even open her eyes. Dark hair fell lank and unbrushed on either side of her wan face. There was fatigue in her posture that reminded Taesia of the grandmothers who did laundry at the communal well.

Then she realized: Her sister was asleep.

Somnus was wrapped around Brailee's head like a coronet, stirring as Taesia approached. Umbra rose to meet her sister's familiar, twining around it in greeting as energy passed between them. Taesia barely managed to sink onto the bed before the connection dragged her into her sister's dream.

It was cloudy and insubstantial, the connection weak. Still, she found herself within her sister's body, felt the tingling on her nape at the sound of heavy breathing. They were in the dark place again, and Brailee approached the boy curled up on his side, tears shining like stardust on his face and fingers tangled in his hair. Taesia could barely see him under the haze.

"Please," he whimpered, although she didn't think he was speaking to Brailee. His gaze was fixed on an unseen horizon.

Brailee knelt, the scent of death in her nose. "Let me help you," she said, placing a careful hand on his side.

He flinched. "I don't know where I am. Why I'm doing this. I want it to stop."

"You can make it stop," she assured him. "You don't have to do this if you don't want to."

"I can't stop," he rasped, chest heaving. "He won't let me. I—"

The boy screamed, and Brailee yanked her hand back as he writhed in the dirt. Though Taesia's instincts told her to slide a dagger between his ribs like giving a swift death to a captured animal, her sister's heart ached with empathy.

"How can I help?" she asked. "Just tell me, and I'll do it."

The corner of the boy's mouth shone with saliva. He hauled himself to his knees, swaying with fatigue. He seemed so lost, so broken, that Brailee was overcome with the urge to frame his face in her hands. He sighed and leaned into her touch.

"Kill me," he murmured.

Brailee winced. "No."

Yes, Taesia implored her.

"It's the only way," the boy urged. "The only way to stop it."

"And if it isn't stopped?"

"Then everyone dies," he whispered.

Brailee's heart sank. She glanced at the Conjuration circle and its layers of rings, realized there was now a fourth being constructed.

But she had barely registered his words when he blinked and his eyes began to glow gold. Baring his teeth, he grabbed her wrists and yanked her hands away, squeezing hard enough to make her bones creak.

"It's too late," the boy snarled.

Taesia had seen enough. She yanked as hard as she could at Brailee's consciousness, using the tenuous connection between their powers to make them fall, tumbling out of the dream and to the floor of Taesia's room.

Brailee gasped and struggled to her knees. Somnus floated above her, pulsing in alarm. Brailee stared at her beyond the curtain of her fallen hair, mouth agape.

"Taesia," she whispered. Her eyes watered before she launched herself into Taesia's arms. Taesia held her tightly.

"Where have you been?" Brailee demanded. "What happened? Why are they saying you killed Don Damari? I—I—"

Taesia shushed her and ran a hand down her sister's hair. "It's all right, Bee. It's going to be all right." Thinking back to the dream, she swallowed. "Did you tell Nik what you've seen?"

Brailee shuddered with her next breath. "Yes. He was in Haven Square when the monument was taken. When they said you . . . Taesia, please tell me what's going on."

"I can't now, but once this is over I'll explain."

Brailee stiffened and pulled away. "Of course. I can't help you, so you'll leave me in the dark."

"It's not safe. I don't want to implicate you in anything. But you have to trust me when I say there's a good reason for all of this."

Brailee let out a choked laugh and drew her knees up to her chest. "How can I trust you anymore if you're never *here*? If you don't tell me what's going on?"

"I . . . Bee . . ."

"I'm alone." Tears fell down Brailee's cheeks. "Dante is gone, and you're gone, and Mother and Father are out of their minds with grief, and we're locked up in the villa like prisoners. Dante is going to d-die and you might—"

Her teeth began to chatter. Taesia went to hold her again, braced for Brailee to shove her away. When she didn't, Taesia rested her head on top of her sister's, smelling the verbena soap she loved.

"You're not alone," Taesia whispered. "And Dante and I aren't going to die. I promise."

"He's going to hang tomorrow," Brailee sobbed against her. "And they want the same for you."

"Dante's not going to hang," Taesia said. "Nor am I. Because I'm going to save him."

Brailee stopped crying. When she pulled away again, her face was wet and flushed.

"What?" The single word from her sister's lips reminded Taesia so much of their mother, a question wrapped around a silent command: *Explain.*

"I have a...secret weapon, of sorts." She lifted her shoulder to show Starfell on her back. "And I'm going to use it to save him." *Save all of us*, she added, the jittery feeling that had followed her all day setting her teeth on edge.

Brailee stared at the wrappings around Starfell. "If they catch you, it's all over."

"Then I won't get caught." Taesia's attempt at a smile withered under Brailee's glare.

She was exhausted, her nerves buzzing and frayed, her stomach cramped with both hunger and nausea. But she remembered when they had shared a dream the first time, what Brailee had suggested.

"There's a way you can help," Taesia said slowly. "Do you think you can find Dante in your dreams?"

Brailee considered it. "I haven't succeeded yet. But maybe your added power will help."

"Let's try it, then."

They climbed back onto the bed, lying side by side, familiars entangling. Taesia thought about reaching over to grasp Brailee's hand, but before she could move, she sank back into Brailee's subconscious.

They returned to the universe of color, the swirling, dizzying expanse of possibility. It seemed even brighter than before, the approach of Godsnight likely inflating Brailee's powers. Her sister also seemed much more practiced at shuffling through the hues, reaching for tendrils only to catch a glimpse of an image, or the briefest snippet of sound, before discarding it.

Dante, Brailee thought, or maybe it was Taesia. *Where are you?*

So dedicated, came a low, velvet voice. *Would you like assistance?*

Taesia spotted a dark, glittering tendril and pulled Brailee's awareness toward it. As they got closer, a wave of warmth and comfort traveled between them, something that smelled like fresh parchment and tasted of almond cake. And, very distantly, they heard the echo of a familiar laugh.

Dante.

They took hold of the tendril and the universe of color dissipated, re-forming into the Nexus public library. There was no haze here, everything in crisp, well-defined detail. It was empty and quiet, sunlight filtering through the windows overhead and gilding dust motes.

Sitting at a table littered with books was their brother. His head snapped up and the harsh, frightening look on his face was replaced with something far softer.

"Bee," he whispered.

Taesia wished she had a body in this dreamscape, longing to call out for him, to hold him, to cry. Brailee did all those things as he stood and wrapped her in his arms.

"I finally found you," Brailee whispered.

"Found me? I've been here the whole time." He broke into an easy grin. "Find anything good in the romance section?"

He thinks we're part of his dream, Taesia reminded her.

Brailee stepped back and wiped away her tears. Dante looked as he had the day Don Soler arrested him, the perfect heir of House Lastrider. Taesia was grateful they weren't seeing the truth.

"Taesia's here, too," Brailee said.

Dante frowned and scanned the library. "Really? I thought she was still banned."

"No, I mean..." Brailee tapped her forehead. "Dante, I discovered something about my powers. It's called dream walking."

The happiness on Dante's face began to erode. On the table, the pages of the open books turned rapidly, as if stirred by a sudden gust of wind. "I've read about that. You can enter people's dreams. Enter *my*..."

Brailee jumped as something in the library crashed. "I don't know how long we have before the dream shifts or you wake up."

But Dante's dreamscape was already turning in on itself, either sensing an intruder or responding to its maker's budding awareness. Cracks splintered through the ceiling, and within their dark recesses dozens of eyes opened, staring unblinkingly down at them. The walls of the library shifted to stone and moved inward, the floor rumbling.

Brailee raised her hands and forced the walls to stop. Taesia felt her calling on the universe of color, siphoning possibility through her fingers. The stone crumbled away, debris turning into flowers midfall. Ranunculus—Dante's favorite.

Their brother gaped at the piles of scarlet petals as Brailee grabbed his hand. "Dante, you have to tell us what really happened with Prelate Lezzaro. Tell us how we can help you!"

His eyes filmed over before sharpening with clarity. "You—Tae's here, too?" Dante grabbed her by the shoulders. "Taesia, you can't trust her!"

The nearby shelves toppled over, spilling books everywhere. Their covers flew open, and pages were torn violently from their bindings, swirling through the air in a cyclone.

"Can't trust *who*?" Brailee demanded at the same time Taesia thought it.

The pages coalesced into two shapes, a cloaked figure with its hand held out toward another in the likeness of Prelate Lezzaro. Parchment rustled as he struggled, until the cloaked figure squeezed its hand and his neck ripped to one side. He fell apart in a spiral of loose paper.

"Aunt Camilla." Dante's fingers dug painfully into her shoulders as the library shuddered around them. "She killed Lezzaro!"

The cloaked figure turned and strode toward them, paper whispering with every step as a knife formed in its hand.

Taesia sat helpless within her sister's mind, unable to untangle her confusion from Brailee's disbelief. Even as Brailee lifted her hands to stop the paper figure, even as it grew closer and they saw the too-familiar rendering of their aunt's face, neither of them could process what they were seeing.

Dante got between them, staring down the figure. "I'll help you," he said. "Leave."

The paper fell apart, floating back to the floor. Brailee still stood with her hands raised, chest worryingly tight. Taesia would have reminded her to breathe if she hadn't been mired in the singular horror of what she'd seen.

Why would she do this? Taesia yelled loud enough to break Brailee from her stupor. *Why would she kill him?* Brailee shakily gave voice to her questions.

"Because she wanted the grimoire, but it was gone by that point," Dante said. "But she'd still *read* it, or enough of it, without him knowing."

Why would she kill him over that? They were working together! We were working together! Again Brailee spoke her words out loud even as Taesia sensed her growing unease. Taesia wondered if her sister could peer into her memories of the grimoire, the night she and Angelica had conspired to steal it.

"She made plans of her own he didn't approve of. He was going to stop her. She—" The library groaned with a violent rocking motion, and he grabbed Brailee before they could fall. "She learned about fulcrums, thought maybe if she had the right sort of power, she could find one."

Golden lines lit up the floor, a circle surrounding them with Dante and Brailee in the center, where a fifth realm would be drawn within a depiction of the Cosmic Scale.

Ostium, Taesia thought and Brailee conveyed. *We can't do the ritual without a fifth heir. Aunt Camilla told me about the Ostium fulcrum, that maybe we could use it—*

"No!" Dante shook his head, eyes wide. "No, Tae, whatever she told you, you *can't* let her summon the Ostium fulcrum." The ceiling began to crumple in the corners, the edges of the dreamscape darkening. Dante was waking up. "If a portal is made to Ostium, it'll be a doorway for demons to get through. They'll be unleashed on the city. Lezzaro warned her against it, threatened to prevent her from showing up at Godsnight, and she—she—"

He was flickering now, and above them the windows shattered. Dante pushed Brailee away from the glass downpour, making them stumble to the edge of the dreamscape.

"She wants the fulcrum for herself!" Dante called as the darkness swallowed him and the rest of the library. "Stop her!"

"Dante!" Taesia yelled, sitting up with one hand extended. She only understood she was back in her own body when she realized how hard she was breathing.

Beside her, Brailee held her head in her hands. Taesia touched her shoulder, but Brailee shoved it off.

"What were you talking about?" Brailee demanded. "Aunt Camilla and a ritual and—and *demons* and— Was this what you two were conspiring about?"

"Bee—"

"Tell me," Brailee demanded. "Not later. *Now.*"

Taesia stood from the bed. Her limbs were unsteady, her mind spinning. Reality didn't feel *real* yet, as if part of her were still stuck in Dante's dream.

She wants it for herself. Why? Why would her aunt lie to her, deceive her?

"Please," Brailee whispered. "If Dante was right and Aunt Camilla is to blame for Prelate Lezzaro..." She choked over the words, nightgown fisted in her hands. "Then we have to prove it. We can clear your name *and* Dante's."

Taesia gripped the edge of her dresser, pointedly ignoring her reflection in the mirror above it. Instead she stared at the small jar of lip paint she had used for the gala. Her fingertips paled against the dark wood.

"But instead you're running around like some common criminal and making it all worse," Brailee went on, hoarse with anger. "You'll really do anything to avoid facing responsibility, won't you?"

Taesia's knees threatened to buckle. Her heartbeat sat uncomfortably in her throat, ears roaring as if she'd thrown herself off a cliff with nothing to break her fall.

Slowly, softly, Taesia spoke. She told Brailee about the ritual. About Dante's workroom, and meeting Lezzaro, and trying to convince the other heirs to attempt breaking the barriers.

"It was Dante's idea," she whispered. "If the Houses reversed the Sealing and saved our realm, we could abolish the monarchy and make way for a House-run parliament. Vaega is too entrenched in an institution that relies on piety. The poor get poorer while the rich get richer. Other-Realm peoples are in constant danger." She thought of the raid in the Noctus Quarter, Naela's scream of terror.

"Ferdinand does not have the best interest of the people at heart," she went on. "He cares only about his image and refraining from making difficult choices to protect his so-called legacy as the Holy King. But Dante convinced me that Vaega deserves more. *We* deserve more. A government with no interference by the gods, a government dictated by the people it's supposed to protect."

Brailee slowly moved off the bed. In the dim candlelight she looked like a spirit from the necropolis seeking closure, or vengeance.

"Taesia," she breathed, and the sound of her name contained so much heartbreak Taesia didn't know if she could survive it. "You...you killed Don Soler. And Don Damari. It *was* you."

Taesia shut her eyes against the betrayal woven through her words. She was still falling off that cliff, knowing the end would be gruesome, bloody. "I know it looks bad, but I did it to protect our family. To protect *you*."

"Don't you *dare* say that! How does this make you any better than Aunt Camilla?"

It was a blow, low and hard and breath stealing. Taesia had done what she had because she thought it justified. That every lie out of her mouth was necessary.

Apparently she took after their aunt more than she knew.

"I promise I'll fix this," Taesia said in a rush, reaching for her sister. Brailee moved away.

"*I'll* fix it," Brailee said. "I'll tell Mother about Aunt Camilla."

"What can you do, if the guards won't let you leave?"

"We'll figure something out. Just . . . get away from here before you're caught. Don't make this worse than it already is." Brailee walked out the door as the first sign of dawn touched the sky outside.

Taesia let her go. Something venomous snaked through her, weaving through tendon and bone, leaving stains like the rose trellis on the wall beside her balcony.

You wear masks, Nikolas had told her. *What will you do when all your masks fall? Who will you be then?*

Taesia finally met the eyes of her reflection. She didn't see a hero, or a rebel, or someone who understood what power was. She saw a liar, a traitor, and a coward.

Gritting her teeth, she grabbed the jar of lip paint and hurled it at the mirror. It shattered into jagged pieces, like all her plans, like her sister's heart.

VIII

Angelica woke as the sun rose.

She wasn't sure where she was until she dug her fingers into the sheets of her bed. Then she wondered how she had possibly managed to get back to the villa, let alone to her bedroom, without causing a scene.

Cosima.

Angelica drew in a sharp breath at the reminder of cool river water and warm hands. She sat up and noted the nightgown she wore, the brown stains under her fingernails, her hair in a heavy braid over one shoulder.

She did not feel powerful, but she felt *something*. It held no name and no shape, but it had a purpose, enough to coax her out of bed and go about her morning routine as if nothing were out of the ordinary. As if it weren't Godsnight, as if her god did not plan to use her, as if she hadn't pried into a mage's body in a frantic bid for control.

She paused at the sight of the scrap of parchment she'd left on her vanity, the one with the little drawn heart. Slowly she picked it up and slipped it into her pocket.

Rather than wait for maids to deliver her breakfast tray, she gave in to the restlessness igniting her nerves in quick and painful flashes. She went downstairs, nodding at the servants dressed in Mardova red and blue. They were oddly hushed, as if they knew Angelica was facing her death today.

She passed the fresco on the wall, the one depicting the four elements. Gently she traced the gilded wyvern surrounding them, a protective circle. Her chest began to ache.

Keep it together, she urged herself.

Unsure what exactly her body needed, she wandered the villa in a daze. She stopped to admire the bookshelves full of titles her father had once collected. As a child she would pull them off the shelves, pretending to read them to imitate her father's actions. When she told him what they were about, he indulged her made-up plots with amused smiles and solemn nods.

Ten years. Ten years without seeing his smile.

Angelica's breathing began to stutter. A terrible weight sat on her shoulders, her fingers itching for an instrument. For her violin.

Her teeth clenched as desire tore up her insides. Holding a hand to her stomach, she turned and headed for the gardens.

The land surrounding the villa was filled with walls of flowering shrubs, a serpentine creek, and a large gazebo facing the olive and fruit trees. Angelica raised the hem of her dress as servants opened the doors and she stepped outside, blinking in the early morning sun.

She followed the path wending through bursts of flowering green euphorbias and purple clouds of agapanthus, surrounded by the sleepy drone of insects. Eventually she noticed a figure standing at the railing of the gazebo, gazing sadly at the glittering creek. Miko.

Angelica turned to head back inside, but she was spotted. Miko gestured for Angelica to join her, and reluctantly she obeyed.

"I've hardly seen you lately," Miko said once she was near. The shade of the gazebo fell over them, forming a rumpled shape on the ground as the sun continued to rise. "And now I see you up so early on such an important day. Are you all right?"

Angelica watched the swaying boughs of the trees. A couple months ago they had been heavy with the thick purple bulbs of plums, ready to be plucked and bitten into. Her mouth watered at the thought of their tart, sweet juice on her tongue.

Then she remembered the organ at her lips, puncturing its outer skin to the blood beyond, and shuddered.

"I'm fine," Angelica murmured.

They stood in silence a moment, the breeze tickling Miko's draping sleeves and the bow on the back of her dress. Angelica noticed her eyes were downcast, her lips pressed together.

"Are…" Angelica cleared her throat, roughly finishing, "Are *you* all right?"

Miko quickly hid her surprise in favor of a small yet heartfelt smile, putting a hand on Angelica's arm and squeezing slightly. "I'm rather homesick today."

Miko had gone back to Azuna only once since she'd immigrated to Vaega, but that was a long time ago. She often spoke fondly of the seasonal festivals her family had attended back then, how they gave thanks to the elements rather than the god who had created them. She and Adela liked to laugh at the irony of who she had ended up marrying.

When Miko and the twins had been incorporated into the House, Angelica had made it clear she wanted nothing to do with them. It had taken her a long time to realize her bitterness was merely her missing her father. Just because someone new resided in the places he once had, that didn't mean his memory was gone. Otherwise why would her mother have kept the bookshelves exactly as they were, or spare his portrait wistful, fond glances whenever she passed it?

"I'm sorry," Angelica muttered.

"It's all right. It will pass." Miko took a deep breath, inhaling all the scents the garden had to offer. "Besides, I am needed here most. You and Adela need support."

Angelica frowned. In what ways had Miko supported her?

As the last curve of the sun parted from the horizon, it dawned on her: her bedroom. Adela hadn't reprimanded her for the mess she'd made of it when her instruments were taken away because she'd never found out. Miko must have ordered everything to be fixed.

As if Miko had sensed her thoughts, she said, "I apologize that Eiko and Kikou took your instruments. It was your mother's idea, but I warned her against it." She shook her head ruefully. "I'm afraid I don't know where the rest of them are."

The rest . . . ? Angelica clenched her hands into fists, released them. The piccolo. The one her father had gifted her, the one that had been destroyed at the gala. The one she had woken to find returned to her.

That *Miko* had returned to her.

"It's a pity," Miko murmured. "I enjoy listening to you play." She brightened a little. "But you sing as well, don't you?"

Not since her father died. That had been their routine, August asking her to sing his favorite operas, Angelica more than happy to oblige. He would close his eyes and smile as he listened, offering the occasional critique.

She'd once found any excuse to sing. While taking a bath, while completing her studies, while walking through the villa and making the most of its acoustics.

But every year her throat closed in a little tighter, the once ever-present urge clamped behind sealed lips and forgotten melodies.

"Will you sing for me?" Miko asked.

Angelica opened her mouth to refuse, then stopped. She did owe her for both the bedroom and her piccolo. She let out a frustrated huff and focused on her breathing, drawing it up from her core, her lungs and belly expanding.

She sang the first song that came to mind, her favorite aria from *The Gossamer Road*. When she plucked out the notes on her instruments, they were clear and shining, newly polished coins clinking together. When she pulled the notes from her diaphragm, they were thicker, richer, ringing with vibrato.

Miko closed her eyes with a smile as the aria swept through the garden. Angelica stared into the middle distance as her lips shaped the words of mourning, feeling them acutely as she thought back to her father's laughter, a childhood in which she didn't know she was nothing but a plaything for the gods.

What do you want? What do you need?

A tear escaped as she closed her eyes, pushing the notes up and out, her chest swelling with song. It was easy to see how music was like a spell, something that controls you without ever being seen. It called out for more, to feed an intangible craving, to douse her burning desire.

The golden light of Haven Square. The scream ripped out of her. The braiding of elements in the practice arenas. The empty stepwell in the Deia basilica. The gilded wyvern surrounding the elements.

Were they all the same thing? Could she reach through the realm's fabric and pry open a door, the way the other heirs had wanted to do from the beginning?

Angelica exhaled notes like a bird tucking in its wings and diving, a freefall of glissando and sforzando, forte to fortissimo. They hung around her like planes aligning into a perfect pattern, lines and curves of a universe breathed into life. The Cosmic Scale.

As the song crescendoed, her body lurched forward as the door pulled open wider, yanking her through the cosmos like a star gone astray. Angelica's eyes shot open as she gripped the gazebo's railing, gasping for breath.

"Angelica!" Miko gripped her elbow. "Are you all right?"

Angelica turned to her, but Miko was frowning down at something. Following her gaze, Angelica froze.

Her violin case lay on the gazebo floor.

With shaking hands she knelt and opened the clasp, lifting the lid to reveal the polished wood and gleaming strings. Angelica nearly sobbed, her skin suddenly itching, burning for release.

"How did...?" Miko looked at her not with the fear and uneasiness of the soldiers in Haven Square, but with concern. "Angelica?"

She couldn't answer, could barely do anything more than hug her father's violin to her chest and watch the rising sun, heralding the beginning of the end.

No—heralding something, but not an end. Not if she could stop it.

Nikolas was woken with a gentle shake from a nurse.

"I'm sorry to bother you, my lord, but there are soldiers asking for you," she whispered.

Nikolas took in his mother's gaunt, sleeping face before glancing at the window. The sunlight was thin, but it was assuredly morning. His mouth dry, he followed the nurse into the receiving room, where his task force stood at attention.

"What happened?" he demanded.

Taide stepped forward with a small bow. "There's been another incident, my lord."

Taesia?

"Another landmark's gone missing."

The Four Gods Fountain had been a structure crafted of bronze atop a steep hill, each god facing a cardinal direction: Thana and her veil, Nyx and his crown, Deia and her sword, Phos and his wings. But it had vanished in the early hours of dawn, leaving no trace of the large structure other than a ring of darkened stone where it had sat within a deactivated Conjuration circle.

Without rampaging spirits, the area was far less damaged than Haven Square had been, and therefore swarming with curious citizens the city guard tried to keep back. This time there was no Don Damari to breathe down Nikolas's neck, and no one had been appointed to replace him yet.

He knelt beside the Conjuration circle and recognized the same glyphs. The university's linguistics department hadn't been as much use as he'd have liked, though they now had a cipher key to translate certain symbols, such as the ancient ones used for the gods, which he spotted within each quadrant.

His eyes narrowed. The Four Gods Fountain had been built so that each of the gods had been staring in the direction of their respective basilicas at each of Nexus's four main districts. The symbols in the circle followed the same pattern.

"Komi," he said, drawing the soldier over. "Do you have a map on you, or can you find someone who does?"

It took a few minutes until he was presented with a map of Nexus and a pencil. Nikolas searched for the exact locations where each landmark had gone missing. He circled the university in the northern sector, the bridge to the south, Haven Square to the east, and now the fountain in the west.

One circle in each of Nexus's four sectors. Perfectly equidistant.

"Nikolas."

He jumped. Angelica stood a few paces away, breathing hard after scaling the steep hill where her carriage couldn't venture. Her violin case was slung on her back.

"What are you doing here?" he demanded, standing.

"I heard about the fountain and..." She swallowed. "I did something this morning, something like...like Haven Square, and I don't know if they're connected."

"What are you talking about?"

She seemed to realize how many people were staring at them. "Not here."

He reluctantly followed her down the hill. He couldn't stand Angelica's dramatics right now, not when his mother was injured and he would be facing a god's judgment in a few hours.

She told her carriage driver to take a break somewhere else. Then she opened the door and impatiently gestured for Nikolas to get inside. "Angelica—"

"Shut up." She climbed in after him and slammed the door behind her. "Listen—"

But someone knocked on the door nearly as soon as it was closed. Sighing in vexation, Angelica opened it to tell them off.

They both started at the sight of Risha. She looked between them suspiciously.

"What are you doing?" she demanded.

Risha woke to her bones aching, a dark, swirling power rising all around her. It felt like the barrier to Mortri, stubborn and spiteful.

It had begun yesterday, a trickle of discomfort up her spine, her fingers hot and prickly as if they were waking from numbness. She ignored it as best she could as the maids dressed her, wrapping her in a black ghagra choli trimmed in gold, fastening a wide gilded hoop to her nose connected by a thin chain to her ear. When she came downstairs, her mother burst into tears.

"You're so beautiful," Darsha said with her hands framing Risha's face. "You will be marvelous today, and you will make the perfect bride after."

Her family thought Godsnight would be a way for her to demonstrate the Vakaras' power for king and country. If her father knew the truth of what she was about to do, it would have broken his heart.

"We will see you at the palace," Rath told her. "Please be safe, meer piaara."

Risha hugged him tightly, fighting against tears. Saya had frowned when Risha turned to her. As if she could already tell something wasn't right. Risha couldn't hold back a sob as she held her sister close, fingertips digging into her back, desperate to not forget, at the end, what this felt like.

"I love you," Risha whispered. *I'm sorry.*

"Risha—"

But she turned away, let the servants lead her to the carriage that would take her to the palace, where she would prepare. Darsha hugged her one last time, and Risha found comfort in her familiar scent and warmth, wishing she had been better to her mother, that she'd found a way to show her she loved her. But then Risha was entering the carriage and leaving the villa behind.

They hadn't gotten far when Risha heard a distant commotion. They were still in the western sector, where her villa and the Thana basilica lay. And Lillum Street. But she dismissed that thought as she pulled back the curtain and frowned at a couple of children running in the direction of the Four Gods Fountain.

She ordered the driver to follow them. A minute later they stopped at the base of the hill leading to the fountain. A restless crowd had formed above.

As she stepped out of the carriage to figure out what was going on, she spotted Angelica shoving Nikolas into her own carriage.

She started after them, then paused. She held her hand in a loose fist, watching the pulse beat frantically at her wrist, until she breathed out and knocked.

When the door whisked open, she demanded, "What are you doing?"

Angelica beckoned her inside. Risha knew she shouldn't, that this wouldn't lead anywhere good—Angelica could be trying to kill them off preemptively, for all she knew—but she couldn't stop from climbing in. The space was cramped with all three of them, Angelica pointedly moving her knees away whenever they touched another's.

"Is this really necessary?" Nikolas asked.

"Shut up and listen, Cyr." There was disquiet in her eyes, which made Risha square her shoulders. It took a lot for Angelica to show weakness of any kind.

"Conjuration," she whispered. "It wasn't just a way to commune with the gods, a trick that got warped into something else."

Risha felt Nikolas stiffen beside her. "Then what is it?"

Angelica licked her cracked lips. "It was Ostium's magic."

Nikolas inhaled. "Angelica—"

"I said *shut up*, Cyr!" she roared. She took a moment to compose herself, the temperature within the carriage rising as she clutched the violin case to her chest.

"That night in Haven Square," Angelica went on. "I managed to tap into something, an element possibly linked to whatever Conjuration really is. The grimoire called it *quintessence*, something that originated from Ostium. And today, when the fountain disappeared..." She stroked the violin case. "I think Conjuration is the lost magic from Ostium, and it's only possible in Nexus because we have some connection to it."

"Connection?" Risha repeated. "Like what?" She wasn't sure why she was entertaining the idea, but what if...

What if they had something to represent Ostium after all?

Angelica shook her head. "I'm not sure." Risha noticed she was shivering. Unthinkingly, Risha moved to sit beside her, which made Angelica tense. But after a moment she began to relax from the heat of Risha's side against hers.

"What do you think?" Risha prompted gently.

"I think one or more of the gods did something to Ostium's," Angelica said. "I asked Deia if she had...had eaten, or..." For a moment she shut her eyes tight, and Nikolas's pale eyebrows furrowed. "But no. She told me 'all I have left are remains.'"

"Remains," Risha repeated. "Like...the god's body?"

"Some part of them could be in Nexus," Angelica agreed.

Suddenly Risha was transported back to the Godsnight Gala. Facing vengeful spirits and screeching corpses, she had delved into her power and felt something beyond them, something cold and large and unbearable. The eye that affixed to her, calling for recognition.

Risha must have made a sound, since the other two looked at her sharply.

"The Bone Palace," she whispered. She turned to Nikolas. "If Deia really has their remains...if she hid them in Nexus..."

Nikolas's eyes widened as the same revelation crashed down on him. There were stories, of course, of the palace having been constructed from actual bone.

But they'd all thought the bones had belonged to beasts, not a god.

"That's why Conjuration's only possible in Nexus." Nikolas swore. "Still, even if we could somehow use this for the ritual, it won't stop our gods from claiming us. We have to try to break the barriers on our own."

"If our powers haven't been enough to do that all this time, what makes you think we'd be able to accomplish it now?" Angelica spat. "Do you think love and friendship or whatever the fuck you believe in is enough to stand against the gods?"

Risha was still reeling from the idea that the remains of a god were hidden within the palace, so she could hardly blame Nikolas for dropping his head into his hands and squeezing his eyes shut for a solid minute.

Eventually they snapped back open. "The sketch," he said, fumbling something out of his pocket. "The one from the grimoire. Draw it."

Angelica frowned but did as he asked. She drew on the blank side of a crumpled map, marking each of the realms and adding Ostium to its center. Nikolas grabbed it back and flipped it over. Staring at the map, he inhaled sharply.

"No," he whispered. "No, no, *no*."

"Nik?"

His face had turned ashen, gaze flitting between four circles on the map, one in each sector. At first Risha thought they were random until she realized they must be the sites of Conjuration attacks.

As they watched, Nikolas connected each circle with lines. He then drew a shaky circle within the center and linked it to the others.

When he was done, they were left staring at a Conjuration circle with the Bone Palace in the very middle, an exact replication of the Cosmic Scale.

"Someone already knows about the remains," Risha whispered. "Whoever's been stealing these landmarks...that's their prize."

"And Conjuration performed in the middle of Godsnight means the ritual will happen whether we like it or not," Angelica said, her voice oddly calm.

Risha rubbed her prickling fingers together and tried not to listen to the low, mournful march of her heartbeat, or the way Nikolas's and Angelica's pulses echoed within the close space of the carriage.

Whatever it takes.

IX

The morning of Godsnight was crisp. Taesia shivered in Julian's jacket as she crouched on the roof of her aunt's house, gazing out at Nexus as the sun turned the city into a playground of light and shadow. To the west was the dome of the Gravespire. To the east rose the minarets of Nyx's basilica.

To the north, the Bone Palace glimmered white and pristine, towering over the stage built before it. A stage that would transform into a gallows.

Where Nyx would inhabit her, mind and body, if she could not get Dante free in time.

My general.

Dante had used her like a general to help fulfill his dream. But she had instead been the vehicle for his downfall. She had tried to make up for it in her own ways, flourishing in her own autonomy.

But every turn and detour brought her back kicking and screaming to the dread that lived with her like her own shadow.

Umbra uncoiled from her ring and wrapped around her arm. The air felt strange on her skin, the city crawling with an energy that trembled through the soles of her feet and up her legs. The Cosmic Scale would come into alignment soon. She didn't have much time.

She slipped through an open kitchen window of the Lorenzos' ivy-choked house. A couple of servants screamed, their arms and aprons coated in flour.

"Get out," Taesia ordered. They rushed to obey.

She stalked through the house her father had grown up in, strides eating up the floor where he had once run and played. The footman rushed to demand what she was doing, but with a flick of her hand the shadows flung him into a closet.

Taesia entered the sitting room where she had often taken refuge. The massive mirror above the mantel held her reflection as she stood taking up the doorway, tall and ragged with her hair down, face smudged with dirt, Starfell peering over her shoulder. She was wreathed in shadows, eyes scorching against the darkness.

Camilla met her widened gaze in the mirror, bright blue against Taesia's black.

"Ah," her aunt said. "I was starting to think you'd never come."

But Taesia couldn't respond. She was too fixated on what else met her eyes in the mirror, the sinister grin plastered on a crimson face.

Demon.

It was one thing to be told nighttime stories of things lurking between the realms, hiding under your bed to drag you into nothingness. It was another to see one up close, draped in red fog that enveloped Camilla like a shroud. Like a parasite.

Her aunt turned to face her. In her arms she carried Lezzaro's grimoire. Black chains wove around her forearms and those of the demon, connecting them. One of Camilla's hands was bandaged, and there was a swirling point of darkness on the demon's abdomen.

Umbra quivered as the demon's energy flooded the room, turned the air thin and metallic. Taesia struggled to breathe.

"You really shouldn't have gotten that boy involved in this," Camilla scolded, as if Taesia had broken one of the Azunese vases lining the hallway. "Luckily, you have me to help clean up your messes."

Taesia held on to the door frame, fighting against the urge to run. A strange clicking sound filled the room. The demon was laughing.

She finally found her voice. "What...boy?"

"The Hunter, of course."

"Julian? What— Did you do something to him?"

"I *tried* to. If he'd been in the compound, I wouldn't have had to rope that poor woman into things." Camilla shuddered. "Gruesome."

The floor nearly gave out under her. She remembered Marjorie Luca the night she had fed Taesia almond cake and tea with brandy, her infectious laugh, her bright, rosy demeanor.

"What the fuck are you talking about?" Taesia forced herself to take a step inside the room, then another. The demon watched her hungrily. "Is this...Are you even Camilla Lorenzo?"

"Oh, darling," Camilla sighed. She set the grimoire on the table and crossed to her drink cart, the demon trailing after like an obedient ghost. "Please don't be dramatic about this."

"Tell me what's going on!" Taesia roared.

Camilla, unfazed, poured herself a tumbler of sherry. "It was only a matter of time until he discovered things he shouldn't have." The demon rested long, wicked talons on her aunt's shoulders. Long hair floated around it as if it were underwater, its eyes glowing black. "I couldn't risk it."

She should have stayed with Julian, made sure they were safe. But then she wouldn't have shared the dream with Brailee, and—

"We know you killed Lezzaro," she blurted.

"And?" Camilla leaned against the mantel, sipping her drink. "He unfortunately had more honor in him than I'd anticipated. A disagreement, that's all."

"That you *murdered* him over, when he was absolutely right. If we open a portal to Ostium, demons will get through." Taesia put a hand on Starfell's hilt. The demon noticed and bared a row of sharp teeth.

"That's why we have the Houses, is it not?" Camilla drawled. "They can fend off the assault while I get the Ostium fulcrum. I'm willing to deal with a little collateral damage if it means obtaining it."

"And do *what* with it?" Taesia snarled. "It's not about the ritual, is it?"

Camilla studied her drink a moment. "It's about protecting family," she said softly.

"How's allowing Dante to be thrown in jail protecting him?"

"He was careless that night, being seen by multiple witnesses. It was easier to let him take the fall while I continued the work out here. But I armed him with tools, and now it's up to him to wield them."

Camilla polished off her sherry, then set the glass down hard on the mantel. "I tried to warn my brother not to marry a Lastrider, told him he'd be happier with a naive merchant's daughter, but he wouldn't listen. But though you may have Nyx's blood, you also have Lorenzo blood, and I did what I could so you and your sister would be safely locked up in the villa come Godsnight."

Damari. Camilla had told her what he was doing in the Noctus Quarter, ensuring Taesia would lash out at him.

And Don Soler—Camilla had spoken of giving him a lesson, planting the seed of an idea in Taesia's mind and trusting it would grow.

"I knew that wouldn't be enough to hold you, though." Camilla smiled, and it was prideful. "You're more Lorenzo than Lastrider. Dante was too soft, but you—you understand sacrifices need to be made. You don't hesitate to cut down weak links. It should have been you I confided in from the start."

"Why?" The single word was quiet, pleading, almost childish. "Why are you so desperate for the Ostium fulcrum? How do you even know if it can be summoned? Was Damari...was that a test to use the astralam bones?"

Camilla gave her a pitying smile. "The bones were merely to keep you busy. I've had my methods planned ever since I was able to read parts of the grimoire without Lezzaro knowing. That's how I learned about Ostium, the fulcrums, and how to summon my own demon."

Camilla reached up to stroke the demon's cheek. "I chose Shanizeh specifically. Her power lies in telekinesis, the movement of physical objects without physical touch. When I bound myself to her, she told me the truth of her kind. How they were once priests of Ostium, a realm in which portals were crafted and exalted. But their god was murdered, and they used their magic to fling themselves into the universe, where they were corrupted by the unfiltered energy of the Cosmic Scale and twisted into beings we call demons. They were the ones who made the portals between realms. But without Ostium as the cornerstone, those portals collapsed."

"The Sealing." Taesia couldn't feel the words on her numb lips.

"Yes." With a flick of Camilla's fingers the grimoire opened to a familiar two-page spread of the Cosmic Scale. "Each realm wasn't born out of *nothing*. The gods needed anchors from which to expand their worlds, a seat of power. The fulcrums. Ostium's god is long gone, and no longer able to activate their fulcrum. But because Lezzaro's Conjurers have thinned the barriers adequately, I have one chance to bring the fulcrum through and activate it once more. One narrow window as the realms align."

Camilla looked up at her with gleaming eyes. "You said so yourself: With Ostium's power, we can undo the Sealing."

"That's not why you're doing this, though, is it?" Taesia demanded. "What is it you want? Power? Are you planning to usurp Ferdinand, or—or are you working *with* him, or—"

Finally her aunt's composure cracked. Her face paled, her mouth tightening. Taesia knew after years of seeing Nikolas's grief that her aunt was returning to something raw and aching.

"I'm not helping *him*," Camilla spat. "He's the reason—" She closed her eyes a moment, controlling herself. "No, I'm not working with Ferdinand. All he's ever done is hurt my family."

"Then why go through all this trouble to summon the fulcrum? You say you want to protect us, but how is unleashing demons going to do that?"

But Camilla only gave her another pitying smile. "Darling, you're too young to understand now, but one day you will. I'll tell you the entire story, then."

Camilla strode toward her. It reminded Taesia too much of Dante's dream. "You're capable of more than your brother could fathom," her aunt said. "If the Sealing is undone, the Houses become stronger. Isn't that what you wanted?"

Taesia kept shaking her head. Umbra formed into a dagger in her other hand.

"Come with me," her aunt said, placing a cool hand against Taesia's cheek. Those black chains around her forearm swayed. "Together we will see the barriers broken. Dante will be saved. Your family will be untouched. We can even cull Ferdinand in the process."

It was everything Taesia had wanted. Everything Dante had wanted.

She stared at the woman who had been as good as a mother to her all her life, who'd given her advice no one else was willing to offer, who'd allowed her to be unapologetically herself.

Somewhere in the city, the bell towers tolled ten times. The world around her seemed to bend and sigh, the shadows growing thicker, darker.

And in her mind she saw Marjorie Luca's smiling face, splattered with blood.

When Taesia raised her shadow dagger, the demon grabbed her and flung her into the mirror. It shattered like a scream, and she landed on the floor with a grunt of pain. Umbra flickered in warning as the demon grabbed her again. Taesia slashed at the dark spot on Shanizeh's abdomen, making the demon screech and recoil.

Taesia lunged for the door. The demon's aggravated clicking and her aunt's cry followed her into the street as she ran in the direction of the Bone Palace.

Of the stage set to end them once and for all.

X

Nikolas only returned to the villa to retrieve the Sunbringer Spear. Armor was laid out on his bed, a gilded cuirass and greaves and vambraces. The pauldrons on either shoulder curved upward, reminding him of the summit of Deia's Heart. It was the same set he had worn in the Phos basilica. All he'd wanted then was to feel power return to his body, the relieving warmth of Phos's attention. To spread wings luminous and golden.

Servants came to help him into the armor, but he turned them away and left it on the bed. The bracelet Fin had given him weighed lightly on his wrist, like it was all the armor he needed.

On his way to the carriage, he found his father in the sun room. Waren stared out the window, gray hair disheveled and clothes askew, older than Nikolas had ever seen him. He turned and spotted Nikolas in the doorway.

For a moment Nikolas thought he might say something. Maybe demand to know where he had taken Madeia, or order him not to particripate in the exhibition after all and spare them the humiliation.

But Waren stared at his son and said nothing. Looking through him, beyond him, to a life he had been denied. One in which Rian wore the armor Nikolas had forsaken, ready to win a crown on behalf of Solara and their god.

Nikolas couldn't believe he had once wanted to make this man proud.

He turned away. Whatever Nikolas did today, it wouldn't be for his father, or his House, or his god. It would be for himself and those who were depending on him.

Even if he fell, there would be honor in trying.

*   *   *

Nikolas had to warn the king about the Conjuration circle around Nexus. Even if they were too late to stop the exhibition or the ritual, they could at least get citizens away from the palace square to avoid casualties.

He could hear the crowd even several streets away. The din traveled straight into his chest, rattling his heart. It was the roar of people equally hungry for divine magic and death, for the delectable drama about to unfold.

It made him want to scream.

The carriage paused as the gates to the Bone Palace opened, and Nikolas pulled back the curtain. A large stage had been erected in the square, a mass of people already assembled around it and spilling out into the streets and alleys. Many had even climbed up onto roofs for a better view. Guards, royal and city alike, stood stiff and watchful. Viewing boxes rose on either side of the stage—one for each House and their own guards.

Nikolas was sweating by the time he stepped into the massive courtyard. He shivered as the air blew cold against the back of his neck, the sky overhead darkening as heavy clouds rolled in. His fingertips began to glow. Lux pulsed above his shoulder.

The Cosmic Scale was aligning. If he closed his eyes, he could feel the edges of their world stop against the barrier to Solara, grinding together like stone.

His unit waited by the lemon grove, staring out at the square with uneasy frowns. Nikolas approached them and caught Gem's attention first, their eyes widening.

"My lord." They didn't point out he was wearing the same clothes as when they'd fetched him from the hospital, though they gave him a concerned once-over. "We weren't able to determine anything new about the missing fountain. We figured the best thing to do was come here and await your orders."

They all stared at him, expectant. A pain formed in Nikolas's throat as he stared back at Komi's kind eyes, the determined slant of Gem's mouth, Taide's squared shoulders. Even Paris was here, though he stood with arms crossed and eyebrows lowered, clearly uncomfortable without his partner.

Nikolas wondered if he was a fool for dismissing Julian when they needed him. But no matter how hard he tried, he couldn't forget the way Julian had punched through a piece of building like it was made of sand, or the way he'd blanched every time they came near a Conjuration circle.

He took a deep breath and addressed them all. "The fact you've followed me this far is…It means more than I can say. Your dedication and your effort haven't been in vain. I have one last order for you, and whether or not you follow is entirely up to you." They waited, and the pain in his throat intensified. "I need you to help get citizens out of the palace square, as far away as they can get."

Nikolas expected confusion, uncertainty. But all of them, even Paris, saluted with fists against their sternum.

"Thank you," Nikolas whispered as the ground shivered under their feet, a warning his time was running out.

He hurried into the Bone Palace. He barely spared a glance at the columns of vertebrae, nor the ribbed vaulted ceiling of the atrium, even with Risha's revelation fresh in his mind. The guards didn't stop him; he didn't wear his armor or even the crest of House Cyr, but the spear on his back was testament enough to who he was.

"Tell the king to meet me at the safe room," he ordered the nearest ones. "Now!"

They ran. Nikolas's long legs ate up the marble as he walked as fast as he could without outright running. He entered a part of the palace where starkness gave way to rich furnishings and walls in warm colors, carpet runners dampening the sound of his strides.

He'd only been here once before, when his family had been brought to the safe room. He expected the hall to be empty—the guards moved fast, but Ferdinand didn't—and rocked to a halt when he met five royal soldiers standing before the heavily locked doors.

"Where is His Majesty?" Nikolas asked. "Is he already inside?"

The soldiers looked at one another rather than answer him, which was his first sign something wasn't right. His skin prickled as they seemed to come to a conclusion and unsheathed their swords.

Three charged at him. Nikolas bristled with a storm of light as the channels of his power began to open, shaping Lux into a ball of energy and hurtling it at the oncoming soldiers. It blew them back into the wall where they slumped at its base, the plaster cracked.

"What are you doing?" he demanded of the remaining two. "I'm Nikolas Cyr, I'm here to protect the king!"

They said nothing as they pressed in. The hall was too tight to properly use his spear, so Nikolas shot Lux out again, hitting one soldier in the face hard enough to break his nose while the other he disarmed and smacked in the head with her own sword pommel.

Panting, Nikolas took the Sunbringer Spear in hand and faced the locked doors. Power seethed along his fingers, Lux looming bigger and brighter overhead. He punched one hand out and the energy condensed, breaking through the doors with a resounding crunch of wood and metal.

He ducked through the opening and froze. A lone man stood in the middle of the stark room, dagger held out before him. Seeing Nikolas, he lowered it.

"Nik," Fin rasped.

Nikolas stepped toward him. "Fin? Why are you...?"

The question died on his lips. Fin wasn't dressed in his usual clothes, nor the outfit of a palace servant. He wore formfitting trousers and a jacket of blue and silver, with polished boots and a ring on one finger, small golden hoops in his ears. Something Nikolas would find in his own wardrobe.

An outfit of nobility.

You've made sure they won't come tonight? King Ferdinand had asked at the gala, followed by Don Cassian's *He will not be a problem.*

I've felt that, too, Fin had said at the festival. *Wondering how less complicated things would be without me here. If the world would be a better place for it.*

Fin saw realization dawn in Nikolas's eyes. "I can explain."

"Who are you?" The question landed flat and low.

"Nik—"

"Who are you?"

Fin swallowed. "My full name is Vincenzo Accardi. But I'm still Fin. I'm still the same person you met."

"Are you?" Nikolas's hand tightened around the spear's stock. "Because I've heard all my life the king has no heirs. That he would determine who among the Houses would next rule Vaega."

Fin reeled back. "What? No, he's going to publicly claim me as his heir after Godsnight," he argued. "He's never said anything about the Houses ruling."

Nikolas's chest fractured as if a hammer had been swung into it. The bracelet's charm slid against his skin, the tree that looked like the one growing at Deia's basilica.

"All this time," Nikolas whispered. "All this time, and you said nothing."

Fin reached for his hand, but Nikolas yanked it away. "I'm sorry. I'm *sorry.* I was going to tell you, but I was scared, and I didn't know how you'd react. My father keeps *everything* from me, Nik. I'm a fucking prisoner in this palace, and I always have been. Do you know how long it took me to figure out how to escape my guards to get into the city? He couldn't even hire a mage to teach me—I had to learn on my own."

Fin turned his face away. "I was...lonely. Whenever I caught a glimpse of you, I wanted so badly to approach you. To get to know you. I wanted to show you my toys, or my new dagger, or to give you a hug after your brother died. Eventually I got good at stealing the servers' uniforms."

All those moments in or near the Bone Palace when he'd felt as if someone were watching him. Nikolas struggled to breathe.

"But my father promised he'd finally announce me as heir after today. I didn't say anything because I didn't want him to go back on his word, didn't want to risk losing a chance at a normal life. And maybe that makes me a coward, but—"

"It's a trap," Nikolas breathed.

Fin frowned. "What?"

Nikolas staggered back. The unconscious soldiers in the hall, Fin alone in the safe room, the king promising his son a title while the Houses congregated—

"The exhibition. Dante's execution. He wanted it to be a show, but it's *not*."

"What are you talking about?" Fin reached for him again, but Nikolas caught his wrist, Fin's pulse tripping beneath his thumb. "Nik?"

It was so painfully clear he didn't know how he hadn't seen it before. All this time Ferdinand had been playing the Houses against one another, ramping them up for this. Ferdinand was never going to name an heir from a House, not when they held so much magic, when the end result would be more infighting and power grabbing.

He'd always meant to lead them to an execution, not a coronation.

"He's planning to kill us," Nikolas whispered. "All of us."

Fin's eyes were round, a shade so blue it tickled Nikolas's memory. Outside, the bell towers rang eleven times. The earth felt brittle and warm, energy swarming up through his stomach and pooling in his chest. Phos's feathers encased within the Sunbringer Spear crackled.

"Do you realize what you've done?" Nikolas tossed Fin's hand away. "If you'd told me earlier—if the Houses knew what the king was hiding—"

Fin looked like he'd taken a cudgel to the head. "Nik...I didn't know, I swear—!"

He didn't have time for this. He had to warn the others.

Fin yelled his name as Nikolas ran down the hall. Nikolas ignored him, ignored the fluttering panic inside him, and focused only on the energy—the ball of bright, pulsing light in his abdomen. He'd felt it when he attacked the soldiers, so unlike his weak attempts with Maddox and the Solarian refugees. It made Phos's feathers flare brighter, the dizzying possibility of strength.

Remembering what Maddox had told him, he siphoned the energy through Lux, his familiar growing and burning sharper as it built the energy up higher between them. It allowed Nikolas to dive deeper into the power growing with the alignment of the Cosmic Scale.

His body bent through space with a crack and pop, flinging him up, out, until he was on the roof of the palace. He ran along its edge, gaze on the square before him. Something was happening—something had gotten the clamoring crowd riled. Across the square came a storm of shadows, reaching greedily toward the palace.

Taesia.

Lux flashed, his power blinding, shooting through him like knives.

He screamed as heat rippled along his back, as two large, golden wings burst from his shoulder blades.

He launched himself into the air. With a flap of his wings, his body twisted through time and disappeared with a crack that echoed through the courtyard.

XI

Standing on the roof of the tallest building overlooking the palace square, Taesia stared at the crowd and absorbed the din of their excited chatter, using it to stoke her rage and panic. It roared into an inferno once she caught sight of the gallows waiting beyond the stage.

They wanted magic, a distraction from their fear-driven lives, and they wanted blood—to see her brother dangle from a noose and proclaim it the end of the Conjurers' reign.

Her anger was not at them. It was at the man who had orchestrated the entire thing. It was at the gods and their pointless war. It was at her aunt for deceiving her. It was at herself for not being able to stop this sooner.

How absolutely foolish she had been to think this city and its politics were not her destiny. To want freedom, to roam and experience and simply *be*.

What a privileged thing to want. What a privilege to regard her fortunes and dismiss them, instead of using them for the tools they were.

And now they were gone.

But she still had one tool left.

The shadows answered her silent call, pouring in from the streets even as the sky grew dark with clouds, even as Risha and Angelica assembled on the stage below. Their eager whispers sounded like pleased laughter.

It was the spectators crouched on the nearby roofs who noticed her first. They pointed and cried out, turning the heads of those in the square. She heard her own name fall from their mouths, each syllable filled with alarm.

Slowly, making sure they were watching, Taesia reached back and grabbed Starfell's hilt. The wrappings slipped away as she pointed its glittering black blade down at the square.

"Bring Ferdinand Accardi forward," she bellowed, the shadows magnifying her voice, "or I bring the palace down stone by stone." To give her threat weight, a shadow struck out at the gallows and smashed it to pieces.

Pandemonium. She smirked as the crowd roiled like a disturbed ant colony. The darkness at her back spread, a vortex of shadow that split itself into tails creeping across the sky. She'd come up with the idea after remembering the gala, the impossibly large train of her shadow cloak and how unnerved the gentry had been by the tendrils snaking around their ankles.

Those tendrils now chased spectators from the roofs, inching toward the Bone Palace to carry out her intent. She needed to get as many citizens away from the square as possible before her aunt's plan went into effect. Before the gods came calling.

A tingling sensation went down her spine as the bells tolled eleven times. The sky churned restlessly as the earth shivered.

Godsnight was here.

A loud *crack* split the air. "Taesia!"

A shaft of light cut through her shadows. Taesia hissed at the pain of it, flinching back, and almost missed Nikolas landing on the roof beside her. He was burning so bright her eyes watered, and she had to blink the tears away to see the large, golden wings bracketing his body.

Her breath caught at the sight of him, tall and fierce like the Solarian warrior he'd been trained to be. "Nik...your wings..."

"Taesia." He grabbed her wrist, his skin uncomfortably warm against hers. "Stop this. You're playing right into what they want!"

"What are you talking about?"

He stared at her, eyes so intent and luminous she could hardly maintain contact with them. "The king. He has a son. He's kept him hidden because he plans to assassinate the Houses *today*."

It was absurd. It made no sense.

But it had to be true, for Nikolas to look this despairing.

Taesia's lips twitched. Then she broke into laughter.

"Fuck," she breathed between giggles. "*Fuck*. This is nothing but a three-way race. The gods, the king, my aunt—place your bets on who'll kill us first!"

He frowned. "Your aunt?"

Her shadows continued to chase citizens from the square as she told him about Camilla. "If she succeeds, we'll have a swarm of demons to deal with," she said. "And if we fight against them using our power, it might set off the ritual."

"It'll be set off anyway," he said. "There's a Conjuration circle around the city. Once it activates, there's nothing we can do to stop it." His gaze drifted back to the palace. "Even if Camilla is stopped and we tried to undo the Sealing, we can't. We need someone from Ostium, and Ostium doesn't exist anymore."

"My aunt said demons came from Ostium. They're . . . priests, or holders of magic, who were distorted by the Cosmic Scale. But it's not like we can politely ask one of the demons she calls down to help us."

His face suddenly turned blank. He whispered, "I have to bring him here."

"What? Who?"

Nikolas turned to her, and she had the sudden urge to kiss him, hold him close, the way she used to when he was this frantic and upset. But that was already a lifetime ago. "Taesia—"

The ground heaved and she staggered, kept in place by his solid grip. "It's started." Starfell glimmered with a swirling purple light. "Why haven't we been possessed yet?"

"I don't know, but I can't waste any more time." His wings beat once, stirring her hair as he launched back into the sky. "Help the others!"

He turned with a booming *crack* and was gone. Taesia peered through the shadows toward the stage, searching for Risha and Angelica. She couldn't see them, but she could *feel* them, the dark seductive call of Mortri and the heated fury of Vitae.

Starfell thrumming with unused energy, Taesia launched herself off the roof and let the shadows envelop her.

The irony of his mother being laid up in the infirmary Julian had stolen from to provide her medicine was completely lost on him. He was too focused on checking her pulse, the too-shallow rise and fall of her chest, the pain etched across her wan face.

The Hunters' infirmary wasn't for family members, but he hadn't known where else to go. When the captain had barged in and found Julian hunched protectively over his mother's body, she'd taken a deep breath and ordered the medics to do whatever they could to save her.

Marjorie was now sewn up and bandaged, but she had lost a lot of blood, her skin ashen and cold. She hadn't woken up yet, and Julian refused to leave her side until she did.

Kerala laid a hand on his shoulder. He barely felt it. "Luca. Tell me what happened."

Every time he tried to talk his throat closed up. He tried his best to tell her about the woman and the demon attached to her. Kerala said nothing, eyes fixated on the far wall.

"A grimoire," she said at last. "And you didn't think to turn it in once you realized what it was? That it might end up falling into the wrong hands?"

His heart gave a sudden, mournful *thump*. He was going to get discharged at best, and imprisoned or executed at worst.

But so long as his mother made it, he didn't care.

"I'm sorry," he whispered. He was too tired to argue for his safety. Let Kerala decide what she wanted. He would accept it without question.

Kerala left, claiming she needed air to think. The morning stretched on, a strange itchiness traveling across his skin, his bones aching in a way they hadn't since he'd experienced growth spurts.

Eventually his mother's eyes fluttered open.

"Ma," he croaked.

It took a moment for Marjorie to find him. "Jules," she slurred. "Where'm I?"

"You're safe. We're safe. The medics are going to take care of you." He took her hand and placed it against his cheek. "I might . . . I might not be here when you wake up, but I'll be all right. I love you, Ma."

She tried to ask something, wrestling with the way her body wanted to drag her under again. Eventually sleep won out, and he carefully placed her hand upon her chest, some of the tension finally leaving his shoulders.

He found Kerala outside the compound. She was glaring at the Hunters who were in the middle of corralling the fenris into a large iron cage, ready to transport it back to its habitat. He was supposed to be among them, he realized. It certainly would have made the process easier; the wolf-beast was dragging its paws, lifting its upper lip in irritation as the Hunters tried to coax it forward with the promise of raw meat.

The captain looked at him, arms crossed over her chest.

"Do what you have to," he whispered.

Her face tightened. But as she opened her mouth, a startling *crack* echoed across the wide, empty street. The fenris jerked and growled, pulling on its lead as the Hunters fought to restrain it.

Julian and Kerala shielded their eyes as a brilliant light shone above them. It dimmed to reveal the glowing figure of Nikolas Cyr landing on the cobblestone, large wings tucking close to his body.

"Julian," he called, his voice as booming as the crack that had signaled his arrival. "We need you."

Julian gaped at him. Kerala seemed just as bewildered, but was quicker to recover.

"Go, Luca," she ordered.

"But—"

"You still have a duty to uphold, so up-fucking-hold it."

He barely managed to nod before hurrying to Nikolas, the Sunbringer Spear a blaze of orange and gold above his shoulder.

"My lord—"

"Stop," Nikolas snapped. "Listen to me. I'm not here because I want to be, but because I have to be. Because you have to be part of the ritual." He dropped his voice. "The way you've reacted to the Conjuration circles... You've been able to sense things from them, haven't you?"

There was no point in hiding any longer. "I have an... ability," Julian said softly, glancing at the fenris, "called beastspeaking. I can sense their emotions, their intentions. When I touched the circles, I was able to sense things from them, too."

Nikolas inhaled sharply. "And at Haven Square..." His tone was grim, resigned. "Julian. Are you descended from demons?"

Julian could do nothing but stare at him. Whatever played across his face—fear, resentment, trepidation—softened Nikolas's own expression.

"Ostium," Nikolas said. "Have you heard of it?" Julian nodded, recalling what he'd read last night. "It was once another realm in the Cosmic Scale, and their magic was Conjuration. When it died, so did the portals between the realms. We wanted to perform a ritual to undo it, but the gods..." Nikolas's familiar wrapped around his neck like a torque. "The ritual needs five heirs, not four. You're the fifth."

That itching, cold sensation scurried across Julian's shoulders again. He closed his eyes and felt the Cosmic Scale beyond the barriers of their world in a way he never had before, as if something made those barriers thinner, weaker. The whole city thrummed with tension.

But it was too much to take in, to understand, to acknowledge what Nikolas wanted him to do. He was Julian Luca, a commoner, a Hunter, who had no business with heirs or gods.

"Taesia needs you," Nikolas said.

Julian opened his eyes. There was pain and even anger in Nikolas's expression, but he remained resolute, his wings expanding to take off again.

"My mother," Julian blurted. "Marjorie Luca. I need your word that nothing will happen to her. That she'll continue to get care."

Another flash of pain in Nikolas's eyes—and something like understanding. He turned to Kerala. "Please see it done. And send Hunters to the palace square immediately. A woman named Camilla Lorenzo plans to unleash demons on the city. She herself has already summoned one."

Julian didn't recognize the name, but he knew without a doubt it belonged to the pale-eyed woman with her crimson demon, blade coated in his mother's blood.

He reached for the fenris with his mind, soothing it to the point that he could pull the restraints off its body. The Hunters demanded to know what he was doing, but Nikolas ordered them to stand down. They looked between their captain and the glowing godspawn, visibly torn.

Kerala did nothing to stop Julian from hauling himself over the fenris's back, tangling his fingers in its soft fur. Its muscles shifted under his thighs, its mind recognizing him, recognizing the instinct to *run*.

"Give him your weapons," the captain ordered one of the Hunters, who hesitated before handing over her longbow, quiver, and sword. As soon as Julian slipped the bow over his shoulder his doubt began to settle into resolve, grounded by its shape and weight.

Nikolas launched himself into the air, showing the way. Julian put his head down and bade the fenris to move. It sprinted down the street, following the streak of gold toward the palace square.

Underneath the fenris's paws, the ground shivered. Julian smelled the faint sting of sulfur in the air. The city was turning brighter despite the storm clouds hiding away the sun.

Conjuration. The power that hid between his muscle and tissue. The power that was going to destroy Nexus from the inside out.

The roar of the crowd made the stage tremble. Their voices were bounced back by the buildings surrounding the palace square, a tornado of sound, calling for the heirs to entertain them. There were even impatient mur-murs from the seating arranged within the Bone Palace's courtyard for the more composed, if no less excited, gentry.

Banners in House colors waved in teases of red and black and white, but the balconies were surprisingly empty. None had been erected for the Lastriders; the Mardovas were only represented by a tight-lipped Adela; and as Risha watched, Waren Cyr climbed slowly up to his bal-cony, stony-faced as always.

She couldn't make herself look at her family. Instead Risha turned to the balcony where King Ferdinand should have been sitting, but he was nowhere in sight. Again Risha thought of Jumari Chadha's warning, and the dread within her rose higher.

After speaking to the others in the carriage, she had gone to the flower shop on Lillum Street. Risha had found Jas in the basement sitting with elbows on his knees, talking quietly with Natsumi. At the whisper of her hem on the stairs, he'd risen to his feet.

"I need your help," she'd said.

"Anything."

That one word had solidified her determination. She could not let the gods carry out their war. She could not let the realms fall into the hands of a being who craved nothing but power.

She had one chance. If it failed, she knew what she had to do.

"Do you still have Leshya's necklace?" she'd asked him. He nodded. "You need to use it the same way you did at the Godsnight Gala."

Natsumi had also risen to her feet, frowning in confusion. "You want us to do that again?"

"Yes. But instead of calling on multiple spirits, you need to direct all that energy toward one spirit alone." She'd told them all she had learned in the carriage, about the Conjuration circle, the remains of the fifth god hidden within the palace. That they needed the power in those bones if they had any hope of breaking the barriers.

That perhaps, if the energy of Godsnight and the Conjuration circle was potent enough, the fifth god could be resurrected.

The Revenants had been silent a long time. Jas had asked, "Are you sure?"

"Yes. And if it doesn't work...if the gods' will is too strong for us..."

She would not let any of them become mindless vessels.

Jas's eyes had been pinched, and even Natsumi had looked concerned.

"You don't have to resort to that, Risha. We'll do whatever it takes to help you."

"Whatever it takes," Risha had whispered back.

She now rested a hand on the bone knife at her belt. In the florist's basement she had changed into the black leather outfit of a Vakara necromancer, knowing she couldn't fight properly in her ghagra choli.

Risha took a deep breath as a ringing voice cut through the din, an announcement echoing through the square. She could barely hear it over the thundering of her heart, the world going hazy and gray.

Please, she thought at Jas. *Please make this work.*

A hesitant touch landed on her shoulder.

"My lady," said one of the guards, "your name was called."

Risha straightened her spine. When she stepped onto the stage, the cheers and jeering coalesced into a sheet of indeterminable sound, washing over her like a sudden downpour.

She had tried everything to resist this moment. She had wanted so badly to follow her father's rules, to do only what was expected of her. But every stride she had taken had led her farther down the path to the inevitable.

Risha did not want a crown. She did not want power. She did not want to die.

I don't want to die.

The thought nearly broke her in two. Her knees threatened to buckle and she gasped, wanting nothing more than to turn back, to run up to the Vakaras' balcony and have her family's arms around her again.

A sound crept into the back of her skull, low and humming and sending a spark of pain down her neck. A torus of cold air began to circle her feet.

Do not be afraid, my blood, Thana whispered, and the crowd roared again as another figure ascended the steps. *This is what you were born for.*

Across the stage, Risha met the blazing eyes of Angelica Mardova.

The palace square faded around her as Angelica stared at Risha. Wind whipped at the Vakara heir's feet, her hair flying as a murky aura surrounded her. It was already beginning.

Angelica ignored the crowd. Somewhere above, her mother was watching, no doubt fisting her hands into her skirt hard enough to tear the fabric.

The locks Deia had constructed inside her were still there. There might be no way to open them on her own.

So she had to do whatever she could to redirect it. If she couldn't open the doors to her true power, she would have to try and steal Deia's.

She stopped several paces from Risha. Angelica was dressed simply in leather breeches and a red doublet, her braid a weight on one shoulder and her violin slung over the other, Cosima's note in her pocket.

"Well?" Angelica demanded when Risha didn't move, didn't speak. "Aren't you going to tell me we can still stop this? That you have some new ridiculous idea?"

Risha's face fell. "Angelica...I'm sorry."

"Sorry for what?"

Risha shook her head. Angelica remembered the night of the gala, staring at the Vakara heir and wondering what would happen if she burned her out of existence right then and there.

Maybe she should have done it and saved herself the trouble.

Nikolas still hadn't made his appearance. She could already feel the base of her spine aching, the palms of her hands growing hot. She released a shaking breath.

Swinging her violin case off her shoulder, she knelt and unclasped it. The sight of the polished spruce and maple helped settle her unease, and she straightened with the instrument perched under her chin and bow held at the ready.

It was then she realized the crowd wasn't yelling in fervor or contempt; they were *screaming*. Above them the sky began to darken with something more unnatural than clouds.

Something's wrong, she thought even as the ground shuddered, the air around her twisting into tongues of flame. There was something she had missed, something other than the gods' wrath, the fate of the realms. It was the feeling of being led into a room and having the lights go out.

She looked up at her mother at the same time an arrow flew into Adela's shoulder.

Angelica's scream caught in her throat. Adela staggered nearly off the balcony, allowing herself only a second to be startled before she snapped the arrow shaft and let it dissolve to ash, teeth bared. Angelica followed her glare to a group of blue-uniformed soldiers, their weapons out as they headed for the House balconies.

A husky laugh slipped into her mind, tumbled out of her own mouth. Deia's presence landed on her shoulders, clawed its way into her chest.

I'll never tire of the games mortals play, the god crooned in her head.

Angelica bent over double as her breath seared in her lungs. The crowd was riotous, and she soon saw why.

Taesia Lastrider emerged from a cloud of shadow. Guards immediately set upon her, and she fought them off as if she had been born with the strange black blade in her hand, throwing one into the outer wall of the palace's courtyard with her shadows and kicking another back into the churning crowd.

"Risha!" Taesia yelled. "We have to get away!"

But Risha was holding her head as the torus of wind around her expanded and picked up speed. Taesia turned to Angelica, frantic and wild-eyed.

"My aunt," she called. "And the king. They're going to—"

But fire clawed through Angelica's body, her skin flaring red. Deia's voice surrounded her, drowning out the crowd and Taesia's cries.

See now what your sickness can do, Deia said as the doors to her power banged open.

Taesia already knew she was too late. Risha and Angelica were in the throes of pain, one glowing a deep, inverted black and the other a sinister red. Taesia's stomach cramped at the warring energy, bloodthirsty, vicious. She threw a hand up as Risha's cold wind combated with the fearsome heat of Angelica's flames.

Taesia scanned the balconies. Ferdinand's was empty, the others seized upon by soldiers. The arrows being shot at the stage were either deflected by the wind or consumed by fire. She covered herself in shadow to avoid detection.

"Fuck," she breathed. She tried to get close to Risha, but was pushed back by her torus. "Risha! They're trying to kill you!"

But Risha's eyes were fully black, the pain on her face replaced with steady purpose.

"You do not get to say who will and will not die," she said, her voice layered over another's, deep and resonant—Thana. "That is for me to decide."

Risha extended her arms, fingers curled like claws. With the same movement she'd used at the Godsnight Gala for her corset, she brought her hands together and the ground beneath the stage cracked and splintered. Shards of white and yellow emerged from the earth far beneath them, bones both human and beast, fitting themselves across Risha's body like armor. Ribs clamped over her torso and scapulae fitted across her chest and back like plate steel. Phalanges lined her arms and thighs in interlocking patterns.

Taesia backed away, Starfell's tip scraping the ground. On the other side of the stage, Angelica laughed with a similar dual voice, her entire body aflame as her eyes smoldered the bright orange of sunset.

"THANA," Deia called. "KEEPER OF THE DEAD. YOU MUST BE SO TERRIBLY BORED, SO TERRIBLY LONELY IN THAT KINGDOM OF SOULS."

"MY KINGDOM WILL GROW INTO AN EMPIRE," Thana said through Risha. "AND YOU WILL SOON LEARN ALL THE WAYS IN WHICH I TORTURE WAYWARD SOULS."

The sky growled with thunder as the two gods launched themselves at one another with a clash that threatened to break the world in half.

XII

On the morning of his execution, Dante worked as quickly and efficiently as he could in the darkness of his solitary cell.

With no chalk on hand, he took a large splinter of wood he'd hidden in his pallet and opened a gash on the side of his wrist. Using his blood, he crafted a circle and symbols inside it, the same five-pointed star he'd watched his aunt draw in Lezzaro's safe room.

"Come on," he muttered to himself, sweat dripping into his eyes as his hands shook. "You can do this."

He still couldn't be sure if he'd really spoken to his sisters through a dream. If he hadn't—if they hadn't gotten his warning—

The circle was done. Gritting his teeth, he pressed a bloody handprint to its center.

It didn't matter he wore lightsbane; this was a magic that transcended his own abilities, a spear thrown into the celestial jumble of the Cosmic Scale. It blazed immediately to life, the circle glowing a menacing, red-veined black.

The pain along his palm and wrist throbbed in time with his heartbeat. Dante yelled as it spread and stabbed, gnawing at his body like teeth. Power drained out of him, feeding the circle eager for his blood, his sacrifice. The name of the one he wanted flashed through his mind, over and over until it was as if he'd learned no other word than this.

A quiet laugh reached his ears.

Dante shuddered and forced his gaze up. A shadow floated shapeless above the circle, contained by the lines of blood binding it in place. A pair of green eyes burned from the center.

"You summoned me from sleep." The voice was soft and melodious in his ears. "I was having a nice dream."

Dante forced a trembling grin to his face. "Well, I'm in a bit of a nightmare."

The shadow reached out and was blocked by the circle. "What do you want?" it said, almost petulant.

Dante's shaking grew worse the longer he held his bloody hand to the circle. If he removed it, his connection would be lost and he would be faced with the backlash. "I need your help. I need…power. Power beyond my capabilities."

"Is that so." The shadow moved a little closer, eyes burning into him. They were an impossible shade of green, like the brightest jade. "Speak your name, and I will speak mine."

It took him two tries. "D-Dante Lastrider."

The shadow breathed in, as if savoring the smell of something divine. "Dante Lastrider." The sound of his own name made his heart quicken. "I am Azideh."

"Azideh," Dante whispered back, the first time he had shaped the name on his lips since Camilla had shared it with him.

Once the demon's name was spoken, he began to take shape. The shadow stretched and elongated into a pair of muscled thighs, a sloping abdomen, corded arms; naked, imitating Dante's form. His skin was so dark blue it was the near-black of deep water, veined in red. Horns sprouted from his head and twisted together in a crown of bone within his tousled black hair, his neck slender, his fingernails long and sharpened.

Azideh crouched before him. Dante was panting now, sweat trickling down his ribs. He stared into the demon's eyes, black pupils slitted like a cat's, and saw his own terrified face looking back at him.

"I will give you the power you seek," Azideh said, carefully gripping Dante by the chin. The demon's touch was soft yet commanding, making him startle as if burned by static shock. "*My* power. But it will depend on your offering." The demon grinned again, teeth gleaming in the black glow around them. "What can you offer me, Dante Lastrider?"

"I have nothing," he croaked. "Except my life."

Azideh's thin eyebrows lifted a fraction. "Offering that will result in great power indeed," the demon whispered. He ran a nail gently down Dante's cheek, barely refraining from breaking the skin. "But to do so is to forfeit your life to me. I will be able to reap it when your business with me is done. No matter what you do, your death will be by my hand."

Dante wondered if he could have done more, tried harder to get the offering he needed. But his body was weak and in pain, and there were no other options.

"Do you accept these terms?" Azideh asked.

"Yes," Dante whispered.

"Then it is sealed."

The demon pressed his mouth to Dante's. It was cold and all-encompassing, diving straight into his heart like a crossbow bolt. His sound of pain was swallowed by the demon as thin black chains wrapped around Azideh's arms, slithering up Dante's body to curl possessively around his neck.

Gradually his weakness began to burn off like fog. When Azideh released him, he gasped in a breath and it felt like his first. The shadows around him gathered at his wrists, pulling and tearing until his shackles broke.

Nox re-formed between his hands. Dante laughed as his familiar twirled happily. The shadows whispered across his skin as if to imitate his joy.

Azideh's hands fell upon his shoulders, chains rattling. "Take now my power," the demon murmured in his ear, "and my strength, in whatever form you wish."

Dante stood. He could sense the demon at his back, smiling and restless.

The door to his cell opened.

"It's time, Lastrider. Let's go."

Officer Ybarra took a half step inside before she froze, caught under the stare of the demon. "What the fu—"

"*Go home*," Dante said. As he spoke, his voice altered—lower, chiming, measured like a song. It had an immediate effect on Ybarra, whose face slackened. "*Go home to your husband and wait there until you know you're safe.*"

Ybarra, under the demon's power, didn't even bother to nod before she turned and blankly walked out of the cell.

Dante faced the thick, impenetrable shell of the Gravespire and held out his hands. Azideh held his out alongside him, his strength suddenly becoming Dante's, muscles taut and veins popping.

Dante yelled and punched the wall. It exploded outward in chunks of glittering sandstone.

"Persuasion for the man who charms others to do his bidding," Azideh whispered. "Strength for the man who had it taken away."

Dante caught his breath as he stood on the edge of the hole, gazing down at Nexus. Wind whipped through his cell and fluttered his hair.

To the east, flashes of light and the growl of rumbling earth cut through the dark, storm-filled sky.

"Taesia," he whispered.

With the shadows coming at his silent call, Dante leapt from the Gravespire and dove into the city below.

From his place in the air, Nikolas saw the Houses surrounded by soldiers in royal blue. Rath Vakara shielded his youngest daughter from the soldiers' blades as Adela Mardova created rings of elements around herself as if she were a planet. A line of golden light shot across the square, and the shapes of glyphs formed under their feet.

"*Shit.*" Nikolas looked down at Julian, riding astride the wolf beast. "It's already started!"

Julian put his head down and rode faster. Nikolas used his lightspeed ability to fly on ahead, landing at the mouth of the palace square. The ground shook as two figures fought in the Bone Palace's courtyard, and he already knew those black- and red-pulsing bodies belonged to Risha and Angelica. His hand tightened around his spear, but he was as empty as he'd been in the basilica, when he had called upon Phos to bless him.

His unit was somewhere in the bedlam of frightened citizens and overwhelmed guards. He wanted to help them, but he had to make sure Julian made it to the heart of the Conjuration circle.

"Nikshä!"

His father landed in front of him, golden wings extended. He and his sword were splattered with blood, eyes lit with furious intention.

"What is this?" Waren demanded, pointing with his sword at the spreading lines of the Conjuration circle. "Why haven't you stopped it?"

"I—"

"The Vakara and Mardova heirs have been possessed by their gods." Waren eyed Nikolas's wings. *Why haven't you?*

The raging flame that was Angelica fell to one knee and slammed her hand on the ground as a tower of granite rose under her. The cobblestone was snaked through with cracks and canyons; as Risha ran past, bones flew out of the fissures and formed a staircase before her. She ran up to meet Angelica height for height, the two of them disappearing under a nimbus of red and black as the earth shuddered again.

Waren stood utterly still against the panorama of chaos behind him. Something in his stonelike expression cracked.

"So it is to be a true Godsnight," Waren whispered. "A blessing of the gods while Ferdinand turns against us. My own soldiers—"

His breaths came heavier as he aimed his sword at Nikolas's heart. "An infected limb must be severed to save the body," he said, so quietly it was nearly lost in the din. "If Phos will not inhabit you, then I will offer myself instead and claim what is ours."

Nikolas barely managed to block his father's swing, metal rasping against metal.

"Father!" The word burst out of him with everything he had been keeping locked in his chest, but even then he knew it would not be enough.

"You cost me my heir!" Waren howled. "You cost me my wife's sanity. You cost me a crown, and our god's power. No more. *No more!*"

Waren broke free and swung. Nikolas winked out of time and appeared behind him, but his father's reflexes were expertly honed. Their blades screeched as Waren turned and deflected, using the advantage of a sword against a spear's broader reach to get into Nikolas's space. He left a shallow gash on Nikolas's unarmored side before Nikolas could launch himself into the air. Waren followed.

"The people are in danger!" Nikolas yelled as he continued to block the onslaught of his father's attacks. "I'm not the one you should be fighting!"

But his words were pointless; Waren was panting and wild-eyed, the same maddened heartbreak as when he'd found Madeia bleeding on the floor. He hurled a ball of light at Nikolas, aiming to pluck him from the sky. Lux stretched into a shield to deflect it.

Nikolas glanced down and saw Julian and the fenris emerge from the mouth of the street. He spun away from his father's sword and called down, "Get to the courtyard!"

Another ball of light slammed into Nikolas's side, making him crash into the nearest roof. He tumbled and nearly fell over the edge, wings flickering with distress. Waren landed before him, sword shining as lightning arced overhead.

"Once you're gone, Phos will choose me," his father was mumbling. "He will fill me with power, and the other Houses will fall, the king will fall, and they will have no choice but to worship us."

Nikolas got to his feet and held the Sunbringer Spear before him. The Conjuration circle was glowing brighter below. A strange blackish light had surrounded the palace, and he only had a second to think about Fin still inside when his father made his move.

Their blades clanged as first Nikolas, then Waren was pushed back.

"Stop this," Nikolas gasped. "*Please.*"

But there was no chance of reasoning with him. There never had been.

Waren yelled and lifted his sword, planning to stab it through Nikolas's chest.

Lux pulsed and dove in front of him, pushing Waren far enough away for Nikolas to swing the spear up and drive the blade deep into his father's neck.

Waren choked and dropped his blade. It slid off the roof as his father staggered back, clutching at the glowing spear, its radiance throwing his face into stark relief. His eyes caught Nikolas's, and for one instant, they shone with clarity.

Then his father's wings sputtered out and he fell after his sword. Nikolas yanked the spear back as Waren tumbled over the tiles and disappeared from sight.

Nikolas fell to his knees and retched, but Lux pulsed frantically before him, silently telling him to get back up.

He couldn't stop to think, react, scream. He had to keep fighting. He had to help the others.

Nikolas flapped his wings in one strong gust to take to the sky. It was difficult to tell if his eyes stung from tears or blood.

XIII

Julian left the fenris at the mouth of the street and gave it an order to return to the compound, unwilling to let it be harmed in the mayhem. He began to wade against panicking citizens and guards, royal soldiers battling the heads of Houses in the middle of the square.

A hand grabbed him. He turned with sword raised and faltered when he saw Paris.

"Julian, fuck!" his partner panted. "Please tell me you're seeing this, too."

A glyph flared to life beneath their feet. The sky flickered with lightning as a loud, echoing boom emanated from the courtyard. A buzzing ache had begun in Julian's head.

"Thana's bloody rotting grave," Paris muttered at his side. His partner's hands twitched toward his dual swords. "I can barely tell who's fighting who."

"I think that's the point." Julian swallowed. "I have to get to the courtyard."

"What? Why?"

"I can't explain now. Will you help me?"

Paris nodded solemnly, shoving the citizens toward the alleys as they made their gradual way across the square. With every new glyph and symbol that lit up, Julian felt as if a knife went through his head.

He sensed something else, too. Faint and dark, cool and heady as midnight, open and airy like a field in spring. The center of the circle. The Bone Palace.

Something waited for him there, and he had to answer its call.

* * *

Nikolas tucked in his wings as he dove toward the palace's courtyard.

It was already in ruins. The gentry had fled, chairs overturned in their haste. The fountain was shattered, and Angelica gathered the water spurting from the broken pipe to strike out at Risha. The lemon grove was on fire, the promenades smashed apart. The Bone Palace cast a sinister black light on the skeletons emerging from the cracks, remnants of the mausoleum coming to join the fight.

By the gates, Taesia fought with her new sword against a royal guard eager to subdue her. Nikolas landed as she finished the guard off with a blow to the chest.

She turned to Nikolas, speckled with blood and shadows roiling around her. For a moment Nikolas wondered if she'd been possessed by Nyx, then realized this was her own power.

She read his thoughts, as always. "Nyx hasn't claimed me. He may have chosen Dante instead. Why hasn't Phos claimed you?"

Nikolas shook his head, tasting blood and bile. His side ached where his father's sword had opened him.

Taesia's face twisted as she turned toward Risha and Angelica. "We have to stop them."

"Julian hasn't come yet?"

"Julian? Why Julian?"

"He's the fifth heir."

"*He's* the fifth—?" He couldn't discern the emotion in her eyes. "How?"

Cobblestone and granite crashed around them through flashes of red and black followed by thunderous blasts of magic. Nikolas formed Lux into a shield as a piece of granite fell toward them.

A hunk of earth smashed into it, throwing it off course and shattering it into harmless bits of stone. Nikolas whirled around. Fin stood with his hands outstretched, eyes wide.

"You can't be here!" Nikolas grabbed his shoulders, but Fin planted his feet.

"I'm getting you out," Fin insisted. "Nik, I didn't know my father's plan, I swear—"

"What is this?"

Taesia was staring at Fin much the same way Nikolas must have stared at him in the hall, taking in his clothes, his jewelry. Fin tensed under Nikolas's hold as she stared at him, a sigh of revelation escaping her.

"So that's what she meant," she whispered. "When she said she'd tell me the whole story later. All that bullshit about protecting family." A grin stretched across her face, toothy and mirthless. "Hello, cousin."

Cousin? Nikolas looked between Fin and Taesia, bewildered, until he noticed it.

Fin's eyes. Blue, piercing, crystalline. The only other person he'd seen with eyes that shade was Camilla Lorenzo.

A woman who, Taesia had explained, had her sights set on gaining the Ostium fulcrum. To gain power perhaps not for herself, but for her son.

Taesia's laugh was wild. "This is beautiful. Truly. I planned to kill your father today." Her sword gleamed in the red fires purling off of Angelica. "But I can settle for you instead."

She stalked toward them. Nikolas stood between her and Fin, wings splayed.

"The *fuck*, Nik," she growled. "You know what he is! If we'd known he existed, the Houses could have started working together much sooner! We could have stopped this!"

"Nothing could have stopped Godsnight," Nikolas retaliated. "You know that."

"I can offer you a full pardon," Fin said from under Nikolas's wing. "As soon as... *this* ends."

Taesia's nostrils flared, a sign Nikolas knew well. "A full pardon," she repeated, her words nearly eaten by the commotion. "Does it look like I care about a *full fucking pardon* right now? Your father wants us *dead*. Your mother wants to—to turn you into a god!"

Her voice rose, harsh and shaking. Nikolas grabbed her shoulder and squeezed hard. "Exactly. Our fight isn't with him, it's with *them*."

"My... mother?" Fin repeated. There was bewilderment on his face and the spark of something like longing. "You know who she is?"

Though his betrayal sat like a lodestone in Nikolas's chest, Nikolas softened as he turned toward him. "Get out of here, Fin."

The prince shook his head stubbornly. "Not without you."

"You're going to get yourself killed if you stay here."

"I—"

But there came another horrible sound, only this time it wasn't behind them—it came from above.

Its appearance had first gone unnoticed, but now Nikolas saw the way the fabric of the realm had torn above one of the palace's balconies, a circle of black with a starry sky beyond its perimeter. Someone stepped through, onto the balcony above the courtyard.

A boy with pale hair and golden, glowing eyes stood at the railing, gazing down with a small, unfeeling smile. Something within Nikolas kicked and thrashed in denial, in madness, in hope, wondering if this was another dream, another torture crafted by his guilt-ridden mind.

"Rian," he breathed. Lumin magic pumped stalwartly through his body as his brother stood there, radiant and otherworldly. All the strength he had missed these last few years threatened to turn him drunk with it. His wings stretched eagerly, begging him to take flight.

"How is this possible?" Taesia demanded behind him. "How is he *here?*"

We buried an empty casket, his mother had said, what he thought had been the words of grief turned delusion.

Rian Cyr, the true heir of their House. The one his father and Phos had chosen.

Nikolas took a few steps forward, wings burning brighter. This time it was Taesia who held him back even as her eyes bored into the glowing boy above them, disbelieving.

"Rian," Nikolas breathed. His face was blank with shock. "*Rian.*"

How is he alive? Taesia thought. *How is he* here?

The boy's eyes flickered. Then Phos's voice boomed through the courtyard as his own wings flared out on either side of him, a radiant white sword forming in his hand.

"THE REALMS ARE MINE. SURRENDER OR FORFEIT YOUR LIVES."

Taesia swore and lifted Starfell, but Nikolas grabbed her arm.

"Phos is controlling him!" Taesia said. "He has to be stopped before he kills the others!"

"*No!* I have to—let me—"

"Taesia!"

Her heart contracted painfully as she turned toward the mangled gates. Brailee's dress was torn and stained, her hair loose, a bruise on her forehead.

"What are you doing?" Taesia demanded, shrill with panic. "Why are you here?"

"They attacked the villa," Brailee sobbed. "I tried to warn them about Aunt Camilla but they— The guards turned on us, tried to k-kill us, the servants. Mother fought them back and got us out, but the voice told me to come here, that I had to—"

Brailee shuddered and stared up at Rian. Her expression was wiped away, and she stumbled forward like a sleepwalker.

"He..." She tripped, and Taesia caught her. "He's here. Rian...?"

Without the haze he'd layered over his dreamscape to protect his identity, Taesia now recognized the boy from Brailee's dreams. All this time and neither of them had realized, the connection to him too warped.

"I'm getting you out," Taesia said. "You shouldn't be here."

Brailee stared at her as if she had spoken a foreign language. Before she could answer or Taesia could haul her out of the courtyard, her sister screamed and convulsed.

"Bee! Brailee!" Taesia held her sister as she sank to the ground. She called out to Nikolas for help, but Brailee shuddered again and opened her eyes.

"Ah," she sighed, "My heir. We meet at last."

Taesia froze. It was not her sister's voice, but the midnight words of Nyx. She recognized it from the basilica, and before, that low sweet voice leading Brailee through her dreams.

Somnus pulsed beside Brailee as her back arched, her mouth open in a silent scream. Holding her like this, Taesia briefly sensed the universe of color beyond Brailee's consciousness, the dizzying realm of possibilities at her fingertips, ready to be brought to life with a single snap.

The courtyard exploded with shadows. Brailee choked on them even as they lifted her up, swathing her body like armor, like a dress made from the finest velvet.

Then the shadows lifted, and Brailee stood calm, quiet. With a twitch of her fingers a sword cut from the night sky appeared in her hand, radiant and ephemeral.

"Bee?"

Taesia's voice was tremulous, uncertain. Brailee turned her head slightly, cocking it to one side.

"My general," Brailee said under the dulcet voice of Nyx. "I told you this was not your fight to win."

The astonishment within Taesia turned to rage. "Bastard," she snarled, lunging forward only to be stopped by Nikolas. "Let go of her! *She's not yours!*"

"You are all mine," Nyx said, turning to acknowledge the others.

Thana and Deia were still locked in their own fight, a war between death and life. "BUT THERE IS A BIGGER THREAT YOU HAVE OVERLOOKED."

Rian stared down at her, smile broadening.

"THERE YOU ARE," he drawled, and his voice, like Brailee's, was overlaid with something darker. "AT LAST I WILL SEE MY HANDS AROUND YOUR THROAT, MY LOVE."

"PHOS," Nyx growled. "YOUR GREED IS TRULY INSATIABLE."

Phos laughed, and it echoed across the courtyard. "IT WAS DEIA WHO KILLED THEM." Rian gripped the railing of the balcony, the palace's black glow beaten back by his luminosity. "SHE IS THE ONE TO BLAME."

"AND YOU WERE THE ONE TO WHISPER IN HER EAR! *YOU* WERE THE ONE TO CONSUME OF THEM!"

"BECAUSE I KNOW WHAT I DESIRE," Phos said grimly. "UNLIKE SOME WHO ARE CONTENT TO SIT BACK AND WATCH THEIR WORLDS SUFFER."

Nyx forced Brailee to lift her dark sword. "Stop," Brailee whispered, and it was her own voice, so small and soft Taesia could barely hear it. "Please. He's suffered so much."

"HE IS THAT BOY NO LONGER," Nyx answered. The shadows crawled over her, ready to snuff out Phos's light. "HE MUST BE STOPPED. KILL HIM."

Brailee might have fought back, but her body betrayed her, leaping through the shadows toward the god of light.

He met her halfway, blinding and beautiful, and when their swords met, it split the sky into night and morning.

XIV

Nikolas held Taesia back as Brailee lifted a sword with a constellation shining across its blade, her eyes drowning in black. Nyx made her launch upward on a gale of shadow as Rian dove down in a streak of gold.

When they clashed Nikolas and Taesia fell to the ground, the earth shuddering beneath them. Brailee and Rian sailed overhead, a comet and its tail, tentacles of shadow ripping apart the palace's balconies and throwing them at Rian. Rian easily dodged and re-formed his sword into a spear. It hurtled toward Brailee's chest, but she managed to knock it away with her own weapon. Using the same power she wielded in her dreams, she formed metallic bars into existence and slammed them into Rian, forcing him up against the side of the palace. He gave a low laugh before his light flared brighter and the bars crumbled away.

"We have to stop them!" Taesia scrambled to her feet. "We have to get them all out of here before—Nik!"

He was already shooting up into the air. "Rian!" he yelled. "Don't let him control you!"

There was no sign of his brother in the formidable scowl on Rian's face. It was all Phos, the greed and corruption of an angry god. Brailee answered it with her own hard frown, Nyx driving her to meet Rian blow for blow.

Nikolas tucked in his wings and dove straight at Rian. He was so busy with Brailee that Nikolas managed to grab him, sending them tumbling through the air and crashing into the palace wall. The breath went out of him, his body crying out in pain.

"Rian!" His arms tightened around his brother's torso, keeping him place. "I know you're in there. I know you remember who you are! Who I am!"

Rian's head turned, and all he saw were furious golden eyes. He was shoved back by the force of Rian's wings, falling until he could right himself.

"YOUR BROTHER IS GONE," Phos said, standing within the ruins of the wall as blood trickled from Rian's forehead. "I MARKED HIM AS MINE FROM THE START, AND MINE HE WILL REMAIN."

Understanding rose within him. The gradual decline of Nikolas's Lumin magic as Rian's strengthened. The way his power had snuffed out once his brother was gone.

Nikolas shook his head. "You have no right to him."

"HE IS MY BLOOD. MY HEIR."

"So am I!" The Sunbringer Spear hummed in his hand, but he refused to point it at Rian. "Rian, listen to me. Mother hasn't been the same since you...you were taken. She's sick. She needs to see you, to know you're alive!"

Rian's eyes shuttered and Nikolas saw a hint of pale blue, the barest second of fear. Then Phos returned, launching into the air.

Nikolas saw the light building in his hands and dove. Taesia and Fin were in the blast range, Fin's mouth open in surprise when Phos released his attack.

Nikolas spun and flung his hands out. A sheet of gold unfurled from his palms, the shield rising in time to absorb Phos's energy. Nikolas's feet skidded against the uneven ground, Fin holding on to him from behind to keep him upright.

Through the pain jolting up his arms, through the heartbreak of what Phos had done to his brother, a pure note rang through him. His shield bore no holes. Taesia and Fin were safe.

Desperately he turned his attention away from Phos and to the power flowing over the arena. The alignment of the Cosmic Scale. Somewhere within its shape was the portal to Solara, the barrier standing firmly in his way.

He brushed up against it, was repelled back. Nikolas's shield faltered and fell.

"Nik." Taesia's hand wrapped around his arm.

"I can't do any more than this," he panted. His side panged; he might have cracked a rib or two. "The barriers..." *Julian, where are you?*

"We can't undo the Sealing so long as the gods are determined to kill one another. Right now we have to worry about them surviving this."

"Nik!" Fin shouted.

The sky above them began to churn and split apart into a dizzying vortex, yawning open like a mouth seeking to devour. Already he could see shapes within, screeching and growling and cackling. Nikolas's heart beat a horrified tempo and the hairs along his body stood on end.

"Camilla," Taesia whispered.

Nikolas lifted the Sunbringer Spear. This was about more than survival; it was about protecting the others, making sure they all got out of this alive.

I am not going to die, he thought. *And neither will anyone else.*

Thana's power had stitched itself through her so completely Risha wasn't sure where she ended or began, if she had ever been born or walked the earth in her own body, if she had ever raised the dead or if someone else had sung her back to life.

It didn't matter. Her torus grew wild and untamable, the chill wind of the pathway to Mortri, carrying the scent of grave soil. Below her lay the remains of beasts and humans and royalty, centuries of death and destruction built over one another in layers of ruin.

Deia matched her in speed and strength. No—her name was Angelica Mardova, a girl about her age, born and groomed for this fight just as she had been. She burned bright against the dark, a monster wreathed in flame.

Inside her, Thana hissed in revulsion. There had once been a time when the two gods could meet across the realms, in the infinite stretch of the universe. They had been near to what humans called sisters, and they had constructed the bridge between life and death through the power of Ostium, one ruling over the elements while the other watched over the souls that traveled from the other realms.

It hadn't been until much later Thana realized she had received the lesser of the two. Deia was free to do as she pleased while Thana was stuck in Mortri, weighing souls and torturing those who deserved retribution. To keep the rivers flowing and the kings of the dead satisfied and glutted on spirits.

She wanted *more*.

And she was going to take it. Just as Deia had murdered their eldest sibling, taking their bones and fashioning herself a cradle of power.

Risha crafted a spear of bone and threw it. Angelica raised a hand and blew it away with a gale, her fingers dancing as a rope of water formed around her arm, extinguishing the flames.

"YOU CANNOT COMPREHEND THE POWER YOU SEEK," Deia told her. Always that condescending tone, that small smirk. "YOU KNOW YOUR PLACE, AND IT IS NOT HERE AMONG THE LIVING."

Risha bared her teeth. Behind her loomed the vast barrier to Mortri, closed even against Thana's power.

Open it, Jas, Risha thought furiously. *Hurry.*

She could sense him and the others nearby making use of the Conjuration circle, making use of Leshya's bones as they concentrated on the Bone Palace. The marble glowed a steady, uncanny black, and deep within its recesses she felt it—the eye fixed upon her, the trapped spirit. A fifth god, unnamed, unknown, unworshipped.

If they were woken, would it be enough to complete the ritual? To call upon Ostium's lost magic and break the Sealing?

She could almost hear Jas calling for her, asking for more time, more power. She sent out a silent summons, reaching for the necropolis, for things buried and forgotten. They answered her immediately—bodies crawling out of their graves, rising through the ground to do her bidding. They joined the remains from the mausoleum in the tattered robes of kings and queens and consorts.

"I WILL SHOW YOU POWER," Thana whispered.

Angelica's face hardened in disgust as the spirits closed in. They scuttled and crawled and lurched toward her, whispering, moaning, weeping. Thana pressed them forward, urging them to overwhelm Deia, devour her inch by inch.

Angelica sent out a flame like a volcano erupting. It flooded the courtyard with red and orange, burning bones down to char and ash.

Thana took her opening. She made Risha dart forward, knife in hand, ready to stab it through Angelica's heart.

Angelica was faster. She stomped her foot and the ground heaved upward, throwing Risha back. She landed painfully on her side, jarring her momentarily from her body.

Thana's thrall ebbed. In that moment she saw the mess of the courtyard, the fire and the spraying water, the broken-up earth and jagged bones. Streaks of black and gold clashed in the sky, but Nikolas and Taesia were by the gates.

Risha's breath caught. If all four of them were here, if the awakened bones weren't enough to replace a fifth heir and complete the ritual...

"Risha!" she heard Jas calling. "Just hold on!"

·But he couldn't mask the strain in his voice. The Revenants, even with Leshya's necklace, would not be enough.

Risha got to her hands and knees. Blood and sweat dripped from her face. Angelica stood waiting for her, eyes red, death written in the line of her mouth.

Death.

Risha reached out with her power the way she had in the mausoleum, mapping out the veins and organs that led to the heart. Her own pulse came first, loud and frantic as she stood. Expanding her range, she caught Angelica's heartbeat.

A memory. Risha, twelve years old, picking over a table of food at a party when she realized the girl standing next to her was the Mardova heir. She'd been petite yet powerful, her presence taking up nearly the entire room.

"Don't eat that one," Angelica had muttered as Risha reached for a pastry. "It's filled with something bitter."

Risha had snatched her hand back. "Thanks."

She'd smiled. Angelica had blushed and turned away with a frown, as if angry at herself for instigating conversation.

Risha came back to herself with a small gasp. Her body shook, eyes welling with tears. Angelica's heart pounded beside her own.

Child, Thana growled inside her. *Stop this.*

But Risha continued to spread her power outward, toward the nimbuses of light and shadow above. She grasped Brailee's heart—*ah, Brailee, so he's chosen her instead*—and recalled the moment she had first met her, a small child with missing baby teeth and a shy demeanor, the way she had become such fast friends with Saya; she grasped Rian's heart—*Rian, oh gods, how are you alive*—and was transported to a hot afternoon in a garden, raising her eyebrow as the youngest Cyr performed handstands to show off for her sister.

Their lives filled her, incapacitated her. She fought for breath even as she kept stretching, searching.

Nikolas's gaze had met hers across a room at a dinner party. His shoulders had been hunched, visibly uncomfortable.

"I don't like these things either," Risha had whispered when she came to stand beside him. "They're always boring."

Nikolas had picked at his fingernails. Lux had peeked over his shoulder, and Risha had giggled in delight.

"O-oh, sorry," Nikolas stammered. "I'm still learning how to keep it still."

"Don't be sorry. I like it." She'd held out her hand, the little familiar twirling above her palm. "It's cute."

The memory faded and she saw Nikolas now, fully grown and framed in golden wings. Risha sobbed and added his heartbeat to the others, nestled beside her own, before reaching for the last one.

A girl had stepped out of the shadows with a smirk that fell when Risha didn't react.

"I didn't scare you," she'd pouted.

"You're from House Lastrider," Risha had guessed. "You're a Shade."

Taesia's eyes had widened slightly, and she had looked Risha over in a way she wasn't used to, something like calculation mixed with curiosity. It had made her feel strangely special.

"House Vakara?"

"Yes."

"Then you're a necromancer. No wonder I didn't scare you." Taesia had grinned then, full of teeth and the promise of mischief. "How many things have you brought back from the dead?"

"Uh…" At that point, it had only been a few insects.

Taesia had grabbed her hand, pulling her toward an alcove. "There's a dead moth at the window. Can you revive it? I want to see!"

And Risha had followed, drawn to her like she herself was a moth and Taesia the light.

She pulled back from the memory and felt tears on her face, warm and wet as blood. Taesia's heartbeat joined the others.

The tethers of their lives wove around her fingers as if she were constructing a spell with string. One thought, one snap, and they would fall as if she were merely banishing a spirit. This would all be over. The paths to the other realms would remain blocked, but at least the gods wouldn't have the chance to destroy them.

Necessary deaths to secure new life.

Angelica shaped a flame into a ball of inferno. She stepped forward, ready to unleash it.

You cannot do this! Thana howled, fighting against Risha's iron will.

Risha cried out from behind gritted teeth as her legs buckled. All the life contained in her chest bore her down, an unbearable weight.

Her fingers trembled, ready to curl into a fist. To snuff that life out in one simple movement.

I'm sorry, she thought. *I'm sorry.*

"Risha!"

Someone was climbing through the debris, trying to reach her. She knew his face, knew his name, but she was six people in one, facing a towering wall of flame as her god raged inside her.

"—thought I knew what I had to do—"

"—don't want to hurt him—"

"—almost time, it's coming, it's ready—"

"—why didn't he tell me—"

"—she's going to die, this is all my fault—"

And then her own soul, her own memories, her own thoughts swarmed her mind with black roses.

"Jas." The whisper escaped her dry lips.

He ignored the chaos of the courtyard and ran to her, stretching out a hand.

"Don't do this!" he yelled. "Risha!"

Angelica released her flames, seeking to burn Risha and Thana to dust.

No! the god wailed inside her, fighting to get out, locked within the prison of Risha's body.

Risha was about to clench her hand when Jas leapt before her, standing between her and the tower of flame.

Jas didn't even have time to scream. One second he was there and the next he was ash, scattered by the raging torus of her power.

The lives within her rushed back out. She was left with the dreadful beating of her solitary heart as it cracked and shattered into pieces.

As Julian and Paris finally made it to the courtyard, he saw the massive hole in the sky that flickered with lightning. But his attention honed in on Taesia, a glittering black sword in her hand and shadows at her back. Blood stained her clothes and matted her hair, her expression murderous.

She spotted him. "Julian!" She approached him, limping slightly. Gone was the godlike girl; this Taesia was already halfway beaten. "Nik was telling me— Is it true? You're the fifth heir?"

"What's she talking about?" Paris asked as he stared at the mayhem.

But Julian didn't know how to explain. He could only meet Taesia's incredulous stare until a boom made them all look up. Under the swirling vortex, a girl wearing shadowed armor battled a boy with wings and golden eyes. They clashed and separated, flying in and out in a sort of dance, as if they had done this many times before. Taesia lifted her sword and Julian readied an arrow.

A blast shook the courtyard, followed by a cold, sharp wind that blew them up against the courtyard wall.

"Julian!" Nikolas yelled. "Do it!"

Julian nearly gagged on the putrid wind as he forced himself away from the wall. The sensation he'd followed through the square was stronger, now. It loomed above and around him, a storm not yet unleashed. It strained against its barriers like a restless animal, a burning eye that couldn't blink.

Standing within the heart of the Conjuration circle, Julian allowed its strange, uneasy attention to fill his body and ignite whatever swam within his blood.

Ostium. He still didn't know what it meant, what it encompassed, but he opened himself to it nonetheless. The presence raised its head and the black light around the palace flared brighter. Something began to stir from within, a door unlocking and swinging from its latch.

No—there were *multiple* doors. One swung outward, into the universe. The other three swung inward, leading from lands dark and bright and cold. The ley lines that had once been so alive, dead for so long, pulsed under his feet.

"It's working!" Nikolas shouted. "Taesia, try to break the barrier to Noctus!"

A loud, booming laugh broke his concentration. Julian's eyes snapped open to find the winged, glowing boy in the air above them, grinning at Julian in obvious delight.

"THERE YOU ARE," he whispered in a strange, two-toned voice. "THE FIFTH PIECE."

The earth shuddered hard enough it nearly knocked Julian off his feet. The lines of the spreading Conjuration circle spilled light onto the Bone Palace and washed away the black.

The girl wreathed in shadows leapt at the boy, but he dodged and kicked her, sending her crashing to the ground like a fallen star.

"Brailee!" Taesia sprinted to her side and turned the girl over, checking her pulse with bloody, shaking hands.

"Now my ritual is complete," the winged boy sighed. "And their remains are mine. Soon I will bridge all four realms. And then..."

Another heaving groan. The Bone Palace and its courtyard were trapped within the same light that had enveloped the monarchs' monument as the Conjuration circle came to its completion.

Angelica didn't know where the Parithvian man had come from. She watched him burn, saw the silhouette of his body in the flames before he was simply gone.

The part of Angelica that was still conscious cried out in horror.

But Deia was annoyed. They hadn't hit Thana and now her vessel was screaming, her torus blowing outward and the ground frosting over.

Angelica tried to fight against the possession, but her god had taken her over too completely. She was a crumb amid the feast of Deia's power. Her doors had been blown open, her magic let free, but without her instruments she didn't have the control necessary to wield it; only Deia did. Her violin and bow dangled from one hand, useless.

Give it back to me, Angelica snarled, pounding against the barrier of Deia's will. *Give me back my body!*

Deia laughed and sent a rope of water to pierce the torus of Thana's vessel, wrapping it around her neck. The vessel choked as water flooded into her nose and mouth.

STOP!

Angelica had wanted power, craved it, thought it was the only thing that would make this wretched city hers. She thought back to Cosima's fingers in her hair. Her mother's hands against her face.

Angelica managed just enough leverage to pull the water away from Risha. Risha coughed and fell to the ground, the wind still thrashing, making Deia's flames gutter. Angelica made use of the opening and brought her violin up, setting the bow across the perfectly tuned strings, releasing a full note that held the flames back.

Obstinate, Deia growled.

Deia prepared another ball of inferno and advanced on Thana's vessel. The Cosmic Scale was already beginning to wane; there wasn't much time left to end this.

Angelica played her violin furiously, fingers numb as she swept the bow in large gestures, trying to beat back Deia's blaze.

You cannot win like this, her god whispered. *Release the full force of your sickness, my blood. It'll be over so much sooner if you do.*

Angelica raged, pouring all of it into her violin, into the wrathful song she played to drive Deia to distraction and split Angelica's magic away from her.

The god laughed. *Pitiful.*

The song changed, turning sharp and spiteful. Angelica's fire was wrenched away from her again, and Deia poured all of it through the violin, using it to amplify what was already too strong to stop.

The inferno that would burn Risha—Thana—from the universe for good.

Angelica fought even as she walked forward, as she played, as the broken courtyard filled with the high whine of the violin. Tears fell and were instantly dried by the crackling heat.

She thought of her father taking her to the opera. Miko standing in the garden, asking Angelica to sing.

Sing.

It was a word her father had spoken often, smiling as he asked her to indulge him.

Will you sing for me tonight, Angel?

The building pressure in her core, the way she had felt a door crack open as she reached the highest note.

Sing.

It took all her might to wrench her jaw open. A single note came out sweet and pure, high as struck crystal.

What are you doing? Deia snarled.

The courtyard trembled as she stepped forward, the wall of fire behind her growing larger, hotter, singeing her skin. Still she held her note even as she played the violin, making it climb higher, into the finale of the aria she loved.

The violin exploded in flame.

Deia yelled in wordless rage as Angelica's magic sputtered and failed in her grasp.

Angelica gulped in a breath. The world creaked and bent around her. The Cosmic Scale was waning, but she felt it here, in her chest, at her feet, in the dark doorway forming before her, powered by whatever lay within the palace that wanted out.

The power of Ostium. Expansive and intangible.

Risha was getting to her feet. Her blackened eyes glared at Angelica as she lifted her hands, the bones along her arms re-forming into blades. Behind her, the air coalesced dreamily, hazy, as if swimming with heat.

Stop, Deia commanded.

Angelica's voice pierced the air again and the portal solidified. Before Deia could attack again, Angelica quickly followed it with a current of wind and blew Risha back.

She only had time to catch the shock on Risha's face before Risha was shoved into the portal. It closed with a snap, and Risha was gone.

NO!

Deia's scream shook her to her core. Angelica fell to her knees, coughing up blood that touched her lips and splattered the ground. Her god clawed at her, resisting the pull of the Cosmic Scale as it started to slide out of alignment.

The doors to her magic shut one by one.

"Julian, don't stop!" Nikolas shouted even as he launched himself at the boy who looked so like him. "As long as we're all here, we can still—"

But the ley lines Julian had connected to felt scrambled, no matter how the presence within the palace strived to feed him its power, no matter how hard Julian fought to maintain his connection with it. He nearly buckled under the burden.

Something was missing. Some*one* was missing.

"Julian." Paris squeezed his arm. "Hang on."

His connection to the presence wavered. Pain lit up his spine, along with a torrent of emotion—not human, not logical, but made of gnashing teeth and furious purpose.

Tilting his head back, he peered into the madness of the portal above. Within it floated shapes of different colors, all wreathed in unnatural power, all drifting toward the palace as if drawn by a lure. Beasts of a wholly different nature.

Julian was many things he'd never wanted to be, but he couldn't forget who he was at his core—a Hunter with a responsibility to protect.

Inhaling deeply, he opened himself up further to this new power. It felt like ripping himself apart at the seams. The earth kept shaking with the force of the Conjuration circle and the portal seemed to grow with it. If he didn't stop the demons from coming through, he was going to die here, die in blood and violence like his father.

The power of Ostium danced along his fingers. He used it to magnify what he already sensed within himself, the bitterness in his blood, the ability he had scorned since he'd learned of its existence, that unwelcome connection to beasts.

The boy who looked like Nikolas turned, sensing the surge of energy. He scowled and flew toward Julian, but Paris stood between them with dual swords in his hands.

"No you fucking don't," his partner warned.

"FASCINATING," emanated a voice that was clearly not the boy's own. "THIS POWER YOU WIELD. I WONDER WHAT ELSE YOU MAY USE IT FOR."

"You won't get a chance to find out," Paris said, twirling one of his swords. It flashed in the lightning overhead.

The boy launched himself at Paris. His partner blocked the first two attacks but missed the third, yelping as he danced back with a long, bleeding slash across his stomach.

"Paris," Julian called, barely a whisper as he shook under the strain.

"I'm gonna rearrange your face," Paris growled, sliding back into the offensive. "Where the fuck is His Brightness?"

Julian saw Nikolas emerge from a pile of rubble he'd been thrown into, his face and hair streaked with blood. With a flap of his wings he flew across the courtyard to reach them.

It distracted the boy enough for Paris to knock his glowing sword away. It spun through the air in a golden disc, and Paris barked a victorious laugh.

"See? Two's better than one," Paris goaded, bouncing readily on the balls of his feet. "Now let's see you—"

The boy grabbed the Sunbringer Spear in Nikolas's hands and spun them around, shoving its blade into Paris's chest.

Paris looked down, startled, and slowly dropped his swords. He fell to his knees as Nikolas yelled and wrenched the blade out, turning against the boy once more as they were lost within a nimbus of light.

Julian's insides twisted as his mouth formed a soundless howl. Heat and darkness engulfed him, blood leaking from his ears.

Above, he heard the demons' laughter as they began to descend.

The presence inside him exploded outward, heat peeling away his skin, his human shell, all the things that made him Julian Luca.

I am a man. My name is Julian. I live in Nexus.

I am not a monster.

I am.

Monster.

I am a monster.

The words burned away into a scorching white nothing. He felt the darkness out beyond the reachable sky, the cosmos of night, the pinpricks of stars amid weightless galaxies. And within, the furious life forces of the demons. He could sense every single one of them, their breaths, their heartbeats, their flexing muscles, their single-minded lust for destruction.

His mouth filled with coppery blood. His nerves were a riot of pain. Still he concentrated on those life-forms, holding them, trying not to let any slip away.

The power flared and burst out of him.

He felt each and every death. Every life snuffed out by his reckoning. It racked his body, convincing him over and over that he, too, was dying. He would have fallen if it weren't for something propping him up, holding on to him as he screamed and shook.

Eventually it waned. Julian opened his eyes and watched the demons' bodies crumble away into nothing, raining dust and ash. Inside his chest his heart still throbbed, reminding him he was alive, alive, monstrous but alive.

Kneeling over Brailee, Taesia hadn't first been aware of what Julian was doing. But then a wind kicked up, as well as a curious pulling sensation in her stomach.

She turned and found him standing near his fallen partner. Julian Luca, a Hunter, a soldier, standing with arms outstretched as a pale green light surrounded him. Black veins had spiderwebbed across his body, sharpened teeth bared against fury or pain or both.

Taesia covered Brailee with her body while the power stormed and thrashed, let loose against the demons like perfectly aimed arrows.

But she couldn't stop staring at him. He was a furious star fallen to earth, or something risen from the depths of an unknown world to seek vengeance. She wondered if this was how he'd felt, watching as she killed and laughed and exposed herself to her power.

But he did not laugh. He bore it like he bore everything—grim, determined, worn like a mantle of duty.

She stumbled to her feet as he began to shake. She rushed to hold him up despite the ache that sank into her arms from touching him.

"Hold on," she told him. "Just hold on."

Eventually the light ebbed away. Julian was covered in sweat, shivering against her. When he turned his head, she inhaled sharply. His irises were bright green, pupils narrowed to slits.

"Julian," she whispered.

"Taesia." His voice was hoarse, rumbling. "I didn't want…"

"I know." She squeezed his hand. "But you did well. It's my turn, now."

He frowned through his fog. "What…?"

"Risha is gone—I don't know where—which means we can't break the barriers. But the portal needs to be closed before more demons show up."

"Camilla Lorenzo," he said slowly.

"Yes. Find her while I keep Phos distracted."

She let him go and walked to the center of the courtyard. The shadows were a living thing, trailing between her limbs and over her skin and clothes, braiding through her hair. They whispered of all they could do, all she could use them for. A frisson of excitement stole through her.

"YOU ARE NOT NYX'S CHOSEN," Rian said, Phos's deep voice layered over Rian's younger, higher timbre.

"Yeah, well, fuck that guy." She was suddenly surrounded by the scent of cloves. "He said this wasn't my fight, but he was wrong." She pointed Starfell at him. "Let's go, light bastard."

Julian couldn't stop Taesia before she rushed at the boy, the courtyard filled with a spiral of gold and black. Although he'd been drained, something still thrummed under his skin, familiar and known.

Once the light subsided, he knelt by Paris's body. His eyes were still open in shock, and shakily Julian closed them. There was nothing he could do for his partner now except ensuring his death hadn't been for nothing.

Julian reached for an arrow. Most had spilled out of the quiver, but there was one left. He aimed it at the winged boy, but they were moving so fast, a blur of sun and shadow, that he couldn't get a good shot.

A flash of red caught his attention, and his breath caught. A figure stood on top of the half-broken wall surrounding the courtyard, watching the portal with hungry eyes.

Eyes that had met his over the wounded form of his mother.

Camilla Lorenzo.

Julian smelled the stone beneath him, the blood on his clothes, the stink of magic blasted into the walls.

And he could smell *her*, rotten, foul, her demon a beacon of wrongness.

He turned toward the woman, longbow in one hand, arrow in the other, and began to stalk his prey.

XV

Dante found his aunt standing on the palace's outer wall, her demon concentrating on flowing its crimson energy through her. She was staring at the wreckage of the courtyard, drawn and tense.

And above: infinite blackness like the depths of Dante's cell, maddening, unending.

Dante landed on the wall, Azideh at his back. "Camilla!"

She turned in surprise and spotted Azideh.

"Well," Camilla said with false lightness. "I see you finally succeeded."

"You sold me out. You told me you would get rid of the evidence!"

She tutted. "I sent you to the Gravespire for your own protection, I taught you how to summon your own demon, and yet here you are ungrateful for it."

"Please, don't do this," he begged. "Lezzaro warned you against this for a reason. Innocent people will be killed!"

"The demons have been dealt with for now." Her eyes narrowed. "Though *how*, I—"

The ground rocked beneath them, and Dante noticed the thick, glowing line that encircled the palace. Glyphs burned within the inner perimeter as if drawn by a giant's finger dipped in gold paint.

"Something else is happening," Camilla muttered. "The heirs are fighting one another. I thought the exhibition would be enough of a distraction, but they may have attempted the ritual after all."

Worry for Taesia pinched his chest. He was wasting time. Dante shot out his hand, and Nox streamed past in the shape of a blade. Camilla cursed as Shanizeh got between them and deflected the attack.

"*You will close the portal*," he spoke in Azideh's power, that chiming quality infused in his words.

But his aunt shook her head. "A demon's power cannot affect another's. And you cannot stop this. Shanizeh will locate the fulcrum, and it'll be ours."

"*Ours?* Don't you mean yours?" Dante stalked forward, all the weeks of his imprisonment building in him like a fever needing to be broken. "I wanted to abolish the monarchy, but all this time you've just wanted the power of a god. You have no idea what the power of another realm could do to this one!"

"Not unless it's properly *wielded*." She sighed. "You may have wanted to abolish the monarchy, but that was never my intention. I only wanted Ferdinand gone. Once that happens, I will ensure Vaega is ruled by someone who actually *is* holy, who not only holds royal blood but also the key to the universe."

Azideh's strength rushed to his legs, made him a blur as he grabbed her. She gasped.

"What are you talking about?" he demanded. "Are you so hungry for the throne you'd put us all in danger?"

"I don't expect you to understand," she whispered, "that a mother would do anything to create a better world for her child. Even if it means some things need to be broken in the process." She held a hand to his cheek. "And I will always put my family first."

Dante tightened his grip, but something flew by over their heads. Taesia, wrapped in shadows, was fighting a boy with wings that wasn't Nikolas. Instead, Nikolas stood across the courtyard, protecting another man who wielded broken bits of earth as weapons.

Following his incredulous gaze, Camilla wrenched out of his hold as her eyes widened in horror. "Why is—?"

The last word was barely out of her mouth when she stumbled back, an arrow blooming from her chest.

Dante followed its angle to where a man stood holding a longbow. His tawny brown skin was riddled with black veins, and he glared at Camilla with bright green eyes like Azideh's, the pupils contracted into slits.

Azideh stirred like a cat arching its back in warning. The man locked gazes with the demon—for one second, two, a moment that expanded and contracted with the startled breath that escaped him.

Then Shanizeh grabbed Camilla and tumbled off the side of the wall.

"Shit!" Dante jumped and landed in the mess of the palace's courtyard. He tried to find any sign of his aunt or her demon, but instead—

"Brailee!" He collapsed beside her, pulling her out of the crater in the shape of her body as shadows purled off her skin. When she opened her eyes, they were pitch-black, winking with hidden stars.

"Dante," she coughed out. "Help me up. I need...to stop him..."

The boy who was undoubtedly possessed by Phos. The boy who looked staggeringly like Rian Cyr, though that couldn't be possible. "No. You need to get out of here."

"Dan—"

"*Get away from the palace*," Dante said, his voice chiming with Azideh's influence. "*Now.*"

Brailee's eyes cleared as she gained her feet and ran toward the square against her will.

"Dante!" she screamed.

He gritted his teeth and turned away, trusting that the demon's power would get her to safety. He opened his mouth, ready to call up to Taesia to repeat the spell, when Azideh snarled beside him.

"This magic is too strong," the demon said. "We will both die if we remain."

"I can still—"

"*Go*," Azideh said, and the word was wrapped in steel and power. Dante fought against it, clutching his head as it rang with pain.

But he was still new to the demon's presence living alongside his own, unable to drive him back. Like Brailee, he found himself running toward the square, away from where his sister fought for her life.

Starfell locked against Rian's sword of light, sparks flying from the contact and stinging Taesia's skin.

"It's no use," Phos drawled. "You cannot fight me without your god."

"Watch me," Taesia growled. She rushed in again, and Phos laughed through Rian's mouth, the two of them twirling in a cyclone of light and darkness.

She was, after all, a weapon. She had fashioned herself into one, helped along by Dante's forging. This was her place—to hunt, to fight, to kill. To be a general.

The thought made her pause long enough for Rian to kick her away.

The shadows caught her before she could fall. She stared at Rian, at Nikolas's brother, at the boy she thought was dead. She remembered holding Nikolas in her arms as he cried, consumed with grief.

She would not be the source of that grief.

Starfell's blade swirled with the same iridescence as when she'd held the vertebrae in the bone dealer's shop. A promise of something beyond the barriers, beyond her own skills, beyond the need for subtlety or restraint.

She had grown up a middle child of House Lastrider, a spare, a descendant of Nyx, forced into a life of accepting duty and carrying it out without complaint. But she had complained. She had fought. And she had picked any fight for the thrill of it, to break out beyond her borders and get a taste of what life could have been, if the circumstances of her birth had been different.

But they hadn't been different, and there was no point in running any longer.

Taesia Lastrider was a girl of shadows and secrets, who had inherited her god's hatred and bloodlust and now needed a way to forge them into something new.

As Nikolas launched himself at Rian again, she looked up at the open portal, the new shapes beginning to writhe within its depths.

Brailee was no longer in the courtyard. She told herself it was for the best; her sister should have had no part in this. And now, with Brailee gone, she could do what needed to be done.

"Nyx!" she shouted. "Use me as a vessel!"

Nikolas spun away from one of Rian's attacks. "Taesia, what are you—?"

"Go on!" she yelled, her voice hoarse and crackling with exhaustion. "You said I'm your general, didn't you? Come and use me, then!"

A cool presence climbed up the base of her skull. Her body tensed, a heavy weight settling in the bowl of her hips and the cradle of her chest.

I thought you refused me, came the god's amused whisper. *That you would rather die.*

A girl can change her mind, she thought.

If I claim you, we will be linked. Is that truly what you wish?

It wasn't. It absolutely wasn't. But all her life she'd been running from the chains of duty only for them to drag behind her. She might as well pick them up and wear them as jewelry.

Taesia bared her teeth in a grin. *What are you waiting for?*

A velvet chuckle. She was drenched in black, starry and veined in purple, an expanding celestial void coming to claim her. She threw her head back as the pain reached its crescendo before disappearing altogether.

When the shadows lifted, she felt calm, steady. Powerful.

"Taesia!"

She didn't know who called her. Enmeshed within Nyx's power, there was nothing beyond the air rushing in and out of her lungs, the easy manner of the shadows waiting at her fingertips.

Fight him, Nyx whispered, and now she felt it in every part of her body. The urge to drive her sword into Rian's heart prickled her skin. *End him.*

Taesia honed in on the darkness. Held it inside her like a thing living and growing.

Once she felt she had control over it, she smirked.

"Sucker," she muttered.

Taesia lifted Starfell above her head in both hands. At once she sensed the diseased edges of the portal, the disturbing power of Ostium's fulcrum trying to get through. The forged astralam bones, flooded with Nyx's power, pulsated.

"WHAT ARE YOU DOING?" Nyx snarled out loud, using her voice underneath his.

"No!"

Somewhere on her left, Camilla's stare dropped from the shivering portal to Taesia's sword. She was clutching her bloodied chest, teeth stained crimson.

Camilla's demon charged at Taesia. Something crashed into it before it reached her, sending them sprawling across the courtyard.

"Julian!" Taesia yelled, hands tightening around the hilt as she struggled to maintain connection to the portal and fend off Nyx's vie for control. "Keep the demon occupied!"

He looked up from where he crouched above the demon, and though there was something of a demon in him now as well, she still recognized Julian beyond it, her stalwart Hunter. He nodded, and it filled her with relief and determination.

With a snarl, he and her aunt disappeared.

Shanizeh grabbed Julian and tried to claw her way through his stomach. He unsheathed his sword and used the motion to ram the pommel into her abdominal wound, the one he'd made in his mother's apartment. The demon hissed and writhed.

Julian rolled away, unharmed. Camilla Lorenzo was not so fortunate. She was favoring one leg as she approached him, one hand clutched around the arrow he'd embedded in her chest. There was a point of darkness on the demon in the same place, as if she were absorbing the wound.

"You." Camilla's bright eyes narrowed on him. "So it's true. There really is an heir to Ostium."

Julian wasn't an heir to anything, but he didn't bother wasting breath to say so. He rushed at the woman only for Shanizeh to grab him again. She lifted him high into the air, far above the courtyard.

Shanizeh grinned with a high, clicking laugh. Julian fought against her, bow hanging uselessly from his shoulder, his quiver empty of arrows.

Although the magic of Ostium had waned from his body, he was still left with the enhanced awareness of his own. It was the same power that had speared into those demons and taken their lives. The same power he had cursed for as long as he had been cognizant of it.

He didn't curse it now.

With his new acceptance came calm, and he stared into the demon's eyes. Beyond them he caught a haze of images: a glimpse of the universe's terrifying expanse, the looming white towers of some unfamiliar city, a shrine with a precise Conjuration circle glowing within. Under the barrage, Shanizeh's grin faltered, and her grip loosened slightly.

Julian stabbed his fingers into her chest, into the swirling point of darkness a mirror to its master's.

The demon howled.

The ground cracked and gave way under Taesia's feet, making her sink deeper. She kept Starfell pointed at the center of the portal. It swirled and shuddered, the cosmos beyond full and sharp like snapping teeth.

Stop this, Nyx warned her. *Focus on the fight.*

This is my *fight*, she bit back. *Not yours.*

Taesia sobbed as her arms screamed from the power shooting into the marrow of her bones. The shadows pushed against her, keeping her upright, shielding her from the combating powers of the Conjuration circle and the portal, the haunting presence crouched within the palace.

Close.

The portal shrank. Julian must have broken the demon's concentration.

Starfell was cold and bright in her hands, stinging her palms, but she didn't dare let go, not when Julian was risking his life to give her this opportunity.

With one final yell, she pushed her powers along with Nyx's through the blade. It shot up and slammed the portal closed like a door.

Taesia gasped and fell to her knees. Almost at once Nyx faded from her, taking with him the strength she needed to stay upright.

We lost this chance, he whispered. *But there will be others. I'll be back for you, my general.* Then he was gone, leaving her hollow and weak.

Despite its biting cold, she cradled Starfell to her chest. The Conjuration circle flared even as the Cosmic Scale waned. The storm overhead brightened—or perhaps it came from the lines and sigils under her body as she toppled to the ground, unconscious.

Julian tumbled through the air when Shanizeh let him go. Yet still he was calm, centering his balance and grabbing the edge of the broken courtyard wall.

It nearly wrenched his arm out of its socket. He snarled in pain and hoisted himself up, refusing to let go of his longbow despite having run out of arrows. As long as he held it, he could remember his name. He could remember his father teaching him how to craft, how to shoot.

He could remember he was more than what his blood wanted him to be.

A blast of darkness shot up from the courtyard. Above them, the portal sealed itself. Camilla Lorenzo screamed in rage, or fear, or both. She began to quickly limp across the courtyard, hand outstretched for the young man being protected by Nikolas Cyr. But Shanizeh swooped down and collected Camilla in her arms, and both woman and demon disappeared in red smoke.

The golden glow of the Conjuration circle was beginning to fill with a deep, sinister purple. A ring of dark light circled the Bone Palace, the courtyard, and at least half the square. And he was inside of it.

Taesia.

Her name was a spark in the darkness, guiding him forward. Julian leapt down into the courtyard as the light engulfed him.

Something was dragging her backward. Angelica flailed weakly, thinking Deia had somehow managed to crawl outside her body.

She was hauled through the broken courtyard wall and into the square. Everywhere she looked she saw carnage, bodies, blood. She tried to call out, but her voice was wrecked.

"I'm here," said the voice of the person half carrying her. "I'm here, Angel. You're going to be fine."

Angelica was leaned against the wall of an alleyway. Her mother's front was drenched in blood, her grim face freckled with it.

There came a deep, humming sound, the ground rolling under their feet. They held on to one another as four lines of glowing black crept into the square amid the golden Conjuration circle, aiming for the Bone Palace.

Angelica leaned forward, but her mother caught her shoulders.

"It's no use," Adela whispered. "It's over."

"Nik," Fin panted behind him, "we have to get out of here."

Nikolas shook his head, as much to deny him as to shake the sweat and blood from his eyes. "Not without Rian."

His brother hovered in the air, having knocked him down again. Risha and Angelica were gone. Taesia was passed out in the courtyard. He'd lost sight of Julian, and Paris was . . .

Nikolas gritted his teeth and was about to take to the sky when the ground rolled and pitched, bathed in a harsh light.

Phos laughed through his brother's mouth.

"IT's TIME," he said.

Fin stepped in front of Nikolas, holding up a spear he had fashioned out of stone. But Phos only laughed again as the earth groaned, the light searing.

Nikolas threw up his arms as Fin cried out. Then the world itself was screaming, breaking, crumbling apart into nothing.

Azideh's power wore off as soon as they were out of the heart of the Conjuration circle. He found Brailee there, on her knees and sobbing. Nyx had left her, leaving her too drained to get back up.

Dante wrapped his arms around her, shielding her against the light that swept over the square. The city shook as the Bone Palace began to sink into the ground. It was like watching a landslide, like something tumbling beneath an ocean's wave. Unstoppable.

The two of them watched the Bone Palace disappear, swallowed whole by a hungry, ruthless god.

When it was over, the world was eerily still and silent. Dante numbly stood and pulled Brailee up with him, and she took a few faltering steps forward. The guards and soldiers either had been knocked out or were looking around in astonishment, and somewhere behind them Dante heard his mother calling their names.

A battered figure limped up to his side. Angelica Mardova, her arm slung around her mother's waist as the two of them stared at the carnage.

Brailee stopped at the edge of the giant crater. The palace, the courtyard, and most of the square were gone.

And so was Taesia.

XVI

Risha Vakara had asked for death to take her, and this time it accepted. Or at least, in every sense of the word save for physically. She held a hand to her chest, felt her heartbeat push up against her palm as if to reassure her that her body had not yet perished.

But something had happened to her. Angelica had been striding toward her, singing, her violin breaking.

And then she had been pushed back into nothing.

A portal. It was the only thing that could explain the sensation of stepping from one place to another, the disorienting fall, the way she'd hurtled through space fast enough she hadn't been able to catch her breath.

She caught it now, sitting in a dark, mineral-scented cave. The smell was undercut with something sulfuric, like the Conjuration circle in the basement of the flower shop.

Her fingers twitched. *Jas.*

She should have stuck to her original plan. She should have ended them all while she'd had the chance.

If she had, Jas would still be alive.

"Pathetic."

Thana loomed above her—not an image, but the god herself, her presence an aching threat.

But she *couldn't* be here, not tangibly. Unless—

"You denied me victory," the god hissed, face twisted in fury.

"You lied to me," Risha snarled back. "I'm not your puppet. I never will be again."

One of Thana's four hands grabbed her by the chin, squeezed hard enough to make her jaw creak.

"DISOBEDIENT CHILD," the god whispered. "WE SHALL SEE ABOUT THAT."

The god left her there, shivering and alone. Risha hugged herself as the tremors grew worse, as a fearsome cold spread through her limbs, as the revelation took hold.

Since the Sealing, the gods could not physically cross over into other realms. And they had not been able to break the barriers.

Which meant she was not in Vitae anymore.

Her teeth chattered as the air glimmered beside her. Risha watched as a pale outline formed in the shape of a man. He looked down at his hands, curling and uncurling his fingers, the cave wall faintly visible through his chest. The ghost turned to her, confused.

"Jas," she whispered.

He was not quite gray, not quite colorful—an indistinguishable blend of life and death. His eyes widened when he found her.

"Risha." He knelt before her and tried to take her hand, his touch barely substantial. "How...Where are we? I thought I..." His expression darkened.

"I died," he whispered.

Her tears fell. He tried to brush them away, but his thumb was a caress of cool air.

The portal. It must have taken not only her, but Jas's lingering spirit as well, his ashes scattered around her.

"Risha," he said again, "where are we?"

She glanced at the entrance to the cave, then back at him. Together they walked, body and ghost, to where a faded red light was spilling into the cave.

Risha took in the sight before them. Massive stalactites dripped amber and blood, a wide river rushing by in churning waves of gray limbs leading to a massive gate of obsidian. All around her was the same sensation of the necropolis's pathway, threatening and tantalizing.

All this time wanting to cross over, to break the barrier, and now she was in Mortri.

And all she wanted was to find her way back.

Risha turned to Jas. He stared dismally at the river, holding himself stiff as if resisting its lure. He was the first spirit who had crossed over since the Sealing; the river wanted to be fed, to carry him through the gates to Thana's judgment.

But Risha wouldn't let him. They would find their way back to Vitae—together.

She held out her hand. Jas's sorrow gave way to determination as he took it. His gray skin, when it touched hers, was a whisper.

Hand in hand, they walked into the realm of the dead.

Taesia opened her eyes to a star-strewn sky.

When she tried to move, she bit back a yelp. Someone knelt beside her. "Easy."

She nearly flinched away. At first she didn't recognize the face peering down at hers, but a name fell from her lips all the same.

"Julian."

Black veins were still spread across his skin. But at the sound of his name they began to shrink back, his eyes returning to their normal hazel.

He helped her sit up, one of her hands still stubbornly clinging to Starfell's hilt. They were at the base of the Bone Palace. It towered high above them, glimmering in the starlight.

Nikolas was getting to his knees, his face bloodied and his wings gone. Beside him, Fin peered up at the palace in consternation.

"Where are we?" Nikolas rasped. He looked at Taesia. "What happened?"

The courtyard lay in ruins before them, ringed by the broken-off edge of the palace square. They were perched on a hill above a city burning with light. There were screams in the distance, bloodcurdling and frantic.

Beyond the city was a field of dark, swaying grass and an endless cosmos of stars and inky black.

Taesia's stomach tightened as Umbra curled around her arm, humming with power. All around her was the scent of cloves.

"We're in Noctus," she whispered.

A cry sounded behind her. They turned and found Rian—Phos—dragging King Ferdinand from the palace steps and pushing him to his knees. Behind them lay the bodies of Ferdinand's advisors. They must have been cowering within the palace all this time.

Rian grinned, eyes still burning gold.

"Father!" Fin made to get up, but Nikolas held him back.

"Let him go, Phos," Nikolas demanded.

"I DON'T THINK I WILL," he said. He grabbed Ferdinand by the hair and slit a knife of light across his throat.

"NO!"

Fin struggled against Nikolas, choking on his cries. Ferdinand keeled over, motionless.

All this time, Taesia had wanted to see him fall. And now he was gone. Just like that.

Rian strode toward them, wings unfurling. As he spoke, his voice fluctuated between boy and god. "BENEATH US LIES THE RUINED CASTLE OF THE ROYAL FAMILY OF ASTRUM. THE FAMILY WITHIN IS DEAD. THE KING OF VAEGA HAS NOW JOINED THEM."

He approached Fin. Nikolas blocked his way, the Sunbringer Spear held across his body.

"Don't do this," Nikolas whispered. "Rian, *please*."

But Phos easily knocked him aside. Fin recoiled as Rian crouched before him, smiling.

"YOU WERE RIGHT, NIKOLAS," Phos said. "YOU ALSO HAVE POWERS THAT WILL BE OF USE TO ME. I HAVE NEGLECTED YOU FOR FAR TOO LONG."

Taesia inhaled sharply as Nikolas's eyes began to flicker.

"Nik," she called, scrambling to get to her hands and knees. "Nik! Don't!"

"DO AS I SAY," Phos crooned, wrapping a hand around Fin's throat, "OR I KILL HIM."

Nikolas had tensed as he fought against it. But at this he gave in, his eyes lighting up gold.

"Nik!"

His face had fallen into an eerie, blank calm. He rose to his feet, abandoning the spear to yank Fin up, holding his arms behind his back. Fin struggled against him, stomping his foot as a piece of stone rose into the air, but Phos slapped him and cut the spell short.

"I WOULDN'T DO THAT IF YOU WANT ME TO KEEP POOR NIKOLAS AROUND." Rian turned to Taesia. "THE SAME GOES FOR YOU, LASTRIDER."

Julian's hand tightened around her arm as she lunged forward. "Why are you doing this?" she demanded. "What's the point?"

"THE POINT?" Phos raised one of Rian's pale eyebrows, then walked to where Nikolas had dropped the Sunbringer Spear. When he picked it up, something within it flared in response, brightening the blood along its blade.

"THE POINT," he said quietly, turning to survey the city in chaos below, "IS THAT SOON, I WILL BE THE ONLY GOD WHO CAN CROSS BETWEEN THE REALMS. THE POINT IS THAT ONCE THE OTHER GODS ARE FINALLY DEAD, SOLARA WILL CLAIM THEM ALL. WITH MY NEW PRIZE, I WILL HAVE FREE REIN OF THE COSMIC SCALE, AND SHAPE WORLDS AS I WISH."

Prize. Taesia looked up at the Bone Palace. She couldn't feel it any longer, but she knew the presence it contained was still there, fighting for release.

Rian turned back to them, wings burning against the darkness.

"It will begin here," he said, and though his voice was now his own the words were not, the god's hold on him absolute. "With the fall of Noctus under a wave of blazing light."

BRIGHT ENDINGS, BRIGHT BEGINNINGS

Rian took in their terrified faces and felt something deep within him flinch.

It is their punishment, said the Voice in his head. Phos. His god. The one who had saved him years ago, given him a new life after his old one had been burned to ash. *They deserve this*.

He was fed memories not his own. The fight against Nyx had reminded Phos of so much—of the times they had pretended to spar like humans, testing the limits of their powers. When they had been more to each other than enemies plotting across the universe. He remembered the glowing feathers of his wings against ice-pale fingers, hair dark as the night sky soft under his touch. The way he had once promised that the two of them were destined to create more worlds out of nothing. Gods of entire galaxies, entire planes.

The bone-shattering betrayal that had followed.

But Rian couldn't help but wonder. He glanced at the man who called himself his brother.

Nik.

His chest ached. He was so tired. So hungry.

You have done well, and earned some rest, Phos whispered. *When you wake, we will begin.*

Rian couldn't help but smile. He looked out at the unfolded cosmos, wings beating gently against his back.

Soon, the night would end.

And the sun would finally rise.

The story continues in...

THE MIDNIGHT KINGDOM

Book TWO of THE DARK GODS

Coming in June 2023

ACKNOWLEDGMENTS

All books are a journey. This one was an odyssey.

I first got the idea for *The City of Dusk* over a decade ago. It started with the name Lastrider—the project's name for several years—and all I had was the premise of four noble houses with cool magic powers. It took a few years until I began to expand on the world, the characters, and the plot, and a couple more after that to start writing.

Since then, the book has undergone heavy construction. I'm talking wrecking-ball heavy. Each draft had new innovations and new problems and new things to cut—like chipping away marble to figure out the shape hiding within. That's why there are a lot of people to thank, because without them I would have never found the shape and would have simply walked into the sea.

First and foremost to my editor Priyanka Krishnan, who remained patient and persistent while I wandered down many roads going "Is this cool? Does this make sense?" until we finally found the right one. This is without a doubt the most ambitious story I've ever tackled, so thank you for guiding me through it while pushing me to keep doing better. The end result is something I'm immensely proud of, and I hope you're proud of it, too.

A truckload of gratitude and roses to the Orbit team for their hard work and support, including Hillary Sames, Tiana Coven, Rachel Goldstein, Paola Crespo, Stephanie Hess, and Tim Holman. For the amazing cover and interior design, endless thanks to Lisa Marie Pompilio, and to Ben Zweifel for helping bring Nexus to life.

A cocktail for my agent Victoria Marini, who's always there to hold my hand while sternly talking me down from the aforementioned walk into the sea.

To Traci Chee, for all your encouragement and advice and insight, and for sitting with me on a bed in Canada while we sketched the Cosmic Scale and you helped me figure out what to call it. To Emily Skrutskie, for tolerating me flinging draft after draft at you, for brainstorming with me when I was stuck (admittedly and embarrassingly often), and for coming up with the name Sunbringer Spear.

To Katy Rose Pool and Akshaya Raman: thank you for all the wine and venting and cheese. Never-ending wine pots to the Cult for being on this wild journey with me: Kat Cho, Mara Fitzgerald, Melody Simpson, Christine Lynn Herman, Amanda Foody, Amanda Haas, Axie Oh, Alex Castellanos, Meg Kohlmann, Janella Angeles, Ashley Burdin, Claribel Ortega, and Maddy Coli.

Thanks to E. K. Johnston for providing cabins and to the Unicorn Crew (you know who you are), especially those who asked if I was okay while I was writing the Deia-becoming-a-giant-spider scene. Special shout-out to Margaret Owen for participating with me in this One Long Yell we call life (and for making me eggs).

To the readers and the booksellers: you're amazing. I love you. I wish I could make you all cookies.

And as always, thank you to my family for all your support and enthusiasm and love, cat and human alike. Mom and Dad: thank you for getting me to this point. I love you more than I can say.

meet the author

TARA SIM is the author of *The City of Dusk*, as well as the Scavenge the Stars duology and the Timekeeper trilogy. She can often be found in the wilds of the Bay Area, California. When she's not writing about magic, murder, and mayhem, Tara spends her time drinking tea, wrangling cats, and lurking in bookstores.

Follow her on Twitter at @EachStarAWorld, and check out her website for fun extras at tarasim.com.

WANT MORE?

If you enjoyed this and would like to find out about similar books we publish, we'd love you to join our online Sci-Fi, Fantasy and Horror community, Hodderscape.

Visit hodderscape.co.uk for exclusive content from our authors, news, competitions and general musings, and feel free to comment, contribute or just keep an eye on what we are up to.

See you there!